D0564162

The
Unexpected
Dragon

Also by Mary Brown

THE UNLIKELY ONES
STRANGE DELIVERANCE

THE

UNEXPECTED DRAGON

Pigs Don't Fly
Master of Many Treasures
Dragonne's Eg

MARY BROWN

Published by arrangement with
Baen Publishing Enterprises
P.O. Box 1403
Riverdale, New York 10471

First SFBC printing: October 1999

Visit the SFBC *online at http://www.sfbc.com*

Contents

Pigs
Don't
Fly

This one is for my little brother,
Micky-Michael,
and my half-sister,
Anna,
and their families.

Acknowledgments

Thanks, as always, to my husband Peter, for his care and patience.

Belated thanks—sorry, folks!—to Bobby Travers and his daughter Joanna for smoothing our way out here.

Thanks, too, to Margaret and Barry Shaw for their help with Christopher.

I am also grateful to our *alcalde,* Don Carlos Mateo Donet Donet, for his assistance and encouragement.

Last, but never ever least, thank you Samimi-Babaloo, my Sam—just for being yourself!

Part I

AN END

1

My mother was the village whore and I loved her very much.

Having regard to the nature of her calling, we lived a discreet distance away from her clients, in a cottage up the end of a winding lane that backed onto the forest. Once the dwelling had been a forester's hut, shielded by a stand of pines from the biting winter northerlies, but during the twenty years since she had come to the village it had been transformed into a pleasant one-roomed cottage with a lean-to at the side for wood and stores. Part of the ground outside had been cleared and fenced, and we had a vegetable patch, three apple trees, an enclosure for the hens, a tethering post for the goat and a skep for the bees.

Inside it was very cozy. Apart from the bed, which took, with its hangings, perhaps a third of the space, there was a table, two stools, hooks for our clothing, a chest for linen and a dresser for the pots and dishes. Above the fire was the rack for drying herbs or clothes, beside it a folding screen that Mama sometimes used when she was entertaining if it was too cold for me to stay outside—though as I grew older I preferred to sit among the pungent, resinous logs in the lean-to, wrapped in my father's cloak, thinking my own thoughts, dreaming my own dreams, where witches and dragons, princes and treasure could make me forget chilblains or a runny nose until it was time for Mama to call me back into the warmth and the comfort of honey-cakes and mulled wine in front of the fire.

Then Mama would sit in her great carved chair in front of the blaze—a chair so heavy with age and carving it couldn't be moved—a queen on her throne, me crouched on a cushion at her feet, my head against her knee, and if she were in a good mood she would talk about Life and all it held in store for me.

"You will be all I could never be," she would say. "For you I have worked and planned so that you may have a handsome husband, a home of your own, and a dress for every season. . . ."

That would be luxury indeed! Just imagine, for instance, a green dress for spring in a fine, soft wool, a saffron-yellow silk for summer, a brown worsted for autumn and a thick black serge for winter with fresh shifts for each. . . . A man who could afford those for his wife would have to be rich indeed, and live in a house with an upstairs as well as a downstairs. Even as I listened the dresses changed in colour in my mind's eye as quick as the painted flight of the kingfisher.

Mama's planning for me had been thorough indeed. On a Monday she entertained the miller, who kept us regularly supplied with flour and meal for me to practice my pies, pastry and cakes; Tuesday brought the clerk with his scraps of vellum and inks for me to form my letters and show my skills with tally-sticks; on Wednesday Mama spent two hours with the butcher and once again I practiced my cooking. On Thursday the visit of the tailor-cum-shoemaker gave me pieces of cloth and leather to show off my stitching; Friday brought the Mayor, who was skilled with pipe and tabor so I could display my trills and taps and on a Saturday the old priest listened to me read, heard my catechism, and took our confessions.

Sunday was Mama's day off.

She had other visitors as well, of course, besides her regulars. The apothecary came once a month or so, sharing with us his wisdom of herbs and bone-setting, the carpenter usually at the same interval, teaching me to recognize the best woods and their various properties, and how to repair and polish furniture. The thatcher showed me how to choose and gather reeds for repairing the roof, the basketmaker, also an accomplished poacher, instructed me in both his crafts.

All in all, as Mama kept telling me, I must have been the best educated girl in the province, and she covered any gaps in my education with her own knowledge. It was she who taught me plain sewing, cooking and cleaning, leaving the refinements to the others. She insisted that as soon as I was big enough to wield a broom, lift a cooking-pot or heat water without scalding myself, that I kept us fed, clean and washed, and throughout the year my days were full and busy.

During the spring and summer I would be up before dawn—taking care not to wake Mama—and into the forest, cutting wood, fetching water, looking to my traps, gathering herbs and then home again to collect eggs, feed the hens, and weed the vegetables. Then I would milk the nanny and lay and light the fire, mix the dough for bread, sweep the floor and empty the piss-pot in the midden, so that when Mama finally woke there was fresh milk for her and a scramble of eggs while I made the great bed and heated water to wash us both; then I changed her linen, combed and dressed her hair and prepared her for her visitors. Once the ashes were good and hot they were raked aside for the bread, or if it was pies or patties I would set them on the hearthstone under their iron cover and rake back the ashes to cover them.

Once Mama was settled in her chair by the fire it was away again for more wood and water and once I was back there were the hives to check, a watch on the curdling goat's milk for cheese, digging or sowing or watering in the vegetable-patch and perhaps mixing straw and mud for any cracks in the fabric of the cottage. Then indoors for sewing, mending, washing pots and bowls, followed by any other tasks Mama thought necessary.

Once the gathering, storing and salting of autumn were over, my outside tasks during the winter were of a necessity curtailed, although there were still the wood- and water-chores, even with snow on the ground. There were the stores to check: jars of our honey, crocks of flour, trays of apples, salted ham, clamps of root vegetables, strings of onions and garlic, bunches of herbs, dried beans and pulses. That done, it was time for candle-dipping, spinning, carding wool, sharpening of knives, restuffing pillows and cushions, sewing and mending, mixing of pastes and potions and repairing of shoes.

Then came the time I liked best. While I dampened down the fire and made us a brew of camomile flowers, Mama would comb her hair and sing some of the old songs. We would climb into bed and snuggle down behind the drawn hangings for warmth, and if she felt like it my mother would either tell me a tale of wicked witches and beautiful princesses or else, which I like even better, would tell once more of how she had come to be here and of the men she had known. Especially my father.

I had heard her story many times before, but a good tale loses nothing in the retelling, and I would close my eyes and see pictures in my mind of the pretty young girl fleeing home to escape the vile attentions of her stepfather; I would shiver with sympathy as I followed the flight of the pregnant lass through the worst of winters and sigh with relief when she reached, by chance, the haven of our village, and my heart filled with relief when I re-heard how she had been taken in by the miller and his wife. Once her pregnancy was discovered, however, there was a meeting of the Council to decide what should be done with her, for now she was a Burden on the Parish and could be turned away to starve.

"But of course there was no question of that," said Mama complacently. "Once I had discovered who was what, I had distributed my favors enthusiastically to those who mattered, and all the important men of the village were well disposed to heed my suggestion for easing their . . . problems, shall we say? Of course much was tease and promise, for there is nothing more arousing to a man than the thought of undisclosed delights to come. . . . Remember that, daughter. You had better write it down some time. Of course I was far more beautiful and accomplished than the other girls in the village, though I say it myself, even though I was four months gone. I still had my figure and my soft, creamy skin, and of course every man likes a woman with hair as black and smooth as mine. . . . You would say, would you not, child, that my skin and hair are still incomparable?"

"Of course, Mama!" I would answer fervently, though if truth were told her hair had grey in it aplenty, and her skin was wrinkled like skin too long in water. But she had no mirror but me and her clients, and who were the latter to notice in the flattery of candles or behind drawn bed-curtains? Besides, those she entertained were mostly well into middle age themselves and in no position to criticize.

"So by the time the meeting of the Council came round it was a foregone conclusion that I would stay. It was decided to offer me this cottage and food and supplies in return for my services," continued Mama. "Of course I laid down certain conditions. This place was to be renovated, extended, re-roofed and furnished. I was also to entertain six days a week only: Sunday was to be my day of rest.

"At first, of course, I was at it morning, noon and night, but eventually the novelty-value wore off and my friends and I settled to a comfortable routine. Your elder half-brother, Erik, was born here and three years later your other half-brother, Luke. . . ."

Erik now was a man grown with a shrewish and complaining wife. Dark, long-faced, with tight lips, he had teased me unmercifully as a child. Luke I remembered more kindly. He was apprenticed to the miller and had the same sandy hair, snub nose and gap-toothed smile. It was obvious who his father was and he even resembled him in temperament: kind and a little dim.

And now came the part of Mama's story of which I never wearied.

"Some dozen or more years ago," she would begin, "your half-brothers were fast asleep and I was all alone, restless with the spirit of autumn that was sending the swallows one way, bringing the geese the other. It was twilight, and all at once there came a knocking at the door. It had to be a stranger, for there was fever in the village and I had forsworn my regulars until it had passed. . . ."

"And so there you were, Mama," I would prompt, "all alone in the growing dusk. . . ." Just in case she had forgotten, or didn't feel like going on. So vivid was my imagination that I felt the shivers of her long-ago apprehension, imagining myself alone and unprotected as she had been with the October mist curling around the cottage like a tangle of great grey eels, slither-slide, slither-creep. . . .

"And so there I was," continued Mama, "determined to ignore who-ever, whatever it was. But again came that dreadful knocking! I grasped the poker tight in my hand, for I had forgotten to bolt the door—"

"And then?" I could scarcely breathe for excitement.

"And then—and then the door was pulled open and a man, a tall, thin man, stood in the shadows, the hood of his cloak pulled down so I could not see his face. You can imagine how terrified I felt! 'What—what do you want?' I quavered, grasping the poker still tighter. He took one step forward, and now I could see his cloak was forest-green, and the hand that held it was brown and sinewy but still he said nothing. Then was I truly afraid, for specters do not speak, and of what use was a poker against the supernatural?"

I gasped in sympathy, crossing myself in superstitious fear.

"I think that my bowels would have turned to water had he stood there silent one moment longer," she said, "but of a sudden he thrust one hand against his side and held the other out towards me, saying in a low and throbbing tone: 'A vision of loveliness indeed! Do I wake or sleep? In very truth I believe the pain of my wound has conjured up a dream of angels. . . .' "

How very romantic! No wonder Mama was impressed.

"The very next moment he crumpled in a heap on my doorstep, out like a snuffed candle! What else could I do but tend him?" and she spread her hands helplessly.

And that was how my father had come into her life. At once she had taken him into both her heart and her bed—what woman wouldn't with that introduction?—and nursed him back to health. For an idyllic month, while the village still lay under the curse of a low fever, my father and mother enjoyed their secret love.

"He was both a courtly and a fierce lover," said my mother. "A trifle unpolished, perhaps, but not beyond teaching. He was always eager to learn those little refinements that make all the difference to a woman's enjoyment. . . ." and my mother paused, a reminiscent smile on her face.

"And what did he look like, my father?"

But here always came the odd part. Perhaps the passage of years had played strange tricks with my mother's memory for my father never looked the same for two tellings. At first he was tall, then recollection

had him shorter. Dark as Hades, fair as sunlight; eyes grey as storm
clouds, blue as sky, brown as autumn leaf, green as duck-weed; he was
loquacious, he was taciturn; he was happy, he was sad; shy, outgoing . . .
I was sure that if ever I loved a man I would remember every detail
forever, right down to the number of his teeth, the shape of his fingernails, the curl of his lashes. But then Mama had known as many men
as there were leaves on a tree, so she said, and always tended to remember them by their physical endowments rather than their physiognomy.
In this respect she assured me that my father was outstanding.

I hated the sad part of my father's story, but it had to be told. One
frosty day, as my mother told it, the men from the village came and
dragged him from the cottage and carried him away, never to be seen
again. "They were jealous of our love," she said, and she had never
ceased hoping that he would return, her wounded lover who came with
the falling leaves and left with the first frosts.

He had left nothing behind save his tattered cloak, a purse full of
strange coins, and a ring. Mama said the coins were for my dowry, but
that the ring was special, a magic ring. She had shown it to me a couple
of times, but it looked like nothing more than the shaving of a horn, a
colorless spiral. It would not fit any of my mother's fingers, and she
would not let me try it on.

"He wore it round his neck on a cord," she said, "for it would not
fit him either. He said it was from the horn of a unicorn, passed down
in his family for generations, but it did nothing for him. . . ."

She had tried to sell it a couple of times, but as it looked so ordinary
and fit no one, she had tossed into a box with the rest of her bits and
pieces of jewelry—necklace, brooch, two bracelets—where it still lay,
gathering dust.

My days were not all work and no play, though I mostly made my
own free time by working that much harder. I had two special treats. If
the weather was fine, summer or winter, I would escape into the woods
or down by the river, lie under a tree and gaze up into the leaf-dappled
sunshine and dream, or sit by the river and dangle my toes in the fast-
running water. This would be summer, of course, but even in the cold
and snow there were games to play. Skipping-stones, snowballs, imaginary chases, battles with trees and bushes . . . Away from the cottage I
was anything I chose and could forget the confines of my cumbersome
flesh and flew with the birds, swam with the fish, ran with the deer.
Gaze up into the rocking trees in spring and I was a rook, swaying with
the wind till I felt sick, my beak weaving the rough bundles they called

nests. Dangle my fingers in the water and I was a fish, heading upstream into the current, the river sliding past my flanks like silk. Given the bright fall of leaves and I ran along the branches with the squirrels and hid my nuts in secret holes I would never remember. Winter and I sympathized with the striped badgers, leaving the fug of their setts on warmer days to search for the scrunch of beetle or a forgotten berry or two, blackened into a honey sweetness by the frost.

But the thing I loved most in the world to do was write in my book.

This had grown from my very first attempt at writing my letters, many years ago. Now it was thick as a kindling log and twice as heavy. At first the clerk had formed letters for me in the earth outside, or had taught me to mark a flat stone with another, scratchy one, but as I progressed he had shown me how to fashion a quill pen and mix inks, so it was but a short step to putting my first, tentative words on a scraped piece of vellum.

As parchment or skin was so expensive I sometimes had to wait for weeks for a fresh piece, but I practiced diligently with my finger on the table to ensure I should make no mistakes when the time came.

For the Ten Commandments, my first page, the old priest provided me with a fine, clear page, but by the time I finished it was as rough and scraped as a pig's bum. My next task was the days of the week, months and seasons of the year, followed by the principal saints' days and festivals of the Church calendar. Then came numbers from one to a hundred. This done, the elderly priest dead and another, less tolerant, in his place—he never visited Mama—I was free to write what I wished, whenever I could beg a scrap of vellum from the clerk. Down went recipes for cakes, horehound candy, poultices, dyes and charms.

I do not remember what occasioned my first essays into proverbs, saws and sayings. It may have been the mayor, once chiding me for hurrying my tasks. "Don't remove your shoes till you reach the stream," he had said, and this conjured up such a vivid picture of stumbling barefoot among stones, thorns and nettles that down it had to go. Not that it cured me of haste, mind, but it was an extremely sensible suggestion. Then there were my mother's frequent strictures on the behavior expected of a lady: "Do not put your chewed bones on the communal platter; reserve them to be thrown on the fire, returned to the stock pot, or given to the dogs." Or: "A lady does not wipe her mouth or nose on her sleeve; if there is no napkin available, use the inner hem of your shift."

She also gave me the benefit of her experience of sex; pet names for the private parts, methods of exciting passion, of restraining it; how to deal with the importunate or the reluctant, and various draughts to prevent conception or procure an abortion. Down these all went in my book, for I was sure they would one day prove useful, though she had explained that husbands didn't need the same titillation as clients. "After all, once you're married he's yours: you will need excuses more than encouragements."

When the pages of my book grew to a dozen, then twenty, I threaded them together and begged a piece of soft leather from the tanner for a cover and a piece of silk from Mama to wrap it in. A heated poker provided the singed title: *My Boke*. At first Mama had laughed at my scribblings, as she called them, for she could not read or write herself, but once she realized I was treasuring her little gems of wisdom and could read them back to her, she even gave me an occasional coin or two for more materials, and reminded me constantly of her forethought in providing me with such a good education.

"What with your father's dowry and my teachings, you will be able to choose any man in the kingdom," she said,

And that was perhaps the only cause of friction between us.

A secure, protected, industrious childhood slipped almost unnoticed into puberty, but I made the mistake one day of asking Mama how long it would be before she found me the promised husband, to be met with a coldness, a hurt withdrawal I had not anticipated. "Are you so ready to leave me alone after all I have done for you?" I kept quiet for two more years, but then asked, timidly again. I was unprepared for the barrage of blows. Her rage was terrible. She beat me the colors of the rainbow, shrieking that I was the most ungrateful child in the world and didn't deserve the consideration I had been shown. How could I think of leaving her?

Of course I sobbed and cried and begged her on my knees to forgive me my thoughtlessness, and after a while she consented for me to cut out and sew a new robe for her, so I knew I was back in favor. Even so, as year slipped into year without change, I began to wonder just when my life would alter, when I would have a home and husband of my own, as she had promised.

And then, suddenly, everything changed in a single day.

2

That morning Mama was uncharacteristically edgy and irritable. She complained of having eaten something that disagreed with her, and although I made an infusion of mint leaves and camomile, she still seemed restless and uneasy.

"I shall go back to bed," she announced. "And I don't want you clattering around. Have you finished all your outside jobs?" I had. "Then you can go down to the village and fetch some more salt. We're not without, but will need more before winter sets in. Wait outside and I'll find a coin or two. . . ."

This was always the ritual. Our store of coins, which Mama always took from passing trade, were hidden away, and only she knew the whereabouts. I didn't see the need for such secrecy, but she explained that I was such a silly, gullible child that I might give away the hiding place. I couldn't see how, as I scarcely spoke to anyone, but she insisted.

I picked up an empty crock and dawdled down the path towards the gate. It was a beautiful morning, and I was in no hurry to go. I hated these visits to the village, but luckily only made them when there were goods we could not barter for—salt, oil, tallow, wine, spices. I enjoyed the walk there, the walk back and would have also enjoyed gazing about me when I got there, but for the behavior of the villagers. When I was very young I did not understand why the men pretended I didn't exist, and women hissed and spat and made unkind remarks and the children threw stones and refuse. Now I was older I both understood and was better able to cope. When I complained, Mama always said she couldn't comprehend why the women weren't more grateful: after all, she took the heat from their men once a week. Like everyone else, she said, she provided a service. But that didn't stop the children calling after me: "Bastard daughter of a whore!" or worse.

"Here, daughter!" I turned back to where Mama stood on the threshold. She would never come outside. In summer it was "too hot", in winter "too cold." In autumn it was wasps and other insects, in spring the flowers made her sneeze, and through all the seasons it was a question of preserving her complexion. "I wouldn't want to be all brown and gypsyish; part of my attraction to my clients is my pale, creamy skin. You had better watch yours, too, girl: you're becoming as dark as your father. What's acceptable on a man won't do on a woman."

Now she handed me some coin. "Watch for the change: I don't want any counterfeit. And if I'm asleep when you return, don't wake me. I shall try and sleep off this indisposition."

"If you're really feeling ill I could fetch the apothecary—"

"Don't be stupid: I am never ill! Now, get along with you before you make me feel worse—and for goodness sake straighten your skirt and tie the strings on your shift: no prospective husband would look at you twice like that! Do you want to disgrace me?"

I kissed her cheek and curtseyed, as I had been taught, and walked away sedately till I was out of sight, then hung the crock over my shoulder by its strap, hitched up my skirts and scuffed my feet among the crunchy, crackly heaps of leaves along the lane, taking great delight in disordering the wind-arranged heaps and humming a catchy little tune the mayor had taught me for my pipe.

It seemed I was not the only one fetching winter stores. Above my head squirrels were squabbling over the last acorns. I could hear hedgepigs scuffling in a ditch searching for grubs, too impatient for their winter fat to wait till dusk, and thrushes and blackbirds were testing the hips and haws in the hedges and finishing off the last brambles, while tits and siskins were cheeping softly in search of insects. A rat, obviously with a late litter, ran across in front of me, a huge cockchafer in her mouth.

The sun shone directly in my eyes and shimmered off the ivy and hawthorn to either side, making their leaves all silver. I passed through a cloud of midges, dancing their up-and-down day dance—a fine day tomorrow—and on a patch of badger turd a meadow-brown butterfly basked, its long tongue delicately probing the stinking heap. My only annoyance was the flies, wanting the sweat on my face, and the wasps, seeking something sweet, so I pulled a handful of dried cow parsley and waved that freely round my head.

I purchased the salt without much notice being taken, for a peddler had found his way to the village, and the women and children were crowding round his wares. So engrossed were they that the miller passing by with his cart had time to give me a huge wink and toss me a copper coin. "Don't spend it all at once. . . ."

Money of my own! A whole coin to spend on whatever I wanted! At first I thought to buy a ribbon from the peddler, but that would need explanations when I returned home, and somehow I didn't think Mama would approve of her clients giving me money. Lessons and food were different. Food! I had just reminded myself I was hungry. I looked up at the sun: an hour before noon. Still, if I bought something now I needn't hurry home, and Mama could enjoy her sleep. I peered at the tray in the baker's. Ham pies, baked apples, cheese pasties . . . The pies looked a little tired and I had had an apple for breakfast, so I carried away two cheese pasties.

One had gone even before I reached the lane again, but I decided to find somewhere to sit in the sun and thoroughly enjoy the other. There was a bank full of sunshine a quarter mile from the cottage just where the lane kinked opposite one of the rides through the forest, and I seated myself comfortably and enjoyed the other pasty down to the last crumb, wiping my mouth thoroughly to leave no telltale grease or crumbs. I found a couple of desiccated mint leaves in the hedge behind and chewed those too, just in case Mama spotted the smell of onions, then burped comfortable and lay back in the sunshine, the scent of the mint an ephemeral accompaniment to the background of autumn smells: drying leaves, damp ground, wood smoke, fungi, a gentle decay.

I sniffed my fingers again, but the scent of mint had almost gone; strange how the pleasant smells didn't last as long as the stinks. I must put that thought down in my book. "Perfumes are nice while they last, but foul smells last longer"? Clumsy. What about: "Sweet smells are a welcome guest, but foul odors stay too long." Still clumsy; it needed to be shorter, more succinct, and could do with some alliteration. "Sweet smells stay but short: foul odors linger longer." Much better.

As soon as I had time to spare I would write that down. The trouble was that it took so long; not the actual writing, now that I was more used to it, but the preparation beforehand. First, I had to be sure I had at least a clear hour before me, then the weather had to be right: too hot and the ink dried too quickly; too wet and it wouldn't dry at all. It had to be mixed first of course to the right color and consistency, and the quills had to be sharpened and the vellum smoothed and weighted down and the light just right.

But then what joy! I scarcely breathed as I formed the letters: the

full-bellied downward curve of the *l*, the mysterious double arch of the
m, the change of the quill position for the *s*, the cozy cuddle of the
e—each had its own individual pattern, separate symbols that together
made plain the things I had only thought before.

Magic, for sure. First the letters themselves, precise in shape and
order, then the interpretation into words and meaning and lastly the
imagination engendered by the whole. The old priest had once given
me a saying: "God created man from the clay of the ground: take care
lest you crack in the firing of Life." I had dutifully copied this down,
but once it was there it took on a new dimension. In my mind I could
actually see little clay men running round with bits broken and chipped
off them, crying out that the Almighty Potter had not shaped them
right or had made the kiln too hot or too cold, and—

"Hey, there! Wake up, girl!"

Suddenly the sun had gone. I opened my eyes and there, towering
over me, was the awesome bulk of a caparisoned horse, snorting and
champing at the bit. Still half-asleep I scrambled to my feet and backed
up the bank, wondering if I was still dreaming.

"Which way to the High Road?"

The horse swung round and now the sun was in my eyes again. I
dropped down to the road, and was seemingly surrounded by a party of
horsemen who had obviously just ridden along the ride out of the forest.
Hooves stamped, harness jingled, men cursed and I was about to panic
and run for home, when the face of the man on the caparisoned horse
swam into view and I felt as though I had been struck by lightning.

He was the handsomest man I had ever seen in my life. It was the
eyes I noticed first, so dark and deep a blue they seemed to shine with
a light all their own. Dark brows drawn together over a slight frown, a
high, broad forehead and crispy dark hair that curled down unfashionably
to his collar. His skin was faintly tanned, his nose straight; there was a
little cleft in his rounded chin and his mouth—ah, his mouth! Full and
sensual, wide and mobile . . . I remembered afterwards broad shoulders,
wide chest and long, well-muscled legs, but at the time I could only
stare spellbound at his face.

Someone else spoke, a man who was probably one of his retainers,
but the words didn't register. I couldn't take my eyes off his master.

The mouth opened on perfect teeth and the apparition spoke.

"I asked if you knew the way to the High Road."

"She's maybe a daftie, Sir Gilman. . . ."

I shook my head. No, I wasn't a daftie, I just couldn't speak for a
moment. I nodded my head. Yes, I did know the way to the High Road.

I was conscious of the sweat pouring from my face, an itch on my nose where a fly had alighted, could feel an ant run over my bare toe—

"If you follow the lane the way I have come"—I pointed—"you will come to the village. If you take the turning by the church you will have to follow a track through the forest, but it is quicker. Otherwise go across the bridge at the end of the village, past the miller's, and there is a fair road. Perhaps four miles in all." I didn't sound like me at all.

He smiled. "And that is the way to civilization?"

I stared. Civilization was here. Then I remembered my manners and curtsied. "As you please, sir. . . ."

He smiled again. "Thank you, pretty maid. . . ."

And in a trample of hooves, a flash of embroidered cloth, a half-glimpsed banner, he and his men were gone clattering down the lane.

I stood there with my mouth open, my mind in a daze. He had called me "pretty maid"! Never in my wildest imaginings had I conjured up a man like this! Oh, I was in love, no doubt of it, hopelessly, irrevocably in love. . . .

I must tell Mama at once.

I hugged his words to my heart like a heated stone in a winter bed as I raced home, near tripping and losing the salt. Flinging open the door and quite forgetting she might be sleeping. I rushed over to the bed where she sat up against the pillows.

I grabbed her hand. "Mama, Mama, I must tell you—Mama?"

Her hand was cold, and her cheek, when I bent to kiss it, was cold too. The cottage was dark after the bright outside and I could not see her face, but I didn't need to. She couldn't hear me, couldn't see me, would never know what I had longed to tell her.

My mother was dead.

3

At first I panicked, backing away from the bed till I was brought up short by the wall and then sinking to my knees and covering my head with my arms, rocking back and forth and keening loudly. I felt as if I had been simultaneously kicked in the stomach and bashed over the head. She couldn't be dead, she couldn't! She couldn't leave me all alone like this! I didn't know what to do, I couldn't cope. . . . Oh, Mama, Mama, come back! I won't ever be naughty again, I promise! I'll work twice as hard, I'll never leave you, I didn't mean to upset you!

My eyes were near half-shut with tears, my nose was running, I was dribbling, but gradually it seemed as though a little voice was trying to be heard in my head, and my sobs subsided as I tried to listen. All at once the voice was quite plain, sharp and clear and scolding, like Mama's, but not in sentences, just odd words and phrases.

"Pull yourself together . . . Things to be done . . . Tell *them*."

Of course. Things couldn't just be left. I wiped my face, took one more look just to be sure, then ran as fast as I could back to the village. Luckily the first man I saw was the apothecary. As shocked as a man could be, he hurried back with me to confirm my fears. He examined Mama perfunctorily, asked if she had complained of pains in the chest and shook his head as I described her symptoms of this morning, as best I could for the stitch in my side from running.

"Mmm. Massive heart attack. Pains were a warning. Must have hit her all at once. Wouldn't have known a thing."

Indeed, now I had lit a candle for his examination I could see her face held a look of surprise, as though Death had walked in without knocking.

"Will tell the others. Expect us later." And he was gone.

Expect us later? What . . . ? But then the voice in my head took over again.

"Decisions . . . Burial . . . Prepare . . . Food."

Of course. They would all come to view the body, decide how and when she should be buried, and would expect the courtesy of food and drink. What to do first?

"Cold . . . Water . . ."

The fire was nearly out and there was a chill in the room. For an absurd moment I almost apologized to Mama for the cold, then pulled myself together, and with an economy born of long familiarity rekindled the ashes, brought in the driest logs and set the largest cauldron on for hot water. With bright flames now illuminating the room, I checked the food. A large pie and a half should be enough, with some of the goat's-milk cheese and yesterday's loaf, set to crisp on the hearth. There were just enough bowls and platters to go around, but only two mugs; I could put milk into a flagon and what wine we had left into a jug and they could pass those round. Seating was a problem; the stools and Mama's chair would accommodate three, and perhaps two could perch on the table or the chest. The rest would have to stand.

The water was now finger-hot, and I turned to the most important task of all. Crossing to Mama's clothes chest I pulled out her best robe, the red one edged with concy fur, and her newest shift, the silk one with gold ribbons at neck and sleeve, and the fine linen sheet that would be her shroud.

The heat from the fire, which had me sweating like a pig, had relaxed her muscles, so it was an easy enough task to wash her, change the death-soiled sheets, pad all orifices and dress her in her best. That done, I combed and plaited her hair and arranged it in coils around her head, but was distressed to see that the grey streaks would show once I had the candles burning round the bed. She would never forgive me for that, I thought, then remembered my inks. A little smoothed across with my fingers and no one would notice. . . .

I crumbled dried rosemary and lavender between the folds of her dress for sweetness, then went outside and burned the soiled sheets and the dress she had been wearing when she died. Outside it was quite cool, the sun saying nearer four than three, and the smoke from the bonfire rising thin and straight: a slight frost tonight, I thought. On the way back in I gathered some late daisies and a few flowers of the yellow Mary's-gold, and placed them in Mama's folded hands, then set the best beeswax candles in the few holders we had around the bed, ready to light once it grew dark.

I looked at her once more, to see all was as she would have wished and to my amazement saw that Death had given her back her youth. Gone were the frown lines, the pinched mouth, the wrinkles at the corners of her eyes. She looked as though she were sleeping, her face calm and smooth, and the candle I held flickered as though she were smiling. She was so beautiful I wanted to cry again—

"Enough! Late . . . Tidy up. Wash and change . . ."

I heeded the voice, so like hers—but it couldn't be, could it?—and a half-hour later or so I had swept out and tidied, washed myself in the rest of the water, including my hair and my filthy clothes, hanging out the latter to dry over the hedge by the chicken run, and had changed into my other shift and my winter dress. Mama would be proud of my industriousness, I thought. But there was no time for further tears, for I could hear the tramp of feet down the lane. My mother's clients come to pay their last respects.

Suddenly the room, comfortably roomy for Mama and me, had shrunk to a hulk and shuffle of too many bodies, with scarce space to move. The only part they avoided was the bed.

They had all come: mayor, miller, clerk, butcher, tailor, forester, carpenter, thatcher, basket-maker, apothecary; all at one time my mother's regular customers. The new priest was the only odd one out. In spite of their common interest I noticed how they avoided looking at one another. At last, after much coughing, scratching and picking of noses, the mayor stepped forward and everything went as quiet as if someone had shut a door.

"Ah, hmmm, yes. This is a sad occasion, very sad." He shook his head solemnly, and the rest of them did likewise or nodded as they thought fit. "We meet here to mourn the passing of someone who, er, someone who was . . ."

"With whom we shared a common interest?" suggested the clerk.

"Yes, yes of course. Very neatly put. . . . As I was saying, Mistress Margaret here—"

"Margaret? Isabella," said the miller.

"Not Isabella," said the butcher. "Susan."

"Elizabeth," said the clerk. "Or Bess for short."

"I thought she was Alice," said the tailor.

"Maude, for sure . . ."

"No, Ellen—"

"I'm sure she said Mary—"

"Katherine!"

"Sukey . . ."

I stared at them in bewilderment. It didn't seem as though they were talking about her at all: how could she possibly be ten different people? Then, like an echo, came my mother's voice: "In my position I have to be all things to all men, daughter. . . ."

The mayor turned to me. "What was your mother's real name?"

I shrugged my shoulders helplessly. "I never asked her. To me she was just—just Mama." I would *not* cry. . . .

"Well," said the priest snappily, "You will have to decide on something if I am to bury her tomorrow morning. At first light, you said?"

They had obviously been discussing it on the way here.

"It would be . . . more discreet," said the mayor, lamely. "Less fuss the better, I say."

"Aye," said the butcher. "What's over, is over."

"What I want to know is," said the priest, "who's paying?"

They all looked at me. I shook my head. I knew there were a few coins for essentials in Mama's box, but not near enough to pay for a burial and Mass.

"I don't think she ever thought about dying," I said. This was true. Death had never been part of our conversations. She had been so full of life and living there had been no room for death. I thought about it for a moment more, then I knew what she would have said. "I believe she would have trusted you, all of you, to share her dying as you shared her living."

I could see they didn't like it, but there were grudging nods of assent.

"What about a sin-eater?" said the priest suddenly. "She died unshriven. Masses for a year and a day might do it, but . . ."

More money. "There isn't one hereabouts," said the mayor worriedly. "I suppose if we could find someone willing we should have to find a few more coins, but—"

"I'll do it," I said. "She was my mother." I couldn't leave her in Purgatory for a year, even if I was scared to death of the burden. "What do I do?"

But no one seemed very sure, not even the priest. In the end he suggested I take a hunk of bread, place it on my mother's chest and pray for her sins to pass from one to the other. Then I had to eat the bread.

It near choked me, and once I had forced it down I was assailed by the most intolerable sense of burdening, as though I had been squashed head down in a small box after eating too much.

They watched me with interest.

"Is it working?" asked the priest.

"Yes," I gasped, and begged him for absolution.

"Excellent," said the priest, looking relieved. "We shall repair to the church, choose the burial site and you may confess your mother's sins and I shall absolve her."

It was cold inside the church for the sun was now gone and twilight shrouded the altar, mercifully hiding the mural of the Day of Judgment which, faded though it was, always gave me nightmares. To be sure, there were the righteous rising in their underwear to Heaven, but the unknown artist had had an inspired brush with the damned, their mouths open on silent screams as they tumbled towards the flames, poked and prodded by the demons of the Devil.

The priest led me through Mama's confession—it was very strange confessing unknown sins for someone else—and he told me to confess to absolutely everything, just in case. Some of those sins he prompted me with I had never even heard of.

"Now you may either say a thousand *Hail Marys* in expiation, or perhaps find it more convenient to make a small donation," he said hopefully.

As it happened I had the change from buying the salt still tied round my waist in my special purse-pocket, so he gave me a hurried full absolution to our mutual satisfaction. Immediately it seemed as though the dreadful heaviness left me, just like shucking off a heavy load of firewood after a long tramp home. Now Mama could ascend to Heaven happily with the rest of the righteous.

We came out into a dusky churchyard, and found the others grouped in the far corner against the wall.

"This'll do," said the mayor. Next to the rubbish dump. "It'll take less digging and is nicely screened from view. Why, you could even scratch the date of death on the wall behind. Pity she couldn't lie next to your father, girl, but of course his bones were tossed to the pigs long ago—"

"My *father?*" I could not believe what I was hearing. My father had been driven away by jealous villagers and dared not return; my mother had told me so.

"Of course. Led us a merry chase, but we caught him about two mile into the forest, and—"

"She doesn't know," interrupted the miller, glancing at my face. "Happen her Ma told her something different." He looked at the others. "No point in bringing it up now."

I could feel something crumbling inside me, just like the hopeful dams I had built as a child across the stream, only to see them crumble with the first rains. I had cherished for years the vision of a handsome soldier-father forced to leave his only love, my beautiful mother, and now they were trying to say—

"Tell me!" I shrieked, the anger and bewilderment escaping me like air from a pricked bladder, surprising them and myself so much that we all jumped apart as though someone had just tossed a snake into our midst.

So they told me, in fits and starts: apologetically, belligerently, defiantly. At first it was just as Mama had related it, there had been fever in the village, the stranger had sought refuge at our cottage and they had enjoyed their secret idyll. Then everything had gone wrong. Houses left empty by fever deaths had been looted, and as they reasoned no one in the village could have been responsible, they had searched farther afield, and had found some of the bulkier objects hidden in a sack at the rear of our dwelling. My father had run; they had pursued him into the forest where a lucky arrow had brought him down. Although he was dead they had had a ceremonial hanging in the village, then had chopped him in pieces and thrown the pieces to the pigs.

So the man whose memory I had cherished, the father who my imagination had made taller, handsomer and braver than anyone else in the world, was nothing more than a common thief!

"I don't believe you, any of you! You're all lying, and just because Mama isn't here you're—you're—" I burst into tears. But I knew they were telling the truth; they had no reason to lie, not after all this time. But the anger and frustration would out, and I switched to another hurt. "And I won't have Mama buried next to the midden! She must have a proper plot, a proper marker, a decent service and committal, just as she deserves—"

"Now look here, girl," interrupted the butcher angrily. "Don't you realize we have to pay for all this? Now your Ma's dead you have nothing, are nothing. Of all the ungrateful hussies—"

"Easy, Seth," said the clerk. "She's upset. None of this is her fault. It's up to us to do the best for—for . . . I'm sorry, girl, I don't think I remember your name."

"My name?"

"Yes," said the tailor. "Always just called you 'girl,' as your mother did."

There were nods, murmurs of confirmation from the others.

"Well?" said the priest.

I stared at them all aghast. I could feel myself falling. . . .

"I haven't the faintest idea. . . ." I croaked, then everything went black.

4

They brought me round with hastily sprinkled font water.

I had never fainted before in my life and I felt stupid, embarrassed and slightly sick. Their faces swam above me like great moons, in the light from the miller's lantern. For a moment I could remember nothing, and then it came back like a knife-thrust: Mama was dead, my father a thief, and I had no name. In a way the last was the worst. Without an identity I was a blank piece of vellum, a discarded feather, the emptiness that is a hole in the ground. I felt that if I let go I should float up into the sky like smoke, and dissolve as easily. I was deathly frightened.

Then somebody had a good idea. "You must have been baptized." Of course, else would I not have been allowed to attend Mass.

They helped me to my feet and we all repaired to the vestry, where by the light of the lantern and the priest's candle, the fusty, dusty, mildewy parish records were dragged out of a chest.

"How old are you?"

But I couldn't be exact about that either, till the miller suggested the Year of the Great Fever, and there was much counting backwards on fingers and thumbs and at last the entry was found, in the old priest's fumbling, scratchy hand.

"Here we are. . . . Strange name to call anyone," said the present priest. Only the clerk, he and I could read, and I bent forward to follow his finger. There it was, between the death of one John Tyler and the marriage of Wat Wood and Megan Baker. The cramped letters danced in front of my eyes, but at last I spelled it out.

No date, but the previous entry was June, the latter July.

"Baptism of dorter to the Traveling woman: one Somerdai."

"Somerdai . . ." I tried it out on my tongue. "Summerday." And Mama had called herself one of the Travelers. All right, she had given me an outlandish name, but at least I now existed officially. And, according to the records, I was seventeen years old, and knew something more of Mama's origins. All at once I felt a hundred times better, and was able to invite them all back for the funeral meats almost as graciously as she would have done.

It did not take them long to demolish everything. I closed the shutters, made up the fire and lighted the candles around Mama; they threw our shadows like grotesques on the whitewashed walls and made it look as though Mama sighed, smiled and twitched in a natural sleep.

The mayor accepted the dregs of the wine jug, drained them and brushed the crumbs from his front. Clearing his throat, he addressed us all.

"I now declare this special meeting open. . . ."

What meeting?

"Having determined to settle this little matter as soon as may be, I think it is now time to for us to agree on our previously discussed course of action."

My! They had certainly been busy amongst themselves, either on the way here or in the churchyard. . . . But what "little matter"?

"Firstly, Summerhill, or whatever your name is—I should like to thank you on behalf of us all for the refreshments." Everyone murmured their approval. "We have already agreed to attend to the burial of the— the lady, your mother, and to defray all costs." He cleared his throat again. "Now we come to the distribution of the assets. . . ."

"My hens," said the butcher.

"My goat," said the tailor.

"My bees," said the clerk.

"The clothes chest—"

"The hangings—"

And suddenly they were all shouting against each other, pointing at our belongings, even gesturing towards the padded quilt on which Mama lay and touching the gown she wore.

I was horrified, but as they quietened down it became obvious that everything I had thought we owned, Mama and I, belonged in some way or other to her clients. They were just loans. If I had ever thought about it at all, which I hadn't, I should have guessed that the finely carved bed, the elaborate hangings, some of the fine clothes, could not have been gifts, like the flour, meat and pulses.

Now the butcher was on his feet. He was the man I had always liked least of Mama's clients, not only because he sometimes tried to put his hands down my front.

"Comrades . . . Quiet! I know what we all have at stake here, but we cannot leave the new whore entirely without."

Surely they couldn't mean that I—

But the mayor took over, with an uneasy glance in my direction.

"Normally, of course, we could have left all this for a day or two until everything settled down," he said. "But under the circumstances—"

"With her losing her job and all—" said the butcher.

"—we shall have to make a quick decision," continued the mayor.

My heart gave a sudden lurch of thankfulness. They hadn't been thinking of me as a replacement after all. But the mayor's next words hurt. "Normally we might have offered young Summer-Solstice here the job, as her mother's daughter, but under the circumstances I don't believe she would attract the same sort of custom. . . ."

"Oh, come on!" said the miller, always ready with a kind word. "She's not that bad! A nice smile, all her teeth, small hands and feet, a fine head of hair . . ." Even he couldn't think of anything else.

"Mama wished me to become a wife, not a whore," I said stiffly. Whores were special, but wives came in all shapes and sizes, so I had a better chance as the latter, especially with my learning and dowry—come to that, where was it? Mama had never said. And when I found the coins, how did I set about finding this elusive husband I had been promised? With winter coming on, it would be better to leave it until New Year. If what they had said about the furniture going to the next whore was true, the cottage would seem very bare. I had a few coins left of Mama's, and perhaps if they let me keep a couple of the hens and I could persuade the carpenter to knock me up a truckle bed, I could manage with what was laid aside. But I should have to buy some salted pork—

". . . so, if it is convenient, shall we say noon tomorrow?" asked the mayor. "Although your brothers are not here now, they will attend the interment in the morning, and your eldest brother let it be known his wife would not be averse to the dresses. . . ."

I had lost something in his speechifying, but that pinched-nosed sister-in-law of mine was not going to wear my mother's dresses, and I told him so.

"Why not? They're of no use to you. Your ma was tall and thin."

"I still would not like to see another in her dresses—"

"Nonsense! Why waste them? The new whore, Agnes-from-the-Inn, would fit into them nicely, too. No point in wasting them."

So that sandy-haired, big-bosomed wench was to be the next village whore! "No," I said.

"As she's getting everything else," said the butcher, "including this cottage, why not chuck the dresses in as well? Not yours to dispose of, anyway."

"This place? But it's ours—mine, surely?"

The mayor shook his head. "Goes with the job. So, as I said a moment or two back, I can expect you out by midday tomorrow?"

"I can't! I've nowhere to go!" This just couldn't be happening! All in one day to lose my mother, the shreds of my father's reputation and also find I possessed a ridiculous name, then to be turned out into an unknown world with nothing to my name and nowhere to go—

I burst into tears; angry, snuffly, hurt, uncontrollable, ugly tears. Now Mama had always taught me that tears were a woman's finest weapon. She had also tried to teach me how to weep gently and affectingly, without reddening the eyes or screwing up the face, but all my tears produced were embarrassment, red faces and a rush for the door, just as if I had been found with plague spots.

"Back at dawn," called out the mayor. "We'll bring a hurdle for the body. . . ."

The priest was the last to leave. "Not even one coin for the Masses?" I shook my head.

I heard their footsteps retreating, then one set returning. The miller poked his head round the door.

"Just wanted to say—will miss your Ma. She was a lady. Sorry I can't take you in like your brother, but the wife wouldn't stand for it." He turned to go, then stopped. "Thought you might like to know; years after your dad—died—someone else confessed to planting those stolen goods. Said he was jealous. Dead and gone, now . . . Hey there: no more tears! Could never abide to see a lass cry. Here, there's a couple of coins for your journey. And don't worry, you'll do fine. I'll see the grave's kept nice," He sidled out through the door. "Sorry I can't do more, but you know how it is. . . ."

"Yes," I said. "I know how it is. . . ."

Alone, I sank to my knees beside the dying fire, my mind a muddle. Shock and grief had filled my mind to such an extent I was incapable of thinking clearly. All I wanted was for Mama to be back to tell me what to do, for I felt an itching between my shoulder blades that told me I had forgotten something, and could not rest till it was seen to.

A log crashed in the hearth and I started up. Mustn't let the fire die down, tonight of all nights—But why? Of course: tonight was All Hallows' Eve, the eve of Samhain. Tonight was the night when the unshriven dead rode the skies with the witches and warlocks and the Court of Faery roamed the earth. . . . Tonight was the night that, every year, Mama and I closed and locked the shutters and doors early, stoked up the fire and roasted chestnuts and melted cheese over toasted bread, thumbing our noses at those spirits who moaned and cursed outside, wanting to take our places and live again. But it was the fire that kept them away, so Mama said, that and the songs we sang: "There is a time for everything," or "After Winter cometh Spring," and "Curst be all who ride abroad this night."

I rushed outside and brought in all the wood I could gather. Why bother to save any for the new whore? Let her seek her own. And she had no daughter to fetch and carry as Mama had done: they would soon be sick of her. I even emptied the lean-to of our emergency supply, running back and forth under an uneasy moon, till the room was overflowing with faggots and logs. Tonight we would have the biggest blaze ever, Mama and I.

By the time I had finished I was quite light-headed, even addressing the still figure on the bed. "There you are, Mama! Enough to set the chimney alight!"

"And everything else . . ." came a voice in my head. "Everything must go with me. . . . Nothing left."

Was that what she wanted? Everything burned? But wasn't that what her people, the Travelers, did? Hadn't she told me once that when a chief died his van was piled with his belongings, his dogs and horses were sacrificed and all consumed in a great pyre? Then if that was what she wanted, that was what she should have.

I approached the bed again. "You shall have a bonfire fit for a queen." I told the silent figure. "They shall not have your bed, your dresses, your chair; I promise."

"Open . . . Fly . . ."

I frowned; what did that little voice mean: *Fly?* What was to fly? There was a moth doing a crazy dance round one of the guttering candles and I moved my hand to bat it away, upon which it swerved over my head and made for the shuttered window, beating frantically against the wood. Then I understood.

"Sorry, Mama . . ."

Ceremoniously I flung back the shutters onto the night, then wedged open the door. Coming back to the bed I blew out the candles, one by one, then knelt to pray. I prayed for a safe journey for my mother's soul, reminding God that her sins were all absolved. Then I leaned over for the last time and kissed her brow.

"All ready, Mama. Go with God." As I did so it seemed a little breeze stirred the hangings, and I distinctly felt a rap on my head—the sort Mama used to make with her knuckles when I had completed a task after a reminder. A moment later the door crashed shut. She had gone.

I refastened door and window, then bethought myself of my own arrangements. If I were to be away from here before they discovered what I had done, then I must pack up all I needed for my journey quickly. Clothes, food, utensils, blanket, money . . . Money. Where had Mama put my dowry? Frantically I searched all the places it could be and came up with nothing. It must be somewhere; Mama wouldn't have made it up. I wished it was light again, for the cottage was full of shadows and every corner looked like a potential hiding place. I must find it, I must! I couldn't face the wide world with the few coins left in Mama's box and the couple the miller had left me.

Opening Mama's box, however, I discovered her bracelets, necklet and brooches, and the horn ring my father had left behind. I took them over to the bed, fastened the brooch and necklet, and then tried to force the ring onto her fingers, one after the other, but it wouldn't go: her fingers were too fat. Strange, she had long, slim fingers. I put on the braclets, deciding I would take the ring with me, wearing it on a string round my neck. It might bring me luck, I thought, and without thinking slipped it onto the middle finger of my right hand, while I bent forward to adjust the bracelets on Mama's wrists to their best advantage.

As I placed her hands once more crossed upon her breast, I noticed something strange; although I was certain I had washed her thoroughly there was what looked like a sooty residue caught under the fingernails of her right hand—All at once I knew where the dowry would be. Rushing over to the fireplace I felt high up in the chimney, first to one side, then the other. At first all I got were scorched fingers and a fall of soot, but at last on the left-hand side my scrabblings found a ledge, and on the ledge a bag of sorts, which I snatched out to drop on the floor with a clink and chink of coin.

I fell to my knees on the hearth and gazed with excitement at the pile of coins that had burst from the split leather pouch that had contained them. I had never seen so much money in my life! And all the coins looked like either silver or gold. . . . All in all, a fortune. Hastily wiping my sooty fingers I began to examine them, one by one. All but two were strange to me, the inscriptions and symbols utterly alien. A scrap of singed paper fluttered to the floor. It was so brittle with age and heat it crumbled to pieces in my fingers even as I read it: "Thomas Fletcher, Mercernairy, his monnaies." There followed a list I could not follow, then "Ayti coyns in all."

So my father had been named, and could write, after a fashion! That surely was where I had got my learning skills. But eighty coins? There were less than half, surely, for even with the confirmation of my tally sticks there were forty-seven missing. I glanced over to the bed where my mother lay in all her finery, extra dresses and shifts spread around her, and my eyes filled with tears, remembering the silver coins and a couple of gold that had purchased them. At the time I had wondered where they had come from, and now I knew. But how was I to know that my father hadn't wished it so? After all, she had been his beloved, and I shouldn't grudge a single coin. Before me lay enough still for a fair dowry, even if the coins would have to be weighed for their metal content only, as they were foreign. But there still a couple of our own coinage: I could manage for a while on those.

Before my eyes the piece of paper crumbled into ash, the pouch also, as if they had been just waiting for me to find them and were now dead like my mother. Carefully I packed the coins inside my waistband purse, determined as soon as possible to make them a separate hiding place.

As I tucked them away I noticed for the first time the ring upon my finger. I couldn't remember putting it there, and absent-mindedly tried to pull it off to tie round my neck, as I had originally intended. But it wouldn't come. There it was, settled snug on my finger as if it was part of the very skin. . . . Suddenly I tingled all over and everything became brighter and sharper, as if a veil had been pulled away.

As if a stranger I saw all the cracks in the wall, the shabbiness of the room; I heard the crack of the fire, the creak of furniture as if it were talking to me; for the first time smelled the sweetish-sickly odor of decay coming from the bed so strongly I had to pinch my nostrils and swallow hard. There was a taste of soot and ashes in my mouth where I had licked my fingers and the hearth beneath my hands was rough with grit and dust.

But there was something else as well. Not exactly hope, that was too strong a word, but a sort of energy I had not known I possessed. Something enforced the knowledge that I was alone for the first time in my life, but also that I would manage somehow or other, that I wasn't a complete idiot, that life held more than I had expected.

I rose to my feet. There were things to be done and as my inside time clock told it was near midnight, the sooner the better. Outside, when I went to check that the goat and chickens would be safe, the moon was riding clear of cloud, the stars were bright and a crispness to the air confirmed frost.

I loaded up the sledge I used for wood with what I thought necessary, did a last check, then piled wood around the bed, sprinkling it with oil the better to burn. I opened the shutters for a draught and left the door open. That done I made a last check, then gazed around the cottage that had been my home, expecting nostalgia.

Nothing. Nothing at all.

It was just a place that two people had lived in, an empty shell with now no personality left. A room, nothing more, as empty of life as the still figure on the bed, the living and memory seeping from it as surely as the body became cold in death. No, there was nothing for me here now.

"Goodbye, Mama," I said, and threw a lighted brand from the fire towards the bed.

Part II

SUMMER'S JOURNEY

5

Someone had opened both shutters and door, and pulled back the bedclothes; the light was shining in my eyes and I was freezing—

I came to with a start. I was in a forest, so had I fallen asleep while collecting wood? Realization came as bitter as the early morning taste in my mouth, as I struggled out of the blanket I had wrapped myself in.

I was in the woods somewhere between the village and the High Road, I was alone, and I was hungry and needed to relieve myself. First things first, and as I squatted down I glanced around the little dell in which I had hidden myself the night before. Last night's frost still silvered the grasses and ferns, but the rising sun promised a warm day. Already a cloud of midges danced above my head and a breeze stirred the almost leafless trees. A pouch-cheeked squirrel darted across the glade ahead, and I could hear the warning chink of a blackbird as I scrambled to my feet. Otherwise everything was quiet, except for the tinkle of a stream away to my right.

So, I hadn't been followed. So far . . .

I cringed when I remembered my escape of the night before. Once I had been sure the cottage was blazing merrily, the flames lighting up the night sky until I feared the conflagration would be spotted in the village, I had set off down the path, dragging the loaded wood sledge behind me. Sighting the way had been easy, with the fire behind and the moon above, so I had not needed my lantern. But where had my caution, my fear of the night, gone? As I remembered it I had strode through the village as if it were a midsummer day, singing some crazy song I couldn't now remember, almost asking those within doors to come out and discover the suddenly-gone-made girl who made the cottage a funeral pyre for both her mama and all those goods that now belonged to someone else, and who was now disregarding the terror of

All Hallows' night and marching down the road with the demons at her heels and the witches swooping around her head.

But no one had appeared. Doors remained bolted and barred, shutters firmly closed. Those who had heard my wild passage had probably hid beneath the bedclothes, crossed themselves and been convinced that at last all their fears walked abroad in ghastly form and that to look on such would snatch what little wits they had away forever. And in the morning, when they saw what remained of the cottage, with luck they might think it had all been a ghastly accident, and that I had been immolated with Mama. Of course, once the embers had cooled down and they could rake through the ashes they would probably realize what I had done and make some sort of search for me—but by that time I hoped to be well away beyond their reach.

My stomach gave a great growling lurch, reminding me it had had nothing since I couldn't remember when. I didn't remember eating a thing last night, so those cheese pasties must have been the last thing to comfort it. I scrabbled among the wreck of my belongings on the sledge—it had tipped over twice last night and scattered everything—and at last found twice-baked bread, cheese and a slice of cold bacon. Washing it down with water from my flask, I refilled the same from the stream nearby, determined next to sort out the things I had brought. But I was still hungry. I couldn't think straight without something else in my stomach. After all, to someone who was used to breaking her fast with gruel, goat's milk, bread and cheese, ham, an egg or two and honey cakes, this morning's scraps were more of an aggravation than a satisfaction.

Searching among the debris I found a heap of honey cakes I had forgotten about. I gobbled down one, two, three. . . . That was enough; I should have to go easy. I couldn't be sure when I would come upon the next village. Well, perhaps just one more: that would leave an even number—easier to count.

Feeling much better, the stiffness of the night nearly gone, I spread out my belongings on the grass. The sledge looked the worse for wear; too late I remembered it was due to be renewed as soon as possible: the carpenter had promised to make new runners. I should just have to hope it would carry my belongings as far as the High Road, then I would have to think again. Even now, there must be at least something I could leave behind the lighten the load.

An axe for chopping wood: I couldn't do without that. Tinder, flint and kindling, also necessary. Lantern, candles, couldn't do without those either. The smallest cooking pot, with a lid that would double as a griddle, a ladle, large knife and small one, spoon, two bowls and a mug. Essentials. Water flask, small jug, blanket, rope, couldn't do without those, either.

Clothes? I was wearing as much as I could, but surely I still needed the two spare shifts, ditto drawers and stockings? My father's comfortable green cloak, pattens for the wet, cloths for my monthly flow, comb, needles, thread and strips of leather for mending clothes and shoes. Packets of dried herbs and spices, seeds for planting when I finally reached my destination—onion, garlic, chive, rosemary, dill, bay, thyme, sage, turnip, marjoram—and a small pestle and mortar.

Which brought me to the food. A small sack of flour—bread to eat if nothing else—a crock of salt, bottle of oil, pot of honey, jar of fat, pack of oats. And for ready consumption two cheeses, a hunk of bacon, two slices of smoked ham, some dried fish, two loaves and twelve honey cakes.

Which left my writing materials, tally sticks and the Boke. Those came with me if nothing else did.

I surveyed the articles laid out on the grass with dismay. There was nothing, absolutely nothing, I could leave behind. Somehow or other I would have to pack them better, and trust the sledge would at least get me as far as the High Road. Then perhaps I could find a lift, or could repair the runners well enough to get me to a village.

The sun was already clear of the trees: I had better get moving. Setting to work I found the packing much easier and the result neater and better balanced, especially when I utilized one of the double panniers I had also dragged along for the eatables, salt and flour, and I reckoned I should get along much faster now.

Perhaps the pannier would be better balanced if I distributed the food more evenly: it must be ten o'clock, and I should travel better with a nibble of something in my stomach. That bread was already stale, so if I ate a crust and a slice of cheese—or two . . .

"Proper little piggy, ain't you?" said a voice.

I whirled around on my knees, sure I had been discovered. But there was no one in sight, the forest was in the same state of suspended alert and there was no sound of footsteps. I decided I must be light-headed and had imagined it. I took another bite of cheese, and—

"Some of us ain't eaten for two days," said the same voice. "Chuck us a bit of rind, and I'll go away. . . ."

Dear God! It must be one of the Little People, of which I had heard from Mama. I crossed myself hastily. What had she said about Them? Mischievous, usually only out at night, not to be crossed lightly. With shaking fingers I cut a piece of rind and threw it as far as I could, then hid my eyes, remembering that They don't like to be looked at either.

"Mmm, not bad at all," said the voice again. A very uneducated voice, I thought, then wondered if They could read minds. "How's about a bite of crust, while we're at it?"

Obediently I threw the crust, and this time there were distinct crunching noises, then silence. I decided I could risk a peep. Surely It had gone. . . .

At first I thought It was an Imp, a black Imp, then I saw that What-ever-it-was had taken the form of a dog. At least I think it was meant to be a dog. I shut my eyes again.

"Garn! I ain't that bad-lookin', surely?"

"Of course not," I said, still with my eyes shut tight. Heaven knows what would happen if I looked at it straight in the eye. "If—if there is nothing else, may I please go my way?"

"I ain't stoppin' you," said the Thing. "Though I thought as how you might like a bit of company, like."

"No thanks," I said hastily. "I'm fine, thanks."

"Pity," said the Thing. "Could be a lot of use to you, I could. Fetch and carry, spot out the way ahead, general guide, guard dog . . ."

"Guard dog?" I said, suddenly suspicious. "You did say 'dog'?"

" 'Course. Don' look like a cat, do I?"

I scrambled to my feet and stared at the apparition. "I've seen you before somewhere. . . ."

" 'Course you have, in the village; seen you a coupla times, too."

I stared across the diplomatic space that still separated us. Of course he was a dog, how had I ever thought otherwise? But dogs don't talk. Especially this one. He resembled nothing so much as a scrap of rug you might leave outside the door to wipe your feet upon. He was like a furry sausage, a black and grey and brown sausage. One ear was up, one down; there was a tail of sorts and presumably mouth and eyes hidden under the tangle of hair at the front. The nose was there and underneath four paws, big ones like paddles, but set under the shortest set of legs imaginable. I remembered now where I had seen him before: chased down the village street by the butcher, those stumpy legs going like a demented centipede.

All right, he wasn't a figment of my imagination and he wasn't one of the Little People, but there was still something wrong. Dogs don't *talk*. . . .

"Where you goin' then?"

"To—to seek a new home. My mother died yesterday."

"Makes two of us—lookin' for somewhere, that is. Never had a place to set down me bum permanent-like. Folks is wary of strays."

Dogs don't talk. . . .

All right, if he wasn't the Devil himself—which was just possible—and he wasn't of Faery stock, then this must be magic. A very powerful magic, too. Surreptiously I first crossed myself again, then made the secular anti-witch sign, the first two fingers of my hand forked. Nothing happened; he still sat there, but now he indulged in a fury of scratching and nipping, then hoofed out both ears with a dreadful, dry, rattling sound.

"Little buggers lively 's mornin'. . . . Tell you what: I'll just come with you as far as the road—that's where you're headed, ain't it? Keep each other company, like."

"No . . . Yes, I don't know. . . ." I said helplessly.

DOGS DON'T TALK!

"Aw, c'mon! What harm can it do? You and I will get along real well, I know we will. 'Tween us we'll make a good team ''

The scream would out. It had been sitting there at the bottom of my throat like a gigantic belch and I could hold it back no longer. It escaped like the tuning wail from a set of bagpipes, only ten times as loud.

"Go away, go away, go away! I can't stand it anymore! Dogs don't talk, *dogs don't talk,* DOGS DON'T TALK!"

And I ran away across the glade, screaming like a banshee, until there was a *thud!* in the middle of my back and I fell face down in a heap of leaves, all the wind knocked out of me.

"Shurrup a minute, will you? Want the whole world to hear? Got hold of the wrong end of the stick, you has. Just sit up nice and quiet-like, and I'll explain. . . ."

I did as I was told, emptying my mouth of leaves and pulling twigs from my hair. The dog sat about six feet away, his head on one side. Close to he was even tattier. I felt like a feather mattress that has been beaten into an entirely different shape.

"Now then you says as how dogs don't talk. Well o' course they does. All the time. Mostly to each other, 'cos you 'umans don't bother to listen. You expects us to learn how you speak, but when we tries you tells us to shut up. Ain't that so?"

I nodded. I had had nothing to do with animals, except the goat, hens and bees—Mama wouldn't have a dog or cat in the house: she said they were messy, full of disease, and took up too much space. Some of the dogs in the village were used for hunting, others as guards, a couple as children's pets, but I had never heard anything from their owners save a sharp word of command, though I had seen kicks and cuffs in plenty. Certainly no one talked to them.

"We don' only talk, we sings, too. P'raps you heard us sometimes o' nights, when the moon is full and the world smells of the chase and we can hear the 'Ounds o' 'Eaven at the 'eels of the 'Unter?"

Indeed I had. Some nights it seemed that the dogs of the village never slept, and even where we lived we could hear the howling and baying and yelping.

"Lovely songs they are too," he said. " 'Anded down from sire to dam, from bitch to pup. . . ."

"But why," I said carefully, "can I now understand what you say?"

"Now, I could spin you a yarn as fine as silk and tell you as 'ow I was the magickest dog in the 'ole wide world, and you'd believe me. For a while, that is, till you found as you could talk with other animals, too. No, I won't tell you no lies, 'cos I believe we got business together, you and I—" He nipped so quickly at whatever was biting him that I jumped. "Got the little bugger. . . . Truth is, lady, that why I can talk to you and you to me is all on account of that there bit o' Unicorn you carries round with you." And he scratched at his left ear, the floppy one, till it rattled like dry beans in a near-empty jar.

I was lost. "Bit of a *Unicorn*?" Unicorns were gone, long ago.

"The ring you wear, you great puddin'! That what you got on that finger of yours. Bit of 'orn off'n a Unicorn, that is. Now you can understand what all the creatures say if'n you pays a bit of attention. Din' you know what you got?"

I sat looking at the curl of horn on my finger in bemusement. It still looked like nothing more than a large nail-paring, almost transparent. I tried to pull it off but it wouldn't budge. Indeed, it now felt like part of my skin. I tried again. "Ouch!"

"Once it's on, it's on," said the dog. "Only come off if'n you don' need it no more, or don' deserve it. Very rare, these days. . . . Come by it legal?"

I nodded, remembering my mother telling me how my father had worn it round his neck. So perhaps he hadn't needed it anymore—or hadn't deserved it. But I wouldn't think about that. Nor that it wouldn't fit my mother. But why me? Perhaps I needed it more than them, specially now I was on my own. Indeed, it had a comforting feel, like something I had been looking for for a long time and had found at last.

"Well," said the dog. "We'd best be goin'. Day ain't gettin' any younger, and we've a ways to travel to the Road."

"I'm not sure I want . . . What I mean, is . . ." However I said it, it was going to sound ungracious, but I had no intention of sharing my dwindling rations with a smelly stray dog with an appetite even bigger than mine.

"Come on, now: you *needs* me. I can be your eyes and ears, I can. Best thief for fifty mile. Nab you a bit o' grub any time; never go 'ungry with me around. 'Sides, I'll be comp'ny, someone to talk to. Nighttimes I'll keep watch, so's you can sleep easy. No one creeps up on me, I can tell you!" He put his head on one side, in what I supposed he thought was an engaging manner. "What d'you say? Give us a trial. We can always part comp'ny if'n it don' work. . . ."

Some of what he said made sense, if he stuck to what he said. And I wouldn't really be any worse off, unless he decamped with all the food. He made it sound, too, as if all the advantages were on my side.

"And just what do you get out of it?"

He hung his head, and I could scarcely hear what he was saying. "P'raps I'm tired o' bein' on me own. P'raps, just for once, I should like to belong. Never had a 'ome, nor one I could call boss." He looked up, and there was a sort of defiant guilt in the one eye I could see. He shook his head as if to free it of water. "Got me whinging like a sentimental pup, you has. C'mon, let's get started; with all that fat you're carryin' it'll take us twice as long. . . . Now what's the matter?"

Just exactly what he had said: that was the matter. The words were carelessly cruel but none the less accurate. He had put into words a fact that everyone—me, my mother, her clients—all knew but never mentioned. The children in the village shouted it out often enough, one of the reasons I hated shopping there, but I could always pretend they were just being malicious. That was one of the reasons the mayor last night would not have accepted me as Mama's replacement; the reason the kind miller had run out of compliments past hair, smile, teeth and the size of my hands and feet.

The fact was I was fat. Not fat, obese. No, admit it: gross. I was a huge lump of grease, wobbling from foot to foot like ill-set aspic. I couldn't see my feet for my stomach, hadn't seen them for years; I had to roll myself in and out of bed, was unable to rise from the floor without first going on hands and knees and grabbing bedpost or chair. I couldn't climb the slightest rise without panting like a heat-hit dog; had lost count of my chins and got sores on my thighs with the flesh rubbing together.

And I had been unable to stop eating, which made it worse. Surprisingly Mama had made no attempt to stop me: she had even encouraged my consumption of honey cakes, fresh bread and cream after that time I had asked her about a prospective husband—

"Missin' your Ma, eh?" said the dog sympathetically. "Understand how you feels; felt the same myself once . . . Are you all right, then?"

We had struggled on for perhaps another half mile when the dog stopped suddenly, his good ear cocked.

"Shurrup, and listen."

Gratefully I put down my burdens. I could hear nothing. Perhaps a kind of rustling and stamping far ahead, a sort of cry . . .

The dog was off through the undergrowth like a flash, his legs a blur of movement. He was gone what seemed like hours, but could only have been a matter of minutes, and arrived back literally dancing with impatience. "C'mon, c'mon! I got us transport!"

"A—a cart? Another sledge?"

"Nah! The real thin'! I got us a 'orse!"

6

That's—that's a horse? You're joking!"

A creature with four legs, sure, head and tail in the right place but the mess in between—was a mess. From what I could see, shading my eyes against the sun, it was swaybacked, gaunt, hollow-necked, filthy dirty and with a hopelessly matted mane and tail.

"Sure it's a 'orse. Got all the essentials. Needs a bit of a wash and brush-up p'raps. . . ."

It would need more than that. As I walked cautiously forward, fearing it might run at the sight of us, I saw that it wasn't going anywhere. It had got itself hopelessly entangled in the undergrowth by bridle, tail, hoof and the remains of a slashed girth and saddlebags that had ended up under its stomach. Its eyes widened with alarm as we approached and it made a token struggle against the bonds that held it, only to become more enmeshed than ever.

I halted a few feet away and spoke soothingly, using the words I had heard the villagers use to their workhorses, for I had never had cause to deal with one before and wasn't quite sure how to begin. The horse showed the whites of its eyes, as well as it could for the sticky tendrils of bindweed that clung to mane and ears.

"Speak to it nicely," said the dog. "Just like you would to me."

"You mean—it can understand me?"

"O-mi-Gawd!" he said. "Din' I tell you about the ring? 'Course it understands, but it's a bit scared right now and may not listen. Nice and easy, now." He walked nearer. "Now stand still, 'Orse, and 'er ladyship 'ere will see to you. . . ."

"Get away, get away! I'll kick you to death—"

"You an' 'oose army?"

I had understood this plainly enough, so I walked up to the horse more confidently and stretched out my hand. It made a halfhearted snap, but seemed quieter, though it still trembled till the branches and twigs which held it fast shook like wind-troubled water.

"Look," I said, "at my finger. I wear the ring of the Unicorn and that means we can understand each other. All I want to do is help. If I release you, will you promise not to run away till we have talked?"

It looked at the ring, at my face, and back at the ring. The shivering stopped, and I gathered it agreed, though I heard nothing definite.

It took a long time, and I was sweating as much as the horse by the time it was released and stood free. I picked away the last of the bramble and bindweed, and tried to comb out the worst tangles from mane and tail with my fingers. Standing free it didn't look much better. There was a long gash across its rump where someone had tried to slash the girths that held the now-empty saddlebags, but these had only loosened, not broken. I slid them up from under the belly and restrapped them.

"There, that's better. . . . Stand still a moment and I'll put some salve on the cut and the graze on your shoulder." In my belongings, dragged along behind as I followed the dog to his " 'orse," was a pot of one of the apothecary's favorite healing balms, a mixture of spiderwebs, dock-leaf juice and boar's grease. I smeared some gently on the broken hide, and found another gash on one hock, which I treated the same way.

"There," I said, standing back. "Near as good as new. . . ."

"I thank you, bearer of the Ring," said the horse. It had a soft, gentle voice, quite unlike the dog's raucous voice. "I am in your debt—"

"Then you can help us carry 'er things," said the dog, who had been remarkably quiet during the last half hour or so, not surprising when I found he was chewing on the rest of the cheese I hadn't packed well enough.

"Thief!"

"There was ants on it . . . All right, all right! Won't do it again. Well, what about it, 'orse? Gonna 'elp?"

The horse glanced from one to the other of us. "I don't know. . . ."

"Of course I can't ask you to help if you belong to someone," I said. "That would be stealing. Is your master hereabouts?"

"All gone, all gone . . ." It started shivering again. "I ran away."

Obviously some disaster. "Calm down! Well, if you don't belong to anyone, what did you plan on doing, boy?"

I was interrupted by a loud snigger from the dog. "Blind as a bat, you is! 'E's a she. . . ."

I felt as though I had been caught in a thicket with my drawers down, and apologized profusely.

"My name is Mistral," said the horse, "and among my own people I am a princess. I wish to go back to where I came from, of course."

Anything less like a princess of anything I had yet to see, but I hadn't had much experience of horses. "And where was that?"

The horse hung her head. "That I do not know. They stole my mother when she had me at her side, and would not leave me to escape. She told me of our people, of how we lived, and of my inheritance. But she died, they killed her with overwork, and I was sold as a packhorse. That was a year, two, ago. All I want now is to find my way back to my people. . . ."

"And you have no idea where that is?"

"No, except that south and west feels right."

"Well," said the dog, "if'n you goes on your own you could be picked up by anyone; best you can get from that is 'eavier burdens or a knock on the 'ead for the glue in your bones and a tough stew or two. Then there's wolves if'n you're thinkin' o' goin' the long way round. Now we offers you a bit o' protection-like, a step or two in the right direction, reg'lar food and all in exchange for carryin' a light load for this lady. What d'you say?"

"And you go south, south and west?"

The dog must have seen my mouth open to say we had decided nothing like that, for he jumped in before I could say anything. " 'Course we is! With winter comin' on, 'oo'd be idiot enough to go north? North there is snow, west there is storms, east there is icy winds, so south we goes. Right, lady?"

Weakly I nodded. Put like that it seemed like the only road to take.

"Right," I said. "And—and if you agree to come with us, then I will care for you as best I can and try and put you on the right road for your home. Is that fair?"

"Without you I should probably have starved to death, or worse," said Mistral. "I accept. And now, perhaps, we should load up. The sun starts to go down."

Indeed it was well past its zenith. Hastily I started to pack our belongings on the horse, only to be brought up short by her patient explanation of weight distribution, top-heavy loads, etc., so the light was already reddening as we set off. Even then she seemed curiously reluctant to go the way I wanted, the way the dog assured me led straight to the High Road.

"We'll have to go past *there*," she said. *"There,* where it happened."

"Where what happened?"

"Yesterday . . . sun-downing. Men, horses, swords. Panic, fighting, blood . . . No, I can't go that way again!"

"Windy," muttered the dog.

"They came out of the trees, the sun behind them. Couldn't see . . . Noise and pain. I ran this way. . . ." Indeed I could see we were now following the road she must have taken: branches broken, shrubs torn by her wild progress, grass trampled and leaves scattered.

"Look," I said. "Whatever happened, happened yesterday. It sounds as though it was an ambush, but they will all have gone by now. It's perfectly safe, I promise. . . . Go forward, dog, and reconnoiter."

"You what?"

I explained, and he ran on ahead. The ground started to slope downwards towards a little dell and Mistral was breathing anxiously.

"Down there . . ." she whispered.

The dog came running back, his tail between his legs. "You ain't goin' to like this, lady: 'old your nose. . . ."

But I could already smell the stench of death, and hear a great buzzing of flies, the flap of carrion crow. There were four of them, lying sprawled in the random carelessness of sudden death, naked except for their braies. Their eyes had already gone, and the crows rose heavily gorged, the men's wounds torn still further by cruel beaks. I shouted and ran at the birds till they flapped to the nearest tree; they would be back, and there was nothing I could do about the clouds of flies, the ants, the beetles. I moved among the corpses, holding my nose, but there was nothing to say who they were, where they had come from, save a scrap of torn pennant under one twisted leg—

My heart gave a sudden, sickening lurch. Staring at the scrap of silk I suddenly recalled what I had completely forgotten until this moment: a tall, beautiful knight on a huge horse, who had smiled a heart-catching smile and called me "pretty." So much had happened since that encounter that he had not crossed my mind again—until this bitter moment. And I had sent him down this road. . . . No, no, it couldn't be! Life couldn't be that cruel!

Frantically I ran among the corpses in the dell, no longer squeamish, turning the lolling heads from side to side, seeking my knight. One head, already severed from the body, came easily to my hand, and I was left holding something that was shaped and heavy as a cabbage, but crawling with maggots. . . .

He wasn't there, he wasn't there! I ran up from the dell, farther into the forest, but there was no other stink of death, nor flies, nor carrion. I ran back to the horse, Mistral.

"What happened to him, where is he? Where is your master, Sir— Sir . . ." But I had forgotten his name.

"Who? What man?"

"He was a knight and rode a black horse—you must remember!"

"They killed the men and took the horses and the baggage. I ran away. That's all I know."

"All of them?"

"I don't know. I only saw my corner of it."

Maybe they had taken him for ransom. Perhaps they had ridden him away into the forest on his fine black horse, to bargain with his folks for far more than the horses and baggage they had stolen—I held the tattered piece of blue silk in my hand and prayed for his safety.

The dog nudged my knee. "Better find a place to kip for the night soon: near sundown."

I gestured towards the bodies. "We can't just leave them like this. . . ."

"You gotta spade and a coupla hours? No. Don't worry 'bout them. This track is used by those in the village; they'll deal with the remains. Bury them the way you 'umans do things. To my way o' thinkin', better leave bodies to the birds and foxes to pick clean."

I muttered a prayer, crossed myself. "Right: lead on, dog."

About a half-mile farther along, as it grew too dark to see underfoot and my feet felt swollen to twice their usual size with the unaccustomed walking, the trees suddenly thinned and we found ourselves at the top of a steep bank. The moon rode out from behind some scummy clouds and there beneath us was a luminous strip of roadway, wide enough for six horsemen to ride abreast.

"Is that it?"

"Well, it's a road," said the dog. "Give or take . . ."

"It runs north/south," said Mistral.

"Come on, then," and in my eagerness I started to slide down the bank towards the shining expanse.

"Not so fast, lady," said the dog behind me. "You doesn't travel a road like this at night—"

"Scared?" and I slid down to the bottom, giving my right ankle a nasty jar, but determined to continue our journey now we had found what we were looking for.

"—'cos it's too dark to see," continued the dog, as the moon disappeared again.

"Neither do you travel alone," said Mistral. "There is safety in numbers. Look what happened to me."

A night-jar churred above my head and I lost one of my shoes in the scramble back. The dog retrieved it for me, all slathery from his mouth.

Scrabbling around in the dark, for I was now afraid of the risk of a lantern, I found the ham and the rest of the honey cakes, sharing a third, two-thirds with the dog. Afterwards, snugged down in my blanket, I listened to Mistral cropping the grass, sounding in the night like the tearing of strips of linen, and felt strangely comforted by the proximity of the two animals, even though the promised guard-dog, alert to every danger, the one who had promised to stay awake so I could sleep easy, was snoring heavily long before I closed my eyes.

I woke early and now that we had reached the road I was eager to be on my way. Not only impatience but also the knowledge that we were still within a half-day's travel of the village by foot, and those on horseback could travel much faster. I had no intention of being called to account for burning down the cottage and everything in it, and at mention of the villagers' possible vengeance the dog, too, looked thoughtful, then volunteered to scout out the road beneath us.

He was gone some twenty minutes, and arrived back to announce that all was clear as far as eyesight.

"Been a group of people past in the last twenty-four hours," he reported. "Mule turds, dried piss. Doubt if there'll be others on the road today."

I decided we'd risk it, and the sooner we were away the better. A quick snack of cheese for the dog and me and we all scrambled down the bank and onto the road.

My memory of the highway from the night before had been of a broad ghostly ribbon winding away smoothly into the distance, but the reality was far different. The surface was stony and uneven, marred by wheel-ruts and loose flints big enough to turn one's ankle, and it twisted and turned like a pig's tail, to follow the contours of the land. Nor was it the same width all the way. Sometimes it narrowed to pass through a gully or across a bridge, like the one that spanned the river that flowed away from our village; at other places it widened or split in two where the ground was obviously boggy after rain.

After an hour of this I felt I had had enough, even though Mistral matched her pace to my waddle—the dog scurried about like an agitated beetle, up and down, back and forth, till it made me dizzy to watch him—and I called a halt. The sun was shining in my eyes, sweat running into my eyes until they stung; my feet were swollen, my thighs sore with rubbing together and my stomach was howling-empty.

But unpacking the food gave me a shock. I hadn't realized how much I—we, I thought, scowling at the dog—had consumed. All that was left that didn't need cooking was a rind of cheese, a slice of cold bacon and one squashed honey cake. I threw the rind to the dog and ate what was left almost as quickly, while Mistral munched philosophically among the scrub at the side of the road, lipping at leaves I wouldn't have thought edible. Obviously her wasted look was partly due to starvation.

The dog, too, found something edible: he crawled out from under a bush crunching on an enormous stag beetle. I felt sick.

"Better get goin' " he said. "Only done a coupla miles . . ."

"Oh, do stop grouching!" I cried in exasperation, all the more annoyed because I knew he was right. "Grumble and grouch and eat, that's all you do all day! Matter of fact, that's what I'll call you from now on: 'Growch'! So there . . ."

He spat out stag-beetle bits, then hoofed his right ear and inspected the results. "Never had a name before," he said. "Thanks." He tried it out. "Growch, Growch, Growch . . . Not bad."

And I immediately felt mean: how would I have felt if I had been christened "Grumble?" Even though "Somerdai" was odd, it had nice connotations. But the dog seemed happy enough; I think he liked the subdued barking noise his name made.

We progressed better for the next hour or so, heartened by the various pieces of evidence that others had traversed this way earlier—a scrap of cloth, more droppings, a midday cooking fire. I began to feel much better, as if a great load had left my mind. I was no longer confined by routine, everything was new and exciting and different. All I encountered from now on would be fresh to my senses and would have to be dealt with by me alone, no one to tell me what to do. In a way daunting, in another exciting. I hoped I was equal to the challenge. But why not? With my education and God's help even I could have a stab at Life. True, not everything was on my side, and I now had the added responsibilities of the horse and the dog, but the former at least was more of a help than a hindrance.

So it was with a sense of lively anticipation that we topped a rise shortly after midday to see, spread beneath us, a huddle of roofs that meant safety and food. The air was still, and the northerly drift of house fires stained the deep blue sky like snarls of sheep's wool caught in a hedge.

I forgot my discomforts and hunger as we wound our way down into the valley beneath, and even though the journey was longer than I thought, due to the bafflement of distance in the clear air and the twists of the road, it was not much after two in the afternoon by the time we reached the outskirts of the sizable village. It must, I calculated, hold at least five times as many people as ours, if not more. Even without my tally-sticks that would mean well over a thousand: more people than I had ever seen in my life!

I stopped to enquire if a caravan of people had passed by of the first person I saw, an old crone catching the last of the sun outside her hovel.

"Went this way yesterday and on again this morning. Left the blind idiot behind."

My heart sank. The sun was now dipping away behind the hills to our right and there was no way we could hope to catch them up. That would mean we should have to shelter here for the night and think again in the morning. I asked if there was a traveler's rest place.

"Not as such. Ask at the inn down the road for stable space."

We trudged down the main street till we came to the tavern she had indicated, a mean-looking place with a tattered bunch of hops hanging over the doorway. I was not reassured by the surly landlord telling me he was short on both food and ale.

"Blame them as came through yesterday," he said brusquely. "More'n usual for this time o' year. Can do you a stew tonight and there's space in the stable out back."

"How much?"

He named an outrageous price, but Mama had taught me how to bargain and the matter was settled for a couple of coins. I begged a crust of bread in anticipation of the stew, which I shared with Growch, then bedded Mistral down in the dilapidated stable, collecting together some stray wisps of hay for her. Growch I left on guard, mindful of the packs I had stored away under the manger. I reckoned the threat of a horse's kick and a dog's bite would be enough to deter even the landlord or his wife, were they inquisitive enough to try and inspect my belongings.

I decided to take a walk through the village while it was still light. In the distance, from the direction of the church tower, came shouts of merriment and I made my way in that direction. Turning a corner I saw that the space in front of the church was crammed with people all apparently enjoying themselves heartily. Children were screaming and running about, playing tag, and over to my left folk were dancing to the strains of a bagpipe.

I caught the sleeve of a woman passing by with her friends. "Is it a festival? A Saint's Day?"

She stared at me and shrugged. "Not as I know. We just come to see the fun. Got a blind idiot in the stocks over there, been pelting 'im all day. Come night we drums 'im outa town, as the rules say."

I knew these "rules." Anyone liable to be a burden on the parish was got ride of, quick. I remembered what the old crone had said.

"Is this the man that was picked up on the road by the caravan yesterday?"

"The same. Now, if'n you'll 'scuse me . . ."

I peered over shoulders in the direction the woman went, but was too short. Might as well see what was going on. We had the small-brained in our village, more than one, but people were generally kind enough to them. After all they were part of the community, somebody's relatives. Of course the worst ones got smothered at birth. This one must be something special.

Using my elbows I squirmed through for a better view. A few minutes later I was at the front, staring at the pathetic figure dropping over the stocks. He was naked except for a short pair of braies, and his hair and body were matted with filth.

Someone picked up a rotten apple, obviously used before for target practice, and chucked it, but it fell short.

I stared hard at the pilloried man. There was something familiar about that tall figure. But what did some disreputable blind idiot in the stocks of an out-of-the-way village have to do with me? I edged nearer: now I was only a couple of feet away. Look up, I begged him silently; let me see your face. . . .

I found I was twisting the horn ring on my finger, unreasonably agitated, as if something unexpected was about to happen.

And then it did.

Someone threw a stone which struck the man in the stocks a painful blow on the shoulder and he lifted his head and howled like a dog at his tormentors.

"Leave me alone! What have I done to you that you should torture me like this?"

My gasp of horror and recognition was lost in the jeers and catcalls of the crowd. How could I have been so blind? That filthy, disheveled, near-naked creature in the stocks had been wearing silks and riding a tall black horse the last time I had seen him.

It was my beautiful knight, Sir Gilman!

7

Horror, exultation, anxiety: all three emotions chased through my mind at the same time. Horror at his condition, exultation at his survival of the ambush, anxiety as to how I was to get him out of this terrible mess. Indulge in the other two later, I told myself: concentrate on the last. Come on, now: it's up to you. No one else can save him. You fell in love with him at first sight, remember? You never believed you would see him again, he was just someone to fantasize about. Well, here he is, just like all the stories you used to tell yourself. In those stories you got your hero out of the most impossible situations: what would your heroine do to save him?

I rushed to the foot of the platform on which stood the pillory and shouted up at him: "Sir Gilman! Sir Gilman? Can you hear me?"

But his face, bespattered with grime and with a two-day growth of beard, showed no recognition, his blue eyes staring past my right shoulder.

Behind me I heard ribald comments, requests to move myself, but my whole being was concentrated on the figure before me. I noticed a huge bruise on his right temple, extending from his hairline right down to his eyebrow; it was a livid, raised purplish-blue, and I recalled what they had said of him: "Blind idiot." Had the blow to his head robbed him both of his sight and his wits? I tried his name again, but there was no reaction.

"Move aht the way, yer silly cow!"

"Shift yer fat arse, and let's get a sight o' the action!"

A hand grasped my arm. A stout man with a colored sash round his waist frowned down at me. "Now then, lass . . ."

I twisted the ring on my finger in my agitation, opened my mouth to say something, but found I was speaking words out of the air instead.

"Are you in charge of—of this travesty, sir?"

"I'm the bailiff, yes, but—"

"Then kindly release my brother at once!" Now I knew what to say, what to do; it was just like my stories. I jingled the few coins in my purse. "I have been seeking him three days now. I am sorry if he has been a nuisance, but . . ." and I tapped my forehead significantly. "You know how it is."

He nodded. "And you come from . . . ?"

I mentioned the name of our village and even spoke the first deliberate lie of my life. "Of course, the mayor, our cousin, has been worried sick! He has always been very fond of—of er, Gill, and even lent me his horse to seek him out, and I have bespoke stabling for us all tonight at the 'Jumping Stag' down the road. . . . And now, if you would please release him, I promise to be responsible for the silly boy!" and I pressed a couple of coins into his hand.

He glanced at me keenly out of eyes like currants, pocketed the coins, and turned to address the restless crowd.

"Listen here, my friends . . ." and as he spoke I climbed up to the pillory and whispered in Sir Gilman's ear.

"Don't fret! I've got you out of this and we'll sort things out in the morning. . . ." I didn't want him disclaiming all knowledge of me.

He swung his confined head in my direction. "Who am I!"

"I know who you are, but you must be patient. Say nothing, just take my hand when you are free, and I will lead you to safety."

The bailiff took keys from his pocket and I led my knight down from the platform and through a clearly discontented crowd, already armed with sticks and stones to drive him out of town. These expulsions often meant the death of the victim, I knew that; I also knew that the bailiff believed little, if any, of my story. Still he had the coins in his pockets and it was too late to send a horseman to the village to check tonight. Tomorrow I determined to be away at dawn.

I led Sir Gilman through darkening streets to the stables behind the inn, lucky to be unfollowed.

"What the 'ell's that?" said Growch.

But Mistral recognized him and crowded back in her stall. "He brings danger! He led the others—"

"Rubbish! He's in need of care and attention. He's no threat to anyone. Just stay quiet while I see to him."

I went to the inn and begged a bucket of washing water, but had to part with another small coin. I gave my knight a strip wash, even taking off his braies to rinse them out, and he stood quiet as a felled ox, even when I rinsed his private parts, which I noted were ample. But Mama had always said that the criterion was less in inches than in the performance.

Apart from his trousers he wore a pair of tattered boots, and that was all. I should have to make him something to wear, but in the interim I put my father's green cloak over his shivers and went to fetch the promised stew and a helping of bread. It was tasteless and stringy, but I added salt and a sprinkle of dried parsley and thyme to make it edible. I fed him with soaked bread until he pushed aside my hand and said: "Enough."

That was the first word he had spoken since his release, but as if a dam had been broken he now started with how's and why's and when's until I shushed him. "Enough for now. It's night and you should sleep. Rest easy. Does your head still hurt?"

"Very much. What happened to it?"

"I told you: in the morning. Lie still, and I'll put salve on it and give you a sleeping draught," remembering of a sudden the vial of poppy juice I had brought with me.

I led him out to piss against the wall, but two minutes later, after I had tucked him up in the straw, he was snoring happily. I fended off questions from the others, merely asking the more reliable of them to wake me at false dawn. That done, the rest of the stew shared between Growch and myself and a few strands more of hay scrounged for Mistral, I lit my lantern and settled down with scissors, needle and thread to turn the better of the two blankets into a tunic for my knight.

A round cut-out for the neck, plus a strip cut down the front for ease of donning; seams sewn down the sides, with plenty of room for arms; laces threaded through holes in the neckline and rope bound into an eye at one end, knotted and frayed at the other for a belt . . .

I opened my eyes, lantern guttered, stiff and sore, to find Mistral nudging me.

"An hour before dawning . . ."

We crept through the outskirts of the village till we found the road south and once out of sight of the village I cut an ash-plant stave from the roadside, thrust it into my knight's right hand, put his left on Mistral's crupper, and determined to put as many miles as I could between us and possible questions or pursuit.

We made about four miles before a growling stomach, the proximity of a nearby stream and the knight's questions decided me it was time to break our fast. As the thin flames flared beneath the cooking pot and the gruel thickened around my spoon, I answered Sir Gilman's questions as best I could. His name and station, the ambush, his blow on the head, that was all I really knew. And he knew no more. Even what I told him raised his eyebrows. "You are sure?"

I reassured him, but did not remind him of our meeting in the forest the day before, lest he remember a hideous fat girl he had courteously called "pretty." . . . Indeed, I was careful to avoid any physical contact except by hand or arm, so that he wouldn't guess at my bulk.

After I had explained twice all that I knew of his circumstances he was silent for a moment or two, spooning down his gruel which I had sweetened with a little honey.

"So I am a knight. But of what use is my knighthood without sight or memory? Where can I go? What can I do? How can I manage without my horse, my sword and armor, money? How do I even know which road to take?" He flung the bowl and spoon away and buried his face in his arms. I longed to put my arms about him, to thrill to the feel of his helplessness, but I knew better than to try. Instead I went over to Mistral and talked quietly to her.

"All I know is this," she said slowly in answer to my questions. "I was hired as a packhorse to carry his armor—and heavy it was. This was in a town many miles north of here. In winter it was very cold in that town, and the people's talk was heavy and thick, not like yours or his. When he set off he said farewell with much of your human embraces and tears with a young woman who seemed reluctant to let him go. Since then we have traveled south by west, and I gather there were many more miles to go. That is all I know."

"Who are you talking to?"

"No one, Sir Knight," I said hurriedly. "I was thinking aloud."

"And what conclusion have you come to?" he said sarcastically. "I for one am tired of walking in this stupid manner and eating food for pigs. I demand you take me to someone in authority and see that I am escorted—taken . . . That I am properly cared for till I regain my memory, and can return to my home. Wherever that is . . ."

He was being rather tiresome. After his experiences of the last few days, how on earth did he think that anyone would believe his story, even with my word as well? Folk would think we were trying it on. If he could have remembered where he came from, even, it would have been a simple matter of sending a messenger to his home, requesting assistance, and then waiting a week or so for grateful parents or family to rescue him. As it was, he was lucky to be still alive. Patiently I tried to explain this to him, but he was not in a receptive mood.

"Still," he said magnanimously, "I am grateful for your help, girl.

You know my name: what's yours? And why are you here? Where is *your* home?"

What a wonderful tale I told! The only really true fact was my name. He learned of loving parents dying of fever, leaving their only child with a huge dowry, traveling south to find her betrothed—

"But why did you not wait till he could send for you?" he asked reasonably.

"Ah," I said, thinking rapidly. "The fact is, my parents did not entirely trust his family, although they paid over the dowry. They said, before they died—" I crossed myself for the lie: he could not see me. "—that it were better I arrive unannounced. Then they could not turn me away."

"Sounds chancy to me. Which way do you go?"

"I was just coming to that," thinking again as fast as light. "I am not in any hurry to reach my new home, so I thought we might try and find where you live first. You were traveling south, so why don't we both go that way and hope you recover your memory on the journey? I have very little money, but we'll manage—if you don't expect too many comforts. As for walking—it will do you good, help you recover. What do you say?"

"It seems I have little choice." He still sounded resentful. "But you will promise to speed my return when I regain my memory?" He sounded so sure.

"Of course! But in the meantime . . ." I could see so many problems ahead if we continued as we were. "It would seem strange if we travel together and I address you as a knight and no relation. We may have to share accommodations, so I think it best—until you regain your memory—if we pretended we were brother and sister, traveling south to seek a cure for your blindness. If you didn't mind I could call you Gill and you can call me Summer. . . . No disrespect intended, of course."

He sighed heavily. "Again I see no help for it. All right—Summer," and he suddenly smiled that heart-catching smile that had me emotionally groveling immediately. "Any more pig food? A drop more honey this time, please. . . ."

That night we were dry and cozy enough in a small copse off the road, with the slices of ham fried with an onion and oatcakes, but in the morning as I prepared gruel again, I had an argument with Growch. This precipitated another confrontation with Sir Gilman—Gill, as I must remember to call him. It still seemed disrespectful.

Growch:—"Is that all, then?"

Me:—"You've had as much as anyone else."

Growch:—"Gruel don't go far. . . ."

Me:—"We've all had the same."

Growch:—" 'E's 'ad more'n me. . . ."

Me:—"He's a man. He needs more."

Growch:—"You gave 'im some o' yours; I saw you."

Me:—"So what? I wasn't very hungry."

Growch:—"Favoritism, that's what it is. Ever since 'e joined us you been 'anging round 'is neck like 'e was the Queen o' Sheba, 'stead o' a bloody hencumbrance. Don't know what you sees in 'im. Can't see a bloody thing; can't hunt, can't keep watch, all the time—"

Me:—"Shut up! Otherwise no dinner . . . Go and catch another beetle."

"You're doing it again," said Sir—said Gill, irritably.

"What?"

"Talking to yourself." I loved the way he spoke, with an imperious lilt to his voice—I must practice the way he pronounced things—but I wasn't too keen on some of the things he said, especially when I had to explain something awkward, like now.

I decided the truth was best. Some of it, anyway; he didn't look the sort of man to believe in magic rings, unicorns and such.

He wasn't. "What you're telling me, Winter—sorry, Summer—is that you possess a ring your father gave you that enables you to understand what the beasts of the field say?"

I nodded, then remembered he couldn't see. "Yes, more or less. It heightens my perceptions."

"What utter rubbish! There are no such things as magic rings, and as for conversing with animals . . . Does not religion teach that animals are lower creatures, fit only to fetch and carry, guard, or hunt and kill?"

I didn't think so. What did religion have to do with it anyway? I knew that Jesus had shown his friends where to fish, and had ridden on a donkey into Jerusalem but I didn't remember him talking about hunting and killing. And hadn't he somewhere rebuked one of his followers for holding his nose against the stink of a dead dog in the gutter, and said something like: "But pearls cannot equal the whiteness of its teeth"? It showed He noticed things, anyway.

But Gill hadn't finished. "I'm surprised you should try and deceive me in this way! I had thought you to be an intelligent girl, but now you're talking like a superstitious village chit!"

He was so persuasive that for a moment I began to doubt the ring, my own powers. Had I made up what Growch and Mistral said to me, a mere delusion bred of my loneliness and anxiety? I glanced down at the ring to make sure it still existed, and found it no longer a thin curl of horn but rather a sparkling bandeau, glittering like limestone after a shower of rain.

"Whats 'e on about?" asked Growch. I opened my mouth, but daren't speak back. The dog cocked his head on one side. "Like that, is it? Don't 'eed 'im. "E'll get used to the idea. You can think-talk, you know, long as you keeps it clear. Easier for us, too. Try it: tell me to do somethin' in your mind," and after I had successfully demonstrated that Growch would turn a circle and Mistral nod her head up and down, I felt much better.

I remembered something my mother had once said: "Don't expect them (men) to have any imagination, except what they carry between their legs. Don't forget, either, that they are always right; even if they swear black's white, just agree with them. No point in aggravation . . ."

This exchange had only taken a few moments—that was another thing: this communication by mind was much quicker than speech—and I was able to answer Gill almost immediately. "You are quite right, of course; and yet . . ."

"What?"

"Would you not call the commands you teach your dogs, horses and falcons a sort of magic?"

"Certainly not! Their response is limited to their intelligence. And they are our servants, not our friends and equals."

He really could be rather stuffy at times, but I had only to gaze across at him to renew my adulation. Torn and bruised he might be, my beautiful knight, with a three-day growth of beard and blind to boot, but he was all my dreams rolled into one. Nay, more: for what dreams could have prepared me for the reality! And the very best thing of all was that he was so helpless he needed me, fat, plain Summer, to tend him. And he couldn't see my blemishes; that was perhaps even better. To him I was just a voice, a pair of hands, and I could indulge my adoration unseen. It was just as if Heaven had fallen straight into my lap. All I could further hope was that it would be a long time before he regained his memory. In the meantime he was mine, mine, *mine!*

By midday we had made eight or ten miles and it started to cloud over. It had been gruel again for lunch, there was nothing else, and I was eager to press forward, especially as Growch's nose told him of smoke ahead, borne tantalizingly on the freshening breeze. Gill grumbled constantly and the weather worsened, so it was with a real sense of relief that we glimpsed the roofs of a village away on a side road to our right. I had given up hope of catching the caravan ahead of us, and was now resigned to spending the night in a stable. Money wasted, but at least we could stock up on provisions, even if it meant breaking into my dowry money. Needs must, and I thought I could recall at least two coins of our denominations.

We still had a couple of miles to go when it started to rain, hard. Leaning into the wind, my cloak soaked, my feet slipping and sliding in the mud, dragging behind me a reluctant knight and complaining animals, I had to think quite hard about my blessings. But then, in which of the stories I remembered did the heroine have it all her own way? On the other hand, reading and hearing of privations was quite different from enduring them.

Three quarters of an hour later the animals were rubbed down and fed, dry in a warm stable, and my "brother" and I were ensconced in front of a roaring fire, our cloaks steaming on hooks, our mouths full of lamb stew and mulled ale. I wanted nothing more than to nod off with the warmth and the food in my belly, but there were things to be done. Upon enquiry I found a cobbler and leather worker and a barber, and by suppertime Gill was washed, shaved, trimmed, and had mended boots, a leather jerkin and woolen hose, and we had paid for our food and lodging in the stable. That took care of the silver coin in my father's dowry, which left only the gold one of our coinage. The others were all strange to me, though mainly gold. These I would keep untouched, for unless I could find an honest money changer, as rare as bird's teeth, they would have to be handed over to my future husband intact. If I chose a sensible man, he would know what to do with them.

And when would I find this husband of mine, I wondered, as I lay quiet on my heap of straw, listening to the gentle snores of Gill and the snorting of Growch, who seemed to hunt fleas even in his sleep. When I had left home my plan had been to join a caravan, travel to the nearest large town, engage the services of a marriage broker and be wed by Christmas. Now I was promised to the service of a man who had lost his memory, had pledged assistance to a horse who had forgotten where she came from, and was lumbered with a dog nobody wanted—and they had preference over my plans, I realized. I was beginning to understand the meaning of the word "responsibility."

The weather had cleared by morning. By diligent enquiry I found that the larger caravans of travelers came past about once a week in either direction during the summer months, but far more rarely during autumn, scarcely ever in winter. The one we were pursuing hadn't stopped at the village, and I realized now that they had a two-day start and we should probably never catch them up. The nearest town, we were informed, was two days travel south—nearer three for us, I thought—but I wasn't going to waste money waiting for the next party of travelers or pilgrims. We had been safe from surprise on the road so far, and with Growch and Mistral as lookouts we could probably make it as far as the next town, where three roads met: a better chance to find traveling company.

But first I had to change my gold coin to buy provisions, and I knew it was a mistake as soon as I handed it over at the butcher's in exchange for bacon and bones for stew. He took the coin from me as though it were fairy gold, liable to disappear at any moment. He held it up to the light, turned it over and over, tested it on tongue and teeth, showed it to the other customers, then called his wife to a whispered conference.

Apparently satisfied it was real, he turned suspicious again and demanded to know where I had got it, implying with his look that no one as tatty-looking as I was could possibly have come by it honestly.

The real story was so preposterous—renegade father, a dowry of strange coins found stuffed up a chimney just before I sent my Mama's body up in flames and fled—that I realized I should have to make something up, and could have kicked myself for not thinking it out earlier. Embarrassed, unused to lying, I foundered.

"It's . . . it's . . ." In my distress I found I was twisting the ring on my finger and all at once, so it seemed, a story came out pat.

"It is a confidential matter," I said glibly, "but I am sure there is no good reason why I should not tell you." I looked around: the place was filling rapidly, and even the local priest had turned up. "My brother is blind, but he heard of the shrine of St. Eleutheria where it seems miracles have occurred, and there was nothing for it but that he must travel there. My father wished him to travel in comfort of course, with a proper escort, but my brother insisted it must be a proper pilgrimage, each inch on foot, dressed poorly and eating the meanest viands on the way." I smiled at the priest. "You will agree, good Father, that this shows true religious intent?" The priest nodded, and I could see him trying the obscure saint's name on his tongue: I hoped it was right.

"As the youngest daughter," I continued, marveling at when I was ever going to find the time to confess all my duplicity, "it was decided I should accompany him to find the way. But my father was determined we should not want on the way, whatever my brother said, so he gave me a secret hoard of coin to smooth our passage. But no one must tell my brother," I said, gazing round at the assembled company in entreaty.

"It would distress him to think we could not manage on the few copper coins he holds. . . ."

The priest gave us his seal of approval. "I shall pray for you both, my child," he said solemnly. "Take good care of the change: we are good, honest people here, but farther abroad . . ." and he shook his head.

After a deal of counting and re-counting I pocketed a great deal of coin, more than I had ever handled before, and made sure to give the priest a couple of small coins for prayers. On to the vegetable stall for onions, turnip, winter cabbage; the merchant for more oil, the miller's for flour and oats and a small sack to carry everything in, and lastly the baker's for a loaf and two pies for the day's food. The cheese at the inn was of excellent quality so I bought a half there, then had to shuffle all round to get it packed tidily on Mistral's back.

Everywhere I went in the village I found my invented tale had preceded me, and folks nudged each other and nodded and smiled as I went past. It seemed everyone came to see us off, just as if we were a royal procession. Quite embarrassing, really, especially as I couldn't explain to Gill what all the fuss was about.

We made reasonable progress, stopping a little later than usual for our pies and bread and cheese. I had indulged in a couple of flasks of indifferent wine, but it was warming and stimulating, so that when we resumed I endured the discomfort of a blister long after it would have been prudent to stop, so that when it finally burst I found I could hardly walk. Cursing my stupidity I unpacked salve and was just applying it when both Growch and Mistral pricked up their ears.

"Someone coming," said Growch.

I was ready to pull off the road and hide, but Mistral reassured me. "Cart, single horse, coming fast so either empty or certainly holding only one man . . ."

By the time I had put on my shoe again I could hear it too, and after a minute or two a simple two-wheeled cart came into view, carrying a few hides. The driver pulled up beside us.

"Got problems?" he asked.

I recognized him as one of the men from the village. He had been in the butcher's when I was trying to change the gold coin, and afterwards I had seen him outside the inn just before we set off. He had a cheerful open face, a smile which revealed broken teeth and eyes as round and black as bilberries. I remembered what the priest had said about the villagers being honest, and smiled back.

"Not really," I said. "We're slowed down a bit because I've blistered my heel."

"Well now," he said, "seems as I came by just when needed! Couldn't ha' timed it better, now could I? We'll all get along fine if you an he"—he nodded at the knight—"Just hops aboard the back o' the cart and you ties your horse to the tailgate. That way we'll reach my cousin's afore nightfall. He's got a small cottage on the edge of the woods a few miles on, and he'll welcome company overnight. By tomorrow you'll be in easy reach of the next town. That suit you?"

It suited me fine. The heavy horse he drove seemed more than capable of taking our extra weight—after all the cart was nearly empty—so I tied Mistral securely to the back and guided Gil to sit so that his long legs dangled free of the road, then pulled myself up beside him.

It was sheer bliss to be riding instead of walking, and the countryside seemed to slip by with satisfying speed. The only complaints came from Growch, and after I saw how fast those little legs of his were working, trying to keep up, I leaned down and hauled him up by the scruff of the neck and sat him beside us.

I relaxed for what seemed the first time in days. Soon, with the sun already dipping red towards the low hills to the west, we should be snug in some cottage for the night, with perhaps a spoonful or two of stew to warm our bellies.

The driver pulled to a halt, and skipped down to relieve himself. "Best do the same yourselves," he said cheerily. "Last stop before my cousin's. I'll help your brother, lass, and you disappear in them bushes."

I needed no encouragement: I had been really uncomfortable with the jolting of the cart over the last mile or so. I clambered down and looked about me. The road was deserted and the land lay flat and featureless, except for a dark mass of forest a couple of miles or so ahead. The nearest shrubs were a little way off, and as I trotted towards them the ring on my finger started to itch: I must have caught one of Growch's fleas or touched a nettle.

Squatting down in blissful privacy I looked up as a flock of starlings clattered away above my head, bound for roosts in the woods. It was suddenly cold as the sun disappeared: even my bum felt the difference as the night wind stirred the grasses around me and I stood up hastily and pulled up my drawers.

Suddenly there was a shout from the direction of the roadway, a clatter of hooves, frantic barking and the creak of wheels. Whatever had happened? Had we been attacked? Had the horse bolted? Had my beloved Gill been abducted? Hurrying as fast as I could, all caution forgotten in my anxiety, I tripped over a root and fell flat on my face. Struggling to rise I was immediately downed again by a hysterical dog.

"C'mon, c'mon, c'mon!"

"What's happened?"

"Come-'n'-see, come-'n'-see, come-'n'-*see*!" was all I could get out of him.

"I'm coming!" I yelled back at him, skirt torn, face all muddy, shaking like a leaf. "Get out of the *way*!"

The first thing I saw as I arrived at the roadside were the long legs of Gill waving from the ditch as he tried frantically to right himself. I rushed forwards and grabbed an arm, a hand, and by dint of pulling and tugging till I was breathless, managed to get him back on his feet again, spluttering and cursing.

"Are you all right?"

"No thanks to that cursed carter! Just wait till I see him again—till I get hold of him," he amended.

"The carter? Oh, my God! Where is he?"

"Gone," said Growch, back to normal, his voice full of gloom. "Gone and the horse and all our food with 'im. Waited till you went behind those bushes then tipped your fancy-boy into the ditch. Chucked a stone at me and was off down the road like a rat up a drain. Got a nip at 'is ankle, though," he added more cheerfully. "Now what we goin' to do?"

8

What, indeed! As for this "we," it was down to me really, wasn't it? So, I could cry, scream, yell, kick the dog, run off down the road in vain pursuit. I could refuse to go any further, abandon both my knight and the dog, do my own thing. I could tear my hair out in handfuls, creep away into the wilderness and die; I could become a hermit or take the veil. . . .

I did none of these, of course. Instead I sat down by the roadside and considered, steadily and calmly, the options left to us. I was aware that despair was only just around the corner; I was also aware just how much I had changed. A few days ago, while Mama was still alive, I would have been totally incapable of coping. Then, if even the smallest thing went wrong, my fault or no, I had run to her skirts and asked for forgiveness, aid, advice, whatever; I had been whipped, scolded, but given my course of action. Now I was on my own.

No, not on my own. I had the others to consider. Without me they would probably perish, except perhaps for Growch. Had the unaccustomed responsibility brought this mood of somehow being able to deal with it all? Or had my "magic" ring wrought the change? It had certainly tried to warn me of danger when it prickled and itched on my finger. I glanced down at it wryly. In the stories I remembered one twist and straw would be spun into gold, a table spread with unimaginable delicacies—But of course! I still had all my money safe, so we wouldn't starve. We might have lost our transport, food, provisions, utensils and, saddest loss of all to me, my Boke and writing materials, but what was that against our lives and some money?

And my ring did give me the power to communicate with Growch and Mistral: why not send out a call to her to escape back to us if she could, however long it took? Given the choice, I would rather have her back than regain our goods. If the carter turned her loose perhaps she would find us. Shutting my eyes and praying that my thoughts had the power of travel I sent her a message, wondering at the same time if I wasn't being foolish to hope.

And while I was about it, an ordinary prayer wouldn't do any harm. So I made one, and Gill joined in with an "Amen."

Rising to my feet I dusted myself down, retrieved Gill's staff, put one end into his right hand and took the other in my left.

"Right! Hang on tight. I'll try and keep to the smoother part of the road, but it will soon be dark and we must seek shelter."

"Where?"

"There are woods a mile or so down the road."

"And what do we do for food?"

"I'll find something."

"Not more of your stupid 'magic,' I hope!"

"If you must know, yes, I have tried to reach Mis—the horse."

"What rubbish! She's miles away by now. You'll never see her again."

"Wait and see. . . ."

And in this way we set off down the road in the gathering gloom, a sneaky wind fingering my ankles and blowing up my skirts indecently. Then just as we reached the shelter of the first trees, it started to rain. It was now almost too dark to see, and we sheltered uneasily, unwilling to lose our footing venturing farther into the forest. But the rain came down harder, and while the firs and pines provided some protection, the oaks and beech had lost most of their leaves by now and were useless as shelter.

From the distance came a growl of thunder, a gust of wind shook the branches above us, increasing our wet misery with a few hundred more drops, and we struggled on, Gill falling on every tenth step and Growch tripping me up on every twentieth. If we didn't find better shelter soon we could die of exposure—

A vivid flash of lightning flared through the trees, followed almost immediately by a tremendous clap of thunder and—

And something else.

A frightened cry. An owl? Something trapped? Someone in distress? It came again. The high-pitched whinny of a terrified horse. This time I recognised it at once.

"Mistral!" I shouted. "Mistral, where are you?"

An answer came, but from which direction? I plunged forward, forgetting Gill, and we near tumbled together.

"Mistral, Mistral! Here, we're here!"

But it took a few minutes more of stumbling around and calling before she found us. I flung my arms around her trembling neck, dropping my end of Gill's staff.

"What happened? Are you all right? How did you escape?" I had forgotten about thought-speech, forgotten that Gill would hear me.

She told me that when the carter had rattled off down the road she had resigned herself to her fate, but once she heard my thought-call—yes, she *had* heard it—she struggled to free herself, but alas! I had fastened her too securely to the tail of the cart. Then she had tried to bite through the rope, with little success until the cart had bumped over a particularly deep rut, when the chewed rope had at last parted, and she had galloped back to find us.

"Brought the food back with you?" asked Growch hopefully.

"Everything is just as it was. He didn't stop to investigate." She paused. "But now I am so tired and wet. . . ."

"Now you're back everything will be fine," I said. "I'll light the lantern and we'll find a snug spot in no time at all!"

"And eat," said Growch.

For once I was in full agreement with him. "And eat."

I held the lantern high to try and get our bearings and saw what seemed like a reflection of our light off to the right. I blinked my eyes free of moisture and looked again. As I watched, the lantern or whatever it was swung slowly from side to side. Yes, it wasn't my imagination.

I stumbled forward, never considering any danger I might be heading for. "Is there anyone there? Help, we need shelter. . . ." and grabbing Gill's hand I made off towards the other light.

The trees shuffled away into the shadows on either side and we found ourselves in a small clearing. A flickering lantern held by a small man threw dances of light onto a queer, humpbacked building, no taller than me, that crouched for all the world like a giant hedgehog beneath the trees. It must be a charcoal-burner's hut, I thought, and certainly not big enough to hold us all. A wisp of smoke trickled from the roof.

The small man bowed. "Welcome travelers. It is not often I have the pleasure of welcoming visitors so far into the forest. Pray take advantage of my humble dwelling, for methinks the weather can only worsen." He spoke in a creaky, old-fashioned way, as though speech came seldom to his tongue. He was elderly, and looked to be dressed in skins; the hand that clutched the lantern was gnarled like a bunch of twigs.

"Thank you, sir, for your kind offer," I said formally. I looked at the low doorway. "But there are four of us, and I fear . . ."

"Plenty of room: You will see."

One of us wasn't waiting; Growch pushed past and disappeared behind the hides that covered the entrance and I found myself pulling Gill in with me. Inside it wasn't a bit what I expected.

Somehow the roof seemed higher—perhaps we had come down a step or two—and the space far greater than I had imagined. It was quite roomy, in fact. The floor was clean sand, the walls wattle and daub; there were piled skins to sit on and a merry fire burned in the center, the smoke curling up tidily to a hole in the roof. To one side of the fire a cauldron simmered and on the other meat was skewered to a spit, browning nicely. A pile of oatcakes was warming on a flat stone, a flagon of wine stood by a jug and wooden bowls and mugs were piled ready. The tantalizing smell of the food was almost more than I could bear without drooling.

I guided Gill to a pile of skins and sat him down, hanging his sodden cloak on a hook in the wall. Growch was already steaming, as near to the fire as he could get, and biting at his reawakened fleas. I heard a munching sound and there was Mistral behind me, lipping at a bunch of winter grass.

It was all rather unexpected, but then I was still unused to much of the refinements of the world. Perhaps houses could, and did, stretch to accommodate extra guests; far more likely, I told myself, my eyes had deceived me outside and I had thought the place much smaller than it obviously was; if not, then we must be in some underground chamber.

Our host came forward, rubbing his hands together with a dry, whispery sound. "Help yourselves to refreshments, my friends. There should be more than enough for all."

Indeed there was. Gill and I spent the next half hour or so crunching into the delicious spicy meat, throwing the bones to Growch, and chasing the last of a thick, hearty broth with oat bread. Then with a mug or two of wine to follow I leaned back and relaxed. The fire still chuckled merrily, apparently without need of fuel, although our host threw a handful of what looked like powder into the flames and instantly the room was full of the scents of the forest.

He was much taller than I had thought, nearly as tall as Gill. How could I ever have thought him smaller than me, I thought muzzily. It was difficult to make out his features properly, too. He seemed to have greyish hair and bushy eyebrows, big ears like ladles and small, round eyes so deeply set I couldn't make out their color. I thought at first his nose was as round as an oak-apple, but in the firelight it suddenly seemed sharp as a thorn and twice as long. His mouth was hidden by an untrimmed beard, but one moment he seemed to have long, sawlike teeth, then none at all.

The food and the wine and the fire were getting to me, I thought: I must pull myself together. Glancing to one side I saw that Mistral's eyes were closed, her head drooping; Growch was staring vacantly at the fire and Gill had his head on his chest. I pinched myself on the hand, surreptitiously, to try and keep awake, catching at my ring as I did so. It seemed very cool to the touch.

I looked up at our host. "I thank you, from all of us, for your food and shelter."

"A pleasure, young traveler. As I said, it is rare for anyone to venture this far into my territory."

"Your territory?"

"Indeed. I said so. This forest is my domain."

Surely all land and the people thereon were owned by the lords of the manors? Even in our village we owed ours work in his fields and tithings.

"You are a lord?"

He chuckled, a sound like wind in the trees. "Lord of the Forest, yes. All around you are my trees, my shrubs, my bushes. My birds, my wild creatures. Every living thing . . ." He sounded quite fierce.

"It—it must be a big responsibility," I said weakly.

He shrugged. "Everything usually runs smoothly: I see to that. Besides, who is there to challenge my authority?"

Certainly not me, I thought noting the scowl, the beetling brows.

"And now," he continued, "I should like to ascertain just how you come to invade my territory. You seem an ill-assorted company, if I may say so. This young man . . ." Gill was fast asleep, too far gone even to snore. ". . . is a relative, perhaps?"

In the silence that awaited the answer to his question, short though it was, I suddenly became aware of all sorts of sights and sounds that had been hidden before. The uneasy prickle of the ring on my finger, the rush of wind and thunder of rain outside, the fire that needed no wood, the unnatural stillness of my companions. Even the shelter in which we found ourselves was seeming to change: the walls were closing in, the roof becoming lower. It's all a big illusion, I thought; he is trying his magic on me and if I tell him the wrong thing—

Before there had been a great compulsion to tell the truth, but now outside reality and I had erected a kind of barrier between the Lord of the Forest and us. So, I told him the story I had told everyone else, lying as though it were the truth.

At the end of it all he humphed! as if he knew it was untrue but couldn't fault the telling. I was beginning to relax again when he suddenly switched his attention to something else.

"That's an unusual ring you have on your finger. A pity it is so undistinguished. Not worth much, I should say."

"It is worth the love of my father, who gave it to me. Were it made only of thread, still would I treasure it. Of course, because it is part of the horn of a—" Horrified, I stopped myself, the ring itself now throbbing like a sore on my finger.

"The horn of a what? Some fabled creature who never existed, save in the imagination of man? I am surprised you believe in such fables. Still," and now his face was all smiles, benign, kindly, "I am willing to exchange it for something far more valuable, just because I am grateful for your company. See here. . . ." and from his pocket he drew out a handful of jewels; gold, silver, green stones, red ones, blue, purple, yellow. "Rings, brooches, necklaces, bracelets: take your pick! Just slide that old piece from your finger and I will give you two for one! How's that?"

"It won't come off," I said flatly. "Not even if I wanted it to. Which I don't. It was my father's gift, and I shall keep it. Sorry."

Of a sudden I felt a great squeezing, as though the breath were being taken from my body by an unwelcome hug, and the walls were so close as to squash me up against the others. Instinctively I took hold of Gill's sleeping hand and cuddled Growch close. Above me Mistral's mane hung like a curtain before my face and I grabbed a handful with my free hand.

Then sleep came down with a rush like a collapsing tapestry.

A drop of rain plopped onto my nose, the aftermath of the storm. Opening my eyes, I blinked up at the trees above. I was cold and *very* hungry. I had been lying uncomfortably on a heap of twigs and stones and my hip and back ached. I sat up; where was the fire? A tiny charred ring in the grass. Walls had gone, roof disappeared. I let go Mistral's mane, Gill's hand, moved away from Growch. Whatever had happened? In a little heap beside the remains of the fire lay a pathetic heap of small, burnt bones: mouse, rat, vole? By them a small pile of desiccated skins crumbled to dust, and blew away on the morning breeze together with half a dozen acorn cups.

Gill stretched and yawned. "What time is it? I'm hungry."

"Hungry?" said Growch. *"Hungry?* I could eat an 'orse!"

"You can talk! I haven't eaten for twenty-four hours," said Mistral.

I gazed at them all. "But don't you remember last night? The food? The little man?" But none of them had the slightest idea what I was talking about.

9

After that, all I wanted was to get away back to normality, and I never thought I should be so glad to see a plain old ribbon of road again. We had no idea exactly where we were, but with the aid of a watery sun headed west by south; even so it must have been at least an hour of stumbling progress before we were free of the forest.

All the while I wondered about what had really happened during the night. As far as we four were concerned we shared the experience of seeing the flickering light between the trees, but after that the others remembered nothing but disturbed dreams. Only I recalled a gnarled old man first small then tall, a room that expanded then contracted, a fire that needed no fuel, food and drink. . . . And in the morning the Lord of the Forest had gone, if he had ever existed. So had his shelter. I might have believed myself the victim of hallucination, except for that tiny ring of charred ground, the little chewed vermin bones, the acorn cups. Magic of a kind, but not nice.

How many other travelers had succumbed, I wondered? If it hadn't been for my ring, the ring he had coveted, the ring that I realized had bound us all together as I gathered the others around me, we too might have been bones on the forest floor. I glanced down at the circle on finger: it was the color of my skin and nestled quietly now. Whatever had threatened was behind us now, but I wouldn't rest easy till we were away from the forest completely. The trees still crowded the road on either side, dank and dripping, their rain-laden branches drooping down like disapproving faces, and no birds sang.

A half hour later we were out in the open. Standing once again in the blessed sunshine, I offered up a silent prayer for our deliverance. It was a chilly morning, last night's rain still lingering in pockets of mist that swirled about our feet and slithered down into the valley below. The countryside was spread out like a checkered quilt beneath us, and some five miles or so distant I could make out through the haze the snaking of a river that curled round the smoke of a fair-sized town. I even imagined that I could hear on the freshening breeze the faint ting-ting of a church bell.

There was little enough dry wood about, but with the aid of the kindling in my pack I soon had a fire going, and spread our cloaks on bushes as I hurried up the first solid food we had eaten for hours—bacon, fried stale bread, cheese and onions eaten raw. It seemed like a feast, but I still mentally gagged when I remembered the 'food' of the night before and could swallow but little, busying myself instead finding choice bits of fodder for Mistral.

We reached the town by midday, and I managed to find an inn which provided both stable room and pallets in the attic. After hearing that a caravan from the east, heading south, was expected within the next couple of days—a rider coming through had reported passing it—I determined to stay until they arrived. Far better to travel in company after the misadventures of the last few days. It meant spending money, but at least we could tidy ourselves up and have the choice of provisions before the others arrived.

I took our washing to the river stones and beat it clean, bought hot water to cleanse ourselves and took Gill once more to the barber, investing in a razor which I thought he could use if careful. I also bought him a cloak with a hood, at horrible expense, and a silken scarf to tie around his eyes: although he could still see nothing, he complained of headaches and a cold prickling in the eyes themselves. The bump on his head was scarcely visible now, but I gave it more salve, just in case.

After decent food and a good night's rest I felt a hundred times better and much more optimistic. I sat Gill out in the sunshine while I caught up with the mending, and tried to jog his memory regarding his family, his home, anything relevant, but he still shook his head sadly.

"I don't remember, Summer: I'm sorry." I could not bear to see someone who should be so haughty and sure of himself brought so low. I tried to recall anything I could of that scene of carnage in the woods and suddenly bethought myself of the scrap of silk I had rescued. Digging it out from the baggage I showed it to Mistral, who sniffed at it, identified it as belonging to the knight's train, but knew nothing of color or shape, as I understood it. I took it to Gill, tried to describe the blue and yellow and what looked like a beak, but he still shook his head. I was sure I could recall a bird's head on the shield I had glimpsed that first day when he asked the way, and tried to combine it all in a drawing, but it was hopeless. Still, I asked about the town as best I could with the scrap of silk, but met with no success there either.

I was making my way back to the inn at dusk, after a wasted afternoon's questioning, when I came across a scuffle of small boys throwing stones up onto the roof of a deserted cottage, shouting and yelling with enjoyment. Looking up, I saw the feeble flapping of wings—obviously they were trying to finish off an injured bird. Even as I passed the bird fell off into the gutter, where it was scooped up by greedy hands and held on high by the tallest boy.

"Mine! Mine!" he chanted. "Pigeon pie for supper!" He was a thin, starved-looking child of about nine, and I couldn't blame him for capturing his supper, but as he put his hand around the bird's neck something made me put out a hand to stop him.

"Stop! Don't kill it. I—I'll buy it off you. . . ." I said impulsively, cursing myself for a soft-pate even as the words were out. What on earth did I want an injured pigeon for?

The boy hesitated, his hand still ready to wring the bird's neck.

" 'Ow much you given' us, fatty?"

I flushed with anger—but then I was fat, wasn't I, and he was as skinny as only starvation can make one.

"Twice as much as it's worth in the market. Only I want it alive—to fatten it up." I reckoned an alley-wise kid such as this would appreciate that argument. I pulled some coins from my pocket and jingled them invitingly. Immediately his eyes glowed fiercely, and I realized I had made a mistake: I should have only produced the two small coins I was willing to part with. I held out my other hand. "Give me the bird. Please."

He clutched the bird closer. "Four pennies, then."

"Rubbish! It's only worth one in that condition, and you know it." To my alarm I sensed the other children closing in around me. There were at least a half-dozen, and I knew I could never escape by running. The alley we were in was narrow and twisting, and if they made a concerted attack I would have no chance. They could crack my head open with a stone with as little compunction as they would wring the bird's neck and share the coins between them, and none the wiser.

If only I had thought to at least bring Growch with me! Nothing to look at, he still had a fearsome bark, a worse growl and very sharp teeth. I took a step back, which was a foolish thing to do. "I—I'll give you another half-penny on top, and that's my last offer."

But still they crept closer, so near that one child nudged my elbow. I took a further step back till I was up against the wall. My heart was beating like a tambour at a feast, and I felt like chucking the money in my hand away as far as I could and taking a chance on running. If only I could reach the end of the alley . . . I lifted my hand, but suddenly there was a small frightened voice in my ears.

"Help me!" The ring on my finger tingled briefly. "Help me. . . ." It was the bird. Suddenly I felt a surge of anger and stepped away from the wall. "Give me the bird! At once! Or I'll . . ."

"You'll what?" But it was the boy who backed away.

"Just wait and see! Well?" I spoke from a confidence I did not feel but even as he shook his head my deliverance was at hand.

A black blur erupted at the far end of the alleyway and charged towards us, bringing its own cloud of dust, the little legs were working so fast. Then there was a nipping and a snarling and a yarling and a yelping and a barking and a biting and boys were scattering everywhere to escape. The pigeon's tormentor dropped the bird in his flight and I snatched it up and made for safety, closely followed by Growch.

We fetched up near the inn and I paused for breath. He spat a fragment of cloth from his mouth, tail wagging. His eyes were bright as blackberries and he smelt as high as hung venison. I made a mental note to dunk him in water whether he liked it or not.

"Luckily I was only dozin' when you called," he observed. "Saw that lot off pretty sharpish, din' I?"

"I called you?"

"Yes, you yelled 'help!' in my ear. Took off like a flea on a griddle I did. What's that you got?"

Once again the ring had worked, and only a thought this time. . . .

"A . . . a pigeon," I said and loosened my fingers a little, aware that I was holding the bird far too tight. "I think it has a broken wing."

"Supper?"

"Certainly not! Don't you ever think of anything except food?"

"Yes, but I ain't seen nor smelt any likely bitches recent. . . . Don' I get anything for helpin'? A reward, like . . ."

He was disgusting, but I bought a pie and gave him half, stuffing the rest into my mouth with relish. "Mmmm . . . Good."

"Might justa well been your bird. Pigeon pie, weren't it?"

"Of course not! Pork and sage," I said, before I realized he was teasing. The bird shivered in my hands.

Upstairs at the inn I examined it more closely. It was a handsome bird in an unusual coloring of soft pinky-brown and buff. On its leg was a tiny canister, locked tight. So, it was a homing pigeon. But from where?

One wing lay splayed and crooked and I touched it gently, using slow
thought for my question.

"Is this where it hurts?"

"Yes. Broken I think. Falcon strike, two days back. Hungry . . ."
The voice in my head was faint but clear. A mug of water and some
oats later and the voice was strong enough to guide me as I bound and
strapped the wing with a splint of wattle and strips of cloth while he
mind-guided my clumsy fingers into the most comfortable position.

"That'll take a while to heal," I said. "Where are you from?"

"South. A town tall with towers. I am a messenger."

"I can see that." I touched the canister on his leg. "How far have
you come?"

"From north fifty miles or so. The same again three times to go."

"Well, you can't fly for a while. . . . South, you said?"

"Yes, and a little east."

"Is your message urgent?"

"It is a message of love from my mistress' betrothed."

Urgent enough to the one who waited. "We travel south," I said.
"But not as fast as you could fly. I don't know how long you will take
to heal, but you are welcome to travel with us if you choose. I can make
a box for your transport."

Of course my dear Gill thought I was quite mad when he found out
what I was doing sitting on the settle by the fire that night, weaving a little
basket from withies I had gathered from the riverside by lantern light. (With
Growch for company this time.) When I explained about the injured pigeon
he snorted most unaristocratically and asked whether I was thinking of
gathering any more encumbrances to hold up our journeying.

Of course I loved my knight most dearly, and could not now imagine
the day when I could not refresh my heart by gazing at his beautiful
face; marveling at the high forehead, straight nose, and those darkly
fringed eyes, so blue in spite of their blindness—but I did wish sometimes that he would grumble a little less.

"Anything the matter?"

"Of course not. I'll just finish this, then perhaps I could ask the
landlord for some mulled ale. You'd like that?"

"I should prefer a decent bottle of wine."

"Certainly." Wine was twice as dear. "I know how you must hate
all this idleness, but perhaps the caravan will arrive tomorrow. . . ."

The travelers straggled in at midday the next day, some fifty of them.
The inn and all the other lodging places in town were full that night and

we had to share our pallets with a husband and wife and their three half-grown children. I doubled up with the wife and Gill with the largest boy. The latter grumbled that Gill took up too much room, while I found myself on the floor a couple of times, the wife having a thin body but a restless one, and the sharpest elbows this side of a skeleton.

The caravan did not waste time and was determined to set off again next day. I had had the forethought to stock up with provisions the previous day, so not for me the frantic buying of everything eatable. I already had flour, oats, cheese, salt pork, dried beans, honey, a small sack of onions and vegetables and a dozen apples, but I did remember to buy some barley for the pigeon and truss of hay for Mistral in the morning.

I judged there would be room for barter on our travels, for I noticed a couple of goats and a crate of hens were traveling with us, part of a merchant's entourage. Milk and eggs would be a treat, although it was late in the year for laying.

Like all so-called "safe" caravans, this one was in charge of a captain and men-at-arms, six of the latter in this case. The captain's job was to determine our rate of progress, decide when and where to halt and to keep us safe from marauders. Our captain was a very large man called Adelbert; he looked quite outlandish, wearing skins and a huge helmet decorated with a pair of bull's horns sticking out on either side. He had a habit of hunching his broad shoulders and thrusting his head forward if anyone dared to question his decisions, that made him look more taurine than ever. His men were a surly bunch, too. They conversed with their captain in a guttural patois I didn't recognize and kept themselves well apart from the rest of us.

Before we set off the following morning "Captain" Adelbert explained his terms. In return for his guidance and protection he demanded a penny a day from each traveler, or sixpence a week in advance. Wagon and carts double, but no charge for horses, asses or mules. I was only too happy to relinquish my worries to someone else, so handed over money for Gill and myself. A week at a time would do.

That first day there were forty-seven of us. Besides the captain and his men, Gill and me, there were the merchant, his wife and four attendants, five lay monks returning south after pilgrimage to another monastery, our room companions of the night before, another family consisting of four generations and thirteen assorted people, a trader and his assistant, a clerk and a troupe of jugglers going south for winter pickings. Captain Adelbert himself led the caravan, two of his men brought up the rear, and the other four patrolled out on either side.

Our pace was of necessity that of the slowest amongst us. We were ruled by a rigid routine imposed by our leader, who became increasingly autocratic the farther south we traveled. We rose an hour before dawn, broke our fast and were on the road as the sun came up. We traveled for four hours, then broke for a meal—not longer than an hour: the captain had a very efficient sand-glass, which to me always traveled faster than the sun—then we were on the road again till dusk, another three hours, perhaps a little more. We camped where he stopped us, unless we were in reach of a town, then it was first in, best served. If we were camping out then we built fires for our evening meal, sometimes combining with others for a joint meal, which was a nice change: the merchant and his wife were too aloof, but the other families and the jugglers became good companions. If the weather was wet we supped cold and soon huddled beneath what shelter we could find.

Luckily we had few really cold days; farther north by now all would be huddled in front of roaring fires, waiting for the snow. I think this was the first thing that made me realize how far we had already come, for by the beginning of December I must have been at least a hundred and fifty miles south of my old home, if not more.

I began to enjoy my life outside, to look around me more. I started to notice weather signs, to see trees, rocks, stones, streams as separate entities. I delighted in the colors of the falling leaves—red, yellow, brown, purple, orange—was forever running off the road to supplement our diet with mushroom and fungi, and was the first of the humans to hear and see the skeins of geese winging south, though I must admit it had been our little pigeon who had alerted me.

He was healing slowly but well, and I didn't need to alter the splint of his wing. Seen at close quarters he was extremely handsome, his pinky-brown plumage set off by creamy beak and legs and bright eyes as red as rubies. He was in no doubt we were heading in the right direction for his home, though he found it difficult to explain why.

"Don't know for sure . . . Something inside my head pulls me the right way." He scratched behind his left ear, or where I supposed it to be, with a delicate claw, then followed the itch all around his neck. "You see, when I am taken away from home and then released to carry a message I climb slowly in spirals, looking all the while for familiar landmarks. If there are none, which means a long journey, I climb until the tug inside comes and I know which way to go." He settled down in his basket, fluffing out his breast feathers. "Of course if I am within ten miles or so of home, then I can see my way, and will be home, weather and hawks permitting, between strikes of the church of the tall tower, which is nearest my loft."

Three hours was the usual interval between strikes of the bell, if the priest was awake, to coincide with the church Offices.

"What does it look like, the earth, from so far above?" I asked hesitantly.

I had put his basket and our baggage on a rock while we took one of our halts, so that Mistral could graze unburdened, and now the bird looked up and then down and around. For a while he said nothing, then: "Stand you up and look down on this rock. This is a mountain. That clump of grass over there is a forest. Scratch a line on the ground and stick two or three twigs along it and you have a river with a town beside it. The ants you can see are the people . . ."

For an instant I could feel the currents of air beneath my wings, stroking my feathers, and glancing down watched the moving map beneath unfold, instinct pulling me farther and farther south—

"You all right?" asked Growch. "Got a funny look on your face, like you was goin' to be sick. If'n it's the bacon, I don' mind finishin' off that bit for you. . . ."

Gill had been remarkably silent about my exchanges with the animals ever since Mistral had found us in the forest; of course I now mostly used thought-communication, but sometimes forgot and used speech. I don't for a moment believe he thought I was really talking to them, or they to me, but he suspected there was something special between us and was no longer sure enough of himself to ridicule it.

The fresh air, plain food and walking miles every day did appear to be helping his memory a little; odd things, like: "I remember having my hair cut when I was a child, and the smell as the pieces burned on the fire," or: "My mother had a blue robe with a gold border," and: "I fell out of a tree when I was six and broke my arm." All endearing memories that made the child he was more real to me, but not really helpful as far as finding out where he lived. Still, it was a hopeful sign.

The caravan changed its character, size and shape as various travelers left or joined us. Among the former were the jugglers and the large family, but the farther south we went, the more our numbers swelled. There were more merchants, with or without wives and attendants, a merry band of students, a couple of pardoners, craftsmen and masons looking for work during the winter and even a dark-skinned man wearing a turban who had woven silk mats and hangings in his wagon.

Of course as the road became more traveled, the deeper the ruts and the more chance of being held up for repairs to wheels or axles. Then we would all stand round cursing the inaction while the Captain organized repairs and restless horses steamed in the chill of December mornings. In spite of this we still managed an average of some fifteen miles a day.

At this time we were traveling through broken countryside: small hills, stony heath, straggly old woods half-strangled with ivy, isolated coppices and turbulent streams. The road, from its usual width of twenty or thirty feet, had shrunk to a wagon's width. Earlier in the day we had come to a crossroads and Captain Adelbert had insisted on taking this narrower right-hand road, saying it was a short cut. I began to wonder if he had made a mistake. It had obviously rained heavily here in the last twenty-four hours, for in many places the horses were splashing through shallows and I had to lift my skirts to my knees and paddle. Once I actually had to carry the smelly Growch twenty yards when he pretended he couldn't swim—it was easier than arguing.

It was getting dark, with a lowering sky overhead, but there was no sight of a suitable camping site. The countryside looked even more inhospitable, outcrops of rock and tangled undergrowth crowding down towards the narrowing road. To make it worse Adelbert's men were harrying the train, trying to make us close ranks and we were soon almost treading on one another's heels. The wagon ahead of us snagged on an overhang and came to an abrupt halt. I was bursting to relieve myself, so dragged Gill and Mistral off the track and behind some rocks, just as the monks behind us closed up.

Our departure went unnoticed in the general hubbub, and I was able to squat down in peace. That was one of the only advantages of Gill's blindness: I had no need to hide myself. He took advantage of the break also, and I was just leading him back to Mistral when the ring on my finger started to itch and burn, and a moment later all hell broke loose in the direction of the road.

Shouts, screams, the thunder of hooves, the frantic barking of a dog, sickening thuds and crashes— Whatever in the world had happened? Making sure Gill had hold of Mistral's mane, I pulled at her bridle to lead her back to the road, but she dug in her hooves and refused to budget, wordless terror coming from her mind to mine. Well, if she wouldn't move I would have to come back for her, but I must see what was happening.

Just as I stumbled towards the rocks something thumped me hard in the stomach and down I went to my knees. Growch was tumbling all over me, stinking of fear.

"Get back, get back!" he barked over the increasing din. "Hide, quick! It's a massacre!"

10

I woke with a sudden jerk, as though I had plummeted down a steep stair, and gazed around wildly. Mistral blew soothingly through her nostrils.

"All safe: sleep . . ."

I lay down again, chilled through to the core of my being, glad for once for the smelly warmth of Growch against my back. Gill was breathing heavily beside me and above the stars shone clear. I closed my eyes, tried to doze off again, but even if I managed a moment or two I soon jumped into wakefulness, fighting the hideous images that crowded sleep.

We had camped beneath an overhang of rock off the road—somewhere. It had been too dark to see, I had not dared light the lantern, and sheer luck and Growch had found this comparatively sheltered spot. We had eaten hastily of broken meats—some sort of pie, I judged—then had wrapped ourselves in the extra blankets and tried to sleep. Gill had dropped off first, but then he hadn't seen what I had. . . .

When Growch had cannoned into me crying "Massacre!" I had not at first believed him, despite the shouts and screams, the clash of weapons. At first I thought it was a minor ambush and that Captain Adelbert and his men were fighting off the attackers, glad that we were out of the way. I saw two monks flee past our hiding place, pursued by a man on horseback waving a sword. It was obviously not safe for us to emerge.

I crept back to Gill. "It looks as though the caravan has been ambushed. It's not safe to move until it's all over. . . ."

But the noise seemed to go on for ever. The screams of anguish and pain were the worst, and I held my hands over my ears; I saw Gill do the same. Perhaps through his dim memory he was reminded of the ambush in which he had been caught.

At last it grew quiet, as far as the screaming was concerned, but I could still hear the tramp of hooves, the crunch of wheels, men's voices, curiously exultant voices. The battle was over; someone had won. I crept forward for a better look. Nothing to be seen, just an empty road. I was about to step out for a better look when there was a fierce tugging at my skirt.

"No! Not yet," growled Growch. "Let me take a quick sken first."

"But—"

"No buts! You ain't got the sense of a newborn pup!" and he crawled forward on his belly and disappeared. I waited for what seemed an age, shivering a little from both fear and excitement, but he came back so stealthily that I heard and saw nothing until a wet nose was pressed into my hand, making me jump. He was shivering, too.

"What's happened? Is anyone hurt? Is it over?"

"S'over all right. They'll be movin' off soon, I reckon. Got what they wanted." He lay down, panting. "All dead."

"I can smell the blood," came the frightened thought from Mistral.

"Like a slaughterhouse," said Growch, still shivering. "Move back a bit: they'll be coming past in a minute or two."

"Who? Who will be coming past? You haven't explained anything! Who is dead? Who attacked us?"

"Never trust no one," was all he would say. "Never trust no one. . . ."

Impatiently I moved for a better view of the road, crouching down behind a rock, mindful through my curiosity of Growch's warnings. Two minutes later I nearly burst out of my hiding place with relief, for here rode our Captain on his stallion, leading behind him two pack horses laden with unwieldy packages. So we had beaten off our attackers! I opened my mouth to cry out, but then I saw the sword hanging from his hand, thick with congealing blood. Instinctively I shrank back; if I leapt out at him too suddenly he might use it without thinking. A moment later and his six men followed, one nursing a gash on his arm, but all chattering and laughing among themselves. Each one led two or three laden horses, and on one I saw the silken rugs from the dark merchant's cart. And surely those two piebalds were the ones who had pulled one of the other merchant's carts? And wasn't that mule the one belonging to one of the pardoners? Where were the others?

I craned forward; the horsemen passed, but there were no others behind. Their voices still carried clearly.

"Din' take too long. . . ."

"Pity about the younger woman—"

"Should'a thought o' that before you chopped her!"

"Whores aplenty where we're goin'."

"Why didn' we take one o' the wagons?"

"Captain says as we're goin' cross-country."

"Three cheers for 'im, anyways! More this time than last!"

" 'E says enough to lay up for the winter. No pickin's worth the candle till spring."

"What about those that ran?"

"Two-three at most. One o' the monks—"

" 'Prentice—"

"Din' see the fat girl and 'er blind brother. . . ."

"Quite fancied 'er, I did. Like an armful, meself. . . ."

"Won't none of 'em get far. Not with the bogs all around."

"Shit! Dropped a bundle. . . ."

"Coupla blankets. Leave 'em. Got plenty. . . ."

Their voices faded as the road bent away, until there was only the dull clops of hooves and a tuneless whistling, and soon both were lost in distance and the growing dark.

I sat down heavily, my mind whirring like a cockchafer. Had I heard aright, or was it all some horrible nightmare? Had our captain, the man we all trusted, led us all astray and proceeded to massacre everyone for the goods we carried? And was it his living, something they did regularly?

Growch slipped past me. He was back in a couple of minutes, looking jauntier. "All clear. You can come out now. Not much to see, though. Or do . . ."

He was right, about the second part anyway. They were all dead, all our companions, strewn along the road for two or three hundred yards like broken dolls—

But dolls never looked like this. Gash a doll and you have splintered wood; wood does not bleed, and there was blood everywhere. My shoes stuck in it, clothes, faces, limbs were caked with it. Dark blood, pink, frothy blood, bright blood—my lantern showed it all. Who would have thought blood would have so many different shades?

And the flies—It was December: where had they all come from? Greedy, fat, blue-black flies crawling everywhere over the carrion that lay cooling in the dark. And in the morning would come the kites, the crows, the buzzards. . . .

Gill was at my side as we picked our way through the corpses, but of course he could see nothing. Growch sniffed his way from corpse to corpse, but there was no life left. We came to the end of death, and there, on the narrowest part of the roadway, a great tree blocked any further progress. At first I thought it had fallen, then I saw the axe marks. So, this had all been carefully planned, and by the look of the tree this way had been used before, this sudden death had come out of the dusk to other travelers.

I must leave word, warning, at the nearest town, I thought distractedly, but first we must get away from here ourselves. Mistral wouldn't come near, and the pigeon cowered in his basket. Taking Gill's hand once more I led him back through the obscenity of bodies, the bile rising in my throat and threatening to choke me. I found I was muttering: "Oh God! Oh God!" over and over as I turned from slashed limbs, contorted bodies, gaping wounds and from the faces that wore death masks of surprise, terror and pain.

Behind me Gill stumbled and cursed. "What the devil—?"

He jerked his hand from my grasp as he fell to one knee, groping in front of him.

"I kicked something: a flagon of wine, a bladder of lard?"

This time I was sick, though there was little save bitter water to spit out. The thing he had stumbled over was a severed head.

"Let's get outta here," said Growch. "Nothin' left but stink o' death."

True enough. The assassins had stripped the caravan of everything: clothes, goods, weapons, valuables, harness, horses and mules, even all food and drink. There was no reason to believe they would return, and they were probably miles away by now, but I still felt uneasy. They had said three others had run off, but if it were true about the bogs they were probably drowned by now.

As if to echo the dread and fear that still lingered among the corpses, a thick miasma of mist started to rise from the ground around us, curling round my ankles with cold fingers.

I took Gill's arm. "We must move. There is nothing we can do for these poor souls save give them our prayers." And we bowed our heads, the muttered prayers sounding loud in that unnatural stillness. There was only one way to go; that was down the road we had come by, for none of us wanted to linger near the slaughter longer than we could help. Even a mile or two would make a difference, for who knew what ghosts might not rise from those poor unshriven souls, to harry us through the night?

Growch slipped off ahead, and I extinguished the lantern: I could not risk the murderers seeing a light, though common sense told me we would never see them again. I knew the dog's and horse's ears were sharp enough to pick up any danger, but we walked forward cautiously, a step at a time, Growch came running back.

"No sign of anyone for miles, but there's a bundle what they musta dropped just ahead. Over to the right . . ."

Two new blankets, still smelling of sheep oil and practically water-proof. I strapped them on Mistral's back. They had been someone else's property, but that person was now dead: no point in leaving them there to rot. There was also a small sack of various broken foods: no point in wasting that either.

We stumbled forward for another mile or so, then Growch had found the rocks we were now sheltering beneath. I shared out the broken pies and bread and cheese and covered us with the new blankets, and then tried to sleep for a few hours.

And was still trying.

But the sights and sounds of the carnage we had left behind were still sharp and shrill in my imagination, too clamorous for sleep. Why did it have to end like that, the journey I was becoming so used to, was even beginning to enjoy? I had become accustomed to walking all day, to spending the occasional night huddled under the stars, to cleaning and mending and patching and gathering wood and cooking. I had met more people in the last few weeks than I had come across in the whole of my life before, seen more villages, towns, hills, rivers, forests and fields than any lord could own in one holding. Of course I had been bone-weary at times, hungry, cold and burdened with responsibility but, given the choice, I would not have retraced one step. Had not my father traveled the world, and Mama been one of the Travelers?

No, I would not have gone back—until now.

Right now I would give almost anything to be back in my own village, under any conditions—even working in the tavern, or as kitchen maid to the sharp-tongued miller's wife. I wanted desperately for life to be ordinary again, safe and predictable. I didn't want responsibility for anyone or anything but myself; I didn't want to think, to plan, to *lead*. I wanted to have all the decisions made for me. No more choices, please God! I couldn't cope, I couldn't, especially if they were going to turn out like this.

I snuggled into the scratching, uncomfortable-because-new blanket, more awake than ever. Gill was now snoring loudly, Growch smelt like a dung heap and I was sure I was starting a miserable cold. . . .

I awoke with the sun full on my face.

"What time is it? Why didn't you wake me?"

"I thought you needed the sleep," said Gill gently, putting out a tentative hand till he found my shoulder, then patting it. "You do so much for us: you deserve a lie-in once in a while. We couldn't manage without you, you know. . . ."

And suddenly, somehow, it all seemed worth it.

11

We regained the crossroads at midday. It was empty. The road north by which we had originally come stretched back into the distance, a straight arrow. The turnoff that had proved so disastrous, we left thankfully. There remained two ways: southeast and southwest. I sent the turd expert down first one then the other.

He came trotting back triumphantly. "Not thataway," he said, indicating southeast. "They went along some twelve hours back, then camped for the night and struck off 'cross the moor."

I turned to Mistral and the pigeon. "Does this southwest road seem all right to you?"

Unfortunately I had used human speech, and Gill stared towards me irritably. "Do we have to consult—pretend to consult—the impedimenta every time anything is to be decided? Or can't you make a decision on your own?"

"Animals have a much better sense of direction than we humans have," I said stiffly. "And I *do* communicate with them, whatever you may think!" And I explained about Growch's foray down the roads. "If you still aren't convinced, we can waste time going down the southeast road till we find the relevant horse droppings and you can feel and smell them for yourself!"

He shook his head and sighed. "No. I believe you somehow manage to tell them what you want, better than most. Now, can we go?"

I turned to Mistral and the pigeon once more. "What do you say?"

She snuffed the air. "We got the right way, for me."

"It will do," said the pigeon. "If only I could fly up and take a look . . ."

"Patience," I said, "you are healing nicely."

"I know . . . Not fast enough." He paused, and preened himself shyly. "They—the others—have names. I should like a name too. If you wouldn't mind. If it's not too much bother . . ."

"But of course!" I suddenly realized that the name had been there all the time. "I have been thinking of you as 'Traveler' all this while. Will that do?"

He crooned to himself. " 'Traveler' . . . Thank you."

We camped off the road that night, and made reasonable progress the next day, without seeing another soul. The same the day after, though by midday we were down to a handful of flour and two wrinkled apples, so it was with relief that I saw the outline of roofs and a church tower some distance ahead. The land around us became cultivated, there were sheep in a fold guarded by two dogs and I could hear wood being chopped in a wood to the west. Small tracks came to join the highway from left and right: it all pointed to a fair-sized town.

Indeed it was so prosperous that on the outskirts were two or three large houses standing in their own walled grounds, which must mean this was a peaceful area too. We were passing the last of these mansions when I stopped abruptly. My ring was tingling and I thought I heard something—no, not heard, rather felt.

"What was that?"

"Bells ringing for afternoon Mass," said Gill, as indeed they were.

"No. Something else. Listen. . . ." There it was again: a sad, cold, dying call.

"Came from over the wall," said Growch, ear pricked. "Somethin' shufflin' about."

"Anyone there?" I called and thought, "Answer me!"

There was a longish pause. "Help. . . ." The sound was faint, drawn out like a thread. "Sooo . . . cooold . . ."

I had to find out what It was, what It wanted. I looked about, but the pebble-dash walls surrounding the house were some ten feet high. No way could Gill lift me up—besides he'd discover just how fat I was—and there were no handy trees to climb. I followed the wall till I came to a small gate, but it was firmly bolted. Still—

I called Mistral and explained what I wanted. We managed it on the third attempt as she bucked me up high enough to grab the top of the gate, climb over and drop to the other side. The first thing I did was to draw back the bolts to ensure a swift exit, just in case. Then I looked about me.

I was in a small formal garden, with apple and pear trees, leafless now, graveled paths, boxed alleys, square and diamond-shaped plots edged with rosemary, a scummy pond and the remains of a camomile lawn. All winter-dead and desolate. The house beyond was shuttered and quiet too.

I peered around in the gathering gloom. Nothing moved. And yet—I started back. Over there, at the edge of the shriveled lawn a rock moved. Rocks don't move, I told myself firmly. But It did it again and I backed away.

"Heeelp . . ."

Talking, moving rocks? If it hadn't been for the positive feeling in the ring on my finger I think I would have fled, but instead I approached It cautiously, ready however to run if It jumped up and tried to bite. Seen closer It was a sort of rough oval, almost black, with orangey-brown patches. I stretched out my hands to pick It up and It suddenly sprouted a smooth head, four scrabbling claws and a stumpy tail. I sprang back: perhaps It did bite!

"Caaarefuuul," came the mournful, slow voice again. "Faairly fraaagile. Chiiip eaaasily . . ."

I squatted down to look more closely. "What are you?"

"Reeeptillia-cheeelonia-testuuudo-maaarginaaata . . ."

It was talking Latin, and that was not my best subject. I understood Church Latin and some market Latin—both understood wherever one went in a Christian country of course, whatever local language the native people spoke—but classical and scientific Latin were beyond me. "Er . . . How can I help you?"

"Cooold . . . Fooorgotten. Neeeeeed fooooood. Sleeeeeep . . ."

It was getting more and more difficult to understand. Obviously as the house was shut up It could expect no help from there. At least I could see It-whatever-it-was-in-Latin got some warmth. "You'd better come with me." I bent to lift It, my hands closing round a cool, horny shell. "Don't stick your claws in . . ." but I was brought up short by a sharp tug. I put It down again. "What's this?"

"Chaaain. Caan't escaaape. Caaan't buuurrow . . ."

Looking more carefully I could see that a thin chain was looped through a hole pierced in the rear of the shell and then went to an iron staple driven into the ground some eighteen inches away. It was an easy matter for me to lift the chain over the staple and release it, but I could see how constricting it had been, for the creature's walking 'round had worn a deep circular trench, the limit of the chain.

I looked around, but there was nowhere I could put It that wasn't just as exposed, and no food that I could see.

"What do you eat?"

"Greeeeeens. Fruuuit . . ."

I sighed. "And where do you come from originally?" but even as I asked I knew what the answer would be.

"Sooouth . . ."

Another one! Whatever would Gill say? I stooped to wrap the chain around Its shell and started to lift It, but was arrested by a hiss of pain. "Toooooo faaast . . . Huuurts heeead."

Slow and steady then, I wrapped him in my shawl and left by the side gate; I couldn't bar it again. There was nothing to steal in the garden, and anyone wanting to rob the house was perfectly capable of climbing the wall.

"What you got?" asked Growch. I showed him. "Hmmm. Smells like dried grass and shit."

Gill asked the same question and I placed It in his hands. He ran his hands over the shell and his face lit up. "Ah! A tortoise! Had one when I was a boy. . . . Laid eggs, but never came to anything. Ran off one August and we never found it again. . . ."

I was delighted. He had not only identified the strange creature, but it had also touched off another piece of memory, however irrelevant. And I had heard of tortoises, but never seen one before.

I hesitated. "Do you mind if we take it with us? I believe its kind live farther south. . . ."

"Of course. Tortoises can't stand winter here. Ours used to bury itself in cold weather. Where did you find it?"

I explained. "It feels as though . . . I think it's hungry. I believe they eat greens, but there aren't many to be found right now. . . ."

He was delighted to be consulted. "Some sops of bread in milk. Ours used to love that."

So that was one problem solved: bread and milk as soon as we reached a decent inn. I wrapped the tortoise in a piece of sacking and tucked him up on Mistral's saddle.

"Food soon. You may find your perch a bit rocky, but you'll get used to it. What do we call you?" I wasn't going to make the same mistake as I had with Traveler, the pigeon.

Now he was warmer his speech wasn't (quite) so slurred or slow. "Back at hooome," he said, shuffling around a little as if he were embarrassed, "the ladies called me Basher. Could hear me for miles," and he gave a little sound, which, if he had been human, I would have interpreted as nothing more or less than a snigger.

* * *

By the time we reached the town proper it was near dark and we were lucky to knock up an inn with reasonable stable accommodation, which we shared with the animals, snug enough on fresh hay. I was lucky also with chicken stew, bread and mugs of milk for Gill and myself, and Basher the tortoise had his first meal "for three or four mooonths," he said. He didn't eat much, but as he said: "Little and oooften. The shell is a bit cooonstricting on the stomach." Like armor must be, I thought.

"How did they come to forget you?" I asked.

"Neeews came. Somebooody ill. All left. Forgooot me."

I fingered the chain wrapped around him. "Shall I take this off?"

"Please. Dooon't want to be reeeminded."

I found there was a catch, easy enough to unfasten, and it now looked just like a gold necklet, something used as an expedient rather than something permanent.

"Who put this on you?"

"Maaan drilled hole. Huuurt. Lady put on chain. Laaaughed . . ."

"Do you want it? It looks as if it might be gold, enough to buy us more food and lodging."

"It's yours. Paaay for my travel . . ."

In the morning we found the town full of people, and the landlord told us many had come from roundabout for the feast day of the Eve of St. Martin, the last chance of fresh meat before the spring. There was a traditional fair to held on a piece of common land and dancing on the green in front of the church. "Be glad when it's all over," he grumbled. "House is full of the wife's relations. We'll dine early tonight, if you don't mind. Everyone'll be at the fair later."

I didn't know whether to stay another night or no: it rather depended on whether the tortoise's necklet was indeed gold. I remembered Mama's strictures on trading and bargaining, and went to three different coin and metal traders. It was indeed gold and the middle one offered the best price but was too inquisitive: "Who gave it to you? Where are you from? Where are you bound for?" and in the end the last man, an elderly Jew, exchanged it for enough moneys to keep us in food and lodgings for many a day, and without too much haggling.

So much money, in fact, that I decided to sleep another night in the town and also visit the fair. I had never been to a fair before. I had been partly persuaded to find in my travels round the town that our acquaintances of a few weeks earlier, the jugglers, were to perform that night.

When told of the disaster that had overtaken us at the hands of Captain Adelbert and his men, the juggler's eyebrows rose into his thatch of fair hair, and his mouth made a great "O" of surprise. He crossed himself several times in thanks for his deliverance and promised us a free show that evening. I left him going into the church to give a donation for his lucky escape, for I was reminded to report the caravan master's perfidy to the authorities.

This took longer than I had expected, as everything had to be written down, and as it was a holiday the town clerk was nowhere to be found and I had to be content with his deputy, who was mighty slow with pen and ink. I could have done better myself. Then they had to have Gill's corroboration, for what it was worth, so we were only just in time for our midday meal—rabbit and mushroom stew, dumplings, bread, cheese and ale—and the fair was already in full swing by the time Gill and I arrived. I had wanted to leave Growch behind, but he had promised he would sneak out and follow us anyway.

"Like a couple of unweaned pups, you two! Not fit to let out on your own . . ." So he trailed a few yards behind us.

I took hold of Gill's hand, and because this was a leisure time, not leading him to relieve himself or across obstacles, the touch of his skin sent little shivers of excitement rolling up and down my spine. Routine flesh to flesh contact became, in my case, imbued with all sorts of undertones and overtones that had my palm sweaty in a minute, and I had to wipe it a couple of times and apologize.

It was difficult in any case to thread our way through the crowds that milled more or less aimlessly among the stalls, tents, platforms and stages that filled the common ground. Like me, I suppose, they wanted to see everything before making up their minds what to spend their money on. As it was afternoon, over half the crowd consisted of children: tonight husbands would bring their wives, young men their sweethearts and the singles would seek a partner.

We found our friends the jugglers easily enough and, as promised, had our free show, though I could tell Gill was bored, his blindness making a mockery of the tumbling balls, daggers and clubs. I found some musicians and we listened to those for a while, then I bought some bonbons which we shared. I described a couple of wrestling falls for him, as best I could, also the greasy pole contest, which to me was hilarious, but again irritated Gill because he could not watch the humor.

The further we went, the more I realized how much these entertainments relied on visual enjoyment—morris dancers, animal freaks, the strong man, a woman as hairy as a monkey, a "living corpse," and all the throwing, catching, running and contests of strength. The only real interest he showed was when I found a stall selling rabbit-skin mitts, and I treated him to the biggest pair I could find.

I was reluctantly leading him back, when I came across a treat I could not resist. Outside a tent hung a sign saying: THE WINGED PYGGE. To reinforce the words (for most could not read) there was a lurid poster depicting something that looked like a cross between a huge bat and a plum pudding with a curly tail. Perhaps I would have lingered for a moment, yearned for a while and then walked on, but at the very moment we stopped, the showman flung aside the flaps of his tent and strode forward, ready to capture the passing trade with his spiel.

"My friends, lads and lassies, youngsters: I invite you all to come in and see the marvel of the age!" His restless little eyes darted amongst us, noting those who had paused, those who would listen, those who were customers. "Here we have a magic such as I dare swear you never have seen! A horse may swim, an eel walk the land, but have you ever seen a pig fly? No, of course you have not! But here, fresh from the lands of the East—the fabled lands of myth and mystery—at great expense I have managed to purchase from the Great Sultan Abracadabra himself, the only, original, once-in-a-lifetime Flying Pig!"

The crowd around us was growing, their eyes and mouths round with speculation and awe. The showman knew when he was on to a good thing.

"Here is your chance to see something that you can tell your children, your grandchildren, your great-grandchildren, knowing they will never see the same! And how much is this marvel of the senses, this delectation of the eyes, this feast of the consciousness?" He had captured them as much with his long words as with his subject, I realized. "I am not asking the gold I have received from crowned heads, nor the silver showered on me by bishops and knights. . . . No, for you, my friends, I have brought down my price, out of my respect and fellow feeling, to the ridiculous, the paltry, the infinitesimal sum of two copper coins!"

The crowd hesitated, those at the fringe began to break away, but immediately the showman drew them back into his embrace with a dramatic reduction.

"Of course this ridiculous price includes all children in the family. And for the elderly, half price!" Some people who had been leaving turned back, but others remained irresolute. Down came the price again.

"All right, all right!" He spread his arms in supplication. "But this price is just for you: you must not tell your neighbor how little you paid, else will I starve. . . . My final offer: one copper coin, just one, for the treat of a lifetime! Come on, now: who will be first?"

Should we, shouldn't we? After all, I would have to pay for Gill and he would see nothing. I nudged Growch with my foot.

"There's supposed to be a pig with wings in there," I nodded towards the tent. "Be a dear and check up for me. I don't want to waste money if it's a con."

He slipped away towards the back, presumably to squeeze under the canvas unseen. A steady trickle of people were now paying their coin: soon the tent would be full. Growch nudged my ankle.

"Well?"

"Dunno. Honest I don'. There's summat in there. . . ."

"Is it a pig?"

"Could be . . ."

"What do you mean 'could be'? It either is or it isn't. Which?"

"Looks like one, but don' smell like one. Don' smell o' nuffin, really. Nuffin as I recognizes."

"Perhaps somebody washed him. Unlike some I could mention," I added sarcastically. "Does it have wings?"

He scratched. "Sort of. Bits o' leathery stuff comin' out o' its shoulders. Like bat wings . . ."

That decided me. I bargained for Gill's blindness but got a "takes-up-the-same-space-don't-he" answer. Inside it was dark and stuffy, lit only by tallow dips. Tiptoeing, I could see a small stage hung with almost transparent netting that stretched from floor to ceiling and was nailed to the floor. To stop the creature flying away, I thought.

There was a rustle of anticipation. The showman reappeared, on the stage this time. He was carrying a large cage which he set down before him, and then started another harangue.

"You've got your money," I thought. "Why prolong it?"

"Once in a lifetime . . . marvel of the age . . . far lands of the East . . ." It went on and on, and the thirty or so people in the tent started to grow restive, shuffle their feet, mutter to one another. A baby began to cry and was irritably hushed.

"Get on with it," somebody shouted from the back.

The showman changed his tack. "And now, here is the moment you have all been waiting for! Come close, my friends—not too close—and wonder at this miracle I have procured solely for your mystification and delight!" And with this he opened the cage, groped around in the interior and finally hauled forth, by one leathery wing, a small disreputable object that could have been almost anything.

It could have been a large rat, a mangy cat, a small hairless dog or, I suppose, a pig. A very small, tatty pig. Pinkish, greyish, whitish, blackish, it certainly had four legs, two ears, a snout and a curly tail, but even from where I stood I could understand Growch's earlier confusion.

There was a murmur of astonishment from the audience, which quickly grew to ooh's and aah's of appreciation as the showman plucked at first one stubby little wing and then the other, extending them until the creature gave very pig-like squeals of protest.

"There now, what did I tell you? Never seen anything like this before, I'll be bound! Worth every penny, isn't it?" He brought the creature nearer to the front of the stage and the crowd pressed forward, making the tallow dips flare and the net curtains bulge inwards.

I held on tight to Gill, explaining what I had seen as best I could.

"Sounds like some sort of freak to me. . . . Are you sure those wings aren't sewn on?"

He wasn't the only one to express doubts. Once the first wonder had worn off there was muttering and whispering all about us, one man going so far as to suggest that there was a manikin sewn up inside a pig's skin.

"Let's see it fly, then," shouted one stalwart, encouraged by his wife. "You promised us a flying pig, so let's *see* a flying pig!"

His cry was taken up by the others, and for the first time I saw the showman discomfited.

"Well now, the creature does fly, I can certify to that, but it strained its wings last week, and—" but the rest of his words were drowned in a howl of protest.

"You promised . . . we paid good money . . . cash back . . ."

It was probably the last that decided him. Retreating to the back of the stage, he held the creature high above his head.

"Right, then!" He seemed to have recovered his equilibrium. "A flying pig you shall see! Stand back!" and he threw the creature as high as he could, as you would toss a pigeon into the air. For a moment it reached the top of the tent and seemed to hang there, desperately fluttering its vestigial wings. Then, abruptly, they folded and it spiraled to the floor, to land with a sickening thump and a heart-rending squeal.

Quite suddenly it was over. The creature was stuffed back in its cage and we found ourselves out in the sunshine. For no reason that I could think of I found my eyes were full of indignant tears. It was so *small!* I told Gill what had happened. He shrugged his shoulders.

"They would have done better to wire it up and suspend it in the air," was his comment. "I'm getting hungry: shall we go?"

I took Gill to Mass and then we ate a rather scrappy supper, everyone in the inn eager to be off to the evening's festivities. There was to be a bullock roasted in the churchyard, maybe two, and all you could eat for two pence. I was in two minds what to do. Part of me couldn't get the images of that pathetic little pig out of my mind and wanted to see him again, the other part knew that Gill would be bored and unhappy if I dragged him round the fair again.

My dilemma was solved in the most satisfactory way. One of the landlord's cronies came dashing into the inn for a quick ale before the festivities started, grumbling that their best tenor had dropped out of the part-singing with a sore throat.

"We'll just have to cut out 'Autumn leaves like a young girl's hair' and 'See the silver moon.' Pity: they're very popular. . . ."

From the corner by the fire came a soft humming, then a very pleasant tenor voice started to sing the descant from "Autumn Leaves." It was Gill; I had never heard him sing before and my heart gave a sudden bump! of unalloyed pleasure.

Everyone turned to listen.

"Can you do 'Silver Moon'? 'The bells ring out'? 'Take my heart'?" and a half-dozen more I had never heard of. Gill reassured the landlord's friend he knew all but two.

"Then you've saved us all! You come alonga me, we'll slip into the church for a quick practice, then you're part of our singers for tonight. No arguments: there'll be plenty to drink and eat. Blind, are you? Pity, pity . . . Don't worry, we'll look after you!" and he took Gill's arm and whisked him away before one could say "knife." At first I was dubious, but one look at Gill's face reassured me. It was full of animation: at last he had found something he could do for himself, I realized, and wondered for a moment whether I was coddling him too much. No man likes to be smothered, Mama used to say. . . .

Which left me free for an hour or so. At first I pretended to myself that I was just going to have a general look around, perhaps buy a ribbon or two, arrive at the barbecue in time for some roast beef and then stay to listen to Gill sing, but my feet knew a different route. Before long I found myself once more outside the "Flying Pygge" tent listening to the showman's spiel. This time I pushed my way to the front, determined to be near the stage. And the silly thing was that I didn't know why, though there was a prickling in my ring that told me that somehow it was important.

I stopped the speech in mid-flow. "My penny, sir!"

He stopped and glared at me, and I realized he had not yet reached his "special reduction" bit. Blushing, I prepared to step back into the crowd, but he recognized me, and seized on his opportunity.

"See how eager this—this young lady is to see the show! Don't I remember you from this morning?"

I nodded.

"And you have come back because you marveled at the show, never having seen its like before? And you told all your friends about it, so I have had two more performances than usual?"

I nodded again. Anything, but let's get a move on!

He beamed. "There's your proof, then," he said to the rest. "Can't wait to see the performance again . . . The young lady perhaps forgets that the price is *two* copper coins, but I think that this time, as a special treat—and don't tell your neighbors—I shall do as she suggests and reduce the entrance to just one penny. . . ."

Once inside I rushed to the front as if blown by a gale and clutched at the curtains. The showman brought out the cage and far away in its depths I could see two sad little eyes staring out, and a great shudder shake the small frame. "It's not fair, it's not fair!" I thought angrily and, impelled by I knew not what, I bent down while the showman had his back turned and ripped up a section of the curtain nearest the bottom of the stage. Looking at the pig as he hung in the showman's hands I willed him to see what I had done. All the while the ring on my finger was pulsing like mad.

The pig was held on high, then hurled towards the ceiling. Once more it appeared to rise a little, then hover, but it was only an illusion, for down it came to land with a crash and a whimper right in front of me—

I ripped up the rest of the curtain, snatched the pig into my arms and, using surprise and my considerable weight, carved my way through the astonished crowd and out into the darkness. I could hear the howl of the showman behind and ran until there were a couple of stalls between us. Then I set down the pig and gave it a little shove.

"Now's your chance to escape! Run, run away as fast as you can!"

But the stupid creature wouldn't move. . . .

12

I took a quick glance behind. The crowd were still pouring out of the tent, getting tangled up with the tent flaps, guy ropes and each other. I hesitated, then darted back and picked up the creature from under the noses of our nearest pursuers and set off once more. If the silly animal hadn't the sense it was born with—!

I ran in the direction of the town, dodging between strollers, around trees and bushes, tents, wagons and stalls until my heart was banging in my ears. I was wheezing like an old woman and could hardly draw a breath. My feet felt like balls of fire and the salty sweat was stinging my eyes till I could hardly see. Behind me I could hear the thud of pursuing feet and cries of "Thief! Stop thief!"

Twice I tried to rid myself of my burden but each time part of it became entangled with my clothing some way or another, and I was scared to pull too hard lest I damage its fragile wings. At one moment it felt as heavy as lead, at another as light as a farthing loaf; it seemed to change shape with every step I took: now long and thin, now short and fat; round, square, oblong—

"What the 'ell you *doin'?*" Growch was dancing alongside. "Got the 'ole town after you . . ."

"Don't—ask—questions," I panted. "Help me get away!"

He swerved off to one side and a moment later I heard a loud crash. Risking a backward glance I saw he had cannoned into a stall selling cooking pots; those that survived the fall were rolling about on the grass, bringing some of my pursuers down. But not the showman: he was in the van of about twelve yelling, shouting villagers. I then saw a blackish blur run between his legs and bring him crashing to the ground, also bringing down another who upturned a stall of fruit and vegetables in his wake. The rest of the pursuers lost interest in the chase and began to fill pockets and aprons with the spoils.

Slowing down I gained the outer streets of the town and sought the temporary refuge of a deserted doorway, panting, disheveled and exhausted, the pig-creature still clutched beneath my arm. Growch came trotting down the alley, tail jaunty.

"Well, that stirred 'em up! What was you doin' anyway?"

"Tell you later . . . Thanks, anyway. Let's get back to the inn."

I crept into the stable, looking fearfully behind, and deposited the creature in the manger.

There was a long moment of silence.

"W - e - l - l," said Growch. "Don't look any better close to. What you want to pinch that for?"

Mistral blew down her nostrils then sniffed, trying to catch its scent. "Strange . . ."

"Those supposed to be wings?" asked Traveler.

"Claaaws like mine . . ." mused Basher, awake for once.

Indeed, its cloven hooves did have tiny hooks embedded in the horn. Those must have been what caught in my clothes when I tried to put it down earlier.

"What *are* you?" I whispered, as if the whole world were asleep and the answer was a secret.

Was it a pig? The snout seemed too long, the bum too high, the skin hairless. The backbone was knobbed as though it hadn't eaten for ages and the tail had a little spade-like tip. The ears were small, and then there were the wings. . . . Scarcely stretching beyond the span of my hand, they were leathery like those of a bat, but without the claw-like tips. He was stretching them out tentatively right now—there was no doubt it was a he—but when folded they tucked away in a couple of pouches on either side of his shoulders. It was a freak—

"I am a pig. At least I think I am. . . . When I came out of the egg—"

"Egg?"

He looked at me. "Yes. Does not everything come from an egg?"

I didn't think so. As far as I knew horses, cows, sheep, dogs, cats, rats, mice, people and—yes—pigs were born bloody and whole from their dams. But on the other hand hens, ducks, birds, snakes, lizards, fish, frogs and toads laid eggs. But he wasn't one of the latter. It was all very puzzling. Perhaps he was a new species.

"Some creatures come from eggs," I said cautiously. "Are you absolutely sure you did?"

"I remember being in a tight place and fighting my way out with my nose. Then there was my mother and my brothers and sisters; they were all pigs. But they picked me out and sold me because of these things," and he nodded along his back to where his wings were folded away. "A man said pigs do not have wings. Said I was a freak. Called me not a pigling but a wimperling, because I cried so much when they tried to stretch my wings. So I suppose that is what I am."

"A Wimperling?" I shook my head. "I'm afraid I've never heard of one of those." It looked sadder than ever, its big brown eyes with the long lashes seeming ready to shed tears any minute. "But I'm sure you're not on your own," I added hastily.

"Thank you anyway for rescuing me. I hope I shall not get you into trouble?"

I hope not, too, I thought. Pig stealing was punishable by hanging. "Of course not. Er . . . Now you are here is there anywhere I can take you? Drop you off?" I waited for the dreaded word "south," like Mistral, Traveler, Basher and Gill, but it didn't come.

Instead: "I do not know where I belong. Nowhere I suppose. Perhaps I might travel with you a while? I shall be no bother. And I eat anything and take up but little space. . . ."

What could I say? After all, I had stolen him from his owners and so I was now responsible for his well-being. But what about Gill? What would his reaction be when he learned I had burdened us with yet another responsibility? And another thought: how long would it be before they traced the stolen pig to me? After all, I was scarcely invisible and there were plenty of people to remember.

First things first. I must hide the little thing securely—from both the villagers and Gill. I made a space under the manger behind our baggage.

"Just for tonight. We'll be away early in the morning. Are you hungry?"

The Wimperling shook his head, but Growch muttered: "Starving, I am. What about all that roast beef?" and my stomach gave a growl of sympathy. I decided that my best cover was to go out again, in my hooded cloak this time instead of the shawl, and try and look as though I had been listening to Gill's singing all the time. Trying to be insignificant was easier than I thought; everyone was so busy enjoying themselves that no one gave me a second glance. Growch and I chewed the rather tough meat—the roasted ox was down to skin and bone by the time we got there—and I was able to listen to the last couple of songs, in which Gill comported himself very creditably.

Afterwards Gill's newfound friends escorted us back to the inn, roistering noisily. On the way I heard a strange tale of a long-haired witch who, accompanied by a pack of fierce hounds, had stolen a flying pig and rode up into the sky on him. . . .

"Wake me an hour before dawn," I said to Mistral.

In any event I was awake long before, spending most of the night tossing and turning, my snatched dreams full of visions of the hooded hangman. We were away long before anyone else was stirring. Gill, of course, had no idea it was still dark. Unfortunately it was a damp, misty morning, threatening rain. The dropleted air smelled of wood smoke, night soil, last night's bad ale and wet wool as we groped our way out of the town, but once on the road again it was wet leaves, damp earth, the complicated decay of December.

A fine, hazy rain started to fall, too light yet to do anything but lie on top of everything like an extra skin. Growch, as usual, grumbled like mad, but Mistral was easy, plodding forward at walking pace, her load balanced so the tortoise and pigeon were basketed on one side, the pig in a pannier on the other. I made sure Gill walked on the former side.

I had bethought myself the day before to renew our dry goods and buy more cheese, so we breakfasted by a quick, small fire on gruel, oatcakes and honey. I dowsed the fire as soon as the food was cooked, pleasant though it was, because I was still afeared of pursuit. I had made extra oatcakes for our midday meal, to be eaten with the cheese, and without thinking I handed them to Gill to tuck away under Mistral's blankets while I finished scouring the cooking pot. There was a sudden sharp squeal and a shout of anger.

"Summer! Come here. . . ."

Oh *no*! I had thought to get away with it a while longer. "Coming . . ."

"What is *this?*"

"What's what?"

"You know perfectly well what I'm talking about—"

"Oh, that!"

"Yes, that!"

"Um. It's a pig. Sort of. A very little pig. It'll be no trouble. . . ."

"And where did it come from?"

"Er . . . the town. Last night. It's come along for the ride."

"That's a ridiculous thing to say, and you know it!" He frowned in my direction.

"As you're determined on being flippant, I suppose you are now going to suggest to me that it's another of your talking animals and that it stood by the roadside and begged a lift? Tchaa!" he snorted. "Well, it can come right out of there and—What's *this*?"

Damnation, hell and perdition! He had been fumbling inside the pannier and he must have found—

"Where did you get this animal?"

"I told you—"

"You stole it! This is the creature we went to see yesterday afternoon, the one you told me had wings! You were the 'witch' they were all talking about last night!"

I wanted to giggle: he looked so—so *silly,* when he was angry, not at all like his usual handsome self. More like a cross little boy.

"I didn't exactly *steal* him; it was more of a rescue."

"Don't play with words! Don't you realize this could be a hanging matter?" Suddenly he looked scared. "And they might say I was aiding and abetting you—"

"Nonsense!" but my heart began to beat a little faster. I had never thought my deed might involve anyone else.

The pig's head popped out of the pannier like a puppet on cue. "I told you I don't want to be any bother. Let me out and I'll—I'll just disappear. No bother . . ."

"You just stay right where you are!" All this was beginning to make me quite angry. "I said you could come with us and I meant it." I turned to Gill. "This animal was being badly mistreated. If I had left it where it was it would have died. After that stupid story about a witch, no one is going to come after us. And as for anyone recognizing the animal, I'll—I'll make it a little leather coat so you can't see the wings. Satisfied?"

He looked dumbfounded. I had never shouted at him before. Growch sniggered. "All right, whatever you say. But don't blame me if we get caught."

"I won't." I shouldn't get the chance: everyone would be too busy blaming me.

We made damp progress during the rest of the morning and ate our midday meal on the move. Only a few weeks ago I hadn't been able to walk more than an hour without having to rest for another; strange how easily one became accustomed to a different life-style. Besides, it helped that I had lost at least a little weight; my clothes no longer fitted as tightly as before and I didn't have to lever myself up from the ground by hanging on to something. A small victory, perhaps, but it did me the world of good.

Around three in the afternoon it began to rain in earnest, the sort of rain that states its intention of continuing for some time. We pulled off the road to shelter while we donned our cloaks and I adjusted Mistral's load to give the animals maximum protection; it also gave Growch the opportunity to shake himself all over us.

It was lucky we were off the road, for Mistral pricked her ears and gave us warning of horsemen approaching. We crowded back farther into the trees as six horsemen rode by, looking neither to left nor right, mud splashing up from the horses' hooves to mire the fluttering cloaks. of the riders. They went by too fast for me to recognize anyone and they were probably not seeking us at all, but their appearance gave us all a nasty jolt.

Besides, even innocent travelers were wary of sudden strangers, especially when they were as unprotected as we were. Bandits, brigands, mercenaries were none of them averse to slitting a quick throat and making off with the spoils and even opposing armies had been known to break off the conflict for long enough to plunder a caravan and share the spoils, then happily rejoin the conflict.

We waited for half an hour before rejoining the road, just in case, and the downpour grew steadily worse. We found we were plodding, head down, the freshening wind driving into our faces and under our clothes till we were all as blind as Gill and soaked through. There was little shelter to either side and I couldn't have lighted a fire, so we just struggled forward, hoping against hope for a deserted hut, a byre, anything at all we could use to get out of the wet.

To add to our misery there can an unseasonal thunderstorm, lightning crackling down the sky with a noise like ripped cloth and thunder bouncing along the road ahead of us. We even seemed to be walking through the fires of hell, for the road by now was a shallow lake with the rain, and the sheets and daggers of lightning were reflected off it like a burnished shield, till I was almost blinded.

A bolt of lightning split a tree off to our right and as I instinctively started back I thought I could see a building just beyond the smoldering tree. Another flash lit up the sky and yes! there was definitely something there. Grabbing Mistral's bridle with one hand and Gill with the other I started to follow a narrow path that seemed to lead in the right direction. As we drew nearer the building the storm revealed it as a small castle built of stone, but there was no sign of life.

We ended up in front of a massive oaken door studded with iron and with a huge ring set in one side. I thumped on the wood and shouted: "Anyone there?" two or three times, but there was no answer. I tried again with the same result, and a last, greatly daring, twisted the iron ring. At first it was so stiff it would not yield an inch, but when Gill lent a hand it slowly turned and the door, with our weights behind it, juddered open a fraction.

"Once more," I panted, and suddenly it swung wide with a loud groan. As I stepped forward into the stuffy darkness I became aware of two things: my ring was burning like fire and the pig was crying: "No, no, no! It's *bad!*"

13

Too late for any warnings: we were in. The relief was so great that any trepidation I might have had was canceled by the luxury of four walls and a roof. The place was dusty, fusty, stuffy, but it was sheer heaven contrasted with outside. Obviously old and untenanted, except probably by rats, mice and cockroaches, it nevertheless must have once been a place of some consequence.

It was fashioned on the old lines; a great hall on the ground floor with a fire in the center that would have found its way through a hole in the roof, a raised dais at one end for the lord and his guests to dine, and presumably outhouses for cooking and stabling. There were turret stairs leading to two round towers I had noticed from outside, but the stairs had collapsed and there was no way up. There was a stairway at the back, but this led only to the chaos of storm-ridden battlements.

Our priorities were warmth and food. There were plenty of crumbling sticks of furniture—tables, stools, benches—so I soon had a brisk fire burning in the central fireplace, unpacked Mistral and rubbed her down, plonked Gill down on a rickety stool near enough the fire for his clothes to steam and hung our sodden cloaks to dry. Decided to feed the animals first, I gave the pigeon some grain and dashed out in the rain again to pull up some grass for Mistral and the tortoise. I set out some corn for the Wimperling, but he cowered under Mistral's belly, still moaning about things being "Bad, bad!"

Growch, stretched out beside the fire steaming gently and beginning to smell quite high in the warmth, told him quite rudely to shut his trap.

I rummaged in our packs for food, wishing I had had time to stock up better. There must be something. . . . In the end I decided on an experiment. I had plenty of beans and grain, but no time to soak the former. Perhaps the latter would yield to drastic treatment. I put some pork fat in the cooking pot, heated it till it smoked, then dropped in a handful of grain. The results were quite dramatic.

There was a moment's pause and then the pot crackled, spat, popped, and grain cascaded everywhere, all puffed up to three times its size or more. A lot sprang back into the fire, more over the floor and I caught some in my apron. Too late I slammed the lid on the pot. In the end I had a large bowlful of something crunchy and very tasty. I devoured a handful then gave the rest to Gill, under protest from Growch.

"Mmmm," said Gill. "Any more?"

The second and third lot was much better because I remembered the lid. Not entirely filling, but certainly better than nothing. I offered some to the Wimperling, hoping to tempt him out of his terrors, but he wasn't having any.

"No, no, not here! This place is bad. . . ."

"Suit yourself," I snapped, by now quite cross, more so because my ring was still tingling and yet my sight and common sense told me there was nothing wrong. The place was old, but it was empty of threat, I was convinced.

"Seems to be getting colder, Summer," said Gill. He was actually shivering. Suddenly it seemed also several degrees darker in the hall. Of course it would, I told myself: it must be well after the set of a sun we had never seen; time to make up the fire and settle down to a night's rest. I made up the fire, fetched out the blankets, luckily only slightly damp, and wrapped myself up tight. I fell into an uneasy sleep, waking every now and again almost choking with the smoke that no longer found its exit in the roof, but was wreathing the hall with bands and ribbons of greyish mist.

Growch and Gill were snoring, but Mistral was restless, twitching her tail; the pigeon was still awake, and so was the tortoise. There was no sign of the pig. I got up to replenish the fire yet again, but it was no longer throwing out any heat. It sulked and spat and burned yellow and blue around the wood, which smoldered but would not catch. I lay down again but sharp cold rose from the flagstones beneath me, making my bones ache. Flinging the blanket aside I grabbed Gill's stool and hunched as near as I could to the fire, till my toes were almost in the embers and the wool of my skirt smelled as though it were scorching, though it was cool to the touch.

"May I join you?"

I must be dreaming, I thought. I could have sworn somebody spoke. I glanced around: nothing but wreaths of smoke crowding the shadows.

No one there except the animals, Gill and myself. I kicked the fire, hoping for flame, but there was none. It must be well after midnight—

"Greetings! May I join you?"

I whirled around, my heart beating like a drum. "Who—who's there?" It didn't sound like my voice, all high and squeaky. In spite of the cold I could feel myself beginning to sweat. Cautiously I slide my hand towards the bundles and luckily found a candle almost at once. Lighting it in a stubbornly flameless fire was more difficult, but the melting wax encouraged a quick flare. Holding the candle high I stood up.

"I said: 'Who's there?' "

"Only me. Sorry if I gave you a fright." Whoever it was gave a little laugh as though he was perfectly at home.

"Where are you?"

"Here . . ."

The voice came from the shadows on the other side of the fire, and now I thought I could see an indistinct shape among the clouds of smoke that made me cough and squint.

"Do I have your permission to join you?" From what I could make out the figure was small and slight, not much taller than I was. What a strange question though: presumably the place was as much his as ours; we were all trespassers.

"Are you alone?" I asked.

"Alone? I am always alone." Again that light, sneering laugh. "No one has visited this place for a very long time. You must be the first for . . . oh, I suppose at least fifteen years. Before that—Nice to see fresh faces. The last people here were a band of robbers. Not very nice people. No *culture* . . ." The figure came nearer, but the smoke made it seem blurred at the edges. "I ask again: may I join you?"

Why this insistence upon invitation? It was the fourth time. From the way he spoke—

"Is this your place? Do you live here?"

He paused for a moment, then laughed again. "This is my family home, yes. But I don't *live* here. Not exactly. More visitor's rights, you might say."

"Then we are the intruders. Please—" "make yourself at home" I was about to say, but there was an agonized squeal from the shadows.

"No, no, no!" cried the Wimperling. "Don't ask it in! Part of the spell! Bad, bad, bad!"

I felt him creep against my skirts, and nudged him with my foot. "What spell? You're being stupid. He has more right than us to be here. Just be quiet."

"Don't invite him to join you—"

But this time I kicked him quite hard, my irritation getting the better of me, and he scuttled away into the shadows again, with a pitiful cry like a child's. I was instantly sorry, of course, but turned my pity into a welcome for our visitor.

"You are most welcome. Please come and join us."

"Us?"

Couldn't he see? "My—my brother and our animals. They are all asleep. Except for the pig."

I could have sworn he hissed between his teeth. He moved forward, however, and now I could see him more clearly.

To my surprise our visitor was little more than a youth, perhaps a year younger than myself, with the beginnings of a fluff of beard. He was fair, with unfashionably long hair curling down to his thin shoulders, and likewise his clothes were unfamiliar. A long tabard reaching to below his knees, complemented with old-fashioned cross-gartered hose and set off with a short, dark cloak, fastened to one shoulder with a gold pin. In his left ear he sported a gold earring, and there were rings on his fingers and a twisted bracelet on his right arm. He carried, of all things, a tasseled fly-whisk, which he waved in one languid hand.

I vacated my stool. "Please . . ."

He smiled and sat down, showing small, pointed teeth. "I thank you, fair damsel."

Unaccountably flurried, I found a backless chair and joined him by the fire. We stared at one another across the cold flames. I was shivering, but he seemed perfectly comfortable.

"You said this was your family's home? Do you live nearby?"

"I regard this as my home. Do you know any stories?"

I blinked at the change of subject. "Why, yes, I suppose so. My mother was a great storyteller. But first—"

"Nothing like a good story to pass the time." He wriggled on the stool like an expectant child. "I hope you have a *great* story to tell me." He stroked his almost nonexistant beard. "A story is almost my *favorite* thing in the world. . . ." Close to, he was very, very pale, almost chalk-like, the skin near transparent. Obviously he didn't get out much. Contrasted with him, Gill and I looked disgustingly tanned and healthy. So far he had made me feel uneasy, uncomfortable: I couldn't say I liked him at all, but we were intruding in his home, and I thought I should try and make myself agreeable.

"Would you like something to eat? There isn't much, but—"

He turned on me a look of fury. "What makes you think I am hungry

for your disgusting comestibles? Of what use are they save to make you
better able to— Never mind. . . ." With a visible effort, it seemed, he
settled back on the stool and gave another of those rather unpleasant
sniggers. "Don't mind me; I am my own company much of the time, and
it makes me forget the social niceties." He waved that absurd fly-whisk
in front of his face. "Quite warm for the time of the year isn't it?"

As I was practically freezing and it seemed to be getting colder and
colder, I didn't know what to say to this. I changed the subject.

"You said this was your home?"

"I have lived here all my life." He leaned forward and quite deliberately passed his thin, white hands through the blue flicker of flame in
the fireplace. I reached forward to snatch at him, but the fingers were
white and unmarked as before. Suddenly I wanted to wake Gill, Growch,
all of them. "Very fond of this place I am," he mused.

"I am sorry we intruded. I did call out. . . ."

"I heard you, but—but I was some way away at the time. Don't
apologize. You are more welcome than you know. It is rare that I can
welcome strangers these days. . . ." He stroked his beard once more,
once more came that disconcerting giggle. "Of course in the old days
this place was quite, quite, different. . . ."

A story was coming, I was sure of it. *His* story. I leaned forward
on the chair, my chin in my hands, as I used to do when Mama had
conjured up a fresh tale for my delight.

The stranger smiled, showing those pointy teeth again. "The story
starts many years ago—I *am* enjoying this: it is many years also since
I had the chance to tell it—when the country was wilder and less civi-
lized than it is now. It all began when a great chief who had fought in
many wars and gathered much plunder decided to build for himself and
his new wife (part of his booty) a home in which to settle down and
raise a family. He was now well into middle age and wearied of battle."
The stranger almost absent-mindedly passed his hands through the
flames again, and this time it seemed for a moment as though his thin,
white fingers were lapped in fire. "He chose this site, near the highway,
topping a small rise, surrounded by forest and near enough a stream for
water. He annexed a thousand acres of the forest for his hunting and set
those slaves he had captured to building this castle. By the time it was
completed his eldest son was nineteen, the second seventeen, the youngest . . ." For a moment he hesitated. "The youngest near sixteen."

There was a movement at my side: Gill had woken and was propped
on his elbow, listening. Quickly I explained what had happened. The
stranger frowned petulantly: obviously he did not care for interruptions.

"To continue . . . The finished castle was furnished in the most exquisite way possible. The Lord had brought with him hangings, gold, silver, silk, wool, carved chests of sandalwood, pelts of wolf and bear, timber and pottery, all part of his conquests, and his wife, children—even his servants—were dressed in the finest of materials."

My eyes half-closed, I could see it all: the splendor, the comfort, the ease of living . . .

"It seemed nothing could ever mar this idyllic existence: a united family, devoted servants, a fine home, but all was not as it seemed." He shifted on his stool, stroked his wispy beard, flicked the fly-whisk, toyed with his earring. "From an outsider's point of view the three sons were all their father could have wished for. The eldest, tall and fair-haired like his father, was skilled at arms, a womanizer and a prodigious quaffer of ale; the second son was dark like his mother, merry and careless, with a fine singing voice. It was the third son who was different. Outwardly unlike either parent, except for his father's fairness and his mother's eyes, he was slighter, more refined in manner, a great reader and penman. His ideas were in advance of his time; he wanted his father to annex more land, build onto the castle, expand a common holding into a kingdom! But his parents were not interested." He frowned. "They should have known better. . . ."

I glanced around. All the animals were awake too.

"His father's hairs were grey now, and when he wasn't in the saddle with his falcons he was dozing by the fire. The mother died of a low fever and the two eldest boys ran wild, promising each other how they would enjoy life after their father's death, filling the castle with wine, women and song! They laughed at the youngest son, gibed at his bookish ways, his ineptitude at the hunt, his miserable showing with the two-handed sword, his distaste for wenching, his lack of prospects as the youngest. By law the estate should be divided between all three equally on their father's demise, but he knew he had little chance of a fair deal with two such brothers."

The stranger was still scowling, now biting at his nails between sentences. He really was absorbed in his story, I thought. The ring on my finger was now colder than I was. Biting cold . . .

"The youngest son smoldered with anger, with frustration, with contempt for his weak father, fear of what would happen when his brothers inherited. It was as he feared. His father was scarcely in his grave when the two eldest brothers filled the castle with whores and roisterers. Week-long, month-long, they caroused and capered till the air was thick with the stench of scorched meats, sour wine and stale sex!" He rose to his feet and paced back and forth, the smoke from the fire swirling round his fingers like an extra cloak. "Driven to near madness, the youngest son consulted a witch, then sought certain plants in the forest. Taking them up to the turret room where he spent his days he brewed and distilled them until he had a vial of liquid the color of blood and clear as wine. He tasted—Ach! Bitter! Too bitter to mix with anything. He added more water, cloves, honey; much better.

"Waiting for another night of feasting the youngest son crept down with the vial beneath his cloak to join the revelry. He watched until the servants had been dismissed and the eldest brothers were too drunk to notice his actions. He then proposed a toast to a long life and a happy one, taking care to open a new bottle and add his poison to the brew. It did not take long: within five minutes they were slumped at the table, no longer breathing. The young man then went out to the kitchens and stables and threw out the servants, not caring where they went. Coming back into the hall he gloated over the bodies at the table, then remembered his two young sisters, asleep in the other turret. Taking a knife he crept up the stairs and cut their throats as they slept. It was like slaughtering two suckling pigs. . . ."

I shivered, not from the cold this time. I saw out of the corner of my eye that Gill had made a grimace of distaste; he liked the story no better than I did. I liked even less the way it was being told—there was a sort of gloating about the stranger that I found scary.

"Coming back to the hall the young man noticed with horror that one of the brothers was groaning. Obviously diluting the poison had weakened it, so he took his brother by the hair, tilted back his head and slit this throat. Then he did the same to the other, just in case, and the bright blood spurted onto the linen cloth, quite ruining it." He sounded more regretful of the spoiled napery than the murders—I shivered again I could swear that a fine mist was stealing through the high slit windows of the hall and under the door, to thicken the smoke that already seethed around us.

The young man reseated himself, rubbing his hands together with a dry, whispery sound like the shuffle of dead leaves. "A good story, don't you think?"

Gill sat up and rubbed the sleep from his eyes. "And all this happened right here? Then I am surprised it has not been pulled down long since! Such places are accursed! If we had known . . .

"But we didn't and it has done us no harm," I said briskly, as much to convince myself as him. "I presume the young man was taken and hanged for his crimes?"

"No, it was not at all like that," said the stranger. "No one came near the place—the servants were all gone, if you remember, and this place is very isolated—so the young man's crimes went undiscovered. At first he delighted in the solitude, the peace, but after a while the silence began to oppress him and he found he was talking to himself, just to hear another voice. He even invented conversations with the corpses at the table. . . ."

"They were still there?" I queried, aghast. Something too terrible to name was nagging at the back of my mind, but as yet I couldn't put a name to it. But when I did—

"Oh, yes. He left them as they were, a reminder of his victory. As time went on and none came to investigate, he loosed the horses, hounds and falcons and the corpses were chewed by rats till nothing but the lolling bones, strands of hair and scraps of clothing were left." He sighed. "After a while even talking to the dead began to pall, so the young man traveled to the nearest town, seeking company. He had not eaten for weeks and he thought perhaps the lack of food had made him transparent, for all passed him by as though he did not exist and none answered his pleas for help. In the end he went back to his dead family, for that was all he had left. After many years, at infrequent intervals, travelers— like yourselves—sought shelter. Then the young man was happy, for he persuaded them to tell him stories, tales to remember that he could hug to himself during the long years when no one visited." And he hugged his arms around his knees, much as that other young man must have done all those years ago.

"And the bodies?" I asked, glancing about me fearfully.

"Oh, they eventually crumbled into dust," said the stranger indifferently. "It all happened over two hundred years ago. Even the bodies of the last travelers are dust. . . ."

"The last travelers?" said Gill sharply, while a rising panic threatened to choke me. "Why did they not leave?"

"They didn't know any stories," said the stranger discontentedly. "The young man wove his spell about them, but still they didn't understand. He even offered to break the chain that held them, let them out one by one, but they still wouldn't play fair. So . . ." He fell silent.

"And so?" prompted Gill, and in his voice I heard an echo of all the horrors that were threatening to envelop me entirely.

"Eh? Oh, the usual thing happened. When they found they couldn't escape they went mad. Killed each other. The only exciting thing was betting on the survivor. Not that he ever lasted long on his own . . ."

Gill rose to his feet. "Then, with all these bloody murders, I'm surprised the place isn't haunted!"

"Oh, but it is," said the stranger. "It is haunted by the ghost of the youngest son. He still waits here for those who have a tale to tell."

I could feel the hair rising on my scalp. "Then—then why aren't you afraid?" I backed away, my chair overturning with a crash.

"Afraid? Why should I be afraid?" He smiled at us sweetly. "You see—I *am* the ghost!"

14

It is impossible to describe what happened in the next few moments. For one thing, I was too frightened to do anything except open my mouth and yell; for another, everything happened on top of itself.

I screamed, Gill fell over something and brought me down with him, the animals panicked and yelled as well and the stranger rushed round and round bleating trivialities like a demented sheep. That made it worse. My expectant terror had anticipated that he—It—would turn into something shrieking and gibbering, wearing a linen sheet, dragging Its chains and blowing like the east wind through a fleshless mouth—

Instead he—It—seemed to flow around us like the smoke from the fire, never touching us but making little patting, placatory gestures, tut-tutting in that high, mellifluous voice, soothing as if the terror I felt had an origin other than Itself. Apart from Its outlandish dress, It looked disturbingly normal, capering around us with Its senseless blandishments.

"No need to panic . . . didn't mean to alarm you . . . all a joke really. Want to be *friends* . . . you must stay awhile . . . don't run away . . ." It went on and on till the whisperings were as thick in my ears and nose and mouth as the air I breathed and I would have promised anything if it would just stop for a minute and let me *think*. . . .

So this—this creature—purported to be a two-hundred-year-old fratricide! This pale, frail youth walking and talking like anyone else . . . No, it just wasn't believable. It was a joke: in bad taste, to be sure, but still a joke. Well, I would call Its bluff.

"That's a—" My voice was coming out like a bat's squeak. I tried again. "That's a good act of yours. . . ." Better. "I congratulate you. But perhaps if you dressed differently, tried a few screams and howls, colored lights . . ."

It stopped rushing about and looked at me doubtfully. "What do you mean? I can't change myself. It's how I was—am! You don't like the story? I can't change that either." It seemed really put out. "You want special effects? Well, perhaps I can arrange some of those. Wait just a minute or two. . . ." and It turned and walked up to the other end of the hall.

There was a violent nudge at my ankle.

"Get away, quick!" whispered the Wimperling. "Now's our chance!"

"What for? I want to see what he's doing—"

"No, you don't!" and this time he gave me a sharp nip. "If he weaves a strong enough spell he can keep us here forever! Didn't you listen to his story?"

"Of course I did! But he's not a *real* ghost; ghosts don't look like that. He's just a storyteller, playing a game—"

"Game, my arse!" growled Growch, shivering so hard his teeth clattered. "You've lost yer senses of a sudden; let's go!"

I looked round at the others. Mistral had backed away into a corner and the pigeon and the tortoise had hidden their heads. I suddenly felt betrayed by them all. Even Gill looked disturbed, afraid, but I knew there was no harm in the youth: how could there be? All I wanted was to see what It would do next. Even my accursed ring was hurting so much I wanted to tear it off.

All right: if I couldn't have my fun, then I would teach them all a lesson! Striding over to the horse with the blankets over my arm, I rolled and stowed them, snapped shut the cages that held Basher and Traveler and fetched the cooking pot and slung it over the other goods. Lucky I hadn't unpacked all our gear. If I'd had to start at the beginning my temper would have gotten even worse.

Running over to the door I flung it open with a crash, letting in a howling gale and lashing rain.

"You are scared shitless? You want to go out in that? Then go, and good riddance! Me, I'm staying here."

They cowered away from me as though I had struck them, all save the Wimperling. He stood his ground.

"We're not going without you," he insisted. "But don't you *see* what danger you're in? There is no more substance to that—that *Thing* than the shadows which surround him!"

"Rubbish!" I snapped, and went back over to Gill, still standing by the cold fire, moving his blind head from side to side like a wounded animal.

"Summer? Is that you? What's going on?"

"I'm here. . . ." I took his hand, if possible even colder than mine and clammy with fear. "Don't worry; there's nothing to be scared of. The stranger has promised us some magic. Special effects, he said. Ah, it looks as though they are starting now."

Beyond us, on the dais where once the high table had stood, came a reddish glow. I moved down the room, dragging the reluctant knight with me, and out of the incandescence I could hear the high mannered voice of the stranger.

"Come nearer, nearer! That's it, right at the front. No, you won't need that candle. . . . Now, watch!" It sounded just like a showman at a fair.

As I stared at the red light, which shifted and swayed like smoke, now brighter, now dimmer, I thought I could discern the outlines of a table, a bench, shadowy figures seated in front of dishes and goblets.

"Closer . . ." urged the voice, now almost in my ears. The smoky dimness swirled back like a curtain and everything became clearer. There was no sound and the outlines wavered now and again like wind on a tapestry, but I could see distinctly two men seated at the table, obviously enjoying the remnants of a feast. A silent carousal, I nevertheless added imagined sounds to myself. They chewed at lumps of meat, quaffed their wine, tossed back their heads and laughed, clapped one another on the shoulder. They both seemed to be dressed in the same quaint way as the stranger, but their outlines were so changeable it was difficult to be sure.

"Not perfect," said the languid voice in my ear, "but memory is not infallible. Watch this: enter the villain!"

Behind the two men I saw the stranger, a flagon of wine in one hand, a vial in the other. He was as insubstantial as the others but I saw part of the story he had told enacted before my credulous eyes. The vial was tipped into the flagon, the men drank a toast and then their heads sank to the table as though they were asleep, and the stranger tiptoed away with a silent giggle. The wavering picture remained thus for a minute or two and I explained to Gill what I had seen.

"It's very clever," I said. "I don't know how he does it!"

"I don't like it," muttered Gill. "Please can we go?"

"It's pitch-black, blowing a gale and raining torrents outside," I said. "Besides, I want to watch. . . ."

The men in the illusion were very still, but then one of them moved a little, choked, flung out an arm. The figure of the stranger appeared again, but this time he carried a knife, a knife that already dripped blood. A hand came out, plucked at the hair of the man who had moved, jerked back his head until the throat was stretched tight, and then slit it from ear to ear. At first a thin beaded seam where the knife had entered and then a great gush of blood that fountained across the table—The stranger turned to the second man—

"No, no!" I screamed. "I believe you, I believe you!"

I pulled at Gill's hand, my heart thumping, and turned to run, but now, between us and the open door at the other end of the hall, stood the grinning figure of the stranger, the murderous ghost, knife still in hand, and now he seemed of a sudden more substantial than anything else around us. Even the animals huddled by the door were assuming a dim and cloudy aspect, seeming to have lost their colors like well-leached cloth.

It smiled that sickly-sweet smile at us again. "Well, I gave you your special effects: did you like them? You must admit I have played *my* part: now it is *your* turn to entertain *me*." The last words were as sharp and threatening as the knife he carried.

"Let us go, we haven't harmed you. . . ." Why, oh why, hadn't I listened to the Wimperling?

"You haven't done me any good, either! That illusion-making takes it out of me." The tone was as sulky and whining as a child's. "Tell me a story, you promised me a story. Lots of stories! I'll let you go when you have told me a story—if I like it, that is. If I haven't heard it before." He moved closer, tossing the knife in the air and catching it. "Come on, we haven't got all night. . . ."

I backed away, still clutching Gill's arm, looking desperately for a way to escape, but the ghost was still between us and safety, and now he seemed to be taller, broader than before. I fetched up against the wall, side-stepped and seemed to find another I couldn't see, only feel—like cushioned stone. I moved the other way and there was another barrier. It seemed as though we were surrounded—was this what the Wimperling had warned me against? Was this the invisible "chain" that had trapped all others who visited the hellish place? There was only one thing for it.

"Just one story and you will let us go?"

"If I like it well enough."

"What—what kind of story?"

"Oh, knights and ladies, witches and dragons, giants and ogres, shipwrecks and sea monsters, spells and counter-spells—Heaven and Hell and the Four Winds!"

Up until that very moment I had known dozens of tales; ones my mother had told me, stories from the Bible the priest told us, tales we had heard on our travels, ones I made up for myself (the largest amount). I could have sworn that with a minute or two's thought I could spin a yarn to satisfy any critic, but all of a sudden my mind was completely empty. I couldn't even summon up the magic formula that started all stories, that first thread drawn from the spinning wheel that has all else following without thought.

"Well? Why haven't you begun?"

"I—I . . ."

"Get on with it! I warn you, I'm beginning to lose my patience! You're just like all the others: no fun. . . ." The voice managed at the same time to be both petulant and menacing. " 'Once upon a time . . .' "

That was it! I looked once more at the ghost, who had stretched and expanded until his head nearly touched the beams overhead, a thin wraith like a plume of colored smoke, a genie escaping its lamp. I opened my mouth to start, hoping now that the rest would follow. My ring throbbed mercilessly.

"Once—"

"No!" It was another voice, a small voice but one made sharp and decisive by some sudden determination. It didn't sound like the Wimperling at all. "He'll have you if you do! Don't say another word. Just get ready to run. . . ." And with that I saw the most extraordinary sight.

A roundish object suddenly launched itself like a boulder from a catapult. As it reached a height of a couple of feet from the ground it seemed to waver for a moment, then there was a snap! and a crack! like a pennon flapping in a gale, and wings sprouted on either side, a nose pointed forward, a tail balanced back, and the pig rose to ten, twelve feet in the air and then, yelling like a banshee, swooped down and passed right *through* the ghost's body, just where its stomach would be!

The ghost-thing wavered and twisted and began to thicken and shrink back to its normal size, but where the Wimperling had flown through there was a great gaping hole, a sudden window through which everything once more looked clear and sharp. But the hole was beginning to close up again, to heal itself even as I dragged Gill forward. Then was a buzzing above our heads like a thousand bluebottles and the Wimperling zoomed above our heads, yelling, "I'm going to try it again, but my strength is failing. . . . As I go through, run for your lives!"

He arrowed down once more on the now normal-sized figure and as his flailing wings beat aside the trails and tatters of vapor that made up the creature, Gill and I ran hand-in-hand right through what remained. For one heart-stopping moment there was resistance, a sudden darkness, a frightful stench, then we were near the open door. Now the darkness was only that of night; the resistance, the wind; the smell that of rain. Never had I been so glad to face a storm before!

I grabbed Mistral's bridle with my free hand and we all ran down the path away from the castle, unheeding of dark and wind and rain. Some fifty yards away I stopped and counted heads.

"Oh, God! Where's the Wimperling? He must be . . . Wait there, the rest of you!" and I ran back to the castle door, my heart thumping with renewed terror. Growch, to do him credit, was right at my heels. I stepped into the hall and there was the ghost, still gathering pieces of itself together, gibbering and mouthing threats; there, too, was the little pig, trying vainly to drag its battered body towards the door. Growch hesitated only a moment then rushed forward, barking and snapping hysterically. Seizing my chance I dashed forwards, snatched up the pig, tucked him under my arm and, shouting to Growch to follow, escaped down the path once more.

As we moved off into the storm we could hear a wailing cry behind us, full of reproach and self-pity.

"Come back, come back! I wouldn't have hurt you. . . . all I wanted was a *story*!"

After that it was hard going, for all of us. The weather cleared for a while after that dreadful night, but the Wimperling lay for days in his pannier in a sort of coma, hardly eating anything. Tenderly I greased his sore wings and saved the choicest pieces of food, and gradually he started to pick up. Gill, however, caught a chill and could not shake it off; night after night I heard his cough get worse. Mistral, too, coughed and shivered; Basher the tortoise retreated into his shell and refused to eat, and Traveler's wing wouldn't heal. As for me, my stomach and bowels churned for days and I had to keep dashing off the road to find a convenient bush.

The weather grew steadily colder, with a biting east wind that snapped at our faces, bit at our heels, snatched at our clothes and blew a scud of leaves and grit into the food. The fires wouldn't light and if they did the hot embers scattered and threatened to set fire to everything. To add to our miseries, we seemed to have lost our way. All the roads were mere tracks between villages, and however much we asked for directions south and followed the road indicated, we still twisted and turned until, as often as not, we ended up facing north again.

The lodgings and food we found were poor and mean, and we were charged far too much: they knew, of course, that we had no choice but to pay what they asked. I began to think we were accursed, except that the ring on my finger was quiet—never again would I ignore its warn-

ing—and that of course Gill and I had made confession as soon as we
could and been absolved. But the days themselves ceased to have individual meaning, apart from the labels of the Saint's days as we passed
through various villages: Barbara, Nicholas, Andrew, Lucy, Thomas . . .

After a particularly hard day—we hadn't seen a village for forty-eight
hours and were on short rations—and five hours walking without rest, it
started to snow. Just the odd flake floating prettily down, but the sky
above held a grey cloak that was gradually spreading from the northeast
and the air smelled of cold iron. I shuddered to think what might happen
if we were caught without cover; we had escaped any heavy falls so far
south, but that searing east wind canceled any advantage of distance.

But it seemed our luck had at last turned, for the next twist in the
road revealed below us what seemed like a fair-sized town, with at least
five or six streets, a large square and two churches. For the first time
in days I could feel my cold face stretching into a smile.

"Warm lodgings and a fair supper tonight, for a change! Come on,
it's downhill all the way. . . ."

By the time we reached the outskirts the snow was falling with that
unhurrying steadiness that meant that, like an uninvited relation, it was
here to stay. Because of the weather there were few folk around; those
that were were engaged on last-minute precautions: putting up shutters,
stabling beasts, hurrying home with a bundle of kindling or a couple of
pies. We enquired for an inn, but the first we found was closed for the
winter, as we were informed by the slatternly girl who answered my
knock, slamming the door in my face before I could ask for further directions.

The snow was now so thick that we found the square by luck only;
I caught at the sleeve of a man hurrying past with a capon under his
arm and a sack over his head for protection.

"An inn, good sir?"

He paused for a moment, blinking the snow from his eyelashes,
then pointed to the other side of the square, gave us a left and a right
and a left. "Martlet and Swan," he said and was gone, swallowed by
the swirling snow.

Now we were the only ones moving in a world of white. We found
the first turning right enough, but I had a feeling we had missed the
second. I could scarce see more than a few yards; the snow was clogging
our footsteps and weighting our clothes. I took a last left turn, but it
seemed as though we were right on the outskirts of town again. I was
just about to turn and retrace our steps, knock at the first door that
would open to us, when I caught sight of the inn sign swinging above

my head. Snow had already obliterated most of the sign, but I could make out the "M-A" of the Martlet and the "S" of Swan, so I knew we were on the right road.

It was larger than the inns we had frequented so far. Double-fronted, the door was locked and barred and there were no lights to be seen. I knocked twice, but there was no answer. On the right, however, the gates were open onto a cobbled yard. We passed under the archway into lights, bustle, activity. On the far side a wagon had just been unloaded and was now being tipped against the snow, while its cargo of sacks was being hurried into shelter. Two steaming draft horses were being led into stables on the right, and buckets of water were sluicing down the cobbles. To our left the door was open onto firelight and the enticing smells of food.

Everyone was too busy to notice us, until I spied out the man who seemed to be directing operations, a well-fed man with a long, furred cloak and red hair, on which the snow melted as soon as it touched. I went over and tugged at his sleeve.

"Sir! Sir? You have lodgings and stabling for the night? For myself, my brother and the animals . . ."

The face he turned towards me had a pleasant, lived-in look, but he seemed to be puzzled.

"Lodgings?"

"Why, yes." Quickly I explained how I had been directed here. "And I saw the sign outside—only a couple of letters, but it was obviously the right place. You aren't full up, are you? I'm afraid my brother is not at all well, and we are cold and hungry. . . . If you are, perhaps you could direct us somewhere else, but . . ." Then I am afraid I started to cry. I couldn't help it. It had been a long, hard, frustrating time since we had fled the castle and the ghost.

He looked at me for a moment longer, then he smiled, a full, heart-warming smile. "Never let it be said . . . Come on, let's look at that sign of mine." Hurrying me out into the street, he gazed up at the nearly covered letters. " 'Martlet and Swan' . . . Dear me: I must get that cleared. No matter, little lady: you found me." And he smiled again, and I knew we were home.

Before I knew what was happening, and with the minimum of direction from the landlord, Gill, his blindness noted, was being led away towards that enticing open door, and I, having insisted, was bedding down the animals with the help of the young stable boy. A rubdown and unloading for Mistral, followed by bran-mash; sleeping Basher tucked away in the box under the manger. Grain for Traveler and the run of the stall. Chopped vegetables and gruel for the Wimperling and a large bone for

Growch: everything I asked for, diffidently enough, appeared as if by magic. But then the inn was obviously not full: Mistral had a commodious closed stall to herself, and there were only the draft horses and a brown palfrey to occupy the rest of the large stables.

The stable boy lighted me over to the side door, now closed, after fastening the yard gates and bolting them. He was obviously glad to be back in the inn, and after a dazzled look around the large kitchen in which I found myself I agreed with him wholeheartedly.

It was the largest kitchen I had ever seen, stretching the length of the stables which matched it across the yard. And there were *two* fires; one obviously incorporating some kind of oven, the other a large spit. Two long tables, one for preparation of food, the other for serving. Cupboards and shelves full of pots and crockery, long sinks for scouring and cleaning, wood stacked waist-high, clothes drying on racks, herbs, onions and garlic swinging gently from strings, hams and bacon hanging from hooks in the smoke-blackened ceiling, baskets of eggs and vegetables, jars of pickles, preserves and dried fruits . . .

And everyone merry and busy, not a long face or laggard step among them. And the nose-tickling smells . . . My mouth was watering as I followed a beckoning finger and found, behind a hastily slung screen, Gill immersed in a large tub of hot water.

"You all right?"

He couldn't answer, for at that moment one of the giggling maids who were scrubbing him put a cloth across his mouth, but he looked happy enough. The landlord poked his head behind the curtain.

"I thought it was the quickest way to warm him up. He'll feel better with the grime of the road away, too. You're next."

No arguments, I noticed. A moment later my clothes were taken away to be washed and I was relaxing in the hot, herb-scented water, my hair combed and rinsed. A brisk rubbing in warmed towels and someone handed me a clean shift and wrapped me in a blanket, shoving my feet into felt slippers a size too large.

I looked around for Gill, but he had evidently preceded me, for by the time one of the servants had ushered me into a parlor at the front of the house, he was already tucking into a bowl of thick vegetable soup. A small round table in front of a blazing fire was laid with linen, bread platters, spoons and knives. I sat down and was instantly served. As I supped I gazed around the comfortable room. Red tiles on the floor, shuttered window, tapestry, huge sideboard decked with pewter and silver, linen chest, a rack of wine . . . What a strange inn!

Hot baths, clothes washed, expensive surroundings—I hoped to God my purse would cover the cost! And where were the other guests? True, there was a third place laid at the table: we should have to wait and see. I must discuss terms with the cheerful landlord as soon as possible. I finished my broth and the bowl was whipped away,, to be replaced by steaming venison-and-hare pasties, the juice soaking into the bread platter beneath. A pewter goblet of wine appeared at my elbow as I leaned over to cut Gill's pasty and guide his fingers.

"May I join you?" It was our host, changed into a crimson wool robe and a white undershirt, his feet in rabbit's-wool slippers. He should *never* wear that shade of red with his color hair, I thought abstractedly, even as I welcomed and thanked him for his excellent hospitality. I had better tackle him straightaway, I thought, even as fruit tarts and cheese were placed on the table. He gave me the opening I needed. "I trust everything is to your satisfaction?"

"Everything is just fine, sir and we are most grateful, but I am afraid we cannot afford—"

He frowned, then smiled. "I had forgot. Perhaps I had better explain. That notice, so helpfully cloaked by the snow, does not read 'Martlet and Swan', but rather 'Matthew Spicer, Merchant.' The inn is two roads away, I'm afraid, but the natural mistake has given me the opportunity to enjoy your company. As my guests, naturally so no more talk of money, little lady!"

15

Those weeks we spent in Matthew's house were like another world to me. Not only were we cosseted, fed, warm, entertained and cared for—we were *safe*. We had only been on the road some seven weeks or so, and yet it seemed to me that I had spent an eternity footsore, usually hungry and cold and always anxious. Not anxious for myself so much as the others. And to have that burden of responsibility taken, however temporarily, from my shoulders was like shucking off a load of wood I had carried, and immediately feeling I could bounce as high as the trees.

My mother had taught me a trick when I was little; lean hard against a wall, pressing one arm and shoulder as tight as I could. Count to a hundred then stand away from the wall. Your arm rises up of its own accord, like magic! I felt like that released arm.

Of course on that first evening there was a lot of explaining to do. At first I had felt like grabbing Gill's arm and rushing out into the night, so embarrassed was I at mistaking a rich merchant's house for an inn, but our host soon made us feel at home.

"A natural mistake, little lady, in all that confusing snow! And what would you have done in my place? Confronted by a damsel in distress, what could any Christian do but take her and her brother in?" He chuckled. "Besides, the servants tell me it is getting thicker by the moment out there. Six inches settled already, and by morning it will be two or three feet. No, it was Providence that brought you to my door, I'm convinced, and Preference will keep you here! But of course," he added hastily, "if after a while you tire of my hospitality, you are perfectly free to go elsewhere."

"But we cannot impose on you like this! You must allow me to—"

"Now you're not going to spoil our new acquantanceship by talking about money, I hope! Money is one thing I don't need. Companionship

I do. As a widower without family I find I do not make friends easily, and strangers such as yourselves will give me an interest to take me out of my usual dull routine. So, you will be doing *me* the favor by staying for a while. . . . Ah, mulled ale! Just what we need."

It was piping hot, redolent with cloves, cinnamon and ginger. I stretched out towards the fire, dazed with heat and food and drink. I hadn't felt as good as far back as I could remember—in fact since before my mother died, when we had stoked up the fire, told stories and eaten honey cakes, while the wolf wind of winter had howled down the chimney and keened under the door, making the sparks at the back of the chimney glow into patterns among the soot.

"Perhaps for a day or two, then . . ." I said weakly. He *had* sounded as though he meant it.

Gill was seized with a fit of coughing and clenched his fist against his chest with a look of pain. I leaned over and rubbed his back but the merchant went into action at once.

"Time we got your brother to bed. That cough sounds bad. Tomorrow we shall engage a doctor, snow or no snow."

He led us up a winding stair to the next floor and pointed to the left. "That is the solar. And here . . ." to the right: "the bedroom."

It was a long, commodious chamber, strewn with rushes, hung with tapestries, dominated by a huge bed that would have slept six with ease. A huge fire burned in the hearth; candles were glimmering on a table by the fire and on two blanket chests against the walls. Two heavily carved chairs stood on either side of the fireplace and a series of hooks on one wall provided hanging space for clothes. Between the two shuttered windows was a small *prie-dieu*. A low archway at the far end was protected by a curtain.

"For washing and the usual offices," said the merchant, following my gaze. "I shall show your brother. Come, sir," and he led him away.

I moved over to the bed but let out a stifled gasp as I saw the covers move, and a moment or two afterwards a naked man and woman slipped from beneath the covers and unselfconsciously donned the clothes they had left on the floor. The woman bobbed a curtsy.

"I believe the chill is off the sheets now, mistress, but a maid will be up in minute or two to renew the hot bricks. . . ." and with that the pair of them disappeared downstairs, leaving me open-mouthed. What luxury! Was this the way it was done among the rich? Come to think of it, many times at night my mother had insisted I retire first "to warm up the bed for my old bones. . . ." A maid scurried in with hot bricks wrapped with flannel, which she exchanged for those that must have already cooled. The bed looked very inviting, piled high as it was with furs.

The merchant came back with Gill, now shivering. "Into bed at once. Shall we put him on this side? No, I think it better if he is in the middle, then with you and me on either side he will keep warmer." He helped Gill under the covers and slipped into bed beside him. He nodded at the curtained recess. "Take a candle with you, little lady," and I headed for the *garde-robe*.

When I returned another maid was handing Gill a posset; she waited till he drank it then snuffed all the candles but two slow burners, in case we needed to relieve ourselves during the night. She bobbed away, but I hesitated. I knew it was the custom for a host and his lady to share their bed with guests, but even in the ill-assorted places in which Gill and I had slept we had never shared a pallet. In the open we had slept with more intimacy, but the animals had been there too. . . .

Matthew Spicer propped himself on his elbow. "Something the matter?"

"Er . . . No. That is . . . I think I'll just stay here by the fire for a while. I—I'm really not tired—"

"Nonsense, young lady! You've been yawning and blinking for the past two hours!" He scrambled out of bed and came over to me, the long night-shift flapping round his ankles. "It's something I've done, isn't it? Or not done . . . Tell me." For a successful merchant, he had the least self-confidence I had ever seen. But perhaps women made him nervous. Mama had always said that men like that were a pain to begin with but sometimes made the best lovers. Eventually.

"No, no! You've been kindness itself. It's just that—" I glanced over to the bed: Gill was snoring softly. "You see, even at home I never shared a bed with my brother, and on our travels I slept separately also. I have never shared sleeping space with a man. Perhaps I'm being silly, but—"

He struck his forehead with the palm of his hand. "Of course, of course! Being a widower I don't have someone to remind me of the niceties. Come to think of it, if we had people staying overnight they were always married couples who shared. Since then all my guests have been men. Do forgive me! I shall have a pallet made up for you immediately. I— Whatever in the world is *that*?"

"That" was Growch.

He must have escaped from the stables and somehow infiltrated into the kitchen, for in his mouth was a large piece of pastry. He was soaking wet and smelled like a midden, but he rushed to my side and sat on my feet, growling softly through the pasty, his eyes swiveling from me to the merchant, the servants who were in pursuit, and back again.

He "spoke" through his full mouth. "Found you! What's goin' on then?"

"Nothing is 'going on'! You've no right up here! Why couldn't you stay where you were put?" To Master Spicer: "I'm sorry, It's my—our dog. I left him in the stables, but he's been spoiled, I'm afraid, and is not used to being on his own." To Growch I added furiously: "Just get back to the stables right now, and behave yourself!"

"No way! Needs lookin' after, you does. . . ." He belched, having swallowed the pastry whole. "My place is with you." I could see him eyeing the fire greedily. "Never tell what mischief you'll get into without me. No, here I am, and here I'll stay." He looked up at me through his tangle of hair. "Send me back down there again and I'll howl all night, full strength. Keep yer all awake . . . Promise!"

I turned to the merchant apologetically—my exchange with Growch had taken no more than a couple of silent seconds. "I'm sorry if he has been a nuisance. May he stay up here for tonight? I'll—I'll make some other arrangement tomorrow."

He considered. "I have no objection, though in the morning he might reconsider his decision. I happen to share the house with a rather large cat. . . ." He smiled. "Saffron will sort him out. In the meantime he could do with a bath. While they make up your bed."

No sooner said than done. Up came a large tub, in went Growch, and by the time his outraged grumbles had subsided, the bed was made up and he was clean and combed—probably for the first time in his short life. In the meanwhile Matthew Spicer sent for more wine and little spiced biscuits and we sat by the fire together. He didn't ask any questions, but I decided I had better tell him our names and our story. Not the real one of course: I used the one I had told everyone so far, but this time I killed off our parents and for some reason didn't mention my "affianced," or the dowry.

"You have had a hard time, Mistress Somerdai. That *is* a pretty name, by the way: most unusual. If I may say so, it suits you. . . . I see your bed is made up. We shall talk further in the morning."

Shyly I knelt before the *prie-dieu* to give hearty thanks for the temporary haven we had found, then cuddled down in the pallet by the fire. I lay awake for a while, tired though I was, listening to the gentle contrapuntal snores from the bed, and the occasional stifled cough from Gill. There was a soft *flumph!* from outside as a load of snow slid off the roof to the yard below. The fire crackled pleasantly but there was another, less endearing sound: Growch was scratching his ears, flap-flap-flap and snorting into his coat as he chased fleas made lively by the heat. It seemed a bath wasn't enough.

I raised myself on one elbow, my head swimming with the need for sleep. By the light from the night-candle and the fire I could see that my scrawny little black dog was black no longer. He looked half as big again, now his cleaned coat had fluffed out—though nothing could lengthen those diminutive legs—and he was not only black, but tan and brown and grey and ginger and white also.

He sneezed six times.

"Can't you stop that?"

He glared at me from under a fuzzy fringe. "Sneeze or scratch?"

"Both."

"Listen 'ere . . . Never mind. All I can say is, if'n you 'ad these little buggers chasin' around, you'd scratch."

"You wanted to be beside the fire! And don't pretend it was all concern for my welfare, 'cos it wasn't! Anyway, why the sneezing? Caught a chill from the unexpected bath?"

"Nar . . . Stuff they washed me in: smell like an effin' whore, I do."

In the morning Gill was definitely worse, tossing and turning in a fever, his cough hard and painful. Matthew Spicer shook his head. "He needs treatment right away." He flung open the shutters: snow was still falling. He closed them again, and shook his head. "Don't worry; one of the servants will get through."

Up and dressed—my clothes returned clean, mended, pressed—I slipped across the cleared yard to the stables. The others were fine; Mistral had been given fresh hay, Basher was still asleep, and I found grain in the bins for Traveler. The Wimperling's nose peeped out from a nest he had made for himself.

"Everything all right?"

I told him about Gill, and the merchant sending for treatment.

"Don't let him bleed the knight; he needs all his blood." I wondered what on earth he knew of doctoring, but let it pass. After all, he had been right before.

"Are you hungry?"

"A little grain will do. I've had a nibble of hay already."

The "apothecary" arrived an hour or so later, in a litter. I don't know what I had expected, but it was certainly not the small, scrunched-up man with the brown skin, hooked nose and black eyes whose candle-lit shadow on the stairs was the first I saw of him. The stooping silhouette with the grotesque reaping-hook nose at first made me cross myself in superstitious fear, but face to face there was nothing to alarm, quite the reverse. The black eyes sparkled with a keen intelligence, the mouth curved easily into a smile and the thin, hunched shoulders and long, clever fingers emphasised everything he said: a shrug of the body, a wave of the hands more expressive than mere words. These he spoke with a heavily accented touch, at first a little difficult to follow.

Matthew Spicer introduced him with pride. "My friend Suleiman, who comes from the East and specializes in many things, including medicine. We have worked together for many years. He has for a long time been my agent in Araby, but now he has been caught by the weather, providentially for us, I might add! I know of his healing powers and salves of old, and he has consented to treat your brother, Mistress Somerdai." He noted my expression of doubt—so did the visitor. "You couldn't do better, I assure you!"

This was soon evident, at least in Suleiman's meticulous examination of Gill. The Arab first questioned his patient thoroughly, asking for all the symptoms, their duration and severity, before he even touched his body. Then he felt his forehead, looked in his eyes and ears with a little glass, put a spatula in his mouth and peered down his throat, then counted the pulse at his wrist.

He glanced up at me. "Your brother has a high fever; to bring this down is our first priority, but first we must find the seat of it. I believe it is in the chest, and I shall now listen to this."

"How?" I was by now too interested for politeness.

"Watch." From the folds of his capacious red robes he brought forth a metal object shaped like a Madonna lily with a hollow, twisted stem. He held it out to me. "Copied from the horn of a rare antelope in the sands of the desert." He held a silver cup to Gill's mouth and asked him to cough, looking gravely at the sputum. "Too thick . . ." Then he placed the wide end of the metal object on Gill's chest, the thin end in his own ear, and listened intently. Repeating this on various parts of the knight's chest, he asked him to sit up and repeated the process on his back. He then beckoned to me. "Do as I did and listen; make sure the instrument is firmly against his chest."

At first all I could hear was a shush-beat, shush-beat which I realized must be the heart, then as Gill breathed in there was a gurgling wheezy noise, as he breathed out a whistling bubble. Incredible!

Master Suleiman took the instrument from me and held it to his own chest. "Listen to the difference. . . ." The steady heartbeat, somewhat slower, but no wheezing, no whistling. "You understand? Your brother has a deep infection in the lungs, hampering his breathing: it is almost as though he drowns in the ill humours that have gathered. So, we can only cure the fever by eradicating its cause: the lung infection. I shall return to my rooms and prepare certain medicines—"

"You're not going to bleed him, then?" I blurted out, remembering what the Wimperling had said.

He shot me a sharp glance from under dark brows. "Sounds as though you are no friend to leeches?"

"A—a friend of mine . . . He says it takes away your strength."

"Perfectly correct. I sometimes wish we had a method to pump blood *in* instead of taking it *out*." He looked over at Gill, manfully trying to stifle another bout of coughing. "We'll soon ease that. . . . Keep my patient warm, no solid food, plenty of drinks. I shall prepare herbs to be steamed over water on a low boil, to soften the air he breathes in here. Please see the fire does not smoke too much. I shall also prepare an expectorant, a potion to reduce the fever and a sleeping draught."

For once I didn't think of cost: whatever he needed, Gill must have. "Will . . . will he be all right?" I asked, hesitantly, fearfully.

Suleiman glanced at me sympathetically. "I tell the truth. He is very ill, your brother. I have seen men die in his condition and I have seen them live. His advantages are his youth and strength—and, I hope, my medicines. And a prayer or two wouldn't come amiss."

For three days my knight seemed to hover between life and death, but gradually the fever abated, his breathing grew easier and the cough-ing less painful. I did not leave his side save to tend the animals, relieve myself and wash. I even ate my meals by the bedside, though I have no memory of their content.

Suleiman called twice a day, Master Spicer fussed and cosseted, the maids washed and dried the patient, gave him fresh linen and night clothes daily. I dozed in fits and starts on a stool by the bed, trying always to be ready for the turn of the sand-glass for the regular dosings, to see the fire was kept topped up, to be ready with cooling drinks and a damp sponge to wipe away the sweat.

On the morning of the sixth day from our arrival Suleiman came in, examined his patient, then crossed the room and flung the shutters wide.

"The sun is shining, the wind has dropped, the temperature is rising and my patient is recovering! Some fresh air will do us all good." He glanced at me, dazed by sudden sun and ready to drop. "I have the very thing for you, Mistress Somerdai. . . ." and he handed me a vial of thick, greenish liquid. "Half of this in a glass of wine—now!—and I guarantee you will be a new young woman before you know where you are!"

I hadn't the strength to resist and downed the bitter-tasting liquid without a murmur. I don't know about feeling like a new woman, I thought, but if I just lie down for a moment or two and close my eyes I'm sure I will. . . .

"Time to wake up," said Matthew Spicer, gently pinching my ear-lobe. "I'll bet you are hungry. Hot milk and honey has been recommended. Sit up and take a sip."

I did as I was told, opening gummy eyelids, considering how I felt. Apart from an unpleasant taste in my mouth, soon dispelled by a sip or two of the milk, remarkably fit.

"What time is it?"

"A little after two in the afternoon."

"I must have slept over four hours! Sorry . . ."

"Four? More like twenty-eight. You took that draught yesterday morning."

"Yesterday? But I can't have. . . ."

"You did!" said another voice, and there, sitting in one of the large chairs by the fire, wrapped in blankets, sat Gill. A pale, thin Gill, but the hectic flush was gone from his cheeks. He smiled in my direction. "Sleepy-head Summer!"

My heart turned over with love and longing. It was a long time since I had had the chance to study him at leisure. Being on the road had been such a struggle just to survive, especially latterly, that I had grown accustomed to an unshaven, grumbling, blind man who needed all my spare attention. Now he was washed, shaved, fed and at ease, and I found once more I was seeing him as I had that first day, and all the old adoration rushed to the surface, so that I had to hide my face lest Matthew Spicer saw my confusion.

"And in case you are worrying about your menagerie," said the merchant, chuckling: "Don't! The horse and the pig—that one will never fatten—have been given mash, the pigeon grain and reptile left to sleep. When we have some time you must tell me how you acquired such a motley collection! As for your dog—" he nudged a recumbent form lying in the hearth: "—he has been bathed again and near eaten his weight in leftovers. . . ."

Growch was stretched out in a nose-twitching, leg-paddling dream. His curly coat of black and tan, ginger and grey, his white chest and paws, all gleamed in the fire and candlelight, and his stomach was so

full it was stretched as tight as the skin on a tabour, the thinner hair on
his belly showing the pied skin underneath.

"He met Saffron, my ginger cat, on the stairs," continued the merchant. "And he retreated at once, as I knew he would: Saffron makes
two of most dogs, especially in his winter coat. However, I think you
will find they have come to some agreement. Your dog is allowed inside
as long as he recognizes who is boss. . . . And now, Mistress Somerdai,
when you are dressed and have broken your fast, perhaps I may show
you something of my house?"

Through the archway at the top of the stairs was the solar, a pleasant
room with a deep hearth, set with benches on either side. The floor was
polished oak, partly covered with two large rugs the merchant told me
had come from a place called Persher; these were pleasant underfoot
and partially muffled the creak of the floorboards. Two carved chairs
stood by the window, and leather-topped stools provided further seating.
On one side of the curtained doorway were hooks for cloaks; there were
two chests, one containing cushions for extra comfort, the other a set
of games: chess, draughts, backgammon and dice.

In the center of the room was a table, the top inlaid in marble to
represent a chess or draughts board; a hanging cupboard contained three
precious books: a psalter, a breviary, and a delightful Boke of Beestes.
Eventually I read this from cover to cover more than once, carefully
examining the delightfully illustrated initials, head- and tail-pieces, marveling all the while at the strange creatures—spotted, dotted, patched,
striped; furred, feathered, scaled; toothed, beaked, tusked, clawed—that
curled, writhed, marched and snaked across the pages. There were creatures I had never heard of, others I couldn't believe in—gryphons, mer-
men, crocodiles, elephants—and yet, amongst them all were tortoises!
Very strange . . .

The walls of the solar were part paneled, part painted, these latter
in patterns of yellow suns, moons and stars on a pale blue background.
Just as the bedroom windows overlooked the yard, the window in the
solar looked out over the street in front, and it was this window that
was the most curious item in the room. There were the usual shutters,
of course, but now no one need freeze to death to look out on the busy
street below, for the merchant had installed proper windows that opened
outwards for summer and remained closed in winter—all of glass! Not
just plain glass, either: he knew a man who restored stained-glass in
churches, and the window was filled with a higgle-piggle of colors, all
small pieces like a patched cloak—red, blue, yellow, green, purple and
even some that had been part of trees, creatures, faces—so that one

looked out on the street through colors that discolored the folk below, and yet when the sun shone these same pieces threw a rainbow of light onto the polished floor. Like a spring lawn sown with wildflowers . . .

Down the stairs and there were the long kitchens at the back where the staff lived, ate and slept. At the front was the room where we had dined on that first night: "Near the kitchens so the food doesn't get cold," my host explained, and, next to it, with a separate entrance and shuttered counter to the street, the shop where the merchant did his day-to-day business.

A long counter held weighing scales, paper, wax and string. Behind this were piles of small sacks, neatly tied and labeled and above them shelves reaching to the ceiling, filled with bottles, jars, pouches, boxes of all shapes and sizes and parcels. Behind the counter was the merchant's assistant, a small, pocked man called Jacob. But it was the smell of the place one remembered. All through Matthew Spicer's house little teasing scents met one on the stairs, hid in chests, fled down nooks and crannies, popped up in the linen, but here was the source, the heart of it all.

There were herbs in plenty—rosemary, thyme, dill, fennel, sage, rue, peppermint, balm, bay, basil, but it was the scent of the exotic spices that overlay all. Cloves, ginger, cinnamon, cardamon, nutmeg, mace, saffron, pepper, cumin, all combining to tickle the nose with their pungency and invite their flavors to match their aromas.

Matthew Spicer was a member of the Guild, and he explained that most of his goods came from the East to a place called Vennis, a magical town that floated on the sea like an anchored island. From there the goods traveled overland to the nearest western port and again took ship across the Mediterranean to a southern port. From there it came by road to the merchant's house, the bulk being stored in the large sheds at the back of the yard, to be packed into smaller containers ready for distribution to various large towns and cities through the country, and even farther north.

It sounded like a long and complicated business, and I said so.

"Certainly it is," he said. "Sometimes it can take up to three years between ordering something and its delivery."

"And what if one of the ships founders, or your wagons are attacked? Or the spices spoil in transit?"

"Luckily that doesn't happen very often. God is good." He crossed himself. "Also, there is a very good profit margin. I am not poor." He sighed. "But money isn't everything. I lost my wife seven years ago, God rest her soul, and I have no family to carry on the business."

"You could marry again. . . ."

"I could, yes, but if I found a woman who pleased me, who knows but that she might refuse me?" He attempted a smile. "I am not very good at understanding the fair sex, I'm afraid, and I am no longer a young man."

I presumed him to be in his early forties. Not stout, but not slim either; not handsome, but not ugly: he had a pleasant, lived-in sort of face. His reddish hair was thinning slightly but his teeth were still good. I spoke to him as I thought Mama would have done.

"I am sure any woman you chose would be only too pleased to accept your offer. Youth is only an attitude of mind, after all, and you are the kindest man I know."

His face brightened. "You really think so? You have cheered me more than I would have thought possible!"

What with Gill's illness we had missed any Christmas festivities, but with Suleiman as another guest we four celebrated the New Year in style: the rooms decorated with sprays of evergreen, sprinkled with rose water, alive with candles; Mass (except for Suleiman), then back to a veritable feast. Chicken stuffed with dates and olives—two fruits I had never tasted before—a baked ham stuck with cloves and glazed with honey, root vegetables in butter with a touch of ginger, small pastry cases full of meat and spices, the latter so hot they made you feel you breathed fire, roast chestnuts, rice with apple, apricot and other dried fruit and a soft, sheep's-milk cheese.

And to drink a toast to the rebirth of the year, an ice-cold sweet white wine that came, like the silken hangings, from a place called Sissilia . . .

I had anticipated taking our journey up again within days, but the visit to church had not done Gill any good—except spiritually, of course. He started to cough again, and Suleiman insisted that he stay quiet and within doors for a week or more at least. This meant that we fell into a certain routine. After breaking our fast we would, Gill and I, go into the solar, where I would take up sewing and mending, which our clothes sorely needed.

I was surprised to find just how much thinner I had become, and the chore of sewing was mixed with a secret delight in being able to take in my clothes as well as patch and repair them. I regretted that my things were so shabby and worn, but they still covered me well enough and I could not afford to indulge in non-necessities. Gill was a different matter. He had been used to so much better, whether he remembered it or not, and as I had taken to exercising Mistral and Growch if the weather was fine, I took the opportunity of buying some rough woolen cloth, burel,

and fitting my knight for longer braies and a new surcoat. The town was
a pleasant place and obviously Matthew Spicer was held in high regard,
for once folk knew we were staying with him—and news travels faster
than a grass fire in a place like that—we were welcomed with smiles and
cheerful greetings. I suspect, too, that I was given a special price for my
cloth, and for the repair of our shoes which was also essential.

One morning Matthew—he has asked us to dispense with the more
formal address—came into the solar looking helpless, a length of fine
green wool over his arm. He hesitated for a moment, then asked if I had
much sewing in hand.

"Why, no. I have only to finish attaching the ties to these braies. Is
there something you would like me to do?"

"Er . . . yes. There is, actually. If you're sure you don't mind? I
have a sister, married to a Dutchman, and she writes in her letters that
she finds it difficult to buy wool in this particular color." He held the
soft wool against my shoulder. "Yes, the shade is just right! Her coloring
is near yours, and I wonder . . ."

"Yes?" I encouraged, indulgent of this successful man who could
yet be so diffident.

"If you could make her a surcoat," he said, all in a rush. "Something
simple and serviceable, nothing fancy? You and she are much of a height
and size, and if you make generous seams and hems . . . But perhaps I
ask too much?"

"Of course not! I only hope I can do this beautiful material justice."
I fingered it: strong and hard-wearing, it was still fine enough to hang
practically creaseless. "A lovely color: like fresh mint."

He was obviously pleased. "Again, if it's not too much trouble, she
would need two undercottes; I have some fine linen dyed a soft brown
which would go nicely. . . ."

It was the least I could do. He had been so kind to us both: a man
in a thousand.

During the time I sewed, Gill would be practicing on a small lute
Matthew had found, or on my pipes, although he soon became bored
and restless; sighing deeply, drumming his fingers on the furniture,
yawning. Then I would coax him to sing: "Winter's weary winds," "Silk
for my sweetheart," or, if Matthew joined us, tenor, baritone and soprano
would essay a round: "The beggars now have come to town," or something similar.

Afternoons I would read while Gill rested, though if there were a
hint of warmth and sunshine I would take a stroll with Growch—who
had become so used to Matthew's majestic cat, Saffron, that they would

now share the solar hearth together. In the evenings we played chess or draughts or backgammon, Matthew against Gill and me. Not surprisingly, Gill was familiar with all the games, and once recalled a chess set he had had, each piece carved in relief, birds for red, animals for white. If Suleiman joined us the men would swap rhymes and riddles while I stayed quiet and listened, for it was not proper for women to assume an equality with men in this sort of area.

If enough wine had been consumed after Suleiman went home, then Gill and Matthew would sing again, each trying to outdo the other. First Gill might chant the "Gaudeamus igitur," Matthew follow this with the drinking song: "Meum est propositum in taberna more" and both finish with the sentimental "My mistress she hath other loves."

We had further snow in mid-January, but by the end of the month Suleiman pronounced Gill fit enough to travel. He had been taking more exercise each day and almost looked as good as new. But Matthew was a puzzle: the nearer the time came for us to leave, the more restless he became. Then one night it all became clear. Gill had just retired and Matthew roamed around the solar, then abruptly followed Gill. I stretched and yawned, enjoying a few more moments before the fire, when suddenly the curtain was flung back and Matthew appeared, looking thoroughly upset. Had something happened to Gill? I rose to my feet in alarm.

"Whatever's the matter?"

He hesitated, then came towards me. His face was all red. "I'm not sure. . . . Perhaps you can explain?"

"I don't understand. . . ."

"I—I approached the man you call your brother upon—upon a certain matter, only to be told that you and he were not related at all." He really did look most upset. "I think I deserve an explanation!"

16

So I gave him one.

Not the real, entire, whole truth. He wouldn't have believed me. He heard about the knight passing through our village one day, being ambushed the next and wandering about blinded until I found him by chance and had promised to try and find his home, when it was obvious no one else either believed his story, such as it was, or was willing to help.

I told Matthew how Gill couldn't even remember his name, that all I could recall was an impression of his standard. I even brought out the scrap of cloth I had kept, but he shook his head. No help there. From there it was an easy progression to explaining away the "menagerie" as he called them. My dog, fair enough, a horse to carry our gear, no trouble there. The pigeon? Found wounded, a carrier, unusual color, might breed from him. Satisfactory. The tortoise? Abandoned, feed him up and sell him off. Fine.

The pig was more difficult. Runt of the litter, got him for next to nothing. Foraged off the land as we passed, always a useful standby for barter. He accepted that, too, and I breathed a sigh of relief. No need for him to know we "talked" among ourselves: animals didn't in Matthew's circle, in spite of all the folk tales of talking foxes, mice, bears and fish. People should pay more attention to stories: they didn't make themselves up.

I thought I had gotten away with it beautifully, but there was obviously something still bothering our host. He umm'd and aah'd and then came to the point.

"And you had no hesitation in—in helping this man, Sir Gilman?"

"Of course not! I had nothing to keep me in the village, I had some money put by, and thought I would like to see a little of the world before I settled down. Besides, if you had seen him that first time, all handsome

and elegant, just like a prince in a fairy tale! He was so utterly unattainable, that when I saw him again, all threatened, maimed and desolate,
it was like being given a present! Even beaten up and dirty as he was,
he was still the handsomest man I had ever seen in my life! And with
him being blind, it was like an extra bonus, because—" I stopped. I had
given myself away well and truly this time.

He looked at me in a way I couldn't fathom. "Because what?"

So I told the truth. What did it matter, now? "Because he couldn't
see me; he couldn't see how fat and ugly I was. And, please God, he
never will. I don't ever want him to know what I look like: I couldn't
bear it!" I paused: he was looking most odd. "There, now I've told you.
I would be obliged if you don't disillusion him." I looked down at my
feet—yes, I could just about see them now—feeling very uncomfortable;
I hated remembering my ugliness, my obesity.

"But he didn't give me time to feel sorry for myself. "Fat?" he
said. "Ugly? Whatever in the world gave you that idea? A little on the
plump side, perhaps, a comfortable armful for any man, but ugly? Not
at all! You have lovely greeny-grey eyes, a straight nose and—"

"Please don't!" I cried. "You're only making it worse!" I lost all
discretion: kindness and tact could go too far. I *knew* what I looked like:
hadn't I seen my reflection in the river often enough? Piggy eyes,
squabby nose, double chins and all? And Mama had sighed, but added
that my superior education and dowry would "go a long way towards
overcoming" my other deficiencies. "You know perfectly well that in a
million million years I could never attract a man like Gill, that the only
time I will ever be able to hold his hand, care for him, gaze unhindered
on his beautiful face, is now, when he's blind!"

"You—you love him, then?"

"Of course I do! How could I not?" He is the sort of man every
woman dreams about, and I am lucky, *lucky,* that even part of that dream
has come true! I don't *want* to find his home, I don't *want* him ever to
see again, may God forgive me!" Suleiman had examined his eyes and
could find no obvious cause for the sudden blindness and loss of memory, except the blow to the head. He had advised him that memory might
return gradually and he could even regain his sight one day as quickly
as it had gone, if the circumstances were right—what circumstances he
wasn't prepared to say. "I shouldn't have said that, I know I shouldn't,
but each day I have him as he is, is one day snatched from heaven!"

Matthew looked completely different: older, greyer, sort of crumpled. "I did not realize. . . ."

"And neither does he!" I said quickly. "He treats me like a sister since we decided on the story we told you earlier: it is easier to travel that way."

He gathered his robes tightly around him as if he were suddenly cold. "Don't worry: your secret is safe with me. . . ."

The next time we were on our own I asked Gill how he had come to betray our true relationship.

He laughed. "You won't believe this, Summer, but he actually came and asked me, as your brother and next of kin, if he had my permission to pay court to you! Of course I couldn't say yea or nay, could I? So I had to tell him we weren't related. Anyway, I gather you must have talked your way out of it. Pity: you could have done worse, I imagine, and he seemed very taken. . . ."

Just imagine what my mother would have said! She would have considered him the perfect catch. "You should have had more sense!" I could hear her scolding. "What future is there traipsing around the countryside with a blind and helpless knight, handsome though he may be, when there is absolutely no future in it? Here is a comfortable home, a good-natured husband who is bound to die before you and leave you with his wealth; you just haven't the sense you were born with!" and then she would have given me a good beating, and it would have been no use pointing out that I had no idea Matthew felt that way.

Too late now, and it wouldn't have made any difference if I had known: my heart, for however short the time, was given to Gill. I was truly sorry if I had hurt Matthew, but I hoped it wouldn't spoil our last few days with him.

I needn't have worried; he was quieter than usual perhaps, and spent more time at his work, but there were no sulks, no reproaches, although I sensed he was under strain and would be glad when we were gone. Suleiman was going to supervise a consignment of spices further north and it had been agreed we would accompany him as far as the crossroads on the main north-south highway, for we had indeed come much too far east for our purpose.

So we set off at Candlemas, in a fine drizzle, all save Mistral safe under cover of one of the wagons, with Matthew out to see us go. I watched him dwindle on the road and then vanish as we turned the corner towards the countryside. I said a short prayer for his future well-being: I felt sorry for him, but had no regrets as to my decision.

"Nice to be on the road again," said Gill. "Perhaps this time I can get nearer home. . . ."

I think the animals felt the same way. The rest and food had bene-fited them all: Mistral had filled out and her coat shone with regular brushing; Basher was eating a little and still sleeping a lot, but Traveler's wing was almost healed and he was taking short flights with increasing regularity. The biggest change of all was in the Wimperling. He had grown almost out of recognition; he was three times as big as before, easily, and tubby with it. No more lifts in the pannier for him: he would have to walk with the rest of us. There seemed to be changes in his shape as well. His nose was longer, the claws on his hooves were bigger, his rump was higher than his head and the vestigial wings were vestigial no longer, in fact they looked definitely uncomfortable. In fact he looked so odd that the first thing I did that first night on the road was to fashion him a sacking coat that at least hid the worst of his strangeness. Funnily enough, though, other people didn't seem to notice he was any different from a normal pig. Very strange . . .

Too soon our journey in comfort came to an end. At the crossroads, the third day after we had set out, I loaded up Mistral once more, checked and double-checked that everything was where it should be, then turned to say good-bye and thanks to Suleiman. He handed me a parcel.

"You'll have to find room for this," he said. "It's from Matthew."

Inside were the green woolen dress and undershifts I had made for Matthew's sister. "He must have made a mistake. . . ."

Suleiman smiled. "No mistake. He has no sister, never had." He handed me a small leather purse. "He said this was for the extra care of your knight." Inside were five gold coins. "He asked me to remind you that love cannot feed on thin air, and that the rain and wind are no discriminators. . . ."

Less than an hour later we were lucky enough to catch up with a small caravan of pilgrims and journeymen; the weather fined up, the road was easy, other travelers joined us. We became friendly with our companions of the road, swapping experiences and comparing dogs and horses: I even remember boasting that Growch was the cleverest dog for miles and that our pig could count to twenty—and this last idiocy got us into real trouble.

It all started about two weeks after we had left the crossroads. It was around midday, the sun was shining, a soft breeze came from the south, the grass was looking greener than it had for months, little shoots were pricking up through the earth, buds were starting to uncurl on bush and shrub, birds were becoming much more urgent in their courting and I was planning ahead for the next two days' meals. Someone ahead was singing a catchy little tune, behind us a baby was being hushed; Gill was whistling the same tune as the singer, the pigeon was giving his wings a tryout on Mistral's back and—

—and they came out of the woods on our left with a clatter of arms and thud of hooves. A dozen or so men, mounted and in half-armor, all in burgundy livery. They clattered to a halt and their leader drew his sword.

"Halt! Halt, I say! Stay right where you are, or it will be the worse for you!"

Panic does all sorts of strange things to people. Some freeze in their tracks, others run, it doesn't matter where; others scream and scream; some faint, others wet themselves. Remembering the last attack in which I was involved, I was about to run to the shelter of the tree—we were at the back, and I could probably have made it—but was brought up short remembering Gill and the others.

At least they weren't killing anybody yet, but a couple of the soldiers cantered down to our end and rounded up the stragglers.

"Move along there, now: not got all day . . ."

Now we were circled by restive, sweating horses, stamping their hooves, tossing their heads till the harness jingled. Behind me someone was groaning in terror. I reached for Gill's hand, whispered what was happening, conscious of Growch's unease, of the Wimperling rock-steady at my other side. My ring wasn't sending out signals, either.

The leader of the troupe stood in his stirrups and addressed us.

"Just shut up, the lot of you, and listen to me! I mean you, you miserable worms! I am Captain Portall from the Castle of the White Rock—look, if you aren't quiet I shall be forced to make you. . . ." and he raised his sword threateningly. "That's better. . . ." He gazed around us, his expression adequately conveying just what a sorry lot we were, how far below his normal consideration, and just how wearisome he found the whole business. "Now, as I said, I am from White Rock Castle, and my lady Aleinor is bored—even more bored than I am in talking to you peasants." He brushed at his drooping mustache with a mailed fist. "And when the lady is bored we all suffer! And her husband and four sons being off on some crusade or other doesn't help; she wants cheering up, does the lady, and that's what I'm here for." He looked at us all once more, even more despondently. "Now, what I want to know is, which of you likely lot has the skills to entertain a lady? And you can drop that sort of thought," he said threateningly at a ribald snigger from somewhere at the back. "I mean singing, dancing, tumbling, juggling, minstrelsy, tricks, that sort of rubbish. Trifles to amuse, tales to entertain, ballads to hearten—something to make her *laugh,* dammit! Come now, half-a-dozen volunteers . . ."

Such was my relief at realizing that we were not about to be hacked to death, robbed or raped that I paid little attention to the captain's speech. Everyone else began to relax also, picking up whatever they had dropped, gathering their scattered belongings, chattering among themselves.

"Well, that's that! I said to Gill confidently. "We should be on our way—"

"I meant what I said!" suddenly shouted the captain. "Unless I find volunteers to accompany me back to the castle to entertain the Lady Aleinor, there will be . . . trouble! And I mean trouble! I want half-a-dozen right now: if not, I shall start stringing you all up, one by one!" He leaned from his horse and grabbed a man by his ear. "And we'll start with this one!"

A woman and girl started wailing, and everyone seemed to shrink into little family and friends groups. The circle grew smaller as the horses closed in. Fear became something you could touch and smell.

"Well? I'm waiting. I shall count to ten. One, two, three . . ."

"I've done a bit of juggling in my time." A man pushed forward. "Nothing fancy, mind . . ."

"You'll do." Captain Portall released the ear he was holding and rose in his stirrups once more. "Who else? You'll get a meal and a handful of silver if you please the lady. Come on, now. . . ."

"Should have mentioned that earlier," muttered a man to my left. He raised his hand. "I know a ballad or two might suit her."

One by one we got a tumbler and his son, a teller of tales, a man who could twist himself into impossible positions.

"Is that all? I'm disappointed, very disappointed! Singers, tumblers, a juggler, contortionist, story-teller: can't any of you do something *different*?"

To my horror one of our fellow travelers piped up with: "That girl over there, the one with the blind brother, she's got a dog what does tricks and a pig that counts. . . ."

I could have sunk straight into the ground! What a fool, what an utter idiot I had been to boast in such a way the other night! And it was lies, all lies—

But the captain on his horse was towering over us. "A counting pig? Now that *is* different. Never come across one of those before. Right, that's enough! Get them all organized, men! This the pig? I'll take him, then." And before I knew it he was down, had heaved up the Wimperling onto his saddle bow and remounted. "Heavy, isn't he?" and he turned and trotted off.

What could we do but follow? We couldn't desert the pig.

Our anxious way took us down a broad ride of the wood for perhaps a half mile, the fallen leaves of the autumn before muffling the thud of the escort's hooves, the chinking of the harness echoed by the chattering of a jay as it jinked away to the left. About twenty minutes later we came through thinning trees into the afternoon February sunshine and saw a picture that might have graced a Book of Hours.

Perhaps a couple of miles away, girdled by the neatest fields I had ever seen, rose the towers of faery. Perched on a grey-white outcrop of rock, from where we stood it looked insubstantial, a building from the edges of dream. There were four towers of unequal height, one much taller than the others. The castle itself was built from white stone, just whiter than the rock from which it rose; silhouetted against the clear, blue winter sky it looked like something one could cut from card.

As we drew nearer we could see the crenellations along the walls and even small figures patrolling the perimeters, and the road along which we traveled curving up towards a drawbridge and portcullis, over what looked like a moat of some kind. On our travels we had glimpsed other castles in the distance, most of them squat and frowning, with solid grey foundations and the hunched look of a sick animal, but this was quite different. Apart from its coloring, the way it seemed to spring upwards out of the rock, there were colored flags fluttering from the gateway, and the thin sound of a trumpet announcing our arrival.

We were traveling through fields plowed or already sown, through orchards of fruit trees beneath which not a single weed could be seen—unlike the unfamiliar orange groves outside the last town we had visited, the goat's foot trefoil beneath their trunks a yellow so bright it seared the eye—and past the twisted, bare branches of dead-looking vines, that later would cluster with heavy grapes. There was also an avenue of pollarded oaks, their knobbed branches giving no hint of the summer lushness to come. Everything neat, everything tidy, not a wavy line in the plowing, not a weed in the fields, not a dead leaf on the paths. Perhaps I had an untidy mind, but I would have welcomed a little disarray, a hint that outside belonged to nature as well as man.

Small houses were clustered at the foot of the White Rock, all as spic and span as the rest, and these we passed, together with the huge communal bread ovens, as we trudged up the sudden steep ascent to the castle proper and clattered over the short drawbridge. I peered over the edge as I passed: as I thought, a dry moat, and judging by the stench and the brown streaks down the walls that had not been evident from a distance, showing that refuse from the kitchens and garde-robes was allowed to flow unchecked, it was evident that there was no constant source of water. The creaking of the portcullis preceded us, but it needed only to be drawn halfway for us all to squeeze beneath.

We found ourselves in a large, cobbled courtyard, full of noise and bustle. Horses were being curried and exercised, wagons loaded and unloaded, soldiers were practicing with short swords, others examining armor and mail newly come from the sand barrels that were rolling up and down a short slope. A bowyer was stringing bows, a fletcher feathering arrows, an armorer busy at his anvil. Stable boys were shoveling ordure into an empty cart and a couple of cooks were gutting and jointing venison. The noise was indescribable.

Captain Portall dismounted his troop and started issuing orders as to our disposition. He lifted the Wimperling from his saddle with a look of distaste: the pig had just let loose a series of little popping farts.

Once down, the Wimperling nudged me. "We must be together. . . ."

"Right!" Captain Portall turned to me. "You and you—" he pointed to Gill: "—over there in one of those huts. Animals in the stables. Gerrout, you mangy hound!" and he aimed a kick at Growch, who was trying to christen his boots. "Whose is this?"

"Mine," I said firmly. "Just like the horse and the pig. All part of our act. And if you want a decent performance for your—your lady tonight, you'll see we are kept together. To rehearse," I added. "It is a couple of months since we have performed together. I presume you want us to be at our best?"

It worked. Ten minutes later we were snug in a stall at the end of the stables nearest the entrance, and a sullen stable boy was bringing hay, oats, mash and buckets of water.

"Two more buckets," I said firmly, twisting the ring on my finger to give courage. "This time of hot water. And towels. Hurry, boy."

Then I had to explain everything to Gill: where we were, what we were supposed to be doing.

"But we are performing nothing until we are clean and presentable: it's obvious the Lady Aleinor places great store on everything being just so. She also wants entertainment, so we've got to prepare something to please her. Besides, we could do with the silver she is offering."

"Have you ever done anything like this before?" asked poor, bewildered Gill.

"There's always a first time. . . ."

"And a last," muttered Growch. "Glad I'm not part of this farce."

"Oh, but you are," said the Wimperling unexpectedly. "We all are. That's why we couldn't be separated."

"Well, what we goin' to do, then? *She* said you could count, whatever that means: I heard her. What about me? The 'orse, the tortoise, the pigeon? Them," indicating Gill and me.

"Be patient," said the Wimperling. "And listen. . . ."

17

It was both hot and smoky in the hall. Although there was a huge modern hearth, tall and wide enough for half a dozen to stand upright, there seemed to be something amiss with the chimney, or perhaps the wind was in the wrong direction, for as much smoke came down and out as went up. The torches smoked in their holders on the walls, the candles on the tables smoked; an erratic wind would seem to have taken possession of the kitchens as well, for the bread was burned, the meat tasted half-cured, the fowls were charred on one side and nearly raw on the other and the underdone chickpeas, lentils and onions sulked in a sauce that reeked of too much garlic and was definitely full of smuts.

But we were too hungry to care much. The ale was good, the smoked herring and eels very tasty and the cheeses of excellent quality. We were seated at the very bottom of the left-hand table, and it was a good place from which to see everything. The edge off my hunger, and Gill well provided for, I had time to gaze around, and a word or two with our neighbors identified who was who.

There must have been upwards of a hundred and fifty people in the hall, counting servitors. The level of conversation was deafening, and this, coupled with the hysterical yelping and snarling of hounds fighting for bones and scraps in the rushes, the roar of flame from the fireplace, the clatter of knives, the thump of mugs impatient for refill and the intermittent screeching of a cagefull of exotic multicolored birds, made hearing a sense to endure rather than enjoy.

So I used my eyes instead. At the top table, raised some two hands high from the rest of us, sat the Lady Aleinor with a neighbor, Sir Bevin, and his wife on her right, and on her left her sister and her husband on a visit. Also on the top table were her daughter, a pudding-faced girl of twelve or thirteen, her chaplain, steward and Captain Portall. Below the salt ran the two long tables, seating about thirty on each side, crammed elbow to elbow on benches with scarce room to lift hand to mouth. At the ends nearest the top table were accommodated the more important members of the household: reeve, almoner, chief usher, head falconer, armorer, apothecary, head groom and verdurers; between them and us were the middle to lower orders: smiths, farriers, bowyers, fletchers, coopers, dyers, gardeners, soldiers, hedgers, cobbler, tinder-maker, trumpeter, clerk, wine-storekeeper and all my Lady's maids, her housekeeper, tirewoman, sewing ladies and her daughter's nurse-companion.

The table manners of those nearest us left much to be desired. Those sharing two to a trencher were using their hands rather than their knives, and even those who had their own place were tearing at the bread and meat instead of cutting it neatly. There was much munching with open mouth and unseemly belching, and few were using cloths to wipe their fingers and mouths: it appeared sleeves were more convenient for the men, hems of skirt or shift for the women. Not that the manners on the top table were much better, though the Lady Aleinor did at least lick her fingers one by one before applying them and her mouth to the linen tablecloth.

We had not yet seen the lady close to and were bowing respectfully when she entered the hall, so I had only had a quick impression of a tall, slim woman in rich red robes and an elaborate headdress of linen, lawn and ribbons. Now I could see her more clearly I saw she was handsome enough, but her face was marred by a discontented expression—much as my mother used to wear if bad weather kept her customers away too long. The lady was obviously bored.

The hall grew hotter, noisier, smokier, but at last the tables were cleared, the hounds kicked into silence, a cover put over the squawking birds and water brought for finger-washing. The steward rose to his feet, banged on the top table for silence, and announced that the entertainment would begin. A young varlet, one of the two cadet-squires who had been serving at the top table—much more palatable food than we had been served with, I noticed—walked down the room and picked out the first of our "volunteers."

After a whispered conversation he walked back between the two lower tables, bowed to the lady, and announced that Master Peter Bowe would sing a couple of ballads: "Travel the Broad Highway" and "Lips Like Cherries." He had a pleasant enough voice, but it was suited to a smaller place than this vast hall, whose timbers reached up into a ribbed darkness like leafless trees. However the Lady spoke to her steward and he was rewarded with a couple of silver coins.

Next it was the turn of the juggler, who was reasonably dextrous. He was certainly good at improvisation, for he had only what lay around to toss and catch; eventually, one by one, he had two shriveled apples, a goblet, a large bone and a trencher all in the air at once. He, too, received two silver coins.

The teller of tales was found to be hopelessly drunk and was thrown out, so it was the turn of the tumbler and his boy. Once the man had obviously been very good, but he was well into middle age and I could tell by the grimaces that he suffered from rheumatism, and both his spring and balance were faulty. The boy did his best to cover for his father's deficiencies—one day he, too, would be very good—but in the end he was dropped heavily; judging by his resigned expression as he rose to his feet, rubbing his elbow, it wasn't the first time and wouldn't be the last. They were given three coins.

Now it was the turn of the contortionist, but I had to miss his performance to slip outside and collect Mistral and the others, for we were next—and last. I brought them in by the kitchen ramp, for the steps up to the main door would not have done: too steep. Leaving them just outside, I rejoined Gill for the applause and coin for the contortionist. The varlet walked up to us, I whispered to him, he went back and announced us.

"My lady . . ." a deep bow: "for your entertainment I present travelers from the north, the south, the east, the west: fresh from their successful performances all over the country, I crave your indulgence for brother and sister, Gill and Summer, and their troupe of performing animals!" Another deep bow, a ripple of interest.

Smoothing down the dress Matthew had given me with nervous fingers I led Mistral towards the top table, Gill on her other side, flanked on either side by a sedate dog and a sedater pig. Traveler was perched on Mistral's back. We all looked our best, I had seen to that, and the animals wore colored ribbons—a sad good-bye to my special ones, I thought. (We had had to leave Basher behind, for there isn't much lively capering to be got from a hibernating tortoise.)

Reaching the dais we performed the only trick we had rehearsed together: we all knelt—man, girl, horse, pig, dog. Traveler bowed his head.

Applause. Encouraged, I rose and addressed the lady. "First we shall show you a roundelay. . . ." and pulling my pipe from my pocket I gave Gill the note and he began singing the "Bluebell Hey." For a dreadful moment I thought it wasn't going to work, then my dear animals obeyed my unspoken instructions. Mistral and the pig revolved slowly, majestically, and Growch began to chase his tail. No matter they were not in time with the music: we were receiving applause already. Traveler rose into the air and gracefully circled the top table. . . . Then it happened.

It is well-nigh impossible to house-train birds, and Traveler was no exception. On his last circuit, obviously full of grain, he let loose and an enormous chunk of pigeon-dropping landed unerringly on the bald pate of the lady's chaplain. There was a long drawing in of breath and then total silence. I stopped playing, Gill stopped singing, Growch stopped chasing his tail. Mistral and the Wimperling stood like statues.

We all gazed at the Lady Aleinor. She rose to her feet, her face suffused with color. If she had said: "Off with their heads!" I would not have been surprised. I twisted the ring on my finger, still cool and calm. The lady's eyes seemed ready to pop out of her head, and the silence was something palpable, a thing you could touch and weigh. She opened her mouth—

And laughed.

And she went on laughing. Not a genteel titter behind her hand, as I had been taught, but a gut-wrenching belly laugh, the sort my mother had produced one day when the butcher had risen from her bed in a temper, tripped and landed bare-arsed and bum-high with his nose in the dirt.

What's more, she went on laughing. She laughed until the tears spurted from her eyes, she laughed till her ribs ached and she had to double up to stop the ache, till she had to cover her ears for the pain behind. And the more indignant the lugubrious chaplain became, trying to wipe the yellow mess from his bald head with the tablecloth, the more she laughed.

Her sycophantic household took its cue from her, and soon the whole place was rocking with guffaws and the very flames of the torches and candles were threatened by the shouts and table-thumpings. The most relieved face in the hall, apart from mine, was that of Captain Portall, who had promised amusement for his lady.

The noise, however was upsetting Mistral, however I tried to calm her, and Traveler was no better. Growch, too, was starting to growl at the lymers, brachs and mastiffs who had started up again with their baying and yelping, so I grabbed the horse's bridle and led them back to the courtyard. Growch, of course, took advantage of this to snatch a rib bone from a distracted greyhound on his way out.

Picking up a leathern bucket I had appropriated earlier I rejoined Gill and the Wimperling, the latter of whom seemed totally unmoved by the hullabaloo around him. In fact his snout was working happily above exposed teeth, almost as though he were laughing too. As I re-entered the merriment was dying down, and the lady leaned forward and addressed us.

"I hope the rest of your act is as stimulating: I declare I have not been as diverted for months! Of course—" she waved her hand dismissively: "I realize it was but a fortuitous accident. Presumably the rest of your performance owes more to skill?"

I bowed. "My lady . . . First my brother will sing a ballad dedicated especially to yourself. An old tune, but new words." I gave Gill his note, and he began to sing:

> *"When I hunger, there is meat;*
> *When I tire, there is sleep;*
> *I am cold, there is fire;*
> *I am thirsty, there is wine.*
> *But when I love, unless you care,*
> *I am poorer than the poor.*
> *Hungry, thirsty, sleepless, cold.*
> *But smile, lady, and I am full;*
> *Touch me and I am warm;*
> *Kiss me once and I*
> *Need never sleep again. . . ."*

It was a touching song, and Gill sang it as if he held a picture of a secret love tight behind his blind lids. So heartfelt was the throb in his voice that it gave me goose bumps. The lady seemed to like it too.

Now for the culmination of our act: I crossed my fingers and went down to the Wimperling.

"Ready?"

"If you are . . ."

I upended the bucket and lifted his front hooves onto the top, catching one of my fingers on the funny claws that circled them. "We will have to clip those. . . ."

"I think they are meant to be there . . ."

Gill finished his song to sentimental applause from Lady Aleinor, which everyone copied. So, the lady decided what amused and what did not. In that case, the Wimperling and I would play to her alone.

"And now, my lady, we present to you the wonder of this or any other age: a pig who counts. As good as any human, and better than most. Would you please give me two simple numbers for the pig to add together?" I saw her hesitate, and gathered that tallying was not her strong point. She would probably be furious if we exposed her weakness so I played it safe. "Perhaps we could start more simply: if you would place some manchets of bread in front of you in a line, so that your guests may see the number, then I will ask the pig to guess correctly. He cannot, of course, see what is on the table."

She looked more pleased and lined up five pieces of bread. I thought the number to the Wimperling, then made a great fuss and to-do with waving of arms and incantations.

Obediently the Wimperling tapped with his right hoof on the top of the bucket: one, two, three four . . . There was a hesitation, a ghastly moment when I thought everything was going to go wrong, then I saw from the gleam in his eye that he was enjoying himself . . . five.

Applause, again, and from then on in it was easy. Shouts from those on the top table who could count: "Three and two . . . Six and one . . . two and four . . ." The lady was counting frantically on her fingers to keep up with her guests, then nodding and beaming as though she had known the answer all the time. Her daughter intervened in an affected lisp.

"Does the creature subtract as well?"

It could, if my mental counting was swift enough.

We finished, by prior agreement with the Wimperling, by me asking him a leading question: "You are a pig of perspicacity: tell me now, O Wise One, who is the fairest, the most generous, the most beloved lady in this castle?" I went along the tables, touching each woman on the shoulder as I passed, and each time the Wimperling shook his head—a pity, for some of the ladies were really far prettier than our hostess. At last, and last, I came to the Lady Aleinor. At once the pig drummed both hooves on the bucket, squealed enthusiastically and nodded his head.

Everyone clapped, as they knew they had to, and the lady was so pleased she snatched the purse of silver from her steward and threw it to me. As I shepherded Gill back outside, the Wimperling trotting behind, I counted the coins: twelve!

"Told you it would be all right," said the Wimperling happily.

We had almost reached the stables when there were running footsteps behind us. It was the varlet who had introduced us earlier.

"You are invited to dine with the rest of the household at dawn," he panted, "and the lady requests that you and your brother—and the wondrous pig—attend her at noon in the solar. I am to come and fetch you at the appointed hour."

Back at the stables I requested more hay and made comfortable resting places for Gill and myself, then went to say goodnight and congratulate the animals.

"You were absolutely marvelous, all of you! The lady liked our performance, and we have a purseful of silver to prove it! She wants to see Gill and me and the Wimperling again tomorrow morning, but we shall be on the road again just after noon, I expect."

"Tonight was one thing," said the Wimperling, "but tomorrow might be different again. . . ."

"Oh, stop being such an old pessimist!" I cried. "You were the star of the show, remember?" and in my euphoria I raised his front hooves, bent down, and kissed him fair and square on his pink snout.

Bam! I felt as though I had been struck by a thunderbolt. Once when combing my hair at home by the fire, I had leaned forward to sip at a metal dipper of water and had the same sharp prickling, but this was a thousand times worse. I must have jumped, or been thrown, back about six feet, my lips numb and feeling twice their size, my hair standing up from my head. But this was as nothing to the effect it had on the pig. He leapt up at the same distance I had back, his wings creaked into action as well and bore him still further until he cracked his head against the rafters and came plummeting back down to the floor.

We stared at one another in horror. The feeling was coming back to my lips, but I still had to put up a hand to convince myself they weren't swollen. They tingled like pins and needles, only far worse.

"What *happened*?"

He shook his head as though his ears were full of ticks. "I don't know. . . . I feel as if all my insides have turned over. Most peculiar. I'm not the same as I was, I know that!"

"I won't do it again, I promise!"

"No, don't. It's just that . . . I don't know. Very strange. . . ."

I had never seen or heard him so confused. After a moment or two he slunk off into a corner under the manger and hunched up. I thought he would sleep, but when I settled down on my bed of hay he was still awake, his eyes bright and watchful in the light of the lantern that swung overhead.

When we entered the solar a little after noon, the Lady Aleinor was seated in a high-backed chair by a roaring fire; like all the chimneys in the castle, this one smoked. The lady's daughter was on a stool at her feet, the nurse and two tirewomen stood behind the chair.

Though the room was sumptuously furnished, it did not have the cozy, lived-in look of Matthew's solar: it was a room to be seen in, rather than used. Candles were lit because the shutters on the one window at the back were tight closed.

The lady received us graciously. We were invited to move into the center of the room—though not asked to sit down—and she started to question us: where we trained the animals, where we were bound, etc. From anyone except a fine lady like herself it might have seemed an impertinence, but we had been long enough together for the brother/sister story to come out like truth. It was more difficult to answer questions about the animals, but I did emphasize (in order that our performances were worthy of reward) the years of training, the bonds of familiarity that had to be forged, the difficulty of communication—and here I mentally crossed myself and touched my ring.

"But surely the whip speaks louder than words?"

I was shocked—would I have been before I wore the ring of the Unicorn? I wondered—but did my best to hide it. Her ways were obviously not ours.

"You may use a whip when breaking in a horse, my lady, or beat a dog, but how can you use punishment to train a pigeon? Our training is accomplished by treating the animals as if they were part of our family and rewarding their tricks, not punishing their mistakes. It has worked well, so far."

Her eyes flashed as though she would argue, then once more she was sweetness itself. "Would you let me see what else your pig can do? I am sure there were tricks you did not show us last night. . . ." I almost looked for the honey dripping from her tongue.

I was deceived, I admit it, even as a warning message came from the Wimperling. "Don't intrigue her too much. . . ."

"Hush!" I thought to him. And to the lady: "I am sure we can find something to divert you. . . ." Back to the Wimperling, quick as a flash: "Can you keep time to a song? Find hidden objects if I tell you where they are?"

He answered reluctantly that he thought he could: "But don't overdo it!" Why? More tricks, more money, and we should be away from here in an hour or two with enough to keep us going for weeks.

I asked Gill to sing "Come away to the woods today" which was a song with a regular, impelling beat, and my pig trod first one way and then the other in perfect time, to polite applause from the lady and her daughter.

"Now the pig on his own," demanded Lady Aleinor, dismissing

Gill's song, which privately I thought wonderful, as a mere trifle. "Come on girl: show us what else he can do!"

"Very well. Perhaps, my lady, if you would hide some trifling object—yes, that needle case would do fine—while the pig's back is turned—so, then I will ask him to discover it."

And behind a cushion, under a chair, beneath the sideboard, in the wood-basket—he found it every time. After I had told him where to look, of course.

The lady watched him perform with a gleam in her eyes. "Very good, very good indeed! Anything else he can do?"

I was about to open my mouth and rashly volunteer his flying abilities, when his thoughts struck into my mind like a string of sharp pebbles to the head. "No, no, *no*! Don't tell her that! Tell her I am tired, anything! Let's get out of here!'

Confused, I stammered out an excuse. She looked at me coldly. "Very well, you may go now and rest. But I shall expect another performance tonight. I have sent out messengers to others of my neighbors and I look forward to an even better exposition of the pig's power." She saw my face. "What's the matter, girl? A few coins? Here you are, then. . . ." And she tossed a handful of silver at my feet.

Automatically I bent to retrieve it, then straightened my back. "It is not a matter of money, my lady, thank you all the same. Last night you were more than generous, and we had not planned to stay longer than midday today. We must be on our way as soon as possible."

Another flash of—what?—from those hooded eyes, then the pleasantness was back again, on her mouth at least. "Of course, of course, but I couldn't possibly let you go without one more of your marvelous performances! You can't let me down after I have invited extra guests! Please say you will do this last favor? One more treat for us all and then you may go on your way. . . ."

It would have been more than churlish of me to refuse, in spite of the warning signs I was getting from the Wimperling. Gill, poor dear, had no idea of the conflict that was going on and added his voice to the lady's plea.

"Of course we must oblige the Lady Aleinor, Summer: it will be no hardship to stay one more night, surely?"

I could hear the Wimperling almost screaming at him to stop, stop, stop! but of course he couldn't hear the pig's thoughts as I could, and he went on with a few more complimentary sentences until I could have screamed also. There was no doubt as to the outcome now, and I picked up the coins and we made our way down the winding stone stairs to the courtyard. Up had been much easier for all of us, and the Wimperling nearly ended by rolling down the last few twists. Once in the courtyard he started to say something, but I hushed him, using our midday meal in the hall as an excuse. Right at that moment I didn't want any prognostications of doom and disaster, so I saw him back to the stable before hurrying back for what was left of the meal.

I purposely lingered over the last night's leftovers, plus a thick broth, a blancmange of brawn and custards of potted meats, but I couldn't put off the reproaches forever. Even so, it was a little past two by the time Gill and I regained the stable, whereupon I immediately found a stool for him out in the sunshine, and returned alone to face the agitation I had sensed at once.

They all had something to say, but it was Growch who was noisiest. "What's all this, then? 'E tells me——" he nodded towards the pig: "——that we're all in danger! Danger from what, I'd like to know? Last night you was full of how well we done, and now 'e tells us the Lady-of-the-'Ouse is poison! In that case, why don't we all go, right now? O' course, if I was just to nip into the kitchens and fetch a bone first . . ."

"I think we should go," said Mistral restlessly. "But our companion tells us we must perform again tonight."

Traveler flapped his wings. "Listen to the pig: he is a wise one."

Thank the Lord the tortoise was still asleep! "What's all this, then?" I asked the Wimperling. "We have a purse full of money and will get more tonight. All we have to do is one more performance and we can leave in the morning. What's one more day? The more money the better."

"If it is only one more day . . . I do not trust her. I can read her heart a little way and it is full of wickedness, guile and greed. I cannot see what she intends, for I believe she does not yet know herself, but it is not good for any of us, of that I am sure."

"You have no proof——"

"No, Summer, but in this you must trust me. Tonight when the performance ends we must be ready to leave, all packed up. If we don't, tomorrow may bring disaster to us all."

I shook my head. I just couldn't believe she meant us harm. And yet—I recalled those flashes of spite from her eyes. Perhaps . . . "It would be too dark to see. Besides, the portcullis will be down."

"Stays up for them as was guests and isn't stayin' over," said Growch. " 'Sides, we've traveled at night before. Moon's near full."

"I shall have to ask Gill," I said weakly.

"Consult 'im? When've you ever consulted 'im? You tells 'im what to do an' 'e does it! Couldn't 'ave got this far without you, an' 'e knows it!" Whenever he got particularly agitated Growch's speech went to pieces. "Consult 'im indeed!" And he emphasized his annoyance by kicking up a shower of hay with his back legs.

"You've all had your say: why shouldn't he?" I was angry, largely because I wasn't sure that they weren't right.

"Becoz-'e-don'-know-nuffin!" said Growch. "Not-nuffin!'

"That's only because he's blind," I said quickly. "You try going around for a while with your eyes tight shut and see how you get on! Anyway, I shall ask him just the same. We're all in this together."

And before I could change my mind I went outside and suggested to a dozy Gill that we leave that night. Of course I couldn't give the true reason, and, understandably, he couldn't see why we didn't postpone it till morning. I decided to wait and see what the evening brought, but packed everything ready, just in case.

We made a good job of our performance that night, repeating much of what we had done the evening before, but adding a couple more tricks to the Wimperling's repertoire. Led by the lady, we received prolonged applause, a purse from her and another from one of her guests. When we returned to the stable there was disappointment: none of the guests was leaving that night and the portcullis remained down.

Right, first thing in the morning then, when the first wagons came up with provisions. If we were ready in the shadow of the wall, we would sneak out as soon as the portcullis was raised. . . . I willed myself to wake up an hour before dawn.

I woke on time, loaded up our gear and we were ready in the darkest part of the courtyard a good quarter-hour before we heard the first wagon rumble across the drawbridge. The driver called out; two yawning soldiers ran across and started to wind up the portcullis with enough creaks and groans to awaken the dead. I shivered: my teeth were chattering both with the early morning chill and with dread.

Three wagons passed through, steam rising from the horses' and the drivers' mouths. I grabbed Gill's hand and Mistral's bridle, and we had almost reached the first plank of the drawbridge when two sentries I hadn't seen stepped out and barred our progress, their spears crossed in front of us.

"Sorry girl, sir," said one of them peremptorily. "None of you is to leave the castle. Orders of the Lady Aleinor . . ."

18

I stared at them in horror. "But why?"

They looked at one another and then the spokesman said: "We don't ask questions of the lady. All we know is, orders were sent down yesterday midday as you weren't to be let go."

"Doesn't pay to disobey," said the other soldier. "We just does as we're told. Sorry an' all that . . . Enjoyed your performance, by the way: that pig's a good 'un. Would he do a trick for me?"

"No, no," I said distractedly. "Only for me . . ." Which was the best answer I could have given, although I didn't realize it at the time. "Er . . . Under the circumstances, perhaps it would be better if—if the lady didn't think we were trying to leave." Scrabbling in my now full purse I handed out a couple of coins. "I think she might be annoyed if she thought we didn't appreciate her hospitality."

On our dispirited way back to the stables I noticed a boy from the village unloading his wagon and eyeing us speculatively: he had obviously seen the exchange of coin. I clutched my purse tighter and hurried past.

I was all for requesting an instant audience with Lady Aleinor, demanding to know the reason for our confinement and insisting on instant release, but Gill urged caution.

"I reckon that might make her more determined to keep us a while. She seems to be a very contrary lady. . . . After all, where's the harm of a few more days? Personally I'm growing a bit tired of singing love ballads to a woman I can't see, but at least it means more money, and we are fed and housed. Not that the food is all that good, but—"

"The most important thing is to be very, very careful," said the Wimperling. "We must find out what she has in mind. Don't force the issue: corner any vicious animal and you relinquish the initiative."

"I want to go," said Mistral impatiently. "This place is bad, and—"

There was a rustling noise from farther down the stable and silhouetted against the open door was the figure of the boy I had noticed earlier. "Hullo . . ." he called out tentatively.

I was in no mood to be polite. "What do you want?"

He hesitated for a moment then moved towards us, twisting a piece of straw between his fingers. He was dressed in a rough, patched jerkin, trousers tied beneath the knee with twine, and was barefoot. He was also filthy dirty—I could smell him from where I stood—and his thatch of hair could well have been fair if it had ever been washed. He could have been any age from twelve onwards.

"To see if I can help. I heard what was going on. Gather you want out of here?" His speech was country-thick but in the lantern light I could see a bright intelligence in those grey eyes.

I temporized: who knew where his real interest lay? "Maybe we do—but why should you help?"

"No love for the Lady 'Ell-an'-All," he muttered. "Killed my father she did," and he glanced over his shoulder as if he, too, was afraid of being overheard.

"Killed him?" and once he started telling us, I thought his story to the animals at the same time as he told it.

"We live in the hamlet beneath the castle. Two rooms, patch of ground behind. Lived there happy, father, mother, self and three young sisters. Father was a forester for the lady, mother helped in the fields with the girls, weeding and picking stones. I was a crow-scarer, then a shit-shoveler. Still am. Bad winter last year, after the lord and his sons went off. Not much food. Pa helped himself to a hare—"

"A poacher?"

"First time he ever done it. We needed the food, and there were a glut of 'em. Kept helping theirselves to our vegetable clamps. Pa caught this one with the dog, on our patch at the back. Someone saw him, told the Lady 'Ell-an'-All. No excuses, no trial. Hanged the dog, old Blackie, castrated my father—"

"Oh, my God!" It was Gill. "How barbaric! My father—My father . . ." He put his hands to his head. "I don't remember. . . ."

"And then she had his eyes put out," continued the boy, stony-faced. "My father stood it for six months. Last August we came in late, found he'd cut his throat. With the trimming knife. They let him keep that."

I put my hand on his arm, but he shook it off.

"Don't want no sympathy. Understand why he did it. Less than half a man . . . Anyway, if you means harm to the lady, then I'm your man."

I didn't know what to say. We still didn't know if our position was serious. It might just be that all the lady wanted was a couple more performances. Even as I tried to persuade myself that the situation didn't warrant any panic, I got a strong signal from the Wimperling to enlist this boy on our side.

"Thank you," I said formally. "We don't wish personal harm to the lady, but we do wish to leave here as soon as possible."

"If she's taken a fancy to you, here you stay."

"We've given her what she asked—"

"Obviously not."

"Look," I said. "First we have to find out exactly what is going on. I don't quite know how you can help, but—"

"You'd be surprised. Bet I can get you all out of here in twenty-four hours." He hesitated. " 'Course, there'd be a price. . . ."

I thought rapidly of what we could afford. "Ten silver pieces. If we need you, that is . . ."

His eyes gleamed. "Done! I'm getting out myself, soon as I can, but can't leave Ma and the sisters without. See you later. . . ."

"But I don't understand," I said.

Gill and I were in the lady's solar again, having requested an audience after the midday meal. She had us standing in the center of the room as before while she reclined by the fire. There was more light in the room today, for the shutters at the window had been flung back on a sunny sky. The room must face south, for low bars of February sunshine slanted through the window and across the floor, specks of dust dancing like midges in the beams. Outside I could see a forest of leafless trees stretching to the horizon, while black specks rose and fell lazily above the branches, a soft breeze carrying the quarreling cries of nest-building rooks.

I had come straight to the point and asked why we had been refused permission to leave. She had gazed at us through half-closed lids.

"I should have thought that would be perfectly obvious."

But when I said I didn't understand, she seemed to come to life and sat up, arms gripping the sides of her chair. "You are not an idiot, girl. If I say you are not to leave, it is because I wish you to stay. And why? Because, for the moment, I find you and your animals—diverting. Life can be *so* boring. . . ." Leaning back in her chair she closed her eyes. "And now I shall rest for a while. I expect more entertainment this evening. Some new tricks, please. . . ." And she let her voice die away, as if indeed it was too tiring to try and explain further to peasants such as ourselves.

"But I don't want—*we* don't wish to stay," I said. "You told us we might leave if we gave an extra performance, which we did. We do have a life of our own to lead, you know, and—"

She rose to her feet in a sudden swirl of skirts, the cone-shaped headdress she wore wobbling dangerously.

"How dare you! How *dare* you! What matter *your* wishes, *your* little lives? All that matters here is what *I* want! This is *my* castle, *my* demesne! Within its bounds I have jurisdiction of life and death over everyone—*everyone,* do you hear?" She was almost hysterical, red blotches on her neck and face, her eyes snapping sparks like fresh pine bark on a fire. She rushed forward and struck first me and then Gill hard across the face. My eyes smarted with the sudden pain, for one of her thumb rings had caught my lip and I could taste the salt of blood. Gill swayed on his feet and would have fallen had I not caught at his arm and steadied him.

"God's teeth! What was that for, lady?"

"Impertinence, blind man! And there's more where that came from if you do not both watch your tongues. I will not be disagreed with, do you hear?"

I was so angry with the way she was treating us that given a pinch of pepper I would have sprung forward and given her a dose of her own treatment, but the presence of Gill gave me pause. That, plus the possible danger to the animals. God knew what she could do if further provoked.

"We have no wish to cross you," I said, as meekly as I could. "But we would like to know when we can leave. If you could let us know how many more performances you require? And if you have any special tricks in mind . . . Of course, it will take time to teach them all—"

"There is no need to teach them all fresh tricks: I am only interested in the pig! Any fool can make a horse turn, a dog obey, a bird fly in circles. You combine them cleverly, I agree, but it is only the pig that has real intelligence. Your brother has a pleasant enough voice, I dare say, but singers are a dozen a week, and you know it! No, the rest of you may leave as and when you wish, but the pig stays!"

"But—but he can't!"

"What do you mean 'can't'? If I say he stays, he stays." She looked at us for a moment, then changed her tactics. Sitting down once more, she smoothed her skirts, turned the rings on her fingers. "Of course you will be recompensed. I realize your pig is a means of livelihood and that you are seeking a cure for your brother's blindness, which will need special donations. I will give you what I reckon it will cost for a further three months' travel. Now, I cannot say fairer than that, can I?"

"You don't understand! It's not just—just what he could earn us, he is *part* of us: I couldn't leave him behind. Besides, he won't do tricks for anyone else, only me."

"Well, you can stay for a while, too. Just till you have taught me how he works."

The woman was mad! "But I can't teach you—"

"Can't? Or won't?" She rose from her chair again, as angry as before. She narrowed her eyes. "Everything can be taught—unless it's some form of magic. . . . Magic? Yes, I suppose that could be the answer. If so," and now her voice was full of menace: "I could have you denounced as a witch! And you know what that means: trial by fire, earth and water and lastly, being burned at the stake. . . ."

"I'm no witch!" I felt the ring of the unicorn cold, cold on my finger. Was that a form of witchcraft? It had never occurred to me, being as it was a gift from my dead father which helped me understand the speech of animals and also warned me of danger, gave me courage—yet perhaps to the lady, to the gullible majority, it would seem like a form of magic—

Suddenly I was terrified. Death came in many forms: illness, accident, war, pestilence, age, famine—but to be burned at the stake! God, please God, sweet Jesus, Mary, Mother of Sorrows, No! I was trembling; the lady saw it, and smiled gleefully.

"Then if it is not magic, it is trickery, and that can be taught. Right? And if you do not wish to teach me, and your—companions—are so precious to you, then perhaps *they* can be persuaded to persuade you. . . . Pigeons' necks can be wrung, a horse can be hamstrung, a dog hung by its tail, a man—"

"Stop it, stop it!" I had my hands over my ears. "Leave them alone! They have no part in all this! You said they could all go. . . ."

I should not have been so vehement. I realized from the gleam in her eye that she now knew I was vulnerable to the threat of harm to the others.

"Certainly not! I have changed my mind. They can all be hostages to your good behavior. And just so as there will be no mistake, we can start the lessons right now! Go fetch the pig!"

There was nothing I could do but obey. As I led the Wimperling back I told him what had happened. "What are we going to do?"

He looked worried, as worried as I felt, the loose skin over his snout all wrinkled up in perplexity. "The only thing we can do is go along with what she wants for the moment and trust to luck. You had better make plans with that boy to escape if you can. In the meantime give me something simple to do—count to five, perhaps—give her some gibberish to learn, then say I can only adapt to a new mistress slowly and tomorrow she will learn more."

So it was decided, but unfortunately it didn't turn out quite as we had planned. . . .

At first it was all right. I gave the Lady Aleinor some rhyming words to repeat—taking great pleasure in correcting her twice—and obediently the Wimperling tapped his hoof five times. She practiced it half a dozen times, but in the middle of the nonsense the pig sent me an urgent message.

"Take a look out of that window. Remember everything you see."

I wandered over and did as I was bid. A sheer drop of some forty feet to the dry moat below; beyond that the forests, with a stretch of greensward in front of the trees.

"What are you doing, girl?"

I walked back. "Turning my back on the pig, lady, just to prove I am not influencing him. I just thought—"

"You do not think! You do as you are told. Come back here and teach me some more."

"The pig is tired, it will take time for him to get used to—"

"Rubbish! We have been at this less than an hour! Do as you are told!"

"He won't—"

"He *will*! You can make him." She paused, and her next words came honey-sweet and loaded with sting. "Unless, of course, you would rather I summoned my soldiers to give your brother here a painful lesson. They are experts, I assure you. . . ."

The Wimperling flashed me a warning. "Do as she says! Simple addition: two and one, two and two. She can't count."

And so it went on, until the Wimperling himself took a hand, sinking to the ground with a groan and puffing and panting, rolling his eyes round and around.

"There! I told you so!" For a heart-stopping moment I believed he was indeed ill, but as I rushed forward and knelt distractedly at his side, I saw him wink.

"Tell me, quickly, what you saw from the window. . . ."

So, as I fussed over him, I described the scene outside.

"Mmm . . . Doesn't sound too promising. Don't look so worried! We'll find a way out of this."

The Lady Aleinor at last seemed persuaded she could go no further today. She sank back in her chair, still repeating to herself the rubbish I had taught her.

"Very well," she said after a moment. "What does it eat?"

"*He* eats most things," I said. "When I get back to the stables I can ask for—"

"The stables? The creature stays here. It's mine now, and I shall look after it."

I was devastated. How in the world could we all escape together when we were down there and he was up here? Together we had a chance: apart, none.

"But—but he needs exercise, grooming, companionship, light. . . ."

"All of which he will get. My soldiers will escort him out twice a day—the exercise will do them good as well. A nice trot around the castle grounds . . . Now, you can go. Attend me tomorrow at the same hour."

"But—but I . . ."

"Do you want a beating? No? Then get out! The creature will soon adapt to its new surroundings. As soon as you have taught me all I need to know you may leave. But if there is any more argument or backsliding I shall have to reconsider. Just remember what I said about the expendability of your other animals. . . ."

Back in the stables I sobbed in despair, trying to explain to the others the mess we—I—had gotten us into. Gill patted me awkwardly on the shoulder, Growch whined in sympathy and Mistral and Traveler shifted from foot to foot in anxiety. I felt terribly alone. I had not realized before how much I had relied on the simple common sense of the Wimperling, his stoicism, his comfortable, fat, ugly little body. Not that he was so small anymore . . . Only a few weeks ago I had been able to tuck him under my arm, and now he seemed near full-grown. One of the nicest things about him was that he never grumbled, and now he had been taken from us I felt utterly helpless: I couldn't even think straight.

"There's the boy," said Gill. "He said he could get us out of here, remember?"

"But that was before she took the Wimperling," I wept.

"Let's see what he got to say, anyways," said Growch. "Ain't nuffin more than we can do today: gettin' dark already."

So it was, and we had missed the midday meal. I found, too, that no one was going to rush to feed the animals, and in the gathering gloom I had to find my own oats and hay, and fill the buckets with water from the well in the courtyard.

It was even more obvious that we didn't exist when we went into the hall for the evening meal. Word had obviously got around of the lady's displeasure, for we were elbowed away from the table, were not offered a trencher, nor any ale. In the end I snatched what I could for both of us and we ate standing; rye bread, stale cheese and a couple of bones with a little meat left on them.

Worse was to come. The Lady Aleinor brought in the Wimperling, an animal so bedecked with ribbons and bunting as to be practically unrecognizable. She made him go through what I had taught her in front of the whole assembly, mouthing the rubbish she had learned; she had a little whip in her hand with which she stroked his flanks: if she had actually struck him I don't know what I would have done.

The applause was loud and sychophantic, and as soon as she had done I rushed forward to give him a reassuring hug before they dragged me away. He managed some quick words: "See the boy! If the rest of you can get away, I think I can manage as well. . . ."

Slightly reassured, we all spent a better night, and in the morning, after feeding and watering the animals and snatching some bread and cheese from the hall for Gill and myself, we settled down to await the boy and his wagon. He brought winter cabbage, some turnips, a barrel of smoked fish and some firewood for the kitchens. Once he had unloaded he picked up a shovel and started to clear the far end of the stable.

"Down here as well, please!" I called out, as if I had never seen him before. He walked down the aisle, trailing a barrow behind him, and bent to shovel out Mistral's stall.

"Well? Thought about it, then?" All the while he spoke to us he never stopped his steady shoveling. "Still want out?"

"Yes, yes; we do. Are you willing to help us?"

"I said so, didn't I? Ten silver pieces you said? Good. How many are there of you?"

I pointed to the others. "And our packages." I mustn't forget the tortoise, either. "The—the pig has been taken into the castle."

He shook his head. "Can't help you there. There's no getting it out now. One of them out there—" he jerked his thumb over his shoulder: "—told me as how you had taught the lady some magic words?"

"Not really," I said hurriedly. "Just the words I always use to direct his act. She's a slow learner. . . . What about the rest of us, then?"

He carried on shoveling. "Dog can slip through the portcullis any time: bars are wide enough. Pigeon can fly over, right?"

"And my brother? He's blind."

"Him and your packages can go in the back of the wagon. I'll back it up to the door at the end of the stables tonight. He'll have to sit under a load o'shit, though, but I got a cover."

"And me?"

"Got a cloak? Right, then. Pin up your skirt and I'll bring a pair of my pa's braies. Be a tight fit, but . . . At dusk, won't matter as much. Get you a hat as well. Find a sack of something to put over your back, walk out t'other side from the soldiers. Dirty your face a bit, too."

"What about the horse?"

"Swap her for mine. Blanket over her, bit of muck on her quarters and head, sack on her back. I'll let on mine's lame and I'm borrowing."

"Tonight?"

"Quicker the better. We'll all meet behind the castle, in the forest. Follow the wood trail. Clearing about quarter-mile in."

"But . . . will it work?"

He stopped shoveling and grinned. "Got to. Else I don't get my money, do I?"

There was much to do. Everything, including the tortoise, to be parceled as small as possible, Traveler and Growch to be briefed as to our meeting place, Mistral to be dirtied up, Gill to be encouraged—

"Hidden in a manure cart? I couldn't possibly. . . ."

—and in between as much food as possible to be filched from the hall and kitchens.

Promptly at midday I was summoned once more to the Lady Hell-and-All (as I now thought of her). More instruction included the Wimperling "finding" lost objects. He was deliberately slow, earning one sharp reprimand and a slash with her jeweled girdle at me for not teaching her properly. In between I managed to convey to him what we had planned and where we were to meet.

"But what about you?"

"Have you forgotten? I can fly. . . ."

I thought he was joking, trying to make me feel better.

The afternoon seemed interminable, though there was only now some three hours till dusk. I checked and re-checked that all was packed and prepared; noted that the sky was clear and remembered there would be a helpful moon; worried lest we didn't get away quick enough, for the lady's soldiers and her scent-working lymers and brachs could pick up a trail easily enough if she discovered us missing too soon; I also prayed: hard.

In between I paced the courtyard restlessly, watching people come and go, all busy, all employed on some task or another. Soldiers drilling, squires practicing with wooden swords, wood being stacked, slops emptied, weapons being cleaned and sharpened, horses groomed and exercised, dogs fighting, chickens being plucked for the evening meal . . .

I felt terribly conspicuous, as if everyone could read my mind, knew what I was planning, but in fact no one took the slightest notice of me. Most were too busy, but as for the others, all knew I had incurred the lady's displeasure, so it was as if I didn't exist at all. If there had been any dungeons in the castle, I should have been shut away in those; being denied the gates, the courtyard was as good a prison as any.

At long last the sun started to sink behind the castle walls. The boy's was one of the last wagons to enter through the gate, and to my dismay he was directed, not to the stables, but to picking up empty water casks. This meant he was half-loaded. He then backed the wagon as near as he could to the stable door and muttered: "Can you get your dog to start a fight?"

Get Growch to fight? It had been with the greatest difficulty I had restrained him during the last few days, and now he needed no further bidding. He chose a pack of hounds near the gateway, slipped on his short legs beneath their bellies, and with a couple of sharp nips here and there and a heap of shouted insults had them in a trice snapping and barking and snarling and biting at one another, in an unavailing attempt to catch him. As soon as the pace got too hot, even for him, he careered through the open gates and across the drawbridge, yelling the dog equivalent of "can't-catch-me!" Half-a-dozen hounds tore off in immediate pursuit, which meant at least the same number of servitors went in pursuit, to ensure the lady's precious dogs came to no harm.

The chase was enlivening an otherwise boring afternoon, and more and more people were breaking off what they were doing to cheer, laugh or shake their heads disapprovingly. A couple of the horses who were being groomed chose that moment to display temper, snapping and kicking out at their handlers, scattering the rest of the dogs and some hens and ducks, whose squawks added to the commotion.

"Load up now!" hissed the boy, and in a fumblingly long moment I had Gill and our packages up and into the back of the wagon, and a tarpaulin hastily thrown over the whole. I threw Traveler up, and after a couple of abortive flutters he took wing and wheeled out of the gate, heading west. "Bring out the horse!" and in a moment he had exchanged her in the traces for his own animal, stooping to fiddle for a minute with his horse's off-hind hoof. He then thrust a bundle into my hand: "Change into these!" And a moment later was nonchalantly loading up a couple more casks and roping them down. All this had taken perhaps three minutes. "See you in the forest," he muttered, and led Mistral and the wagon towards the gateway, his own horse limping behind.

I watched them, my heart in my mouth, but no one took the slightest notice, and in a minute they were trundling across the drawbridge and away, just as the last of the protesting hounds were being led back to the courtyard. I heard a derisive bark from the far side of the moat and knew Growch was safe.

But I was wasting precious time. Ducking back into the stables I opened the package the boy had given me, tucked up my skirt as best I could and struggled into the braies, a very tight fit. I shoved my hair up under the broad-brimmed straw hat—why the hell hadn't I thought to braid it up!—and wrapped my cloak around me. Picking up the sack I had earlier filled with hay I flung it over my shoulder and stooped over as though I was carrying a much heavier burden.

It was perhaps twenty yards from the stable to the gateway, but it seemed like a million miles. I had to walk slowly, I had to hunch up to keep my face hidden, and with the broad brim of the hat I could only see a couple of paces in front of me. At last I could see the penultimate wagon ahead trundling through the gateway, and hurried a little to pass through in its wake. I had my hand out ready to hang on to the tailgate when everything went horribly wrong.

I had hurried too much in changing and hadn't fastened my skirt up securely. It started to drop down and, bending to retrieve it, I felt my hat fall off and my hair cascade down round my face. There was a shout off to my left and I dropped the sack and was panicked into running, my heart thumping like a drum. A soldier slipped from the shadows, stuck out a foot and I landed flat on my face in the dust, winded and bruised.

I was hauled to my feet, none too gently.

"What's all this, then? Trying it on again, are we? We'll just see what the lady has to say about all this. . . ."

19

The lady had a great deal to say, or rather scream, the words punctuated with slaps, punches and pinches which I was helpless to avoid, being held firmly by the two soldiers who had brought me upstairs. I was almost blinded by tears of rage and pain and at first I only half heard the little voice in my head. There it was again: "Courage; we'll soon be out of this. . . ." Then I realized the Wimperling must be in the solar as well.

The lady eventually ran out of breath and went back to her chair, her face crimson with rage and exertion. "After all I've done for you, you ungrateful little whore! Oh, I see I shall have to teach you a real lesson this time? Misbegotten little tart! You can't say I didn't warn you. . . ." She turned to the soldiers. "Go and wring the neck of that pigeon of hers, then take it to the kitchens and bid them make a little pie of it: I shall start my meal with it tonight. Then bring her brother here: we'll see how he likes losing his tongue as well as his eyes. . . ."

"Oh, *no!*" The words were out before I realized that the others had gone, were hopefully safe for a while, but she enjoyed my reaction, clapping as if she had just performed a clever trick and was applauding herself. Her tongue flickered back and forth between her teeth, a snake tasting the air for my terror.

"I'll show you just who is in charge here! If you don't want your brother to lose other parts as well—a hand, his ears, his balls perhaps—you will swear on God's Body not to dare cross me again!"

We were alone now—where *was* the Wimperling? The fire smoked abominably, my face hurt and the soft flesh on my upper arms throbbed where she had pinched and nipped with unmerciful nails. My loosened hair was plastered across my face, and I lifted my hands to braid it back, but she half-rose from her chair on an instant.

"No tricks, now, or I'll call the guard!" I let my hands drop again and she subsided. Just then the Wimperling appeared from behind her chair, festooned as before with ridiculous ribbons and bows. He gave me a reassuring wink; I could see his ears were cocked, listening to something I could not hear.

"Not on their way back yet," he said to me. "On my count of three run across to the window and open the shutters as wide as you can!" He started to take deep breaths. The lady's expression changed; she bent down to caress him.

"But you can't—"

"Don't argue!" he said. "Just go. Trust me. . . . One, two, three!"

I should perhaps have rushed to the window without risking a glance back. As it was I nearly knocked myself senseless on the corner of the ornate sideboard just to glimpse the lady rise from her chair and call out, the Wimperling circling her warily with exposed teeth—he had real tusks I noticed—all the while hissing gently.

I reached the window without further mishap and looked round wildly for the fastening. Of course! There was a heavy bar that dropped into slots on either side. I tried to lift it, but it wouldn't budge. Swearing under my breath, I heaved and heaved again. One side started to move, the other was stuck. Helplessly I shoved and pulled, then realized that one shutter hadn't been closed properly and was catching against the bar. I slammed it shut with the heel of my hand then hefted the bar once more. It came loose so easily it flew up in the air and narrowly missed my feet as it crashed onto the floor. I tugged the shutters open as hard as I could till they crashed back against the wall and suddenly the room was flooded with dusk-light and there was a great gust of welcome fresh air.

"Right!" I yelled, and turned back to an incredible sight. The Wimperling appeared to have grown to twice or three times his normal size: he was blowing himself up as one would inflate a bladder, and looked in imminent danger of bursting. I could hardly see his eyes, his tail stuck straight out like an arrow and his wings were unfolding away from his shoulders, because there was no room to tuck them away.

The lady's eyes were almost popping out of her head, but she was still making valiant attempts to reach me, thwarted by the pig's circling motions. I took a quick peep out of the window; we couldn't possibly escape that way. It was a sheer drop down to the dry moat and I didn't fancy suicide.

The Wimperling took a last, deep, deep breath, adding yet more

inches all over, until his tightly stretched skin looked as if it were cracking all over into tiny, fine lines like unoiled leather.

I could hear footsteps on the spiral stair.

"Bolt the door!" cried the Wimperling. "Then watch out!"

As I ran to the door I saw him charge the Lady Hell-and-All, knocking her flying into the hearth, shrieking and cursing. I threw both bolts
and dashed back, the lady being occupied in trying to extinguish the
smoldering sparks that had caught her purple woolen dress, doing less
than well because the bright-edged specks were widening into holes and
then crawling like maggots this way and that in the close weave.

Somehow the Wimperling had managed to heave himself up onto
the windowsill, and was now balanced precariously on the edge. He was
so fat he could barely squeeze his bulk through the frame.

"Hurry up, Summer!"

"What? Where?"

"On my back," he said impatiently. "Hurry!"

"You can't—"

"I *can*!"

I tried to scramble up, but whereas the windowsill had been on a
level with my waist, with the pig's bulk on top his back was at chin-
height and I kept slipping off. Now behind us we could hear a hammering
on the door, the lady was still screeching and any minute she would
rush over and snatch me back—

I grabbed a stool, climbed on that and found myself lying flat on
the pig's back.

"Arms round my neck and hang on tight! Here we go-o-ooo!" and
before I could take a breath there was a sudden sickening plunge and
we were away. I felt a shriek of pure terror wind its way up from my
stomach and escape through my mouth, the sound mingling with the
screech of disturbed rooks and the rush of air past my ears. There was
a sudden Whoosh! of sound and then a Crack! as of flags snapping in
a sharp breeze, and we were flying!

A steady rush of air came from the Wimperling's backside and his
wings spread out from his shoulders, balancing us on our downward
path away from the castle. The moat slid away from beneath my frightened eyes; there were the trees of the forest, the patch of greensward
rising gently to meet us. . . .

It was a terrifying, wonderful few moments. The wind blew my hair
all over my face, I felt utterly insecure, my teeth were chattering with
fear, yet there was enough in me left to appreciate just what I was ex-

periencing. The world was spinning, I was a bird, I was going to the moon, I would live forever, I was immortal, omnipotent—

The hiss of escaping air behind us stopped suddenly, started again, then deteriorated into a series of popping little farts, and in an instant we were wobbling all over the sky. The world turned upside down and a moment later we landed on the strip of grass in front of the trees with an almighty crash that rattled my teeth and knocked all the breath from my body.

For a moment—a minute? longer?—I lay fighting to regain my breath, then sat up and felt myself all over. Plenty of bruises and bumps, but nothing broken. Where was I, what was I—?

The Wimperling! Oh, God, where was he?

I gazed around wildly, saw what looked like a shrunken sack lying a few yards away. "Wimperling? Are you all right?" I crawled over and poked the heap.

"Yes," said a muffled voice. "No thanks to you. I was underneath when we landed. . . ."

He sat up slowly, shook each leg in turn, then his tail and ears and took a deep breath. Immediately he looked less like a sack and more like a pig.

I shook my head admiringly. "How did you *do* it? The flying, I mean?"

"Improvisation. I don't think I'd try it again, though: not easy enough to control emission. Without it, though, I couldn't have managed you as well—my wings aren't strong enough yet."

There was a sudden shout from the direction of the castle. I looked back and could see the lady hanging out of the window we had just left, waving her arms and shouting, and around the corner of the castle came a party of foot soldiers, trotting purposefully our way. I scrambled to my feet.

"Quick! We've got to find the others. Something about a firewood trail . . ."

"I saw it on the way down, as well as I could for mouthfuls of your hair," said the pig tranquilly. "Off to the left." And he set out at a fast trot, with me stumbling behind. We swerved into the undergrowth and it was hard going, for the bushes were thick and overhead branches became tangled in my hair while roots tripped my feet. But the Wimperling kept going and soon we burst out into a twig-strewn ride.

Behind us we could hear shouts, the lady's fading screams, and we ran as fast as we could down the ride into the forest, me fearful lest we had missed the others. The trees swung on either side and there were stacks of part-chopped wood, two charcoal-burner's huts and—yes, they were all there, Mistral already loaded.

Growch came bouncing to meet us. "Hullo! Got away all right, I see. Didn't I do well? Saw that lot off, I did."

Gill fumbled for my arm. "You all right? That cart . . . I smell terrible." He did.

I mind-checked the others: all well. Even Basher was awake, and grumbling. "A-a-all that bouncing . . . Chap ca-a-an't sleep. . . ."

The boy was dancing about impatiently. "Hurry! I must be away before they come. Wind's from the east—them to you, which'll help you with the dogs. I'll try and head 'em off. . . ." and he swung a smelly sack from his hand.

"Thanks!" I panted. I had a stitch in my side from running. "Why the extra help?"

"Catch you and they catch me," he answered succinctly. "If they screwed your arms out of their sockets you'd tell. Have to."

I pulled out my purse from under my skirt and poured coins into my hand. "Ten silver pieces: one, two— Hey! What are you doing?" To my consternation a dirty brown hand had snatched the purse and scooped the coins from my hand.

The boy stepped back well out of reach. He pulled a knife from his belt, and I bent down to restrain a growling Growch.

"Why?"

"For my Mam and sisters, remember? Reckon they need the money more'n you. You got the pig: reckon he can earn for you. Better get going: the lady has a long arm. Take the path to your right, then first left to the stream. Walk in the water to confuse the hounds till you come to a grove of oaks. After that take the path either to the east or south. Lady's demesne finishes at the road you'll find either way. Twenty miles or so. Get going, will you?"

"Wait!" I called, as he made for the shelter of the trees. "What's your name?"

"Dickon. Why?"

I should have been furious with him, risked setting Growch on him, fought him myself for the money, but in a queer way I knew he needed it more. It was a shame, but I still had some of Matthew's money left: we'd manage. "When are you leaving?"

"Soon as the weather brings the first leaves on the beech. Go and get myself 'prenticed. Come back for the family once I'm earning."

"If you go north, seek out . . ." and I gave him Matthew's name and direction. "Say we sent you. He's a kind man but a canny merchant. He might fix you up with something. Treat him fair and he'll do the same."

"Thanks. I—" But there came a flurry of shouts and barking behind us and we fled one way, he the other.

At first it was easy, in spite of the deepening dusk. Behind us we could hear the hounds and then a sudden whooping, hollering sound and gathered they had picked up a scent. I only hoped it wasn't ours, but the sounds seemed to be away to our left, no nearer. We nearly missed the path to the stream, it was so overgrown, but at last we found ourselves splashing ankle-deep in freezing water, and by the time we managed to identify the grove of oaks the icy chill of my feet had crept up to my stomach and chest. It was near full dark; Mistral, the pigeon and the tortoise were fine, but Gill, Growch and I were so cold that all we wanted to do was light a fire and roast ourselves by it, forgetting bruised feet, turned ankles and scratched faces and hands.

But there was no way we could risk that. Far away I could still hear the mournful belling of the hounds, though the distance between us seemed to be increasing. I hoped Dickon was safe back home. Even if he had laid a trail, eventually when it came to an end they would cast back, though they would probably wait now until morning: the lady would not thank them for losing any of the hounds, even to catch us. And I knew she would be even keener to do that now she knew the pig could fly. . . .

We stumbled on as best we could through the long night, halting only for a quick snack of the bits and pieces I had managed to bring with me. We had the advantage of clear skies, a near-full moon and the prickle of stars, but it was still hard going. There were no rides here and the undergrowth hadn't been cleared for years. Fallen trees, hidden roots, sudden dips and hollows, the tangle of briars, an occasionally stagnant pond—all contrived to hinder our halting passage.

The noise of our progress effectively drove away most of the wild-life, though tawny owl hunted relentlessly. There was the intermittent scurrying in the undergrowth as some small animal was disturbed, and we almost fell over a grunting badger, turning the fallen leaves for early grubs. Towards dawn I called a halt under some pines and we hunkered down in an uneasy doze. There was nothing much to eat for breakfast but the rest of what I had brought from the castle, and that was little enough: the bread stale, the cheese hard, the pie so high only the Wimperling and Growch would touch it. Luckily there was grazing for Mistral, some seeds for Traveler; Basher had dozed off again.

It was a long day. Once or twice we heard the far-off sounds of men, dogs and even horses, but even these receded after a while. At the midday halt Mistral and the Wimperling foraged as best they could, the pigeon found some thistle heads, and Basher, thankfully, had decided to hibernate again. Gill and I just had to tighten our belts and trudge on. Luckily that afternoon I found some Judas' Ear growing on elder: it was a tough fungus with little taste, but after dusk I risked a small fire—during the light I reckoned smoke could be still seen from the turrets of the castle, but a tiny red glow in a hollow was more difficult to spot at night—and chopped the fungus into the pot with oil, salt, a pinch of herbs and a little flour and water and it made a filling enough mess. I also made some oatcakes to eat in the morning. Of course we were still hungry, but at least our stomachs didn't grumble all night.

And this was the pattern of the next two days. Luckily the sun shone and we took whatever promising trail we could, though very often these animal tracks started going east or south, and then wandered all over the place, sometimes even circling right back, and the undergrowth was too thick for us to wade through, unless we found bare ground beneath pine or fir. Twenty miles straight it might be, crooked it was not. I wondered how far we had really come: probably halfway only.

I looked for more fungi and found a few Scarlet Cups, better for color than taste, some Blisters, and a few Sandys. This time I boiled them up with a dozen or so chicory and dandelion leaves and the last of the flour. Growch dug up a couple of truffles and I added these and the result was quite tasty. Gill and I were down to one thin meal a day, though the animals fared better with their foraging, and the Wimperling it was who found us both some shriveled haws and the handful or so of hazelnuts the next day. But we were all weakened and weary by the evening of the fifth day when the trees started to thin out and at last we could walk straight with the setting sun to our right.

I don't think any of us quite believed it at first when we found ourselves actually stepping on a proper road, able to see in all directions and with no pushing and shoving along a trail. I looked back. Nothing save anonymous trees: it could have been anyone's demesne. I felt like putting up a great notice by the side of the road saying: "Beware! The Lady Aleinora is an evil Bitch!" But what good would it do? Most who passed here would not be able to read, and for those who did the castle was twenty miles away from this side.

I hadn't realized how tired I was: we were on a road, pointing in the right direction, but we had no food and no shelter: I didn't feel I could go a step further. Growch nuzzled my knee sympathetically, but it was Traveler who called to be let out of his cage.

"I'll fly a little way and see what I can see. . . ."

He was back in ten minutes, to report a hamlet some two miles ahead. I don't know how we made it but we did, just before dark. We had to knock them up, the food was poor, the shelter minimal, but at that stage we couldn't be choosers. We ate, we slept, and the next day we did the same. On the second day we were on our way again, wending from hamlet to hamlet. The weather remained dry, the village folk were hospitable, the food adequate, but I was worried at how far east we were veering, although there was no alternative except the occasional track. Even Traveler, who was a definite bonus, could see no alternative way, fly as high as he could.

The countryside was changing, too. It was becoming more rocky and the road more undulating, and we passed through scrub and pine as the land gradually rose. On either side mountains rose in sympathy, at first blue and distant, then nearer and sharper each day, till we could clearly see the tall escarpments, the towering crags, the black holes of faraway caves, the skirts of pine that clothed their waists. Above our heads we could hear the complaint of flocks of crows and sometimes see the mighty soar of eagles, their great wings fingering the winds we could not feel.

Understandably Traveler became wary of flying too far with so many predators about, but one day he came winging back to report a "town of sorts" off to our left. Three or four flights away, he said, but a pigeon's flight was variable, relying as it did day by day on weather conditions: wind, rain, cloud, sun and the type of flight needed to suit each variation.

"Can we reach it before nightfall?"

"Up the hill, down the hill, round the next hill, turn east, twisting road between high escarpments, down to the valley . . . Yes."

"And what's it like, this town?" A town meant proper shelter, a full replenishment of our stores, mending of shoes, a warm wash—everything we had sorely needed for the past two weeks.

"Difficult to say. Never seen anything like it. Lots of tents, few buildings. Many people and animals. No castle, no church. Big road leading off to the south."

And that is what decided me. This was the road we needed, and if it meant going through the "town" Traveler had described, then that was the way we had to go, although many times during that long day I cursed the pigeon's directions. Birds fly, they don't walk, and their "up" and "down" meant little to them, but a hell of a lot to those on foot. The narrow path we followed that crawled and looped what seemed a million miles towards the valley floor nearly finished us all off: it was so frustrating being able to see our goal one moment, and then having to turn away from it. That, plus the falling rocks, the blocked paths we had to climb around, the streams that poured on our heads or meandered across the track . . .

I had already lit the lantern and fixed it to Mistral's crupper by the time we reached the valley floor. Ahead was a short walk through well-trodden scrub to the perimeter of the "town," marked by a regular series of posts set into the ground, a very shallow artificial moat and a couple of temporary bridges. Beyond we could see a score of small stone buildings, a mass of tents, a half-ruined amphitheater and a slender temple, the broken columns throwing exquisite shadows in the moonlight. Obviously once this had been the site of an earlier civilization. And now?

We were stopped at the nearest bridge. Not by a soldier, but by a fussy little civilian with a mass of papers in his hand, a quill behind his ear and an ink pot in his pocket. His very officiousness calmed any fears I might have had, and before long I was trying not to smile at his earnestness. Here was normalcy: no shrinking houses, ghosts or wicked ladies.

"What have we here, then? There are only two weeks left, you know: you're late!" He consulted his lists. "Do you know just how many models we have had this year? Nearly two hundred! And of course now accommodation is at a premium. . . . Do you have a sponsor? No? Still, there is always Mordecai, the Jew, or Bartholomew. . . . I believe they are both short this year. Now, how many are there of you? A man, a lady and a horse . . . And what's this? A pig? and do I see a dog? Well, I don't think I've seen a pig, this year, but of course dogs are two a farthing. You have a pigeon? And a tortoise? Now that *is* a novelty! This might make all the difference. Quite a call for exotic creatures like that, especially for breviaries. Haven't by any chance got a coney or a hedgepig, I suppose? Pity; both in short supply this year. Seven of you, then: lucky number, seven . . . Come far? Now, that will be nine of copper: two each for the humans, one for the animals."

I was completely confused. "Models," "sponsors," a tortoise to make all the difference? Instead of the expected normalcy, this place sounded like a madhouse. But the word "models" gave me a clue: perhaps this place contained artists who wanted various creatures to draw and paint, human and animal?

"How many artists here this year?" I asked diffidently, to make sure I was on the right track.

"Artists? A few more than last year . . ." So now I was right. "Now, let's have your names. . . ." He took them down.

"What—what are the rates?"

"Depends on your sponsor. You haven't been before? No, well if you follow me I will try and find someone to take you on."

He led us across the wooden bridge to a squalid huddle of temporary huts, a line of tethered horses, mules and donkeys. Small cooking fires burned in the deepening gloom and people scurried back and forth carrying washing, water, pots and pans, babes in arms.

"This is the poorer end," said our guide, wrinkling his nose. "Not organized at all, this lot . . . Farther in are the stores, stables, cooking and washing areas. Plus of course the hiring place, market and artists supplies . . . Stay here: I won't be long." And off he strode with a purposeful air, papers flapping.

"What *have* you got us into this time, Summer?" said poor Gill.

He might well ask!

Our guide, Master Fettiplace, returned, and led us a few hundred yards to a row of orderly tents. "Let me introduce you to Master Bumbo—" a small, bustling, bald-headed man, with a snub nose red from wine and a potbelly to match. "He is willing to take you on, providing terms can be agreed."

"No reason why not!" cried our new sponsor. He beamed at us all, but the smile did not reach a pair of small, black, calculating eyes. He would drive a hard bargain but we had no option. He had a large black mole on his left cheek, from which sprouted three bristly hairs: this should not have made him any less likable, but somehow it did.

"Come along, come along, all of you!" said Master Bumbo. "Let's get you settled in. You'll be hungry and tired, I have no doubt. . . . Er, you did say you had a tortoise . . . ?"

I sized up Master Bumbo, and decided it would be a battle. But we needed the money. . . .

"Of course," I said. "A trained one. As are the horse, the pigeon, the pig and the dog. Very expensive animals. They will do exactly as I say: stand, sit, walk, fly, or be perfectly still. But they only obey me. We do not come cheap, my brother and I. . . ."

"Of course, of course! My commission is small, very small—and in return you will have bountiful accommodation, free, and one good meal a day. And of course your fees for posing . . ." He walked along the row of tents, disappeared into one; there was the sound of an altercation and a moment or two later a tawdry female came flying out, followed by half a dozen cushions, a blanket and various pots and pans. Master Bumbo returned with an ingratiating smile and a bruised lip. "As soon as you like . . ." The tent smelled like a whorehouse, and showed signs of the hasty eviction of its former occupant: underwear, pots of perfume, a torn night dress. I handed these gravely to our sponsor.

"You mentioned a meal. . . . I think we will take today's now. And if I may accompany you to the cooking lines, I believe we shall have better service when we need it. Precooked meals, or will they cook our own?"

"Er . . . Either. They are not cheap, but who is these days?"

I decided to build our own fire. Hanging our lantern on a hook, I saw there was rush matting on the floor and a few rather tatty cushions. We had our own bedding, so that was all right. "Is there a bathhouse?"

"Over there." He pointed. "Again, not cheap . . ."

Right. We would pay for hot water once, and I would wash the clothes, myself; there must be a stream nearby.

He tried again. "Fodder for the animals a hundred yards to your right—"

"Not cheap," I said gravely.

"Er . . . No. Your horse can join the lines down—"

"My horse," I said, "stays here, behind the tent. She's trained, remember?"

And so the first small victory was mine, but it didn't remain that way for long. Every day it swung first one way then the other, as first Master Bumbo then I gained advantage. Of course he tried to cheat us, and I retorted by snatching the odd freelance for any of us I could.

The "town" was as I had suspected: a winter retreat for artists where they could paint, draw or sketch in peace with everything provided— from the latest tube or pot of Italian Brown to the row of whores' tents behind the temple. They had all the scenery they needed—a river, mountains, forests, romantic ruins—and all the models imaginable; black, white, brown; tall, short, wide, thin; dwarfs and giants, men, women and children; the beautiful, the ugly and those in between. They had animals of all shapes and sizes (but ours was the only tortoise), the flowers of the field carefully painted on wood and cut out to be placed where they wished and all the impedimenta of indoor life—pots, pans, candlesticks, stools, chairs, tables, hangings, goblets, knives etc. There were costumes and armor, swords and spears, in fact everything an artist could need. At a price.

Why in this hidden valley? I had thought we were miles from anywhere, but in fact the road Traveler had seen led straight to an important crossroads, and was only ten miles from the nearest town. The whole venture was run by an Italian, who had another such project in his own country, held in the autumn. Signor Cavalotti, whose brainchild this was, believed that exchanges of ideas and techniques were essential to the development of art; indeed, I was told there had been significant advances in perspective and the mixing of paints in the ten years the two "towns" had existed.

Well, Signor Cavalotti may have had high ideals and thought he was a philanthropist, but the consortium who ran this caper was very far from being either. Everything was very highly priced, but those who came off worst were probably the models like us. It went like this: the artist paid the model, who then relinquished some seventy percent to the sponsor; he in turn paid ten percent for food, five percent to pitch the tents, and then perhaps twenty percent to the consortium for the privilege of sponsorship. Probably the artists spent more than everyone else—space, canvas, paints, props, costumes, models, food, accommodation—but then they had the money to start with.

Most of them were sponsored by rich families or the church—I counted at least a dozen altar pieces and triptychs in various stages of completion—and many had private means. There was a handful of students and apprentices, but most of these were under the patronage of the artists themselves. Useful to be able to take credit for the important bits and have an unpaid lackey to fill in the background.

Master Bumbo had very little idea how to promote his models—he had ten others besides ourselves—but in spite of his laziness, incompetence and avariciousness Gill's good looks provided us with two St. Sebastians and a disciple; I got two crowd scenes, very background, and Basher was fully occupied with two young monks composing a bestiary and an artist creating a series of panels on popular legends. One artist was interested exclusively in birds and their plumage and anatomy and was very pleased with the (private) sittings with Traveler.

And what of the Wimperling in all this? All in all, he earned more than the rest of us put together. Master Bumbo gave up on him after the first day: he was, after all, a rather ugly pig—but I had better ideas. A German artist who had used poor Mistral in an allegory for famine recommended a Dutchman who was looking for "odd" creatures, and I saw why when I peeped round the corner of his screened off area. He was painting the pains of Hell on a large canvas, and very frightening they were, too. Fires, flames, smoke; imps, demons, devils, trolls, dragons: all delighting in torturing, beheading, raping and disemboweling the hapless sinners who cascaded down from the top of the canvas in a never-ending stream. And everywhere there was an inch or so of space capered creatures from a wildly demented imagination, gleefully cheering on the destruction.

These creatures could never have existed: birds with fish heads, lizards with horses' hooves, cats with six arms and two heads, mouths with thin spindly legs, spiders with human faces, torsos with heads in their stomachs, a pair of legs with wings—It was this last that gave me the idea. Withdrawing quietly before the artist noticed me, I returned later with a fully briefed Wimperling.

The artist was a thoroughly unpleasant little man, hunched and smelly, so much I had already heard, but I wasn't prepared for the brusque way he dismissed me before I had opened my mouth.

"Unless you've got an extra pair of tits or balls I don't want to know: bugger off!"

But I wasn't going to be thrown out just like that. Instead I dared his wrath and looked critically at the lizard-like thing with wings he was trying to draw.

"You've got the wings wrong," I said. "They should be more leathery and the tips less scooped. . . ."

"What? What do you mean? How do you know anything about Wyrm-wings?"

"Look" I said, and the Wimperling carefully extended one wing. "And if it's claws and hooves you are after, just look at these. . . ." The pig lifted one hoof. "And as for fangs—" Obligingly the Wimperling bared his teeth. I hadn't realized just how sharp they were till now. The pig folded himself away again. "What do you say?"

"Christ-on-the-Cross!" breathed the artist. "Do that again!"

The Wimperling obliged.

"How much do you want for it?" snapped the artist, his eyes even piggier than the pig. "I'll give you what you want. Within reason . . . Ten gold pieces?" His fingers were crawling towards the pig with desire, his sleeve smudging the charcoal sketch I had criticized.

"He's not for sale," I replied firmly. "But I am offering him to you as a model: exclusive rights, of course. At a reasonable price."

"For the rest of the time here? Nine days? One gold coin."

"Two. He's worth far more, and you know it. *Exclusive* rights, remember: you'd better keep him hidden away." I was calculating on his artistic greed in this: I didn't want anyone else to know about the wings. I needn't have worried: the artist's "find" was far too precious to share, and at the end of our two weeks the artist had dozens of sketches of every part of the pig's anatomy, from the tip of his fanged snout to the end of his spade-tipped tail and everything in between.

I supposed this was the way to assure immortality, I thought, looking at the sketches, remembering the other drawings and paintings of all of us, even my crowd scenes. Some day, many years hence perhaps, people would look at a pigeon's wing, a horse's flanks, a scruffy dog, a tortoise in a bestiary, the wings on a creature from hell, a woman bending over a basket, a saint's agony, and maybe wonder at the originals they were created from. But only we would know, and we wouldn't be there to tell them. It was a shivery thought.

But once more on the road, with the warm wind lifting the hair from my forehead and the prickly-sweet perfume of the gorse on the hillsides tickling our noses, all such somber thoughts were chased away.

"I can smell spring," said Gill, lifting his blind eyes to the sun. "And after spring comes Summer!" and he smiled at his own little joke, a smile to lift my heart and renew my love.

20

It was true, Spring had arrived, and with it came an uplifting of the spirit, a healthy optimism that had nothing to do with reality. I would wake in the mornings, stretch the creaks from my bones (for the nights were still cold), sniff the crisp dawn air and feel as though I had drunk a bucketful of chilled white wine.

As we traveled further and further south, I delighted in plants, trees and herbiage that were strange to my northern eyes. All seemed brighter, bigger, pricklier; citrus trees with evergreen leaves sprouted little dots of white bud; bushy grey-green cacti and succulents were tipped with barbs like daggers; a yellow cascade of mimosa poured over stone walls, and miniature iris and crocus speared up through the scrub under olive and carob. Of course I had to ask the names of all these, but there were plants I recognized, though their flowering was at least a month ahead of ours at home.

I found the pale tremble of pink-white-purple wood anemones, petals ready to fly on the slightest breeze; heart-shaped leaves of deepest green hiding the thick, soft scent of violets; the perfumed cream of wild jonquil; shaggy coltsfoot and tender celandine, days-eye, lions-tooth—the last two demanded daily by an awakening Basher, together with the tender young leaves of chicory and clover.

As we passed through villages and hamlets the pink smoke of almond blossom clothed the slopes of the hillsides, though the knobbed vines were still bare. I experimented with the new-grown herbs: wild mint (good with lamb and goat), young and bitter shoots of asparagus, pale among its prickly adult cage, the tasty tips of nettle, and thyme and rosemary (excellent with all meats and fish).

And the birds and animals echoed this burgeoning promise. Sparrows, thrushes, blackbirds, green- and goldfinch, tits, siskin, flycatchers, brambling, all were busy picking and pecking for insects, snails and young shoots, twigs, hair, moss and mud for nests. Wrens scuttled along old walls, tree-creepers sidled up the bark, and against the eaves of buildings the house martins were already building new nests or repairing last year's, dark mud against pale. In the trees the russet squirrels were dashing about with their usual indetermination, all mouth and ruffed tails; shy roe deer leapt among the ground elder and sweet cicely, the hinds already heavy with young; the jaunty scuts of coney were glimpsed flashing through the undergrowth, we could hear the crash and grunt of swine, the faraway howl of wolf and scream of vixen; the shepherds who walked their sheep and goats along the slope often carried new-dropped lambs, their wool still sticky with pale birth blood, the ewes reaching up anxiously to nuzzle their young, the dogs chewing at strings of afterbirth as they followed the flock. Above our heads came the first sweet babble of the ascending larks, and if you searched carefully you could find in nests soft with down and moss the incredible promise of eggs blue as the sky, or scrambled with speckles and blotches, like a child's scribbles.

The first flies came to torment us, yolk-yellow butterflies quivered on the scarcely less bright gorse and broom, mornings showed the sil-ver-slime trail of snails, clouds of midges danced about our heads, bees buzzed from flower to bush; from the groves of pines crept processions of striped caterpillars: I picked up a couple, disturbing the caravan of their passage, and was well rewarded with a crop of white blebs which itched intolerably till an old crone in one of the hamlets took pity on me and threw a jug of sour wine over me: I stank for days, but the irritation was gone.

In the ponds and ditches humps and strings of spawn showed where frog and toad had been: some had already hatched into flickering life and sun-warmed lizards ran along the stones. Fish began to spawn, a flurry among the stones of streams, three or four males to every female, or so it seemed.

The farther south we went, the more the countryside changed: arid, mountainous, yet conversely in the valleys, more fertile. The air was clearer, colors brighter, contours sharper; the people wore more colorful clothes, too: patterned skirt, red scarf, purple jacket although the elderly were still in a contrast of black, for mourning: who at their age had not lost a member of the family? We passed repainted shrines and gaily clad processions for St. Joseph's day, disregarding the rigors of Lent, and then the hearty celebrations for the new Year of Grace on March 25, a fiesta full of green branches, embroidered shawls and colored ribbons.

The going became easier the farther south we went, perhaps because our feet had become accustomed to the rubs, bumps, flints, pebbles and stones of the highways. More and more we traveled in company, too many for ambush or treachery. Many languages were distributed among the mighty campfires each evening; men spoke of ice, fog and snow in islands to the north and west, even in summer; of sand, sun and people black as ink to the southlands, of great temples of stone and creatures as tall as a house and with horns of ivory; when they spoke of the east they told of beasts of burden who never drank, yet carried houses upon their backs, of heathens who sang to their gods from tall towers, of men as yellow as a canary bird who fought like devils. The west was full of great grey seas, ships with bird's wings that skimmed the waves to deliver their cargoes of cloth and wine, spices and silk, of great sea monsters who devoured a ship in one mouthful, and of the sea maidens with long hair and fishes' tails who sang the mariners to destruction on the rocks.

All this talk was heady stuff: it whetted my appetite to see more of the world before I finally found a husband and settled down. If men could travel around the world, why not a woman?

Travel seemed to improve the health and well-being of us all. Gill became tan-skinned, his step was bolder, he lost his gauntness. Mistral grew rounder and sleeker, her tail and mane longer, her hide lightened to a creamy color. Basher ate till he filled his shell and developed an extra ridge on his carapace, demanding a short walk each day to exercise off the excess. Traveler declared himself fit and wing-whole again, taking longer and longer flights and dancing back in brightened browny-pink feathers to wheel and dive above our heads. The Wimperling grew stouter and stronger by the day, until he was fast becoming the largest pig I had ever seen, and I felt lighter and fitter every day.

But it was Growch who took full advantage of all spring had to offer. One day the caravan in which we currently traveled was joined by an abbess and her servants, bound to take healing waters. She rode in a litter with silk curtains and was too superior to mix with the rest of us. Not so, apparently, her dogs. With her in the litter, fed on a diet of chicken and milk and sleeping on silk cushions, were two small, long-haired bitches, silky hair trimmed, curled, plaited and beribboned; they were exercised four times a day by the lady's attendants, waddling around like small brown sausages, their long black claws clip-clipping on the road, their plumed tails cleaned every time they excreted, their hair combed free of tangles by their mistress herself, using the same comb she used on her own hair, it was rumored. Growch's inquisitive nose and eyes found them the first time they set paws to ground, although his first essay was beaten back by the lady's attendants.

"Stripe me like a badger! What little chunks of sweetness! Plump and petted and just ready for it! You've no idea—"

"Now just you keep away from them," I said severely. "We don't want any trouble. The lady's servants will chop you in half if you—"

"Garn! Got to catch me first! 'Sides, I can have 'em away any time I choose. They fancies me, I can tell. . . ."

And apparently they did, to my amazement, for first one and then the other managed to escape from the servants and disappear from sight in the undergrowth, hotly pursued by a dog I promptly disowned. The abbess was distraught and insisted on staying behind until her "darlings" turned up again. . . .

Growch rejoined us two days later, some fifteen miles further on, absolutely shattered, his belly dragging on the ground. He was even filthier than usual, and declared himself starved.

"You don't deserve a thing!" I said, giving him a hunk of cheese and some stale bread. "You're absolutely disgusting! Er—what happened to the bitches? Did their owner get them back?"

" 'Ventually. Servants caught one, t'other went back when she was hungry. Not before we'd had a coupla nights of it . . . I can recommend a threesome. Never enjoyed one before," and he smacked his lips, whether from the cheese or fond memory I wasn't sure.

"I'd never seen dogs like them before," I said, remembering their snub noses, plumed tails and flouncy way of walking.

"Come from a place east, long-a-ways," said Growch, scratching furiously. He smelled like a midden, and I determined to dump him in the next stretch of water we came to and scrub him, hard. "Nice manners—none of this nonsense of equality between the sexes—just the right height with them little bow legs, and virgins as well . . . Not that that made much difference once they got goin'—"

"Shut up!" I said automatically. "I don't want to know!" I wondered whether the pups would look like him: probably a mixture. The abbess would have a shock. "They had nice faces. . . ."

"Faces? *Faces*?" He leered. " 'Oo the 'ell was looking at their faces?"

We were holed up for five days by howling winds and driving rain, which Basher assured us were normal at this time of year. "Good for the young heather shoots," he said. Traveler took advantage of the downpour to sit in puddles and air his wing-pits to the rain.

"Gets rid of the ticks," he explained.

I decided to take the opportunity of tidying us all up. We had taken a large loft above the stable in a hospitable farmhouse and there were a couple of rain butts in the yard below, now overflowing, so we were allowed unlimited bucketfuls and paid for two cauldrons of water heated over the kitchen fires.

First I scrubbed Growch—who immediately went out and found something disgusting to roll in—then the Wimperling and Mistral, combing out the tangles in the latter's mane and tail. With fresh water I washed our winter clothes, hoping that now we could wear our lighter things. With the hot water I found an old tub and first submitted Gill and then myself to a thorough going over. I remembered thinking it was a good job he was blind, else he would have seen my blushes as I washed those parts difficult for him to reach. . . .

I felt wonderfully fresh myself after I had bathed and washed my hair, changing into a clean shift and my thinner bliaut, surprised to see how winter storage had stretched the material: it was far roomier than I remembered, and I had to take it in an inch or two down the side seams.

I finally caught Growch and washed him again, threatening permanent exile in the rain if he did it again.

Being a stock farm we were staying in, there was no lack of leather and I bought some and busied myself stitching fresh boots for Gill. I used my mother's simple recipe: triple leather soles turned up at the sides and hemmed for a lace that fastened at the front, the whole stuffed with discarded sheep's wool for comfort and warmth. While I was about it I also made us sandals for the warmer weather: thick soles, a single band across the instep, a toe thong to go between the big toe and its brother, and a loop at the back to thread with a lace that tied round the ankle.

When we took to the road again we found that the wind and rain had washed the world as clean and fresh and new as we were. The grass was greener and taller, all the trees were in leaf, the woods were full of birds shouting, singing, quarreling, wildflowers and weeds had sprung up overnight and the stones and rocks sparkled and glinted like jewels in the sun.

Now many roads joined the highway and wandered off again and the houses were whitewashed against the summer sun. People were smaller, darker and spoke with a harsher patois and used their shoulders, hands and their faces to express themselves, like actors in a play.

Our little group was just one of many traveling the roads, but I could see that while we were nothing out of the ordinary, the Wimperling did attract attention. He was so large that I could see by the speculation in many an eye that they were measuring him for chops, sausages, brawn, roasts and bones for soup. I was careful to keep him by my side at night, though I believe he was more than capable of taking care of himself.

By now I was content with our little group, used to all their idiosyncrasies and fond of them all, but I knew it couldn't last. One by one the animals would leave us when they found whatever haven they were seeking, and each departure would diminish me. Once I had been alone except for my beloved Mama; now it seemed I was friends with all the world via a dog, a horse, a pigeon, a tortoise and a pig. I couldn't bear the thought of losing any of them, and when the time suddenly came for the first of them to leave us, I was unprepared.

One fine morning Traveler ate a handful of grain, pecked disgusting grit from the roadside, drank from a puddle and rose in the air to scan our road southward as usual. But this time he was gone longer than usual, so long in fact that I began to gaze anxiously up in the sky for eagles or falcons but could see none. I was beginning to get really fidgety when I saw him skimming back across the trees as he slowed his wings, starting to curve down at the tips, and waver a little as he gauged the wind. He skidded down in front of us, trembling from both excitement and exhaustion.

"I've found it! It's there! I had begun to think it wasn't—I hadn't—"

"Calm down!" He was so elated his beak was gaping and I was afraid his heart would stop. "Here, take a sip of this," and I poured some water from my flask into my horn mug. "That's better. . . . Now, tell us!"

It seemed he had flown higher than usual to surmount a range of hills to the southeast and had seen through the haze a large town and a ribbon of river, much like others on our journey, but as the mist cleared and he flew closer the sun touched the towers and pinnacles with gold, and he knew he had found his home town.

"I flew on and on, just to make sure, but there was no need. The knowing in my body, the thing that tells me where to go, it was pointing right at the city. . . ."

"What's going on?" asked Gill. "Why have we stopped? Don't tell me you are talking to your animals again. . . ."

"Hush! Let him finish. What then? You're sure it's the right place?"

"Sure as eggs become squabs . . ."

"Did you go near enough to find your home?"

"Not enough wing-time. Tomorrow, perhaps."

"Summer—"

I turned back to the pigeon. "Just a *minute*, Gill! Will you . . . Will you go on your own, then?" I was suddenly scared that the time had come to say goodbye, and I wasn't ready, not yet.

"No, of course not! I need you to tell the lady about the broken wing so she understands why I was so long."

"Very well . . . The message on your leg is for her, if I remember?"

"Yes, I told you. From her lover."

"Then she will forgive the delay, I'm sure. How far away is this town of yours?"

He considered. "For you, three, four days," and began to nibble at the tender shoots of grass by the roadside, tired of talking.

I knew Gill still didn't believe I had any real communication with the animals, but I reported exactly what the bird had said. There was a silence. "I'd like to say I'll believe it when I see it," he said carefully. "But you know that's impossible. I'll say this, though; if we find this town, *and* his home, *and* the lady he speaks of, then I will ask your forgiveness for doubting you. If . . ." He suddenly grinned. "Ask him if the lady is pretty." And he grinned again, not really expecting an answer.

"He says he doesn't know the meaning of the word 'pretty' as applied to humans," I translated after a moment or two. "He says she is smaller than me and that her hair is straight and pale. He says she has a quiet voice and gentle hands."

He thought about it. "Well . . . Tell you what, as long as there's a town ahead, she can be tall or small, fat or thin, dark or fair, just so long as we have a day or two in comfort again. No reflections on your cooking, Summer, but it will feel good to have my feet under a table again, eat a great chunk of game pie and drink a quart of ale."

"Well in that case," I said stiffly, "the sooner we get going the better!"

We arrived at our destination mid-afternoon of the fourth day, guided all the way by an ever more excited pigeon. After a couple of his disastrous "shortcuts," we kept to the roads; the flight of a bird takes no account of hills, rivers, stones or forest.

Once we had entered the town by the west gate and paid our toll, Traveler disappeared. He had obviously flown straight on, but like all the towns we had been in, there was no straight way anywhere; side roads, crooked lanes, blind alleys, and everywhere choked with traffic: horses, mules, carts, wagons, litters, pedestrians laden and unladen, children, cattle, sheep, pigs, dogs and cats.

He eventually returned and tried to guide us, soaring above us one minute, on a ledge the next, but several times we lost sight of him altogether. I became more and more conscious of the curious glances we were attracting: a blind man holding on to a horse's tail, and a scruffy dog, large pig and fat girl all scanning the rooftops like stargazers.

It seemed to take hours, but at last Traveler led us, fluttering just above our heads now, down a quiet street near the river, with high-walled houses on either side and a tall church at the end just striking the office for three hours after noon, echoed by others near and far.

Traveler came to rest atop a large double gate and fluffed his feathers. "It's here. . . ." I could feel his anticipation and anxiety as if it were my own and shivered in sympathy. Lifting my hand I knocked firmly: no answer. Somewhere down the road a dog, awakened from his siesta, barked for a moment. I knocked again, and there was a limping step, a creaking bolt and a face peered out at us, the chain still prudently fastened. Traveler hopped down to my shoulder.

"Yes?" said the door porter. He was almost bald and nearly toothless but had fierce, bushy eyebrows.

"I wish to—to see the lady of the house," I said, conscious that a name would have been better, but of course names meant nothing to a bird. "About a pigeon. This one," and I touched Traveler with my finger. "I believe he is one of hers. He has a message to deliver."

The porter stared out at us, at our travel-stained clothes, our generally tatty appearance, and I didn't blame him for his next remark.

"My mistress don't entertain rogues and vagabonds. Why, you don't even know her name, do you? Besides, how do I know it ain't all a trick to get in and rob us all? Could be anyone's pigeon you got."

"This color?" and stroked Traveler's wing. "Pink pigeons don't come in dozens. Besides, only your mistress has the key to the message strapped to his leg. . . ."

He thought about it. Finally: "I'll go and see," and he shut the gate again.

We waited for what seemed an age. I urged Traveler to fly over the gate and find his mistress, but he refused.

"We go in together," he said firmly.

Once more the shuffling steps approached the gate, but this time one half was flung open. "Mistress Rowena is in the garden at the back. Leave the beasts here." I took Gill's hand and followed the way that was pointed out to me, across the cobbles and down a narrow alleyway at the side of the house to a garden full of sun and sleepy afternoon scents.

Square beds were planted centrally with bay or evergreen, fancifully trimmed, and edged with box or rosemary. In the beds themselves were the long runners and green tips of miniature strawberries, the soft faces of violet and pansy, the tight buds of clove carnations. Beside each bed ran a little canal of water, probably fed from the river I could see glinting at the foot of the garden, beyond a lawn starred with daisies, camomile and buttercups. Against one wall were trellises for the climbing roses,

on the other were tall clumps of dark Bear's Braies and pale fennel, and
behind was a thick hedge of oleander.

At the top end of the garden fat, lazy carp swam in a pond plated
with water-lily pads and there, tossing pinches of manchet into their
hungry mouths, was Traveler's owner, who turned to meet us with a
smile. She was as the bird had described: small, slim, with icy blond
hair hanging straight down her back with a blue and gold fillet binding
her brow, to match her deep-sleeved dress. Her face was pale, as were
her lashes, brows and blue eyes.

Her smile revealed white teeth as small as a child's, with tiny points.
A cat's smile, I thought. She held out her hands and reached for Traveler,
fluttering nervously on my shoulder, and pinioned him in her soft white
hands.

"My servant, Pauncefoot, told me you had found one of my birds,
but I never expected it to be my Beauty! Where did you find him?" and
she put her cheek against his head, crooning softly.

I started to explain how I had rescued him, about the broken wing
and how long it had taken to heal, but as soon as I mentioned the message
on his leg I could see the rest didn't matter. Still nursing the bird she
fumbled in her purse pocket and drew out a tiny key, as fine as a needle
and in a moment the leg ring was open and she was unrolling a thin
strip of paper between finger and thumb. For the first time I saw a tinge
of color in her cheeks as she read the few words it contained. She looked
at us, smiling that cat smile.

"He comes at the end of this month, as he promised. . . ." Her eyes
were dreamy. "I knew he could not stay away. He was my father's apprentice. When he asked for my hand, my father stipulated that we spend
a year apart and he sent Lorenzo north on business, with the added
proviso that we should not communicate with each other. He still thinks
Lorenzo is after my money. . . ." She cuddled Traveler closer. "I thought
of a scheme to circumvent my father's dictum. Lorenzo took two of my
pigeons with him: a grey, and Beauty here. They gre arrived back in
October confirming his love, and he must have sent Beauty soon after.
My father will know nothing of the message. He had bribed the servants
to intercept any letters, but he never thought of the pigeons." She turned
to me. "I cannot thank you enough: with my father ill I cannot ask you
to stay overnight, but perhaps with these—" She handed me some coins,
one gold, I noticed "—I can combine my thanks with assurance you
may find good lodgings."

At first I was shy of accepting, but looking at the well-cared-for
garden, her clothes, the tall house behind, I realized she could well afford

it. "Thank you . . . The pigeon: his wing has healed, but he may not be able to manage such long flights as before. You will . . . ?"

"Still care for him?" she supplied. "Of course. Somehow he guided you here with my message—I can always breed from him. I have a couple of females the same shade. . . ."

I turned to go but suddenly Traveler—I couldn't think of him as "Beauty"—flew from her arms onto my shoulder. I turned my head to see his ruby eyes regarding me steadily. "Thanks," he crooned. "I shall always remember you, all of you. . . ." And he leaned forward and pretend-fed me, as an adult pigeon would a squab, then sprang from my shoulder and flew to the pigeon loft against the house wall.

I heard his owner draw her breath in sharply as she watched his flight, but my eyes were suddenly too blurred to see the expression on her face. She called out peremptorily to a gardener's boy raking the gravel between the flower beds. "Shut the loft door! Hurry . . ."

Out in the street again, the doors shut behind us, the coins jingling satisfactorily in my pocket, I should have felt satisfaction at a task well completed, a wanderer having found his home, but I didn't. I felt uneasy, depressed, somehow all *wrong*. I opened my mouth to say something and the ring on my finger, dormant so long, gave me such a sudden painful jolt that I cried out instead. At the same time a voice full of terror rang in my mind: "Help me! Help me. . . ." It was Traveler. What in the world had gone wrong?

Obeying an instinct stronger than thought or caution I turned and began to beat on the closed gate: "Let me in!" but there was no answer, and all the while I could sense the feather-flutter of Traveler's fear in my mind. I threw myself against the gate, but it wouldn't yield; by now the others, with the exception of course of Gill, had also "heard" the pigeon's panic. They needed no urging to help my assault on the gate. Growch barked hysterically, setting off other dogs down the road, the Wimperling added a shoulder-charge to my efforts and Basher even battered his head against his basket, but it was Mistral who got us in.

Turning, she aimed two vicious kicks at the gate panels, which gave on the second blow, allowing me to reach in and slip the bolts. As I reached the garden again at a run, I saw the gardener's boy hand a feebly fluttering bird to his mistress. Grabbing his wings cruelly with one hand she put the other hand around his neck, the tendons on her wrist already tightened to twist his head off.

"Stop!" I cried. "In the name of God, stop!"

21

She paused, her fingers still cruelly tight on Traveler's wings and neck. "Get out! What business is it of yours?"

"But you promised. . . ." I was bewildered. "You said you would care for him. . . . I don't understand!"

"It doesn't matter whether you understand or not!" she hissed. "It is *my* bird, to do with as I will! If I wish to wring the wretched thing's neck because it has betrayed me—"

"Betrayed you? How?"

She showed her small, pointed teeth in a grimace. "He is *my* bird, he does as *I* say, he owes *me* all his devotion! I saw what he did to you: he has never done that to me!"

She was jealous! Jealous of an affectionate gesture the poor bird had given me. . . . She must be mad. Feeling in my pocket I tossed her coins to the ground in front of her.

"Take your money: I don't want it! Instead, I'll take back a bird you obviously don't want either."

White lids came down over pale blue eyes, but not before I had seen the sudden gleam of cunning, so quickly veiled. "Very well," she said slowly, but her fingers were almost imperceptibly tightening round the bird's neck. At the same moment the ring on my finger gave me another sharp shock and my hand jerked forward, the ring now pointing at the Lady Rowena.

She screamed as though she had been stung and dropped Traveler, who lay at her feet, fluttering feebly, scrabbling round in the dirt in helpless circles. I picked him up gently and held him close. "It's all right now. . . ."

His owner backed away from me, crossing herself, her eyes wide with an emotion I couldn't fathom. "Witch! What have you done?" I moved towards her and she crossed herself again: I realized now the emotion she felt was fear. "All right, all right, take him! I wouldn't have kept him anyway: there is a knot in his wing, and I never keep anything that isn't perfect. . . ." And she spat at me, the phlegm landing in a yellow gobbet at my feet. "Now get out, before I call the servants to have you thrown out, or summon the soldiery and have you all arrested for theft and witchcraft!"

We went.

When I told Gill what had happened he actually put out a finger and stroked the still-trembling bird. "Poor little thing," he said. It was the first time I had seen him ever evince any interest in any of the animals: his usual stance was indifference. "What will you do with him now?"

"The first thing to do," said the Wimperling, "is to get out of this town right now, before she pulls herself together and does get us all thrown into jail. A woman like that cannot bear to be bested."

We took the southern gate from the city, not stopping even to eat. A trembling Traveler sat on my shoulder, looking back at the towers and pinnacles from which he had hoped so much, now bathed in the magical light of a yellow-orange sunset. I smoothed his feathers.

"Don't worry," I said. "We'll find you somewhere better. . . ."

"But that was my home," he said with sad, unassailable logic.

The Wimperling looked up. "A home is not one place," he said slowly. "A home can be a place where you are born and brought up, a place you like better than any other; it can be a dwelling where your loved one lives, a house in which your children are raised, or somewhere you have to live because there is no other. A home is made by you, it does not create itself. It can be large or small, beautiful or ugly, grand or mean. But in the end it is only one thing: the place where your heart is. And you don't have to be there in your bodily self; you can carry it with you in spirit wherever you go. . . . Like love," he added.

I thought about what he had said later that night when we had found a farmhouse and paid a couple of coins for well-water and a share of the undercroft with their other animals—goats and chickens. What did "home" mean to the bird, the tortoise, the horse, the knight? For them it was where they were born, where their own kind lived, simple as that. Growch and I were on the lookout for comfort and security, in my case a husband, and in his case I suspected he would settle wherever I did— and wherever it was, and with whom, there we would call "home."

But what about the Wimperling? He was the philosopher, but he had never indicated where he wanted to go, where his heart lay. Born from an egg (if his memory was to be believed), raised as the runt of a litter of piglets and sold into a life of performing slavery—where did *he* want to go? South, he had said, but I believed he had no clear direction. I must ask him. If he went on growing at his present rate he would have to go and live with the hellephunts, which I understood were as big as houses, or live by himself in a cave, for no sty would hold him.

We traveled south and west for six days and the terrain grew gradually wilder; the roads more tortuous. Now the hills were of limestone, striped by tumbling streams fed by the snow water that still lingered on the high peaks. Pockets of reddish earth were starred with the scalding yellow of gorse and broom, pink-plumed spears of valerian and blossom from wild cherry. The pines and fir were showing a new, tender green at their tips, and the air was full of the scribble-song of siskins; orioles swung above our heads, gold and blue; flycatchers, wagtails and bee-eaters chittered and bobbed ahead of us on the road, and from far away I could hear the strange call of the hoopoe. Bees droned on the bushes, all on the same soporific note, ants marched in lines across our path, wasps were after anything we ate and the dusk was full of the piping of pipistrelles—the airy-mouses of legend.

And above and beyond all this there was a teasing, ephemeral scent that came and went with the southern breeze: a smell that could have been wet rocks, a drying lake, salted fish, dried blood but was none of these.

"It is the ocean," said Traveler, soaring high above us.

"It's the Great Water," said Basher, now stuffing himself from dawn to dusk with heather shoots, clover and young grass till his scales shone and his voice no longer was drawn out, thin and feeble.

"It's the sea," said Mistral, her pink nostrils flaring as she snuffed the wind. "But not my sea. This is a little sea; mine is endless and comes crashing in from the far corners of the world and the foam is like the manes of my people as they outrun the waves. . . ."

"Can you see this Great Water from your home?" I asked Basher curiously.

"It is a glint in the sun, far, far away, but you can taste it in the breeze and the salt sometimes touches the air like seasoning." He scurried away among the undergrowth, his long black claws clicking on the stones. "Thirsty-making . . ."

Southward still we went, leaving the great snow-tipped mountains behind. The land was gentler, there were farms, orchards, tilled fields, small towns. The midday sun burned Gill's and my faces, arms and legs and we shed clothes till he only wore a pair of shortened braies and an open shirt, and I kilted my skirt between my legs, glad that he could not see my bare legs.

One night, when sudden warm rain and a gusting wind that chased up and down like a boisterous child made us seek shelter, we found a ruined chapel on a little hill. Once there had been a settlement of houses nearby, but these were deserted and had fallen into disrepair, like the chapel. There was no clue as to what had happened to the previous inhabitants, but beneath the chapel walls were more than the usual number of untended graves. Perhaps one of the sudden pestilences had decimated the villagers and they had abandoned their homes; perhaps marauders had carried off the women and children: who knows?

It was near dusk when we sought shelter under the crumbling tower of the chapel, and I found enough broken sticks of furniture in the deserted houses to build a good blaze. There were no church vessels to be seen, nor any crosses, and the once-colorful murals had faded to blisters of pale brown and yellow—an arm, a leg, part of a flowing robe   so the place had obviously been de-consecrated, and I had no hesitation in building a fire to cook our strips of dried meat and vegetables.

The smoke rose upwards and then wavered as the gusts of wind from the round-arched windows caught it and blew it like a rag. Soon enough the pot was bubbling and the seductive smell of herby stew set my—and Growch's—stomach rumbling. I pulled the pot to one side and lidded it, to simmer till the ingredients were softer, and set about cutting up the two-day-old bread to warm through.

Suddenly there was a wild flutter and commotion above our heads and debris showered down amongst us. I was glad the lid was on the pot: I didn't fancy stewed pigeon shit.

"What in the world . . . ?"

Traveler took wing and circled our heads "I'll go and see. . . ."

He was gone some time, and there were more flutterings, scrapings and dried excreta, which luckily burned well. The noise subsided, there were a couple of coos and soft hoots and he rejoined us, feathers ruffled and disheveled, but he looked brighter, less despairful, than he had since we left his hometown.

"There are couple of dozen of my kind up there— wild ones, with little civility, but they are thriving. They have been in the tower since any can remember, and manage well enough foraging off the land. I have promised we will douse the fire as soon as possible, for the smoke is choking the young squabs who cannot leave their nests. I shall talk to them again in the morning."

With the morning came the sun again, and I built a fire in the open for oatmeal porridge and cheese and toasted bread. At dawn Traveler had disappeared up into the chapel tower again, and I saw him perched on a ledge with some of the other grey pigeons, or flying around the tower in formation, his pinky-brown color the only dissonance in the otherwise perfect unison of their wheeling and turning.

I scrubbed out the cooking pot with grass and sand from the nearby stream, filled the water bottle, packed everything up, washed my hands, feet and face, and helped Gill to do the same, but Traveler still did not reappear. I went into the chapel again and called him, and eventually he came fluttering down to land on my shoulder, his feathers a little disarranged.

"Time to go," I said, stroking the soft feathers on his neck and scratching him under his chin. He shuffled about on my shoulder.

"Do you mind . . . Do you mind if I stay?"

I looked up at the tower above; little heads peeped down, there was a ruffling of neck feathers, a warning "hoof!", a croon or two, the plead-ing cheep of a squab. "Are you sure? They don't look very friendly to me."

"They know I am different: it will take time. But there are more hens than cocks and rats got at the eggs last year. The ropes the rodents used to climb with have rotted and gone, but the flock needs building up. I think it will be all right. . . ." He sighed. "I hope so."

"But you don't know how to forage the countryside as they do," I objected. "You will go hungry."

He straightened up and preened himself. "Then I shall just have to learn, won't I? I have all the summer to learn, and by winter I will be no different from the others."

"This wasn't what I meant for you. . . ."

"I know that, but you cannot decide my life for me: only I have the right to do that, now that you have freed me. Do not worry, I shall be fine. It is better that I take this chance while I can for I may not find a better. Living is better than not-living, whatever it brings. . . ."

"Good-bye," I said and kissed the top of his head. He sprang away and flew up to the rafters.

We had not gone far down the road, however, when there was a rush of wings and he was circling above us. "May you all find what you seek. Remember me!" And he was gone, leaving me feeling as empty as though I had had no breakfast.

"We have a dovecote at home," said Gill unexpectedly. "Their coo-ing was the first thing I used to hear when . . ." He trailed off. "I don't remember any more."

But at least he was recalling more and more; inconsequential little fragments maybe, but one day they might all fit together like a tapestry. And if I was missing the pigeon so much, what would it be like when my beloved knight finally found his home?

It was about a week later that we came to a place on the road where the land sloped sharply down to the south and there, a glittering shield that stretched away as far as the eye could see, was Basher's Great Water. I sniffed the air and there it was again, that tantalizing salt smell that was like no other, even mixed as it was with pine, heather, wild garlic and gorse. I started to point it out to Gill, before I remembered he couldn't see.

Mistral was also snuffing the air, as was Growch, and Basher stopped chewing the chicory leaves I had put for him in his basket.

"It's here," he said. "Here, or hereabouts. We've found it. . . ."

"You're sure this is the place?"

"Smells right. There should be land sloping to the sea, way off in the distance. Lots of heather, sandy soil for the eggs and hibernation. Pools or a stream, trees for shade. Rocks to keep the claws strong. No people. Lots of lady tortoises."

"From what I can see—"

"Oh, let meee doooown," he said impatiently. "Let meee see . . ."

Holding him to my chest, I scrambled down the steep slope to level ground, Growch beside me. I stood and looked about me for Basher's specifications. The sea was about three miles distant and there was no sign of human habitation. The soil was sandyish, rocky, there was the sound of a stream off to the right and there were both pines and heather in abundance. Gorse, broom, wild garlic, oleander, fan palms, Creeping Jesus, the huge leaves of asphodel, thyme and rosemary—"Looks all right," I said cautiously. "But I can't see any other tortoises."

"I can!" helped Growch, who had christened every bush in sight and was now foraging farther down. "There's more movin' rocks down here: 'ow the 'ell do you tell if'n they're male or female? Looks all the effin' same to me. . . ."

"Females larger, flat shells underneath," said Basher succinctly. "Males undershells curved concave. Makes sense. Think about it . . ."

But I was about to get a demonstration. Growch came panting back.

"Two females down there. Tell you what, don't like bein' up-ended! Cursin' like 'Ell, they is!"

By the time we got there they had righted themselves again, their pale brown patched shells disappearing into the undergrowth at speed.

I put Basher down and immediately he was off, pausing only to eye the disappearing females with an experienced eye and turn in scurrying pursuit of the larger. A moment later there was a resonant tap-tapping noise, a pause, then a sort of triumphant mewing. Cats? No, just a tortoise enjoying himself; as I came nearer I could see him reared up at the back of the female, his mouth open on pointed pink tongue. "M-e-e-w!" Oh, what bliss! How I've missed thiiiis! Hey—"

With several violent jerks from side to side, the female disengaged herself and charged off once again, Basher in pursuit. Then once again the tap-tapping, pause, and "M-e-w! Bliss . . ."

"Basher! Are you all right?"

"Couldn't be better! Thanks for eeeeverything . . ."

"Basher, wait . . ." There was something wrong, something about him, about the female . . . Oh, God! They were a different species! He was black and gold with a shell that frilled out at the back, they were pale brown shaped in a perfect hump. . . . I ran after him. "Wait! They're a different species! Come back, and we'll go on further. . . ."

"No fear!" His voice was rapidly diminishing. "This'll do me. Color isn't everything. . . . Their parts are in the right place!" Tap-tap. "This is far better than freezing to death! May you all find what you seeeeek. . . ."

When I rejoined the others, my heart heavy, Gill was listening, his ears cocked. "That tapping noise: reminds me of the cobbler mending my boots. . . . Is he all right?"

"Yes," I said. "He has—what he wants." What he thinks he wants, I added to myself. But there would be no eggs to hatch into little black and gold tortoises: his would be sterile couplings. Why couldn't he have waited till we found the right place? And yet, like Traveler, he seemed to be content with a substitute, and they had both said it was better than being dead. . . .

Were none of us to find what we really sought, I wondered?

"Half a loaf is better than none," said the Wimperling unexpectedly. "Especially when you're hungry."

"Talkin' of bein' hungry," said Growch: "Ain't we stoppin' for lunch today?"

22

We had come as far south as we could, without crossing into another country. As one accommodating monk explained when next we sought food and lodging (overnight stay in the guesthouse, sleeping on straw; stew and ale for supper, bread and ale for breakfast and please leave a donation, however small), our country was a rough square, bounded to the northeast by one kingdom, the southeast by another and the south by a third. The other boundaries were sea, but there was still a lot of the square to explore. He drew everything in the dirt with a stick so I could understand.

Because he was a monk I told him a bit more of the truth than I had anyone else, and once he understood I was looking for Gill's home he worked out roughly for me the way we had come, like the right-hand side of a tall triangle. He suggested that I travel along the ways that led from east to west till I came to the sea, then either completed the triangle by going northeast, or bisected it by going straight up the middle.

That seemed good advice, but there was not only Gill to consider. The Wimperling contemplated for a moment, then said he had felt no tuggings of place so far, and was content to continue as I suggested. Growch scratched a lot—warmer weather—and said that as long as there was food and company he wasn't bothered. But it was Mistral who was keenest on the idea. She said that the distance south seemed about right, and if there was a real sea to the west of us, that would be right too.

Not having told Gill about consulting the others, of course, he was happy enough to fall in with the idea, so we walked the many miles west during those spring days in a sort of dreamy vacuum. Mistral became more and more convinced we were heading in the right direction and I knew I wasn't about to lose Gill, for he had suddenly recalled that he couldn't see any mountains from his home—which was comforting to me, as we were leaving the highest ones I had ever seen to our left as we traveled. The range seemed endless, rearing purple, snow-fanged tips so high that the sun hid his face early behind them, the shadows stretching cold in our path.

But even the biggest mountains come to an end, and gradually they sank away the farther west we traveled. By now we looked like a band of gypsies, brown and weatherbeaten, our clothes comfortably ragged, although I tried to keep Gill as smart as possible by trimming his hair and beard regularly, and I kept my hair in its plaits. Mistral was shedding her winter coat, and I could have stuffed a mattress with the brown hair that came out in handfuls when I tried to brush her. Growch evaded all attempts to wash, brush or trim anything.

But it was the Wimperling that was changing faster than anyone else—so much so that his name seemed too childish to fit the long-as-me-and-growing-longer animal that trotted away the miles beside us. He was taller, too, near up to my waist, and his knobs and protuberances were growing more pronounced as well. The claws on his hooves were real claws, the tip of his tail more like a spade than ever and his wings were bigger as well.

He was shy of showing them off, preferring to flex them behind a tree or large rock or in a dell, but I saw them once or twice. They resembled bat's wings more than anything else, but they were proper wings, not extended hands and fingers like the night-flyers. I began to feel embarrassed in villages or with our fellow travelers, for fear they would think him some sort of monster and stone him to death, but for some peculiar reason they seemed to see him as just another rather largish pig: they even looked at him as if he were much smaller, their eyes seeming to span him from halfway down and halfway across. It was most peculiar, but the Wimperling merely said: "They see what they expect to see. . . ."

"But why don't I see you like that?"

"You wear the Ring." And quiet it was now, almost transparent, with tiny flecks of gold in its depths.

As he had no objection, every now and again the pig gave a simple performance in a village square, to augment our dwindling moneys— nothing fancy, just a bit of tapping out numbers, no flying, and Gill and I would sometimes literally sing for our suppers.

Growch disappeared a couple of times—I caught a glimpse of him once on the skyline at the very tail end of a procession of dogs (five hounds, two terriers, three other mongrels), following some bitch in season, but he had little success, I gathered, spending more time fighting for a place in the queue than actually performing. Being so small, he was a master of infighting, but he would have needed a pair of steps to most of the females he coveted. He remembered with nostalgia the two little bitches with plumed tails he had successfully seduced way back.

"Don't make them like that round here. Some day, p'raps . . ."

I hoped so. Fervently. Then perhaps we would all get some peace.

The terrain became flatter, more wooded, and every day I peered ahead to try for my first glimpse of the sea. Now and again I thought I caught a teasing reminder of that evocative sea smell, and Mistral was forever throwing up her head and snuffing the breeze. Now she had shed her winter coat she was a different creature. Her coat was creamy white, her mane and tail long and flowing, and the sharp bones of haunch and rib were now covered with flesh. Her step was jauntier, her chest deeper, her head held high and proud; she was no longer just a beast of burden, and sometimes in the mornings when I loaded her up I felt a little guilty, as though I were asking a lady to do the tasks of a servant.

At last one morning she sniffed the air for a full five minutes, and she was trembling. "It is here," she said. "Over the next ridge, you will see . . ."

And there, glittering in the morning light, some five miles or so distant across flat, marshy land, was her ocean.

"You are sure?"

"I am certain. This is the place. This is where I came from."

I looked more carefully and there, sure enough, some two miles away, were other horses, mostly white, some with half-grown brown colts, grazing almost belly-deep in grass. Perhaps because we were not as high as when we had seen Basher's Great Water, this sea seemed different: steely, clear, sharp against the horizon. And the smell was subtly different, too; colder and saltier.

"Right," I said, my heart strangely heavy. "Let's go and find your people, Princess." And taking Gill's hand I followed the sure-footed Mistral towards the shore. As we drew nearer the sands, I could see that the grassy stretches I had taken for meadows were in fact only wide strips of green, full also of daisies, dent-de-lions, buttercups and sedge, bisected by narrow channels of water, so that the ground was sometimes treacherous underfoot and we had to take a circuitous path.

Growch took a flying leap into the first channel we came to, after what looked like a bank vole, which disappeared long before we hit the water, and we had to spend the next five minutes or so fishing him out, as the banks were too high for a scramble. When we finally landed he was soaking wet and, choking and hawking and spitting, he managed to let us know that the water was: "salty as dried 'erring, and twice as nasty!"

Now we were in a marshy bit—it didn't seem to bother Mistral, and for the first time I noted that her hooves were wider than usual in a horse—and Gill and I took off our shoes and boots, squelching with every step. The Wimperling and Growch were even worse off, and when the horse noticed our difficulty she led us off to the right and firmer ground, through a thicket of bamboo twice as tall as Gill.

At last we emerged on a firm stretch of sand and there in front of us was the sea, stretching on right and left as far as the eye could see. From here I could see white-capped waves that looked like the fancy smocking on a shirt, but moving towards us all the time, like never-ending sewing. A cool breeze lifted the hair from my hot forehead and flared Mistral's tail and mane.

I lifted the packs from her back, undid the straps and took off the bridle, laying them down on the sand. Strange: I had never thought how we were to manage our burdens when she was gone; share them out, I supposed now. I looked at the pile with growing dismay—we had taken her bearing of our goods so much for granted.

"There you are," I said. "You're free now. . . ."

In a moment she was flying across the ribbed sand away from us and towards the foam-fringed edges of the sea, then turning and galloping along the shoreline, her hooves sending up great gouts of water until she was soaked and streaming. Then she came thundering back and wheeled round us, her hooves whitening the sand as they drove out the water, the prints hesitating before they darkened again into hoof-shaped pools.

"This is wonderful," she neighed. "It's been so long, so long. . . . And now I'm free, free, free!" and away she galloped again, until she was only a speck on the horizon.

I sighed. Was that the last we would see of her?

"Let's walk down to the sea," I said to the others. "I have a fancy to paddle. And I want to taste it, too. I've never done either."

It was farther than I thought, nearer a mile than a half, but the long walk was worth it once I got there, for it entranced all my senses. The regular shush, shush, shush as the waves broke on the shore like a slow-beating heart, the faraway scream of a sea bird; the limitless horizon seeming to curve down at either side as if the world were round; the unutterably strange and pleasurable feeling of walking along the water's edge, the yielding sand spurting up between my toes, the sharp taste of salt on my tongue, the smell of water and mud and weed . . .

I stepped into the water and it lapped around my ankles like the warm tongue of a calf or pup. I had been so certain it would be cold that I threw away all caution and kilted up my skirt till my behind was bare and waded further in, until the water was round my knees, up to my thighs. I lifted my skirts higher, and now it was round my waist, but also noticeably colder, too.

Suddenly I began to feel the power of the sea. What at first had been a gentle push against my knees, my thighs, now became a more insistent thrust against the whole of my body. At first the sensation was pleasurable, then a stronger wave actually lifted me from my feet, knocked me off balance, and I tipped back into the water.

Help! I was drowning! There was a roaring in my ears, my hair was floating round my face, I swallowed a mouthful of water, I couldn't breathe, I didn't know which way was up. Desperately I flailed with my arms, paddled with my legs and, perhaps five seconds later, though it felt like forever, I was once more standing upright. I coughed and choked, dribble running from my mouth and nose, my eyes stinging, my ears still bubbling and popping.

As soon as I had pulled myself together I turned to wade back to the others—but they were miles away! Surely they had been nearer than that? Now I could see Gill waving, apparently calling my name, saw Growch shaking with barks, the Wimperling running up and down the shoreline anxiously, but I could hear nothing for the freshening breeze, which was whistling in my ears and making the waves angry, so that they swished past me with foam on their lips.

I set off towards the others as fast as I could, but I was now hampered with the drag of wet clothes, and fast as I tried to go the sea seemed to beat me, and I could see the others retreating even as I watched. The water was definitely pushing hard at me now, even when I was only thigh and knee deep, and twice I nearly stumbled and fell, but at last it was only round my calves, and I thought I was safe. But then came another hazard; as I reached the shoreline the waves no longer pushed, they pulled, scooping back from where they broke and drawing the sand with them so that I almost lost my feet again.

At last I stood on firm sand, chilled to the bone and shivering violently.

Gill groped towards the sound of my heavy breathing. "Are you all right? You were gone such a long time. . . ."

"Look just like a drowned rat," said Growch, with relish.

"I can't swim," said the Wimperling, "else I would have come in after you. Come on, we'd better get going; the tide's coming in fast."

"What's that?" I asked, wringing the water from my hair and skirt as best I could.

"The very thing that means you were on dry sand a moment ago and now are standing in water again," he said, retreating as the water washed over his hooves. "Twice a day the sea comes in, twice a day it goes out. That is a tide. Hurry, there's a way to go till we're safe."

We set off at a brisk walk, the sun and breeze soon drying my exposed skin, though my bodice was damp and my skirt flapped in dismal, wet folds, irritating skin already chapped by salt and sand. The latter had even got between my teeth, making them grind unpleasantly together.

The Wimperling was right: the tide was coming in very fast, and the haven of the fields ahead was still a long way away. We trudged on through sand that seemed to drag at our feet like mud, till my legs were aching and Growch was whimpering away to himself, lifting his feet more and more reluctantly. At last I picked him up and tucked him under my arm, only to have him grumble about my wet clothes.

"Shut up, or I'll put you down!" I threatened. Turning round I glanced back at the sea, to comfort myself that it was at least as far behind us as the fields were ahead, meaning we had come at least half way. To my horror the creeping water was only some twenty yards behind us, creaming forward inexorably like a brown flood. Surely we had not stood still? Even as I watched the next wave spread within a few yards of us. The tide . . .

"Run!" I yelled. "Run!" and I grabbed Gill with my free hand. As we stumbled along I saw we were at last keeping pace with the sea, it was no longer gaining on us, thank God! But now, on either side of us I could see arms of water creeping to surround us; with relief I realized the fields were much nearer, I could see the shrubs tossing in the wind, the heap of our belongings. . . . I slackened speed nearly there.

The Wimperling and Growch had galloped ahead as Gill and I caught our breath, but now I saw them come to a sudden stop, Growch running from side to side and barking hysterically. I pulled Gill forward again and my heart gave a sudden lurch of fear: ahead of us, cutting us off from safety, a swirling mass of water frothed and bubbled and roiled, growing wider and deeper by the second. To either side the arms of water encircled us and behind the tide raced to catch us up.

We were trapped!

23

I was riveted with fear and panic, terrified of coming into contact with that suffocating water again.

"Gill, we're cut off by the tide: can you swim?" I was unable to keep the panic from my voice.

He shook his head. "I don't think so. . . . Is it that bad?"

"Yes, and getting worse every minute!" I glanced back: the water was flooding towards us, and now we had to retreat a step or two from the flood in front as it bubbled and frothed. Without being asked Growch and the Wimperling dashed off in different directions to see if there was any escape to left or right, but returned within a few moments to report we were entirely cut off.

Now we were marooned on a strip of sand some hundred yards long and twenty wide, and it was getting smaller by the second.

"We shall have to try and wade across," I said firmly, twisting the ring on my finger to give me courage: strangely enough it was not emitting any warning signals; a little bit warmer than usual, with a light throbbing, that was all. We must be all right: we *would* be all right, please God! "The water can't be all that deep. Dogs can swim, Growch, so you'll be all right. Now's the time to find if you can paddle as well as you can fly, pig dear." I tried to smile, but it was difficult. "Right, Gill: keep tight hold. Off we go!"

The animals plunged in ahead of us gamely enough, Growch's legs going like a centipede, but the swirling currents were making a nonsense of him swimming in anything but circles, until I saw the Wimperling, who had floundered a couple of times, suddenly spread his wings and float like a raft. He came up alongside the dog, who grabbed his tail in its teeth and they headed in the right direction.

I pulled Gill into the water, but as soon I did so I knew we had no chance. The water deepened after less than a couple of steps and the swirling water clutched at our legs, so that we had to lean sideways as if in a great subterranean wind. We couldn't swim and we couldn't float, and as soon as we took another step we immersed up to our shoulders, our legs flailing helplessly in the water. I lost hold of Gill and we were swept apart, choking and gasping, I grasped his tunic and we were swept together again and somehow we managed to scramble back to our "island" again, now half its size.

I clutched the ring on my finger, shaking so hard it nearly slipped from my fingers. "Help us, please help us. . . ."

Across the widening stretch of water I saw the dog and the pig struggle out of the water and flop down on the sand, completely exhausted. Thank God, they at least were safe. Gill was muttering a prayer, but prayers were a last resort: surely there must be something we could *do*? If only there was something we could cling to and paddle across, if only the tide would suddenly turn—

I gazed around wildly, and suddenly saw what seemed like an apparition racing through the water towards us from our left, throwing up great clouds of spray as it came.

"Mistral! Gill, it's all right, it's all right! Mistral's coming!"

She arrived with a snort and a skid of hooves, her body flowing with water.

"I heard your call. . . ." The ring on my finger gave a sudden throb. "I should have warned you about the tides. Quick, follow me: it's shallower this way." She led us at a trot to a place where the water was wider, but I could see none of the eddies and swirls of deep currents. "It will only be a short swim this way; wade out as far as you can, one on either side of me, and then hold fast to my mane when I tell you." I told Gill what we were going to do, guided his hand to her neck, and after that it was easy, taking only a few minutes to cross what had once seemed impossible, her warmth and steadiness against me giving me back all my confidence, so that once we were safe I flung my arms about her neck and gave her a big hug.

"Thanks, Princess Mistral, thanks a million times!" Once the word "princess" applied to the tatty, broken-down horse I had first known was nothing more than a joke, but now it was nothing more or less than the truth. She was utterly changed from the swaybacked skinny creature who had trudged the roads with us, head down: now she was white as the foam of the sea, sleek as the waves; her eyes were bright, her neck arched, her long mane and tail like curtains of mist. "You are so beautiful now. . . ."

"Thanks to you."

"I did nothing. . . ."

"You rescued me, healed my hurts, fed me, talked to me and burdened me but lightly. I am grateful to you. And now . . ."

"And now you must go and join your kin. We shall miss you." I had seen out of the corner of my eye a mixed herd of horses, colts and foals, led by a great white stallion, moving across the fields to the reeds and shallows. She neighed once and the stallion flung up his head. She turned to me. "Make for that clump of trees; keep to the higher ground. You will be safe now. Remember me: and may you all find what you seek!" And she was gone, cantering up to the other horses and wheeling into the middle of the herd.

She was full-grown now, but I saw with a stab of pity how much smaller she was than the other mares. Her hard life had stunted her growth. Would the great stallion consider mating with one so undersized? Could she carry a foal to full term and deliver it successfully? To me she was the most beautiful of all those beautiful horses, but would they see it that way?

My eyes filled with tears. It was the tortoise and the pigeon repeated again. Why could not their lives be as perfect as they deserved? One robbed of his home and forced to fight a wilder existence, another living in the wrong place, and now one handicapped among her peers by the life she had been forced to lead. If these were to be the precedents, then what in the world would happen to Growch, the Wimperling, Gill and me?

"We keep thirty horses in the stables," said Gill suddenly. "My stallion is called Fleetfoot, but I take Dainty when I go falconing. My tiercel kills rooks and we . . ." He trailed off. "I forget. . . ."

I opened my mouth but was interrupted by Growch's salt-roughened bark. "Better get 'ere quick! The blankets is soaked and yer pots and pans is floating out to sea. . . ."

Midsummer's Day, and we were no nearer finding Gill's home. Yet there seemed no hurry. Deceived by a summer dreaminess we drifted down tiny lanes and dusty highways, the former further drowsing us with the honey-sweet scent of hawthorn and showering us in the pale petals of the hedge rose, the latter a patchwork of blinding white road and the black shadow of forest.

Everywhere color brightened the eye; scarlet poppies shaking out their crumpled petals, gold-hearted daisy and camomile, creamy elder and sweet cecily, sky-blue lungwort, vinca and chicory, pink mallow and bindweed, white asphodel, purple vetches. And all the greens in the world: willow, beech, oak, ash, pine, fir, reed, duckweed, grass, ground elder, horsetail, clover, moss, nettle, sorrel, ivy, bracken—grey-green, red-green, blue-green, yellow-green, shock-green and baby green: both a stimulus and a soothing to the eyes. There was color, too, in the myriads of butterflies, in the dragon- and damsel-flies and even in the barbaric stripes of wasp and hornet.

The spring shrillness of the birds had abated somewhat; at one end of their scales was the brisk morning chirping of sparrows scavenging hay and straw for seeds and the faraway bubble of ascending larks; in the middle, hot afternoons held the sleepy croon of wood pigeons and the evening sky rang with the high scream of swifts scything the sky. We passed lakes and ponds where frogs barked like terriers and sudden splashes marked the recklessness of mating fish; whirring grasshoppers sprang from beneath our feet, bees and hummingbird hawk moths droned like bagpipes, cicadas sawed away incessantly and great June bugs racketed clumsily by.

We were surrounded, too, by the particular scents of summer; not just the dried dung and dust of the highways, the pungent smells of grass and leaves after rain, the thin, evocative perfume of wildflowers, but sudden surprises: pinch of fresh mint, crush of thyme and rosemary underfoot, warm river water, salty smells of fresh sweat, the clean smell of drying linen, the oily smell of resin from fresh-cut logs stacked to dry for winter and the gentle, fading scent of drying hay.

Different tastes, too. Salads instead of stew, fresh meat instead of salted, plenty of eggs and milk, newly brewed ale. Fish and eel and shellfish from the rivers, butter and cheese so light they had practically no taste at all. A deal of vegetables I could collect myself from the fields and woods; hop tips, ground elder, chickweed, dent-de-lion, nettle, wood sorrel, broom buds, ash keys, young bracken fronds and the leaves of wild strawberry and violet. Chopped up with a little oil and salt and eaten with a hunk of cheese and fresh rye bread it made a feast.

Not that we were short of food. If there was a fair, a saint's day or a local fiesta, out would come my pipe and tabor and Gill would sing, Growch would "dance for the lady," answer yes or no and "die for his country." My instructions to him were simple enough; the "dance" consisted of him chasing his tail, yes and no barking once or twice, nodding or shaking his head—"bend your head down as if you had fleas under your chin, shake your head as if you had mites in your ears—you haven't, have you?"—and dying was merely lying down and pretending to go to sleep. But he had a short attention span, and if we really wanted to bring in more than a few coppers then the Wimperling would do some of his tricks.

He was still growing—which was just as well, for he was needed to share with Gill and me the carrying of our bundles—but still people saw him as smaller than he was: in fact one traveler accused us of over-loading him! But he was looking at a pig he expected to see, as the Wimperling reminded me, not the giant he had become.

June became a warm, thundery July. Once I had decided that Gill's home must lie farther north—for he had not recognized many of the plants I had described to him, nor the terrain this far south—I led them first east northeast then west northwest as best my judgment and the countryside would allow, trying to cover both the left-hand side of the triangle the monk had described and the bisection of the whole at one and the same time.

Gill was recalling more and more as the days went by; little incon-sequential things for the most part, like a favorite tapestry; the pool where they bred carp for the table, the time he was scraped by a boar's tusk—sure enough, there was a crescent scar on his thigh. Once or twice he did remember facts relevant to our search. I already knew there were no moun-tains, I realized that if he went falconing for rooks his home was probably surrounded by fields of grain crops and there must be woodland or forest for both the birds and wild boar; now he talked of the Great Forest half a day's ride across the plain where once the king had hunted. Which king? He shook his head. He also spoke of the wide and lazy river that curved round the estate, but again a name meant nothing.

So we were looking for a province of plains, rivers, and forests, and as he never spoke of the sea we didn't travel too far west and kept the mountains to a distance. I continued to question people we met and showed them the sketch I had made of Gill's escutcheon, also the scrap of silk I had kept, but they all shrugged their shoulders and shook their heads.

The breakthrough, when it came, was entirely unexpected.

We had lodged on the outskirts of a largish town overnight, on the promise of celebrations for St. Swithin on the following day. There was to be a fair in the marketplace and dancing in the church yard, plus the usual roasts. I groomed both Growch and the Wimperling thoroughly, a ribbon round the neck of one, the tail of the other. The skies remained clear and as long as the prayers at Mass that morning were efficacious, it would remain that way until harvest, so the superstition went.

We did well in the marketplace, for folk were happy at the prospect of a good harvest, and wished to relax and enjoy themselves. There were other attractions of course, but a counting pig was still a novelty, and I collected enough coins that afternoon and early evening to keep us going for a week or two.

As it grew dusk, great torches were stuck in the ground and lanterns hung from the branches of the trees, and the people gathered to dance away an hour or so as the lamb carcasses turned slowly on the spits set in a corner of the square. A traveling band—bagpipes, two shawm, a fiddle, trumpet, pipe and tabor and a girl singer with a tambourine—performed for the dancers. Round followed reel and back again, until the dust was soon rising from the ground with the pounding and stamping of feet, jumps and twirls. When they paused for breath jugs of ale were brought out from the nearest tavern, and enterprising bakers sent their assistants round with trays of pies and sweetmeats.

As Gill couldn't see to dance I had not joined in, though my feet were tapping impatiently to the music. During one of the intervals I brought out the Wimperling again for a few more coins, then went and joined the line for slices of roast lamb and bread. Afterwards we sat for a while longer, watching and listening. As the evening wore on and it became quite dark, one by one the dancers dropped out, exhausted; couples snuggled up to one another in the shadows, children fell asleep in their parents' laps, babies were suckled, dogs snapped and snarled over the scraps, the church bells sounded for nine o'clock and some went in to pray. Somewhere a nightingale provided a soft background for the girl with the tambourine to sing simple, sad songs of love, of longing, of childhood.

She sang without other accompaniment than her tambourine, just an occasional tap or shake to emphasize a word, a phrase. She sang as if to herself and to listen seemed almost like eavesdropping. It was so soothing that I found myself nodding off, and was just about to gather us all together and find our lodgings, when Gill suddenly gave a great start as though he had been bitten.

"That song . . . !"

Song? A sentimental song of swallows, eternal summer, of home. One I had never heard before, with a plaintive descending refrain.

"What about it?"

But he wasn't listening to me, and when she started on the second verse, to my amazement he joined in, at first hesitantly, as though he had difficulty remembering the words, then more confidently. At first they sand in unison, then he took the harmony in the last verse.

"The sun is warm, the wind is soft,
O'er wood and plain, house and croft;
I long to wake again at dawn,
In the land where I was born. . . ."

Gill looked as though he had awakened from a dream and to my embarrassment I saw that tears were pouring down his cheeks. He rose to his feet.

"The singer . . . Take me to her!"

But she had come over to us. "Congratulations, stranger: you sing well. But where did you learn that song?" Close to she was no girl. The paint on her cheeks, eyes and mouth had disguised at a flattering torchlit distance that she must be at least thirty. "I had thought no one outside my own province knew it. Do you come from there?"

Gill stretched out his hand to her, and it was shaking. Quickly I explained his condition and that we sought his home, and this was the first real clue we had had.

"Tell me, are there great plains, a big river, forests, much grain growing?" I was trying to remember all Gill had recalled.

"Assuredly the land is flat. There are cattle, many fields of grain, great orchards—"

"Apples," said Gill. "And plum and cherry."

She glanced at him. "You are right. And there are wide rivers, and forests stretching as far as the eye can see. Can you not remember your name, now?"

He shook his head. "But I know that is where I come from," and his voice was strong with a confidence I had never head in him before. "My nurse taught me that song when I scarce out of the cradle." He turned to me. "That is the way we must go, don't you see? Oh, Summer, take me there, take me there!" And now his tears were spilling down onto the skin of my arm, warm as summer rain.

"Of course we will!" I turned to the singer. "Thank you so much, you don't know how much this means! We have been searching for nine months, so far. . . . Here, do you recognize this emblem?" and I pulled the scrap of silk from my purse.

She peered at it, listened to what else I could recall of it, but shook her head regretfully. "No, but it is a large country. I come from the southeast, but your—your friend may well live to the north and west. But you can ask again when you get there."

"How far away is it?" asked Gill eagerly. "How long will it take us?"

She shook her head again. "Straight, I do not know. Many days. You will have to ask my husband. We travel as the will and the weather take us, following as best we can fairs and feast days, the larger towns." She turned and beckoned, and the short, dark man who had been playing the fiddle joined us.

Once she had explained, he, too, shook his head. "It lies to the northwest of here, but I can give you no direct route. If you head that way, and take the better roads, it might take a month, perhaps two. It depends on the roads, the weather, your pace, as you must know. If you are lucky, you will reach there in time for harvest—"

"The best time of the year," murmured Gill. "Great feasts, hunting songs, dancing . . . We must start at dawn."

"Yes, yes, of course," I said. "But now we must sleep. In this weather it's better to travel early and late and rest at midday—"

"But not for long! I could walk a hundred miles without rest if I knew home was at the end of it!" Gone was the often sad, sometimes complaining man I had known: here was an impatient young man with hope in his face, as eager for tomorrow as any eighteen-year-old.

The singer and her husband wished us luck, and I emptied the day's takings into her hand. "Pray that this time we were heading in the right direction. . . ."

Gill fell asleep as soon as he lay down in the straw of the stable we occupied that night; all the way back he had been humming the song that had awakened his memory, but I could not sleep. I tossed and turned restlessly. Outside a full moon shone through the gaps in the planking of the walls, its pale light seeming to touch my closed lids whichever way I turned on the rustling straw. I told myself I was relieved we knew the way at last, how happy I was for Gill; in a month, two at most, he would be restored to his family, and my responsibility towards him would end. Then I would be free to pursue my original objective and find a safe, respectable husband and a comfortable home.

And at that happy prospect, I cried myself to sleep.

24

It took us exactly six weeks.

We departed at dawn on the day after St. Swithin's and arrived on the feast day of Saints Cosmos and Damien. It was a long, hard trek, with a hotter August and early September than I could remember. At home with Mama, of course, I was not exposed to the merciless heat of an open road; I had been able to take my ease under the trees in the forest, once my chores were done, and perhaps cool my feet in the river. Even at night we sometimes slept with the door open, the goat tethered nearby to challenge any intruder and give us time to bolt the door.

But now I was walking all day—at least the hours between dawn and two in the afternoon, and then again for a couple of hours in the evenings. Often there were no trees to shade our path, no streams or rivers to cool our feet or to bathe in. In fact water became scarcer the farther we traveled, and often they had none to spare in the villages we passed through. I bought another flask and filled it when I could, sometimes walking a good way cross-country to find a river, after spying out the land to find the telltale signs of willow, shrub and reed which marked its course.

I think the flies were the biggest nuisance. Somehow they always managed to find us, great tickling, annoying things, alighting on any part of our exposed bodies to suck the salty moisture from our skins. They buzzed, they clustered, they crawled; other insects, midges, mosquitos, horseflies and wasps stung also, and unless one flailed one's arms like a windmill all day long, or waved a switch cut from the hedgerows, one was irritated to say the least and, more usually, infuriated and exhausted by nightfall, for they wouldn't even let us alone during the afternoon rest.

No food could be left uncovered for more than a moment because it was immediately attacked. I had never particularly disliked any insect before, except perhaps for the ugly black cockroaches that scuttled and tapped around fireplaces at night, but now I had a personal vendetta against any fly, wasp, hornet, midge, mosquito, horsefly or ant in the country. Gill was not as badly affected as I was—perhaps he didn't taste as good—and Growch's thick coat protected most of him, although he was regularly infested with sheep ticks, which were as difficult to dislodge as body lice.

Strangely enough, they all left the Wimperling well alone.

All around us the country was getting ready for harvest. In the south the grapes were swelling and coloring, often on land that looked too arid to support anything, and we passed olive and orange trees that looked ready for picking, but as we headed north it was the grain that caught the eye and the orchards of apple and espaliered pears that promised delights to come. It was a bounteous time in the woods and wayside, too, and many a skirt of raspberries and blackberries I gathered. Hips, haws and hazelnuts had a month or so to go, but the autumn mushrooms and fungi were coming to their best.

The drought dried many of the ponds and streams that would have provided fish, and sheep and cattle were being fattened for the winter salting, poultry were wilting in the heat and there was little milk, but we managed, though I could feel the lighter clothes I wore were hanging looser by the day, and Gill and Growch looked leaner and fitter. Not so the Wimperling.

He still appeared to eat anything and everything with gusto and to my eyes was bigger than a small pony and no longer as pig-like as before, though it was difficult say exactly what he did resemble. One day I took a piece of the rope we used for tying our bundles and surreptitiously measured him as he lay snoozing. From stem to stern he was as long as Gill was tall, and, if my calculations were right, near as much around the middle.

"No, you're not imagining things," he said, opening one eye. "I'm growing. A lot of it is the wings, though."

I was so startled I dropped the piece of rope. "Wings?"

"Round the middle. Look." And he rose to his hooves and slowly, lazily, extended his left wing. What I had taken for fat was in fact a combination of the wing itself and the disguising pouch he hid it under, grown larger with its contents. The wing itself now extended some five feet away from his body, a warm, living extension of himself, lifting in the slight breeze of evening. "See?"

"I still don't understand how everyone else sees you as small," I said helplessly, more shocked by the revelation than I cared to say. "When—when will you stop growing?"

"I told you: people see what they expect, and to help that I think pig." He didn't answer the second question, I noticed. Perhaps he didn't know.

This was a silly conversation, and I decided to be silly, too. "So if I wanted people to believe me beautiful, all I would have to do was think it?"

"Matthew the merchant thought you were beautiful. . . ."

"But I didn't try and make him think so!"

"So perhaps you are anyway."

"Rubbish! My mother always said—"

"You shouldn't believe all she said. Many mothers tell their daughters they are plain in order to steal their beauty for themselves. Think yourself ugly and unattractive and you will be."

"My mother wouldn't have done a thing like that!" Would she? No, of course she wouldn't. That would have been cruel. Besides I must have been ugly: I was never considered as her replacement when she died. Then had I thought myself ugly, as he was suggesting? No, I remembered my reflection in the river: fat, double-treble-chinned, mouthless, eye-less, disgusting. "Anyway, I'm fat, gross, obese." These at least were true.

"Was."

"Was what?"

"Fat. Didn't you boast once to your knight about how well you were fed by your imaginary family?" How did he know I hadn't been telling the truth? "You said your mother fed you with all the greatest delicacies; it sounded more like force-feeding, and you were the Michaelmas goose. That was another way to make you less attractive than she was. No competition."

"Nonsense! She wouldn't have done a thing like that! It would be wicked!" Why, she had loved me so much she had had me educated for the best in the land, and could not then bear for me to leave her to seek a husband!

Apparently the Wimperling could read my mind. "Most men don't choose their spouses for their education. A pretty face goes further than being able to construe Latin. Child-bearing hips and a still tongue go even farther. And a dowry, of course . . ."

"I have that!" I said, stung with anger. "My father left it for me."

"All of it? Or was some of it gone? And did your mother show you it?"

"No, but—"

"Exactly. Another five years as her slave and there would have been no dowry left, only a grossly fat woman tied irrevocably to her mother's side, a useless human being who could hold a pen, add two and two, sew a seam, cook a meal—and eat most of it—and who would have had ideas far above her station. When your mother died you would have been released from your bondage only to starve, or become a kitchen slut. You would have been the pig, not I!"

"But she didn't know she was going to die!" I flung back at him. "She—she thought she would live a long, long time, and . . . and . . ."

"I know that, don't get angry. I don't suppose for a moment she realized how selfish she was: she just didn't want to lose you. But she went about it all the wrong way. There are people like that, so scared of losing the ones they love that they cling to them like ivy on a wall, not realizing that you have to let go to retain."

I thought about it: poor Mama, she should have realized I would never leave her. If she had found me a husband I would have been happy for her to live with us, or at least have a house nearby.

"But I'm not like that now," I said, subdued. "Life is very different on the road. . . ."

"Yes, and thank the gods for that! But mostly you have your father and the ring he left you to be grateful for."

"My father? The ring?"

"He bequeathed a ring to the child he would never see, a ring he knew he could no longer wear because he did not deserve it. It probably served him well in earlier years, but his life must have been such that the ring shed itself from his finger. The ring on your finger—diluted by age and wearing—is part of a Unicorn, and as such cannot be worn by anyone undeserving of its protection."

How did he know all this?

Again he seemed to read my mind. "Because your tumbled thoughts spill out into the wind sometimes, and before you have a chance to catch them back I can pattern them in my mind. Better than you, sometimes. Besides, I can sense the power. Unicorns—and witches and warlocks, wizards and dragons, fairies and elves, trolls and ogres—are become unfashionable in this modern world of ours. Yet all are still there, if you look for them or need them, although their power is greatly diminished by man's indifference and disbelief. One day they will disappear altogether, and the world will be a sadder place."

I looked down at the ring on the middle finger of my right hand. A sliver of horn, almost transparent, nearly indistinguishable from the flesh it clung to. And yet it had served me well. How else would I have been able to communicate with the others, the animals? I should have rejected Growch, probably misused Mistral, would not have been able to mend Traveler, never heard Basher in his cold misery. And what of the Wimperling himself? Would he not still be a showman's toy if the ring had not sharpened my pity when I heard his cry for help? Or dead?

One way or another, the ring had given them all another chance: me too.

The farther north we traveled, the more soldiery we came across. Not fighting, just minding their own business: wars were things that happened all the time. Some soldiers were quartered in the villages we went through, and there food was scarce: for whatever king, lord or seigneur they served made it a practice to utilize their subjects to supply their troops. Cheaper than having them loll around the castles idle, and out on the borders they were nearer the action, if and when it came.

Apparently no one had fought any battles for at least three years but rumors were rife of imminent attacks here, there and everywhere and hostilities were expected any time. I began to wonder if we should find Gill's home under siege or razed to the ground, but said nothing of my fears, for each day he grew more and more tense, fuller of longing to see his home again—for he was sure, too, that once back his sight would return also.

"It is a fine place, Summer: not a fortress, more a fortified manor house, as I recall. . . . I seem to remember my nurse's name was Brigitte. I think my mother was as tall as my father, but very thin. . . . We have lots of hounds. I seem to remember a friend called Pierre. I don't think I enjoyed my lessons. . . ." And so on.

I tried to keep him as clean, shaved and smart as I could, just in case we suddenly came across someone who recognized him, for I remembered only too well how magnificently he was dressed and accoutered that never-to-be-forgotten day when he had asked me the way to the High Road. Now I doubted even his mother would recognize him, in spite of my care. I bought a length of linen and made him a tunic that reached mid-calf, as befitted his station, but kept it hidden till the time was right. When the light lingered in the evenings I would take it out, to complete the key pattern I was edging the hem and side slits with, in a blue to match his beautiful, blind eyes. . . .

One August morning, around ten of the clock, we came to a confused halt, we and the dozen or so we were traveling with, for ahead of us the highway, which had broadened out considerably during the last few days, was now blocked by a formidable line of the military. A caravan ahead of us had also been halted, for beasts were already tethered for foraging by the side of the road, carts and wagons were drawn up in orderly rows, their occupants either resting or arguing with the captain of the troops, with much gesticulating and nodding and shaking of heads.

Whatever it was, it obviously meant delay. Seating Gill in the shade, I pushed my way forward, asking first one and then the other the reason for the delay, but got only confused replies. "It's the war. . . . Road ahead is blocked. . . . Plague . . . Robbers and brigands . . ." In the end I approached one of the ordinary soldiers, relieving himself in a ditch some way away from the others, a bored expression on his face. I remembered what the Wimperling had said about thinking oneself into what people expected to see, so I tried to project myself as pretty.

"Excuse me, captain. . . ." He turned, shook off the drops and tucked himself in again. I saw the boredom on his face replaced with interested speculation. Perhaps it was working!

"Yes, missy? How can I help you?" His gambeson was food- and sweat-stained, he hadn't shaved for days, his iron cap was missing and his hose full of holes. Most of his teeth were rotting or gone, and he spoke with a thick, clipped lisp.

I smiled sweetly. "I can make neither head nor tail of what is going on, sir, so bethought me to seek one out who surely would." Mama had taught me how to flatter. "One can tell at a glance those worth talking to." I smiled again. "A man of experience such as yourself must surely know *everything*. . . ."

It worked. He grinned self-consciously, then with a quick look over his shoulder to where his captain was still waving his arms about and shouting, he settled the dagger at his belt and took my arm, drawing me away behind a clump of elder bushes, strutting like the dung-heap cockerel he was.

"Well, look here, pretty missy, it's like this. . . ." The Wimperling had spoke true! He had called me "pretty"! "You knows of course we is at war, has been for as long as I can remember. . . ."

"But there haven't been any battles for years. . . ."

"That don't matter round here. 'Readiness is all,' as the captain says, and we can't afford to relax for a moment." He spat on the ground. "Arrogant bastard! Thinks he knows it all because he fought in a couple of campaigns abroad! Still, no use crossing him. Worth a flogging, that is." He peered at me. "What's a nice-spoken lass like you doing here, anyways?"

But I was ready for that. "Traveling north with my father, a spice merchant," I said quickly, conscious that he had moved closer. "He's over there," and I pointed in the direction of the still-arguing captain. "He's also trying to find out what is going on—but I think I am having a better success! Er . . . I heard somebody say something about a renewal of war?" And that was the last thing we needed, I thought.

"Not exactly, but there have been a couple of skirmishes on the border last few days. Still it puts us on alert, and means the border's closed for a while. Usually it's open twice a day for trade and barter: they likes the wine and fruits from the south, we likes their grain, cider and cheese. Everyone gets searched, 'cos that's enemy territory over there, there's a small toll, and everyone's happy. Not strictly official, mind . . ." He sucked his teeth. "Still, none o' that for a week or so." He looked disconsolate: I could imagine in whose pockets the "tolls" went.

Oh, no! Gill, I was sure, could not bear to be patient for so long now he was near his home. Our money was running out, there'd be little food nearby and as for entertaining, with only the soldiers' pay to depend on, we should soon starve.

"Is there no other way across?"

He turned me round to face north, taking the opportunity to put his grimy hands round my waist. My mind shuddered at his touch, my nose wrinkled up at the stinking breath whistling past my left ear, but I kept my body still. He pointed over my shoulder.

"See there, that line o' trees? That's the border between *here*, what belongs to our king, and *there*, what belongs to the king over-water, Steady Eddie, they calls him. Got quite a bit o' land over here: that's what the battles are about. Road across goes through the trees. Left there's thick forest for miles, fifty or so, and their patrols go up and down there day and night." He swiveled me towards the right. "There's the village. T'other side o' that's the river what runs into enemy territory. They got their camp on the banks; we patrols this side, they patrols the other. No way through . . ."

But there had to be: somehow we must cross that border. From the other travelers I had confirmed that what lay ahead was indeed Gill's part of this divided country, so for his sake it was imperative we lingered no longer than was necessary. But how to evade the patrols? Alone, I might have tried to creep through their lines at night, especially with Growch to spy ahead, but a blind man was clumsy at the best of times and the Wimperling's bulk precluded any attempt for the four of us together.

Successfully evading the importunate soldier we ate what little we had left and lazed the day away, but in the evening, to quiet Gill's restlessness, I took him to the tavern in the village for an indifferent stew and a mug or two of thin ale, together with half-a-dozen or so other disconsolate travelers.

And there, in that stuffy, malodorous little ale house, came the answer to our prayers. . . .

25

"**H**ullo, Walter! How many this time? A dozen? Good. Welcome to our side, gents—and lady. . . ."

A trap, a stupid, miserable trap! All we had thought of was crossing the border, too eager to question the ease with which our "safe" passage had been procured. If I had had half the sense I credited myself with we should have been suspicious from the start and never joined this sorry enterprise.

Thinking back, Walter the ferryman had been a shifty-looking individual from the start, but his suggestion of slipping through enemy lines on his raft—at a price—had seemed like the answer to a prayer to all of us. He said that if we set off around three in the morning we could drift past the sentries on both sides, and assured us he had done it many times. Twelve of us had paid the silver coin demanded, and rushed back to gather up our belongings. The Wimperling said that nothing in the world would get him on a raft, he would spread his wings and float past, and Growch said that if he couldn't slip past a sentry or two we could chuck him in the river. Next time . . .

The raft nearly tipped twice, although the river was low and sluggish, for most of the other passengers were frightened of the water and didn't heed instructions to keep to the center and be still, but rushed from side to side, imperiling us all. The boatmen poled us out from the bank with a suck and a slurp and a pungent smell of mud, and once all was settled we drifted downstream through the oily water.

There was a quarter moon, few stars and an absence of sound: no wind, no birds. It was warm and still, the heat of the day still lingering in the heavy air. I trailed my fingers in the river: water warm as my skin. The banks on either side seemed deserted.

All at once the sneaky Walter started to pole us in towards the bank—surely we couldn't be beyond the enemy lines yet?—and I could see a makeshift landing stage through the gloom. The raft slapped against the pilings with a jolt that nearly had us all in the water, sudden torches flared, a dozen hands pulled us from the craft and hauled us up on the bank. By the flickering light I could see we were surrounded by soldiers. Different ones.

"Welcome," said their leader again, snickering. "Line 'em up, lads, and let's see what they got. . . ."

They relieved us of our packs and bundles, chuckling and commenting to themselves all the while. "Sorry-lookin' set o' buggers . . . Which pack belongs to the Jew? Pity they don' close the border more often. . . . Got a blind 'un here, with 'is girl. . . ." One of them gave a couple of coins to Walter, our betrayer.

"Bringin' more tomorrow?"

"If'n I can con 'em. Two lots if possible. Twenty-four hours'll make 'em keener. Don' let any o' these slip back to give a warnin'. . . ."

A moment or two later the Jew broke away from the rest of us and fled into the darkness and another of our companions jumped into the river, where he foundered and gasped and was twirled away on the current, flowing faster here, his mouth open on a yell drowned by a gurgle of water. A moment later he was swept out of sight.

They brought the Jew back five minutes later. He was unconscious and had obviously been beaten. He was thrown to the ground and disregarded, while the soldiery enjoyed themselves opening the packs and sharing out the contents, including our blankets, which they declared "a fine weave—good against the winter," and promptly confiscated. Luckily they could find no use for Gill's new tunic, and by the time they had emptied the other pack they were so surfeited with some golden spices, oils and unguents, jewelry, embroidered cloth, carved bone figures, some fine daggers and a silver crucifix that they tossed my pots and pans to one side. They were momentarily puzzled by my precious Boke, ripped off its cover looking for a hiding place, then tossed the loose pages into a bush.

Anyone who protested was beaten quiet. My pens and inks were scattered on the ground but they took what little food we had, chomping noisily on hastily divided cheese. The ten of us who could still stand were then searched. Rings were pulled from fingers (mine went suddenly invisible), brooches unfastened, earrings torn from ears, embroidered clothes ripped from the owner's back, leather boots pulled off. Ours were too tatty to bother with. Luckily Gill and I looked so poor that our search was perfunctory, and they didn't discover the dowry, or the few coins I had left of ordinary money.

Some of our compatriots were weeping and wringing their hands, but I held Gill's hand and preserved a stoical silence. What else could I do? I was worrying about Growch and the Wimperling, but at least we no longer had Mistral, Traveler and Basher with us: I could well imagine what would have happened to them if we did.

Searching and scavenging done, one of the soldiers ran off in the darkness to return a moment or two later with a man on a horse, obviously in command. There followed what was a well-rehearsed interchange between the captain and his troops. I don't think it fooled anyone.

Captain: "What have we here, then?"

Soldiers: (One, two, three or seven, it didn't matter which: sometimes they answered singly, sometimes together, like a ragged chorus. Suffice it to say they all knew their parts off pat). "Infiltrators, sir! Crossing the border without permission, sir!"

Captain: "Have you examined them and their belongings?"

Soldiers: "Yes, sir!"

Captain: "And?"

Soldiers: "All guilty, sir! Carrying contraband, some of 'em . . ."

Captain: "Let me see the goods."

Here some of our fellow travelers tried to protest, but a stave round the legs, a buffet to the jaw soon silenced them. The captain dismounted and pawed through the heap of spoils, finally selecting the silver crucifix, one of the more ornamental daggers, a ring set with a ruby and the gold coins. "Mmmm . . ." He shook his head. "Obviously stolen goods. I shall have to confiscate these while further enquiries are made." He carried a big enough pouch to hold them all. "Now then, men: what is the punishment for spies and thieves?"

Chorus: "Death!"

I gripped Gill's hand so tightly I could feel my ring biting into flesh. One of the other travelers broke away and flung himself at the captain's knees, scrabbling at his ankles, sobbing pitifully.

"Mercy, kind sir, mercy! I have a wife, three children. . . ."

The captain kicked him away. "So have I, so have the rest of us! You should have thought of that before you entered a war zone." He rubbed his chin. "Mind you . . ."

I think we all took an anxious step forward, for the soldier's voice held a considering tone.

"Mind you . . ." he repeated: "If they were willing to pledge them-

selves against a little ransom, as an earnest of their repentance, men, I
think we might reconsider, don't you?"

Immediately the man still on his knees was joined by three others,
all well-dressed, pledging house, money, jewels, coin or livestock as
bribes. The four were led aside into the darkness, their faces now expressing a hope none of the remainder could hope to match. The captain
gestured at the unconscious Jew. "And him?"

"Caught trying to run off, sir . . ."

"His baggage?"

"Nothing of consequence. Papers mostly, sir." The soldier pointed
to a scatter of vellum.

"Cunning bastard; not worth the investigation. Get rid of him!"

To my horror two of the soldiers came forward, picked him up and
flung him into the river. A couple of large bubbles broke the surface
and that was all.

The captain surveyed the rest of us. "Send the rest of them back: let
their own side deal with them." My heart leapt, but I might have known
it was just a cruel jest. "No, wait: they can either enlist with us or work
as slaves: give them the choice." He turned away to remount but one of
the soldiers who had been eyeing me with a leer went over and whispered
in his ear. The captain turned back, beckoned us nearer. "And what have
you to say for yourselves?" He addressed himself to me.

I kept my gaze modestly lowered, my voice meek. "My blind brother
and I are returning home, sir. We traveled south in a vain attempt to
find a cure for him. We live in this province, we are not spies, and we
have spent all our money in doctor's bills. We are only here because
war does not take account of innocent travelers. . . ."

He stared at me in a calculating manner. "What was in their baggage?"

One of the soldiers indicated the scattered pots and pans, the flasks,
odd bits of clothing. Just these, sir."

"Whereabouts do you come from? What does your father do?"

I had dreaded such questioning. "Our—our father is a carpenter.
We were sent—" I twisted the ring on my finger in my agitation and
out of nowhere came a name I must have heard somewhere, sometime
I could not recall. "We were sent south with the recommendation and
blessing of Bishop Sigismund of the Abbey of St. Evroult," I said firmly,
and raised my head to look at him straight.

He raised his eyebrows. "I see. . . . Let them continue their journey." He crossed himself. "I have no quarrel with the church." He turned
away again, but once more the soldier whispered to him. He turned and

looked at me again. "Very well: I am sure she will cooperate. But no rough stuff, mind." And with that he remounted and clattered off into the darkness.

The importunate soldier came over and took my arm, not unkindly. "You come along o' me, you and your brother."

"Our things . . ." I pointed to the pots and pans.

"Well, pack 'em up, then," he said impatiently. "Coupla minutes, no more . . ."

Well within that time I had retrieved everything, even my torn Boke, and tied it into two bundles. The pans were dented, one of the horn mugs was cracked and one of the flask stoppers had disappeared, but at least we were alive. The soldier plucked up one of the torches stuck in the ground and nodded to us to follow, winking at his fellows as he led us off.

"She'll keep till later!" one of them yelled, and suddenly I realized the implication of the captain's words: "I am sure she will cooper-ate. . . ." and a cold finger of fear and revulsion touched my spine.

He led us to a broken-down hut that must once have housed sheep or goats, for the earthen floor was covered with their coney-like drop-pings and the place smelled of fusty, damp wool. There was no place to sit so we huddled against a wall, and he took the torch with him so we were left in darkness. As we became more used to our surroundings, however, I could see, through the gaps in the wattle and daub walls and the rents in the reed thatch, a certain lightening outside: false dawn preceding the real one.

I tiptoed over to the flap of skin that served as a door and peeked out. To my right, about ten yards away, two soldiers sat cross-legged by a small fire, playing dice. No escape that way. Coming back into the darkness I felt my way round the wall seeking for a weakness, but apart from a few fist-sized holes there was nothing. If only we had been able to reach the roof, now, there was—

I nearly leapt out of my clothes as something damp and cold touched my bare ankle.

"For 'Eaven's sake! It's only me. . . ."

I knelt down and hugged him, tacky though he was. "Where've you been? Are you all right? Where's the Wimperling?"

" 'Ush, now! We're all right. More'n I can say for you . . . Now, listen! I gotta message for you from the pig." And he told me what they planned to do, but when I started to question, he shut me up. "No time to argue: we gotta get goin'. Be light soon," and he slipped out of the door as I felt my way back to Gill and explained, slinging our packs ready as I spoke.

This time he didn't argue about talking to animals but shrugged his shoulders fatalistically. "Just carry on: we couldn't be in a worse position, I suppose."

I felt like saying that it was me, not him, that was liable to be raped, but thought better of it. "It'll be all right, I'm sure: just a couple of minutes more. . . ."

It felt like an eternity, and I kept wiping my hands nervously on my skirt because they were sweating so much. I pulled Gill over to the doorway with a fast-beating heart so that we were ready—ready for the shout that came moments later from over to our left. Peering through a gap in the hide covering I could see a tongue of flame shoot upwards at the fringes of the forest, some quarter-mile away, then heard the drumming of hooves from a couple of panicking horses. The two guards outside leapt to their feet, undecided what to do, but when a second tongue of flame started to run merrily towards the tents of the soldiery and there were more galloping hooves, ours abandoned fire and dice and started running towards the confusion.

Now was our chance. Grabbing Gill's hand I led him, stumbling, out of the hut and to our right, where the river should be. It was much closer than I thought and in fact we nearly fell in, because at the wrong moment I risked a glance behind us, to see a merry blaze had caught the summer-dry grasses at the fringe of the forest and, fanned by the dawn breeze, the flames were creeping towards the encampment. Luckily Gill fell full length as we reached the riverbank, just before we both plunged down the slope into the water, and a moment later Growch appeared to lead us further downstream to where a small rowing boat was tethered in the reeds. Untying the rope I helped Gill aboard, instructed Growch to jump in, and—

"Where's the Wimperling?"

"Right here," grunted a hoarse, cindery voice and he rolled up, panting and covered with smuts. "Don't wait: I'll float. Need to get rid of the smoke . . ."

"You're sure?"

"Just get going! Push off from the bank, keep your heads down and the boat trimmed."

"Trimmed?"

"Both of you in the middle. No looking over the side. The current will carry us away from all this."

It was as he said. I kicked off from the bank and collapsed in an ungraceful heap at Gill's feet, as the boat nudged out into the center and found the current. It seemed my knight had been in boats before, for he told me much the same as the pig: "Sit down in the muddle, Summer, hands on both thwarts—" (thwarts? I presumed he meant the sides) "—and don't lean over the side, either. That's it. . . ."

Slowly and surely we gained speed to almost a walking pace. Over to our left fires were still burning, accompanied by shouts and curses, but everyone was too busy to have noticed our defection, and a moment later we swung round a bend in the river, shaded by trees, and the fire and commotion died away behind us. Gill seemed calm and content, but I was still terrified of rocking the boat, and desperately needed to relieve myself. The Wimperling was floating just behind us, so when I told him he gave the boat a nudge out of the current and I scrambled ashore, and thankfully ran behind some bushes, while Growch christened the nearest tree.

"Do we have to go back?" I asked the pig, gesturing towards the boat, where Gill was happily trailing his fingers in the water. "I—I feel safer on land."

"Not safe yet. Besides, we can travel faster by boat."

"We're not going very fast now," I objected.

"We will, just wait and see. Back you go. . . ."

We swung out into the channel again, and I gripped the sides as tight as I could, till my knuckles turned white with the strain. The Wimperling swam up behind us once more.

"Move towards the bow—the *front*—both of you." I told Gill and we both shuffled forward and it was just as well we did, for a moment later the rear of the boat tipped down as the pig hooked his useful claws into the broad bit. I thought for a moment he was going to try and clamber in, but a moment later there was a flapping noise and his wings lifted out of the water and spread until they caught the now freshening breeze behind us, and we were bowling along in a moment at twice the speed, and the banks of the river were fairly whizzing by.

We traveled this way for the rest of the day, with a couple of stops for me to forage for berries, for we had nothing to eat. We saw no one, and I became used to the rocking motion of the boat eventually. The only creatures we disturbed were water fowl, a couple of graceful swans with their grey cygnets and an occasional water vole. At dusk the Wimperling steered us to the bank again.

"There's a village ahead—you can see the smoke. You can find a buyer for the boat. It'll provide you with enough for some days' food."

"Thank the gods for that!" said Growch. "The sides of me stummick is stuck together like broken bellows. . . ."

And the thought of dry land, food, and perhaps a mug or so of ale, rather than the risk of river water, so filled my mind that I quite forgot the question that had been tickling at the back of my mind since our escape: how on earth had the Wimperling managed to light those fires?

No one questioned where we had come from, where we were going, and there were no soldiers. I got a reasonable price for the boat, even without oars, and that night we slept in comparative luxury in a barn attached to the alehouse. It was fish pie for supper with baked apple and cheese, but everything was fresh and tasty. There was no talk of war and battles, only of the approaching harvest. I tried once more to describe Gill's home and showed them the piece of silk, but they shook their heads.

"Further north's best place for grain and orchards. . . ."

My hopes were momentarily dashed, but Gill's enthusiasm was unabated. He declared he could hear in the villagers' voices the echo of the patois they used near his home, and the more ale he drank the more details he seemed to remember. Wooden toys, servants, fishing, a boat, a blue silk surcoat, a flood . . . After he had downed his third flagon of ale I tried to dissuade him from more, but he declared petulantly that I was spoiling his evening and was worse than a nursemaid, so I mentally shrugged my shoulders and ordered a fourth.

Halfway through he fell asleep with his head on the trestle table, and I had to enlist the help of a couple of the locals to carry him back to the barn and lay him down on the straw, face down in case he vomited during his sleep. I stayed awake for a while, for sometimes when he had drunk too much he woke and the liquor excited that ache between the loins that all men have, so Mama used to say, and he would toss and turn and groan until his hands had accomplished relief: at times like that I couldn't bear to listen, and would tiptoe away till he had finished.

Tonight, however, everything was quiet and peaceful, so I wriggled myself about till I was comfortable and fell asleep at peace with the world—

To awake in the dark with a hand on my bosom and a voice in my ear.

"My dearest one . . . I've waited so long for this moment! I've been thinking of you night and day. Don't turn me away, I beg you, I implore you! I need you, oh, so much. . . ."

My heart was thumping, my breath caught in my throat with a hiccuping sob, and I reached up in wonderment to hold Gill's head with my hands, ruffling the familiar curly hair with my fingers. I had waited so long for a sign, anything to prove he cared for me, and now my whole body was filled with an aching, melting tenderness, a yielding that left me trembling and helpless. His hand left my breast and slipped beneath my skirt, his hand warm on my thigh, and his seeking mouth found mine in our first kiss. . . .

So that was what it was like to be kissed by the man you loved! A little, distracting voice from somewhere was whispering: "Not yet, not yet! He's drunk too much, you only lose your virginity once. . . ." But if he was drunk, then so was I: drunk with desire for this man I had secretly loved so long.

Already he was fumbling with the ties of his braies and I felt him gently part my thighs.

"My sweet Rosamund, my Rose of the World . . ."

26

I froze, like a rabbit faced by a stoat. Rosamund? Who the hell was Rosamund? Not me, anyway. But perhaps I had misheard. . . .

I hadn't.

He nuzzled my neck. "I have waited for this so long, my Rosamund of the white skin, the golden hair! At last you are mine. . . ." and he thrust up between my legs, still murmuring her name.

That did it. In a sudden spurt of anger, disappointment and frustration I kneed him as hard as I could then rolled away from beneath him, got to my feet and ran out into the night. He yelled with pain, then groaned, but I didn't look back: I couldn't. My fist stuffed into my mouth to stifle the sobs, I let the stupid tears run down my cheeks like a salty waterfall till my eyes were swollen and my throat felt all closed up.

I didn't know whether I hated him or myself the most.

Hating him was irrational, I knew that in my mind, but my heart and stomach couldn't forgive. He was drunk, and in his dreams had turned to a suddenly recalled love; he had found a female body and mistaken me for her.

But I was worse, I told myself. Without thought I had surrendered to my feelings and immediate emotions, forgetting all Mama had impressed upon me about staying chaste for one's husband, not succumbing to temptation, etc. All I wanted was to indulge myself with a man I had fantasized about for months—husband, future, possible pregnancy, all had been disregarded in the urgency of desire. And if I thought about it for even one moment, I would have realized that it could never lead to anything else once he returned home, for he was a knight and I was nothing. I cursed myself for my stupidity.

But at the back of my mind was something else, something worse: hurt pride. He had preferred his dreams, his memories, his vision, to me.

In reality I hadn't even been there. Summer was a companion, his guide, his crutch, his eyes: if he had known it was me he wouldn't have bothered, drunk or no. The tears came so fast now they hadn't time to cool and ran down into my mouth as warm as when they left my eyes. They tasted like the sea.

There was a shuffling and a grunt behind me and the Wimperling lumbered out of the barn and looked up at the lightening sky, sniffing. "Another fine day . . . Did I ever tell you about the story of the pig with one wish?"

"Er . . . No." I couldn't see what he was getting at. Surreptitiously I wiped my eyes on the hem of my skirt. "What—what pig?"

"It was a tale my mother pig used to tell us when we were little. Once there was a pig who had done a magician some service, and in return he was granted one wish. He was a greedy thing, so immediately without thinking he wished that all food he touched would turn into truffles, because that was what he liked most. His wish was granted, and for days he stuffed himself so full he nearly burst. Then as he grew surfeited, he wished once more for plainer fare, and he cursed the day he had wished without thought. . . ."

"And then what happened?" I was interested in spite of my misery.

"Well, first he tried to punish himself by trying to starve to death, but that didn't work, so, because he was basically a kind and caring pig, he decided to turn his misfortune into a treat for others, going around touching other pigs' food so they had the treat of truffles. And it did his sad heart good to see them enjoying themselves. . . ." He stopped. "What's for breakfast?"

I smiled in spite of everything. "Not truffles, anyway! And then what?"

"Then what what?"

"The pig."

"Oh, the pig . . . I disremember."

"You can't just leave it like that! All stories have a proper ending. They start 'Once upon a time . . .' and end '. . . and so they lived happily ever after,' with an exciting story in between."

"Life's not like that."

"I don't see why it can't be. . . ."

"That is what man has been saying for thousands of years and look where it's got him! Without hope and a God the human race would have died out eons ago."

"You say that as if animals were superior!"

"So they are, in many ways. They don't think and puzzle and wonder and theorize, look back and look forward. What matters is only what they feel right now, this minute, and if they can fill their bellies and mate and keep clear of danger. And when they dream, and twitch and paddle in their sleep, then they are either the hunters or the hunted, nothing more. No grand visions, no romance—and no tears, either."

So he *had* noticed. I felt embarrassed and went back to his tale. "But the story was a story, so it must have an ending. . . ."

"Well, then, you give it one, just to satisfy your romantic leanings."

I thought. "Because the pig turned out to be so unselfish after all, helping his friends to enjoy the truffles when he could no longer, the wizard reconsidered his spell and then lifted it. And—and the pig was properly grateful to have been shown the error of his ways and never again yearned after something unsuitable. He married his sweetheart pig, who had stayed loyal to him through good times and bad, and they had lots of little piglets and lived happily ever afterwards. There!" I stopped, pleased with myself, then had another thought. "Oh, yes: The strange thing about it all was, that the piglets and their children and their children's children couldn't *stand* truffles!"

The Wimperling made polite applause noises with his tongue. "A predictable tale—redeemed, I think, by the last line. I liked that. And the moral of the story is?"

"Does it have to have one?"

"All the best ones have. Disguised sometimes, but still there."

"Er . . . Don't make hasty decisions: think before you open your mouth?"

"Or your legs," said the Wimperling. "Exactly!" And off he trotted.

Over a breakfast of oatcakes, fish baked in leaves and ale, Gill told me he had had a wonderful dream during the night. "And Summer, it seems my memory is really coming back!"

It was lucky for him he could not see my face, and did not sense the desolate churning in my stomach that made me push aside the fish with a sickness I could not disguise.

"In this dream I was wandering through a building that seemed familiar yet wasn't, if you know what I mean. Then I realized I was in the household where I had served my time as first page, then squire. But I was no longer a boy, I was as I am now, but without the blindness—you know how illogical dreams can be."

I nodded, then remembered. "Yes." In *my* dreams I was slim. And beautiful . . . How illogical could you get?

"Then suddenly I was in a barn—a barn in the middle of a castle,

Summer!—and there, lying in the straw, was my affianced, my beloved, my Rosamund!"

"Rosamund?"

"Yes—I told you my memory was coming back. Any more ale?"

I handed him mine. "Tell me more about—about this Rosamund."

"Ah, what can I say? No mere words could do her adequate justice! I met her when I was a squire and with my parents' consent we became affianced. Her father was a rich merchant and his daughter Rosamund the middle one of three, with a handsome dowry. She is two years older than I, but as sweet and chaste and demure as a nun. We plighted our troth five years ago, but I was determined to earn my knighthood before I claimed her as my bride. I journeyed north to bring her gifts from my parents and say we were ready to receive her, and on my way back I think I . . . That bit still isn't clear. I don't remember."

On that journey back he had been ambushed, and he wouldn't be here if I hadn't rescued him, I thought bitterly. "Is your bride-to-be as pretty as she is chaste?" I asked between my teeth.

"Pretty? Nay, beautiful! Tall, slim, perfectly proportioned. Her skin is white as milk, her cheeks like the wild rose, her hair like ripened corn—"

"And her teeth as white as a new-peeled withy," I muttered sulkily.

"How did you know? I was going to say pearls. . . . A straight nose, a small mouth " He sighed. "Truly is she named the Rose of the World. . . ."

I rubbed my smallish nose and practiced pursing my not-so-small mouth.

He sighed again. "As I said, she is as chaste as a nun, and has never permitted me more than a kiss or two, a quick embrace. . . . But in this dream I had my impatience got the better of me and I threw aside her objections and embraced her long and heartily. It was just getting interesting when—when . . ."

"Yes?" I said sweetly.

"When all of a sudden I was in a tournament and my opponent unhorsed me, to the detriment of my manhood, if you will excuse the expression. . . ." He scowled. "Very painful."

"You got kicked in the balls," I said succinctly. "And woke up. Are you sure it wasn't the fair Rosamund defending her chastity?"

He looked shocked. "Really, Summer! Even in dreams she wouldn't be so—so unladylike! And she was never coarse in her language . . ."

Of course not. "Seeing how much your memory had improved, was there anything else you recalled that we might find useful in our search for your home and family? Such as a name, or a location?"

He looked surprised. "Oh, didn't I say? How remiss of me. I meant to. I remembered my father's name a few days ago, just before we came to the border. But then there was so much to think about, with escaping and all. . . ."

I could have throttled him. "Well?"

"My father's name is Sir Robert de Faucon and our nearest big town is Evreux; we live some thirty miles to the west. My mother's name is Jeanne, and—"

"Why in the world didn't you tell me before!" Of course: the bird on his pennant was a falcon; I remembered it now. And the name was the same. Simple.

"We were trying to cross the border—"

"But your name might have meant something—"

"Yes! A ransom. And we'd still be there."

Very reasonable, but I was sure it had never crossed his mind till now. I simmered down. We would make our way to Evreux, the place that had come so providentially to mind when we were questioned at the border, and from there on it should be easy.

Not as easy as I had hoped. There were fewer travelers on the road and fewer itinerants as well, for these latter were hoping for jobs with the imminent harvest. It was the wrong time and the wrong place for pilgrimages also, so we had to keep to the high roads in daylight and not chance evening walking. We also found these people of the north stingier with their money and their handouts, more suspicious of strangers: maybe it was the war that had been going on for so long, maybe their northern blood ran colder, I just do not know.

We took some money with a performance or two in the cathedral town of Evreux, and confirmed the westerly road towards Gill's home. Now we were so near our objective I would have expected him to be far more impatient to press on than he actually was. Instead he walked slower than usual, complained of blisters, said his back hurt, had an in-growing toe-nail. I pricked and dressed his blisters with salve, rubbed his back and examined a perfectly normal toe. Next day he felt dizzy, had stomach pains, nausea, vomiting and cramps. I treated all these, difficult to confirm or deny, but on the third day, when we were less than five miles from the turnoff that we had been told led straight to his estates, and he said his legs were too weak to hold him, I knew something was seriously wrong.

I sat him down under the shade of a large oak tree, dumped our parcels and asked him straight out what was the matter.

"For something is, of that I am sure. And it has nothing to do with bad backs, blisters or your belly!" I remembered how he had "forgotten" his father's name so conveniently, until I had jolted his memory. "For all your talk of your beautiful lady, you are behaving like a very reluctant bridegroom! One would almost think you didn't *want* to go home!" I was joking, trying to bring an air of ease to a puzzling situation, but to my amazement he took me seriously.

"Perhaps I don't."

"What do you mean? Ever since I first met you we have been trying to find out where you live, and no one has been more insistent that you! We have traveled hundreds of miles—never mind your blisters, you should see mine!—and have gone through great dangers, faced starvation, scraped and scrounged for every penny, crossed innumerable provinces, just so that we can bring you to the bosom of your family once more! You can't mean at this late stage that you don't want to go home, you just can't!"

His blind eyes were fixed unseeingly on his boots. He muttered something I couldn't catch, so I asked him to repeat it.

"I said: what use to anyone is a blind knight?"

Dear Christ, I had never thought of that. How terrible! When first I had rescued him I had thought of nothing but helping him to recover, largely, now I admitted, for my own gratification. His blindness had been an inconvenience for him, but a bonus for me. It had meant I could worship him unseen; feed him, clothe him, wash him, cut his hair and beard, touch him, hold his hand. . . . And all without him realizing how fat and ugly I was. Facing it now, I could see that all I had wanted was his dependence, in a false conviction that that would bring me love. And also boost my own self-importance: was that why I had also taken on a hungry tortoise, a broken pigeon, a decrepit horse? Just so that they would pander to my ego by being grateful to me? Dear God, I hoped not: I hoped it was the gentler emotion of compassion, but how could I be sure? I had had little choice with Growch, and the Wimperling was almost forced on me, but the others? It didn't bear thinking of.

And now my beloved Gill had faced me with an impossible question: what, indeed, was there for a blind knight? Knights fought in battles, competed in tourneys, hunted, went on Crusades—what did a knight know save of arms? Would his overlord, the king from oversea, want a man incapable of warring?

Quick, Summer, think of something. . . .

"There are plenty of things you can do," I said briskly. "People will still obey your commands, won't they? A blind man can still ride a horse, play an instrument, sing a song, run an estate, make wise judgments, and . . . and . . ." I had to think of something else. "Remember what that wise physician, Suleiman, said? He foretold you would regain your memory, as you have, and he also said there was nothing wrong with your eyes that time also couldn't cure. He said you could regain your sight suddenly, any day!"

I don't think he was listening. There was something even more pressing at the back of his mind. "Of what use is a blind husband?"

I was about to observe that most lovemaking took place in the dark anyway, but suddenly realized just how much he must be fearing rejection: some women wouldn't consider allying themselves to a blind man, never mind that to me it would be an advantage. But then, I wasn't beautiful. . . . I remembered that Mama had told me that a man's pride was his greatest emotion. Let's give him a boost and a get-out, however frivolous the latter.

I put my arms about him and hugged him. "Any woman would be crazy to look elsewhere!" I said comfortingly. "A handsome man such as you? Why, if she won't have you, I will!" I added in a lighthearted, teasing way. "We shall take to the road again, you and I, and have many more adventures, until your sight is returned. We'll go back and stay with Matthew the merchant for a start, and—" I stopped, because his hands had sought the source of my voice, and now they cupped my face.

"You know, you are the kindest and most warmhearted woman I have ever known," he said, then leaned forward and kissed me. "And I don't think I shall ever forget you. Tell me, Summer, are you as pretty as your voice? If so, I might even take you up on your offer," and now his voice was as light and teasing as mine had been.

I leapt to my feet, my stomach churning, my face red as a ripe apple, my mind all topsy-turvy. It was the first time he had ever offered me a gesture of affection. Why now? I screamed inside, why now when you are so near home and in a few hours I am going to lose you? If he had told me before of his fears, if he had once shown me any love, then I would have ensured it took twice as long to reach here. And now how I regretted refusing his love-making attempt: what would it have mattered if he had thought me someone else? What would have been simpler than to take what he offered and enjoy it, then perhaps confess to him afterwards?

But all I said was: "You can judge of that when you can see again. But the offer's open. . . ." in my gruffest voice, adding: "Enough of all this nonsense! Let's get you cleaned up, bathed and properly dressed, so you will not disgrace us all. And I must do the animals as well. . . ." and I grabbed Growch, who had gathered the main import of what I had been talking of in human speech, and was about to disappear down the road.

Luckily there was a meandering stream not far away through the trees, and though it was summer-low I managed to dunk the dog and comb out the worst of the fleas, and freshen up the pig. Then I gave Gill an all-over, my eyes and hands perhaps lingering too long on those special parts that would soon belong to another. I trimmed his beard and mustache as close as I could and cut his hair, then gave him a fresh shirt and the new blue-embroidered surcoat.

There was little I could do for myself except bathe, plaiting my hair, donning a fresh shift and the woolen dress Matthew had given me, but I felt clean and more comfortable. One bonus was to find some water-cress to supplement our bread and cheese.

We still had several miles to walk before we reached Gill's home. Once we found the left-hand turning we were bounded by forest on both sides, and the road narrowed to a wheel-rutted track, but after a mile or so we came to a pair of gates that seemed to be permanently fastened back, and through them the road wound among orchard trees and har-vested fields towards a fortified manor house some half-mile away. There were few people about, and no one challenged us as I led Gill slowly towards his home.

It was now late afternoon, but the sun had lost little of its heat and we finished off the water in the flask and I picked three apples from those near-ripe. Then another and another for the Wimperling, who had suddenly decided they were his favorite food. I picked them quite openly, for there were none to see, save a boy coaxing some swine back from acorns in the forest, and a girl with her geese picking at the stubble. Besides, I thought, these are Gill's orchards, or will be some day.

I started to describe our surroundings to him, but I had no need. Now his memory was nearly complete once more, he could smell, hear, taste and touch his own land; at first tentatively, then more assured as he described what lay on either side of us as we passed. Here a copse, there a stream, crabapples on one side, late pears on the other, and he even anticipated the flags flying from the gateway.

As he drew nearer I could see that his memory of the grandness of the manor house was a little exaggerated, like most fond memories. It was nothing special; we had passed much grander on our travels. The original structure was of wood, in two stories, but a high stone wall now surrounded it, embracing also the courtyard, stables, kitchens and stores; outside, small hovels housed the workers, though everything seemed empty and deserted.

"Entertainers?" said the porter at the side gate. "Everyone's welcome today, even your beasts. Round to your right you'll find the kitchens.

Tonight's the Grain Supper: always held on this day, come rain or shine."
And he went back to gnawing at what was left of a large mutton bone.

"This is ridiculous!" protested Gill, as we started off again across
the courtyard, also deserted. "I belong here: this is my home! What in
God's name are we doing creeping round like a couple of thieves? Just
lead me over to the main door—no, I can find my own way!"

"Wait!" I said, catching hold of his arm. "Let's not rush it. You
don't want to give them all heart failure! Let's surprise them gently.
Listen a moment, and I'll tell you what we'll do. . . ."

Leaving Gill and the animals outside, I went to the kitchens and was
given a large bowl of mutton stew and a loaf of the "poor-bread" I remembered as a child, before Mama could afford better: the grain was
mixed with beans, peas and pulses, and this was fresh as an hour ago and
very filling. We ate hungrily, sitting in the courtyard with our backs to a
sunny wall, then I went back and asked to see the steward, asking permission to perform in the Great Hall later. As it happened there were a
juggler and a minstrel already waiting, but we were added to the list.

All that remained was to keep out of the way of anyone who might
recognize Gill, and a couple of hours later I was waiting nervously at
the side door, Gill tucked away in the shadows with the hood of his
cloak pulled well down over his face, Growch and the Wimperling at
his side. As the minstrel sang the song of Roland, I peeped into the hall;
so thick with smoke, I could barely see the top table, but obviously the
thick-set, bearded man must be Gill's father, the thin woman with the
tall headdress his mother. And there, sitting beside Gill's father, was a
slim woman with long blond hair fastened back with a fillet: the fair
Rosamund, if I wasn't mistaken. I wished I could see her more clearly.

Beside me the kitchen servants brushed past, ducking their heads
automatically as they passed under the low lintel, laden with dishes and
mugs, though this was the last course: fruits in aspic, nuts and cheese,
so there was more clearing away than replenishing.

The juggler had passed back to the kitchens a half-hour ago, jingling
coins in his hand, and now the minstrel was coming to the end of his
recital. There was polite applause, the tinkle of thrown coins, and a hum
of conversation as the singer made his way back to the kitchens. Our
turn next: I don't think I had ever felt so nervous in my life.

One of the valets announced us. "Entertainers from the south, with
a song or two and some tricks to divert . . ."

Growch "danced" to my piping, somersaulted, rolled over and over,
nodded or shook his head as required and "died" for his king, then the
Wimperling did some very simple counting; a) because I was nervous

to the point of nearly wetting myself and b) wanting to get it all over and done with, at the same time fearing the outcome—a little like having severe toothache and knowing the toothpuller was just around the corner; it was the last few steps to his door that were the worst.

I finished the tricks to a good deal of applause and dismissed the animals, picking up the coins that were thrown and putting them in my pocket. "Thank you ladies, knights, and gentle-persons all. If I amy crave your indulgence, my partner and I will conclude with a song," and taking a candle branch boldly from one of the side tables I walked back to the doorway where Gill was waiting, his hood hiding his face.

"When I come to the right words," I whispered, "throw back your hood, hold the candles high and march through the doorway, straight ahead. I'll come and meet you."

Walking back to the space in front of the high table I started to sing, beating a soft accompaniment on my tabor. It was an old favorite, the one where the knight rides away to seek his fortune.

> *A knight rode away.*
> *In the month of May,*
> *All on a summer's day;*
> *"I shall not stray,*
> *Nor lose my way,*
> *But return this way,*
> *On St. Valentine's Day. . . ."*

It had several verses, with lots of to-ra lays in between, and I had to sing quickly to turn "Valentine" to "Cosmos and Damien." The ballad tells of how news came to the knight's fiancée that he was dead; she visits a witch and sells her soul to the Devil in order that her beloved will return. And, of course, he returns, the rumor of his death having been exaggerated, right on the day he foretold. Just as she calls on the Devil to redeem his promise she hears the voice of the knight. This was Gill's cue, and his clear tenor rang out through the hall.

> *"I have returned as I said,*
> *I am not dead,*
> *But astray was led. . . ."*

I answered his words with the words of the song:

"Knave, knight or pelf:
Come show yourself!"

Gill threw back the hood of his cloak, held the candles high and stepped firmly forward. There was a hush from the audience, then a muffled scream as his face was illuminated. He hesitated for a moment on the threshold, then threw back his head and marched briskly forward.

And then it happened.

There was a crack! that echoed all around as his head came into contact with the low lintel of the doorway. He teetered for a moment, rocking back and forth on his heels, then dropped like a stone to the rushes.

I ran forward with my heart full of terror and reached his side, kneeling to take his poor head in my arms, looking with horror at the red mark across his forehead where he had struck.

"Gill! Gill . . . Are you all right?"

He opened his eyes, thank God! and stared straight up at me.

"That bloody door was always too low. . . . And who the hell are you?"

27

After that everything became confused.

I got up, was knocked down, rose again and tripped over the Wimperling and Growch, was overwhelmed by a great rush of bodies, flung this way and that, buffetted and elbowed. I saw Gill embraced, hugged, kissed, slapped on the back, borne off, brought back, cried over. Women fainted, men wept, dogs howled; trenchers, mugs, jugs, cups, food, drink littered the rushes. Trestles and small tables were overturned, candles burned dangerously and the clamor of voices threatened to bring down the roof.

Little by little the animals and I found ourselves, from being at the center of the fuss, to being on the fringes of the activity. Behind us was the door to the kitchens. I looked at them, they looked at me, and with one accord we marched off. The kitchens had been abandoned as the staff heard the commotion in the Great Hall, and we found ourselves alone, surrounded by the detritus of the Grain Supper in all its sordidness. Unwashed dishes, greasy pans, empty jugs; bread crusts, bones, fish heads, chicken wings littered the tables and floor, and half-eaten mutton and beef showed where kitchen supper had been left for the excitement elsewhere.

"Well . . ." I said, and sat down suddenly on a convenient stool. There didn't seem anything else to say.

Growch was sniffing round. "Pity to waste all this," he said, helping himself to a rib of beef almost as big as he was.

The Wimperling rested his chin on my lap. "Give it all time to settle down," he said. "He'll remember about us later. In the meantime, why not stock up on a bit of food and drink and find a stable or something to settle in for the night?"

I scratched his chin affectionately. "Why not?"

There were some boiling cloths drying on a rack, so I wrapped up a whole chicken, slightly charred, three black puddings, a cheese and onion pasty and a half-empty flagon of wine, and crept away guiltily to the courtyard. The stables were all full, but I found a small room that must have been used for stores, but was now empty except for a heap of sacks in one corner and a pile of rush baskets. The whole place smelled pleasantly of apples.

We could still hear sounds of revelry and carousing from the direction of the Great Hall, but it was full dark outside by now, so I closed the door and lit my lanthorn and we shared out the food. I had half the chicken and all the crispy skin, and the pasty, and I shared the rest of the chicken and the black puddings among the other two, though the Wimperling said the latter could be cannibalism.

"I thought you said you didn't know whether you were a pig or not," I said sleepily, for it had been a long day and the unaccustomed wine was making me feel soporific. I arranged the sacks to make a comfortable bed for us.

"True," said the Wimperling. "And I'm still not sure. . . ."

"Then pretend you're something else. A prince in disguise . . ."

Growch snorted.

We were wakened at dawn by an almighty hullabaloo. I was grabbed from the pile of sacks and held, struggling, between two surly men; another had hold of the Wimperling's tail and was hauling him towards the door and two others were trying to corner a snapping, snarling Growch. The storeroom seemed to be full of people all jabbering away, pointing at me, the animals. What had we done? Then I remembered the food I had filched from the kitchens the night before: was I about to lose a hand for thieving?

"Is this the one?" shouted one of the men who was holding me.

The steward stood in the doorway, consulting a piece of vellum. "A girl, named of Summer; a pig and a small dog. Seems we've got 'em. Well done, lads." And, addressing me: "Is your name Summer?"

What point in denying it? "Let the animals alone: they've done nothing!" I suddenly remembered. "I demand to see Gill—Sir Gilman, immediately! There's been some mistake. . . ."

He thrust the piece of vellum back in his pocket. "You're all wanted, girl, pig and dog. Do you realize just how long we've been looking for you?" He seemed in a very bad temper, and my heart sank. "Why, not a half-hour ago I sent mounted men out to chase you up. . . . Have to send more to recall them. All this fuss and bother, never a moment's

peace. . . . Well, come on then! They're waiting. . . ." and without giving
me time to tidy my hair or smooth down my dress I was hauled across
the courtyard, in through the main doorway, across the Great Hall—still
full of last night's somnolent revelers, the smoldering ashes of the fire
and a stink of stale food and wine, dogs, guttered candles and torches,
vomit and sweat—closely followed by a man carrying the Wimperling,
who seemed to have shrunk of a sudden, and three others still trying to
catch Growch.

Up a winding stone staircase hidden by an arras behind the top table
and we were thrust, carried or chased into a large solar wherein were
seated four people: the lord of the manor, Sir Robert, his wife, the
golden-haired Rosamund and—and Gill. A Gill close-shaven, handsomer than ever, clad in fine linen and silks. He looked now just as he
had when I first saw him: beautiful, haughty and unattainable.

As we were shoved into the room he rose from the settle where he
had been holding hands with his affianced, a look of bewilderment on
his face as he gazed first at me, then the animals, and back to me again.

"Can it be . . . ?"

The steward gave me a shove in the back that had me down on my
knees and addressed Sir Robert. "Is this them, then?"

Sir Robert glanced at his son. "Gilman?" but Gill had started forward, a look of anger on his face as he helped me to my feet.

"Whether it is or no, you have no right to treat a girl like that!
Leave us, I will deal with this!" The steward and his men bowed and
retreated and Gill looked searchingly into my face. "Is it really you,
Summer?"

Of course he had never seen me, except for that time he had asked
the way, and he didn't know it was the same girl. I blushed to the roots
of my hair that now he should see me in all my ugliness.

"Yes," I admitted finally. "I am Summer. And this is the Wimperling
and that is Growch," hoping he would stop staring at me.

"But I had no idea. . . ." He plucked a dried leaf from my hair
abstractedly, then took my hands in his again. "I thought—I had thought
you were quite different. . . ."

"Blind men have all sorts of strange fancies," I said, then forgot
myself to ask anxiously: "You are all right, then? You can see properly
again?"

"Apart from a slight headache, yes. You and Suleiman were right.
I reckon it was the knock on the head that did it. It all happened so
quickly I still feel confused—"

"And so you should!" came a cool voice from behind him and there stood the fair Rosamund, who pulled his hands from mine and tucked them round her arm, all so gently done that it seemed the initiative had come from him. She gazed at me, a faint sneer on her lips. "I'm not surprised you feel confused! Used as you are to the best, it must have been hell for you to traipse around the countryside with this tatterdemalion crew!" Her cold blue eyes raked me from head to foot. "Still, I suppose the girl needs some recompense, before she and her—menagerie—take to the road again." She paused. "I may well have a dress I need no more, though I doubt it would fit. . . ."

"Enough of this!" It was Gill's tall, thin mother Jeanne who spoke. I had the impression that nothing short of a catastrophe gave her the courage to speak normally, though now of course her beloved Gill's return must have sparked her into fresh resolution. "The girl brought our son back to us safe and sound, and she deserves the very best we can give her. As long as she wishes to stay, she is our honored guest. As—as are her pets! See that they are accommodated in the hall tonight: I myself will find a length of cloth so she is decently clad."

"The hall?" said Gill. "Father, Mother, nothing less than a good bed will do! Why, I am sure my betrothed would be only too glad to share her room with Mistress Summer?"

She looked at me as if I had the plague, then turned to Gill as sweet as honey. "My dearest, whatever you wish. But—" and she flashed me a glance that would have split stone as neatly as any mason's chisel and hammer: "—perhaps we should ask the young person herself? She may have other ideas. . . ."

Meaning I had better. She needn't have worried. The last person in the world I wished to share a bed with was her. Now, if it had been Gill . . . I pulled myself together and addressed Sir Robert and his wife.

"I thank you Sir, Lady, for your kind offer," I said, and curtsied. "The length of cloth would be most welcome, and I can make it up myself. As for accommodation, however, if I might be allowed to sleep in the storeroom where I spent last night, then I can be with our traveling companions, who are used to being with us and have been of great assistance in our travels, as no doubt Sir Gilman has told you." I curtsied again. "I should also be grateful for hot water for washing and some extra thread: I used the last to make Sir Gilman a surcoat."

There! I thought: that should give them something to think about. Polite, accommodating, clean, thrifty and yet independent, with a couple of reminders of the life we had led and how I had cared for Gill . . . I smiled at him. Never mind my ugliness: he still seemed to care about my welfare.

Sir Robert inclined his head. "As you wish. I shall see to it that the room you prefer is made more comfortable. And now, I think it is time to break our fast. . . ."

And while we ate—just below the top table this time: on it would have been too much to ask—the storeroom was transformed. Swept out, sacks and baskets removed, a table, stool and truckle bed installed, hooks for our packages knocked into the wall, two large lanthorns and a pile of straw for the animals—luxury indeed!

After breakfast servants brought hot water, soap, linen towels, and from Gill's mother came a length of fine woolen cloth in blue, needles and thread, a new comb and ribbons for my hair, and even a new shift: too long, of course, but surprisingly, none too tight. I took it up, cut out my new surcoat, mended my old one, washed and indulged recklessly in the bottle of rosemary oil that came with the soap and towels, washed my other two shifts and stitched my shoes where they were coming undone.

The midday meal was at noon, the evening meal at six, and by that evening I had my new surcoat finished, so for the first time I felt comfortable enough to survey my hosts at my leisure. My position just below the top table gave me ample opportunity to look at both Gill's parents and his affianced.

Sir Robert was stout rather than tall; he had fierce mustaches and a rather dictatorial manner, but he always treated me with kindness. His wife was normally silent, looked older than her husband, and her usually careworn expression only lightened when she talked to her beloved son. I scarcely recognized him that evening, for he had had his curly hair cropped short like his father's, to facilitate the wearing of the close-fitting helmet they affected in these parts. I liked him better with it long.

It was the fair Rosamund however who intrigued me most. "Fair" once I judged, but whatever she may have told Gill about her age, she must be at least four or five years older. Already fine lines radiated from the corners of her eyes when she smiled, which was seldom enough, and her mouth had a discontented droop. She was also missing two teeth; perhaps that was why she didn't smile much, that and the fear of deepening her lines.

She had pretty manners however, using her table napkin often to dab away grease from mouth or fingers. Her voice was pleasant enough, her figure good and her walk swaying and graceful and her hands were white and beautifully shaped. Her hair was rather thin—or mine was too thick—but it was her pale complexion I envied most of all; but, come to think of it, if she tramped the roads as we had, it would have reddened and blotched in a most unsightly way.

In all this I was fully aware that I was being over-critical, but I knew she didn't like me, and I hated the way she monopolized Gill, snatching his attention if ever he glanced over at me, and giving exaggerated little "oohs" and "aahs" as he told of our adventures. And it didn't do any good for me to remind myself she had a perfect right to do so.

Several times during the next few days he tried to speak to me alone, and each time he was foiled, usually by her, sometimes by other interruptions. Sometimes I would catch him gazing at me, and if I smiled at him, he would smile back, but it was always an uncertain, puzzled smile. It got to the stage when I started worrying whether I had two noses or was covered in some disfiguring rash.

But life drifted by for a week in this lazy fashion, eating, sleeping, and I let it, for I was in no hurry to leave. A golden September would all too soon give way to October. The mornings even now held a hint of the chill to come, dew heavy on the millions of spiderwebs that carpeted the stubble till it glinted in the rising sun like diamonds; the swifts were long gone, but a few swallows still gathered on the tower tops, and martins on the slopes of the roofs like a scattering of pearls. The leaves of the willow were already yellowing, and across in the forest the trees were a patchwork of color.

Noons were still warm and heavy, the sparse birdsong drowsed by heat, only the robins still disputing their territory in fierce red breastplates. Nights were colder and it was nice to snuggle under a blanket once more and listen to the tawny owls practicing their "hoo-hoos" across the empty fields.

I thought of Mistral; at this time of year, she had told us, the tide sometimes raced in and overwhelmed the fields till even the horses ran from it, their coats flecked with foam from the waves that roared in over the ribbed sands from the other side of the world. I thought of Traveler, safe I hoped in the ruined chapel tower; at this time of year there were still seeds and fruits in plenty, but soon would come the harsh winter, when the weakest would die. I thought of Basher: about now he would be looking for a soft, sandy place to dig himself in for the winter, till that funny shelled body of his was safe for the long sleep. . . .

I thought of them all, I missed them all, I prayed for them all.

And what of the fourth of the travelers to find his "home"? The others had accepted less than they deserved: would Gill, too, be cruelly rewarded? I hoped not, but I sensed there was something amiss, in spite of the fact that he had regained his sight, his home, his beloved.

One night after supper he caught at my sleeve and murmured urgently,

"At the back of the room you sleep in there is a stairway up to the walkway on the wall: meet me there in an hour. I need to talk to you."

My heart gave a great thump of apprehension: what was so important we couldn't discuss it openly?

I found the doorway he described, behind some stacked hurdles, but it was so small I could only just manage to squeeze my way up the dusty, cobwebbed spiral. Obviously it hadn't been used in years and there was a stout wooden door at the top, luckily bolted on my side, but it took all my strength to slide back the rusty iron.

Once out on the guarded walkway I felt a deal better; I had never liked confined spaces, and now I took deep breaths of the welcome fresh air. Not that it was all that invigorating: the night was cloudy, the atmosphere oppressive, as though we waited for a storm. Down in the courtyard the little chapel bell rang for nine of night and I could see one or two going for prayers. An owl hooted, far away in the forest; a dog barked from the cluster of huts beneath the wall. Somewhere a child wailed briefly, then all was quiet once more.

I leaned against the low parapet and rested my eyes on the darkness. I heard quick footsteps mounting the outside stair to my right but didn't turn; for a moment longer I felt I didn't want to know what Gill had to say, didn't want to become involved once more. Whatever it was, I had the feeling it would mean more heartache, one way or the other.

"Summer?"

"Here . . ." I turned and was immediately taken into an urgent, awkward embrace that had my nose squashed against his shoulder and the breath knocked out of me. I pushed him away as hard as I could.

"Are you mad—?"

He stepped back, but regained possession of my hands. "I'm sorry, I didn't mean . . . Look here, Summer, I can't stand this much longer, not being able to see you and speak to you! There is so much we must talk about, and I—"

"Hush!" I pulled my hands from his grasp. "If you yell like that you'll have everyone up here!" for his voice had risen with his anxiety. I looked down into the courtyard but all was quiet. "Now, just tell me—quietly—what on earth's the matter?"

"Everything."

"Don't be so dramatic! You are back home, safe and comfortable, you have your sight back, and are reunited with your betrothed—so what could possibly be wrong?"

He hesitated. "I don't know. . . . It's just that—that everything, everybody's changed. It's not what I expected. . . ."

My breathing slowed down a little. Silly fellow! "You've been away for over a year, you know! But they haven't done anything drastic like moving the house or burning down the forest, have they? Perhaps there are some new faces, old ones gone, different fields plowed, but—"

"It's not that. How can I explain it?" He ran his hand through his close-cropped hair. "Everything looks somehow smaller, shabbier, meaner!" he burst out.

"Shhh . . . That's easily explained. While you were away you'd built up a picture in your mind, that's all—like a dream. Things always look larger in dreams."

"But what about the people? My mother looks older, sort of—defeated. And I don't remember my father's beard having so much grey in it."

"But they are older: over a year older. So are you. . . . Life didn't just stand still, waiting for you to come home. They probably feel the same about you. You are thinner, browner, more restless, and have had enough adventures and mishaps to change anyone. You've got to have patience, time to settle in once again." I patted his arm. "There: lots of good advice! I'm afraid there's no other way I can help. . . ."

He turned away, gripped the parapet, stared out into the darkness. "Yes. Yes, there is."

"How? Do you want me to talk to them? I don't think they would take much notice of me."

"It's not that. . . . It's Rosamund." He exhaled heavily, as though he had been holding his breath, and turned back to me. "You see, I just don't love her anymore."

I was speechless. Of all the things I had expected him to say, this was the last.

"It happened as soon as I saw her again," he hurried on, as if now eager to tell everything as fast as possible. "Perhaps, as you say, I had built up an idealized picture of things in my mind, and especially her. It wasn't only that she looked—looked older, harder; it seemed she had changed in other ways, too. I hadn't remembered her as so overpowering and at the same time sickly-sweet. And I had forgotten her little mannerisms; things that I found once so enchanting now did nothing but irritate me. You must have noticed them, too."

Of course I had. But let him tell it in his own way.

"You know the sort of thing: the little cough to get attention, the way she keeps smoothing her throat to draw notice to its whiteness, how she holds her head to one side when she listens to you and opens her eyes wide like an owl's, the way she sucks her teeth. . . . She's stiff, unreal, mannered, like one of those jointed wooden puppets you can buy. . . . I can't explain it any better."

What could I say? I tried the same arguments I had used before, how it took everyone time to adjust, that he had changed too and there were probably things about him that annoyed her too, and all the while I had the horrible feeling that I knew just what he was going to say next, and I hadn't the slightest idea how to deal with it.

"But you are not like that, Summer! You are young, younger than I, and so full of life! If I had had the slightest idea what you were really like, if I hadn't been blind in more ways than one, then—then I should never have come back! Not unless and until I could have brought you back with me as my wife!"

He couldn't mean it! Not now; it was too cruel a twist of fate! For how many months had I worshiped him in secret, never once letting him know how I felt? If only . . . He couldn't see the tears on my cheek but I tried to keep them from my voice.

"You know it wouldn't have worked. I'm not your kind, would never fit into this kind of life. No, wait!" For he had moved forward to embrace me. "Besides, you could never have broken your betrothal vows. They are sacred things, as sacred as marriage itself, and you know it. The dowry has been paid, she has been accepted into your family, there is no going back now. In the eyes of God you are already wed."

"God could not be so cruel, not now when I have found my one, my true and only love! To hell with the dowry, that can be paid back. . . ." He took me in his arms, and I could smell the acrid sweat of emotion and anxiety. "The contract can be canceled. Come away with me, Summer! We can go back on the road, we managed before. Now I can see again I can find work somewhere farther south where no one will follow us." He tipped up my chin with one hand. "And don't tell me you have no fondness for me: I know you have!" and he bent his head and kissed me, at first soft and then hard and hungry.

It was my first real kiss; I had always wondered where the noses went, how the faces would fit, what it felt like to taste someone else. Now I knew, but even as my whole body seemed to melt against him, part of me knew it was wrong, wrong!

"Stop it, Gill! Let me breathe, let me think. . . . Please!"

He released me and I had to cling to the parapet, I was shaking so much. He took my hand. "I know it's sudden, my dearest one, but don't you see? It's the only way. Please say you will at least consider it. I have some moneys, not a lot, but enough to find us a safe haven for the winter. I swear to you that I will make it worth your while. Why shouldn't we both be happy instead of both miserable?"

There were a hundred, a thousand reasons why, but I couldn't think straight. "Give me time to think. . . . I don't know, right now I don't know." And then the words that must have been spoken so many times in the past by women far less surprised than I: "This is all so sudden!"

He bent and kissed my hands, one after the other.

"Of course, my love, but not more than a couple of days. I am being pressed already by Rosamund to name the wedding date. Tonight is Tuesday; I'll meet you here for your answer the same time on Thursday. In the meantime," he added, "I shall find it extremely difficult to avoid grabbing you and kissing you in front of everyone! I love you, my dearest. . . ."

I staggered back to my room down the stone stairs in a complete daze. At the bottom, by the light of a candle I had left burning, I saw two pairs of eyes staring up at me accusingly. Too much to expect that, between them, they didn't know exactly what had happened.

"I'm going to bed," I said firmly. "Right now. We'll talk in the morning, if you have anything you want to say."

The truth was that for a few precious hours, just a few, I wanted to hug to myself everything he had said, everything he had done, without dissipating the secret joy a jot by sharing or discussing it. If you leave the stopper off a vial of perfume it soon evaporates, and this love potion I had received tonight was the sweetest perfume in the world, and I had every intention of staying awake all night to conserve and savor every drop. . . .

"Breakfast," said the Wimperling succinctly, "is outside the door. As we didn't turn up for breakfast, they brought it to you."

I opened bleary eyes, for a moment lost to the day and hour. Then I remembered. But surely I couldn't have fallen asleep—

"What time is it?"

"Getting on for two hours after dawn, I reckon."

So much for spending the night awake, relishing the declaration of Gill's love! I must have fallen asleep almost at once and been tireder than I thought, for now I was grouchy, headachy, scratchy-eyed. The storm that had threatened last night hadn't broken after all and, like most animals, I still felt the oppression in the air, like a hand pressing down on the top of my head. And there was so much to do, so much to think about. . . .

We ate, what I don't remember, but I know the others had most of whatever it was. All the while the thoughts in my head danced up and down, round and about, like a cloud of midges, and as patternless.

"I'm going for a walk," I said abruptly. "You can come or stay as you wish."

We left the courtyard and passed the cluster of huts below the wall. Ahead stretched the long, straight road that led through the fields and orchards, past the fringes of the forest, to the gates of the demesne. I walked, not even noticing the surrounding landscape, just thumping my feet down one after the other, my mind a hopeless blank. It was an unseasonably hot day and at last sheer discomfort made me turn off to the shade of one of the still-unpicked orchards. I sank down on the long grass, leaned back against one of the gnarled trunks and sank my teeth into one of the small, sweet, pink-fleshed apples they probably used for cider. The Wimperling wandered off in search of windfalls, and the breeze brought faint and faraway the sound of the chapel bell ringing for noon.

Even Growch knew what that meant. "We've missed the midday meal," he said plaintively, sucking in his stomach.

"I know," I said unsympathetically.

"Ain't you got nuffin with you? Bit o' crust, cheese rind?"

"No. You had most of my breakfast, remember? Go away and look for beetles or bugs or something and don't bother me. I need to think," and promptly fell asleep once more, to awake only when the lengthening shadows brought with them a chill that finally roused me from sleep. The Wimperling lay by my side, the freshening breeze lapping his hide with the dancing shadows of the leaves above; Growch was lying on his back, snoring, his disgraceful stomach, pink, brown and black-patched, exposed to a bar of sunshine.

I sat up, suddenly feeling rested, alert, alive once more. I stretched until my bones cracked and twanged, then bounced to my feet and snatched another apple, sucking at the juice thirstily, then another, not caring whether I got stomachache. Time to walk back, or we should miss another meal, and now I felt hungry.

I realized I was enjoying the leisurely walk back, and spoke without thinking. "It'd be nice to be back on the road again. . . ."

Then began the Great Campaign, as I called it later, though the first few words were innocuous enough.

"Nice enough when the weather is like this," said the Wimperling. "But it's autumn already. All right for those with stamina and guts."

"Remember how cold it was last winter?" said Growch. "His Lordship—beggin' your pardon, lady—caught a cold what turned to pew-money?"

"Certainly doesn't like cold weather," said the Wimperling. "His sort are used to riding: never liked walking far."

"Remember how he used to complain about his feet?" said Growch. "Used to whinge about the food, too. . . ."

"That's the trouble with knights," said the Wimperling. "Only trained for one life. Give them a sword, a charger, a battle, and they're happy. In civilian life they can loose a hawk, sing a ballad—"

"Or flatter a lady . . ." said Growch.

"Easy enough for them to get accustomed to being waited on, having the best of everything—"

"Soon enough blame anyone what robs 'em of it—"

At last I realized where all this was leading, refused to listen, stopped up my ears. How *dared* they try and influence what I was going to do! It had nothing to do with them, it was between me and Gill.

The trouble was, their words remained in my consciousness, as annoying and insidious as the last of the summer fleas and ticks. And what they had said, exaggerated as it was, still held a grain of truth. Gill *had* grumbled a lot—but then he had had a right to. But would choice make it any easier for him to bear a simple life? Yes, he did catch cold easily, yes he was a bit soft, but he hadn't been used to the traveling life. Would he be any better prepared now? A small voice inside me whispered that it had been a new way of life for me, too, though perhaps I had made a better job of it, but I brushed the thought aside impatiently: everyone was different.

It was true, too, that the only life he had known was that of a knight, and that in spite of his brave words he would find it difficult to turn his hand to anything else. And that bit about flattering ladies: were the words he had spoken to me merely the courtesies he thought I would like to hear, not meant to be taken seriously? If he found it so easy to be turned from his betrothed, would a week or so in bad weather have him feeling the same way about me?

I got through the rest of the day somehow or other, but at dinner that night I found myself studying Gill's face for signs of what he was really like. Was his chin just a little bit weak, compared with his father's? Had he always looked so petulant when something displeased him, as it did that night when a particular dish was empty before it reached him? And if he now disliked his fiancée so much, why was he paying her such great attention? His fine new clothes certainly suited him: that was the third new surcoat I had seen him in. Who would carry all his gear if we were on the road once more?

That night I couldn't sleep at all. Hoping a little fresh air would help, I crept up the spiral stair to the walls again, but just as I drew back the bolts, greased earlier in anticipation of my meeting with Gill on the following night, I saw that the walkway was already occupied, although it must be near midnight. A man and a woman stood close by, talking softly. I was about to descend again when something about her stance made me believe I recognized the woman, and curiosity kept me where I was.

". . . that makes it so important to risk being seen?" I couldn't identify his voice, and he had his back to me.

"I had to see you! As things are, I have to be with him all the time. . . ." Rosamund's face was as pale as the moon that rode clear of cloud as she turned fully towards the man before her. "Robert, what are we going to do? I'm at least two months pregnant!"

28

I couldn't help a gasp of horror as I realized the implications of what she had just said, but they were so intent on each other that they didn't hear. Once again I knew I should retreat without further eavesdropping, but how could I? This concerned Gill's and my future so closely I *had* to listen.

"Two months, you say?" said Gill's father, after a pause. His voice never faltered: he might have been discussing the gestation period of a favorite horse.

"I have missed two monthly courses, yes. One could have been ignored perhaps, but I have always been as regular as an hourglass, and now there are further signs. . . ." A shrug of those cloaked shoulders. "It will start to show soon."

"Let me think. . . ." He started to pace up and down the walkway, up and back twice, his arms folded across his chest. How like Gill he walks, I thought. He came back to face her. "You were no virgin when I took you," he stated flatly. "How do I know . . . ?"

"Of course it's yours! You know it is. Whatever I did in the past has nothing to do with it."

He regarded her broodingly. "Maybe not, but you were already a practiced whore when you came here. You seduced me with sighs and words and gestures, and I believed you knew what you were doing, that there would be no harm in it. I am not in the habit of soiling my own midden."

"You were as eager as I," she said sulkily.

"Maybe . . . How come you never got caught before?"

"Medicines, herbs; they are not available here."

"Then it was either intentional, because you thought my son would never return, and you wished me to keep you as my mistress—"

"It was an accident. Do you think I wanted to spoil my figure on the chance you would accept the child? No: like you I gave way to something I could not help." She spoke with conviction, and apparently he accepted it.

"Then there are two ways to deal with this—three, if you count being sent home in disgrace. But I shall not do that. Your dowry has been paid, and some of it already spent. The second way is to seek out the witch in the wood, and try one of her potions—"

"I have already tried that. The maid you gave me was pregnant by one of the grooms, so I sent her for a double dose. It worked for her but not for me. Your child is lusty, Robert: it wants to live."

He thought for a moment. "Then it has to be the third way, and no delay. No one knows about this but us, so let's keep it that way, but I shall want your full cooperation. . . ."

She nodded. "You have it."

"Right. The first thing is to get my son to your bed now, tonight— no, listen to me! I will give you a potion that I have sometimes used when my wife has failed to excite me. Make sure he drinks it, and if you cannot tempt him to your bed, then visit his. He will be so befuddled he will not know whether he has or has not performed. He will sleep without memory, but make sure you are there beside him when he wakes. He is a simple man: he will believe whatever you say."

"And the child?"

"There are plenty of seven-month babes. And he could be away. . . . There are many errands I could send him on."

"But your wife . . . She would know."

"She will say nothing. Her only thought is of Gill, what would make him happy. She may suspect, but once the babe is born, she will accept it. And once he, and everyone else, is persuaded he has slept with you then the wedding can take place within the week."

"The sooner the better . . ." She moved forward and rested her hands on his shoulders. "You think of everything. I had rather it had been you, but I promise to make your son a good wife." She was smiling like a pig in muck. "And your son—*our* son—will be the next in line, after Gill. Quite something, don't you think?" She leaned forward and kissed him, and I noticed he didn't draw back, but rather folded his arms around her and returned her embrace. "And perhaps, another time?"

"Get away with you, hussy. . . ." but he didn't sound displeased. "Remember, my son mustn't suffer over this."

"Of course not! I am really quite fond of him. There will be no complaints from that quarter, I swear. I know some tricks that even that girl he traveled with would not know—which reminds me: I fancy he became quite close to her, and I would not wish her to distract him from what we have planned. I have caught him looking at her a couple of times as if he were quite ready to disappear with her again—and we can't have that, can we?"

Oh, Gill, you idiot! I thought, shrinking back into the shadows as far as I could go. She is much cleverer than you thought. . . .

"She shall be disposed of, if you play your part. By tomorrow morning I want to see everyone convinced that my son will be the father of your child."

"Disposed of?"

"An accident, a disappearance: what do you care? No problem. It will be in my interest as well as yours, remember? But first, you must do your part. Tomorrow I will take care of Winter, or Summer, whatever she calls herself. . . . Meet me in the chapel in ten minutes and I will give you the potion."

I started back down the stairs, carefully closing the door behind me, shocked and horrified by what I had just heard. First their arrant duplicity regarding Rosamund's pregnancy: what could I do? Rush and find Gill, tell him what I had heard? I didn't even know how to find him and if I did, would he believe me? I doubted it. Whatever happened, I realized that Gill's dream of running away with me was gone forever. If his father's plan succeeded, by tomorrow morning he would believe he had seduced a virgin, his betrothed, and would be honor bound to marry her as quickly as possible; in cases like these his knightly training would give him no choice, however much he fancied someone else. And had I the right to try and stop it, even if I could? That baby could not be born illegitimate; I was myself, and I knew how it felt, not to have a father and to be jeered at because my mother was a whore. It would be worse in the sort of household Gill's father ran, and I believed both he and the perfidious Rosamund would bring the child up as Gill's. He need never know, and I was sure he would make a good father.

So now the choice I had thought would be so difficult was taken from me. Why was it that with no decision to make, I now felt a great sense of relief? Did that mean that what had happened was for the best, that Gill was not, never had been meant for me? I should always remember his declaration of love, I thought, but now I need never discover he would change, or I would as we traveled the roads. It was as if he were dead to me already: I should just remember the best, and nurse a few sentimental regrets.

"Infatuation," said the Wimperling at my elbow. "Nothing like the real thing. You wait and see."

"What are you doing! You made me jump out of my skin!"

"Just wanted to remind you that we'd better not tarry—yes, I was listening to your thoughts—because I reckon they mean you harm. . . ."

Of course! How could I have forgotten. I had to be got out of the way, and that didn't mean a bag of gold and a lift to the nearest town, I knew that. Headfirst down the nearest well, a stab in the back, perhaps a deadly potion . . . It would have been better to leave right away but I wanted to be sure, quite sure, that there was no chance Rosamund had failed in her plan. I knew in my heart she would succeed, but something within me wanted to twist a knife in the wound already so sore in my heart. Besides, Sir Robert had said he would do nothing until the morning.

During that long night I packed everything securely into two bundles, one for the Wimperling, one for me. The only money we had left were the few coins tossed down for our performance before Gill's miraculous appearance on the first night, but I wasn't worried. The countryside was still full of apples, late blackberries, enough grain to glean to thicken a stew, fungi, and mushrooms. Besides we could always give a performance or two.

The last thing I did was to write to Gill: I felt he deserved some explanation, even if not the true one, and it might also serve to put his father off trying to pursue us. I tore a blank page from the back of my Boke and thought carefully.

"Gill:— I am sorry to leave without a farewell, but it is time I was on my way. Besides, I hate good-byes. Perhaps I should have confided my hopes to you earlier, but I have not had the chance to speak with you alone. . . ."

That should allay their suspicions, I thought.

"I am going back to Matthew, and will now accept his proposal. It will be a good match for me."

I paused, flicking the end of the quill against my cheek. Yes . . .

"Please thank your family for their hospitality. I wish you and your betrothed every happiness, and many sons."

I signed my name "Someradai" as it had been written in the church register at home. After some thought I scratched out "Gill" and substituted "Sir Gilman." There, that would do. I rolled it carefully and tied it with one of the ribbons Gill's mother had given me. I would leave it on the table.

Satisfied that I had done all I could until dawn, I snatched a couple of hours sleep, but was up and ready as soon as the kitchens opened. We might as well take something with us, so I made up some tale about spending the day out-of-doors, missing meals, etc., but everyone was only half-awake, so it wasn't difficult to help myself to a cold chicken, some sausages, a small bag of flour and a string of onions.

After taking these back and packing them, I slipped into the Great Hall for breakfast, as if everything was normal, the Wimperling and Growch with me as usual. We should have to eat as much as we could, for the other food would have to last some time.

I watched carefully as the family appeared, one by one, on the top table. First Sir Robert, yawning hugely, downing two mugs of ale before touching any food. He never even glanced in my direction. Next came Gill's mother, who picked listlessly at a manchet, dipping it in wine, her eyes downcast. Where, oh where was Gill?

At last he appeared, but I would not have recognized him. Even on our worst days on the road he had not looked so disheveled, haggard, outworn. Unshaven, tousled in spite of his cropped head, it seemed as though he had thrown his clothes together in a hurry, and as soon as he sat down next to his mother, he grabbed her arm and started whispering in her ear; no food, no drink, nothing. He didn't glance in my direction either.

Then came Rosamund, and as soon as she appeared she made the position quite clear. In an artfully disarranged dress, she yawned, rolled her eyes; her hair was unbound, her cheeks flushed, and as she made the obligatory curtsy to Sir Robert and his wife she pretended to stagger a little. She sat down next to Gill, and to everyone's fascinated gaze, proceeded to examine her arms and neck for imaginary bruises, smiling contentedly all the while. Above the neckline of her low-cut shift were strawberry bruises; love-marks. She could not have placed them there herself. She appeared to notice Gill for the first time, and her hands flew to her mouth and she gazed away as though she were ashamed.

It was a consummate performance, and it quite halted breakfast.

Eating and drinking were temporarily suspended as elbow nudged elbow and nods and winks were exchanged. The message was quite clear, even to those on the bottom tables, and there was a sigh of envious relief as she suddenly swamped him in her arms, pouting, grinning, cuddling up, murmuring in his ear. He looked half-awake, bemused, bewildered, but she leaned across and spoke to his parents, then she nudged him and, prompting as she went, she made him say what she wanted.

I had seen enough, and even as Sir Robert rose to announce that his son's wedding would take place a week hence, the animals and I were making our way back across the courtyard. Now the plotting was confirmed, I had no intention of finding myself suffocated in the midden or letting the Wimperling crackle nicely on a spit; Growch would escape anyway, but what use was that to the pig and me?

I loaded up the Wimperling and myself as quickly as I could and made our way to the gate. We were in luck; two carts were about to go down to the cider-apple orchards, farthest away from the house, and we accepted a lift; no one questioned our right to leave, though all the talk was of the coming wedding and who would be invited. It had been less than a half-hour since Rosamund's performance, yet it seemed everyone had a topic of conversation to last for days. I tried not to listen.

We were only a quarter mile from the forest when the wagon halted. Getting down I thanked them for our lift, and at a nudge and thought from the Wimperling, asked for the quickest road to Evreux, making sure they remembered the direction I had asked for.

"Now, make for the gates as fast as possible," said the Wimperling and within a quarter hour, breathless, we were on the road again. A couple of foresters were at work clearing the undergrowth, and once again, on the Wimperling's prompting, I asked the road to Evreux. Once out of earshot I asked him why the insistence on that road.

"Because if they come after us, they will waste time looking along that way," he answered tranquilly. "We will take the other road west just to throw them off the scent."

"I see. . . . In the note I wrote to Gill I said we were going to Matthew's, so everything is consistent. Clever pig!"

"But your knight won't get the note."

"Why not?"

"If he had done, then he wouldn't bother any further, and the road would be clear for his father to pursue you uninterrupted. Without it he will worry, perhaps insist he goes out with a search-party. . . . Sir Robert won't have it all his own way, and it will give us a better chance."

I hadn't considered this: the Wimperling was cleverer than I thought.

He must also know who I was writing to. How did pigs know things like that?

"But what did you do with the letter?"

"I ate it. Ribbon and all."

"Did it taste nice?" asked Growch interestedly.

"No."

"Oh."

"But why should anyone come after us now?" I questioned. "Sir Robert and Rosamund have everything as they want it, surely?"

He didn't answer for a moment, then he said: "Just suppose you had been bothered by a mosquito all night, but hadn't caught it? Then in the morning you saw it again, ready to swat? Would you leave it, on the off chance it would disappear, or would you annihilate it there and then, so there was no further chance of it biting?"

"I see. . . . At least, I think I do."

"All that matters to Sir Robert now is that his son is born legitimate, and no one to question it or deflect his son's interest. He is a very proud man, and to ensure this he would do almost anything, believe me."

The Wimperling wouldn't even let us stop to eat at midday; instead we had to march on, chewing at the chicken. I was getting crosser and crosser as we approached the fork in the road we had turned off before, the right-hand fork leading to Evreux, the left to the west. I was about to demand a rest when we came across a swineherd grazing his half-dozen charges along the fringes of the forest.

By now I knew what question we were supposed to ask. He pointed the way to Evreux, but as soon as we left him at the turn in the road the Wimperling directed us into the trees to double back.

"Why? Can't we leave it a little longer? This is a good road, and so far no one had come after us. . . ."

"You've still got a lot to learn about human nature! Do as I say. . . ."

We crept back through the trees till we were almost opposite the fork in the road again, and skulked down behind some bushes. Ahead I could see the swineherd patiently prodding his pigs.

"Now what?"

"We wait."

Nothing happened for five, ten minutes, a quarter hour. Then I heard them: hooves thudding down the road from the De Faucon estate. A moment later two horsemen clattered by, wearing swords but no mail. They halted by the swineherd and one called out: "Seen a girl on the road with a couple of animals?"

The swineherd pointed in the direction we had supposedly gone, but when asked how long ago he looked blank; time obviously meant little to him. The horsemen rode off in the direction of Evreux and in a moment were out of sight.

I stood up. "Gill might have sent them. Why should we hide?"

"They would hardly have come seeking you with an invitation to the wedding armed with swords and daggers! Be sensible. It's as I said; Sir Robert wants to be rid of you."

I had the sense to become frightened. "Then, what do we do?"

"Once they find you are not on the road they have taken, they will come back and take the western road. And if they don't find us, others will be sent out. So, we go back to the estate."

"You must be mad! That's straight back into danger!"

"Not at all. The last place they would look is on their own doorstep. Come on: there's a good five miles to go before sundown!"

29

So, using the road, but dodging back into the forest when we thought we heard anything, we made our way back to the estate. We had one more narrow escape: Growch was fifty yards ahead, the Wimperling the same distance behind, and their danger signals came at the same moment. Luckily I had time to hide, only to find that the first couple of horsemen had ridden back, to meet up with a fresh contingent of four who had come straight from Sir Robert. They halted so near my hiding place I could smell both their sweat and that of their lathered animals.

"Find anything?" asked the leader of the second band.

"They took the road to Evreux, according to a peasant we met, but we went a good five miles down and no sign of them. Another fellow coming back from the town reported a wagon going the other way, but we saw no sign of it."

"Fresh instructions: Sir Robert found a door or something leading up to the walk-away, and has reason to believe the girl may be wise to the pursuit. Go back the way you came, search along the way for more clues. We are taking the western road. Orders are the same: lose 'em, permanently!"

"Jewels still missing?"

"So the lady says."

"How's the boy taking it?"

"State of shock. Can't believe it. I fancy he was sweet on her. Can't say as I blame him: know which one I'd've preferred."

And they rode off in the direction of the fork in the road, leaving me in a state of disbelief. So that was Sir Robert's excuse: I was supposed to have stolen some jewels! I realized that it would have made no difference what I had written; valuables would still have disappeared, and I should have been to blame. So now there was a price on my head, and death the reward. No turning back, however much I might have wanted to.

I wondered when the jewels would conveniently turn up again—or would Gill's father believe it worth the game to leave them buried or whatever, and buy Rosamund some more?

Once we reached the demesne, the Wimperling led us along deer tracks through the forest, at a convenient distance from the manor house. We described a great loop around the demesne, going short of food because I couldn't light fires, though the Wimperling and Growch were quite happy with raw sausages. On the third day the Wimperling declared us free of the de Faucon estate, and we found a road of sorts.

At the first village we came to, two days later, I threw caution to the winds, and spent far more than I intended on bought food, luxuriating on pies and roasted meat. In the next village and the next I recouped some of the results of my spendthrift ways with a performance, but villagers have little enough to spend at the best of times, and now the winter was fast approaching.

Which led to the question of where we were headed.

All I had thought about up to now had been escaping Sir Robert, but now was the time to consider our future. I knew Growch had said he wanted a warm fire, a family and plenty to eat, and I had set off on this whole enterprise with the thought of finding a complaisant and wealthy husband, but as far as I could see, neither of us were nearer our goal, once I had refused Matthew's offer. And what of the Wimperling? He had never asked for a destination, had seemed content to follow wherever we went. But we couldn't just go on wandering like this: if nothing else we had to find winter quarters, and soon.

The question of which way to go came up naturally enough. One morning we stood at a crossroads; all roads looked more or less the same, and I had no particular feeling about any of them, except that south would be warmer, and it might be easier to over-winter in or near some town.

"Which way?" I asked the others, not really expecting an answer, for Growch was a follower rather than a leader, and the Wimperling had never expressed a preference. Now, however, he did have something to say.

"Er . . . I'd rather like to discuss that," he said diffidently. "Perhaps we could sit down."

"Lunchtime anyhow," said Growch, looking up at the weak sun. "Got any more o' that pie left?"

"We finished that yesterday. Cheese, apples, bean loaf, cold bacon—"

"Yes."

The Wimperling chose the apples and I munched on the cheese.

"Right, Wimperling, what did you have in mind?"

He still seemed reluctant to ask. "When—when you so kindly rescued me," he began, "I said I would like to tag along because there was nowhere special I wanted to go. . . ."

I nodded encouragingly. "And now there is?"

"There wasn't then, but there is now. Yes." He sat back on his haunches, looking relieved. "Let me explain. When I was little I was brought up as a pig and believed I was one—in spite of the wings and the other bits that didn't quite fit." He held up one foot, and looked at the claws, much bigger now. "See what I mean? Well, ever since then as I have been growing I have felt more and more that I wasn't a pig. What I was, I didn't quite know, though I had my suspicions. Then, that night when we crossed the border, I thought I knew. And the feeling has been growing stronger ever since."

"Can you tell us?"

He shuffled about a bit. "I'd rather not, just yet. In case I'm terribly wrong . . . But I should like you to come with me, to find out. You might find it quite interesting, I think."

I looked at Growch, who was practically standing on his head trying to get a piece of rind out of his back teeth. No help there.

"Of course we will come. Where do you want to go? How far away is it?"

"One hundred and twelve miles and a quarter west-southwest," he said precisely. "Give or take a yard or so."

I flung my arms about his neck, laughing, then planted a kiss on his snout.

"How on earth can you be so—"

But before I had finished my sentence an extraordinary explosion took place. The Wimperling literally zoomed some twenty feet into the air vertically, then whizzed first right and then left and then in circles, almost faster than the eye could see. As he was now considerably larger than I was, I was tumbled head-over-heels and Growch disappeared into a bush, rind and all.

The whole thing can only have lasted some fifteen seconds or so, but it seemed forever. I curled up in a ball for protection, my fingers in my ears, my eyes tight shut, until an almighty thump on the ground in front of me announced the Wimperling's return to earth.

I opened my eyes, my ears and finally my mouth. "You nearly scared the skin off me! What in the world do you think you're *doing*?" I asked furiously. Then: "You're—you're *different*!"

He looked as if someone had just taken him apart and then reassembled him rather badly. Everything was in the right place, more or less, but the pieces looked as if they might have been borrowed from half a dozen other animals. His ears were smaller, his tail longer, his back scalier, his snout bigger, his chest deeper, his stomach flatter, his claws more curved, and the lumps on his side where he hid his wings looked like badly folded sacks. He looked less like a pig than ever, while still being one, and his expression was pure misery.

My anger and fright evaporated like morning mist. "Oh, Wimperling! I'm so sorry! You look dreadful—was it something I said? Or did?"

His voice had gone unexpectedly deep and gruff, as if his insides had been shaken up as well. "You kissed me. I told you once before never to do that again. . . . Remember?"

I did, now. "Sorry, sorry, sorry! It's just that—just that when one feels grateful or happy or loving it seems the right thing to do. For me, anyway." I thought. "It didn't have the same effect on Gill. And, come to that, I've never kissed Growch. . . ."

"Who wants kisses, anyway?" demanded the latter, who had crept out from his bush, minus rind, I was glad to see. "Kissin's soppy; kissin's for pups and babies an' all that rubbish!" Something told me that in spite of the words he was jealous, so I picked him up and planted three kisses on his nose.

"There! Now you're one ahead. . . ."

He rubbed his nose on his paws and then sneezed violently. "Gerroff! Shit: now you'll have me sneezin' at night. . . . Poof!" He nodded towards the Wimperling. "An' if that's what a kiss can do, then I don' wan' no more, never!"

I turned back to the Wimperling. "Better now?"

He nodded. "Think so . . ." His voice was still deep, and if I hoped he would regain his old shape gradually, I was to be disappointed. "As I was saying, before all—this—happened—" He looked down at his altered shape. "I should like to go to the place where it all started. The place where I was hatched, born, whatever . . . The Place of Stones."

This sounded interesting. "And is this the place that you said was a hundred miles or so to the west-something?"

He nodded.

I wasn't going to miss this, hundred miles or no. "Will you set up your home where you were born?" "Hatched" still sounded silly. Pigs aren't hatched.

"No. It will merely be the place from where I set out on a longer journey, to the place where my ancestors came from."

"A sentimental journey, then," I said.

"An essential one. Without going back to the beginnings I will not have my coordinates."

"Yer *what*?"

"Guidelines, dog. Itinerary to humans."

Growch scratched vigorously. "Me ancestors go back as far as me mum, and I doubt if even she knew who me dad was, and as for me guidelines . . . I follows me nose." And he accompanied the said object into the bushes, his tail waving happily.

"And how far is it to where your ancestors came from?"

"Many thousands of miles," said the Wimperling. "A journey only I can take. But I should be glad of your company as far as the Place of Stones. . . ."

"You have it," I said. We sat quiet for a moment, and I suddenly realized that my conversations had been, for a long time, on a different level with the Wimperling than with the others. He didn't just "talk" in short sentences about the food or the weather, he communicated with me as though we were two equal beings, talking about feelings and emotions, even philosophizing a little. He wasn't really like an animal at all—

"And then you will be free to seek that husband of yours," continued the Wimperling, as though I had just said something. "Will you tell him your real name?"

I gazed at him blankly. "My *real* name? What do you mean? My name is Summer—well, Somerdai."

"The name on the register, as you keep telling yourself. Your birth was recorded by the priest but he never knew the exact date. So he wrote 'Summer day,' only he ran the letters together and misspelled them because he was an old man. . . . But when you saw it written down you seized on the name, as a convenient way of burying deeper the hurt when you learned your real, given name. . . ."

I was stunned. How did he know about the register? But it was my name, it was, it was! If I'd had another, then my mother wold have called me by it instead of "girl," or "daughter" as she always did.

"I know because the memory is still there inside you," he said, "hurting to get out. Thoughts like that escape sometimes when you are asleep because they want to be out in the open. I have become used to your thoughts in the time we have traveled together. You have tried to kill the memory because you are ashamed, but let it go and you will feel better. I know, because I am not what they called me, Wimperling, and when my new name comes I shall be a different person."

A nasty, horrid picture was forming in my mind, however hard I tried to stifle it, cry "Go away! I don't want to remember. It happened to someone else, not me!" A child, a girl of four or five, a fat little girl, was playing on the doorstep as one of her mother's clients came to the door. And the mother said to the child: "Go and play for a while, girl. . . ." And the man said: "Why don't you call her by her given name?"

". . . and my mother said: 'How can I call that shapeless lump with the pudding-face *Talitha* when she is neither graceful nor beautiful, nor will ever be? I was pregnant when—when her father died, and he had made me promise to give her that name if it were a girl. Of course I agreed, never expecting she would be so plain and clumsy!' " I was crying now, hot tears of shame and remembered humiliation. "How could you remind me! I had forgotten, I didn't remember, it *hurts*!"

"And that is why you stuffed the memory away for so long, just because you were afraid of the hurt. But it was a long time ago, and things—and people—change. Now you have let it out, you will heal, believe me, and be whole." He hesitated. "I will not be with you much longer, so please forgive me. I did it for you."

"Yes, yes, I know you did. . . ." I tried the name on my tongue. Now I remembered my father had chosen it, it seemed right. "I feel better already. Thanks, Whimper . . . But you said you weren't. Aren't . . . you know what I mean! What is *your* real name?"

He shook his head. "That's the exciting thing. I don't know yet. It comes with the change, the rebirth if you like. All I know is that I took a form and a name that was convenient at the time, in order to survive. That's how I remember how far it is, counting the steps we traveled when they took me away. And that is how I can guide you there."

"Then what are we waiting for? Let's get going. Come on Growch, wherever you are: we are going to a place full of stones, and you can christen every one!"

"Oh, I don't think so," said the Wimperling. "These stones are—different."

We were now in the last couple of weeks of October, and the weather stayed fine. We made leisurely progress, ten or twelve miles a day, but the terrain changed dramatically with every turn of the road. Villages became smaller, more isolated, there were fewer farms and no great houses or castle. The land became rocky, wilder, less hospitable, and now, instead of dusty lanes, there were sheep tracks, moorland paths, great stretches of heather, thyme, gorse and broom. A barren land as far as crops went, but with a wild beauty of its own.

The winds blew with no hindrance, whirling my hair into great tangles and carrying in their arms gulls, buzzards, crows, peregrines and merlin. The undergrowth hid fox, hare, coney, stoat, weasel and an occasional marten; under our feet the ground was springy with mosses, lichen, heather, bilberry, juniper, cotton grass and bracken, the latter the color of Matthew's hair, Saffron's cat-coat. Away from the paths the going was tough; wet feet, scratched legs and turned ankles the penalty for trying a shortcut.

We came upon a small village, some seven days before the end of the month, and the Wimperling advised me to stock up. They had only had a small harvest, but were eager to have coin to buy in some grain, so I used what little I had left and was rewarded with cheese, salt pork, honey, turnip, onion and small apples, till I could hardly stagger away under the weight. Once away from the village however, the Wimperling insisted I load most of it on his back.

"My strength is much greater now I approach the end of my journey."

"So is your size," I said, for now he was truly enormous: over twice as big as me, length and breadth.

"Ah, but I have much to hide. . . ."

"If you hides it much longer you'll burst," said Growch. "If'n I had that load abroad I reckon me legs'ud be worn to stumps."

"Really? I was under the impression that is what had happened already. . . ."

The next day we topped a rise in the land and there were the Stones in the distance. Not just ordinary stones, but ones of great size and power, even from miles away. I could feel them now from where I stood, both repelling and attracting at the same time. We had already passed the odd standing stone and the stumps of plundered circles, but there for the first time was a veritable forest, a city of stones: circles, lanes, avenues, clumps; grey and forbidding, they pointed cold stone fingers at the sky, now whipped by a westerly into a roil of rearing clouds. Down here at ground level it was still relatively calm, but the heavens were racing faster than man could run.

The Wimperling heaved a great tremble of anticipation and satisfaction. "The Place of Stones starts here. Half a day's journey and we are there."

Briefly I wondered how we were going to find our way back to civilization without our guide, but I held my tongue, sure he would have a solution.

That night we sheltered in a dell, the freshening wind creaking the branches of the twisted pine and rowan above our heads, the latter's leaves near all gone, the few berries blackened. I fell asleep uneasily, with Growch tucked against my side, to wake half a dozen times. And each time it was to see the Wimperling standing still as the stones, his gaze fixed westward, the wind flapping his small ears, his snout questing from side to side and up and down, as though reading a message in the night only he could comprehend.

In the morning the wind had swung to the northwest and it was noticeably chillier. After breakfast, as I strapped the Wimperling's burdens to his back, I noticed how hot his skin felt, as if he was burning from some internal fever; I made some silly quip about burning my fingers, but I don't think he even heard. His gaze was fixed on the journey ahead, and he didn't seem ill in any way, only impatient to be off.

The further we went, the more stones; some upright, others broken, a few lying full length, yet more with a drunken lean like the few trees in this bare landscape, which all grew away from the prevailing westerlies, like little hunched people with their hoods up and their cloaks flapping in the breeze.

More and more stones, and yet we never seemed to get near enough to them to touch. There they were to left and right, ahead, behind, distinguishable apart by their different shapes, height, angle, markings and yet as soon as I headed towards one I found I had mysteriously left it behind, or it had grown more distant. I even felt as though I passed the same monolith a dozen times as if we were walking in circles through a gigantic maze, but the Wimperling still trotted forward confidently and the ring was quiet on my finger.

At last we came to a great avenue of stone, and there in the distance was a huddle of ruined buildings on a small rise. The Wimperling stopped and looked back at us. "There it is," he said simply. "Journey's end."

It didn't look like much to me, and looked less so the nearer we approached. It was the remains of what had obviously been a small farm—cottage, barn, stable and sty—and the buildings were rapidly crumbling. The thatch had gone, apart from some on one corner of the cottage, the broken-shuttered windows gaped like missing teeth and all walls and fencing had been broken down. The place was deserted, no people, no animals and, perhaps because it was the only sign of civilization we had seen in a couple of days, the desolation seemed worse than it probably was.

"And all this in less than a year," said the Wimperling, as if to himself. "They angered the Stones. . . ." Then he turned to us. "You must be hungry and tired. And cold, too. Come with me and don't be afraid. I promise you will feel better in a little while."

I hoped so. Just at that moment I felt I had had more than enough of the mysterious Stones: all I wanted was to find some cozy corner inside where I could curl up and forget outside.

He led us to that part of the cottage adjoining the barn where there was still a corner of roofing. The room itself was about twelve feet square, with a central hearth, but I dragged over enough stones to make another fireplace under the remaining thatch. There was plenty of wood lying about, and I soon had a cheerful blaze going, the smoke obliging by curling up and disappearing without hindrance. I found a stave in one corner and, binding some heather to the end, made a broom stout enough to sweep away the debris from our end of the room. Then I went out and gathered enough bracken to make a comfortable bed for later. The Wimperling showed me where a small spring trickled away past the house, and I filled the cooking pot and set about dinner.

I had the bone from the salt bacon, root vegetables and onion, and was just adding a pinch or two of herbs when the Wimperling strode in with a carefully wrapped leaf in his mouth. Inside were other leaves, some mushrooms and a powder I couldn't identify, but on his nod I added them all to the stew, and the aroma that immediately spread around the room had me salivating and Growch's stomach rumbling. I had a little flour left so put some dough to cook on hot hearthstone. I tasted the stew, added a little salt, then walked outside to join the Wimperling and Growch, who were variously gazing up at a waxing moon, some three or four days off full, riding uneasily at anchor among the tossing clouds, and searching the old midden for anything edible.

"Will it rain tonight?"

"Probably," said the Wimperling. "But we have shelter."

"Is it—time? Are you going tomorrow?"

"No, the time is not quite right. A day or two."

"We haven't got much food left. . . ."

"Don't worry. The food will last."

And that night it seemed he was right. However much we ate—and Growch and I stuffed ourselves silly on a stew that tasted like no other I had ever come across—the pot still seemed full. The Wimperling said he wasn't hungry, but he did have a nibble of bread.

As we sat round in the firelight, the fire damped down by some turves of peat I had found in the barn, I felt sleepier than I had for ages; not exhausted but happily tired, the sort of tiredness that looks forward to dream. Growch was yawning at my feet, stretching then relaxing, his eyes half-shut already.

"Gawdamighty! I could sleep fer days. . . ."

"Why not?" said the Wimperling.

"He'd die of starvation in his sleep," I said, laughing, and stifled a yawn.

"Not necessarily. What about those animals who sleep all winter?"

"Good idea," I said. "Wake me in March. . . ." And as I wrapped myself tight in my father's old cloak and lay down on the springy bracken bed, Growch at my feet, I gazed sleepily at the glowing embers of the fire, breaking into abortive little flames every now and again, or creeping like tiny snakes across the peat, till all merged into a pattern that repeated itself, changed a fraction, moved away, came back. Soothing patterns, familiar patterns, patterns in the mind, sleep-making patterns . . .

When I finally came to I found it was already mid-afternoon, and Growch was still snoring. The fire smoldered under a great heap of ash that seemed to have doubled overnight. I broke the bread, stale now, into the stew, and put it on to heat up. Then I went outside to relieve myself and look for the Wimperling, but he was nowhere about. I went down to the spring for a quick, cold wash, for I still felt sleepy, then combed out my tangled hair. Still no sign of the Wimperling. He couldn't have gone without saying goodbye, surely?

It had obviously rained overnight, for the ground was damp and the heather wetted my ankles as I lifted my skirts free from the moisture. After calling out three or four times I shrugged and went back to dish out the stew, leaving a good half for our companion. I cleaned out the bowls, banked up the fire and went outside again. The wind was still strong, but it seemed to be veering back towards the west and the biting chill had gone.

Something large trotted out of the shadows. "Were you looking for me?"

"Wimperling! Where have you been?"

"Around and about . . . Did you sleep well?"

"Like a babe! Your supper is waiting."

"I'm fine without, thanks." He gazed up at the sky, where the moon seemed to bounce back and forth between the clouds like a blown-up bladder. "Tonight I can sup off the stars and drink the clouds. . . ."

"And what about the moon?" I teased, looking up at where she hung, free of cloud at last. "A bite or two of—Oh, my God!"

I felt as if I had been kicked in the stomach. "I don't understand!" Suddenly I was afraid. "Last night when I went to sleep the moon was three or four days short of full. And now . . ."

And now the moon was full.

30

Yes," said the Wimperling, following my gaze. "You have slept through four days. 'Like a babe' is what I think you said."

Just like that. Like saying I overslept. Or missed Mass.

There was still a clutch of fear in my stomach. "I don't understand! Magic? How? Why?"

"No magic, just a pinch of special herbs in your stew. They slowed down your mind and your body, therefore you needed less breath, less food, less drink. As to why . . . As you said, there was little food left, and I had some things to do while you slept."

I still felt scared that anyone's body could be so used without their knowledge and permission; suppose, for instance, the dose had been too strong? And did one age the same while in that sleep? Did one dream? I couldn't remember any.

As usual, he knew what I was thinking.

"I wouldn't hurt you for the world, you know that. The dose was carefully measured. All it meant was that you and the dog had a longer rest than usual, that's all. And saved on food. No, you haven't gained time and yes, you did dream. One has to. But you don't always remember."

"What—things—did you do?"

"I will show you. When—when I am gone, if you travel due west for two days, you will come to a road that leads either south or east. You will have enough food to last till you come to another village. As to coinage—Follow me!"

He led us back to the room we had slept in, and there, in a heap on the floor, were twenty gold coins.

"It takes time to make those," he said.

I ran the coins through my fingers. "Are they real?" They felt very cold to the touch.

"As real as I can make them. More solid than faery gold, which can disappear in a breath. But you must be careful how you use them. As long as they are used honestly for trade they will stay as they are, although each time they change hands they will lose a little of their value. A coating of gold, you might say. But if they are stolen or used dishonestly, then the perpetrator will die."

"How are they made?"

"White fire, black blood, green earth, yellow water."

None of which I had ever come across, but I supposed anything was possible with a flying pig-not-a-pig. A large flying pig. Very large, Now he almost reached my shoulder: those four days sleep of mine had made him almost twice as big again.

"You will soon be too big for your skin, you know," I said jokingly.

He looked at me gravely. "I hope so. . . . Come and see what else I have been doing. You'd better make up the fire, while you're at it."

"I've been letting it die down. I can light it again for breakfast. It's not cold."

"Don't you remember what your mother taught you? On no account let the house fires go out on the eve of Samhain, lest Evil gain entry. . . ."

"Samhain? All Hallows' Eve?"

He nodded, and I suddenly realized that it had been exactly a year ago that I had made a funeral pyre of our house for my mother and had set out on my adventures. A year, a whole year . . . Somehow it seemed longer. That other life seemed a hundred years and a million miles away. I couldn't even clearly recall the girl I had been then: this Summer was a totally different person. For one thing she had a name—two names, in fact. For another, this person would not have been content to sit by the fire and dream, and eat honey cakes till she burst. In fact, I couldn't now remember when I had the last one. This girl now talked to animals, tramped the roads, thought less of her own bodily comforts and more of others, and had learned a great deal that was not taught in books. And hadn't used one single item of her expensive education that she could recall . . .

I threw a couple more logs on the fire and then followed the Wimperling out and across the yard to where the pigsties had once been, an unusually subdued Growch tailing us. The Wimperling stepped over what had once been one of the walls of the sty, and now in the middle, rising some six feet high, was a newly built cairn of stones.

"Did you build this?"

"Takeoff point," he said.

I looked at him. He seemed so different from the little persecuted pig I had stolen from the fair and run off with tucked under my arm. Not just the size, which was phenomenal; he had also grown in confidence over the months I had known him. He was mature, patient, wise, and had saved us more than once with courage and good advice. I had lost my little piglet to an adult one, and wasn't sure whether to be glad or sorry.

"What are you going to do?"

"You will see. First let me tell you a little of what happened when I was young. . . ."

I sat down on part of the old wall and listened, Growch at my feet.

"This is where I was born. The very spot I hatched." "Hatched" again, as though he truly believed he had come from an egg. "I was raised, as you know, among a litter of innumerable little piglets, although I didn't grow exactly the same and stayed the runt of the litter. As I told you, I would probably have made a fine dish of suckling pig if the farmer hadn't discovered my stubs of wings, and sold me. After weeks of torment you found me, and the rest you know."

"But if you were unhappy here, and pretending to be something you were not, why come back?"

"Because this place is a Place of Power. It was arranged that I start my breathing life here, and also meant that I eventually leave from here for the land of my ancestors. The fact that a farmer built a pigsty over my hatching place was an accident that couldn't have been foreseen. However, once I had been sold, the Stones made sure they left and destroyed what remained of the farm. The Stones are my Guardians, they have watched and waited for a hundred years for my birth and then the Change."

"What?" I couldn't believe what I was hearing. He was fantasizing. "You waited to be born for a *hundred* years?"

"Legends have it as a thousand, but that is an exaggeration. A hundred is the minimum, though, but the warmth of the sty above me accelerated things somewhat and I only had ninety-nine years. This hadn't given my personality enough charge to resist the nearness of the other piglets, so I adapted their bodily conformation to give myself time to acclimatize before the Change. Exactly a year, in fact."

I was utterly bewildered. I had lost him somewhere. Hatching, a hundred years, Stones of Power, a "change," guardians . . . I seized on one question. "You say the stones around us are Stones of Power? What does that mean?"

"Listen. Listen and feel. Where we are now is the centre of it all, like the center of a spider's web. If you hung like a hawk from the sky you would see the pattern. This is not the only Center of Power, of course: they exist in other countries as well. Because of their special magic they have been used since understanding began for birth, breeding, death, religions, sacrifice, healing. I say again: listen and feel. . . ."

I tried. At first, although the night was still as an empty church, I could hear nothing special. Then there was a growl from Growch and I began to feel something. A low, very faint vibration, as though someone had plucked the lowest string of a bass viol, waited till the sound died away, then touched the silent string and still found it stirring under their finger. I put both hands flat on the ground and found I could hear it as well, though the sound was not on one note, it came from a hundred, a thousand different strings, all just on the edge of hearing. I felt the sound both through my body and in my ears at the same time, both repelling and attracting, till I felt as if I had been a rat shaken by a terrier. Beside me Growch was whimpering, lifting first one paw then the other from the ground—

"Understand now?" asked the Wimperling, and with his voice the noise and vibration faded and was still. "That is why I had to come back. Had my life been as it should, my hatching taken place at the right time, had I not become part pig, I should have needed no one. But you were instrumental in saving my life, you have fed and tended me, and now I need you as the final instrument to cut me from my past. I cannot be rid of this constriction without you," and he flexed and stretched and twisted and strove as though he were indeed bound by bonds he could not loose.

"Anything," I said. "Anything, of course. How soon—how soon before you change?" I wanted to ask into what, but didn't dare. I didn't think I wanted to know, not just yet, anyway. In fact, just for a moment I wished I was anywhere but here, then affection and common sense returned: nothing he became could harm us.

He glanced up at the sky. The moon was calm and full and clear and among the stars there ran the Hare and Leveret, the Hunger, his Dog and the Cooking Pan. There were the Twins, the Ram, the Red Star, the Blue, the White. . . . No wind as yet, night a hushed breath, as if it, too, waited as we did.

Around us the ruins of the farm, all hummocks and heaps, farther away the Stones, seeming to catch from the moon and stars a ghostly radiance all their own, casting their shadows like fingers across the heath, so the land was all bars of silver and black like some strange tapestry bearing a pattern just out of reach of comprehension. And yet if one looked long enough . . .

"Five minutes," said the Wimperling. "When the shadow of the cairn touches the nearest Stone. Climb up with me and you will see. . . . That's right. See, there is room for us both at the top."

Growch yipped beneath us, and scrabbled with his claws at the stone but could get no further.

"This is not for you, dog," said the Wimperling. "Be patient." He turned to me. "Do you have your sharp little knife with you?"

"Of course." I touched the little pouch at my waist where it always lay, wondering why he wanted to know.

"Then it is farewell to you both, Girl and Dog. My thanks to you, and may you find what you seek soon." He took a deep breath. "I had not thought partings would be so hard. . . . Are you ready, Talitha?"

"Yes," I said, wondering what was to happen next. The shadow was creeping nearer and nearer to the Stone. . . . "At least I think I am."

"Then take out your knife, and when I count to ten, but not before, cut my throat. One . . ."

31

Two . . ."

"What are you *talking* about?"

"Three . . . Four . . ."

"I'm doing no such thing! How could I possibly hurt you?"

"Five—"

"Listen, *listen*! If I dig this knife into you—"

"Six—"

"—you will *die*! I thought you said you were going to—"

"Seven!"

"I won't, I can't!"

"Eight!"

"Wimperling, Wimperling, I can't kill you!"

"Nine! Do it! You *must*!"

"I love you too much to—"

"Do it *now*, before it's too late! Ten . . ."

And there was such a look of agonized entreaty on his face that I brought the knife out and drew it across his skin. The tiny gash started to bleed, a necklace of dark drops in the moonlight, and I couldn't do any more. I had rather cut my own throat.

"Talitha, Summer—there are only a few seconds left!" His voice was full of an imprisoned anguish. "*Please* . . ."

"I *can't*! Stay a pig: I'll care for you always, I promise! and I flung away the knife, threw my arms around his neck and kissed him.

There was a tremendous bang! like a thunderbolt, a great blast of hot air, and I was toppled off the cairn. The moon and stars were blotted out and I lay stunned, conscious only of a huge tumult in the air, as if a storm had burst right over my head. I could hear Growch yelping with terror, but where was the Wimperling?

I sat up, my head spinning, and saw an extraordinary sight. The body of the flying pig was hurtling around the cairn like a burst bladder, every second getting smaller and smaller. Pony-size, man-size, hound-size, piglet-size, until at last it collapsed at my feet, a tiny bundle no bigger than my purse, and the moon appeared again.

Crawling forward I picked up the pathetic little bundle and held it to my breast, rocking back and forth and sobbing. Once again I had been asked to help, once again it had all gone wrong. At least I had never physically harmed any of the others, but there was my precious little flying pig burst into smithereens, and all I had left was a split piece of hide with the imprint of a face and a string of tail, four little hooves and two small pouches where his wings had been—

"Look up! Look up . . . !" The voice came from the air, from the clouds that were now massing to the west, from the Stones—

The Stones! They were alight, they burned like candles. One after the other their tips started to glow with a greenish light as if they were tracking another great shadow that glowed itself with the same unearthly light as it swooped, banked and turned, dived in great loops from sky to earth and back again. The sky was full of light and there was a smell like the firecrackers I had once seen, and a beating sound like dozens of sheets flapping in a gale.

Again came the voice: "Look up! Look up!" but I could only hug the remains of the Wimperling, little cold pieces of leather, and cry. Growch crept to my feet from wherever he had been hiding, whimpering softly.

"Great gods! What was it? Where's the pig? Are you all right? C'mon, let's get back inside. . . ."

But even as he whined there was a sudden rush of air that had me flat on my back again and there, balancing precariously on the cairn above us, wings flapping to maintain balance, clawed feet gripping the shifting stones was a—

Was a great dragon!

I think I fainted, for darkness rushed into my eyes and I felt my insides gurgling away in a spiral down some hole, like water draining away and out down a privy, and there was a peculiar ashy smell in my nostrils. Then everything steadied, I decided I had been seeing things because of the terror of the night, and cautiously opened one eye. . . .

It was still there.

The great wings were now quiet at its sides, and the scaly tail with the arrow-like tip was curled neatly around its clawed feet. The great nostrils were flared, as if questing my scent, the lips were slightly curved back above the pointed teeth, but the yellow eyes with the split pupils seemed to hold quite a benign gaze. I could see its hide rise and fall as it breathed.

I had never seen a dragon before, but it closely resembled the pictures I had seen, the descriptions I had read, so I knew what it was. Perhaps if I stayed perfectly still it would go away. It couldn't be hungry, for it had obviously eaten the Wimperling. So I waited, scarcely daring to breathe, conscious of Growch trembling at my side.

It cleared its throat, rather like emptying a sack of stones.

"Well?" it said, in a gritty voice. "How do I look?"

I swallowed, surprised it could speak or that I could understand. But of course the ring on my finger . . . Come to think of it, why wasn't it throbbing a warning? To my surprise it was still and warm. Perhaps after all, dragons didn't eat maidens, in spite of what the legends said.

"Er . . . Very smart," I said, my voice a squeak. "Very . . . grand."

It stretched its great wings, one after the other, till I could see the moon shine faintly through the thin skin, like a lamp through horn shutters. "Still a bit creaky, but they haven't dried properly yet," said the dragon. "Everything else seems to be stretching and adjusting quite nicely. Of course I shall have to take it in short bursts for a day or two, but—"

"What have you done with the Wimperling?" I blurted out. "He was my friend, and all he wanted was to return to his ancestors! He never harmed anyone, and—and . . . If you've swallowed him, could you possibly spit him out again? I have his skin here, and I could sew him up in it and give him a decent burial. And if you're still hungry, I have some salt pork and vegetables left. . . ."

He stared at me, and for a moment I thought if he hadn't been a dragon, he would have laughed.

"You want your little pig back?"

"Of course. I said he was my friend. Now I am alone, except for my dog. He—he's somewhere about. . . ." Hiding, I thought, as I should have been.

"You offered me salt pork . . . Pork is pig."

"Not—not like the Wimperling. He was different. He wasn't a *real* pig. You want some? Wait a moment. . . ." and I dashed back inside and emerged with the cook pot and put it on the cairn. "I'm afraid it's only warm. . . ." But there was no sign of the dragon. "Don't go away! It's here," I called out.

"So am I," said a small voice. "But I can't reach it there," and a tiny slightly blurred piglet was at my feet, just the same size as the Wimperling when I first met him. I bent to scoop him into my arms, my heart beating joyously, but as my hands closed over him he was gone, only the scrap of hide I had earlier cuddled in my fingers. Then I was angry. I shook my fist at the sky.

"I don't care who or what you are!" I screamed. "You cheated me! Just eat your accursed stew, and I hope it chokes you. *Where's my Wimperling?*"

A man stepped from the shadows behind the cairn, a tall man wearing a hooded cloak that was all jags and points. I could not see his face and my heart missed a couple of beats. I snatched up my little sharp knife, the one I had thrown away only minutes ago, and held it in front of me.

"Keep away, or I'll set my dog on you!"

"That arrant coward? He couldn't—Ouch!"

Apparently Growch was less afraid of strangers than he was of dragons, for he darted from the shadows and gave the man's ankle a swift and accurate nip before dashing back, barking fiercely.

"Mmmm . . ." said the stranger. "I could blunt all your teeth for that, Dog!" He addressed me. "I mean you no harm, so put that knife away. You weren't so keen to use it five minutes ago, to help your friend."

So he had seen it all. I wondered where he had been hiding. I tried to peek under his hood, but he jerked his head away.

"Not yet. It takes time. . . ."

I didn't know what he was talking about. Just then the rising wind caught the edge of his jagged cloak and a hand came out to pull it back. I stared in horror: the hand was like a claw, the fingers scaled like a chicken's foot. What was this man? A monstrosity? A leper? He saw the look in my eyes.

"Sorry, Talitha-Summer. I had thought to spare you that. See . . ." and held out a hand, now a normal, everyday sort. "I told you it would take time. Better with a little more practice. And it's all your fault, you know. . . . If you hadn't kissed me—not once, but the magic three times—I would have appeared to you only in my dragon skin. As it is, I am now obliged to spend part of my life as a man." He sighed. "And yet it was that last kiss of yours that set me free. If you had but kissed me once there would have been a blurring at the edges every once in a while, human thoughts. Two kisses, a part-change now and again and a definite case of human conscience—which hampers a dragon, you know. But the magic three . . ."

"Wimperling?"

"The same. And different." He came forward and one hand reached out and clasped mine, warm and reassuring. The other threw back the concealing hood and there, smiling down at me, was at one and the same time the handsomest and most forbidding face I had ever seen.

Dark skin and hair, high cheekbones, a wide mouth, a hooked nose, frowning brows, a determined chin. And the eyes? Dragon-yellow with lashes like a spider's legs. Under the cloak he was naked; his hands, his feet, were manlike, but at elbow and knee, chest and belly, there was a creasing like the skin of a snake's belly. Even as I looked the scaly parts shifted and man-skin took their place.

"You see what you have done?"

"Does it hurt?" I asked wonderingly. Down there, at his groin, he was all man, I noted, with a funny little stirring in my insides.

"Changing? Not really. More uncomfortable, I suppose. Like struggling in the dark into an unfamiliar set of clothes that don't fit and are inside out."

"How long can you stay? When did you know what you were meant to be? When—when will you change back? Er . . . Do you want the stew?"

He laughed, a normal hearty man's laugh. "How long can I stay? A few minutes more, I suppose. Until I start changing back into my real self and my dragon-body. When did I know I was meant to be a dragon? Almost as soon as I was hatched, but the piglet bit fazed me a little. I was sure again that night when we crossed the border and I set the forest on fire with dragon's breath—" Of course! The question I had forgotten to ask at the time. "The stew? No, from now on my diet will be different. Here," and he lifted it down from the top of the cairn.

"Like what?" said Growch, already accepting the situation and sniffing around the stew pot. I tipped some out for him.

"Well, back east where my ancestors come from, there is a land called Cathay, and there—"

"And there they has those enticing little bitches wiv the short legs and the fluffy tails!" said Growch, the stew temporarily forgotten. "*That* was the name they used: Cathay!"

"And men with yellow skins and a civilization that goes back a thousand years! You have a one-track—no, two-track mind, Dog: food and sex. There are other things in life, you know. . . ."

"Not as important. Think about it, dragon-pig-man: reckon in some ways as I'm cleverer than you."

Sustenance and propagation, with the spice of fear to leaven it: he could be right.

But the Wimperling-dragon-man ignored him and took my hand.

"Let's walk a way. I don't know how long I can stay like this. Trust me?" And we strolled towards the nearest Stones, an avenue shimmering softly in the moonlight, a soft green, nearly as bright as glowworms.

As we walked I became gradually aware of his hand still clasping mine, of the contact of skin to skin, and my whole body seemed to warm like a fire. There were tickly sensations on my groin, tingly ones in my breasts and I'm sure my face burned like fire. I had never realized that palm-to-palm contact could be so erotic, could engender such a feeling of intimacy.

He stopped and swung me round to face him. "Well, Talitha-Summer, this is journey's end for us. Where will you go?"

"Wait a minute!" I didn't want to say good-bye, and couldn't think straight. "You know my name, but what is yours? We called you the Wimperling, but that was a pet name, a piglet name."

He laughed. "In Cathay they will call me the One-who-beats-his-wings-against-the-clouds-and-lights-the-sky-with-fire, but that is a ceremonial name and you'd never be able to pronounce it in their tongue. My shorter name is 'Master-of-Many-Treasures,' and that does have a Western equivalent: Jasper."

"Like the stone," I said. "Black and brown and yellow . . . I don't want you to go!" Gauche, naïve and true.

He didn't laugh, just took both my hands in his.

"If I were only a man, my beautiful Talitha-Summer, I would stay."

But that made me angry and embarrassed, and I pulled my hands away. "Now you are laughing at me! Don't mock; I am fat and ugly; not in the slightest bit beautiful. . . ." I was close to tears.

"Dear girl, would I lie to you? Look, my love, look!" And in front of us was a mirror of clarity I couldn't believe. I saw the reflection of the man dragon beside a woman I didn't recognize. Slim, straight-backed with a mass of tangled hair, a pretty girl with eyes like a deer, a clear skin, a straight nose and an expressive mouth—a woman I had never seen before.

"You're lying! It's some fiendish magic! I'm not—not like *that*!" I gestured at the image and it gestured back at me. "I'm ugly, fat, spotty. . . ."

"You were. When you rescued me you were all you said, but a year of wandering has worn away the fat your mother disguised you with. She didn't want a pretty daughter to rival her, so she did the only thing she could, short of disfigurement: she fattened you up like a prize pig, so that only a pervert would prefer you. Now you are all you should be. Why do you think Matthew wanted to marry you? Gill leave all behind and run away with you? You're beautiful, Summer-Talitha, and don't ever forget it!"

I reached out my hand to touch the reflection and it vanished, but not before I had seen the Unicorn's ring on my finger reflected back at me. So, it was true.

"Look at me," said the dragon-man, the Wimperling, Jasper. "Look into my eyes. You will see the same picture."

It was so. Dark though it was, I could see myself in the pupils of his eyes, a different Summer. I shivered. Instantly he put his cloak around both of us and pulled me towards him, so I could feel the heat of his body.

"Too much to comprehend all in one day? Don't worry: tomorrow you will be used to being beautiful. And now I must go: it will take me many days and nights to—"

"Don't! Please don't leave me. . . ."

"I must, girl. From now on our paths lie in different directions. Go back to Matthew, who will love and care for you, take the dragon gold to a big city and find a man you fancy, travel to—"

"I want you," I said. "Just you. Kiss me, please. . . ." and I reached up and pulled his head down to mine, my hands cupped around his head. Suddenly he responded, he pulled me close, as close as a second skin, and his mouth came down on mine. It was a fierce, hot, possessive kiss that had my whole being fused into his and my body melting like sun-kissed ice into his warmth.

Then, oh then, we were no longer standing, we were lying and—and I don't know what happened. There was a pain like knives and a sharp joy that made me cry out—

And then I was pinned to the ground by a huge scaly beast and I cried out in horror and scrambled away, my revulsion as strong as the attraction I had felt only moments since.

"You see," said the dragon, in his different, gritty voice. "It didn't work. For a moment, perhaps, but you would not like my real self. Don't hurt yourself wishing it were any different."

I swallowed. "But for a moment, back there, you forgot the dragon bit completely. We were both human beings." I felt sore and bruised inside.

He was silent for a moment, shifting restlessly. "Perhaps," he said finally: "but it shouldn't have happened. It gave me a taste for . . . Never mind. Forget it. Forget me. Bury your remembrances with that scrap of hide you kept. Go and live the life you were meant to lead.

"And now: stand clear!"

He flapped his great wings once, twice, as a warning and I scrambled back to safety, watching from behind one of the Stones. He flapped his wings again, faster and faster, and it was like being caught in a gale. Bits of scrub and heather flew past my ears till I covered them with my hands and shut my eyes for safety. There came a roaring sound that I heard through my hands and a great whoosh!, a smell of cinders, my hair nearly parted from my scalp and I tumbled head over heels.

Once I righted myself and opened my eyes, my dragon was gone. A burned patch of ground showed where he had taken off and in the sky was a great shadow like a huge bat that circled and swooped and filled the air with the deep throb of wings. To my right—the east—the Stones had started to glow again, a long avenue of them, like a pointer.

The shadow swooped once more towards the earth then shot up like an arrow till it was almost out of sight, then it steadied and hovered for a moment before heading due east, following the direction the Stones indicated, head and tail out straight, wings flapping slowly. I watched until its silhouette crossed the moon, then went wearily back to the ruined farmhouse.

I wasn't even annoyed to see Growch with his head inside the now-empty cook pot. I was too tired. His voice sounded hollow.

"I saw you! Doing naughties, you was!"

"Naughties? What do you mean?" But even as I said it I realized what it must have looked like to an inquisitive dog. *Was* that what had happened?

"You know . . . you didn't do naughties with the knight or the merchant with the cat and the warm fires: why with *him*?" He pulled his head out of the pot a trifle guiltily and his ears were clogged with juice. "Sort of fell over it did; din' want to waste it. . . . Why don' we go to that nice place for a while? Likes you, he does, and it's too cold to stay outside all winter. Just for a coupla months . . ."

"Matthew?" I was deadly tired, confused, bereft, couldn't think straight. I must have time to sort myself out, and better the known than the unknown. "Yes, why not?"

32

Easier said than done. It was the beginning of November now, and we were all of three or four hundred miles from the town where Matthew lived, north and east. It took us two weeks to get anywhere near a decent, well-traveled road, and those people we met were usually traveling south as we had done the year before, so we were heading against the flow of traffic. Company and lifts were few and far between and I was burdened with all the baggage, now there was no Wimperling, and what I would have expected to travel before—ten or twelve miles a day—was now only five or six: less if we were delayed by rain.

For the weather had changed with the waning of the moon: cold, blustery, with frequent rain showers. We seldom saw the sun and then only fitfully, and too pale and far away to heat us. To ease my burdens I made a pole sleigh—two poles lashed together in a vee-shape, the tattered blanket acting as receptacle for the rest of the goods—but the majority of the roads were so rutted and stony that the sleigh either kept twisting out of my hands, or the ends wore away and the poles had to be renewed.

Thanks to a couple of good lifts, by the end of November we were over halfway, but every day now saw worsening weather, and at night sometimes, if the wind came from the hills, we could hear wolves on the high slopes howling their hunger. Mostly we slept in what shelter we could find by the way—an isolated farmhouse, a barn, a shepherd's croft—but sometimes I paid for the use of a village stable or a place beside a tavern fire. Careful as I was, the cost of food and lodgings was so high in winter that almost half the dragon gold had gone when disaster struck us.

One night in a tavern I had been paying in advance for a meal when my frozen fingers spilled the rest of the gold from my purse onto the earthen floor. I scooped it up as quickly as I could, but three unkempt men at a corner table were nodding and winking at one another slyly as I did so. That night I slept but little, although the men had long gone into the dark, and in the morning my fears were justified.

Growch and I had scarcely made a couple of miles out of the village when the three men leapt out from the bushes at the side of the road, kicked and punched me till I was dazed, snatched my purse, pulled my bundle apart and flung Growch into the undergrowth when he tried to bite them. They were just pulling up my skirts, determined to make the most of me, when there was the sound of a wagon approaching and they fled, taking with them my blanket, food, cooking things and my other dress.

The carter who came to my rescue was from the village I had just left, and he was kind enough to help me gather together what little I had left and give the dog and me a lift back. I was in a sorry state: my head and arms and face bruised and swollen and my clothes torn, but poor Growch was worse off, with a broken front leg. The tavern-keeper's wife gave me water to wash in, needle and thread to mend my torn skirt and sleeve and a crust of bread and rind of cheese for the journey and I made complaint to the village mayor, but as the thieves had not been local men there was nothing they could do, and I was hurried on my way with sympathy but little else, lest I became a burden on the parish.

Once out of the village I bound up Growch's leg, using hazel twigs wrapped with torn strips from my shift, and poulticing it with herbs from the wayside to keep down the swelling and aid the healing, using the knowledge I had and the feel of the ring on my finger to choose the best. Of course now I would have to carry him, so I discarded any nonessentials, leaving me a small parcel to strap to my back, and my hands free for Growch.

By nightfall, hungry and depressed, I reached a tumbledown hut just off the road. As I walked through the scrub towards it I saw various articles strewn by the way: a man's belt, a rusty knife, a tattered blanket—surely that last was mine? I shrank back into the undergrowth ready to run, but Growch sniffed, wrinkled his nose and demanded to be put down. My ring was quiet, but cold, so I let him hobble forward on three legs to investigate further.

He came back a few minutes later. "We're not dossin' down there tonight, that's for sure. They's all dead an' it stinks to high heaven."

I crept forward, but even before I reached the hut I was gagging, and had to hold my cloak across my face. There, huddled on the earth floor, were the men who had robbed us only this morning, dead and smelling as though they had been that way for weeks. The contorted bodies lay in postures of extreme agony, mouths agape on swollen tongues and bitten lips, arms and legs twisted in some private torture, a noisome liquid oozing from great suppurating blisters on their blackened skin. Surely even the plague could not strike so quickly and devastatingly?

Then I noticed a little pile that was smoking away in a corner, like the last wisps from a dying fire. It was from here also that the worst stench came. Carefully stepping over the bodies, I walked over to investigate. There, dissolving in a last sizzling bubble, were the remains of the coins of dragon gold the then-Wimperling had left for me. I remembered what he had told me: given or used for trade they were perfectly safe; stolen, they brought death and destruction. I shivered uncontrollably, but not from cold.

That night we spent in the open, the first of many. With no money but my dowry left, which coins the country people would not accept, not recognizing the denominations and being suspicious of strangers anyway, I was reduced to begging, to stealing from henhouses, a handful of grain from sacks, vegetables from clamps. It was a wonder I was never caught, but with a dog who could no longer dance for his supper what else could I do? I did find the occasional root or fungi and gather what I could of herbs and winter-blackened leaves, but every day I grew weaker. Growch's leg healed slowly, but he probably fared worse than I did, for I could no longer find even the beetles and grubs that he would eat if there was nothing else. I even tried to trap fish, as I had been taught as a child, but with the frosts the fish lay low in the water and it all came to nothing, even the frogs having burrowed down under the mud.

There were one or two remissions, like the time I came upon a late November village wedding—none too soon from the look of the bride's waistline—and I stuffed myself stupid in return for a handful of coins and a tune or two on my pipe and tabor which I had providentially kept. I took with me a sack of leftovers that lasted us for a week.

But that was the last of our good luck. The weather got even worse and our progress slowed to a crawl. Lifts, even for a couple of miles, were few, and the stripped hedgerows and empty fields mocked our hunger. A couple of times, dirty and disreputable though I now was, I could have bought us a meal or two by pandering to the needs of importunate sex-seekers, but somehow I just couldn't. I do not believe it had anything to do with morals, nor the off-putting stench of their bodies: it was something deeper than that. I had been infatuated with Gill—the Wimperling had been right about that—I had had an affection for Matthew, and—But

I would think no further than that. The recent past I blotted out from memory. Sufficient that it stopped me from greater folly.

I have no clear recollection of those last few days. I know I was always hungry, always cold. My shoes had fallen to pieces but my numb feet no longer hurt on the sharp stones. I was conscious of a thin shadow that dogged my heels as a limping Growch tried to keep up, and I do recall him bringing me a stinking mess of raw meat he had stolen from somewhere and me cramming it into my mouth, trying to chew and swallow and then being violently sick. I also remember a compassionate woman at a cottage door, with half a dozen children clinging to her skirts, sparing me a mug of goat's milk and a few crusts, and finding rags to bind my feet, but the rest was forgotten.

It started to snow. At first thin and gritty, hurting my face and hands like needles, then softer, thicker, gentler, drifting down like feathers to cover my hair, burden my shoulders, drag at my skirt, but provide a soft carpet for my feet. I think it was then that I realized I wasn't going to make it, although some streak of perversity in my nature kept me putting one foot in front of the other. I remember falling more than once, stumbling to my knees many times, and on each occasion a small hoarse voice would bark: "Get up! Get up! Not far to go now . . . We ain't done yet. . . ."

But at the end even this failed to rouse me. The snow was up to my knees, above them, and I could go no further. Even Growch, plowing along in my dragging footsteps and then trying to tug at my skirt to pull me forward, failed to rouse me.

"Come on, come on, now! A little further, just two steps, and two more! Round this corner, that's right! You can't give up now. . . . Now, down here a step or two—don't fall down, don't!" Another tug at my skirt, and this time a nip to my ankle as well. I tried to thrust him away, but he was as persistent as a mosquito. I staggered a few steps, fell again. The snow was like a featherbed and no longer cold and forbidding. If I could just lie down for a few minutes, pull up the covers and sleep and sleep and sleep . . .

"Get up! Don't go to sleep! Up, up, up!" Nip, nip, nip . . .

"Go away! Leave me *alone*!" For the last time I got to my feet and stumbled down the road. "Leave me, go away, I don't want you anymore!" and I fell into a snowdrift that was larger, deeper, softer, warmer than any before. Shutting my eyes I burrowed deeper still and drifted away, the last thing I heard being Growch's hysterical barking: "Yip! Yip! Yip!" but soon that too faded and I heard no more. . . .

* * *

"I think she's coming round . . . How are you feeling?"

A strangely familiar face swam into focus, an anxious, rubicund face with a fringe of hair like the setting sun. I shut my eyes again, opened them. Did angels have red hair? Assuredly I must be in Heaven whether I deserved it or not, for I was warm, rested, lying I suppose on a cloud, and no longer hungry, thirsty or worried about anything. Except—"

"Growch? Where's Growch? Is he here too?"

"She means the dog," said someone, and something walked up my feet, legs, stomach and chest, then thrust a cold wet nose against my cheek and I smelt the familiar, hacky breath.

"Been here all the time—'cept for breakfast 'n' lunch 'n' supper— thought at one time as how you wasn't goin' to make it. . . ."

I put up a strangely heavy and trembly hand to touch his head. *Did* they have dogs in Heaven, then? I'd think about it later. Just have a little sleep . . .

"Fever's down," said another voice I thought I recognized. "By the morning she'll be fine."

And by morning I was at least properly awake, conscious of my surroundings and hungry, though not exactly "fine" just yet, for all the damaged parts of me that had been exposed to the bitter weather started to smart and ache, and I was still very weak.

Of course I had ended up at Matthew's house, thanks to Growch. He had led us both over the last few miles, scenting food and warmth and comfort, and luckily my final collapse had taken place just outside the merchant's house, though it had taken Growch a long time to rouse them from sleep and he had ended up voiceless, for a few hours at least.

At first they were convinced I was dead, so pale and cold and lifeless I had become, but providentially for me Suleiman had been staying with Matthew once more and he found a thin pulse and proceeded to thaw me out.

"Not by putting you in hot water or roasting you by the fire, as my dear friend would have me do," he said. "That would have killed you of a certainty. Instead I used a method I learned when a boy, from the Tartars my father sometimes traded with in hides. A tepid bath, oil rubbed gently into the skin, a cotton wrapping, then the natural warmth of naked bodies enfolding you. The servants took it in turns. Then the water a little warmer, and so on again . . . It took many hours until you were breathing normally, though once I saw you could swallow, though still unconscious, I gave you warm sweet drinks.

"Unfortunately there was a fever there, waiting for your body to warm up, but with one of my special concoctions and poppy juice to keep the body asleep, we managed to pull you through, though it was a close thing. The bruises and cuts will heal soon, but you have two broken toes, and I have bound those together; you were lucky you did not get frostbite as well."

After I had done my best to thank him, I asked about Growch's broken leg.

"Ah, you did a good job there. He still limps a little, but I have removed the splints and renewed the healing herbs. He will be as good as new."

Once I started to eat again properly I made rapid progress and was soon allowed up to sit by the fire in the solar, with a fully mobile Growch at my feet, luxuriating in the idleness, and Saffron, the great ginger cat, actually venturing his weight on my lap, though he was singularly uncommunicative, even when he realized I could talk to him. Of course I was petted and pampered and cosseted by Matthew, who seemed delighted to have me back. Both he and Suleiman could hardly wait to hear of my travels and find out what had happened to "Sir Gilman," so I gave them an edited, but nevertheless entertaining, account of my wanderings.

I had had plenty of time while convalescing to think up a good story, for who would believe the real one? I told them about the ghost in the castle and about our sojourn in the artist's village, and they were suitably impressed, both believing in the supernatural and Suleiman having heard of the other artist's seminars in Italia. When I recounted our stay with the Lady Aleinor, I had a surprise, and further confirmation (to them) of the complete veracity of my story.

"I quite forgot to tell you!" exclaimed Matthew. "The lad who helped you escape, Dickon, came here eventually, he said on your recommendation. He seemed an enterprising sort of lad and brought news of you—though he did embroider the facts a little!"

"Something about you flying to safety on the back of that pig of yours," said Suleiman, but his eyes were speculative. "It was a good tale. . . ."

"Anyway, I decided to give him a chance, for your sake," said Matthew. "Sent him off on one of our caravans with a letter of introduction. He'll be away at least a year, and he may prove useful. We can always do with promising youngsters."

Of course I didn't tell them the whole truth about Gill. I made a great tale of our escape across the border and of the miraculous return of his eyesight, however, the latter gratifying Suleiman.

"A theory of mine proved. One blow to the head: blindness. Another knock, and whatever has been displaced in the brain is jarred back. I expect he will have recurrent headaches for a while, but all should be well."

Matthew looked uncomfortable, but after a while he asked: "And the young man's parents? They must have been glad of his return. . . . He—also had—others—who must have rejoiced?"

I nodded and said, my voice quite steady and unemotional, "His fiancée had almost given him up for dead. They celebrated their nuptials while I was there and Rosamund, a beautiful fair-haired lady, was already with child when I left, I believe. . . ." That at least was true.

"And the rest of your little menagerie?" asked Suleiman. "The horse, the pigeon, the tortoise and the—er, flying pig?"

"The pigeon flew away once his wing was healed and joined a flock of his brethren." Truish. "The tortoise I let loose in suitable surroundings." True, but short of the full facts. "The mare—she grew up into quite a fine specimen and went for breeding." Again, basically true, but not the full story.

But what is truth? I thought to myself. It is always open to interpretation. Even if I had told them everything it would have been colored by the telling, my subjectiveness, and they would have heard it with ears that would hear parts better than others, would remember some facts and forget others, so the story to each would be different. If someone asked you what you ate for breakfast and you answered truthfully: "eggs," that would be truth but still not tell the enquirer how many, how cooked and what they tasted like, though they would probably be quite satisfied with the answer.

"And the pig?" asked Suleiman. "The odd one out . . ."

"He—the pig, died," I said. Another sort of truth. "He just dwindled away. He doesn't exist anymore." I still had the little scrap of hide, shriveled still smaller now though still bearing the imprint of its owner's face and the remnants of his hooves. Stuffed, it wold make a mini-pig, and child's plaything. My eyes were full as I remembered all that had happened.

"Well, it seems all turned out for the best," said Matthew comfortably. "Feel well enough for a game of chess, Mistress Summer?"

Through the colored glass of the window in the solar I watched the sun climb higher in the sky every day as the celebrations of Candlemas gave way to the rules of Lent. Matthew and Suleiman still insisted on convalescence, so I brought out my Boke, one of the few things I had managed to save, and wrote out my adventurings as best I could, but the version for my eyes only. When I had finished, the fine vellum

Matthew had insisted on buying stood elbow to wrist high and my fingers ached. And even then the story wasn't complete.

It ended when the Wimperling "died," for there were still some things I couldn't bring myself to write down, or even think about.

Matthew and Suleiman brought out their maps, planning the year's trade and seeking a faster route to the spices of the East. I studied the maps too, fascinated by the lands and seas they portrayed, so far from everything I knew. At one stage Suleiman mentioned the difficulties of coinage barter and exchange between the different countries and I bethought myself of my father's dowry gift, bringing the coins to show him.

To my amazement and delight he recognized them all and spread out the largest map in the house, weighing it down at the four corners with candlesticks.

"See, these coins all belong to different countries: Sicilia, Italia and across the seas to Graecia. Then Persia, Armenia . . ." and he placed the coins one by one across the map so they looked like a silver and gold snake. South by east, east, east by north, northeast; all tending the same way. "Your father must almost have reached Cathay. . . . He did: look!" And he held out the last and tiniest coin of all, no bigger than a baby's fingernail and dull gold. "Either that, or he was friendly with the traders who went there. These coins follow our trade routes almost exactly. . . . Don't lose them: they might come in useful some day."

I offered the coins, my precious dowry, to dear, kind Matthew when he tentatively proposed marriage to me just before Easter, but he closed my hand over them. "No, I have no need of them; you are enough gift for any man. Keep them in memory of your father."

It was agreed we would be wed when he returned from a two-week journey to barter for the new season's wool in advance. He and Suleiman set off together one fine April morning and I waved them out of sight, clutching Matthew's parting gift, a purseful of coins, to buy "whatever fripperies you desire."

He had kissed me a fond good-bye, and as his lips pressed mine I remembered Gill's urgent mouth on mine. And another's . . .

"Well, then: that's settled," said Growch by my side, tail wagging furiously. "Home at last, for both of us. When's lunch?"

Part III

A BEGINNING

33

"**G**otcha!"

I awoke with a start to find Growch trampling all over me, tail wagging furiously. Night had fallen early with lowering cloud, but I was snug in the last of the hay at the far end of the barn, wrapped in my father's old cloak, and had been sleeping dreamlessly.

"D'you know how long I been lookin' for you? Four days! Four bleedin' days . . . Fair ran me legs orf I did. You musta got a lift. . . ."

"I did. Yesterday." I sat up. "How did you know which way I'd gone?"

"Easy! Only way we ain't been. 'Sides, I gotta nose, and that there ring of yours got a pull, too."

I glanced down at it. Warm, but pulsing softly.

"Got anythin' to eat? Fair starvin' I am," and he pulled in his stomach and tried to look pathetic.

I gave him half the loaf I had been saving for breakfast. "And when you've finished that you can turn right round again and head back where you came from!"

He choked. "You're jokin'!"

"No, I am not. I left you behind deliberately. I even asked Matthew in my note to take care of you while I was away. . . ."

A note he wouldn't find yet, not for a couple of days at least, and by that time I should be aboard a ship for Italia, cross-country to Venezia and ship again for points east. And then to find Master Scipio and present myself to the caravan-master as Matthew's newest apprentice . . .

Once the merchant and Suleiman had disappeared I had had plenty of time to think.

Before, there had always been someone hovering, in the kindest pos-

sible way of course, making sure I wasn't hungry/cold/thirsty/tired/bored.
I hadn't realized how constricted I had felt until they were both gone: the
first action of mine had been to run from room to room, down the stairs,
round the yard and then back again, flinging cushions in the air and the
shutters wide open. Free, free, free! I sang, I danced, I felt pounds lighter,
almost as if I could fly. Growch thought I was mad, so did the cat and
surely the servants.

Once I had calmed down I asked myself why I had acted like that,
and I didn't particularly like the answers I came up with. One of them
was obviously that a year or more traveling the freedom of the roads
had left me with a taste for elbow room; another that I was obviously
not ready to settle down yet. The third answer was, in a way, the most
hurtful: I obviously didn't care enough for Matthew to marry him—at
least I didn't return his affection the way he would have wished.

And why should you expect to love him? I could hear my mother's
voice like a dim echo. Marriage is a contract, nothing more. You are
lucky in that you don't actively dislike him. Just look around you, see
what you will have! A rich husband who will grant your every wish, a
comfortable home, security at last . . . A little pretense on your part
every now and again: is that so much to ask?

Yes, Mama, I answered her in my mind. You had my father, don't
forget, you knew what real love felt like. You, too, had a choice. Didn't
you ever regret not flinging everything aside and following him to the
ends of the earth and beyond? A cruel and unjust death took him away
from you, but at least you had your memories. And what have I got? A
taste, just the tiniest taste, of what life could really be like, what love
meant.

If I married Matthew now, feeling the way I did, I should be doing
him a grave injustice and he was too nice, too kind a man for that. He
would know I was pretending. Whereas if I tried to find what I was seeking
and failed, then I could return and truly make the best of things. If he
would still have me, of course. And if I succeeded . . . But I wouldn't
even think of that, not yet. Besides, the odds were so great, maybe ten
thousand to one, probably more. But I was damn well going to try!

That letter to dear Matthew had been difficult to write, for I knew
how it would hurt him.

I know you will be upset to find me gone, but I find I cannot yet
settle down, much as I am fond of you and am grateful for your
many kindnesses. I hope you can forgive me. I am not sure where
I shall go, but I hope to return within a year and a day, all being

well. By then, of course, you may well have changed your mind about me, but if not I hope I shall be ready to settle down with you.

I have taken the bag of coins you gave me so I shall not be without funds, although I know you intended them for more frivolous purposes. Thank you again for everything. Please, of your goodness, take care of my dog till I return. . . .

There were two things—three—that I didn't tell him. I had spent a few coins in kitting myself out in boy's clothes: braies and tunic, stockings and boots. Also, I had cut my hair short. At first I had been horrified at the result, for now my hair sprang up round my head in a riot of curls, but I soon became used to the extra lightness, and it would be much more convenient. I had taken the discarded tresses with me, for there was always a call for hair to make false pieces and they might be worth a meal or two.

Another thing he wouldn't know was that I had copied his maps showing the trade routes, and the last way I had taken advantage was to use his seal and forge his signature to a letter of introduction to one of his caravan masters, the same one who had engaged young Dickon. Having memorized, unconsciously at the time, the schedules of the routes, I now knew I had a couple of days more to make the twenty miles or so to the first rendezvous. And now here came trouble on four legs just to complicate matters. . . .

"I locked you in deliberately to stop you following! You can't come with me! I'm not even sure where I'm going. . . ."

"Why can't I come? S'all very well tellin' the servants as you're goin' visitin', but I ain't stupid! They tried to keep me in, as you ordered, but I jumped out a window, I did. You ain't goin' nowheres without me. You knows you ain't fit to be let out on your own. Din' I get us to that fellow's house?"

I admitted he had.

"Well, then! There's gratitude for you. . . . I don' care where you're goin', I'm comin' too. Try an' stop me."

"I thought all you wanted was a comfortable home. Matthew would take good care of you. And all that lovely food . . ."

"I can change me mind, can't I? You have. Don' know what you wants do you? Well, then . . . Where we goin'?"

I gave up. "To sleep, right now. In the morning . . . east."

"Where the little fluffy-bum bitches come from? Cor, worth a walk of a hundred miles or so . . ."

Nearer thousands, I thought, as I lay down again. It was a daunting prospect, thought of like that. But otherwise how could my mind and body ever be rid of the ache, the questioning, the unknown, engendered on that never-to-be-forgotten night when my world had turned upside down?

Growch had been wrong there: I did know what I wanted.

Somewhere a dragon was waiting. . . .

*Master
of Many
Treasures*

For my husband
Peter
with my love.
Thanks for
everything!

Acknowledgments

My thanks to the Baen team—especially Jim, my editor Toni, and Hank—for their many extra kindnesses.

Thanks again to Barry and Margaret Shaw for helping us with Christopher.

Special thanks to my friend Ingrid von Essen for her expert research—and for the beer-bottle label!

Sam: I know how you hate all pens, paper, typewriters and word processors, so I'll try and rearrange my schedule next time! Love you . . .

Prologue

It was a difficult journey.

Once in the air he had thought the flight would be easy; after all, he would be flying higher than all but the largest raptors. The thermals, currents of air, clouds, and winds provided his highways, hills and vales, and the skyscape freed him from the pedestrian pace of those on the earth beneath. In that other skin he had once worn ten or fifteen miles a day had been enough, but now he could easily manage a hundred in one stint, though he usually cut this by half. After all, there was no hurry.

No problems with the route, either. Like all of his kind the ways of the air were etched into his brain as a birthright, a primitive race memory he shared with birds, fishes and some of the foraging mammals.

At first the wind aided him on his way and the sun shone kindly at dawning and dusk, for he preferred to return to land during the day for food and rest, ready for the guidance of the stars at night. The sleeping earth rolled away beneath his claws, and his reptilian hide adapted to the cold better than he had expected, not slowing him down with his reduced heartbeat as he had feared.

Rivers glinted in serpentine curves beneath the moon, hills reared jagged teeth, tiny pinpoints of light showed where those wealthy enough burned candles and tapers in castle or church, and he grew complacent, so much so that when the Change came, he wasn't ready for it.

It was that comfortable time between moondown and sunrise and he was cruising at about a thousand feet, ready to do a long glide down in search of breakfast, when he suddenly became aware that something was terribly wrong. Although his wings were beating at the same rate, he was losing height rapidly and feeling increasingly cold.

Glancing from side to side, he was horrified to see that his wings were almost transparent, were shrinking; his heartbeats were quickening, his legs stretching in an agony of tendons and muscles, his clawed forefeet turning into . . . hands?

Then he remembered.

She had kissed him, not once but three times, and so as part of those accepted Laws—Laws that until now he had dismissed as mere myth, though he had jokingly told her of them as truth—he would now have to spend part of his life as a human, earthbound as any mortal.

All right, all right, so he was going to be a man for a minute, two, five, but why no sort of warning? He was falling faster and faster, but all he could think about was there should be some way of delaying the Change, or of controlling it—

He landed plump in the middle of a village rubbish dump, all the breath knocked out of him but otherwise unhurt. For a moment he lay dazed and winded, then the stench was enough to make him stumble to his feet and stagger drunkenly down the main (and only) street, shedding leaves, stalks, bones and worse. Halfway down he realized he was not alone.

A small boy, perhaps five years old, clad only in a tattered shirt, was watching him with solemn brown eyes in the growing dawnlight. By his side was a smaller child, perhaps his two- or three-year-old sister, in a smock far too short for her, thumb stuck firmly in her mouth.

He thrust his hands out in a useless gesture of friendship. "Sorry, children: didn't mean to scare you. Just passing through. . . ."

Fiercely he concentrated on his real self—though what was real anymore?—and to his relief he began the awkward pain of changing back. In the midst of his discomfort he became aware of the children still watching him, their eyes growing rounder and rounder with amazement, and the humor of the situation struck him even as he took a running leap into the air, as clumsy as any heavy water fowl.

"Good-bye," he called, but it sounded just like the rumble of thunder, and he could see now the terrified children beneath him rush for the nearest hut and safety. Never mind, they would have a tale to tell that would keep the village buzzing for months.

After that the weather became more hostile, and not only was he battling against his "changes," which took time to recognize and regularize, but also strong easterlies, snow, and sleet, so it was well after the turn of the year before he saw in the distance his objective, four thousand miles from the Place of Stones of his transformation: a small conical hill set proud on a plain, a hill that shone softly blue against the encircling mountains. . . .

Part I

1

Venice stank. For the loveliest city in the world (so I had been told), center of Western trade, Queen of the Adriatic, she certainly needed a bath. One would have thought with all that water around the smells would have been washed away, but the reverse was true: it made it worse. The waters in the canals were moved only by the water traffic, which stirred but did not dissipate, and all the slops and garbage merely settled a few feet further on.

The city was certainly busy with trade and teeming with merchants and dripping with gold, but she was only beautiful at a discreet distance. Pinch one's nose and one could admire the tall towers, fine buildings, richly dressed gentry; one could feel the sun-warmed stone, listen to the sweet dissonance of bells and the calls of the gondoliers; watch the bustle at the quays as the laden barques and caravels were rowed in the last few yards . . . but keep one's nostrils closed.

I moved restlessly from bed to window and back again: three paces and then another three. It was hot and stuffy in this little attic room, but when I had opened the window some time back the stench had made me gag, so it stayed shuttered. Consequently it was not only stifling but also dark; I had trodden on my dog twice, but couldn't keep still.

Mind you, I was lucky to have a room to myself. Apart from Master Alphonso, the trading captain, all the others—horse master, interpreter, accountant, guards, cooks and servants—had to share. And why was I so privileged? Because I bore papers that proved I was under the personal protection of the wealthy merchant who had financed the expedition, Master Matthew Spicer.

And I was the only one who knew the papers were forged. By me.

I had a couple of other secrets, too, and secrets they must remain, else this whole journey would be jeopardized, and that mustn't happen. I had left too much behind, risked too much, hurt too many people to fail now. This was the most important journey of my life, and to justify what I had done, it must succeed.

A bad conscience and a real fear of pursuit had kept me glancing over my shoulder during our journeying the last couple of months, but at least then we had been moving, whereas for the last two weeks we had been stuck in this stinking city. No wonder I couldn't keep still. I—

Feet on the stairs, a thumping on the ill-fitting door.

"Hey, boy! Wake up there. . . . Cargo's in, we're going down to the quay. Coming?"

Action at last! Telling my dog, Growch, to "stay," I jammed my cap on my head, grabbed my tally sticks and clattered down three flights of wooden stairs to the street below. Outside it was scarcely less hot than my room, but at least there was shade and a faint breeze off the sea. Master Alphonso, the interpreter, and a half a dozen others were milling around, but as soon as I appeared we set off for the quay, through the twists and turns of narrow streets, across the elegant curves of bridges, through the busy thoroughfares, all the while having to contend with the purposeful and the loiterers; carts, wagons, riders, pedestrians, children, dogs and cats impeded our progress. Watch out for the overhead slops—forbidden, but who was to see?—and be careful not to trip over that heap of rags, a sudden thin hand snatching at your sleeve for alms. Keep your hand on your purse and your feet from skidding in the ordure. . . .

Matthew's ship was already being unladen. Because of the press of the sea traffic she was anchored some way out, rowing boats busy ferrying the cargo ashore. A couple of our guards stood over the deepening piles of bales on the quayside, and our accountant started setting out paper, pens and ink on his portable writing desk, ready to itemize the cargo.

I tugged at Master Alphonso's sleeve. "How soon before it is all unladen? When can we go aboard? When do we sail?"

He twitched his sleeve away impatiently. "How many times do you have to be told, boy? When all the cargo is on dry land and checked by description against the captain's listings, then it is taken to a warehouse, opened and itemized, piece by piece. Then, and only then, will it be distributed as Master Spicer wishes. In the meantime the ship will take on a fresh crew and fresh supplies, the new cargo will be listed and loaded aboard. Then if the weather is fair, the ship sets sail. If not, it waits. Satisfied? I shan't tell you again."

In nodded, but inside I was in turmoil. Just how long would all this take? A week, at least . . . I turned away, but he stopped me.

"Just where do you think you're going? You may be Master Spicer's protegé, but that doesn't mean you skip out every time there's work to be done. You're here to learn the business, that's what your papers say, so stop farting around and go help the accountant."

So I spent a long, hot afternoon working my tally sticks at top speed against the accountant's vastly superior abacus, then helped load the cargo for the warehouse. All my own fault; when I had forged Matthew's signature on the carefully prepared papers, I had represented myself as a privileged apprentice, to learn a merchant's trade from the bottom up. This was obviously the bottom. Up till now I had been a supernumerary; now it appeared I was about to earn my keep.

Snatching a meat pie and a mug of watered wine from a stall, I followed the cargo to a warehouse on the outskirts of the city. There the bales were off-loaded, recounted against the existing lists and at last opened to check the contents.

This was the exciting bit. Although Matthew was principally a spice merchant, and some eighty percent of the cargo was just this—mainly pepper, cloves, nutmeg, and mace—he also traded in whatever was out-of-the-way and unusual, sometimes to special order. Thus the rich, black furs would be auctioned off in Venice, the jewelry entrusted to another outlet; some rather phallic statues were a special order, as were certain seeds of exotic plants. This left drawings and sketches of strange animals, two curiously-shaped musical instruments, and several maps. These last were earmarked for Matthew himself, together with a couple of rolls of silk so fine it ran through one's fingers like water.

And who was in charge of these sortings and decisions? A tall thin man with a hawk nose, conservatively dressed, who Master Alphonso whispered to me was Matthew's agent in Venice, responsible not only for distribution and collection of cargo, but also for hiring and firing.

It happened that he and I were the only ones left later: he because he was arranging for warehouse guards, I because I was going back over one of my calculations which did not tally. By now I was almost cross-eyed with fatigue, so was only too grateful when the soft-spoken Signor Falcone came over and in a couple of minutes traced my mistake and amended it.

"Only one error: tenths are important, youngster. Still, well done." His fingers were long and well manicured. "You are Master Summer, I believe?"

I nodded. Relief at having finished without too much blame made my tongue careless and impudent. "Matthew must have great trust in you. I wouldn't—" and I stopped, blushing to the roots of my hair.

"Trust someone so greatly without supervision? Of course you should not, unless you know him well." He regarded me gravely. "But then, you see, I owe him and his friend not only my livelihood, but my education. And also my life."

"Your life?"

He hesitated.

"I'm sorry," I said. "I shouldn't be so inquisitive."

"No matter. At your age I was the same." He hesitated again. "It is not a tale I recount easily. Still . . ." His eyes were bright and dark as sloe berries. He took a bundle of keys from his belt and, beckoning me to follow, locked up the warehouse, nodded to a couple of armed men lounging nearby, and started back towards the center of the city. "Come, we shall walk together. . . ."

It was a strange enough tale, and I forgot my weariness as I listened.

"When I was eight years old I was sold into slavery by a parent burdened by too many children. It was in a country far from here, and I was pretty enough to be auctioned as a bum-boy—you understand what I mean?—but I was lucky. A stranger stopped to watch the bidding and among those who fancied me was an old enemy of the stranger. So, to teach this man a lesson, the stranger bid for me too, and in the course of time he won himself a boy he had no use for. The stranger's name was Suleiman, on his way to visit his old friend Matthew Spicer—I see that first name means something to you?"

I wasn't conscious of having betrayed myself, but I nodded. "I met him while I was at Master Spicer's." I didn't add that it was the gifted Suleiman whose doctoring had saved the life of my blind knight, the man I had once fancied myself in love with.

"Then you will know that he is both wise and kind. He left me with his friend, to care for and educate, to learn to read, write and calculate. There I also learned French, Italian and Latin, for my own language was Arabic. At about the same age as yourself I was sent abroad to learn the ways of trade, and after some years Matthew appointed me his agent here. I have never regretted it, nor, I believe, has he. His is a generous and trusting nature, and such a man's trust is not easily abused. Nor should it be: remember that."

How could I not? For in my own way I had betrayed his trust in worse ways than Signor Falcone could imagine.

We had reached the end of the street where I lodged.

"Your journey starts in a day or two. I do not think you have the slightest idea how far it will take you, nor are you mentally prepared as you should be. About that I can do little, but at least I can see you are physically ready. Do not forget you will be representing Master Spicer, and you need a new outfit for that." He fished in his purse and brought out a handful of coin. He saw my eyes widen with surprise at the gold, and allowed himself a wry grimace. "Call this the Special Fund. For emergencies—and youngsters who need smartening up. Choose good materials, and something neat but not gaudy." He put a couple of coins in my hand. "You will also need travelling gear: leather breeches and jacket; a thick cloak; good, strong boots; riding gloves." Another couple of coins in my hand. "It can be cold at nights where you are going, so a woollen cap, underwear and hose." A last coin. "And a good, sharp dagger. Go to Signor Ermani in the Via Orsini and say I sent you." And he swung away across the square. "And get your hair cut! At the moment you look like a girl!"

It was so late by now that the pie shop around the corner was closing as I went past, but I managed to grab some leftovers and broken pieces for my dog, who was almost crossing his back legs in an effort not to relieve himself by the time I reached my room. So pressured was he that he forwent his supper until he had christened every post and arch within a considerable distance. I trailed after him without fear of marauders, for he had a piercing bark, an aggressive manner, and extremely sharp teeth.

And, after all, when one has bitten a dragon and got away with it, what else has a dog to fear?

That evening, what was left of it, I brought my journal up to date. This was Part Two of my life. Part One was already finished the day I left Matthew's for the second time. It was a bulky volume, bound with a wooden cover, and as I weighed it in my hands I realized how much of an extra burden it would be to carry it any further. It would be better to leave it with someone I could trust.

Part Two was far less bulky. I had already devised a form of shortened words and wrote smaller, so could justify taking it with me. Pen and inks would have to go with me as part of my job, and a couple of extra rolls or so of vellum were neither here nor there.

Next morning I went out in search of new clothes. Neat but not gaudy, Signor Falcone had said, but although hose, breeches and boots were easy enough in shades of brown, the jacket was an entirely different matter. Finding a good, plain one was practically impossible. They all seemed to be embroidered with vine leaves, pomegranates, artichokes,

red and white flowers and even stars and moons, but then Venice catered
mainly to the rich and fickle. The materials, too—silks and satins—were
too fine for prolonged wear, but at least after a search I tracked down
a fawn-colored jerkin with the minimum of decoration, and a green
surcoat of fine wool, without the usual scallops, fringes and frills.

The afternoon I spent in mending my existing hose and underwear,
a chore I detested, but just as I had decided it was candle time, there
was a rush of feet on the stair and a hammering at the door.

"Master Summer? You there?"

"Yes . . ." I was practically naked, so the door stayed shut.

"Master Alphonso says you're to be ready at dawn."

"So soon?"

"Outbreak of plague reported in the south. Report to the quayside
at first light." The feet stumbled back down the stairs.

Plague? Perhaps the greatest fear man had, far more threatening
than battle or siege. Against a human enemy there were weapons, but
the plague recognized no armies but—deadlier than sword, spear or ar-
rowhead, unseen, unheard, unfelt—could decimate the largest army in
the world within days. Either great pustules broke out on the skin and
the victim died screaming, else it was the drowning sickness, when the
chest filled with phlegm and a choking death came in less than a day—

I shivered in spite of the heat, fear closing my throat and opening
my pores. No time to waste. I must call down for water to wash in, then
collect my cloak from the laundry down the road. Once my father's,
then my mother's, it was practically indestructible, being of a particularly
fine and thick weave, though light and soft, with a deep hood. Much
mended and much worn, it was nevertheless better than many new ones
I had seen, but I had thought to have the mire and mud of the journey
to Venice dispersed by a good soak.

So, that to collect, a good scrub for myself—and the dog, if possible—then everything to be packed as tight as could be. Something to
eat, and lastly a safe place to leave Part One of my journal.

I hurried as well as I could, but the last streaks of gold and crimson
were staining the skies to the west when I knocked at Signor Falcone's
door, praying that he had not gone out to dine.

I was shown by a liveried servant to an upstairs room and gasped
in wonder at the fine furniture, glowing tapestries, delicate glass and
silken drapes. My host smiled at my expression.

"Without Suleiman and Matthew a mere slave could never have
afforded all this. . . . What do you want of me, youngster?"

I started to explain about the plague and our early departure, but he cut me short.

"I know all this. We have worked throughout the day to get everything loaded and ready. What is that package under your arm?"

Straight to the point, Signor Falcone! I had rehearsed my story on the way.

"It contains a journal I have been keeping. Before I—before Master Spicer sponsored me I had some amusing adventures, which I have written down plain. If—if anything should happen to me on my travels I should wish Master Spicer to have it. A sort of thanks . . . It might also explain some of my actions more clearly." I was floundering, and I knew it. "Besides, it is too heavy to carry. Please?"

"So, if anything should happen to you on the way—Allah forbid!— this is to be forwarded to Matthew? Otherwise I hold it until your return; is that it? Very well. The package if you please." Going over to his ornate desk he extracted sealing wax and, rolling the stick in a candle flame, dropped the pungent-smelling stuff onto the knots in my package. He motioned to quill and ink. "Write Master Spicer's name there clearly. So. Now come with me."

Taking up a candle I followed him down a short passage into a small locked back room, windowless, full of shelves and nose-tickly with dust. Boxes, scrolls, books, small paintings and other packages lined the shelves, all neatly labelled. He placed my parcel high up on the nearest shelf.

"There, it will be safe till you return. And, should anything happen to me, my servants' orders are to forward everything in here to the name on the label. And now, if there is nothing else you wish to tell me, I think I shall take to my bed, and I would advise you to do the same." Ushering me downstairs, he opened the door on a night of stars, with a thin veil of mist creeping up from the east. "Hmmm. Don't like the look of the weather."

"There's no moon, no land breeze either, but the sky is clear enough."

"Exactly. Moon change and a sea mist. Still . . . off you go, sleep well." He turned to re-enter, then turned back. "I thought I told you to get your hair cut!"

Dear Lord, I had completely forgotten! Surely it would be too late at night now. Taverns, brothels, gaming houses, eating places would be open for business, but barbers . . . Collecting Growch from some odorous rubbish bin, I set out to look.

I was lucky, although it looked very expensive.

A gilded sign above the door hung motionless, announcing to those who could read that Signor Leporello was hairdresser and barber to the greatest in the land. On the door was tacked a list of prices; a trim didn't look too expensive. Telling Growch to wait, I lifted the latch and peered within. A little bell on a string gave a melodious tinkle.

"Hallo? Anyone there?" A couple of candles burned on a side table, otherwise the room was empty. I called again.

A moment's pause, then a bead curtain swung back and a creature teeter-tottered forward on those ghastly wooden-platformed shoes that the fashionable all seemed to be wearing these days. This man—if it was a man—had mismatched hose, red and blue, slashed sleeves and a surcoat flapping with pink and gold embroidery. Topping it all off was a huge green turban with a large purple stone set in the center. Probably real, which made it all worse. Gaudy, but not neat . . .

A waft of oil of violets, the glint of rings as he lit a couple more candles. "And what have we here? A late customer, I do believe. Come in dear boy, come in! A shave perhaps? No, not a shave, definitely not. A trim? Yes, a trim I think. A trim and a wash. Pretty hair like yours should always be clean and dust-free. . . ."

"Pretty hair?" I squeaked. This was obviously the sort of place and proprietor young boys were warned about. "I'm sorry, there is some mistake: I have no money, and—"

"Nonsense! You need a trim and I am in a good mood. Come, it shall be on the house," and before I knew what was happening he had plonked me down on a tall stool, and swiftly plucked a few hairs from my head, holding them to the candlelight. "See these? All different colors. Two shades of red, two of brown, blonde and black." It was true. "All together they are individually responsive to light and shade, like those clear eyes of yours. Now, bend over that basin and we'll begin!"

If there was to be a dangerous moment, this would be it, but my worries soon vanished as he washed, rinsed, rubbed, combed, brushed and clipped. At last he brought me a mirror, and even with its uncertain depths and the flicker of candles I was gazing at a different me. Gone was the tangle of jagged ends and unruly curls. The hair was layered and waved neatly to my head—

"Is he someone I would know? How long ago did you run away from your family—or the convent, perhaps? Come, I've seen all this before, many times. A young girl imprisoned against the unsuitability of her beloved, dresses as a boy, runs away to find him. . . ."

"A—girl!" I stammered, and I must have been as red as fire.

"Why, yes! Oh come!" and he leant forward and lightly brushed his fingers across my chest. "I have been leaning over you for near an hour . . . I happen to have some stretch webbing that will hide those breasts much more discreetly, young lady, and only a silver piece a yard. . . ."

2

The morning was gray, dull, misty, chill. A sulky red sun lurked behind the mist and I was shivering, both from cold and anticipation. Strange to think the Shortest Day was but a week past: it felt more like November.

Dirty water slap-slapped against the piles of the Piazetta as the rowboats came and went, ferrying the last of the cargo aboard. Behind us the square was deserted, or so I thought, but at the last moment a figure came scurrying across carrying a tray of freshly baked rolls and pasties. They were delicious, the meat sending little pipes of steam into the air from the crumbling pastry. The baker was an enterprising fellow baking so early—but then his prices were enterprising too, as I discovered after Growch and I had burnt our tongues.

"Feel better?" asked a familiar voice. I turned to see Signor Falcone, well wrapped against the cold.

"Much!"

"Well try and keep it down. I still don't like the look of the weather; red sky at morning, sailor's warning . . . Still you're safer away from the plague, and the captain has done this run many times."

"Aren't you afraid of catching the sickness?"

He smiled. "It is as Allah wills. If it comes too close I have a small villa in the hills to the north. I usually spend August there anyway: it is pleasantly cool, and Matthew curtails his trade during the hottest months. In fact, the stuffs now in the warehouse are the last but one Master Alphonso will escort back till fall."

I glanced over to where the trade captain was talking to his accountant. "But—but I thought they were coming with us. . . . With me." I should be alone, no one to ask questions of, to depend on. A little fist of panic curled up in my stomach, and I could taste the pasties a second time around.

Falcone patted my shoulder. "Stop worrying. Master Scipio takes over on the other side, and he is a competent man, one of the best. You'll be safe enough with him. Matthew's papers and listings are on board, and mention has been made of you. . . . Have I said how much better you look with your hair cut?" He smiled. "Now, I must bid you farewell, but first I have a commission to execute." He pulled a small, tightly wrapped package from an inner pocket. "This arrived some time back, but I had to be sure it was going to the right person."

I took the package and turned it over. No name, no superscription. "Who's it from? How do you know it's for me?"

"The sender is a mutual friend. And how do I know it is for you? Just answer me one question: what is the name of your dog?"

"My *dog?* Why, Growch . . ."

"Exactly! That was the password, just in case I was not convinced by my own observations. You make a handsome enough lad, but I'm sure the woman underneath is even more attractive." He laughed a little at my stricken face. "Your secret is safe. Our—friend—believes he knows the purpose of your journey and its destination. You are a brave lass: may Allah be with you. Now go: you don't want to miss the boat."

As the rowers pulled away from the quay, my mind was in turmoil. Disguising myself as a boy had seemed a good idea at the time, but in less than twenty-four hours two men had discovered at least one of my secrets. Did anyone else suspect? I felt as though my face was burning as I tried to flatten my chest, pull my long legs in under my surcoat.

Of course even twelve months ago it would have been impossible to think of posing as a boy. At that time I had still been decidedly plump, decidedly female. It had been that last, impossible journey back to the haven of Matthew's home that had fined me down to the weight I now carried, that and the pain of losing the one love I could never replace, the love I had found too late by the Place of Stones. . . .

I had tried, of course I had, to be satisfied with a substitute, but even the kindest of men—and Matthew was certainly that—could not compensate for that searing moment when I discovered what true love really meant.

And that was why I was here, in this rackety little rowboat, heading for—for what? Even I wasn't sure. All I knew was that somehow I must find my love again, see him just once more, for the touch that had fired my blood with an indescribable hunger could never be satisfied by another.

Perhaps I would never find him, perhaps if I did he would spurn me, or be so changed I would matter less than a leaf on a tree but at least I had to *try*! Nothing else in the world mattered.

The rowboat bumped against the towering hull above, a rope ladder dangling just out of reach. Only the most agile of monkeys could have scaled that, what with the overhang and the sluggish dip and sway of the ship, but luckily there was one more bale to be hauled up by hand, and Growch and I went the undignified way, bumped and banged against the ship's sides on what felt like a bed of nails.

If I had expected a fanfare of trumpets to greet me once on board I was to be disappointed. In fact no one took the slightest notice of us at all. We were tipped unceremoniously off the bale, which was then lashed to others on the deck. The whole ship was boiling with activity, and gradually we were pushed into an obscure corner as sailors scurried around getting us ready for sea. Up came the anchor, down came the sails, two men unlashed the tiller and swung it across, and everyone seemed to be shouting commands and countercommands. What with that and the creak of chain, snap of sail, hiss of rope and scream of the gulls overhead, I doubt if anyone would have noticed if I had set fire to myself.

But all this frantic activity didn't seem to be getting us anywhere at all. The ship wallowed uneasily from side to side, the sails flapped listlessly, everything creaked, but we weren't moving. After half an hour or so, a flag was run up on the forward mast, and eventually a rowing barge came astern, took a line and ponderously towed us, tail first, outside of the shipping roads and into clear water.

Peering over the side, I could see how, even here, the contamination of the city behind us reached its dirty fingers into the main. The water was still brown and scummy and I could see flotsam from the sewers float past, plus a broken packing case and the bloated carcass of a goat. I glanced back at the city and now, at last, she resembled the lady I had heard about. She looked to float well above the water, the pale sun gilding her towers and cupolas till she seemed crowned like any queen.

The sails above me filled at last, the tiller was pushed over to starboard, and at first slowly, then with gathering speed, we headed northeast into the open sea. Immediately I had to grab at the side to keep myself from slipping: it was probably only a cant of a foot or so, but it was most disconcerting for me and worse for Growch, for his claws slipped and he slithered straight into the scuppers. We would have to find a place to call our own.

The ship was quieter now, although everyone seemed to have a job to do: trimming sails, coiling rope, swilling down the deck, and I could

see an extremely large lady was shaking out bedding and punching energetically at what seemed to be a feather mattress. Probably the captain's
wife: I had heard they often accompanied their husbands to sea. I had
correctly identified the captain as the man who shouted the loudest and
longest, and decided now was the time to introduce myself. He was a
self-important looking man, stout and short, with a bristling beard and
lots of hair in his ears. He stared at me as I approached.

"Who's this, then?"

I introduced myself, but had to explain who and what I was before
his brow cleared and he nodded his head. Yes, yes, he'd heard I was
coming aboard, but it had slipped his mind, and now he was too busy
to deal with me personally. I would have to see the mate, find myself
quarters, settle myself in. And keep that blasted dog from under everyone's feet. . . .

The mate, when I found him, had even less time for me. I was handed
over to one of the crew, who showed me round in a desultory manner,
and had me peering down the bilges—sick-making—and trying to climb
in and out of a string bag he called a hammock; needless to say I fell out
either one side or the other immediately. Apparently all the crew slept in
these because a) they took up little space and b) they always stayed level,
however the ship swayed. I went down into the hold, where everything
was stacked away neatly, and into the galley, where it wasn't. Pots and
pans, jugs, bottles, a side of ham, bags of flour, jars of oil, dried beans,
strings of onions and garlic, sultanas and raisins, boxes of eggs, all hugger-mugger on shelves and floor. Outside, a couple of barrels rolled from
side to side, and a couple of crates of scrawny chickens were stacked next
to a bleating nanny goat. The cook was snoring it off in a corner.

But where was I to sleep? There were eighteen crew, split into three
watches, so that at any one time there would be six on duty, six asleep
and six relaxing, and I wasn't going to fall out of hammocks all day
and night. Besides, there was no locker in which to stow my gear. I
asked if there was any other space, but apparently not. The captain and
his wife had quarters aft, the mate a tiny cubicle next to the rope locker
and the cook slept in the galley.

The sailor had one useful suggestion. I could either doss down in
the hold, although the hatchway was normally battened down, or find
myself a niche topside, among the deck cargo.

I didn't fancy being shut away, so I inspected the bales on deck and,
sure enough, they were so stacked that there was a cozy sort of cave to
one side, which I thought would do. Even with my gear dragged in as

well, there was room to lie down or sit up quite comfortably, and the
smell of tarred string and sea salt was far pleasanter than bilge water.

I had about got myself settled down when bells rang for noon and
food. I never quite got the hang of those bells; I knew they signalled
change of watches, time passing, but the number of chimes never seemed
to fit the hours, striking as they did in couples.

By the time I had unpacked my wooden bowl and horn mug I was
almost too late; there was only a scrape of gristly stew left and a heel of
yesterday's bread, plus some watered wine, but I wasn't particularly hungry so Growch benefitted. The bread and wine sloshed around uncomfortably in my stomach, for the ship was definitely rolling more heavily
now. Before long, too, there came the pressing need to relieve myself. I
had watched at first with embarrassment, then in increasing awareness
of my own problems, as the crew relieved themselves when necessary
over the side, and had seen the captain's wife empty a couple of chamber
pots the same way. I couldn't do the first and hadn't got the second. Then
I remembered there were some buckets and line in the rope locker. I
pinched the smallest of the former and fastened it to a length of rope long
enough to drop over the side and rinse in the seawater as I had seen the
crew do when they needed water for swilling anything down.

Temporarily more comfortable, I slid my knife under the seals and
string of the packet Signor Falcone had given me and drew out a letter.
I might have known: it was from Suleiman.

"I believe this will reach you before you sail. Do not fear pursuit
for there will be none. Matthew was most distressed to find you gone,
and hopes for your return, but I know better, I think. Something changed
you before you came back to us; I have seen that restless hunger in
other eyes. So, go find your dragon-man—yes, you talked a great deal
in your delirium, but I was the one who nursed you, so it is our secret.
In case you did not copy all the right maps before you left, I enclose
one that is the farthest east that I have.

"Use the gold wisely: you will need as much as you can, the way
you go. May all the gods be with you, and may you find your dream."

There were tears in my eyes as I unfolded the map and found the
gold coins he had enclosed. His understanding touched me deeply.

Sitting back I recalled the time Suleiman had taken the handful of
coins my father had left me and arranged them across a map of the trade
routes, showing how each one—copper, silver or gold—led inexorably
towards the east and the unknown, the very way a certain dragon had
gone, that night when he had left the Place of Stones—

And me.

* * *

Towards evening the weather steadily worsened. The wind blew in gusts, first from one quarter, then another, the lulls leaving the ship rolling uneasily on an increasingly oily swell. Dusk came down early, showing the thinnest crescent moon slicing in and out of the clouds; the cheese I had for supper was causing me great discomfort. At last it and I just had to part company, and I rushed for the rail, only to be jerked back at the last moment by the brawny arm of the mate.

"No puking into the wind!" he hissed. "Else you'll spend all night swilling down both the decks and yourself!"

I made it to leeward just in time, and spent the rest of that miserable night rushing back and forth to the rail. Sometime in the small hours all hands were called to shorten sail, and now I was pushed and cursed at and stumbled over, until in the end someone tied a rope around my waist and wrapped the other end round the after mast, leaving just enough room and no more for me to move between the rail and my improvised quarters.

In the end there was nothing more to come up and I curled up miserably in my cloak, dry-retching every now and again, a sympathetic Growch curled against my hip. In the morning I was no better; I staggered along the now alarmingly tilted deck to fetch food—cheese once more—but it was for my dog. I took a sip or two of wine, but up it came again, and as I was leaning over the rail a huge wave came aboard, near dragging me away back with it, and soaking me to the skin.

Somehow I just couldn't get dry again; rain came lashing down, and the ship was running bare-masted before a wind that had decided to blow us as far off course as possible. The whole vessel creaked and groaned under the onslaught of the waves, and it took three men to hold the ship steady, the tiller threatening to wrest itself from their grasp. I lay half in, half out of my shelter, too weak now to move either way, conscious of Growch's urgent bark in my ears, but lost in a lethargy of cold and darkness of soul and body. Soaked by the rain, tossed to and fro by the motion of the ship, stomach, ribs and shoulders sore and aching, I slipped into a sort of unconsciousness, aware only that I was probably dying. And the worst of it was, I didn't care, even though the ring on my finger was stabbing like a needle.

Suddenly an extra lurch of the ship rolled me right into the scuppers. This is it, I thought. Good-bye world. I'm sorry—

Someone grabbed me by the scruff of my neck, hauled me to my feet and shook me like the drowned rat I so nearly was. A couple of discarded chamber pots skittered past my feet and a voice boomed in my ears in a language I couldn't understand. I shook my head helplessly, muttered something in my own tongue and tried to be sick again.

"Ah, it is so? You come with me . . ." and I was tossed over a brawny shoulder and carried off in a crabwise slant across the deck. A foot shoved hard, a door crashed open and I was spilled onto the floor of a room full of fug, wildly dancing lantern light and blessed warmth.

Dimly I realized that the stout boots and swishing skirts that now stood over me were those of the captain's lady, and that it was her strong arms and broad shoulders that had brought me to the haven of their quarters. Squinting a little through the salt water that still stung my eyes, I saw the captain and mate seated at a center table screwed to the floor, studying what looked to be maps. They had obviously been discussing how far we had been blown off course, but the captain's wife wasn't interested.

I was hauled to my feet again.

"What is this poor boy doing out there? Who is he? Where he come from?" She was speaking my language, although with a strong guttural accent.

The captain rose to his feet. "Ah—an apprentice, my dear, to be delivered to Master Scipio—"

"Then what he do dying out there in storm? No good to deliver dead boy! What you thinking? Get out, both of you! I take charge now—"

"But my dear, we were just—"

"Out! This is now sick bay. Find elsewhere. I take care now. You go sail ship, storm slack soon."

There was a scuffle of feet, a door opened to let in a gust of tempest, shriek of wind. "And you find chamber pots and bring back clean. . . ." The door shut.

I was picked up again, more gently this time, and placed on a bunk in the corner. A large hand felt my forehead, brushed the salt-sticky hair from my brow.

"There, poor boy! You stay still and Helga will care for you, make you well again. Now, out of those wet things and we give wash . . ." and fingers were at the fastenings of my clothes.

I tried to sit up, to protest, but my voice was gone, my hands too feeble to pull my jacket tight across my chest.

"Now, boy, no modestness! I have born and raised six strong boys, and know what bodies is like! Lie still! Once I have . . . Ahhh!" There was a moment's pause. "What do we have here, then?" Rapidly the rest of my clothes were peeled off and I lay naked and exposed, in agonies of shame.

I think I expected almost anything but what I got: a great roar of laughter.

"This is what you call a joke, yes? I feel sorry for skinny lad, and what do I get? A young lady instead . . ." But the voice wasn't unkind, and even as I tried to explain in my cracked voice I was enveloped in a bone-breaking hug. "No talking, that come later. We get you warm and dry first."

A knock at the door. "You wait. . . ." Hastily she flung a blanket over me. "What is it?"

Apparently the return of the chamber pots. "Good. Now you fetch two buckets fresh water. Where are your things?" to me. I whispered. "And boy's things in bales on deck. He stay here. Hurry! What devil is *this*?"

"This" was Growch, a small, wet, filthy bundle that hurled itself across the cabin and onto my bunk, sitting on my chest and growling at everyone and everything, teeth bared.

I found my voice. "My dog. Very devoted. Please don't throw him out. He and I are alone in the world." Weak tears filled my eyes.

"Poor little orphans!" Another hug, for us both this time. "He can stay, but on the floor. Is *filthy*!"

As usual.

The water arrived plus my cloak and bundle. Ten minutes later I was in cold water, being scrubbed clean, my dirty clothes were handed out for washing, and then I was rubbed warm and dry, donned someone's clean shirt and drawers, and was thrust back into bed. A moment later and Growch was in the tub as well, too shocked to protest, and five minutes later he was shaking himself dry in a corner, thoroughly huffy.

Out went the dirty water, in came food, a sort of broth and some real bread. I went green at the thought of anything to eat, but the captain's wife insisted.

"If you going to be sick, better you be sick with something to be sick on. Dip bread into soup, suck juices, nibble bread. Count to ten tens—you can count?—then do again. And again. Try . . ."

I did, and it worked. After a few queasy moments I kept the first two pieces of bread down, and the rest was easy. The last few pieces of bread and broth I indicated were for Growch.

A hammering on the door again, and that loud-voiced martinet who strode the deck of his ship like a small but determined Colossus and ruled his crew with the threat of a rope's end, was heard asking his wife in the meekest way possible if he might have some more maps?

"Take them and be quick about it! Take also a blanket and your eating things. You will bunk with the mate. Now, be off with you! I have work to do. . . ."

I suppose my mouth must have been hanging open, because as he left she turned and winked at me. "Never let them get away with nothing, my chick," she said comfortably. "Out there—" she gestured to the sea, the storm, the tossing deck, "—he is boss. In here, I am, and he don't forget it."

I looked around the cabin. Comfortable, yes, but not luxurious. Not the sort of place one could call home.

"Do you sail with him all the time? I mean, haven't you got a place ashore? And aren't you ever afraid?"

She laughed. "No, yes, and yes. I sail when I want a change, go to new places. I have a home far from here, near youngest son, not yet married. Afraid? Of course. But this not bad storm, only little Levante who blow us off course forty-fifty mile. Rest of voyage routine. My man know this: he only want maps to make him look important." She bustled about, tidying the already tidy. "Now you get some rest. Tell me all about yourself when you wake up." She held up one of the chamber pots. "You or dog want pee-pee?"

I slept all through the rest of that day and the night, and when I awoke at last the storm was off away somewhere else, my sickness had gone, I was hungry for the first time in days and all I had to do was concoct a romantic enough story to satisfy my indulgent hostess. It wasn't too difficult: I remembered my beautiful blind knight, invented parents who didn't understand my love, relived parts of my earlier journeys, including a near rape, and finally sent my betrothed off on a pilgrimage from which he had not yet returned, thus my escapade.

Tears of sympathy poured from her eyes. She sighed, she sobbed as my tears—of hunger: where was my breakfast?—mingled with hers.

"My dearest chick! How often I wish for a daughter! Now my prayers will all be with you. . . ." She dried her eyes, glanced at me. "You are sure you are set on this knight of yours? My youngest son, he is not the brightest boy in the world, but . . ."

I was almost sorry to disappoint her.

One fine evening we sailed between two jaws of land into the mouth of a bay made bloodred by the setting sun. Climbing the hill behind was a beautiful city, with gold cupolas, pierced minarets, palaces and tree-lined streets. Even as we nudged in towards the quay, lights appeared in windows, along streets, moving with carriages or hand-held, until the whole city resembled a rosy hive alive with sparkling bees.

Matthew's ships had a permanently allotted landing stage, so we were rowed in and tied up right on the quayside. Immediately aboard was the Master Scipio I was waiting to meet. Of medium height, with a forked beard, he exuded authority. After a brief courtesy to myself, he took Falcone's papers from the captain and started the unloading with his own team, disregarding the swarm of itinerants who crowded the quay touting for work.

The cargo was checked by myself, now fully recovered, and Master Scipio's assistant, a dark man called Justus, then it was borne away to a warehouse for storage. It was well into the night by the time we finished and we ate where we stood, highly flavored meats on skewers with a sort of pancake bread. At last we went back to the ship for what remained of the night. It was strange to lie down and not be rocked from side to side, and it took a while, tired as I was, to get to sleep.

Added to the lack of motion there was the noise from ashore. Used as I was to the creaking of the ship, the noise of wind and sea, my ears were now assailed by the sounds of humanity at large, determined to wine and carouse the night away. The ship was moored right up against the "entertainment" part of the harbor, and the night was alive with singing, wailing and shouting, wheels, hooves, and musical instruments. I learned later that the captain's wife had stood guard for the rest of the night on the gangplank, armed with an ancient sword, turning back not only those members of the crew who wished to creep ashore, but also any enterprising whore who attempted to board.

Before we went ashore finally she drew me aside and pressed a small packet into my hand.

"Is a nothings," she said. "But pretty enough perhaps. You take it for present. My husband he bring it back as gift when he sail alone. Say it come from wise man down on his luck. . . ." She laughed. "Only truth is, I get gift means he has another woman somewhere. Guilty conscience. Better you have it for dowry," and she gave me another of her bear hugs, which almost had my eyes popping out. "Take care, chick; I so hope you find your man!"

On shore Master Scipio was waiting with his second-in-command, half a dozen guards and a horse master. After briefly introducing me, we went off for breakfast at a small tavern some half-mile from the port. We ate a thick fish stew, more of the pancakelike bread, olives, a bland cheese, and drank the local wine. A street and a half further on were our lodgings; a three-story house in a narrow twisting alley, that almost touched its neighbor across the street at roof level.

Our rooms were little more than cubicles, overlooking a central courtyard where a small fountain tinkled pleasantly amid vine-covered walls. I was lucky enough to have a small space to myself: a clean pallet and a stool, and it was relatively cool.

Master Scipio spoke to us from the stairs. "I have things to arrange. We shall meet again tonight at the same tavern. To those of you who are new to the city, a word or two of advice. Don't venture far and keep your hand on your purse. Don't get involved in arguments on religion or over women, because I won't bail you out. Watch both the food and the drink; if you are ill you are left behind. One last thing: do not discuss our cargo or our destination."

"How long are we here for?" asked one of the guards.

"We start out at dawn tomorrow. Anyone not packed and ready will be left behind," and off he clattered down the stairs. Not a gentle man, but at least one knew where one was with him.

Two of the guards set off almost immediately, to "see the sights," as they put it, but the others lingered. Eventually one, a local man, went off to visit some relative or other, and the others decided to go out sightseeing.

"You coming, youngster?"

I would dearly have loved to explore the city, but after last night's sleeplessness the pallet was more inviting. I took off my jacket and lay back, promising myself a good wash later. My eyes closed. . . .

At the foot of the pallet Growch made a great to-do of hoofing out his ears and nipping busily for fleas.

"Can't you do that on the floor?" I asked sleepily.

"More comfortable up 'ere." He was quiet for a moment or two, and I began to drift off. " 'Ow long you goin' to kip, then?"

"An hour or so. Why?"

"I'm 'ungry!"

"You're always hungry. . . ."

"Can you remember the last thing I ate? No, and neither can I."

"Just give me an hour," I said between my teeth. "One hour . . ."

3

Actually he let me sleep for two and I woke gently and naturally, lying back in a luxury of lassitude. I could hear him on the landing, snapping at flies. He was quite good at it, usually; having such short legs he tried to compensate in other ways, and quickness of paw, mouth, and eye were three of them.

And of course it was Growch who had alerted me to the other of my secrets: the power of the ring I wore on my right hand. One could hardly guess it was there, I thought, lifting my finger to gaze at it. As thin as a piece of skin it nestled on my middle finger as if it were a part of it. I couldn't remove it, either. According to what I had heard, the ring chose its wearer and stayed there, until either the wearer had no further use for it or grew unworthy to wear it.

This latter must have been what happened to my father, who had left the ring, some coins and his cloak as the only legacies to my mother and myself. He had been hunted down and killed on a false accusation before I had ever been born, but my mother—who was the village whore and no worse for it either—had kept the few pieces he left as mementos. She had worn the cloak I now possessed, had spent all the current moneys he had left, but was unable to change the curious coins I inherited, that had so fitted the maps Suleiman and I had studied. Coincidence perhaps, but intuition told me my father had once come this way, too. A good omen.

As to the ring I had slipped on my finger so thoughtlessly the night my mother died, it had been the most magical thing in my life. According to Growch, the first creature I had met after fleeing the village where I was born, it was a precious sliver of horn from the head of a fabulous Unicorn, and as such enabled me to communicate with other creatures and also, as I discovered later, warned of impending danger.

I wondered what sin my father had committed for it to leave his finger; my mother had not been able to fit it to hers either, whereas it had slipped onto mine like bear grease and stuck like glue.

I couldn't have managed without it. Nor, I thought with a wry smile, would I have once encumbered myself with not only a blind knight, but also a dog, Mistral the horse, Traveler the pigeon, Basher the tortoise, and my beloved little pig. . . . No, I mustn't think about the pig.

Be that as it may, the ring had completely changed my life. My mother had had ambitions for me. With the help of her "clients," I had been educated far beyond a village girl's station. I could read, write, figure, cook, sew, carpenter, cure, fish, hunt, brew, farm, spin and weave. She had plans for me to become the sort of woman who could choose her own husband and take a place in society, but the queer paradox had been that she couldn't bear to part with me, so had, knowingly or not, fed me with sweet cakes and honeyed fruits until I was the fattest, most unattractive girl in the province and no one would have me. I hadn't realized it until after she died, and it took a while to become reconciled to her duplicity, conscious or not.

But, as I said, the ring had changed all that. By the time I had learned to communicate properly with all the creatures I met and who needed my help, the original intent of seeking the first husband I could find had disappeared under other considerations.

Not that understanding the animals had been easy. Only one-tenth of animal speech is in sound—barks, neighs, bleats, etc.—and another three-tenths are in body movement, position of head, legs, ears, and feel of coat and fur. The other, and greater part, is thought-talk. This last was the most difficult for me, even with the help of the Unicorn's ring. Animals think in sorts of pictures, colored only by their own thoughts and seen from their own angles, so a bird didn't send back the same images as, say, a dog or a horse. Eventually, though, it became easier, and Growch and I spoke to each other almost entirely by thought.

Dear dog: all he had wanted in the beginning was a real home, a warm fire to curl up by in the winter, regular food and a pat or two, but he had left all that behind to follow me into an uncertain future. He had pretended that his real reason was to find more of those "fluffy bum" bitches he had fallen for in our earlier travels, pampered creatures from Cathay with legs as short as his and no morals whatsoever, but I knew better. He had decided that his real role in life was to keep an eye on me: he was convinced I couldn't manage on my own.

He trotted in now, one ear up, one down, as usual.

"Awake now, are we? 'Ow's about some food, then?"

* * *

We assembled in a small square behind our lodgings in shivering dawn. The sun would soon rise above the rearing mountains, but now the sky was a pale greenish-blue, and the mist lay knee-high in the streets. Breakfast was pancake bread and honey, and as the church bells called out six and a muezzin sang from his tower, the convoy got under way.

A string of heavily laden mules, two wagons, eight mounted guards and horses for Master Scipio, interpreter Justus, horse master Antonius and our guide, a skinny fellow called Ibrahim. Nothing for me: Master Scipio explained that I either walked or hitched a lift in one of the wagons.

"Do you good, boy," he said robustly. "Half day walk, half ride. And you can alternate the wagons. One driver doubles as the cook—you can give him a hand, he'll teach you what foods are best for travelling. T'other wagon is driven by the farrier: knows all there is to know about horses. Right?"

So we were off, all yawning, for we had none of us had much sleep at the lodgings. The guards had straggled back at all hours, full of the local wine and boasting of their winnings and/or conquests.

I reached up to pull at Master Scipio's sleeve.

"Where are we bound?"

"For the trading town of Küm."

"How long will it take?"

"Over the trails we follow, four or five days."

So long! Now that we were finally on our way proper I was eager to complete my journey east as fast as I could. It seemed I would have to be patient.

Our way lay to the northeast, and once we left the city behind the travelling was frustratingly slow. We twisted and turned along trails that followed the lowest contours of the land; the tracks had been there for time immemorial, the easiest for man and beast, and for the most part were within easy reach of water, but were also rutted and broken by the years of travel.

At first the surrounding countryside was relatively well wooded and we were hemmed by low hills, but the further we travelled the wilder became the terrain. The hills grew higher and crowded closer, the trees gave way to low scrub and the sun burned us in the breezeless valleys. It was cooler at night, but we always built a fire, both to cook the evening meal and to deter any wild animal; every evening we heard mountain dogs howling at the moon, sometimes near, sometimes far.

We had brought our own provisions with us, to avoid paying high

prices in the small villages we passed through, and this proved our un-
doing.

On the third night the cook prepared a stew, and in order to disguise
the (by now) high smell and taste of the meat, threw some very pungent
herbs and spices into the pot. I watched him take various packets from
his pockets, but after asking the names of a few, all unknown to me, I
lost interest; besides, he said my watching him made him feel nervous.
He was a taciturn man at best, and poor company if I rode in his wagon.
He wasn't a very good cook, either.

I took a portion of the stew over to Growch and sat down beside
him to eat mine, but two very disconcerting things happened. One, my
precious ring gave a little warning stab, and two, Growch took one sniff
and flatly refused to eat any.

Now, my dog doesn't refuse food. Ever. He can devour stuff that
turns my stomach even to look at.

"What's the matter? It smells all right. A little spicy, perhaps, but
you've eaten worse." I lifted my spoon to my mouth but his tail got in
the way, and at the same time my ring prickled again.

"Don' touch it! S'not good to eat. Don' know why, but somethin'
in there ain't right."

"Are you suggesting it's poisoned?" I tried to laugh it off. I was
hungry.

"Not poison. Told you, don' know what's wrong; all I know is, I'm
not havin' any, and you shouldn' neither."

The ring stabbed again. "All right," I said crossly, as much to it as
to Growch. "Cheese and dates."

"Skip the dates. . . ."

As I went to return our untouched food to the stew pot, I noticed
others doing the same. Not all, by any means. About half the men were
eating heartily, others were just picking. If I had needed any confirmation that it wasn't entirely palatable, I would have had it in the fact that
the cook himself wasn't eating his own food: he had just handed the
guide Ibrahim a plate of dried fruit and cut himself a heel of cheese,
although he scowled when I asked for the same.

It wasn't until we had been on the road for a couple of hours the next
day that the wisdom of avoiding the stew became apparent. One by one
men groaned, clutched their stomachs and disappeared into the brush to
be violently ill. By noon about half were incapacitated, unable to ride,
and had to be hauled up onto the wagons, their horses tied behind.

Master Scipio called me over, his face gray and sweating.

"Here, boy: take my horse. I'm going to rest for a while," and off he disappeared into the bushes, to reemerge some moments later to help me up on the horse and then climb himself onto the nearest wagon.

At first it was just fine to be riding up so high, feeling well and fit while all around were groaning and moaning, but Growch was grumbling that he was wearing his legs down to their stumps trying to keep up with me as I rode from one end of the line to the other, as Master Scipio did, and after a while the high wooden saddle began to chafe and the bottom of my spine felt bruised. I checked up and down once more: half the mule drivers and half the guards were riding the wagons and the guide, Ibrahim, was driving the farrier's cart.

I brought the horse to an amble beside Master Scipio.

"Like to ride again? Or shall we halt and have a rest, water the horses?"

He looked better, but not much.

"Not yet. We won't stop, because if we do we'll never get going again. Keep riding; there's a good camping place a few miles further on. We'll stop there overnight."

The trouble was, we had had to travel so slowly with the overladen wagons that we had made very little progress by the time the sun slid behind the hills and the valley we travelled became gloomy and full of shadows. Once again I implored Master Scipio to take to his horse but once again he refused.

"A mile or so more, that's all, then we can rest, I promise. Ride up to the head of the line and see if you can hurry up those mules. . . ."

I was so sorry for myself and my saddle sores as I rode to the front, noting the weariness of the animals as they plodded on, heads hanging, puffing and blowing, that it wasn't for a moment or two that the growing noise behind me made any sense. It seemed that the hubbub and the prickling of my ring coincided, which meant danger, so I wheeled the horse as quickly as I could (not easy because the track had narrowed to a defile) and pushed him back towards the wagons and Master Scipio.

Our whole caravan stretched back now over a quarter-mile or thereabouts, because of the growing dusk, general weariness, lack of Scipio's incisive leadership and, most of all, the narrowness of the trail. As I kicked my reluctant jade to a faster pace, Growch panting at our heels, the noise—shouts, yells, neighing of horses, clash of swords—made no sense, until I rounded a curve and saw the horde of ragged men armed with spears, swords, clubs, and knives that were creeping out of the bush and attacking the wagons.

Ambush!

My heart gave a *thump* of terror, and the hand that fumbled at my belt for the dagger I kept there was slick with the sweat of fear. My horse had caught the scent of blood and reared suddenly, so that I lost the reins and had to hang on to his mane with both hands as he turned away from the battle. I tried my damnedest to pull his head round, find the reins again, but all of a sudden a figure leapt from the undergrowth, a knife between his teeth, a spear in his hand.

The ring was burning on my finger but I could do nothing but freeze in horror as the spear was lifted in my direction and the man's mouth opened in a howl of exultation. Death stared at me, and I couldn't even pray—

There was a growl, a yelp, a cry of pain, and the spear missed me by a fraction and struck my horse's rump. It reared with a scream of pain, its flailing hooves downed my would-be attacker, luckily missing Growch, then it plunged off again down the track and away from the fighting.

Once more it was all I could do to hang on as I was bounced and jounced like a sack of meal on that horrid hard saddle. I bumped both nose and chin on the high pommel, banged my leg on a rock as the horse swerved at the last moment, and scratched my arm on some branch or scrub that scraped our sides.

Tears of pain squeezed past my closed eyelids: would this never stop? We must have galloped at least—

The animal came to an abrupt halt, forelegs quivering, and the sudden lack of motion did what the flight couldn't. I fell off onto the ground and lay there with my head spinning and everything else hurting, while the wretched animal cropped the grass next to my ear with a sound like tearing linen.

I'm dead, I thought. I must be. No one could have survived that headlong gallop. I'll just lie here and wait for the golden trumpets. . . . Washed in the blood of the Lamb—

Nothing so sacred. I was being washed, but by a sloppy, anxious dog. I sat up gingerly.

"Go away, Growch! I'm all right. . . ."

"Then get up and tell 'em! 'Bout the ambush!"

I opened my eyes. We were in a clearing full of people running towards us. Over to one side a huge fire was flickering. For a desperate moment I thought I had stumbled into the ambushers' camp, but a closer look showed these were respectable travellers. In a moment I was surrounded and a babel of tongues was flinging questions at me till my head hurt worse than ever. I explained in my own tongue, market Latin, a little Italian and a couple of words of Arabic I had picked up (I think these last were profanities, remembering where I had heard them, but no one seemed to mind) and a moment or two later armed men were clattering away back the way I had come.

Someone led me over to the fire and smeared an evil-smelling grease on the more obvious bumps and bruises, and gave me a mug of spiced wine which I downed gratefully. I accepted another and a bowl of rice and chicken. Something nudged my arm, and half the contents of the bowl were on the ground.

"Ta!" said Growch pleasantly, licking up the last grains. "That was fun, wasn't it? That fella din' 'alf yell when I nipped 'im! Quite a battle . . ."

Of course! I remembered now. He had doubtless saved my life when he bit my attacker's ankle, though I didn't know whether he realized it. I tipped the rest of the rice out.

"Here: I'm not hungry. . . . Thanks."

"Nothing to it. 'Ere: why don't you ask for another bowlful?"

It appeared the ambush had been well planned. The stew had been dosed with a powerful emetic, and both the guide Ibrahim and the cook had made good their escape. We had lost two guards and a mule driver and there were several wounded, including Master Scipio, who finally rode in with his arm in a sling. But I was hailed as a hero for riding to seek help and feted with choice titbits and a handful of hastily gathered coin, a whip-round from the survivors.

I felt a trifle guilty as I accepted the coins and blushed when they called me a hero, but as Growch remarked, now was not the time to tell them my horse had bolted from a superficial spear wound and heroism had nothing to do with it.

Master Scipio accepted the offer of our new friends to travel under the protection of their bigger caravan—a friendship cemented in gold I noticed—as far as the trading city. Being a larger party, and with wounded to care for, our progress was of necessity slow, so it was on the third afternoon after our rescue that we topped the final ridge and I gazed down on the city of Küm.

4

But that's not a town," I said, bitterly disappointed. "It's just—just a collection of tents!"

Scipio drew his horse alongside the wagon I was riding in.

"Tents maybe, but still the largest trading center for hundreds of miles." He gestured below. "A plain some three miles wide, the same long, with a river to the east. Mountains all around, yes, but with age-old trails that lead in from Cathay, India, the Middle Sea, the Baltic, the Western Isles . . ." He leant back, let the reins lie slack, as we waited for the wagon ahead to start the narrow trail down. "Looks fine now, doesn't it? But in the autumn when the rains come the river down there is a raging torrent; in the winter the bitter winds blow in from the north, the river freezes over and the sands below are as sharp as hailstones as they whirl across the plain. In the spring the rain and the melting snows from the hills flood the plateau, but when the waters recede and the sun comes out, the grass and flowers grow thick and fast. Then the advance parties come, those who cut and dry the grasses for forage; after them come the men with tents for hire, the cooks, the laundrymen, the farriers, and the men who dig the cesspits. Local villagers bring in fresh fruit, vegetables, chickens, sheep, and goats, and there is a committee of those concerned who ensure everything runs smoothly for when the first of the traders arrive in mid-June. From then until mid-September the place is seething. I truly believe one can find anything in the world down there if needed. . . ." And off he spurred down the hill.

I turned to Nod, my driver. "Have you been this way before?"

"Oh, aye: wouldn't miss it for the world. Just as Master Scipio says: the world and his mate meet here. Nice rest for us too. We can just sit back and enjoy ourselves while the bosses natter and bicker and blather and dicker over every blessed piece of barter." He was chewing on a root of liquorice and spat a brown stream over the edge of the wagon as we began the descent. "I seen stuff there as you couldn't imagine: furs, silks, wools, dyes, carpets, rugs, 'broideries; copper pots, clay pots, glass, china; daggers, swords, spears; paintings and manuscripts, pens and brushes; all the spices you could think of and dried herbs; wines, dried fruits, rice, and tea. There's even bars of gold and silver, precious jewels, children's toys— Whoa, there!" He was silent for a moment or two as we negotiated a difficult turn. He spat out more juice. "Then there's the animals. . . ."

"Lions and tigers?"

"Sometimes. They're mostly to special order. I seen a panther and a spotted cat with jewelled collars, tame as you please, and even once, a helefant, with a nose longer than its tail. . . . No, mostly they's more portable. Monkeys, 'xotic birds, snakes as thick as your arm, queer little dogs . . ."

Oh, no! I thought. Not Growch's "fluffy bums"; keeping an eye on him in that place would be difficult.

"Then there's the slaves. Mostly men, 'cos women and children don't travel well, but you see the occasional two or three. All colors, too: mostly black or brown, but there's some yellows and near-whites. Dwarfs, sometimes, they fetch a good price." He spoke as indifferently as if they were bales of cloth.

We were on easier ground now, and the town beneath seemed to be taking on a pattern. The tents appeared to be arranged in rows rather than haphazardly, and although the number of people running around made it seem chaotic, there also seemed to be a purpose in all they did.

Nod pointed out the various vantage points with his whip.

"To the right there, by the river, is the laundries, below 'em the cesspits, above stables and forage. In the center the living accommodation, to the left the cooking areas. Below us are the money-changers. Top left the brothels. Clear space in the middle, the market, held daily. Doubles up for special entertainment at night."

"What sort of special entertainment?"

"Oh, dancing girls, snake charmers, acrobats—whatever's going. One year there were those belly dancers from Afriky: sight for sore eyes they were. . . ."

It seemed Master Scipio was right: everyone was catered for.

Rent-a-tent came first. We hired four. Scipio, interpreter Justus, horse master Antonius and I shared one, the remaining guards and mule drivers another, larger, and our goods took up the last two.

The sleeping tents were circular, those for the goods rectangular. The poles were bamboo, the canvas thin and light, for no rain was expected at this time of year. Other traders had brought their own, more luxurious, with hangings to divide the interiors into smaller sections for sleeping or entertaining. Some had oriental rugs and silken cushions to sit upon, small brass or inlaid wooden tables, oil lamps and fine crockery, but we had grass matting, stools and wood-frame beds strung with rope, which were highly uncomfortable. I stated my intention of sleeping on the floor, but Scipio pointed silently to a double column of ants, in one side of the tent, out of the other. He then handed me some small clay cups.

"Fill these with water, then put the feet of the beds in them, otherwise we'll have all sorts climbing up. Bad enough with the mosquitoes."

He wasn't joking; I spent a most uncomfortable night, listening with dread for the sudden silence which meant they had found their target. The next night I was given a jar of evil-smelling grease, which helped, but that first day I was as spotty as any adolescent lad.

Even without the mosquitoes, that first night would have kept me wakeful. I had not yet learnt how to fold my blanket so as to even out the rope sling I was suspended upon, the moon shone with relentless brightness through the thin walls of the tent, and the night was full of unaccustomed noise. There were snores from my companions, barking from scores of dogs—including Growch, who was absent without leave—the flap-flap of canvas as it responded to the night breeze, shouts and yells in the distance, and somewhere someone was singing what sounded like an endless dirge full of quarter tones that scraped at my sensibilities like the squeaks of an unoiled axle.

That first day—and many afterwards—was spent visiting tent after tent with the attendant interminable bargaining that seemed so much a part of any sort of trade out here. No price was ever fixed, not even for the food we ate, and even less so for the goods we bought and sold. A great deal of exchange and barter took the place of coin: we exchanged all our wool, for instance, for what seemed to me a minute quantity of saffron and some lily bulbs, but Scipio was more than satisfied.

I had to attend as it was part of my (supposed) training, and if it hadn't been for the endless hospitality—sherbet, yoghurt or mint tea, small sweet cakes or wafers—I should have dropped off long before the sun was high. Nearly everything had to be done through our interpreter, Justus, and one had to go through all the politenesses of enquiry about travel, friends, relatives, weather and health long before one revealed one's true objectives. It seemed such a waste of time, but Master Scipio was insistent that I realize it was the only way to get things done, and was less than sympathetic when I begged off the last visit with an ill-concealed yawn.

"I'm sorry: I didn't sleep very well last night. I'll be better tomorrow, I promise."

"And so you better had; you're here to work, to learn, to become a trader, and a night or two's lost sleep is neither here nor there. A young lad like you should party the night away and then be fresh as new milk in the morning. I don't know what the world is coming to: why at your age . . ." and so on.

They went off on their last visit, I smeared myself with grease, fell on the bed and must have slept for hours, for when I awoke, hungry and refreshed, they were all abed and snoring and it must have been around an hour past midnight. It was Growch's cold nose that had woken me: he was hungry too.

As he had been absent most of the day I wasn't sympathetic, would probably have turned over and tried to sleep again, except that my own stomach was grumbling likewise. I was also sweaty and sticky and needed a good wash. By the sounds outside, the food stalls would probably still be open, so I swung my legs off the bed and we crept out through the tent flap into the moony night.

It was a near light as day, and there was no problem in finding our way towards the cooking stalls. I found one of our guards seated on a long bench by a large barbecue and he invited me to join him in a dish of chicken, lentils and herbs. I sneaked some to Growch, then repaid the guard by buying the wine. While we travelled food and lodgings were paid for out of the travelling purse, so at a place like this we were given a food allowance every day, the same for all. The guards and drivers were either paid their wages at the end of the journey or re-engaged to be paid at the other end on their return, which was the case with our guards and drivers, so they would have little enough to spare. I left him a couple of coins for more wine, then strolled in the direction of the river, hoping it would be deserted enough for a wash.

It seemed, though, that some people worked throughout the night. The forage-and-horse lines were relatively quiet, but the launderers were hard at work, washing and rinsing, beating out the dirt on great flat stones and draping the clothes out on rocks to catch the early sun. Here the river was scummy with dirt, which flowed on down towards the cesspits, where I could hear the noise of digging.

I turned north, past the great tumps of hay and straw to where the land grew rockier and the river flowed faster, and was lucky enough to find a tiny sandy bay which curved round a pool where the water was quieter.

I gazed about me but could see no one, and all the activity seemed to be away south.

"Keep watch," I said to Growch. "I fancy a quick dip—"

"You're mad!" he snorted. "Wouldn' catch me bathin' in that! Un'ealthy, all this washin' . . ."

I stripped right down and plunged into the water, stifling a yell as the freezing mountain water all but numbed me. Summer it might be, but the water didn't know that. After the first shock, however, I luxuriated in the fast-flowing water as it washed away the stinks and grime of the last few days. Even my bruises from the bolting horse had started to fade, I noted. My underwear and shirt joined me in the water: they could dry out on my body, for the night seemed positively hot after the icy water.

My last act before getting clothed again was to pick up a furious, scratching, nipping Growch, and dump him in the deepest pool I could find. . . .

He cursed for a full fluid minute without repeating himself when he reached dry land, but I had a couple of raisin biscuits in my pouch which mollified him somewhat, though he did treat me to an exhibition of the hollow cough he had suddenly picked up, and shivered most convincingly.

"Don' ever do that again! 'Nough to give me my death, that was!"

I suggested a walk, to dry us both off.

"Quickest way to the food tents is straight across," he said, so that was the way we went, though I doubted they would still be serving. Luckily for him we found a couple of stalls still open and I bargained for some skewers of meat, which we chewed as we wandered back towards the sleeping tents.

Growch stopped in midstride. "Listen . . ."

At first I could hear nothing, then the wind picked up the sound. A soft whimpering, moaning, keening, like the sound a child will make when it has been punished and sent to bed, but dare not make too much noise unless it invites more punishment. The breeze changed direction and the noise died away, then I heard it again.

Growch's nose was working overtime. "Back there," he said tersely. His nose was pointing way beyond the rest of the encampment. "Not nice . . ."

My ring was warm on my finger, so there was no danger, and there was something in the sound that called out to me, like the despair of a trapped animal. Almost without conscious thought I started to walk towards the crying. At first, in spite of the moonlight, I could see nothing unusual, but as I rounded an outcrop of rock I saw what looked like a huge cage, or series of cages, like those in which they kept the exotic animals on offer.

But animals didn't sound like this, or smell like this either.

I wrinkled my nose with distaste and beside me Growch was growling, not in anger but rather in a mixture of bewilderment and disgust, as if this was a situation he did not know how to cope with. I moved closer till the moonlight threw the shadow of the bars across me like cold fingers, and I could see the full horror of what lay behind them.

The cages were crowded with human beings, men, women and children, all shackled, and all standing, sitting, or lying in their own foulnesses. Even in the stews of large towns I had smelt nothing like this, and it was not only the excrement but a sort of miasma of despair and fear that came from the unwashed captives that made me recoil in disgust.

Hands were stretched out between the bars towards me, the keening rose in volume and now there were words I could not understand, except that they were pleas for help. Against my will I moved closer and now the chains were clanking, the babble of words grew louder and fingers clutched at my sleeve with a strength I would not have thought possible.

"I can't do anything," I said urgently, although I knew they would not understand. "Let me go. . . ."

But their seeking hands found more and more of me, until there was a prickle from my ring and almost at once a shout and running feet. At once I was released and, looking back, I saw a couple of men with lanterns bobbing in their hands running towards the cages.

"C'mon," barked Growch urgently. "We don't want to be caught by that lot. They'll think we've been tryin' to help 'em escape. . . ."

Dodging in and out of whatever shadow I could find, I ran back to the safety of the lines of tents, my heart beating uncomfortably fast, my mind churning. It was not that I didn't know slavery existed—why, in the very village in which I had grown up, we were less than animals to the lord of the manor, who held the power of life and death, imprisonment or mutilation, as he chose. But there at least we had known the rules and abided by them, and life was comfortable enough if we paid our dues. Besides we knew no other existence; those poor captives back there had been snatched away from homes and families against their will—and what sort of future could they expect?

That they would be exploited there was no doubt. If you paid for something you expected your money's worth. Physical labor, prostitution, degradation, these were the least they could look forward to. Perhaps I should not have minded so much if I hadn't remembered Signor Falcone's far kinder fate—but where were the Suleimans of this world to rescue this batch? And the thousands of others, both now and in the future? How many of these would still be alive in, say, a year's time?

I was saddened and frustrated, and said extra prayers for those poor creatures before seeking what I thought would be a sleepless bed, but I must have been more exhausted than I thought, for I slept like a child.

The following days were spent in more trading. It seemed that you could exchange what you had for something of equal value, and the next day swap that for something you considered to be more valuable, sell half that, find a customer for the rest, use the money for another purchase and so on. In this way our tents of goods were emptied and filled at least three times to my knowledge. Master Scipio did not appear to lose by these deals for he went about with less than his usual degree of taciturnity, though whether this had anything to do with the nightly entertainments he went to, I do not know. Sufficient to note that he, Justus and Antonius seldom came to bed before the small hours.

The pattern of barter and trade soon became easier for me to follow, although I still found the whole process tedious and realized I would never have either the patience of Matthew nor the acumen of Suleiman. But this apprenticeship was the only way to my goal, so I tried my hardest to learn and even earned compliments from Scipio for my diligence. Of course there were still the language barriers, but I was picking up a word or phrase or two of Arabic every day and could refer to our interpreter, Justus, if I had need.

On the fifth day I asked Scipio how much longer we should be at Küm, to receive the answer that we awaited one particular trader to conclude our business.

"We shall do no more trading until he arrives," continued Scipio, "so why don't you take the afternoon off and see the sights? Here, go buy yourself a trinket or two," and he tossed me a couple of coins.

Glad enough not to be shut up in a stuffy tent for hours, Growch and I wandered off into the sunshine. For many this was the afternoon time, which meant we could roam at will without being trampled underfoot, so we stopped for sherbet and barbecued meat on sticks, then watched a basket weaver for a few minutes. Growch decided he was going to investigate what sounded like one of the interminable dogfights that went on day and night, so I just walked where my feet took me, refusing a sweet seller here, a rug seller there, until I found myself at the western edge of the camp, beyond the tents.

Here on the edge of the encampment lived those too poor to hire tents, or nomads who preferred to wander the fringes with their flocks, sleeping under the stars. Among the former were the fearsome men from the far north who had brought their shaggy ponies laden with furs, carvings of wood and bone and metal ornaments in the shape of dragons and strange sea creatures. I had learned from the horse master, Antonius, that they found no trouble in disposing of their wares, exchanging them for salt, dried fruits, linen and presents for their women: combs, polished metal mirrors, needles and colored threads, but that as it was all strictly barter they were always short of cash for food and amusements, and often went to unorthodox methods to obtain it. Of course they could go straight home once the goods were exchanged, but it seemed they stayed as long as they could, loath to return to their cold and barren lands.

They were wild enough to look at, these northerners. Dressed in their outlandish gear of iron skullcaps (some with horns affixed), fur capes and short leather trews, their faces scarred with ritual knife cuts and adorned with straggling moustaches, they would have been fearsome enough even without the assortment of knives and axes they stuck in their belts.

If truth would have it though, they were probably no more fearsome than the adolescent town louts of any large town, swaggering the streets with boasts of their conquests on the field and in bed, swearing that they could drink anyone under the bench. All mouth and cock, as my mother used to say.

They appeared to have arranged some sort of wrestling match and had shouted up a reasonable audience for it, one man busy taking bets on the outcome. It was to be a no-holds-barred free-for-all, with kicking, gouging, biting, hair-pulling and balls-grabbing part of the fun, as a bystander explained to me; he seemed to think all the fights were fixed, but watching the first, in which the loser ended up with half an ear torn off and his face ground into the dirt till he lost consciousness, I wasn't convinced.

Someone came round with an upended skullcap and I tossed in the smallest coin I could find. Another bout was just starting—promising, from the look of the combatants, to be even bloodier than the first—but by now more people, siesta over, had arrived to watch, and being slighter and smaller than most I found myself elbowed out to the fringes, where I could see but little. I had just decided to look for amusement elsewhere when there was a nudge on the back of my leg and Growch, absent till now, said quietly: "Look at that feller over there; pickin' their purses, he is. . . ."

Nearby was a stack of bales, ready for loading onto the shaggy ponies when these warriors decided enough was enough and I moved behind it to watch the thief unobserved. He was younger than most— around seventeen I should guess—and slim, stealthy and quick. I could not help but admire the way he circled the back of the crowd, picking his next victim, then holding back till the people surged forward at a particularly vicious moment in the wrestling to yell encouragement to one or other contestant, then taking advantage of the press of bodies to lift a purse to his hand, weigh its possibilities—I saw him reject two in this way—and then use his sharp knife to detach pouch and contents from its owner. Judging from the bulge at the back of his trews he had been busy for quite a while.

I was so busy admiring his expertise that it wasn't until he had lifted three more purses that I realized that I should do something about it. But what? Shout "Stop thief!"? Thieving was a sin, but did I owe the gullible crowd anything? Besides he was an artist, in his own way, and nearly everyone would steal if the need was great— Stop it, Summer! I told myself severely. Never mind the ethics, just prevent him from further robbery.

I had a word with Growch, then stepped from behind my hiding place and tapped the young man on the shoulder. He jumped about a foot in the air and was about to bolt, but Growch's teeth were now fixed lovingly in his right ankle, and he had no alternative than to follow me to my hiding place behind the bales.

Perspiration was pouring off his forehead and I could smell the acrid sweat of fear. We knew not a word of each other's language but I mimed my disgust at his actions and threatened to trumpet his thefts to all within earshot.

He crumpled at my feet; purses and bags came tumbling from his trews. One by one he offered them to me, his hands shaking, but this was not what I had meant at all. He was obviously terrified, so the purpose of my intervention had worked: there would probably be no more stealing today.

I shook my head vigorously at the pile of purses at my feet and backed away, but he must have thought I wanted more, something special, for he offered me a blue amulet that hung round his neck, then an iron ring set with a red stone, and the more I shook my head, waved him away, the worse he got. I suddenly realized the reason for his fear; thieves could be hung, or at the least their hands cut off—

Something was thrust into my hands, a hard object wrapped in soft leather, and from the look of the thief's face it was his prize possession, the ultimate gift. I unwrapped it, curiously, but all it was was a piece of stone or rock or metal pointed at one end, about two fingers long and one wide. There was a small groove around the middle and wound round this was a piece of gut with a loop at the end so that it could be hung from one's finger. What was it? A weapon? A child's toy?

My puzzlement must have shown, for the thief took it from my hand, gestured to the north and held the stone so that it pointed in that direction. He looked at me, then turned the pointed end to the south, let it go—and it swung back to the north again. He handed it back to me and it worked once again. Sure that there was some trickery I twisted the gut round and round and let the stone twirl—still it ended up pointing north. Light dawned: this was a fabulous navigating instrument that would work even if the sun was hidden or the night without stars. Just think how wonderful it would be at sea, with no landmarks to steer by!

But apparently this stone had other properties, for he held out the iron ring on his finger and the stone swung towards it, then to his iron dagger and it did the same. He shook his head, indicating that it would only work away from iron.

As the sounds of the fight—which I had completely forgotten—rose to a real hubbub of yells and counter-yells, I tried the stone myself on an iron spear, a discarded buckle, then back to the north again, thinking with wonderment as I did so that there must be the biggest mountain of iron in the whole world up there in the frozen wastes—

" 'E's orf!" barked Growch. "Want me to chase 'im?"

I shook my head. The thief was gone with his gains, but he had left behind something more precious to me: a magic stone!

When I returned to our tent and showed it to the others, I could not miss the look of envy on their faces.

"That there is a Waystone," said Antonius at last. "Heard of 'em but never seen one before."

"Look after it well, boy," said Scipio. "It could fetch a penny or two. Want to sell it?"

I shook my head.

"Where did you get it?" asked Justus.

I decided to tell them half the truth: the rest was too complicated. "I had it from one of the northerners. He wanted cash to spend before he left for home."

Luckily they didn't ask me how much I had spent, but apparently they, too, had a surprise for me. Sayid ben Hassan, the trader they had been expecting, had turned up at last, and we were to go to his tent at sundown for the usual courtesies.

"So, spruce yourself, boy; put on something more appropriate. And we don't take dogs."

Obeying Master Scipio's instructions I scared up a clean shirt and the clothes I had bought in Venice, sending the rest down to the laundry via one of the guards. Buying a bucket of water from one of the water sellers I made myself look as presentable as I could, and bribed Growch to be good in my absence with a pie from the stall nearest the tents.

Sayid ben Hassan's tent was at the end of a line. He had obviously brought his own, although the three next to it, full of goods, were hired. It was huge, to my eyes, easily rivalling any others I had seen. Fashioned of some dark-blue material, thicker than the usual canvas, it was layered like some extravagant fancy, the lowest being a sort of corridor, then the next, rising higher, compartmented into small rooms and the third and highest a spacious circle full of rugs, small tables and embroidered cushions.

Incense smoked on one of the tables—a sickly sort of smell, like powder—and water was bubbling in a little burner. A servant came in and made mint tea and remained to serve small dishes of nuts and raisins. Elaborate courtesies followed, meaning nothing but essential to Eastern hospitality. Then out came the cargo manifests from both sides and the haggling began. For once I didn't mind, for there was plenty to look at.

Sayid himself was a tall, slim Arab with a large hooked nose and piercing black eyes. He was dressed simply enough in white robes, but on his wrists were several gold bangles and the dagger at his belt had a jewelled hilt. The servant and the guards outside were all young, handsome men, dressed in short blue jackets and voluminous baggy trews; and the rugs, hangings, cushions, shawls, tables, lanterns and pottery were of the highest quality. I wouldn't mind living in such sybaritic luxury, I thought, but there was something perhaps a little too soft, too cloying, for it to be enjoyed forever.

I dragged my mind back to the haggling and Justus' whispered translations. It seemed that we had raw ivory from Africa and cotton from the same source and he had a mix of spices and silk carpeting of an incredible lightness and color. I let my mind drift again, only to be brought up short by the mention of my name.

"Master Scipio just said that you will be travelling with Sayid to—"

"With him? Why not with you?" I interrupted. Surely I wasn't going to be shuffled off to someone strange yet again?

"I thought you understood that," said Scipio. "We all go only so far, you know. We each have our own territory and our own contacts. I go no further than this." He saw me open my mouth and snapped: "Don't argue! As an apprentice you do as you are told! If you don't wish to continue your journey now you may come back with me for the winter but you will have to start over again next year. Or, if you wish, you can surrender your papers right now and cancel your apprenticeship. It's up to you."

Out of the corner of my eye I could see Sayid listening to what was said, and from the expression on his face I believed he understood much more than people imagined. For some reason I began to blush, and I thought I saw a spark of amusement in the Arab's eyes. He murmured something to Scipio, who looked annoyed.

"What did he say?" I whispered to Justus.

"He said . . . He said he didn't know Master Scipio was in the habit of hiring children to do a man's job!"

All of a sudden I hated this supercilious Arab with his fine tent and expensive accoutrements and would have given anything not to be travelling with him. But what choice did I have? I had come this far in pursuit of a dream, far, far further than I had ever been before. How big was this world of ours, anyway? If I went back now I would be wasting all I had planned and saved for. And it would all be worth it in the end, it had to be!

"I shall be honored to travel with you," I said and bowed to Sayid.

"Good, good," said Scipio. "And now, if the business is concluded I believe Sayid wishes to visit the slave market?"

The Arab nodded.

"Then we shall join you. Come along, boy: it should be an interesting experience for you."

5

We made our way to the open marketplace, cleared now of stalls and lit with flares and torches. A temporary platform had been erected in the middle and there, huddled together as if for mutual protection, were the captives I had seen in the cages.

They had all been washed down, for there was less smell, and now the shackles had been removed and they were roped loosely between the ankles. They looked reasonably well fed; most were dark-skinned, but one or two were lighter. An overseer stood on the platform with them, running the thongs of a whip through his fingers.

Many of those crowded round had merely come to watch, but there was a scattering of genuine traders like Sayid, who had their servants clear a way close to the platform.

The slave master, a fat Arab wearing rich robes, had a thin, drooping moustache and great dark pouches under his eyes. He waited until he reckoned all prospective buyers had arrived, then stepped up onto the platform and the sale began.

But first he had to extol the worth of his wares, the exotic locations they had come from, the distances travelled, the hardships he had had in transporting them, all to bump up the price as master Justus explained as he translated for me. "He doesn't say how many he lost on the way, though," he added.

I shivered, although it was a warm night.

One by one the slaves were paraded around the platform. Bids were called in a leisurely fashion, and betweentimes would-be buyers went up on the platform and examined the slaves as casually as they would choose fruit in a market. Mouths were wrenched open for teeth to be counted, heads inspected for ringworm or lice, joints tapped, eyelids lifted and—embarrassing to me at least—genitals were scrutinized for disease and, in the case of the men, testicles weighed in cupped hands.

"Estimating whether they will be good breeders," said Scipio. "Bit of a hit-and-miss way to do it, I should have thought. I remember . . ."

He turned to Antonius and I missed the rest.

The slave master could have earned his living on the stage. He had a rather high-pitched, whiny voice, but he wiggled and postured across the platform in spite of his bulk, all the while beseeching, cajoling, exhorting. He begged for bids, he pretended horror at their paucity and near wept with gratitude when his price was reached.

Sayid ben Hassan went up to examine four men of much the same height and age. He bid for three and settled for two, having them led off by four of his guards. Once again Justus explained to me.

"He had an order for two good-looking blacks for a widow in Persia. Got fancy tastes, apparently. Told to look for sweet breath and large, er, you-know-whats."

"Why didn't he bid for the fourth one?"

"Foul teeth and a leery left eye."

We were coming to the end; now there were only some four or five scrawny children left. These were going at much lower prices.

"Might survive, might not," said Scipio. "Not everyone wants to take a chance on a child. The next one, though, he's different: fetch the highest price of the night, I shouldn't wonder," and he pointed to a slight, exceptionally beautiful black boy of perhaps twelve or thirteen with huge, lustrous eyes.

"Why?"

He gave me a quick, almost contemptuous glance. "Where've you been, lad? Maybe you missed out on all that, but he's ripe for it. Bum-boys like that will be pampered pets for years, then go to train others. Wait for the bidding. . . ."

And indeed the boy fetched an astronomical sum, sold after brisk bidding to a thin Arab with long slim fingers that could not forbear from caressing his purchase even as he led him away. Another two children went for small sums, and now there was only one figure left. At first I thought it must be a dwarf, so much smaller and squatter he was than the rest. The other boys had been either brown or black, this one was a sort of yellowish color. His hair was as black as the others had been, but unlike theirs it was straight as a pony's tail, hanging over his eyes in a ragged fringe. His body was muscular enough, but his legs were slightly bandy and he scowled horribly.

For the first time the auctioneer seemed less than confident.

"What does he say?" I asked Justus.

"He says the boy is special. He comes from the east, was captured by brigands, nearly drowned trying to escape, was sold to someone or other who lost him in a game of chance. He speaks an unknown tongue, but is fit and healthy and good with horses." He yawned. "That's as may be, but the lad looks like trouble to me. Probably a pickpocket and thief— Ah!"

This exclamation was prompted by the said small boy suddenly bending down and freeing himself from the ropes around his ankles, butting the overseer in the stomach and jumping off the platform into the crowd. Although he seemed as slippery as an eel as he successfully eluded one pursuer after another, he really had no chance in that audience, and was finally hauled back onto the platform, kicking and biting. The overseer grabbed him by his hair, lifted him off the ground and hit him so hard across the face that he at last hung limp and shuddering.

My ring was suddenly warm on my finger, throbbing with my heartbeat.

The auctioneer stepped forward and spoke, but his words were lost in a howl of derision from the crowd.

"He says all the boy wants is a bit of correction and lot of understanding," translated Justus, without me asking. He snorted. "The only thing that child would understand is a rope's end. . . ."

The slavemaster made a last appeal; the overseer lowered the boy to his feet and gave him a shake. The boy turned his head and spat, accurately.

The audience clapped and jeered, but in a good-natured way, the overseer lifted his hand to administer another blow—and the ring on my finger throbbed harder than ever.

Without quite realizing what was happening, I found I was on my feet.

"I offer—ten silver pieces," I called out, astounded to hear my own voice. Now why on earth had I done that? I sat down again in confusion, conscious of the incredulous looks of those around me. Never mind: perhaps the auctioneer hadn't understood, for I was speaking in my own tongue.

But slave-trading auctioneers don't get rich without learning more than one language. He understood all right. He gesticulated, cupped his ear, pretended he had misheard my paltry bid. Then came the histrionics. The very idea that anyone could have the gall, the impertinence to offer a mere ten pieces of silver for this treasure of a boy! High spirited he might be, yes, but with a little judicious discipline . . .

He appealed to the audience: he would be generous. As a great favor he wouldn't ask for twenty-five silver pieces, though even that was a mockery: just this once he would settle for fifteen, although that in itself was sheer robbery . . . the bargain of the day! Now, what about it?

The audience laughed, they jeered, they clapped their hands together, they pointed at me.

"What are they saying?"

"That yours is the best offer he will get!"

As if to underline this the boy tried to kick the overseer where it would hurt the most and almost succeeded, to be rewarded by another blow to the head. My ring throbbed again and I leapt to my feet.

"Stop that! I said I offer ten silver pieces—"

Scipio reached up to pull me down. "Steady on, boy: if you're not careful you really will buy him, and you don't want . . ."

But I was pushing myself to the front. I stepped up on the platform, fumbled in my purse and took out the ten coins.

"My final offer! Take it or leave it!"

The slave trader stared at me. "Twelve?"

I knew enough Arabic to count and shook my head.

Behind us the audience were whistling and jeering. The auctioneer must have realized he was making an idiot of himself by trying to force up the price, because his face darkened and he snatched the coins from my hand, grabbed the boy and thrust him towards me.

"Take the son of Shaitan then," he hissed between his teeth in a sort of market-Latin. "And may Allah deliver me from such again. You deserve each other!"

The boy had sunk to the ground. I touched him on the shoulder and he flinched. Reaching for his hand, I pulled him to his feet.

"Come with me. There's nothing to fear."

I knew he would not understand, but hoped the tone of my voice was enough. The ring on my finger had quietened down, so I was obviously doing the right thing. Not according to Scipio, Justus and Antonius. They were loud in condemnation.

"Complete waste of time and money . . . be off as soon as you look away . . . watch your purse, etc. . . . ."

Luckily Sayid ben Hassan had already left, so I didn't have to undergo his scorn as well. As it was I felt like a mother who has been left with her newborn for the first time: I hadn't a clue what to do next.

I needn't have worried. "What you goin' to do with that?"

Him as well! But that was the spur I needed. "We're going to feed him, wash him and clothe him, Growch: in that order. And you can come along to see he doesn't run off. Right?"

"Right!" If I hadn't named our chores in that particular order he probably wouldn't have been so cooperative.

Keeping a firm hold on the boy's hand we made our way over to the food. I let him choose. He pointed to rice, curd cheese, and yoghurt, mixing it together in the bowl and eating hungrily with his fingers, while Growch and I chose something more palatable. I let him have a second helping, then dragged him towards the river.

All at once he twisted away and was gone, running across the sand like a young deer.

"Growch . . ." But he was already in pursuit, his short legs a blur of determination. They both disappeared behind some rocks, there was a yell, a cry and then Growch's bark.

"Come and get 'im!"

When I reached them the boy was sitting on the ground rubbing his left ankle, where a neat row of dents, already turning blue, showed how my dog had floored him.

I knelt by his side and mimed a slap, upon which he immediately cowered, but I shook my head. "No," I said slowly. "But you must be good," and I made soothing gestures. "And now—" I mimed again "—down to the river to wash . . ."

Half an hour later we were all soaked, for it was obvious the boy and water were virtual strangers, but at least he didn't smell anymore. We found the tailors and menders next to the launderers, which should have been obvious. Now what clothes to fit him with? I looked at his naked body and could see faint marks which were paler than the rest. It seemed that once he had worn short trews of some sort and a sleeveless jacket. I asked the tailor in market-Latin and sign language for what I wanted, adding underdrawers and a short smock, remembering what Signor Falcone had said about the cold to come. We bargained, the tailor fetched a relative to help with the sewing, and the clothes were promised within the hour.

What next? I looked at the scowling little face: I could hardly see his eyes. At the barber's he panicked again once he saw the knives and shears, but this time I had a firmer grip. Patiently I mimed and he consented to sit on a stool, his eyes tight shut, shivering like a cold monkey as the barber snipped and cut his hair into a basin cut, so that at least his eyes, ears, and nape of the neck were free of the wild tangle that had obscured them before.

The barber brushed away the cut hair from the boy's face, neck, and shoulders, then proffered a polished silver mirror. The boy stared at his reflection, his narrow eyes slowly widening, until at last he flung the mirror away before bolting again.

"Probably never seen hisself afore," said Growch resignedly, before taking off in pursuit. This time he didn't get so far, and I led him back to the tailor's. The clothes were ready, and now, washed, barbered and decently dressed, he really looked quite presentable.

But how to keep him from running off? He looked quite capable of taking care of himself, but supposing another slave trader found him? Or if he was caught stealing and had his hands chopped off? Or starved to death because of not knowing the routes? No, I had bought him and he was my responsibility.

But how to convince him of that? How to explain that he would travel with us until he was near enough to his home and people to travel alone? How had things been explained to me as a child, when words were not enough?

Of course! I led him back out beyond the tents until I found a smooth stretch of sand. I motioned him to sit beside me, then pointed at myself, repeating my name slowly and clearly. Then I pointed at him and raised my eyebrows in enquiry. He just grinned as if it were some sort of entertainment, but at least it was the first time I had seen him smile. I tried again.

"Summer, Summer. Summer . . ."

A grunt, then "Umma . . ."

"Good, very good!" I clapped my hands. Did I have one of those salted nuts left in my pouch? I did, and popped it in his mouth.

"Summer. Summer . . ."

"Zumma. Summa . . ."

I clapped my hands again, gave him another nut, then pointed to him. He said nothing, so I cupped one ear as if I was listening and jabbed him in the chest.

A slow smile spread over his face, making his eyes crease up more than ever. He pointed to himself and out came a string of clicks and whines and grunts that sounded something like: "Xytilckhihijyckntug." I tried it out—hopeless! His black eyes crinkled up more than ever. He repeated the word more slowly and again I made a fool of myself, waving my hands in frustration. Again. And again. The only bit I could remember was the last syllable: tug.

I pointed to him. "Tug?"

He grinned again, then nodded. He pointed to me. "Summa" then to himself "Tug," clapped his hands as I had done and held his out for a nut.

So far so good, but now he had become withdrawn again, the scowl was back, and he kept glancing from side to side as if gauging his chances of escape.

Right, if words wouldn't do, it would have to be pictures. I smoothed out the sand, took out my dagger and drew a circle in the sand. The rising moon cast our images long across the ground, so I moved round until what I drew was clear of shadows. Inside the circle I drew a rudimentary tent, then pointed back at the encampment. Then came two little stick figures. I pointed to him and to me and the tent. He nodded his head. Now came the tricky bit. Moving a little way to the west I drew another circle, another tent, another stick figure, then pointed to myself. Then I "walked" my fingers slowly to the first circle. And stopped, pointing at him and then to the east. He took the dagger slowly from my hand, and I had a moment's panic, then he moved away to the path of the rising moon and drew a wavery circle. A tent inside the circle, a line with a little head atop, and his fingers walked back to the first circle the way mine had done. But had he understood so far? I hoped so, for the next bit was the important one.

Taking his hand, dagger safely back in my belt, I walked our fingers to the west, to my circle, then shook my head, making sure he was watching. Back in the center circle I pointed first to him then to me and used our fingers to reach his circle. I looked at him; his brow was creased in thought. At last he took my hand and we went through the same performance, only this time he did the finger-walking and it was he who shook his head at my circle. When we came to his he nodded his head vigorously, pointed at both of us and clapped his hands. I shared out the last of the nuts.

" 'E's got it," said Growch wearily. "The thickest pup in the world wouldn' 'ave taken that long. . . . Now do the bit about you 'avin' the cash an' buyin' the food and all that. . . ."

That night Tug slept at the foot of my bed, ants or no ants, with a watchful Growch stretched across the tent flap in case he did a runner.

The next morning Scipio and company were keen to be on their way. They were travelling back with another trader for extra safety, and I spent most of the day helping them load up, after making a careful inventory of the goods they carried. They set off midafternoon, with just enough time to make their first scheduled camp stop. Tug had stayed near my side all day, helping with the loading and carrying. He was even more anxious than I was to be on our way, and every now and again he would pull at my sleeve and point towards the east. I had no idea how much longer Sayid wished to stay, so I pointed at the sun, mimed it rising and setting twice, and luckily for Tug's faith in me, was exactly right.

That night I had presented myself at Sayid's tent, and one of the guards pointed me in the direction of the tents packed with goods, which suited us fine. It seemed we were not invited to eat with the rest of them, and I felt a little anxious about this, as food and lodging were normally included, but reasoned that once we were on the road things would be different. So we made pigs of ourselves on chicken and rice and slept comfortably on the bales of wool in the tent.

Tucked inside my jacket were my apprentice papers and a note from Master Scipio to the merchant at our next destination; they had been entrusted to me rather than to Sayid, and for this I was both apprehensive and grateful; apprehensive because it seemed that Scipio trusted Sayid about as much as I did, grateful because it meant that even if I was abandoned I had the means, and the money—for Scipio had given me an advance—to make my own way.

The next day, and the next, Sayid did more trading, we slept in the same tent and bought our own food. On the third morning, however, things were different. At dawn the tent was pulled down around our ears, a string of men carried the goods away and we found ourselves on the edge of the camp, shivering in the cool morning air, while a half-dozen grumbling, spitting camels and the same amount of mules were loaded up.

It was the first time I had been near one of these fabled camels, with the floppy humps, long legs and disagreeable manners. Growch had warned me about them: apparently he had been near enough to just escape being badly bitten. From what I had heard, however, they were the ideal beasts of burden over long journeys, being strong, swift, and needing little water: every three days was enough, Antonius had said.

Water: I had seen two or three large containers being loaded onto one camel. Did that mean we should bring our own? I turned tail and ran back to the water carriers, purchased two flasks and a fill from the yawning vendor. Why didn't anyone tell me? As I arrived back I saw my pack being loaded onto an already overloaded mule; hastily I strapped on my flasks.

It seemed we were ready. The camels were loaded, so were the mules, on two of which perched the cook and Sayid's personal servant. The two slaves the Arab had purchased were manacled in the space between camels and mules. The guards and Sayid were mounted on magnificent Arabs, but where was our transportation?

It seemed we were to walk. (Later it transpired that we were to share the mules, but it was an uneven swap: the servant and the cook were loath to set foot on the ground.)

Tug had given a moan of terror when he saw the chained slaves, but I quieted him. During the last couple of days I had spent an hour or two teaching him simple words and phrases, and he had responded remarkably well. Now was the time for another lesson.

I pointed to the manacled slaves. "Tug bad, chains. Tug good, no chains . . ."

"Tug good," he said perfectly clearly, and held out his hand for a reward.

6

Thus began the most arduous part of my journey so far. Our destination, a town called Beleth, was some three hundred miles away, and it took four weeks to reach it. Of those three hundred miles, I reckon Tug, Growch and I must have walked two-thirds. Growch I carried when he was too exhausted to go further. Tug's feet were tough and horny, but after the first day my soft leather boots were the worse for wear and my feet were killing me.

At the first village we stopped at, Tug—yes, Tug of all people!—persuaded me with signs and a few words to buy a pair of the ubiquitous sandals worn there, and after that it became easier. It was Tug, too, who made the first contact with the rest of the caravan that eventually made our presence more welcome. Every night he helped with unloading the camels and mules, assisted with setting up Sayid's tent, brought wood for the cook and led the horses down to drink. He was a marvel with the horses, and before long the guards allowed him to ride their mounts for an hour or two each day. He was even allowed to groom Sayid's own mount, a magnificent white Arab, whose mane and tail nearly reached the ground.

Thus it was we found ourselves welcome in the big tent at night, albeit in the outer corridor with the slaves, and shared the somewhat monotonous food: couscous or rice with whatever meat or vegetables the cook had been able to buy.

We travelled a well-worn trail from village to village, though there were days when we camped out at night. A large fire was always built and the guards would spend the evenings in wrestling with each other or playing endless games of chance. I took these opportunities to teach Tug more of my language; in the meantime he was also picking up a good deal of Arabic. One day I noticed he wore a brand-new knife at

his belt; I decided not to ask him where he got it, although I suspected
he could gamble with the best.

For the most part the weather was fair, although it became pro-
gressively colder, not only because the nights were drawing in, but also
because we were climbing, gradually but surely, into the foothills of the
mountains that loomed ever nearer. Those nearest were green with thick
vegetation; behind, some fifty miles farther away, they assumed a more
jagged and unfriendly look, while those on the farthest horizon reared
so high they seemed to touch the very sky, their sides white with snow.

Was it there, among those unimaginable heights, that my love, my
dragon-man, had his home?

The terrain around us changed in character, too. From sun-baked
earth, scrub, and tumbled rocks, with scant water trickling down deep
canyons, we then travelled grass-covered slopes, with herdsmen tending
their goats along the trail, and through deciduous woods and wind-swept
valleys. As we trekked even higher we were among pines and spruce,
seemingly brushed by the wings of great eagles soaring on the thermals
that sometimes took them beneath us, to dive on some prey unseen. It
seemed the less we saw other human beings, the more vigilant Sayid
became, and the guards closed up every time we traversed any place
likely for ambush, and were doubled at night.

As there were now four guards around the campfires at night, that
mean Tug, Growch, and I moved into one of the smaller cubicles that
led off the main room of the tent. It was so nippy after dark that I wished
I had more blankets, and I envied Sayid the brazier that burned so warm
in his inner sanctum. I envied, too, those guards he chose to share his
luxury: a sort of reward, I supposed, for their devotion. Sometimes it
was one, sometimes two or three. His method of choosing was always
the same; he would tap the privileged one on the shoulder and offer him
a sweetmeat, upon which they would disappear to the cosiness of cushions and warmth, and the silken drapes would be drawn to.

One night I, too, had my chance to sleep soft.

I had rolled myself up in my blanket and was drifting off to sleep
when there was a touch on my head, more of a stroke really, and I opened
my eyes to see Sayid squatting by my side. As I sat up, struggling free
of the blanket, he popped a sugared fruit in my mouth and then another.
Taking my hand he pulled me to my feet, nodding towards the inner
tent as he did so.

I had taken no more than one step forward when there was a sudden
commotion and somehow or other there was a fierce little Tug standing

between us, knife in hand. Shoving me back he hissed: "No! No! Bad . . ." and then followed some words in Arabic I didn't understand.

But Sayid obviously did, for he backed away, a scowl on his face, after a moment choosing one of his guards to accompany him, who gave me a big grin and an obscene gesture before following his master.

"What in the world . . . ?" I turned furiously to Tug. "Why did you do that?"

"I shouldn't ask, I really shouldn't," said Growch.

But Tug was not inhibited, and after a minute or two of a few words and plenty of bodily gestures I realized what I had escaped.

"Yes, yes, thanks!" I said, to save further embarrassment. "Very good, Tug!"

I learned later that it was common practice among the Arabs to seek out their own sex for relaxation when away from women for any length of time and no one thought twice about it but, unprepared as I was at the time, I was both scared and disgusted. Luckily there was also a small bubble of amusement lurking around: whatever would have happened if Sayid had found out I was a girl? It would almost have been worth it to see his face. . . .

After that he was very cool towards me, and I also earned the derision of the guards, so it was perhaps just as well that we had our first sight of the city of Beleth less than a week later.

It lay like a child's toy extravaganza at the foot of a steep valley, probably some three thousand feet straight down from us. I could make out what looked like a large square with streets radiating from it, a palace, big and small buildings, twisty alleys and the smoke of a myriad house fires. I wanted to run down the track straightaway, but Sayid camped where we were for the night and I saw why in the daylight, for it took half a day to bring us all down safe, the precipitous trail winding like the coils of a snake in order to use the safest ground.

Everyone had spruced themselves up that morning, and there was a lot of combing, plucking and twisting of hair, oiling of skin and use of a blackened stick to enhance the eyes, but I decided to leave well alone, except for a clean shirt and the donning of my boots once again.

At noon, or a little past, we clattered across the wooden bridge that spanned the narrow river flowing to the west of the city. We had already passed through neat and obviously fertile fields, the soil dark and friable. At the town side of the bridge we passed under a splendid carved arch set in battlemented walls, and onto a broad street, paved with river cobbles, that led after a half-mile to the large square that dominated the center of the city. All the way along the route we were flanked by laughing children and saluted by well-dressed citizens. It seemed a well organized, wealthy city, and my spirits rose. A proper bed—

"A proper meal," said Growch.

And no more walking, at least for a while.

Everyone dismounted, and I was glad enough to squat down and rest in the sunshine as the unloading began and men rushed in all directions, presumably to herald our arrival. The square must have been a quarter-mile across; at the moment it was full of market stalls, but these looked about ready to pack up for the day. Tall houses, many set back in courtyards, ringed the perimeter, and facing us was the imposing facade of the palace, with—as I learned later—one hundred marble steps leading up to the columned portico, built in the Greek style. Some twenty or thirty soldiers lounged on the steps, and others were tossing a ball about in a corner of the square. All very relaxed and comforting: obviously they were more for show than use.

I glanced up at the houses. They were in different styles, although most were white with flat roofs, and the windows were either tightly shuttered or barred with a fancy fretwork. Smoke rose lazily into the air and there were tantalizing snatches of music, pipes and strings and a tabor. Growch's nose lifted.

"Food . . ." he said.

Just then one of Sayid's guards returned, accompanied by a fat, waddling creature in purple silks and a large turban. He was perspiring freely and mopping his brow with a long scarf, whose color matched his red leather shoes with curved toes. He and Sayid embraced conventionally and exchanged courtesies, then Sayid produced papers, the fat man did the same; another thin man in white started checking the bales and porters appeared from nowhere and started to carry off the items as soon as they were unloaded and checked on both manifests. In no time at all it seemed all that was left to be dealt with were two loaded mules, three loaded camels, the slaves, and ourselves.

Sayid signed to his guards and drivers and the animals were led away. He assigned two guards to the slaves and these also were led away, but in a different direction. Sayid remounted and swung his horse in a long curvette before bowing his farewells to the fat man.

"Hey! What about us?" I ran forward to clutch at his bridle.

He spat on the ground just in front of my boots.

"You go with him," and he nodded in the direction of the fat man, who had sat down on one of the bales, mopping his brow again. He shouted something which sounded nasty, indicated us, then reared his stallion so sharply the bridle was snatched from my hand and I tumbled back in the dirt, then rode away out of the square.

I got up, dusted myself down, and walked over to the fat man who had relinquished the last bale to one of his porters.

I looked at him, he looked at me.

I bowed, he did the same. We spoke together.

"My name is Master . . ."

"And whom do I have . . ."

He had a sense of humor, this fat man, because he grinned when I did. I handed him the sheaf of papers Master Scipio had given me and introduced myself. He read through the scrolls rapidly, then handed them back to me, and bowed again.

"Welcome, Master Summer. I am Karim Bey, accredited agent to Master Spicer, and have been these past fifteen years." He bowed again. "I am happy to welcome you to our city, and hope to make your stay as pleasant as possible."

He spoke my tongue very well, albeit in a slightly archaic manner.

"I am happy to be here," I said. "Tell me, what did Sayid say to you about us?"

"Something to the effect that I had inherited excess baggage . . . Do not mind him. He is a very proud man, he likes his own way. But he is trustworthy, and guards his goods well. And now, if you and—your friends—would please to follow me?"

He led us to a pleasant house down a side street, set in a courtyard draped with bougainvillea and with a fountain tinkling away in the center. He indicated a stone bench covered with a Persian rug. Tug and Growch perched themselves on either side of me. Karim Bey looked at me interrogatively.

"My friend Tug," I said, indicating the boy. "I rescued him from a slave market and am trying to find his people. The dog's name is Growch, and he has been with me on all my travels."

"Where does the boy come from?"

"I don't rightly know. He speaks a language no one seems to understand."

"From his looks he comes from farther north and east. Let me have a word. . . ." He tried various dialects, but Tug shook his head, speaking in his strange clicks and hisses. Karim shook his head, too. "No, the language is unfamiliar to me, and he does not appear to understand any Italian, French, Spanish, Arabic, Turkish, Hindi, or Persian, all languages familiar to me. I will make further enquiries." He clapped his hands. "And now I think we shall eat."

Five minutes later we were tucking into kebabs of meat and red peppers, boiled and fried rice, pastry cases full of beans, peas and bamboo shoots, with a dessert of stuffed dates, peaches, cheese, and yoghurt. There was a chilled red wine, sherbet or goat's milk to quench our thirst.

After dining we were invited to bathe and rest, while Karim Bey made arrangements for our lodgings. We were led to a room in which stood two tubs of warm, scented water, towels, and various oils. Tug needed persuading to the water, but not the ointments: he smelt like a bunch of mixed out-of-season flowers when he had finished. In the next room there were pallets for our siesta, and I persuaded him to take a nap so I could bathe in private, unafraid my true sex would be discovered. I luxuriated in the chance to have a proper soak and wash my hair, the first time since I couldn't remember when.

Around dusk Karim sent one of his servants to wake us up, and announced that we were to lodge with another of his "regulars"—whatever that meant—and that the servant would escort us. He added that he would be seeking my help the next day in the warehouses. More tallying, I thought dismally.

The servant shouldered my pack with ease and led us through a maze of streets and alleys until we arrived at a thick double gate. We found ourselves in a courtyard with a well in the center, stables to the left, living quarters to the right, and a low arch, on either side of which was a washhouse and a kitchen, leading through into what looked like a vegetable garden. Stone steps led up to a galleried upper floor, with half a dozen closed doors.

The servant put down my pack, saluted and left, just as a man emerged from the downstairs living quarters and hurried towards us. He was dark-skinned, black-haired, small and thin, clad in a white jacket, cap and a sort of skirt looped between his legs and tucked into his belt. On his fingers were many rings and a jewel dangled from one ear, though both metal and gems looked too large for real worth.

He was already gabbling as he came towards us, and his speech was the most amazing I had ever heard. He used words from every language I had ever heard, and some I hadn't, though when he found where I came from it settled into a mixture of Arabic, French, Italian, market-Latin, Greek and what I learned later was his native tongue, Hindi. Whatever it was, his sentences had a quaintness that kept me constantly amused.

"Velly welcome, isn't it? Chippi Patel at your service, young sir! Jolly damn glad see you. Room you are taking. Up this, pliss," and he led the way up to the verandah. Stopping at one of the doors he flung it open and ushered us into a small whitewashed room containing two pallets, two stools, two wooden chests, a grass mat, a row of hooks on the wall and a small, shuttered window at the back.

"Habitation of other young sir, Ricardus, happy to share. Boy sleep on mat. Dog too, yes?"

"You are most kind, Master Patel, but—"

"No, no, no! My name Chippi! Mix marriage, Daddy name Chippi, Mummy Patel. Many Patel, few Chippis."

"Very well, Master Chippi—"

"No mater-pater here! Just Chippi . . ."

"Well then, Chippi, my name is Summer, and—"

He took my arm and clasped it fervently, then clapped me on the back. "Happy you meet, Zuma! You happy here. Nice room, nice mate to share . . ."

"No, Chippi," I said firmly, disengaging myself from his clasp (he did smell awfully garlicky) and knowing that if I did not stop this garrulous little man right now I never should get my own way. "We need another. Just for us. For me, my friend Tug, my friend Growch." I indicated us in turn.

"Not friend with dirty pi-dog . . . ?"

"Not pi-dog . . ." I found to my exasperation that I was speaking just like him. "Dog is good friend for many miles. Long pedigree: much money. Not see another like him."

He looked askance at my filthy, tatty animal.

"You right there . . . Now, this room most commodious, and—"

"Karim Bey assured me we should have our own room," I said mendaciously.

That did it. At the mention of the agent's name Chippi scuttled away down the verandah and showed us into another room two doors down, the twin of the first. He had an injured air, but I learned later it was common practice to try to make newcomers share and collect for two separate rooms. Corruption became more rife the farther east we came, but it was all good-humored, played as a sort of game: you won some, you lost some, and within a minute or two Chippi was all smiles again, showing us the washhouse and taking away our dirty laundry, to be returned spotless within hours.

For the next few days I worked busily for Karim, first in the warehouses where I assisted his tally man as goods moved day by day; one morning we would exchange silks from Cathay for pottery from Greece, and in the afternoon check in rice or rugs or rich tapestries. Perishables were usually targeted to the market, but in the main office, full of scrolls, clerks and comings and goings, the rest of the goods were assigned to various caravans, north, south, east or west; orders were taken, part consignments made up, other traders contacted for out-of-the-way requirements. Karim also had an army of scouts distributed throughout the town and outlying villages, ready to report the unusual, and if he thought it worth his while he would send an expert to bargain for whatever it was. He also did his own trading, short journeys only, mainly in small goods and local pottery.

Besides the warehouses, and the office, I was also sent to the market to oversee the trading in the perishables, and by the end of that first week I earned a commendation for my hard work.

"And now we must concentrate on the language. Master Ricardus, he must be much of an age with you, and he was fluent in basic Arabic within weeks, could add and subtract faster than most and bargain with the best. An old head on young shoulders."

"And where is this young paragon now?" I asked, masking my irritation with a smile. I could just imagine this pompous, unbearable young man strutting around dispensing wisdom I didn't want at all hours of the day and night.

"He has accompanied a small caravan some seventy miles south, to act as my agent. It is the second such journey he has undertaken; he made me a good profit the last time. I expect him back within a couple of days."

But in fact he came back that very afternoon. When I returned to our room at sunset, after making a couple of deliveries of orders for ribbons and sewing materials to some small shops down the alleys, Chippi met me at the gate to the courtyard with a conspiratorial smile on his lips.

"Your new friend is back being with us. He has just had a big bath. . . ." He indicated the bathhouse. "At suppertime you will see."

I hurried up the steps, Tug and Growch close behind. I had better have a wash myself, find a clean shirt and comb my hair before I met Wonder Boy. But there was someone in my room already, bending over the wooden chest at the foot of my bed, just about to lift the lid.

"What the hell . . . !"

He straightened up guiltily, then just stared and stared.

"When I heard the name . . . You've come a long way, haven't you, *Mistress* Summer!"

The recognition was mutual.

"My God!" I said, "You . . ."

7

Instantly my mind was whirled back to a stretch of forest in a country hundreds of miles away. It must have been some eighteen months ago but it seemed like a hundred years. So much had happened in between that I didn't even feel like the same girl. Now the scene came back with sudden clarity, and I could see the dirty-faced stable lad who had helped me and my previous friends escape imprisonment and torture, been well paid for his trouble—and then robbed me of the rest of my moneys.

Even then I had somewhat admired his cheek and, remembering he was only stealing to help his widowed mother and sisters, I had told him to seek out Master Spicer, feeling sure that the kind man would give him a better-paid job in his own stables. I recalled Matthew had said the lad had been sent somewhere for "training," but until this moment had thought no more about it.

But the young man standing in front of me now, with his freshly coiffed hair, fine clothes and added inches of height—he must be at least as tall as I—bore little resemblance to the scruffy boy I had thought to be only about fourteen. Amazing what good food and an easier life could do; he must be about seventeen, I guessed, and the only familiar features were the thatch of fair hair—still untidy in spite of the fashionable basin cut with the curled fringe—the intensely blue eyes with their look of sharp intelligence, and the rather greedy mouth.

"What in the world are you doing here, Dickon?"

"Not Dickon anymore: Ricardus. I'm working for Matthew Spicer as a trainee trader and have done pretty well for myself—"

"So I've heard . . ."

"—and Dickon is a common, peasant name. Latinized it sounds far more impressive, don't you think?"

To me he was still Dickon. "How are your mother and sisters?"

A hint of a scowl. "Well enough. Master Spicer secretly sends them a part of my wages. My eldest sister has got married. . . . But what about you? Why are you here? And why dressed as a lad? What happened to the rest of the ragtag you carted round with you?"

"Part of it is still here," I said, pointing to Growch, who was growling softly. "Quiet, boy; you've met him before." I nodded at Tug. "He travels with us to find his people; he was stolen as a slave sometime back." Tug was scowling. "Friend, Tug. Ricardus. Say it . . ." But he wouldn't, and, still scowling, spat over his shoulder, which is neither easy nor a sign of approval.

"Looks a bit of a dimwit to me," commented Dickon. "What of the others?"

"The knight went back to his lady—"

"Thought you were sweet on him?"

"—and the mare, the tortoise and the pigeon found their own kind."

"What about the pig? The one I saw fly. What of him?"

"Nothing," I said defensively. I still didn't want to think about him. "He—went back to his beginnings." Which was true enough, but light on the full details.

"Thought you might have got some money out of it by selling him to a freak show. Pigs don't fly." His eyes were too sharp, too inquisitive.

"His wings were only temporary things. . . ."

"Oh, fell off did they? You should have sewed them on more firmly. . . . Still haven't told me why you're here, though. Must say you've got nice long legs, Mistress Summer!"

I pulled my jerkin down. "*Master* Summer, if you please!" I had had just about enough time to think. "I'm here for the same reason you are: to learn the business. Matthew—Master Spicer—thought I would be safer dressed this way." Why was I blushing?

He grinned, winked. "Way he talked about you, took me in without question on your word, thought he was keen on you. . . . Fact remains, dressed as a lad or not, this is no job for a female. Surprised he let you come."

"It wasn't a question of letting me—" I stopped. Better not tell him too much. Somehow I didn't feel I could trust him. Apart from that brief meeting a year and a half ago, what else did I know about him except that he was a thief, made the most of his opportunities and had become a bit of a snob?

His eyes were narrowed, considering me. "And no one knows of this change of sex, 'cept me?"

"Apart from Matthew, Suleiman—and Signor Falcone in Venice." Two of the three, anyway.

He seemed satisfied. "Must admit you don't look too bad. Bet you don't walk right, though; women walk from the hips, men from the knee."

"You haven't seen me walk," I objected.

"Not yet, but I'll bet you . . ."

"Just wait and see," I snapped. "At least I don't suppose you have ever been propositioned as a bum-boy!"

His eyes widened. "My, you have been living it up! How did you get out of that one?"

I shrugged. "A knife and a few words, carefully chosen . . ."

"I still can't believe Master Spicer sent you all the way out here just to learn the business." He narrowed his eyes again. "Are you sure you weren't sent out on a special mission? As a spy, perhaps?"

"Don't be ridiculous. I just wanted to see a bit of the world, that's all. I haven't the money to travel as a pampered female and I—we—thought this was a good way to do it." What had he been searching for in the wooden chest? Why was he afraid of someone spying? After all, he hadn't known I would turn up until he saw me.

Chippi came bustling up the stairs to announce that the evening meal was ready.

"Ah, the great friends they have met! Two such pretty young fellows, by damn! Much good pals will be. Wife has prepared special dish. Coming down for same, isn't it?"

Tables were set out in the courtyard as usual, but tonight Chippi deigned to sit with us at the table of honor nearest the kitchen. Mistress Chippi wouldn't join us, of course: women were generally of lower status than the menfolk out here. As dark as her husband, but much fatter, she bustled about setting out delicacies for starters: crisply fried savory biscuits, bean shoots, meatballs. Then came the special dish, a steaming heap of meat and vegetables on a bed of boiled rice. I watched how Dickon would cope; he took up one of the soft pancakes Chippi call chapatis, folded it round a mouthful of food, conveyed it to his mouth without so much as spilling a grain of rice and chewed appreciatively.

"Excellent!" He spoke with his mouth full: he hadn't learned everything yet.

It looked easy enough, and I managed quite nicely but, as I leant forward to scoop up another mouthful, a terrible delayed reaction set in.

My tongue, my mouth, my throat, my stomach—they were all on fire! I had been poisoned! My eyes were streaming, I couldn't breathe. . . . Struggling to my feet, choking and gasping, I signalled frantically for a drink—water, wine, sherbet, anything!

Slurping down whatever was offered—it could have been anything for all the effect it had on the terrible taste in my mouth—I could feel a gradual lessening of the burning heat. Perhaps I hadn't been poisoned after all.

At last I could breathe normally again. I mopped my streaming eyes and looked across at Dickon and Chippi—they were doubled over with laughter!

"It's not funny! What on earth was it?"

"Oh, dearie, dearie me!" Chippi blew his nose on his sleeve. "We are larks having, isn't it . . . First time you eat curry, yes?"

"What?"

"Curry. Very hot being. Wife cook it good, yes, Ricardus?"

"Very good," said the objectionable Dickon, tucking in heartily. "You'll soon get used to it, *Master* Summer."

"I will not!" And I kept my word.

For the next few days Dickon initiated me further into the mysteries of merchanting, and I took care not to show him how bored I became, trying to appear interested and attentive. He of course knew nothing of my true reason for taking on the guise of apprentice; my only worry was Tug, who was growing increasingly restless at being confined to the town.

I had a word with Karim Bey on the subject of moving on as soon as possible, pretending eagerness to travel further. He looked shocked.

"But it is entirely the wrong time of year to venture further, Master Summer; everything closes down shortly because the higher routes will soon become impassable. I had thought you would be content to over-winter here, and learn as much as possible for the spring journeys." He must have seen the disappointment on my face. "I myself shall not be sending out any more caravans. However, as you seem so keen, I will try and get you a place with an eastbound trader, if I can find one. You may well find that you end up at the back of beyond, forced to stay until the snow melts, and find it difficult to return. However, that is up to you."

And with that I had to be content. I told Tug we were waiting for a special trader to take us further east, and I think he believed me.

Our daily work had to finish sometime, and in the evenings after supper Dickon, Tug, Growch, and I took to wandering down the myriad side streets and alleys that radiated from the square right through to the edges of town, as haphazardly as the tiny veins on the inside of one's elbow.

Here lay the real life of the city, a place where the great and wealthy never came. During the day one might see town officials bustling about in the city proper, respectable citizens about their business, soldiers exercising, merchants fingering the goods on offer in the market, discreetly veiled ladies taking the air, either on foot or in gilded palanquins, and all around were the workers, those who catered to their whims: servants, both male and female, stall holders, farriers, cooks, children running errands, water carriers, weavers, tailors, hairdressers, beauticians, fortunetellers, launderers, beggars, refuse gatherers, cleaners, night-soil collectors, rope makers, jewellers, wine sellers, oil vendors—in fact all those unregarded people without whom the city could not function at all.

At night, though, it was as if a soft blanket came down on all this bustle and the little side streets and alleys came into their own, for this was where the workers lived. Here they had their homes; here they were born, grew up, loved, hated, became ill, died. Here was all manner of meaner housing; tenements, small one-roomed hovels, stables, tents, holes in the ground or in the walls, shacks and even the bare ground.

Here also were the little family restaurants, minor businesses, brothels, stalls that sold items not available in the open market: strange drugs, stolen goods, information; here there was trade in quack medicines and human beings; much gossip and entertainment; and lastly were the stalls that sold those small, largely useless objects that might just fetch enough to buy the daily bowl of rice.

These alleyways were only dimly lit and the town guard generally gave them a wide berth. It was not wise for a stranger to walk there alone, but I had always felt safe with Tug and Growch, though we didn't go far. However when Dickon heard of our expeditions he insisted on accompanying us, ostensibly as guard, but I suspected he had never dared go alone before and we were merely an excuse. As it was he strutted and postured like a young lord, especially when there was a pretty girl about. He was trying to grow a moustache, none too successfully, and he fancied himself as a lady-killer. In fact on the third evening he thoroughly embarrassed me, suggesting a visit to one of the many little brothels.

"I'm not going to one of those! How could I?"

"You're dressed as a lad. You don't have to—participate. You can just watch, can't you?"

"Certainly not! You can do what you like, but I'm staying outside."

"Suit yourself! Just don't get lost: I may be some time. . . ."

Which left the rest of us wandering up and down the street, pretending to examine the goods at one or another of the stalls, fending off too persistent vendors and generally feeling conspicuous. I had almost made up my mind to trust Growch's sense of direction to get us back to our lodgings, when Dickon reappeared with a smirk on his face and ostentatiously adjusting his clothing.

"I hope it was worth it," I said nastily.

"Of course. I always ensure that I get value for money. Pity in some ways you ain't a lad: I could show you a thing or two in this town."

"If I were, I doubt if I'd take advantage of your offer. I wouldn't want to risk catching something nasty."

"I know what I'm doing—"

"Good for you. Can we go now?"

He didn't repeat the experiment, if that was what it was. After all he certainly hadn't been in there more than a quarter hour, however long it had seemed outside. But perhaps that was the way they did things in those places. I wasn't going to ask.

Two nights later something very strange happened.

We had wandered farther than usual and came at last to a narrow street that twisted and turned like a snake almost under the tall battlements that protected the city. Here were more stalls than usual, some set out on the ground on scraps of cloth, others displayed on stools or tables, yet more in tiny cupboardlike niches in the walls. There was less noise than usual and those who passed by seemed to do so as if in a dream. Even the bargaining sounded muted, the examination of objects slow and unhurried. At one corner the street seemed as light as a fairground, at another full of shadows, much as a candle flame in a draught will flare one moment and be down to a mere flicker the next.

I found myself infected with the same strange lethargy, yet my mind seemed as sharp as a needle. I found I, too, was taking my time at each stall, examining everything minutely, yet no one was pressing me to buy. I looked at small prayer mats, embroidery silks, combs and brushes, painted scarves, brooches and bangles; I picked up a length of silk here, a phial of perfume there. I waved a fly whisk, tried on a pair of felt slippers, tapped a brass tray, turned over some table mats, flicked my finger at a tray of pearls that rolled about like a handful of dry white peas; I bought and ate a couple of sticky, green sweetmeats, passed by painting brushes, colored inks, charcoal, dyes, spices, pellets of opium. . . .

Between a hole in the wall occupied by a man selling sachets of sweet-smelling dried flowers and a conventional stall laden with pots and pans, an old man squatted behind a small folding table on which was displayed a heterogenous collection of what looked like secondhand curios. I bent down to see a small, blue brush jar with a chip, a dented brass bowl, a piece of dirty amber, a paperweight dull with use, some scraps of embroidery, a yellowed piece of carved ivory. . . .

I straightened up, ready to pass on, when the old man lifted his head and looked straight into my eyes. He was nearly bald, what was left of his hair hanging white on either side of his face to mingle with a wispy beard. There were laugh lines at the corners of his eyes, and his whole expression radiated a warmth and good humor, although if you asked me to describe him feature by feature I could not have done so.

He nodded at me as if we were old friends, said something I didn't understand, then indicated the tray in front of him. Obviously an invitation to look closer. I glanced around for the others. Tug was bargaining for some sweetmeats in sign language with some coins I had given him. Growch was flushing out imaginary rats from some rubbish heap, Dickon was chatting up the girl selling rice wine in tiny cups.

Why not indulge the old man while I waited for the others? He seemed pleasant enough, although I had seen nothing that attracted me on the tray, except perhaps that little ivory carving—

Strange. The goods looked different. A pearl, discolored; a chipped blue and white cup; a carved bamboo flute the worse for wear; an old inkpot—surely those had not been there before? Ah, there was something I recognized: the little ivory figure. I couldn't quite make out what it was meant to represent. The old man said something, and as I looked up he nodded, wreathed in smiles.

I smiled back and squatted down in front of the tray.

Now the tray was full, and every object, cracked, chipped, dented, worn or just old, all were carved or decorated with representations of living things. The blue brush jar had a lively dragon wrapped around its base, the brass bowl had raised figures of mice chasing each other's tails, inside the amber, carved as a fish's mouth, a tiny fly awaited its fate. Embroidery covered with lotus blossoms, a paperweight with a grasshopper for a handle, a carved bee on the side of the flute looking alive enough to fly away, a pearl etched with chrysanthemums, a blue and white cup painted with butterflies, and an inkpot decorated with a flock of small birds: broken they all might be, but these objects had an exquisite living grace. And around them all, lively as a kitten, cavorted the ivory carving.

Some part of me, the sensible part, told me there was something very amiss here. Half a dozen pieces, less than interesting, then others, and now both lots together, and all worth a second look. But the sensible side of Summer stayed quiet and the credulous Summer just accepted what she saw.

Or thought she saw . . .

The old man stretched out his right hand and took mine; in his left he held a green bowl of water that danced its reflections in the lamplight as the ring on my finger tingled, but not unpleasantly. He nodded at me again, indicating that I should look into the liquid. I leaned forward and found myself gazing into a swirl of colors. Figures passed through the water; I saw a white horse with a horn on its forehead, a frog or toad, a cat, a black bird, a fish. . . . Then something I thought I recognized: another horse galloping across the sands, a scrabbling tortoise, a pink pigeon, a small elongated dog with short legs, a pig . . . Ah, the pig!

A pig with wings. A pig I had kissed three times. A pig that turned into a dragon.

And the girl in the picture kissed the pig-that-was-a-dark-dragon for the third time, and he turned into a man. A dark man called Jasper, Master of Many Treasures, and my heart broke as he turned back into a dragon again and flew away from the Place of Stones—

Leaping to my feet, I dashed the bowl from the old man's hands. I could feel the stupid tears welling up.

"How could you know? Dickon?" I called over my shoulder. "Come and translate for me, please. I want to ask this old man a couple of questions."

He, too, had risen to his feet, although he still had hold of my hand. He was speaking again, but thanks to Dickon who must have been standing behind me, I now had a translation.

"I mean no harm, young traveller."

"The pictures in the bowl . . ." I stopped. I didn't want Dickon to know what I had seen.

"Before you there was another who wore a ring," said the old man, and now the translation was almost simultaneous. "Many, many years ago. She, too, adventured with animals she was wise enough to call her friends. The rest you saw was what you wanted to see."

"No! I never wanted . . ."

"Then the head denies the heart it would seem. You travel far, girl, to find what you do not want, then?" There was a gentle, teasing quality in his voice, which I now seemed to hear clearer than Dickon's. "It will be a long journey for the seven of you. . . ."

"Seven? Three, you mean." Me, Tug and Growch.

"Three is a lucky number, I agree, but seven is better. She who first wore the ring knew that."

"It's just three," I repeated firmly.

"Life does not always turn out the way you want it. I think you will need help with your journey, extra help."

"You—know where we are bound?"

"I know everything." He picked up the bowl again, and miraculously it was still full of colored water. "Look again. Closer . . ."

Forgetting Dickon, I gazed once more into the bowl. The colors paled, faded, and now there was just a milky haze. The haze steadied, snow was falling and I was in it, flying like a bird between high mountain peaks. But the snow started to drag at my wings, at the same time destroying my perspective of the land beneath, the familiar landscape I should know so well. Mountain after mountain, peak after peak, they all looked alike. The snow grew heavier and now I was weary, blinking away the flakes of snow that threatened to blind me. Each beat of my wings seemed to wrench them from their sockets; if I couldn't find what I was looking for soon I should have to land, but it was unlikely I would find shelter in unknown terrain.

Then, suddenly, I saw it.

A momentary lessening in the blur of snow, and the three fangs of the Mighty One, gateway to my goal, loomed up ahead. A turn to the left and I steered between the first two of the three rock teeth that were so steep that even now they gloomed blackly in the snow that could not rest against their sides.

Over at last and down, down, down into the valley beyond. There was the monastery on its hill, where the saffron-robed monks rang their gongs, sounded their queer, cracked bells and said their prayers to an endlessly smiling, fat god. Finally a switch to the right, away from the Hill of Constant Prayer and the village beneath, and a long slow glide to the Blue Mountain and the cave entrance hidden on the northern face.

Wearily I braked back, my leathern wings as clumsy as the landing gear of a youngling. Wobbling a little, I shoved forward my dragon claws and—

"Jasper!" I cried out, and smashed the green bowl into a thousand pieces. "Jasper! *I* was *him*!"

The old man stooped down and picked up one of the tiny shards of glass. One piece? No, for now all the others seemed to fly into his hand and the bowl was whole again. He tucked it away in his robe.

"And so you now know the way to go," he said. "It is always the last part of the journey that is the hardest."

My mind was in such turmoil that I could think of nothing to say—except thank him.

He bowed. "It is nothing; a breath of wind across a sleeping face, bringing with it a dream of the poppies over which it has travelled. . . . And now, young traveller, you were thinking of bearing something away from my tray."

I was? Yes, perhaps I was. That must be why I was bending over the tray again, and now all the creatures and flowers were real, alive. A butterfly perched on my finger, then flew to the old man's beard; a tiny fly cleaned its wings of the amber that had imprisoned it; a fish swam in the brass bowl that the old man tucked away in his robe; a string of mice disappeared up his sleeve; a tiny blue dragon flew to his shoulder then vanished down his collar; a grasshopper leapt to his head, a flock of tiny birds circled the stall and a bee, heavy with pollen, rested for a moment on my sleeve, before crawling up a fold of the old man's robe, whose lap now held a mass of flowers. . . .

Now all that was left on the tray was the little ivory figure. It was still difficult to make out exactly what it was meant to represent—he looked like a mixture of dog, horse, dragon, deer—but he did have a very intelligent expression.

"How much?"

"He is not for sale. He goes where he wishes." He spoke as though the creature had a will of its own, but then nothing would have surprised me now.

"May I pick him up?"

"If he will let you . . ."

What did he do then? Bite? Disappear in a puff of smoke?

Gingerly I bent forward, picked him up between finger and thumb and put him on my palm. Exquisitely carved, he had the body of a deer, hooves of a horse, a water buffalo's tail with a huge plume on the end, a stubby little face with a minihorn in his forehead and what looked like fine filaments or antennae sweeping back from his mouth. Funny that I hadn't been able to see him clearly before, especially as he was the only perfect piece. He sat quite comfortably on my hand.

"What is it—he?"

"That is for him to tell you. If he wishes."

I waited for something to happen, but nothing did, so with a strange reluctance I put him back on the tray. My ring was warm on my finger.

"Are you coming? The young lass over there says her dad has an eating house round the corner." Dickon spoke over my shoulder. "I'm hungry even if you're not."

All the lights were suddenly brighter, and I could smell sewers.

He nudged my arm impatiently. "You've been staring at that tray for hours. Looks like a lot of junk to me."

I looked down. An old man squatted in front of a tray of secondhand objects, none of which I had seen before. The ivory figure I thought I remembered seeing wasn't there.

I shook my head, as much to clear it as a form of negation. "I can't see anything I want," I said slowly. "Thanks for translating just the same." I bowed to the old man, and we moved away down the street. I felt all jangled inside as if someone had jumped me out of a dream too soon.

We were finishing off an indifferent dish of vegetables and rice when Dickon said suddenly: "What did you mean: 'thanks for translating'? I wasn't anywhere near you."

"Yes you were! I called you over because I couldn't understand what the old man was saying. You were just behind me."

"Was never!"

"You're kidding. . . ."

"I'm not!"

And the more I insisted, the more adamant he became. Had I imagined it all, then? The whole episode was becoming less clear by the minute, but still I clung to an image, a feeling: a dragon—me, him?—flying in the face of a storm to the Blue Mountain.

Jasper . . . lover-dragon, dragon-lover.

He was what this journey was all about, of course. Once upon a time I had rescued a little pig with vestigial wings from a cruel showman. The pig had grown and grown until one day when we found the place where he had hatched out, the pig's skin had been cast away and there was a beautiful, dark, fearsome dragon in the place of my pig.

But why fall in love with a dragon? Because I had loved the pig and the dragon wasn't a dragon all the time. And that was my fault. Three times I had kissed the pig, out of affection and gratitude, and because he was a dragon inside that pig skin I had broken a law of the equilibrium of the universe, and for each kiss the dragon was forced to spend a month a year in human form.

That's how he had explained it to me as he kissed me, made love to me as Jasper the man, just before he changed back into what he called his true self and flew away to the east, where all dragons come from, leaving me sick at heart beside the Place of Stones.

The blind knight had offered me love of a sort, Matthew Spicer had proposed marriage, but it had only been in the arms of Jasper, the Master of Many Treasures, that I had found that overwhelming joy that true love brings.

And that was why I was here, in this strange town many hundreds—

nay, thousands—of miles from my home. I would find him, I had sworn I would. I would sacrifice anything for just one more embrace—

"Your turn."

"I beg your pardon?"

"Wake up, Summer!" said Dickon. "I said it was your turn to pay."

I fished among the small change I kept in my pouch (the greater coins I kept next to my skin) and all of a sudden I drew out an extraneous object and placed it on the table.

"What the hell's that?"

"The old man had it on his tray. . . . Quick, I must take it back," and I picked up the ivory figure and hurried out, leaving Dickon to settle up. Search as I would, however, there was no sign of the old man. Even the street seemed different, better lighted, less twisty, and when I found a stall holder I thought I recognized he said he had seen me standing in a corner talking to myself. Which was ridiculous!

In the end we returned to our lodgings, though I promised myself I would go back the next day and try to find the old man. In the meantime I put the figurine on the chest at the foot of my bed and curled up in bed seeking a sleep that seemed strangely elusive. I tossed and turned, flickered in and out of brightly colored dreams I could not recall, but was at last sinking into deeper slumber when all at once there was a voice in my ears, a tiny, shrill voice that snapped me back into consciousness at once.

"Stop thief! Stop thief!"

8

I sat up at once, my sleepy eyes just making out a shadowy form slipping through the open doorway into the near darkness outside. Stumbling off the bed I made my way over to the door, shut and bolted it. Normally I didn't bother with the bolt, as Dickon and I were the only occupants of the verandah at the moment. Feeling my way back to the chest, I discovered that the lid was open, meaning flint, tinder and candle stub must be on the floor somewhere. I found the first two and was fumbling for the third when that squeaky voice came again.

"To your right a little . . . That's it!"

Needless to say I nearly dropped the lot.

"Who's there?"

Nothing, save Tug's soft breathing and a snore from Growch. Fingers trembling, I at last managed a light and held the candle high. Plenty of shadows but no intruder. Tug rolled up on the floor in his blanket—he still wouldn't use the bed—and Growch curled up at the foot of mine. No one else—

"I'm here. On the floor by your feet. Please don't tread on me. . . ."

I stared down at the ivory figure. Surely not! I must be dreaming.

"Yes, it's me. You can pick me up, if you don't mind. Quite uncomfortable standing on one's head. Thanks."

I found I had picked it—him—up and put him on the chest, right way up. I stared down; no damage from his tumble as far as I could see. But the voice! Surely that would have woken the others, or one of them would have heard the intruder. If there was one. Suddenly I wasn't sure of anything anymore.

"If you could just touch me with your ring for a moment—that's it—then I shall find the transition much easier. . . ."

I did as he said: my ring thrummed with energy for a moment, but there was nothing but good here.

"Dearie, dearie me!" said the squeaky voice. "It's been such a long time! Ivory is pretty to look at but it hasn't the warmth of amber or the manipulation of wood. But with wood there's always the threat of wood-worm of course. . . ."

I sank to my knees in front of the chest; this wasn't happening! That little figure wasn't talking to me, it wasn't, it couldn't!

"Oh, yes I am! I suppose it must be rather disconcerting for you, but if you will bear with me I'll try and make the change to living as quickly as I can. . . ." He thought for a moment. "If you could just hold me in your hands for a moment, warm me up. That's fine. Don't worry about your friends: they can't hear us."

I put him down on the chest again and sat back on my heels to watch one of the most amazing things I had ever seen. It was almost like a chicken breaking from an egg, a crumpled poppy unfurling its petals from the bud; you wondered how on earth it ever fitted inside. Of course this creature's task was different: it had to turn from inanimate to living, but the process seemed about the same.

First I saw the nostrils dilate as the first breaths of air were inhaled, then the nostrils became pinkish and the antennae at the side of his mouth flexed back and forth. Like a chick's feathers, dry little hairs release themselves from the ivory and fluffed up around his face; dark brown eyes blinked and moistened. Then came the ears and throat, the former twitching back and forth till they were set as he wanted. A forked tongue tested the air.

"A little rest: this is tougher than I thought. It's been a long time. Please, excuse the delay. . . ."

He curled back his lips, panting a little, and I could see a tiny row of chewing teeth. Now the process speeded up; tiny hooves stamped, ribs expanded, a rump gave an experimental wiggle and lastly a short tail with an outsized plume gave an exultant wave.

"There! That's better. How do I look?"

"Er . . . very impressive." I didn't really know what to say. The whole process was mind-bending, but as I didn't know what he was supposed to look like, I couldn't really qualify my statement.

He seemed to be reading my mind. "You're quite right! I've forgot-ten the colors, haven't I? Just watch. . . ."

In a way this was the most impressive of all his tricks. From being a dullish creamy yellow, he rapidly developed a uniquely tinted body that glowed like a jewel on the lid of the chest. First came a bright yellow belly, then the fur on his back developed shades of blue, purple, violet, brown and rose, his legs and tail darkened to gray and lastly the plume on his tail fanned out into crimson, gold and green. For a brief moment it seemed that his whole body was lapped by flame, but then he was as before.

"Not bad, not bad at all. I'm particularly proud of the tail: not exactly conventional, but we are allowed a certain latitude. . . . Just a moment. I'd feel more comfortable with a bit more space."

And something that had been beetle-sized rapidly expanded to the dimensions of a mouse.

"Er . . . are you going to get any bigger?" I asked nervously, as the growth seemed to be accelerating.

"Sorry! Not for the moment. Would you like to see just how big I can grow?"

"Not at the moment," I said hastily. "Some other time."

"Very well. I suppose it has taken it out of me a little. . . . Let me introduce myself. My name is Ky-Lin." His voice was less squeaky.

"Ky-Lin," I repeated like a dummy. I found it difficult to cope with what was happening.

"Yes, and you?"

"My name is Summer. Pleased to make your acquaintance."

"A mutual honor."

A little silence, then I plucked up courage. "I'm sorry, but I'm afraid I'm not quite sure to what I owe the pleasure of your company. I found you in my pouch last night, and I was going to try and find the old man tomorrow to return you—"

"Didn't he say that I went where I wanted? Where I thought I was needed?"

"Yoo, but "

"So, I am here. You need me, I think. You have a long journey ahead of you and I believe I might prove useful. The trip sounds interesting and if I comport myself well I shall have earned myself more points."

"Points? For what?" This conversation was very confusing.

"For my Master."

"The old man?"

"No, no!" He looked scandalized. "He is one of the Old Ones, a Master of Illusion, but quite earthbound I assure you. No, I speak of my Lord." He settled back on his haunches. "A long, long time ago there lived a great and good man called Siddhartha, later known as the Buddha. He was so wise and so loving that he gave up all worldly distractions. He had to walk about the world in poverty, preaching of the Divine Way to Eternal Life. He saw life as a great wheel that eventually led to Paradise, which is a way of becoming part of the Eternal. But this way can only be realized by living a perfect life, and as man is not perfect he is given many chances. These take the form of various animal lives or incarnations, accompanied by rewards and punishments—points, if you like. You may be a good horse in one incarnation, and be rewarded by being a man in the next. Or you may be a bad man, and find yourself a lowly insect in another. Do you see?"

I thought so, though it was a novel idea, these many chances to be good. Like all people in my country I had been brought up a Catholic, but since then on my travels had come across many other religions: Judaism, Hinduism, Mohammedanism. It seemed there was more than one road to God. A clever God would understand that just as different countries, different climates, different cultures produced different ideas, so He could tailor these to men's beliefs so that their worship was comfortable to them.

"You are partly following my Lord's teachings," he continued, "because you care about animals. We are taught to go even further; we believe that we must not damage any living thing, because we might be hurting one of our fellows, temporarily on a lower path or incarnation."

"But you—you are not like any creature I have ever seen."

"Because I, and my many companions, were created especially by my Lord Himself to epitomize how many creatures may be one, an harmonious whole. We travelled with Him, as His guards and friends."

"Your Lord, whom you said lived many years ago, has presumably found His Eternal Life: why are you still here, and not with Him?"

There was a longer silence. "I hoped you wouldn't ask. . . ."

"Sorry, I didn't mean—"

"It's all right. You should know." Another silence. "The fact is, I should be perfect, and I'm not. Wasn't."

"Wasn't?"

The words came out in a rush. "I-was-careless-and-trod-on-the-grass. I-was-also-greedy-and-lazy-and-rebellious." He paused. "But the worst was—I-said-I-didn't-want-Eternity. . . . I thought it would be boring. There! Now you know. That's why I'm here. I can't change my shape, but I have to work off my badnesses by helping others, until my Lord Buddha decides I am fit to join Him."

It seemed so unfair to me. Poor little creature! How on earth could you remember not to tread on grass? I reached out a finger without thought and stroked his head, and there was a little grumbling purr, like a cat, but suddenly he twitched his head aside.

"You mustn't indulge me; that is pure pleasure, and I am forbidden anything like that. I've lost a point already, being proud of my plumed tail a moment ago."

"All right." I had made a mistake with my pig-dragon. "And how many points have you got now?"

"I don't know. The trouble is, my last choice was purely selfish, and my Lord recognized it as such. I came across an old man—he was nearly eighty—who wanted help translating Greek and Roman texts. I reckoned he might last another five years or so, but my Lord saw through my deception, and the old man lived to a hundred and ten. It was hard work, too," he added, and sighed.

I found myself trying not to smile. The idea of this vibrant little creature being tied to dusty scrolls for thirty years . . . I had another idea.

"You speak, or understand, other languages, too?"

"Most. My Lord arranged it so we have an inbuilt translator in our heads."

An extra bonus: perhaps he would be able to make sense of Tug's click-clicks, and find out where he came from.

Ky-Lin yawned, his forked tongue curling back on itself till I could see the ridged roof of his mouth. "And now, it is time for sleep. I shall, with your permission, curl up inside the chest, if you would open it up? Thanks."

A last wave of his tail and I found I couldn't keep my eyes open nor my brain fit to think over what I had just seen and heard. As I pulled the blanket up round my ears, I realized that I hadn't asked him who had been the potential thief he had disturbed.

And in the morning there wasn't time.

Karim Bey sent for both Dickon and me shortly after dawn. He had found a caravan that had come in the previous day and intended to leave at midday for points further east, with a special order of furs, perfume and German glass. When Karim told Dickon I had asked to accompany it, he at once volunteered to go too. "Just to keep an eye on a trainee," as he put it.

I was surprised: I thought the distractions of the town would have been more enticing. I wasn't sure whether to be glad or sorry; Dickon was a passable lad, a good linguist, knew far more than I did about merchandising and had always been helpful. But there was something, just something I couldn't put a name to, that made me uneasy in his company. It wasn't his womanizing, though that was annoying enough, nor was it his vanity—how many lads of seventeen or so wouldn't take advantage of good wages to dress well? If I were back in my girl's guise wouldn't I want ribbons and fal-lals? No, there was something else, something *sneaky* about him.

We were hurriedly introduced to the caravan owner, a small and undistinguished character called Ali Qased, then Karim paid out moneys for our food and lodgings and the hire of a couple of mules, making sure we realized that the latter would be deducted from our commissions.

I hurried back to our lodgings for a quick breakfast, an even quicker packing—a sleepy Ky-Lin tucked surreptitiously in the lining of my jacket—and a prolonged and formal farewell to Chippi and his wife, with much head bobbing and wringing of hands from them both.

The sun was high in the sky when we set off, winding away from the city and up again into the hills, this time to the east. Tug was beside himself with happiness that we were at last on the move, and sang tunelessly as he trotted along beside us, disdaining the offer of a ride.

I didn't find things so easy. For some reason I felt out of sorts, with a grumbling stomach, a sort of warning that things might get worse. I was snappy with the others, critical of the journey, couldn't sleep—in fact it reminded me of nothing so much as those times before my monthly loss. It was a shock to realize too that these had not manifested themselves for nearly a year, a fact I had initially put down to the terrible journey I undertook to return to Matthew, after my dragon had flown away and left me.

The lack of a monthly flow had been a boon in my travels as a boy, and I had completely forgotten about it until now. Perhaps I should be worried, I thought; perhaps there was something permanently wrong. Surreptitiously I felt my stomach: a little swollen, but nothing else. If it was pregnancy I was worried about, then there was nothing to fear, of course, for Jasper was the only man to touch me in that way and the nine months needed to make a baby had long gone. Just in case I checked my pack to make sure the cloths I had packed were still there if needed.

It grew rapidly much colder the farther east and north we travelled, with an intermittent icy wind sliding down the ever-nearing mountains, and it was with relief that we mostly found small villages in which to spend the lengthening nights; tents in the open were no substitute for four walls and a roof, however basic. Tug was the only one who didn't feel the cold, merely wrapping himself up tighter in his blanket.

I kept Ky-Lin hidden, as we mostly shared quarters with Dickon, and for some reason I was reluctant to share him. I fed him scraps of rice or dried fruit, because of his taboo on eating or killing anything live.

One night we were on our own, Dickon and Tug foraging for wood for the communal fire and Growch off on an expedition of his own. I set out some raisins and a few nuts in front of Ky-Lin, watching his pleasure as he nibbled at the latter.

"You like them?"

"Mmm. One of my favorites. You know what I like best of all?"

"No."

"Flaked almonds coated with honey, or a nice pod or two of carob. Very bad for the teeth, but quite delicious."

I made a mental note to seek out either or both as soon as I could.

As I watched him I suddenly remembered something I had meant to ask a long time ago.

"Ky-Lin, that first night you came to us . . ."

"Mmm?"

"You woke me up calling out 'Stop thief!' "

He nodded.

"Did you see him?"

He nodded again, mouth full of nut.

"Did you see who it was?"

Another nod.

"Who?"

It seemed ages before he answered. "Got sticky fingers that one."

"Who has?"

"Your friend Dickon, of course! Who did you think it would be?"

9

I don't believe it!" I shook my head. "There's nothing there he would want."

"Have you anything in your baggage he desires?"

I thought through all my belongings: clothes, writing materials and journal, now written in a form of shortened hand and difficult to decipher; tally sticks, a few herbs and simples, my forged papers from Matthew, Suleiman's letter—had Dickon made something that wasn't out of that?—mug, bowl and spoon, plus the lump of glass the captain's wife had given me. This had proved rather disappointing: beautifully shaped and cut, it nevertheless had looked nothing other than dull when I had looked at it one gray evening when we had been on our way to the tent city of Küm. My other treasure from that city, the Waystone, I kept in a pouch about my neck, together with some little scraps of discarded skin that had come from a certain little pig; just a keepsake, I kept telling myself.

But there must be something. Think . . . I went through the list again in my mind. No, there was nothing else—nothing except the maps I had copied, and the one Suleiman had enclosed with his letter. Could it be these he had been looking for?

Ky-Lin was reading my mind. "Could be," he said. "Especially if he has the sort of suspicious mind that believes you are doing something other than just being an apprentice."

I remembered Dickon's accusations of being a spy, or on a secret mission for Matthew. "Let's take a look," I said. I peeked past the hanging leather that served as a door in this poor place; Tug was squatting by the fire, Dickon was talking to one of the village girls.

"All clear." I pulled out the two maps I had duplicated at Matthew's and spread them out on the dirt floor using elbows and knees to keep them flat. Ky-Lin trotted over to sit on the fourth corner.

I pointed to the first, larger map. "Here's where I come from, and that's the route, marked out, that we took to Venice. . . . Here's the sea we crossed to the Golden Horn, and this could be the way we took to Küm. But there are lots of trails leading from there, so we must have used the most easterly. I suppose we could be just about here, now. . . ."

Ky-Lin squinted horribly and shook his head from side to side which he explained helped him concentrate. "The trouble with maps is that they are never used by people who know the routes and know the terrain, so there is no one to update them. Most of them are hopelessly inaccurate, and at best are mostly guesswork. Distances, too, can be very misleading, for who counts his paces or even his days to mark his passage? Ask one caravan master how long it takes from this city to that and he will tell you ten, twenty days, depending on the weather. Another will take a different trail over easier ground and shorten the time by half, yet as the bird flies the mileage would be the same."

"It's marked with mountains and things," I said defensively. An erupting volcano graced part of Italia, a couple of small ships on the seas; there was what looked like a lion and a triangular temple on the coast of Africa, and Cathay was shown with snaky rivers and high mountains. In the corner where Ky-Lin was sitting was a great empty space and the legend: "Here be Dragons." That was one of the reasons I had been keen to have a copy.

"Pictures of them, yes, but are they where it shows them? I think you have a clue here," and he tapped his hoof right in front of where he was sitting. "To the ignorant layman, when you see the word 'dragons,' what would you immediately think of? Yes," he added, crossing my thoughts. "Treasure. Maybe your young friend believes you are on a treasure hunt, with or without Master Spicer's assistance or knowledge. Let me see the others. . . ."

The second of Matthew's maps he pronounced as better, but not much. I produced the one Suleiman had sent.

"Ah, this is more like it. The man who made this actually travelled these routes. I recognize this, and this, and this. . . ." He shook his head, crossed his eyes alarmingly, waved his plumed tail.

"But I can't read these squiggles. . . ."

"Those 'squiggles' are in Cantonese, but even without them I can see places I have visited. See, the Land of the Lotus, the Singing Gardens, the Desert of Death, the City of Golden Towers (not true, they are only gilded), and there are others I have heard of. The country of Snakes, the town of the Three-legged Men (named after an annual race they hold), the Blue Mountain, the—"

"Did you—did you say the Blue Mountain?"

"Yes. Here it is, just beyond the Three Fangs of the Mighty One. This means something special to you?"

All at once all I could think about was the vision the old man had shown me in that magical bowl of colored water, where I had been for a brief moment or two a dragon, steering my way through the Fangs and down to the valley beneath and the Blue Mountain with the hidden cave.

I jabbed my finger down on the map. "It's there, it's true, it's real! *That's* where I must go!" I was almost shouting with joy.

There was a sudden silence. The ivory figurine that had been holding down the map rolled off into the shadows. I looked up, and there was Dickon framed in the doorway.

I don't know how much he had heard or seen, but of course he pretended there was nothing amiss, merely saying that he had come to ask whether I would prefer rice or pancakes for our evening meal, but all the time he was speaking his eyes were darting suspiciously around the hut, glancing at the map I had immediately released so that it had scrolled itself and rolled into a corner.

Poor Ky-Lin, I thought: he will have to start all over again. Even while I was thinking this I was gathering up the maps and stuffing them back in my pack, and all the while chattering away like a demented monkey.

"Hello, Dickon, I didn't see you there! How nice of you to come and ask what I wanted. . . . Let me see, now. We had pancakes yesterday, didn't we? Or was it beans . . . On the other hand I'm a bit tired of rice. My stomach hasn't been all that good, as you know, so perhaps it had better be pancakes. Or do you think they will be too greasy? What do you suggest?"

I continued to rummage around for my writing things.

"I thought I would catch up with my diary of our travels, so I checked the maps to make sure I have the route all planned out correctly. They're not very accurate, though; what's this place called, do you know? Never mind, I'll just mark it as a village. . . ."

And so on, trying to cover my confusion and making it worse.

But he couldn't contain his curiosity for long. "I heard—I thought you were talking to someone . . . ?"

"Me? Now who could I be talking to: there's no one else here. The place is empty. . . ." *Think* of something quick, Summer! "Oh that! You heard me talking to myself, I suppose. Haven't you ever done that? It always helps if you're trying to work something out in your mind, makes it all much clearer. . . ."

I could see he wasn't satisfied, kept looking around the room, but there was nothing to see. "I'll order you rice then. It'll be ready soon."

As soon as he was gone, I rushed over to Ky-Lin and picked him up.

"I'm terribly sorry. I hope it wasn't too difficult to come alive again?"

Almost at once out popped a living nose and mouth. "Easier each time. Give me a few minutes. Go and get your food; if you wouldn't mind bringing me a few grains of rice? I always get particularly hungry after a change. . . ."

The meal was an uneasy one. Dickon put himself out to be charming and entertaining, but I still worried about what he might have seen and overheard. Besides which, my stomach had started aching again and I definitely felt queasy. I couldn't finish all the rice and vegetables and excused myself before the others had finished, longing to just wrap myself in a blanket, lie down on my pallet and try to forget the pain in my guts in sleep. It wasn't particularly cold, but I was shivering.

"Did you remember . . . ? It doesn't matter. You look ill. . . ."

"Oh, hell! Sorry Ky-Lin. Yes. It does matter." I went to the door and called Tug over and explained what I wanted. He had been playing five-stones with the village boys, but he was always cheerful and willing these days. Two minutes later he was back with some rice and vegetables wrapped in a vine leaf.

"You still hungry, Summa?"

I made up my mind. "Tug come with me. New friend to meet."

Tug's eyes were as wide as I had ever seen them as Ky-Lin fluffed out his tail in welcome. But instead of dropping the rice or running off in horror, he instead gave a stiff little bow, then walked over to the creature and placed the food in front of him, standing back to watch him eat.

"Tug, this is a—"

"Ch'i-Lin," said Tug, and gave that jerky little bow again. "*Very* good. Go with Lord Buddha."

"He knows. . . ."

"My Lord's wisdom has travelled to many places, like the wind," said Ky-Lin, chasing the last pieces of rice with his forked tongue. "If I am not mistaken, this child comes from the Northern Plains."

"Can you speak his tongue?" Perhaps at last we should be better able to help him.

"I will try. . . ." And for the next few moments there was an incomprehensible (to me) series and exchange of clicks and hisses, at the end of which Ky-Lin's eyes were crossed and Tug had a broad grin on his face.

"I was right," said Ky-Lin. "The boy is one of the Plainsmen, the great Horsemen. They are nomadic herdsmen, live in tents, and travel many hundreds of miles in a year."

"And how far away is his homeland?" I asked, my heart already sinking in anticipation of his reply.

"Perhaps a thousand miles to the north, perhaps a little more."

It was as I had feared. I had promised Tug, in sign language if not in words, that I would take him back to his homeland, and I couldn't break a promise, even if it meant I went hundreds of miles out of my way. I looked at the hope in his face, and knew I couldn't let him down. How should I have felt if I had been snatched away from home and family at ten or eleven years old, transported hundreds of miles, only to be sold like an animal to the highest bidder? After all, my dragon would wait, wouldn't he?

"Do you know the way there, Ky-Lin?"

"I can guide you in the right direction, if that is what you wish; the way is quite clearly shown on that last map of yours. But I warn you that the country itself, besides being many miles away, is also far vaster than anything you have come across so far. Another thing; it will take many months to reach, and this caravan we travel with is taking us too far to the east."

Which meant we should have to abandon the safety of the caravan and strike out on our own. For a terrible moment I thought I hadn't got the courage; feeling as I did now, I would have been thankful to have just curled up for the winter and hibernated like the red-leaf squirrels near my old home. My ring gave a little throb, and I remembered we had Ky-Lin with us, and we hadn't failed up to now, had we? And we wouldn't: not with the help of God's good grace—and a little luck.

But we should have to be careful not to rouse Dickon's suspicions. He was the last person I wanted to accompany us, but if he got the slightest hint we were to be away on our own he would be sure to follow, especially if, as Ky-Lin had suggested, he believed we were after treasure. And, knowing Dickon, he would stick like a leech.

The following morning I made enquiries that all could hear as to when we would reach the next town, explaining that I needed the services of a competent purveyor of pills for my stomach pains. The answer was three days; once there I would plead indisposition and stay behind. Of course once I announced my indisposition, it miraculously cured itself, as an aching tooth will while queuing for the tooth puller, but I still pretended it was worsening, and this was aided by the fact that apparently I still looked pale and drawn.

In the meantime I introduced Growch to Ky-Lin, only to be informed that he had "known all the time, and just how many more spare parts was I going to invite along on what was, after all, supposed to be a special journey just for the two of us . . ." etc.

I realized that he was jealous, only had been too caught up in my own plans to recognize it, so from then on I made a special fuss over him, even going to the extreme of treating him to a bath and comb. He whined like hell, of course, but secretly I believe he thought any attention was better than none, and we were soon back to our old footing.

The journey that should have taken three days took five, due to torrential rains, but this worked to my advantage in the end, because Ali Qased, the caravan master, was eager to press on immediately before any more autumnal downpours held him up, and as far as he was concerned one sick apprentice more or less would only hold him up.

Using Dickon as my interpreter, he was quite willing I should stay behind until he returned—a guess of a month or more—but he also insisted that I consult the local apothecary, a shabby little man with an obsequious manner and a satchel full of phials of crushed insects, dried bats' wings, unidentified blood, powder of tiger claw, bitter herbs and pellets of opium. He prodded my stomach, shook his head, and went way to make up some pills.

To add color to my "illness," I took to my bed in the small attic room Dickon had found for me. He returned with powder in a twist of rice paper and half a dozen pills, insisting that I take them at once.

"You owe me two silver coins—"

"He's expensive!"

"Yes, but if you take these at once you may be better in the morning and ready to continue the journey. We don't leave till ten."

I fished out the money, then groaned. "I don't think I shall. . . . Now, leave me alone to get some rest."

"When you've taken your medicine. The powder is to be dissolved in water and the—"

"I haven't got any."

"What?"

"Water."

He nodded at Tug, who was arranging some stones on the floor in a complicated game. "Send your slave boy."

I was tired of his attitude towards Tug.

"Once and for all, he's not a slave. I bought him and gave him his freedom. And no, I'm not sending him: he couldn't make himself understood. Go yourself."

"He's a cretin. . . ."

"He's not that either. You just don't understand him."

I might add that Tug was perfectly well aware of Dickon's dislike and played up to it, acting like a village idiot when he was near, so Dickon's remark wasn't entirely unjustified. Now the boy stuck out his tongue and waggled his fingers in his ears.

"Tug . . ." I said reprovingly, wanting to giggle.

"Told you," said Dickon. "All right, I'll fetch you some water. Just stay here till I get back."

What did he think I was going to do? Fly out the window?

As soon as he had gone I scooped Ky-Lin out of my sleeve.

"Quick!" I said. "The medicines. Are they fit to take?"

He sniffed delicately at the twists of paper.

"Mmmm . . . the powder is harmless. Crushed pearl, a pinch of gentian for color, cinnamon for taste. The pills? Sweetener for coating, a little clay for setting; inside rat's blood, burnt feathers and a good dose of opium."

"Yeeuk!"

"You've eaten worse, certainly from my point of view! At least there is nothing to harm you permanently. Try and get away with just drinking the powder: the opium in a pill will make you sleep heavily, and if you want to be away tomorrow as soon as they leave . . . spit it out as soon as he's gone."

But the trouble was he wouldn't go. He watched me tip some of the powder into my mug and add water, stirring it with my finger till it was purple. I drank it down with an expression of disgust, though the taste was not unpleasant.

"I think I'll take a rest now. . . ."

"Pills first."

"In a minute! I'll just see if the drink will—"

"The pills are to be taken at the same time. Go on. Two."

"I am *not* taking two! Suppose they don't agree with me? Do you want to spend the night nursing me?"

"One, then. Now!"

I put it in my mouth, and tucked it quickly under my tongue, making exaggerated swallowing motions. "There! Now you can go and leave me alone."

He still wouldn't leave; instead he paced the floor, small though the room was: three steps one way, two back.

"How can I leave you on your own? Master Spicer would never forgive me if you worsened. . . . You said yourself that heathen boy can't make himself understood. No, my duty is to stay here with you. The caravan can manage without me."

The pill was gradually melting in my mouth. I could taste the bitterness through the coating.

"And Matthew would never forgive me if you broke your apprenticeship just to look after me! I'll be fine in a couple of days. I've enough money to stay here until you come back, and I can spend the time bringing my journal up to date and learning a bit more of the language. I wouldn't dream of you staying behind!"

"Don't tell me what I ought or ought not to do!" Then in a gentler tone: "I consider it my duty to look after you. Don't forget I am the only one who knows you are a girl . . ."

Was this an implied threat?

". . . and you wouldn't want anyone else to find out, would you?"

Yes, it was.

"What harm can it do for me to stay and—you to go?" The pill must be taking effect. I mustn't go to sleep, I mustn't! "After all, I can't go anywhere, can I? Ali Qased said his was the last caravan expected this year. . . ." I yawned uncontrollably.

At last he left, promising to look in again, and the next thing was Ky-Lin hissing in my ear: "Spit it out! Spit it out!"

The pill, what little was left of it, dropped to the floor. I struggled up on my elbow. "Mustn't sleep . . . lots to do. Got to find out—find out—how to get away. Transport . . . food. Can't . . . can't sleep."

"Do-not-worry," said Ky-Lin, close to my ear. "We-will-see-to-it Leave-it-to-us. Sleep-in-peace. . . ."

I didn't hear or see them leave, knew nothing else in fact until a bright light flashed across my eyelids. I tried to open my mouth, my eyes, but nothing happened. It was as if I was frozen to my bed. The light flashed again.

"Perhaps you were telling the truth after all, little witch," said a voice I should recognize. Then more sharply: "Wake up, Summer! Time to get up," and someone shook me, none too gently. I moaned and rolled over, but could respond no further, slipping back down into a velvety darkness.

Then something triggered a thought. Of course I recognized the voice: it had to be Dickon. With a supreme effort I opened my eyes. There was a lantern on the floor, and by its light I could see Dickon going through my papers, my pack open at his side. He held up first one map and then another, frowning and muttering to himself. "Can't see much there. . . . Possible, possible. We're way off track, though. . . ."

He rolled the maps, turned his attention to my journal but, as I had anticipated, he could make little of my scrawl, especially as it had been only recently that the former stable lad had learned to know his letters. "Still, I heard her say there was somewhere she had to go . . . but where, *where*?"

He glanced across at me, but luckily my face was in shadow and I closed my eyes quickly.

"Still, there's nowhere to go from here. Safe enough, I reckon."

At that moment there was a bark on the stone steps that led up to my room; the others were back.

With a speed that obviously owed much to practice, maps and papers were stuffed back in my pack and it was rapidly refastened. A moment later and he was standing over the bed, lantern held high.

Growch rushed in growling, closely followed by Tug. Dickon straightened up.

"Just checking on the patient, for the benefit of a cretin and a scruffy hound," said Dickon. "I know you can't understand, stupid bastards both, but I'll be back to check in the morning."

I heard his steps on the stair and tried to keep awake long enough to tell Ky-Lin, emerging from Tug's jacket, just what had happened, but he shushed me.

"Go to sleep. Don't worry about a thing. We have got it all organized. By this time tomorrow we shall be spending our first night afloat. . . ."

I could have sworn he said "afloat." But we weren't anywhere near the sea. I must have been dreaming.

And two minutes later I really was.

INTERLUDE

He was bored. Restless. Unhappy.

He told himself not to be stupid, that he had everything he needed, that dragons did not admit to boredom, or restlessness. And, most of all, not to unhappiness. Yet how else could he explain why he felt as he did? Dragons usually were only affected by purely physical things: heat and cold, hunger and thirst; and by the pure pleasure, endless delight, of jewels and gems, and the retelling of tales of travel.

But then he wasn't a dragon all the time, was he? Like now. Now he was a man sitting on a deserted beach somewhere, chucking stones into the sea and suffering from indigestion.

And that was another thing: a man ate what a man ate, dragons were different. If one had a fire in one's belly, used regularly or not, one could digest anything, bones and all, but a man's stomach churned on the remains of a dragon dinner.

He gave a snort of disgust. This just shouldn't be happening to him. He had reported back, been welcomed and initiated into the proper rituals, then allowed the treat of inspecting the Hoard. He had been obliged, however, to disclose his Affliction, as he termed it, and been rewarded with consternation and disbelief. Spells had been cast, charms used, lore memory consulted, but all to no avail. Nothing like this had ever happened before; of course it was known that it could, but what mortal maid in her right mind had ever kissed a dragon?

At first, of course, they hadn't believed him, until he had done an involuntary change and back right there in front of them. It was the most exciting thing that had happened to the community since the Blue Dragon had returned hundreds of years back with his jewels and the tales of the witch who had stolen them, and the knight and the girl and the animals who had returned them.

His Affliction had had a mixed reception. Some of them thought it *added to his powers, others that it must inevitably detract from the purity of line they had preserved.*

Five minutes, ten, of thought, and he was still bored, restless and unhappy, and the sea a hundred stones fuller. He might as well admit it; he still hankered after that lass with the long legs who had rescued him from death in his first incarnation as a pig, cared for him, loved him and finally—irony of ironies!—given him the three kisses he would remember forever. That, and the moment of passion when he was caught between man and dragon—Aiyee! That experience had been enough to make anyone's toes curl!

Fire and ice! He must see her again—if only to convince himself that he didn't need to. . . .

It was late spring when he started his journey. Back first to the Place of Stones, where his transformation had taken place, then retracing her route back to that fat merchant she would probably marry. As a man he came down to earth to ask questions, see if she had passed that way, but to no avail. By midsummer he had even dared the servants at the merchant's house, only to find she had disappeared a few weeks before with her dog to parts unknown, and that the merchant, heartbroken, had gone on pilgrimage to Spain.

So, where was she, the girl whose memory still tormented him? North, south, east, west? He tried haphazardly: northern fjords, southern deserts, western isles, eastern mountains—but surely even she wouldn't travel that far. Why run away from a perfectly good marriage anyway? What was she looking for now? What worm was eating her brain this time, silly girl?

He grew crosser and crosser; what right had she to haunt him so? Time he pulled himself together; what he needed was a break, a few months, a year perhaps; time, anyway, that he sought some gifts for the Hoard, part of his dragon duty. Perhaps by then he would be free of what was rapidly becoming an obsession.

So, which way? Somewhere warm for the winter. Africa, India, the isles of the Southern Seas? It didn't really matter. . . .

Part II

Part II

10

I had never thought it would be so wonderful to be one's own mistress again, to be free of caravans, merchants, warehouses, tally sticks, accounts, invoices, bales and bargaining. Most of all it was wonderful to be rid of Dickon. More and more he had constricted my every move and his suspicions had haunted me so much I found myself glancing over my shoulder even now to make sure he wasn't following.

Of course being free was a comparative term. I had the others to think about and care for, Tug to return to his people and my own journey to complete, but at least we could proceed at our own pace.

It was bliss to just lie back against the thwarts of the boat, even hemmed in as we were by peasants, farmers, children, sacks of grain, rolls of cloth, strings of dried fish and crates of chickens. Above us was a cloudless sky, rice fields and stands of bamboo slid past with a lazy regularity, and the smooth water of the Yellow Snake River gurgled and slapped against the hull, accompanied by the flap of sail and creak of rudder.

Ky-Lin, Tug and Growch had done well while I lay deadened by the opium. Ky-Lin had remembered from the map that the river looped briefly towards the town some five miles away and had ascertained that boats travelled regularly both north and south, and in fact we had picked up one this midafternoon. The river eventually turned to the east and Cathay, but by this way, though slower, we should be some two hundred miles farther towards our goal, with little effort on our part. Just as long as the money held out: we should have to be careful and economize where we could. Luckily nobody would charge for Growch, and Ky-Lin was tucked up in the hood of my cloak, both for safety and so he could whisper translations if necessary.

I patted Tug's knee. "Not bad, eh?" He shivered and snuggled nearer, his eyes rolling in fright. "It's all right," I said slowly, hoping he would understand. "Ky-Lin: tell him there's nothing to be afraid of."

But though the magic creature did his best Tug refused to be comforted, and I recalled my own experience with water. The first time I had been in a frail rowing boat carrying me away from marauding soldiers; the second I had nearly been drowned when I was cut off by an incoming tide and the third had been that dreadful storm when we had left Venice, so perhaps Tug was to be pitied. I stretched out my hand but he had bolted to the side and heaved up into the river.

I moved over to rub his back, a thing my mother had done when I was a child in some sick situation, and I had always found it comforting. Remembering my ring had many powers, I drew that gently down his spine too, and wasn't surprised when he turned to me with a weak smile and announced he was: "Better with no tum!" He added: "Like ride horse. Fall off two three time. Learn quick." And after that he was all right.

We travelled from one stopover to another, at each one discharging cargo and passengers and taking on others. I had no word of the native tongue, even having to bargain for our fare with sign language and Ky-Lin's whispers, but the people were kind and cheerful, inviting us to share their meagre provisions. These were usually cooked on a brazier in the well of the boat, although occasionally we tied up for the night by some village or other and dined there in one of the tiny eating houses. In this way we travelled some seventy or eighty miles north, then the boat in which we were travelling turned back and we took another, smaller, which tied up every night. In order to eat I had to buy a small cooking pot, food on the way and have Tug forage for the wood for a fire. This took us another fifty miles, and then we swapped to a string of barges carrying cattle—not an experience to be repeated.

The weather gradually changed as autumn and the approaching north brought colder winds, rain, falling leaves, and cranes winging south. By now we were some hundred and fifty miles further on, but the river narrowed into a series of gorges through which water raced in a torrent, and only the hardiest and most reckless boatman would venture the rapids. It seemed this terrain was unchanged for fifty miles or so, and we decided to finally leave the river and start walking.

We hadn't gone more than a couple of miles or so when I, at least, was regretting it. I had gone soft, what with mule and river travel, and although Tug carried his fair share of the baggage, mine felt to weigh a ton, and we were all hot, sticky, and tired by the time we had walked ten miles that first day. A village gave us shelter for the night, we had a lift on a bullock cart the following day, which was a bit like travelling snail-back, but at least it gave my feet a rest. My stomach, too, had begun to play up again, but only intermittently. For the next three days it rained continuously and we were holed up in a miserable hovel with a dripping roof and I began to wonder if we had offended some local god.

On the fifth day our luck changed for the better. The sun shone warm, we dried out, and I reckoned we could risk a night in the open if we could find some bushes or convenient trees. During the day we had managed to gather some nuts and berries to supplement our diet, and as we were now in sight of a good-sized village, I decided to go in and buy rice or beans. Travelling on the river, the money had trickled away as fast as the water ran, and I had no idea how much farther we had to go.

We had just found a likely camping spot and set down our baggage, dusk was falling and Tug was about to forage for wood, when we heard the sound of pipes and firecrackers from the village. I never got used to the half and quarter tones of eastern music and firecrackers always made me jump, but Tug loved both, so we picked up our packs again and set off towards the celebrations. At the very worst there would be some scraps of food dropping from the tables for Growch to scrounge, and at best we might be invited to share with some hospitable villager.

Although the outer streets were deserted there had obviously been a procession of sorts earlier, for the ground was littered with scraps of colored paper and burned-out firecrackers, but the noise now came from the center of the village, as did a healthy smell of cooking meat and rice. We followed our ears and our noses and found ourselves in the village square.

In one corner a couple of spits were turning vigorously and large pans were simmering over a trench fire; while they waited for the food, the villagers were clapping an entertainment. As usual at these functions, like any other village in the world, certain unwritten rules for social behavior were observed. The elderly were comfortably seated around the perimeter, some with smaller children and babies on their laps, the young men congregated in one corner, the girls in the opposite, parents and middle-aged bustled from one group to another exchanging gossip, and the older children played tag and got under everyone's feet.

But for now all was relatively quiet as they watched the performers. A trio of children, some younger even than Tug, were working acrobatic tricks with a man who was obviously their father, while an older boy twisted himself into knots and did cartwheels round them; in another space a pair of jugglers tossed balls, rings and torches into the air and at each other, while on the fringes waited a great brown bear with a ring through its nose, shifting restlessly from paw to paw. Its owner, a thickset man with a pipe in his hand ready to play the music for the creature to dance to, suddenly jerked at the chain that ran through the ring in the bear's nose, which bit into the soft part of the nostril and made the poor thing squeal with pain. Simultaneously, it seemed, my heart jumped in sympathy and the ring on my finger gave a sudden stab.

The ring stabbed again, and all at once I had a brilliant idea. In what seemed another life my beautiful blind knight with his clear singing voice and the animals with me then had given performances such as these to pay our way. Why not try it again? True, the only original members of our troupe were Growch and myself, and all he had ever done was beg, turn somersaults, and lie down and "die," but surely we could concoct something between us. I asked Tug if he knew any tricks, through Ky-Lin.

"He says," translated the latter, "give him a horse and he is the best in the world. He also says he can turn cartwheels, do leaping somersaults and walk on his hands as well as the children over there. Oh, and he says he dances and plays the pipe also."

I had left my old pipe and tabor behind at Matthew's, but I supposed one could be bought somewhere here. In the meantime . . .

"Growch darling, come over here." But he had found some scraps under a table and was discussing their ownership vigorously with a couple of village curs. I dragged him away.

"What d'yer wanna do that for? Got 'em on the run, I 'ad—"

"Listen to me a moment! I'll buy you all the supper you want if you'll do me a small favor. Do you remember . . ." and I reminded him of our past performances, and tried to get him interested in some more immediate ones.

"Not on yer life! Right twit I used ter look, all ponced up in ribbons an' fings! Said then 'never again' I said. . . ."

"You never did!"

"Said it to meself. Never break a promise to yerself." And he scratched until the fur flew.

"Right. Have it your own way. But the only way we can buy supper—slices of juicy meat with lots of crackly skin, nice crunchy bones filled with marrow—is by earning some money performing here and now."

He hoofed out his left ear, looked at his paw and licked it. "Well, what you goin' ter do, then?"

What indeed. I didn't sing or play their music and couldn't stand on my head.

Ky-Lin spoke softly in my ear. "How about a little magic?"

"Real magic? How?"

"What they will believe is magic. How about a talking dog?"

"Growch?"

"Who else? Listen . . ." and he outlined a scheme so beautiful in its simplicity that I felt at once optimistic. We crept around a corner to rehearse.

I thought I foresaw a difficulty.

"How can I announce us and also name the objects when I don't speak a word of their language?"

"Simple!" said Ky-Lin. "Mime. I'll speak the words and you just open and shut your mouth and wave your arms about. Listen!" and all at once in my ear came my own voice, echoing my persuasions to Growch, awhile back. This was followed by a rapid speech in the language of the country. As he was sitting on my shoulder it was like having an echo to the earlier part. "Convinced?"

With a little more practice it might just work. After all, they could only boo and jeer and turn us out of the village if they didn't like us, and we'd be no worse off. . . .

"Well," I said, patting my stomach, "I haven't eaten so well for weeks!"

"Very palatable," said Ky-Lin, licking the remains of the honey from his antennae.

"Good, good, good!" grinned a greasy-faced Tug, and belched—a habit which seemed to be the polite way to express appreciation in his country. "Do again, more money, more food . . ." He belched again.

"Growch? Are you satisfied?"

But a snore was the only answer. His stomach was so distended with rice, pork, beans and pancakes that it shone like a pink-gray bladder through the thinner hair of his belly. A couple of fleas scurried through the curls quite clearly. Oh, Growch! Still he had done a great job this evening: so had they all.

I curled up on my pallet in the small back room we had hired for the night and let the images of our performance dance behind my closed eyelids, secure in the comfortable discomfort of a just-too-full stomach and the consciousness of a pouch full of small coins . . .

"Illustrious villagers, fathers of industry, mothers of many, older folk with the wisdom of the years, youngsters who will grow strong and tall as their ancestors . . ."

"Move your mouth a bit more," whispered Ky-Lin. "It looks more authentic."

We should have to practice this more; still in the torchlight it probably didn't look too bad.

"Tonight we bring you, from the far corners of the world, an entertainment to delight and mystify. You will see marvels of agility from a prince of his people, feats of intelligence from a dog who learnt his wisdom from the Great Masters of the East, and finally an act so mindbending that you will be telling your children's children of it for years to come. . . ."

It was strange to hear my voice ringing strong and confident, translating the words I gave Ky-Lin in a whisper into the local language. It was the showman's spiel, of course, used throughout the world with only local variations. Grab the attention of your audience, flatter them, then give them an inflated idea of the acts they were about to see, and provide the performers with exotic backgrounds for greater wonder and appreciation.

Puff the acts as they appear and keep the best till last, for that is how your audience will remember you when the bowl comes round for the coins. In this way Tug did his acrobatics, Growch his tricks. Then came the part I was dreading: if it failed we would be laughed out of town.

But it hadn't, the dear Lord be praised! In fact it had gone better than expected. After an introduction, explaining what we intended to do, Tug had moved among the audience borrowing an object here, another there. These he showed to Growch one by one, and the dog had then trotted over to where I sat with my back turned and "told" me what each object was with barks and yips, Ky-Lin, tucked up in my hood, correctly identifying the objects as Tug showed them to Growch. I then made a great thing of rising to my feet and pretending to consider what the dog had "told" me, Ky-Lin eventually announcing it in my voice. To add verisimilitude I had once or twice pretended that I hadn't understood, and made Growch repeat his noises with a little variation, till he had informed me he was giving himself a headache. . . .

Sleepily I began to plan ahead. If we could polish up the act a little, were sure of finding enough audiences, then we should not only not have to worry about money, but could afford some costumes: the more profitable you looked, the more likely you were to attract more money and greater respect.

It may have been the unaccustomed feast that lay uneasy on my stomach, but when I finally did fall asleep it wasn't of our better fortunes that I dreamt: it was of a poor tormented bear, dancing an eternal jig to a screech of pipes, his nose bleeding and his feet sore. . . .

From then on the travelling, though not perfect, became more tolerable. Our first "take" lasted until our next, more polished performance in a larger village. That one not only filled my pouch, but provided a bright costume for Tug (he wanted to wear it all the time) and ribbons for Growch (who never wanted them at all). Now we could afford a lift to the next villages and if, when we got there, they were too poor to pay us in anything except a bowl of rice and a room for the night, then that was all right too. We were moving in the right direction as Suleiman's map showed and my Waystone confirmed.

The only drawback was that the weather was worsening; it was now late fall and we were travelling towards the northerly cold as well. Every now and again a flurry of sleet bore down on the winds, and a chill breath lay over the early mornings. In the countryside the harvests of rice and grain were safely gathered, fodder for the wintering beasts stacked and fruits dried, cheeses stored. The peasants knew that their food had to last until spring so there was little enough to spare for travellers, even if they could pay. One could not eat coin, but two handfuls of rice saved meant another day's bellyful.

As we travelled farther, rumors began to trickle back about a great celebration to be held in one of the principal cities of the province. Ky-Lin (who listened to everything about him) reported that the second and favorite son of the ruler was to be married amid great pomp and ceremony.

"They say it will be a sight no man should miss. There will be enough food and drink to feed the whole city free for a week, and entertainments are to be held day and night. It is also said that those who have such entertainments to offer will be doubly welcome and paid accordingly."

"It might be just a rumor. You know how these things get exaggerated by hearsay."

He waved his plumed tail. "True, but judging by the consistency of the tales, I think we can safely say that there is to be a marriage, there will be celebrations and possibly entertainers would find it worth their while to attend."

"Is it far out of our way?"

"A little perhaps, but that should be outweighed by the fact that as we go towards the city more lifts will be available. The same after the celebrations, for everyone will disperse to their homes again, and that will include those who travel our way. It should bring us nearer Tug's people."

"Can we wait for a day or so more? Just in case . . ."

But it seemed that Ky-Lin was right. The roads became suddenly more crowded; not only with the usual traffic but with other entertainers and even a more prosperous traveller or two, able to afford his own transport, and they were all moving in the same direction. Now we were joined by caravans carrying goods and provisions, and it became more difficult to find food along the way, so we took to carrying and cooking our own, it having been tacitly decided that we would take our chances with the rest travelling to the celebrations.

Along the way we met other entertainers we had come across before—the father with his acrobatic children, two or three jugglers, a sword swallower. Also on the road were cages of exotic animals: I saw two lions, large apes, a striped horse and huge, comatose snakes. And then, in a largish village some seventy miles short of our destination, we came across the dancing bear again.

For once I had managed to secure a room for us in a ramshackle house on the edge of town, but at least it was shelter from the cold. The proprietor had also provided a reasonable meal of rice and vegetables, with even a bit of meat thrown in. It had been a miserably wet, windy day's travelling, but the rain let up in the evening, and we decided to take a stroll, having no intention of wasting a show on such an inclement night, but wanting to see if anyone else was desperate enough to try it.

As I thought, most houses were already tight-shuttered for the night, just a chink of light from their lamp wicks floating in saucers of oil to show they were occupied, and even these would soon be dowsed to save the precious fuel. It wasn't till we came to the ubiquitous square that we saw others had braved the weather. This village boasted the equivalent of a town hall, and on its steps lounged a couple of the village law enforcers, stout cudgels in their hands. In the square itself were half a dozen men, two women and about twenty children, watching the antics of a second-class juggler and a magician whose tricks were of the simplest. The juggler, a thin man with long, yellowed teeth, dropped his last few sticks, grimaced, and, picking up the single coin that had been dropped, disappeared down a side street. The magician continued to pull his colored scarves, open and shut his "magic" boxes, but now all eyes went to another attraction: the bear had emerged with his keeper, the latter obviously well away on rice wine.

The creature looked worse for wear than ever; he was shabbier and thinner than when I had seen him last, and his fur now stuck up in spikes from the soaking he must have got earlier that day. His owner was in a foul mood as well as being too drunk even to play his pipes properly. The worse he played, the more he jerked on the chain that ended at the bear's nose as it refused to respond, even kicking it with his heavy boots till it grunted in pain. A couple of the village curs decided to join in, nipping at the bear's heels till it roared in pain; the owner struck it on the nose with his pipe, the crowd jeered and the bewildered creature dropped to all fours.

The ring on my finger was throbbing, and I could bear the cruelty no longer. I started forward, but Ky-Lin hissed in my ear: "Wait! oh impatient one, wait a little longer."

"We must *do* something!"

"We will. Just be still. . . ."

Eventually the torture stopped. No coins were forthcoming, the dogs found something else to distract them and the bear owner gave a last cruel twist to the chain and led the beast off.

"Now we follow," said Ky-Lin, "if you still wish to help."

"Of course!" But how, I wondered.

We followed them at a discreet distance right to the outskirts of the village, where there was fifty yards or so of open land till thick wood crowded in. The bear and his keeper disappeared into the trees. With open ground to cover we were threatened with discovery.

"I'll go," said Growch. "See what 'e's up to. You wait 'ere."

Five minutes later he was back. "Anchored the bear to a rock in a clearin'," he reported. " 'E's on 'is way back. Better clear out."

We made our way back to our lodgings, but I couldn't settle.

"Can't we take him some food or something? The poor thing was starving." In a corner of our room, also used as a storeroom, there was a pile of root vegetables. I picked out two or three. "These'd do; I'll pay for them in the morning."

Ky-Lin thought for a moment. "We need a clear field," he said at last. "No interruptions. I think I can arrange that. Follow me. . . ."

At a little smoky eating house we found the bear keeper, seated on a stool, arguing with the two law keepers we had seen earlier. They were not inclined to argue back, I could see that, but Ky-Lin had a little magic at his disposal. I heard him chuntering away to himself, and a moment later the stool on which the bear keeper sat collapsed under him, he grabbed at one of the law keepers for support and the pair of them crashed to the floor, fists flying. In a moment the other man had joined in, and the upshot of it all was one rebellious bear keeper dragged away to the village's small lockup to spend the night.

"How did you do that?" I asked Ky-Lin, as we hurried off to feed the bear.

"All matter has its own composition; it just needed disarranging a little," he said, which I didn't understand at all.

Growch led us across the waste ground, littered with rubbish and odds and ends, and through the scrub to a path between the trees, now faintly illuminated by a quarter moon.

"Down 'ere a bit. You'll 'ear 'im afore you sees 'im, more'n like."

I had thought it was the moaning of the wind in the trees, but it was a voice, made clear and stark by the ring on my finger, throbbing once more in time with my heart.

"Oh me, oh my, how miserable I be! How I hurts, how I stings! How dark is the world, how drear . . . I be hungry, I be wet, I be cold! I long to be dead, dead or back in the land that gave me birth. My hills and forests, they call out to me. . . ."

" 'E's mad!" breathed Growch. "Stark, starin' . . . Don' go too near 'im, girl!"

In the clearing, chained to a rock, the bear was weaving his own kind of dance. Moonlight dappled his shabby fur as he swayed from front to back, his paws leaving the ground one after the other and back again, his head swinging from side to side, his eyes crazed and red.

Strangely I felt no fear, and my ring was comforting. I stepped forward and placed the roots on the ground in front of him, then stepped back again. "Food for you, Bear," I said slowly and clearly.

But the animal still swung back and forth, his eyes glazed, his jaw dripping spittle. I went forward again, and this time, in spite of an anguished squeal from Growch, I gripped the dripping muzzle firmly in my hands. "Stop it! We are friends. We have come to free you. . . ."

Gradually he stilled, and a pair of small black eyes looked straight up at me.

"Who are you?"

"A friend." I brought the ring close to his eyes. "We have come to help you."

"How? But how?" The head started swinging again. "I am chained, chained forever! Nose hurts, but keeps me chained . . ."

I hadn't thought about the chain. "Ky-Lin?"

A tiny sigh. "If I thought what I thought just then it would put me back another twenty points. . . . But I'm not going to think it. I am here to help. Now, listen: it is time for a little more magic. This time both yours and mine."

"How? I have no magic. . . ."

A patient sigh. "Of a sort. Just do as I say." He leaned over my shoulder and a tiny puff of smoke escaped his nostrils and drifted towards the bear. A moment later the beast's eyes closed, its head drooped. "He's asleep. Take out your Waystone and stroke it round and round the nose ring—no questions, just do as I ask. That's it: one hundred times, no more, no less. Are you counting?"

A minute, two, three. "Ninety-nine, one hundred. Now what?"

"Hold me close to the nose ring. . . ." There was a *ting* of metal and the ring snapped. "Twist it out of his nose." The chain fell to the ground, the bear opened his eyes and blinked. "Alteration of matter twice in one night: amazing! Just pass your Unicorn's ring across his nose: it'll ease the pain."

The bear was free: groggy, but free. I stepped back and breathed more easily. "Eat the food and then get yourself back to your hills or forests," I said. "Good luck, Bear!"

I was just going to ask Ky-Lin how on earth the Waystone had anything to do with snapping the ring in the animal's nose when I tripped over Growch who had stopped suddenly on the path back to the village. He growled menacingly.

I gazed ahead: nothing unusual. "One of these days you'll give me heart failure," I said. "Move over—"

It was then I screamed. Without any warning a heavy hand clamped down on my shoulder, a voice hissed in my ear.

"Got you! Thought you'd escaped me, didn't you? Well, you can think again. . . ."

11

It was just as well I had no pressing need to relieve myself. I leapt away, Growch growling, Tug cursing, but it was a moment longer before I recognized the shabbily dressed figure.

"Dickon!"

"The same, my girl! I've had the devil's own job finding you, although at the end you left enough clues with your playacting—"

"But why? Why did you follow us? I told you—"

"A pack of lies! *I* know where you're bound, and why! I'm just not going to let you get away with it, that's all! I don't know whether you're in league with Matthew Spicer, or that darkie fellow Suleiman, or whether you're working on your own, but either way I'm going to be a part of it."

"Part of what? Oh Dickon! You're not thinking we're after treasure, are you? I tell you, there's no such thing!"

"You have maps. On it is the legend 'Here be Dragons.' And where there are dragons there is treasure. Everyone knows that!"

"Oh, you silly boy!" I said wearily. "If you could read a bit more you would know that all mapmakers put that when the terrain is unknown. It's their excuse, don't you see?"

"Then why are you headed that way? What's in it for you? What would drag you halfway round the world unless it was a fabulous treasure?"

"That's my business," I said. "Now why don't you leave us all alone and go back where you came from?" I was so utterly fed up with his sudden appearance that had I had a magic wand I would have waved him away to perdition. "I'm leaving, and I don't want to see you again."

His hand snapped down on my wrist. "Not so fast! I'm not letting you— Ow! Let go! Summer . . ."

"You want me to kill?" asked the bear, whom I had completely forgotten. On his hind legs he was taller than any man I knew, and he held Dickon against his chest as easily as I would hug a doll. I thought he had eaten his roots and disappeared, but it seemed he was trying to repay me for his freedom.

"No, no!" I said hastily. "You can let him go. Thank you just the same. He is no threat, just a bloody nuisance."

"You sure?" He sounded disappointed.

"I'm sure." I went forward to help Dickon to his feet, for the bear had dropped him pretty hard on his rear. "Get up, Dickon, and be on your way."

He scrambled to his feet. "You can communicate with that—that beast? I realized when I saw you all that time ago that you had some sort of rapport with the other animals, especially that flying pig of yours, but I thought it was just good training. But that—that Thing," and he nodded in the direction of the bear, now busy polishing off the roots I had brought him, "He's new to you, surely?"

"Best I've ever tasted," mumbled the bear. "Best I've ever tasted. My, oh my, oh my!"

I suppose I hadn't thought about it. My ring could give me access to animal communication, but this time I had just "talked" to the creature without prior reasoning. Well, it had worked.

"Yes," I said. "We can understand one another."

"Well, tell him to disappear," said Dickon, brushing himself down. "You've set him free, I saw you unlock his chain, but that's that, isn't it? Come on, let's get back to that room you've hired. I've got to talk to you. It's important."

To whom? I wondered. It meant that I couldn't get rid of him immediately, not if he had been following us so close he even knew where we lodged. I supposed the least I could do was explain once more and give him a few coins to speed him on his way. The trouble was, he had a very persuasive tongue. . . .

"Very well. You go ahead, you obviously know where it is. I'll just see this creature on his way. Growch, you go with him." I didn't want him searching my baggage again.

I turned to the bear, now cleaning his mouth with his paw of any residue of root.

"All better now? Good. Now you are free, free to go wherever you please. Your master is locked up for the night, but you had better get going so he doesn't catch you again. Why don't you go back home?"

The bear turned puzzled eyes towards me. "Home? Home many, many, many treks away. Not sure where to find. You help."

"Oh dear!" said Ky-Lin. "I should have guessed as much. Sorry, girl."

"What that?" said Bear, his scarred nose questing the air. "Demon?"

Ky-Lin showed himself and Bear seemed suitably impressed. "Good demon."

"I'm afraid he is of limited intelligence," said Ky-Lin for my ears only. "Probably taken too soon from his parents, and the treatment he has suffered would make it worse."

I felt that at any moment I should have a headache.

"Don't you have any idea which way is home?" I asked wearily.

He settled down on his haunches, closed his eyes and began to recite.

"Long times ago, cub with sister. Hunters come, kill mother, take cubs." He stopped, and his head began to sway from side to side again. "First treat good, feed well. Then hot stones to burn feet, make dance. Tie up with chain to stand high. Pipe make squeak, dance, dance . . ." and now his whole body was swaying, his paws leaving the ground rhythmically, one after the other. "Ring through nose, much pain. Sister lie down, not get up any more. Aieee, aieee!" and he lifted his muzzle and roared in pain and anger.

"Hush, now!" I was scared we were making too much noise. "No more pain. You'll find home soon. . . ."

"How? Bears not see good longways. Know from that way," and he nodded west. "Mountains. Trees. Streams. Caves. Honey, roots, grubs. Mother, warm, milk, play, sister, love . . ."

That did it. Love is so many things.

"If we show you the way to go?"

"Lose way without help. You help, Bear help. Show you where is honey, roots." He smacked his lips. "Bear find caves to sleep. Bear protect. Bear come with you."

I saw it was hopeless. "Very well. Bear come with us. First we find home for boy—" I nodded at Tug, who was keeping his distance, "—then we find your home. But we have little . . ." I hesitated, then drew some coins from my pocket. "We have little of these. They buy us food and lodging. You will have to forage for food."

"Is same as man get for dance—you want more? I dance for you. All eat well."

It was an idea, but we should have to move fast if we were to get away from his former master. If he wasn't chained we couldn't be accused of stealing him, I reckoned. I led the way back to our lodgings without meeting anyone. Perhaps the better for Dickon's peace of mind, Bear elected to sleep outside by the woodpile. I warned him to keep out of sight.

"If Bear want no see, no see."

Inside, Dickon had made up the fire in the brazier and was sitting on a stool nervously regarding Growch, who was perched like a hairy statue on top of the baggage. Part of his left lip was snagged back on a tooth, showing he had had occasion to snarl.

"Not very trusting, is he?" said Dickon, sucking the knuckles of his right hand.

"Depends. He takes his duties very seriously."

"I was just trying to be friendly. . . ." There were a couple of neat blue puncture marks on his hand.

"Friendly is as friendly does," said Growch. "Don' call it friendly when 'e puts 'is paw where 'e shouldn'."

I sat on the other stool, a sullen Tug crouched at my feet.

"Now, Dickon, what was it you wanted to say?"

He shifted uncomfortably. "It's a bit difficult. You see, when I left the caravan, I—I sort of resigned."

"You *what*?"

"Chucked it in, said I wasn't going back. You see, I thought that when I found you—"

"Not that stupid business of a treasure again! If I've told you once, I've——"

"I know you have! I just don't believe you. I thought it was worth the risk."

"Well it wasn't! It was just plain stupid of you to throw all that away. Just look at you: where are all your fine clothes, your fancy haircut?" There must be a way out of this. "If I give you some travelling money and a note to Matthew, I'm sure he'd take you back."

"Why? You two got something special going? He'll take me back just to keep my mouth shut? Is that it?"

"I assure you, once and for all," I said through gritted teeth, "what I'm doing here has absolutely nothing whatsoever to do with Matthew Spicer. Quite the reverse, in fact."

"Well, I can't afford to go back, not now. I used all the cash I had in tracing you." He gestured at his rags. "Even had to sell my clothes. Got anything to eat? I'm starving! I'm also broke, and cold. Didn't reckon you'd use the river: clever, that." He stood up. "Thanks for offering some travel money, but how far do you think I'd get before winter caught up?" His tone changed; now it held a wheedling note. "Look, I'll accept all you say about not going after treasure, but you must see that you need me. You're going somewhere, that's plain, and presumably also coming back. So why can't I go with you? If it's no secret, then how can you possibly object? After all, you're only a girl, and you need a man to look after you. . . ."

"I seem to have managed all right so far with Tug and Growch. And now the bear has volunteered to join us." I stood up. "Going somewhere? Yes. I'm taking Tug back to his people, then finding Bear his home; after that, who knows? So, there's nothing in it for you except a lot of travelling with companions you have already found—unfriendly. What's more, we just can't afford you. Back there you spoke the language, you had experience of the routes; here, you're less than we are. We have to work our passage and we have enough mouths to feed already."

"I can work!"

"Doing what? Standing on your head, walking on your hands, turning cartwheels? Or would you fancy a bit of mind reading? Oh, come on, Dickon!"

"No, no, no! Don't be silly, I've seen your act twice—just waiting a good moment to approach you—and I think you could do with someone more polished to choose the objects from the audience. We could establish a code, you and I; if I said 'what have we here?' it could mean a scarf; 'what is this?' a piece of jewelry—"

"Don't be silly! If you spoke in our language folk would believe you were telling me straight out what was in your hand, and you don't speak their tongue. Besides, I don't need your code; Growch manages quite well to tell me what Tug has in his hand. If you've seen us perform you'll know how it works."

"Stuff and nonsense! That cur wouldn't know how to describe—a spectacle case, for instance, or an embroidered purse, whatever primitive language you have going between you. I've seen you identify things like that, so, how do you do it? Mirrors? And where did you learn the language? They seem to understand you."

So he didn't know our secrets, didn't know about Ky-Lin.

"I don't need mirrors; I am told exactly what Tug holds up—by magic."

"Rubbish! No such thing. You can't kid me. It's all a trick, albeit a damned clever one."

I shrugged. "Think what you like. . . . So, what else could you do?"

"Manage the bear. With a bit more training, it'd—"

"He."

"He, then. I'm not in the business of sexing bears. *He* could learn a few more tricks, and we'd—"

"He doesn't like you."

"A bear on a chain doesn't have to like you. . . ."

"He's not on a chain, and he's never going to wear one again."

"Then how are you going to control him? He's vicious, you know."

"He's as gentle as—a lamb. Just a bit bigger, that's all."

"And the rest! That creature isn't safe! You can't control it with—"

"Him!"

"—a softly, softly approach. Now if you'd just let me have a go—"

"No!"

"Why not? We'd increase our profits, buy new clothes, even could hire a wagon to travel in; you'd like that, wouldn't you?"

All of a sudden he had become a part of the "we". . . .

"Of course I would," I said. "But I've freed Bear and in return for trying to find his homeland, he has already agreed to work with us. I don't know yet just what form this will take, but no way will I have a chain put back on him, or try and coerce him into something he doesn't want to do. He's suffered enough."

He looked at me for a long moment, but I couldn't read his expression. Then he looked away and shrugged his shoulders.

"Have it your way. I still think I could be an asset. Let me travel with you for, say, a couple of days: after that, if I don't prove my worth, we'll say farewell. Fair enough?"

"And if I don't agree?"

"I'd follow you anyway. And you wouldn't like any disruption to your plans, would you?"

That sounded like a veiled threat. Welcome me into the bosom of your little family, otherwise I'll throw firecrackers at the bear, interrupt your mind-reading sessions and tell everyone you're a girl. . . .

If I'd had more time to think, had considered how Ky-Lin could perhaps have come up with a better solution, I probably wouldn't have caved in so easily. As it was I was too tired to argue.

"Two days, then. We're off at dawn. Walking—until of course your grandiose schemes come to pass," I added nastily.

He had never been one to recognize sarcasm. Instead he beamed, giving me a glimpse of the handsome lad he had become, in spite of the rags.

"Thanks. I sort of thought you might see it my way eventually. We'll make a great team, you and I, Summer. You want to get ahead in the world, make some money, then I'm your man. You're really quite an attractive girl in your own fashion and if you let your hair grow and—"

"Have you eaten?" I was furious at his condescension. "Here you are!" I flung a couple of coins in his direction. "Don't disturb us when you come back. I'm sorry there isn't another blanket, but you could always go outside to the woodpile and curl up with Bear!"

But as it happened he did wake us, and that long before dawn.

I heard someone stumbling around, knocking over a stool, treading on my foot, groaning. It must have been around four in the morning, and I reckoned he must have spent most of his money on rice wine and was too drunk to keep quiet. Sitting up, I unwrapped myself and lit one of the oil lamps.

"Can't you keep quiet?" I hissed. "Some of us are—why, whatever's the matter? Are you sick?"

Even by the scanty light I could see his face had a greenish cast, and he was swaying from side to side, wringing his hands.

He shook his head, less in negation than in what seemed an effort to clear it of some awful memory.

"No, no, it's nothing like that. . . ." Even his voice was different: he sounded like a child afraid of the dark.

"Then, what? Here, sit down before you fall down. I've got some water—"

He waved it away. "No thanks. It's just that . . . I've never seen . . . Oh, Summer, it was terrible! You wouldn't believe—" and to my complete consternation he broke down and wept noisily. "We must get away, now!"

All animosity forgotten, I went over and laid a hand on his shoulder. "Tell me. Take your time, but I want to know. . . ."

I held my lantern high over the form of the sleeping bear, curled into a ball like any domestic cat, paws over his nose and snoring a little.

"Wake up, Bear," I said. "Time to go."

He opened his small black eyes, blinked, yawned and stretched. "Why go in dark? Wait till sun."

"No, Bear; we move now. Village not safe anymore. There are— there are men who seek to hurt you. Come, quick: we are ready."

"You say go, we go." He lumbered to his feet and had a good scratch, his loose skin moving up and down as if it were an extra coat. "Why men want to hurt Bear? Bear not do wrong. . . ."

No, Bear, I thought: you wouldn't think it wrong. To you it was the law by which you had been taught to live.

Dickon had told me how a man had come stumbling into the eating house where he had been sitting, yelling and shouting, pointing down the street towards the thatched hut where the bear owner had been imprisoned overnight. The clientele had all streamed out and followed the man to a terrible sight. The flimsy thatch on the low roof had been torn away, and inside lay the prisoner, the skin flayed from his back, his throat chewed open.

No, Bear, I said to myself again, you didn't do wrong. But I watched with a squeeze of horror in my heart as the animal completed his toilet by licking the last of the dried blood from his claws.

12

We made the best speed we could that day and the next, but to my great relief no one seemed to have followed us. There was no reason why they should, of course; they would assume that the bear had killed his master and then fled into the wilderness. All the same, I didn't want anyone to see the animal until I had changed his appearance a little. To that end he had a thorough wash and brush and, at Ky-Lin's suggestion, I used some wood dye to darken his mask and paint a broad stripe down his back, like a badger's. In truth though, washing and brushing and good food made more alteration than anything else: after a few days I doubt anyone—even his old master—would have recognized him.

The thought of what he had done still gave me shivers, but once again it was Ky-Lin, the creature who could not even bend a blade of grass, who understood better than I.

"He is a child," he said. "In his last incarnation he was probably a neglected baby never taught right from wrong and died before he learnt. The Great-One-Who-Understands-All would not blame him. He has a chance now to learn from us that we all owe each other something and that includes living together in a social harmony. He was just removing something that had hurt him—like you humans think nothing of swatting a wasp."

I managed a weak smile. "Wasps don't sting you," I said. "They wouldn't dare!"

He fluffed out his plumed tail. "The colors put them off," he said, perfectly serious. "Besides," he added: "Like your Son-of-God, we are taught to turn the other cheek. One good thing has come out of this."

"What?"

"The bear's owner has been sent away before he can compound his crimes. Perhaps the Great One will bring him back as a bear, so that next time he will have learnt and will be redeemed to a higher plane."

I didn't feel I was competent to enter into a religious discussion with Ky-Lin; all I was grateful for was that Bear was gentle and sweet-tempered with us, and willingly cooperated in perfecting our act.

Tug did his acrobatics first, then Bear ambled in, wearing a soft red collar I had made for him, decorated with little bells. Tug coaxed a weird tune or two out of the pipe I had bought for him, the bear danced and when he had finished dropped to all fours. Tug climbed on his back with a shivering, eyes-tight-shut-all-the-time Growch in his arms. Bear rose to his hind legs as Tug climbed up his back and, having perfect balance, the boy stood on the bear's shoulders, holding Growch aloft as Bear slowly clapped his paws together. Needless to say, the only one who needed persuasion, bribes and petting, was Growch.

"S'not dignified," he said, "for the star performer, the talkin' dog, to be 'ung up in the air like so much washin'. 'Sides, makes me all dizzy!"

"But just listen to the applause," I said slyly. "How many of your kind do you know that could be as brave? And just look at all the fine meals we're having, and all because of you. . . ."

After that he didn't grumble as much, but he still kept his eyes tightly shut.

I kept Ky-Lin a secret from Dickon still, and although the latter now took over the job of selecting trinkets from the audience for me, dressed in a multicolored costume I had sewn from scraps of colored silks and cottons I had bargained for, he was still mystified at my "guesses," as he called them.

For the most part Ky-Lin lived either in the lining of my jacket or in the hood of my cloak, though if we had a room to ourselves at night, he would come out and prance around like a tiny pony, all fluffed up and full of energy. Separate rooms were becoming an increasing problem, though, as we neared the city. At most, with the increasing traffic, we were making only a few miles a day, and accommodation in the villages we rested at was becoming difficult to find, bespoke by those who came first. Sometimes we were lucky, sometimes not.

On one of the luckier occasions we were only twenty miles short of the city: we tried the houses on the edges of the village first and, just as it started to rain—a rain that would last for two, soaking days—we found a widow woman willing to rent us her house.

Through Ky-Lin I learned that her daughter-in-law was expecting her first and had taken to her bed, so the woman was going to keep house for her son till the baby appeared. It was less costly to hire than I thought, and I asked Ky-Lin (who had done the bargaining in my voice) just why.

"I told her that on the third day from now she would be nursing a fine, healthy grandson on her knee."

"Wasn't that chancing it a bit? Supposing it arrives tomorrow and it's a girl?"

"It won't and it won't be."

I opened my mouth and shut it again. By now I was learning not to question Ky-Lin: he was always right.

We spent a restful night. The house, if you could call it that, had a largish room, partitioned off by a screen to make a living and sleeping area. Outside was a woodshed, where Bear was comfortable enough. I lit the small brazier and cooked a meal I had sent Dickon out for: ubiquitous rice, beans, and some vegetables. Out of respect for Ky-Lin I kept our consumption of meat to a minimum (except for Growch). Him I kept content with a huge ham bone I had been saving, and Bear was perfectly happy with beans and some pancakes I made.

In the morning it was still raining, so I decided to do some sewing. I thought that my cloak, warm and comfortable as it was, needed tarting up a little for our performances, so had sketched a design of a blue dragon I had seen on a broken-down temple, brought a piece of sky-blue silk and now settled down to cut it out.

Suddenly I felt a cold breath touch my cheek, as though sleet had been chucked in my face. At the same time my ring stabbed like a pinprick and my stomach throbbed in sympathy. I had a vision of great mountains, like those that marched alongside our daily travels, but these were much nearer, rearing up until they filled the sky, the snow glittering on their sides, their tops clouded by the spinning of wind-driven flakes like a permanent veil. I saw a blue dragon, I saw a black dragon—

"Whassa matter?" said Growch. "Look like you seen a ghost. . . . Hey, you all right? That ol' stummick again? Too many of those black beans; been fartin' meself all mornin'."

"Nothing to do with the beans," I said, by now doubled over in pain, "I'll be better in a moment. . . ."

But I wasn't. It was worse by the minute, like I used to get with my monthly show, only sharper.

Ky-Lin whispered urgently in my ear. "Send Dickon out for a drink. Tell him you have woman's trouble and wish to be alone for a while. He'll go if you give him some coin: the rain's eased off a bit."

I gave him enough to get drunk twice over, and dragged myself off to my pallet in the partitioned part of the room. I heard Ky-Lin speak to Tug, and a moment later the boy had brought in both the little oil lamp and our own stronger lantern.

"Lie down," said Ky-Lin. "Take your clothes off and lie under the blanket—"

"Tug?"

"He has known all along you were a girl. You washed him once in a river, so he says, and you all got so wet your outline was unmistakable. He's never questioned it: I need him now to help me. Don't worry: it means nothing to him at his age."

"It hurts," I whimpered like a child.

"Not for long," and he spoke to Tug, and a moment or two later one of the opium pills I had kept in my pouch, just in case, was pushed into my mouth, followed by a draught of cool water.

I undressed with difficulty and lay on my back, as instructed by Ky-Lin. Then I was told to rub my ring in a circular movement round my navel, and whether it was the pill or that, or both, the pain diminished and I felt sleepy and relaxed. I began to fantasize. I saw again the cottage where I was born, the forest and river where I played as a child; I could taste the honey cakes my mother gave me, remembered the little church where the mural of the Last Judgment faded gently on either side of the altar. A knight rode by, a handsome knight; a white horse gambolled in surf no whiter than she; I heard a tortoise rustle away into the undergrowth and the clap of a pigeon's wings; I was flying, and then suddenly the dream changed. A castle whose stones were stained with the sins before committed, a thin, wheedling voice: "Tell me a story. . . ."

"Gently, gently," said a voice in my ear. "Nearly over . . ."

I dreamt again. A dog was barking, his voice ringing through woodland; I flew once more, then crashed to the ground, bruised and breathless; waves dragged at my clothes, I was so cold, so cold—

No, it was only my stomach that was cold, numbing the pain. . . .

"Rest, rest, lie still. Remember the Place of Stones and what happened there a year ago today?"

Yes, yes, of course I remembered! I was looking for a pig, a large pig, who had disappeared. It was All Hallows' Eve, exactly a year since I had left home, and the air about crackled with mystery and magic. And then I had found my pig, my dearest pig, and had kissed him and suddenly there was a stranger in his place, a dark stranger—but no! it was a dragon, a black dragon with claws that could rend me in twain—

"Just a minute more . . ."

And the dragon was the stranger, no stranger, again. And he had

enfolded me in his arms. He had kissed me, lain with me, and a hot
flood of feeling had filled me like an empty skin waiting to be filled
and the pain had been so exquisite that I had cried out—

"Aaahhh . . ."

But when I opened my eyes he was a dragon again and had flown
away into the east, his shadow passing across the moon, and I was
alone. . . .

A warm tongue caressed my cheek and my nose was filled with the
smell of warm, hacky breath. "Better, Summer dear?"

But I wasn't Summer: I was Talitha. *He* had called me Talitha, and
he was . . . he was Jasper, Master of Many Treasures.

"Wake up!" barked Growch.

"All over," said Ky-Lin. "No more pain."

I tried to sit up, but there was a sort of stitchy feeling in my stomach.
Tug's hands raised my head, propped something behind it and fed me
some welcome, warming broth. Then I was lying down again, a blanket
tucked under my chin.

"You can sleep now," said Ky-Lin. "No more pain."

"But I don't want—"

"Yes, you do. In the morning you will feel wonderful. Just breathe
deeply and I will give you some Sleepy Dust. . . ."

My mouth and nose were filled with the scent and taste of fresh
spring flowers, summer leaves, autumn fires, winter snow. . . . I breathed
it all in greedily until I was floating way up, up, up till I could touch
the damp edges of the clouds and twist and turn with the screaming
swifts. Ghostlike, I flew on silent wings with the owls, hung on the tip
of a crescent moon, fell back into a bed of thistledown, a nest lined with
the bellyfur of rabbit, a bed with down pillows—a hard pallet with a
couple of blankets and someone shaking me awake.

"Hey! You going to sleep all day as well?"

"Oh, piss off, Dickon!" I said irritably. "I was having a wonderful
dream. . . ."

"Well, you can't sleep all day! We're all hungry, and you've got the
money. . . ."

And will have to cook it too, I thought. "How long have I slept?"

"You were asleep when I came back yesterday, you've snored all
night, and it's around noon now."

Nearly twenty-four hours! Still, it was as Ky-Lin had promised: I
felt wonderful, relaxed, happy—and now I came to think about it: very
hungry.

"Is it still raining?" A nod. "Well give me a few minutes to get dressed and we'll go to the eating house. My treat."

It was while I was dressing that I discovered something wrong.

"Ky-Lin," I hissed. "What's this around my waist?"

"Just something to keep you warm," came the small voice from under my pillow. "Leave it there for the time being, there's a good girl." He must have sensed my indecision. "Have I ever given you bad advice?"

So I left it where it was. It didn't discommode me at all, but I was a little disconcerted to find out I had started my monthly flow again, which was annoying after so long without.

It stopped raining on the afternoon of the third day, and with the weak sun came the widow woman, almost crying with joy, the rent money held out for me to take.

"It is as I said," whispered Ky-Lin. "Now, open and shut your mouth as you do in our performances. I have something to tell her. . . ."

And to the openmouthed astonishment of Dickon, out came a soft stream of words from my lips and, for a moment hidden from all but the woman, Ky-Lin showed himself.

She fell to the floor and gabbled, the tears of joy streaming down her face, then bowed her way out of the door. Dickon picked the coins up and tucked them in his pouch.

"What was all that gibberish about?"

Luckily Ky-Lin had briefed me.

"It was a prophesy; her grandson will become one of the great sages of the country."

"Still don't know how you do it," he muttered. "However, a nice way of conning her out of the rent."

I bit back an angry retort. Ky-Lin whispered in my ear.

"Right, everyone," I said. "Time to go. We'll steal a march on the rest who have stopped over. With the roads empty we can make good time. Oh, Dickon: leave that money on the stool. Call it a present for the baby. . . ."

We made reasonable progress during the next couple of days, and on the second night, Dickon having gone out scouting the prospects for a performance, Ky-Lin made me lie down on the bed.

"I want to take the bandage off." He seemed uncharacteristically nervous; he had gone a shaky sort of blue color all over. "Let's have a look. . . ."

He spoke to Tug, who slowly and carefully unwound the cloth.

"Mmmm . . ."

"What's the matter?" I tried to sit up; my stomach felt cold.

"Nothing. Nothing at all." His color had returned to normal. "Take a look. . . ."

Sitting up, I gazed down at my stomach; at first I could see nothing and then—

"Hey, Summer! We've got a performance!"

Damn and blast and perdition! Hastily pulling my shirt down and my breeches up, I staggered over to the bolted door. Dickon burst in.

"There's a rich caravan just pulled in and they were enquiring about entertainment; Arabs and Greeks mostly, so you'll have to 'Magic' some of their language. . . ." He sniggered. Little did he know Ky-Lin!

"But it's full dark; must be near nine at night."

"They're camping in the square, 'cos there's no other accommodation. Plenty of light, torches, lanterns. They're being fed now, so we'd better hurry before they decide to kip down for the night."

It was past midnight before we returned to our quarters, but my pouch was full of coins. It had been a treat to have a relatively sophisticated audience, for it was a rich caravan, and they had insisted on us performing twice over. They had travelled from the south, with a special order for the wedding: gold and silver platters, silver-handled daggers and filigree jewelry, and were near two weeks late. Tonight would be their last stop, for with horses and camels they could make the city easily by the next day.

So they were relaxed and generous, and Ky-Lin's Arabic, Greek and a little Persian was impeccable. When we packed up Dickon obviously had a yen to go farther afield, so I gave him a generous advance, knowing full well he had also gathered tips on the way from the audience, and he disappeared for a while in search of his own entertainment.

Growch was on a high; one of the objects held up for my "discovery" had been one of his "fluffy bum" pups, and he had nearly let us all down at this point, completely forgetting to concentrate, even running over to the puppy and investigating.

"Keep your mind on the job!" I hissed at him when at last he reached me.

"Thought I 'ad—my job. Why I came, an' all. Boy pup: pity."

I was so tired when we returned that all I wanted to do was flop down on my pallet and sleep, but there was one other thing to do: look once more at my stomach. I thought I had seen—but no, it couldn't be. I lay down, lifted my shirt and peered down, aware out of the corner of my eye that Ky-Lin was watching anxiously. At first nothing, then—

What looked like a pearl nestled in my belly button. I touched it gingerly: it gave a little to my touch. I tried to prize it out—

"No! Don't touch it yet; it hasn't quite hardened." Ky-Lin had gone quite pale again, and was peering anxiously over my shoulder. "Give it a day or two more. . . ."

"But what *is* it?" It resembled nothing so much as a jewel one might stick in a belly dancer's navel. "And how in heaven's name did it get there?"

"Er . . . I put it there. For safekeeping. Nicely insulated. Warm . . ."

"*What is it?*"

"Actually—well, it's quite simple really. It's a dragon's egg."

13

A . . . what?" I was already asleep; I must be.

"Egg. Dragon's. Not yet set," said Growch succinctly. "Leastways, that's what I thought 'e said." He didn't seem the least surprised or alarmed—but then it wasn't happening to him.

I attempted to laugh it off, all the time nursing a horrible feeling it wasn't a laughing matter. "If this is all a joke, it's not in very good taste. Now be a good creature and take it away, Ky-Lin, and I'll forget all about it."

"I can't 'take it away,' just like that," said Ky-Lin unhappily. "It's yours. Yours and—*his*."

I knew immediately who he meant, but wasn't going to accept what he said. It was impossible! That sort of thing just didn't happen; it couldn't.

"That was what was hurting you, giving you the stomachache. It was ready to come out for the second stage of its development," said Ky-Lin. "Don't ask me how, or why; I'm no expert in this sort of thing, and indeed I doubt it has ever happened before just like this. Humans don't mate with dragons. Normally dragons are bisexual: they can reproduce themselves. Theoretically so can Ky-Lins; that's what my name means: male/female. We never have, though."

I remembered the pain of that embrace by the Place of Stones: the pain and the ecstasy. Had we bypassed the natural laws, my man-dragon and I? Was this, this tiny pearl, still semisoft and shining, a product of a love that had never been seen before, just because I had kissed a creature and made him man, however temporarily?

I gazed down at my navel and, gently, so gently touched the shining pearl. Just in case . . .

"But it's so tiny!"

"Oh, it grows. A fully developed egg, ready to hatch, will be at least as big as a human baby. But, I warn you, this one could take many, many years—longer than you have—to grow and mature. You will never see what it contains. You are just its guardian, for a little while. So, don't get fond of it. Your job is to keep it warm, give it its first few weeks of incubation." He sighed. "You are very privileged."

I didn't feel the least bit "privileged": quite the reverse, in fact. I felt confused, hurt, bewildered, used, somehow *dirty*.

Ky-Lin read part of what I was thinking. "You truly are privileged, dear girl. You may not realize it now but that egg, however it got there, has been a part of you for a year, you nourished it in your body, and whatever happens to it in the future, you will always be a part of it. Also remember, it was created in love."

I looked down again; right now it was tiny, soft, vulnerable. Anyone could squash it, crush it, snuff the little life that lay inside. . . . Without conscious thought my hands curled protectively over my navel, and emotion took over from instinct, realizing ruefully that once more I had conned myself into caring for yet one more burden. Once before they had all been maimed in their separate ways; this time they were all more or less normal, even if they still had their particular needs—except Ky-Lin, of course, though even he was trying to gain extra points towards his redemption.

"And so we are lucky seven," said Ky-Lin happily. "You and I, Growch and Tug, Dickon, Bear and the Egg. Just as the Old One foretold."

I shivered and crossed myself; the Good Lord protect us all and bring us to a safe haven. . . .

Two days later we topped a rise and there lay the Golden City beneath us. They called it golden because the stone used was a warm, yellow sandstone, quarried from goodness knew where, because the surrounding hills and mountains were dark and forbidding. Right now, at midday, the sun made the whole place glow, picking out the various towers and steeples that were gilded with real gold, till the whole scene shimmered with warmth and welcome.

We had a steep descent, but beneath us a wide river curled around the east of the city, a river so wide I could see the boats, like beetles at this distance, scurrying about on the water. To the south the plain widened out, and I could see a wide field, with men drilling and horses being exercised.

It looked like a place full of promise, but it took all of three hours to reach the city gates, the road ahead being crowded to suffocation with caravans, carts, wagons, cattle, horses and travellers on foot like ourselves. Past experience made us head for the side streets once we had passed through the west gate; the city would be crowded already, and the best chance of accommodation was out of the mainstream. We were lucky; entertainers were at a premium, and although I had to pay more than I had reckoned, we found two ground-floor rooms with accommodation in a shed for Bear, breakfast and midday meal included.

After a plain but satisfying meal of rice, chicken, and fruit, we left Bear behind and decided to explore the city. By now it was dusk, and evening fires hazed the rooftops. There was already a chill to the air but it made no difference to those who, like us, were determined to make the most of all the city had to offer. The main streets were paved and bordered with fine buildings, but the streets radiating from the main square were full of bustle, crowd, and character.

The stalls were crammed with all the goods in the world, or so it seemed. Over glowing braziers meat, fish, glazed chicken wings, and nuts sizzled and popped and every available space was filled with beggars, jugglers, fortune-tellers (bones, water, sand, and stones), and pretty ladies plying their charms, which is how we lost Dickon.

The rest of us found ourselves in the huge main square, deserted now except for a few gawpers like us. Ahead of us lay the palace, a heterogenous mass of gilded roofs, towers, tilted eaves, and balconies, approached by wide steps guarded by soldiers in green and gold. Flares, torches and lanterns kept the whole facade brightly lit, and through the screened and fretted windows could be glimpsed figures scurrying to and fro.

"This square is where the main celebrations for the wedding will take place," said Ky-Lin, who as usual had been listening to everything going on around him. "During the next few days, palace scouts will seek out the best entertainers and they will be invited to perform here in front of the prince and his prospective bride."

" 'Ow they goin' to choose us, then?" asked Growch.

"They go around the streets and smaller squares, list those they prefer, then send others for a second opinion."

We had already come across some half-dozen of these smaller squares.

"Do we keep to one or try as many as we can?" I wondered.

"More the better," said Ky-Lin. "That way we reach a wider audience and have a better chance of being noticed. Even if we aren't picked, we can at least earn some money. There are many very good acts here already, so we need to polish up our performances, make some new costumes, and I will provide some powders to burn that will give you a better light, sprinkled on torches. Can you walk on your hind legs, dog?"

" 'Course I can! Well, sometimes. A bit. I could try. . . ."

His legs were so short and his body so long, I sometimes wondered how his messages got from one end to the other. "That would be very nice," I said enthusiastically. "Worth an extra bone or two."

And he tried, he really did; at the end of two days he could stagger at least two yards. . . .

We made—I made—new costumes, we played the small squares and larger side streets from one end of the city to the other, and at the end of four days both Dickon and Ky-Lin recognized the same nonpaying faces at our performances.

Ky-Lin nodded his head in satisfaction. "Definitely scouts," he said.

In the meantime we had been making more money than in all our journey so far and I was perplexed as to where to keep it—by now a small sackful—safe. I daren't leave it in our rooms: quite apart from thieves I couldn't trust Dickon's sticky fingers, and it was Growch who suggested the solution. " 'Oo's the one they're all scared of? That great bear. 'E can guard it daytimes, and when we give performances, 'e can 'ave it tucked under 'is arm or sumfin'."

Which solved the problem.

With only twenty-four hours to go before the grand entertainment we were visited in our lodgings by two palace officials, smartly dressed in gold jackets and green trews, who informed me (through Ky-Lin) that we had been picked to perform in the Palace Square the following evening. It was a great honor, as the acts were limited to thirteen, the Moons of the Year. We were allowed a half-hour only, to give time for all the other acts, so we practiced curtailing Tug and Dear and it made for a crisper performance, which we took round the streets that night, able to boast that we were one of the chosen ones for the following night. Our purse was heavier than ever that day.

Our actual performance seemed to be over before it began. We had to wait through performing ponies, acrobats, contortionists, a magician, and a woman who climbed a ladder of swords and lay on a bed of nails with a man standing on her chest, but eventually the large hourglass was set down again in the sand and it was our turn. By now I had worked myself into such a lather of expectation that I was trembling in every limb, my mouth was as dry as the sands of the desert and I desperately needed to relieve myself.

Once we started, however, I was as cool as a draught of cold water, even remembering to direct our act towards the balcony where the prince had his seat. They said afterwards that the prince, a sophisticated man, was bored by much he saw, but that his prospective bride, an ingenuous girl, clapped enthusiastically the whole way through. Be that as it may, each performance was rewarded by a bag of silver coins, good, bad or indifferent, and was cheered impartially by the large crowd penned behind rope barriers at the perimeter of the square.

There were many acts after ours, but I fell asleep through exhaustion, tucked up against Bear, and only woke when Dickon nudged me. The square was emptying, torches guttering and a chill wind blew away the detritus of the evening.

"Bed," said Dickon. "There are three days till the wedding and after tonight the audiences will pay even better. . . ."

But the morning was to bring a further surprise. Before the first cock had even cleared his throat, another official from the palace, this one with gold braid and tassels, presented us with an invitation to perform that evening within the palace confines themselves. Apparently the prince and his bride-to-be wished a closer look at some of the acts they had enjoyed the night before.

"We've cracked it!" exulted Dickon. "Can't you just see it? We can advertise ourselves as by royal command!"

It was an attractive idea, but I could see it would only complicate matters. As far as I was concerned I had places to go, people and animals to answer to, and that was enough. I didn't want more than would carry us to our next destination, but Dickon wanted it all: gold, prestige, fame.

"Are you coming, then?" asked Dickon.

"Coming? Where?"

"I've just been telling you. Outside the city, on the parade ground, they're having races, entertainments, wild animals. It's a day out. It's a *free* day out. All you want is money for some food. Or, take our own. Hurry up, or all the best vantage points will be taken."

We left Bear in the shed; as the winter advanced, although he had never been allowed his natural hibernation since he was a cub, he nevertheless became more lethargic, and was quite happy to be left guarding the money and snoozing the day away. I hoped that when, and if, we ever found his homeland, he would find a convenient cave in which to sleep every winter till spring.

The races and entertainment were held in the amphitheater to the south I had noticed on first looking down on the city. Cordoned off and edged with a low wall of stones, it was an oval, sandy space perhaps

three-quarters of a mile in length and half that distance wide. Roughly
marked out were four staggered lanes for foot or horse racing, and in
the center a raised circle for wrestling. Seats there were none, but plenty
of boulders and banked sand, so we made ourselves comfortable behind
the ropes, knotted with colored cloths, that kept us from the tracks.

Heats of the footraces had already been run, and the finalists rested
while the children of the city had their turn. All kinds were represented,
from the silk-kilted privileged to the half-naked urchins, and it was one
of the latter I was glad to see that won the junior race, two laps of the
track, to bear a purse back to his delighted parents.

I could see that Tug, too, would have liked to participate, but we
didn't know the rules, so I consoled him with sticky sweetmeats from
a peddler's tray. There was plenty to eat—if you could afford it—for
behind the crowd there were braziers frying and roasting all sorts of
delights, and trays of cheeses, cakes, boiled rice, and fruit. The poorer
people had brought their own food, but we were in a festive mood and
nibbled away all afternoon, fortified by drinks of water, wine, or goat's
milk from the skins of the sellers.

The day wore on. We watched the wrestling—which seemed to be
a near-killing exercise of arms, feet, hands, teeth and nails—and ap-
plauded the finals of the footraces. Then came the chariot races; light,
wicker-framed two-wheeled carts with two horses. There were plenty of
thrills and spills, and special applause when the prince's charioteer won
the top prize. Next was an exhibition of kite flying, great monsters of
birds, flowers, giants, and dragons, but there was little or no wind, so
these were a disappointment. We were about to pack up and go back to
our lodgings to ready ourselves for tonight's performance, when there
was a clamor from far across the field.

A distant thunder of hooves, a murmur from the crowd: "The Riders
of the Plains!" and into the arena galloped a troop of wild-looking horsemen, riding even wilder horses. They circled the arena at an even faster
pace, churning the sand into swirls of smoke, manes and tails flying,
the horsemen uttering wild yells of encouragement until suddenly, with
no apparent signal, they crashed to a rearing halt in the center, shouting
what sounded like a battle cry to my untrained ears.

There was an eruption at my side and Tug sprang to his feet, his
face alight with joy, his fists raised over his head in salute.

"My people, my people! They come. . . ." and he was gone, scrambling over rocks and people with abandon, to disappear into the amphitheater amid the melee of men, horses, sand and dust.

I called after him, but it was no use: he couldn't, or wouldn't, hear.

"Leave him be," whispered Ky-Lin. "He will be back. Just watch."

And watch we did, an unparalleled exhibition of horsemanship. Horses raced, apparently riderless, till their riders twisted up from under their bellies; one horseman balanced on the backs of two, three, four mounts at a gallop; they threw spears at targets as they raced past, hitting them every time; they leapt to the ground first one side, then the other, rode with their heads towards the horse's tail; they fought mock battles; they jumped—one, two, three men—onto the back of a galloping horse until we were exhausted just watching.

The crowd was as stupefied as we were, then on their feet yelling for more.

And Tug? He was in the midst of it all. Running, riding, vaulting, balancing; handstands, yells, two hands, one hand, no hands . . . On the ground he was a rather awkward boy with bandy legs and a usually sullen expression; put him on a horse and he was transformed. I could see now that those bandy legs had been used to riding from the time he could toddle and saw from his face how much being back with his own kind meant to him. I didn't need the confirmation of his words when he finally climbed back to us, tattered, sweaty, and utterly happy.

"Found them! They mine . . . Go home!" He started to speak in the few words of my tongue I had taught him, but soon lapsed into his own language, and I was glad to have Ky-Lin's whispered translation. Dickon stood by, his face a picture of bewilderment, but Growch's tail was wagging furiously: he at last understood what was going on.

"My people come for prince's wedding: special invitation. Prince rides with us, in disguise. . . ." He pointed to a taller man, dressed as the rest, who was sneaking off the field. "His treat . . ." He waved his hand at the rest of the horsemen. "They are of my people, but not of my tribe, although they know of my father. He is chieftain. They return to our lands tomorrow, next day, before snows come and I will travel with them."

"If your father is chieftain, then you . . . ?" I asked through Ky-Lin.

"I am my father's first son, and will be chieftain when he dies."

So, I had rescued a prince among his people, this shabby boy who now squatted before me, took one of my hands in his and pressed it to his forehead.

"I shall always be in your debt," he said simply. "You bought my freedom, fed me and clothed me, treated me with kindness. I shall never forget you. And you, Great One," and he bowed in the hidden direction of Ky-Lin.

"Rubbish!" I said gruffly, conscious that I had difficulty in speaking. I ruffled his hair, just as if he were the young boy who had already shared our adventures, and not a young prince.

Dickon had finally picked up the drift of what was happening. "He's not going, is he? Not before the performance tonight, surely! In the palace, by special request, remember? You don't turn up only with half your act!" He looked scandalized. "Out here they could cut your head off for a thing like that—or at least chuck you in a dungeon and throw away the key. . . . Besides, just think of the money!"

In the excitement I had completely forgotten; although I did not believe we should be punished for turning up without Tug, it would certainly mean a revision of our act. I asked Ky-Lin to explain as best he could.

As we had been talking, we had gradually become surrounded by Tug's fellow countrymen, smelling strongly of horses and sweat. Smaller in stature than most, they were still a fearsome-looking lot, with their yellowish faces, high cheekbones, long hair, fierce eyebrows and drooping moustaches. Like Tug, they had black eyes and bandy legs. They shuffled closer, and I had the distinct impression that they were quite ready to kidnap Tug and carry him away if we had any intention of trying to keep him.

But Tug listened to what Ky-Lin had to say, shrugged his shoulders and nodded. Turning to his people he made a little speech, indicating us, then bowed quite regally in dismissal. The men glanced at each other, then, thankfully, bowed also and moved away.

"I have told them," said Tug formally, "that I have an obligation to fulfill, but shall join them later tonight. All right, Summer-Lady-Boy?" And he grinned, once more the boy I would always remember.

Returning to our lodgings, we washed and dressed in our costumes and made our way as previously directed to the side door of the palace, giving onto the kitchens, armory, stores, laundries, etc. We crossed the large, cobblestoned courtyard and were shown into an anteroom. Like the largest houses I had seen, this part of the building was strictly utilitarian. No fancy clothes, no elaborate decoration, everything meant for use. In the anteroom the other three acts were already waiting, obviously as nervous as we were ourselves. They became positively agitated when they saw Bear, however, and that coupled with the thought of bear droppings on the carpets, made me ask through Ky-Lin if we might wait in the courtyard.

It was chilly out there, so I walked over to one of the braziers to warm myself up. There were some half-dozen of these, crowded by off-

duty soldiers, kitchen porters, and itinerants waiting for the scraps of
the feast now taking place. Obviously they were still eating, for enticing
smells were coming from the kitchens: behind the bland scents of rice
and vegetables came the aromas of fish and meat, sharpened to a fine
edge by the pungency of spices such as ginger and coriander. My stomach started to rumble, although we had all eaten before we came out.
A couple of trays of saffron-colored rice full of niblets of dried fish
were thrust out into the courtyard; you ate, if you were lucky, with your
fingers: the beggars had brought their own bowls.

I managed a handful for Bear and Growch; one of the better-dressed
beggars shouted at me, gesticulating to his friends.

"What does he say?" I asked Ky-Lin, passing him a grain or two
of rice.

"Not to waste good food on animals. Just ignore him."

"It's just that—I'm sure I've seen him somewhere before. . . ."

"Where?"

I racked my brains, but came up with nothing; here, there, somewhere, I was sure of it. "I don't know. . . ."

"Well, don't worry about it: it's our turn next."

It must have been near midnight when we came out into the courtyard again, still dazed by the lights, music, dancing, gold, embroideries,
costumes, decorations, plate, jewelry, and sheer opulence of all we had
seen, touched, heard, smelled, in the last couple of hours. The inner
reality of the palace was like something from a legend; pointless to
wonder where the money had come from to create such luxury: to marvel
and enjoy was enough.

In the vast banqueting hall in which we had been called upon to
perform there were patterned marble floors, thick colored rugs, gilded
pillars, painted walls and ceilings, embroidered cushions, long carved
tables, a silver throne, and men and women guests wearing robes of silk
and fine wools, heavily sewn with gold and silver thread and studded
with jewels. The whole area was lighted to brilliance with oil lamps,
torches and flares, the light reflected from vast sheets of brass, placed
the best for catching the flames.

Behind painted screens musicians sighed and wailed on strings and
woodwind, with the insistent drubbing of a tabor; there was a heavy
scent of incense, sweet oils, of opium and hashish, both cloying and
exciting at the same time.

The prince, on a silver throne, had been gracious enough to lead
the applause for our act, but as an audience the rich guests could not

have been more different from our credulous village spectators. There
was a background murmur of conversation all the while, the applause
was polite and it seemed there was more attention paid to eating and
drinking than to the performance. It was not just us though: all the others
acts were received in the same way, a restrained appreciation for something far beneath such a sophisticated guest list.

Still, the coins we were paid with this time were of gold. . . .

As we came out into the courtyard we all breathed in the clean, cold
night air with relief. All but a couple of the braziers had been extinguished and someone was unfastening the heavy gates for us, just as a
shout came from away to our left, and a figure ran at us, followed by a
half-dozen others. I stopped, bewildered; it was the man I thought I had
seen somewhere before, but now he was yelling out something over and
over again. Ky-Lin hissed urgently in my ear: "Run, girl, run! Tell them
all to run and hide. . . ."

"But why? What's he saying?"

"That's the man you thought you recognized; he comes from the
village where Bear's former master was found dead. They are going to
arrest you and Dickon on a charge of murder!"

14

I opened my eyes: nothing.

I shut them tight again, screwed them up, rubbed them with my knuckles, opened them again.

Nothing. Black as pitch.

If I wasn't so cold and it didn't hurt when I pinched myself, I might have thought I was still asleep and dreaming, or in that muddled half-awake situation children find themselves in sometimes when nothing makes sense. Once—I think I was six or seven at the time—I found myself trying to pull up the earthen floor of the hut in which my mother and I lived, in the mistaken belief that it was a blanket. I had fallen out of bed but the fall had only half woken me, so I thought I was still there. I remembered crying with the cold and frustration, then Mama had leaned over and plucked me to her side again, scolding me heartily for waking her. . . .

I wanted my Mama again, right now, scolding or no. I wouldn't have cared if she had thrashed me—the physical blows wouldn't have counted against the warmth of contact with another human—but she was long dead and I was alone, totally alone, in a mind-numbing darkness that froze my mind and made icicles round my heart.

I hadn't even got the comforting presence of Ky-Lin: he had disappeared together with the others.

In the confusion of that sudden attack in the courtyard we had all become separated. The gate was half-open, I had shouted a warning, and a white-faced Dickon had been first away, followed by a bewildered Bear. I felt Ky-Lin leap from my shoulder, heard Growch growling and barking at my feet and was conscious of Tug trying to fend off my attackers. Somebody had grabbed the boy by his jacket, but he twisted free and punched someone else on the nose. Growch had another aggressor by the ankle and was being shaken like a rat, and a guard tried to catch me by the hair.

"Run, you idiots, run!" I yelled. "Watch the gate!" Which was already being closed again. I started off for the narrow gap that remained; ten feet, five, four. My hands touched the thick oak, I pushed with all my might, Growch squeezed through, then suddenly I tripped, fell flat on my face and was immediately pinned to the ground by half a dozen men. Fighting to keep my head clear, I saw the gate clang to, followed by a flying leap from Tug, who seemed to run up the ten feet or so like a cat scaling a wall, to disappear over the top.

So at least Tug, Growch, Bear and Dickon had a chance of escape, although I had no idea of Ky-Lin's whereabouts. Knowing how violence of any kind was anathema to him, I wondered if he had hidden himself away somewhere; wherever he was, I could certainly have done with his help during the next hour or so.

I had been hauled into the palace again, but this time to a small windowless antechamber, in which I was ruthlessly questioned, my accuser and his friends pointing the finger of guilt; a senior palace official tried to get a statement out of me. Impossible, of course: without a translator we couldn't understand each other at all. In any case I was so bruised, battered and confused by now, that I doubt I could have said anything sensible in any language.

My brain seemed to have gone to sleep, and after three hours we had gotten nowhere. For the moment it seemed it was one person's accusation against my silence, for my accuser was treated no better than I; finally we were both marched along endless corridors, down steps, across a winding walkway and finally into what could only be the dungeons. Then we were separated: my accuser went one way, I went the other, to end up in front of a low, barred door. The bolts were drawn, the door creaked open and I was flung headlong onto a pile of filthy straw; the door clanged shut and the blots were drawn with a dull finality. Something was shouted from outside, and the footsteps marched away, their sound to be smothered all too soon in the darkness of the thick walls.

The stench of the cell was terrible. At first after I got to my feet I wasted my breath calling and shouting, but the air was so thick my voice lost itself in the gloom, and there was no answer. Next I felt my way all around the cell—with, strangely enough, my eyes shut: it seemed easier that way—only to find it was empty of all but a rusty ring on one wall with a chain dangling from it and a small drain in the floor, presumably for excreta. I must have spent an hour trying to find a way out, but in the end had sunk to my knees in the filth, as miserable as I had ever been in my life.

And what of the others? Dickon had got away and was capable of looking after himself, but Bear was too large and clumsy to hide. Tug and Growch would probably come looking for me, but what could a boy and a dog do on their own? And what had happened to Ky-Lin? I had not seen him at all and he was so small that someone might have trodden on him—but I could not bear to think of that.

I had no idea of time, for in that fetid darkness my inside body-clock seemed to have stopped; I found I could no more judge either time or distance.

My ears caught a sound: a tiny, scratching, rustling noise. My God— rats! No, I couldn't stand rats, I couldn't! There it was again. . . .

Rising to my feet I shuffled backwards until my trembling hands touched the damp wall. I listened: nothing, except a distant irregular drip of water. I must have imagined it. I took a deep breath, tried to relax. I counted to a hundred slowly under my breath. No sound— scratch, scritch . . . thump!

I screamed: I couldn't help it. The sound bounced back off the walls in a dead, muffled tone. No one could hear me—I opened my mouth again—

"Steady there, girl," came a small voice. "It's only me. Quite a jump down—"

"Ky-Lin!"

"The same. Now, stand still, and I'll find you. . . ."

There were further rustlings and a moment later something touched my ankle. I bent down and found a plumed tail.

"You've grown!"

He was now puppy-sized.

"It seemed like a good idea. Better for getting around. There was a lot to do before we could get to you."

"We?"

"Tug, Growch, and myself. Bear was willing to help, but we left him guarding the money and baggage. All safe. Now, just listen; in another hour or so—"

"How did you get in?" I interrupted. The door was solid and I hadn't found the smallest space anything could crawl through. "How did you find the others? Where are they? Where's Dickon?"

"In what order am I supposed to answer these questions? Perhaps in reverse. The young man has disappeared: I smelled his fright as he ran—"

Typical Dickon, I thought. Keen for gold, coward for danger.

"The bear went back to your lodgings. I had climbed onto the boy's shoulder when I left you; we had to persuade the dog to follow us: he was all for staying by the gate."

Typical of Growch too: loyal and devoted, whatever the danger.

"We packed your belongings and moved them to a safe place. The boy went away to arrange certain matters and is less than two hundred yards away with the dog. As to how I got in? Through the window."

"What window?" I stared around once more. "I can't see any window!"

"Perhaps because you are not looking in the right place. Besides, there is no moon."

"Where?"

"Look to your right . . . no, much higher, to twice your height. Keep looking; let your eyes get accustomed to the dark. There now: do you see it?"

Yes, now I did. A grayish sort of oblong. Like all things, obvious once you knew where they were, I wondered how I could have missed it earlier. I stared and stared, with growing hope, until I got dancing specks in front of my eyes. Specks . . . and lines.

"But—there are bars across! You might be able to squeeze through those, but I couldn't. Besides, it's miles too high to reach!"

"Don't exaggerate! We've thought about all that."

"You're sure?"

"Sure." He hesitated. "At least . . ."

"At least—what?" Hope received a dent.

"If everything goes according to plan. Don't *worry*! If plan alpha doesn't work, we can always go to plan beta."

"If I don't get away from here before morning they'll probably haul me up for questioning again, and I'll need you to translate. And you can't hide in my cloak if you're as big as—"

"There is another hour until the false dawn, and now is the time when everyone sleeps deepest. That's why we chose it," he interrupted. "And now, if you will excuse me?"

"Don't go!" I was going to panic again, I knew it.

"Courage, girl! We have things to do. Firstly, put the Waystone in my mouth—that's it. Now lift me to your shoulders and bring me under the window. . . ."

He was much heavier now, and the spring he took from my shoulder nearly knocked me to the floor. I stared upwards, and could make out a darker shape against the outline of the window. He appeared to be doing the same he did with the bear's nose ring: stroking the iron bars in one direction. It seemed to take an age.

"Ky-Lin?"

"Shhh . . ."

I shushed, for what seemed a lifetime. At last the scraping noise stopped. "That should do it: catch!" The Waystone dropped into my cupped hands. "Can you climb a rope?"

"I don't know. . . ." I never had.

"Well, now's the time to find out!"

Something touched my face and reaching out a hand I found I was clutching a knotted rope. Looking up, I thought I detected movement, a muffled whisper, but still eight bars stood between me and freedom. It must be getting lighter, because now I could make them out quite clearly.

"Wait for a moment," breathed Ky-Lin. "But when I say 'move!' you move!"

A moment's pause, a straining noise, a muffled thud of hooves, and the first bar snapped cleanly away from the window. Two minutes later another, then a third. The fourth broke only at the top.

"Now!" said Ky-Lin urgently. I grabbed the rope tight, wrapped my legs around it and tried to pull myself up. The rope swung wildly, I made perhaps a couple of feet, banged hard against the wall, let go and dropped heavily to the floor of the cell. I didn't even manage a foot of climbing before banging my knuckles against the slime of the walls and falling down again.

"It won't work. . . ." I was desperate.

"Wait. . . ."

What seemed like a muttered conversation took place above, then Ky-Lin called down: "Wrap the rope around your waist, hold it tight in your hands, and hang on!"

I swung out and in against the wall, almost fainting at one stage from the pain of a bruised elbow, but gradually I was being hauled higher and higher. At last, when I thought the strain was too great and I would have to let go, a pair of hands gripped my wrists and pulled me up the last few inches till my shoulders were level with the window.

"Tug . . . !"

With his hands to help me I tried to wriggle through the space left by the missing bars. At first it was easy, and I was halfway through and could just make out, in the grayness that preceded the false dawn, a courtyard and a couple of the Plainsmen's small horses, ropes around their necks. At last I was breathing fresh air again, and Growch's eager tongue lapped at my cheek. Another pull, I was nearly there—and then I stuck.

That last bar, the one that had only broken halfway, was lodged against my hip, and I couldn't move. Tug tried to maneuver me past it, but it was hopeless. At last Ky-Lin slipped in beside me and pushed sideways as Tug pulled, and with a final jerk I was free, minus some trouser cloth and skin.

But there was no time to feel sorry for myself. I was shoved onto one of the horses. Tug led both out of the gates, then went back to bolt the gates on the inside, climbing back out when he had finished.

"That courtyard is where prisoners' friends are allowed to bring the food," explained Ky-Lin. "They are fed through the bars. For most that is all they get. The boy has bolted the gates so they will think you escaped by magic—or flew away with the dragons—and nothing will be traced back to his people."

The sky was lightening perceptibly as we moved silently through the deserted streets, the horses' hooves muffled with straw, to one of the smaller gates in the city wall. A few early fires smudged the clear, pre-dawn air, a child whimpered somewhere, a dog howled, but that was all.

A smaller gate it might be, but it was still some twenty feet high, bolted, barred and with an enormous keyhole that could only encompass an equally enormous key. I knew these gates were not opened until the dawn call from the muezzin, and feared that if we lingered here my escape might be discovered. Besides which, we were a motley enough collection that any guards would remember, for at that moment two of Tug's people came to join us on horseback, Bear ambling amiably be-hind. Our packs were fastened on the horses.

I gazed fearfully at the gate house, expecting the guards to emerge any moment and tell us to be about our business; instead, Tug dismounted, went over, opened the door and a minute later reappeared with a key almost half his size. Over his shoulder I could see the two guards lying in a huddle on the floor.

"Sleepy Dust," said Ky-Lin, his tail fluffed out. "Good for another hour at least. . . ."

With a struggle Tug and his fellows managed to slide back the bolts and bars and manipulate the key; we slipped through the gate and there was a straight road leading north. Tug stayed behind to close up again and return the key, before scaling the gate and rejoining us on the road.

"Right!" said Tug, in my tongue. "Now ride. Slow first, then faster."

Once the city was out of sight behind a curve in the dusty road we quickened our pace; as we rode we shared rice cakes and a flask of

water but there was no slackening until the sun was at its zenith, when
Tug led us off the road into a stand of trees.

Behind the trees was a tumbledown, deserted hut, and Bear collapsed into the shade, closely followed by Growch. Tug dismounted and
helped me down, bumped and bruised from the ride, my hip aching
from the scrape against the broken bar in the cell. Tug's friends dismounted, took the muffles from all four horses' hooves and led them
over to a nearby stream to drink. Our baggage they put in the shade. I
drank deep of the clear, cold water then lay down in the winter sun,
glad of the transient warmth. I felt I could sleep for a week. . . ."

"Anyfin' to eat?"

I don't think I could have roused myself even for Growch's plaintive
plea, but luckily Tug and his friends had lit a discreet fire and we were
soon eating cheese, strips of dried meat and pancakes.

Tug pointed to the road ahead. "Bear's way," he said. "Keep to trail
during day, not roads. Bear will soon sniff way. We go now." He bent
and put his forehead to my hands. "My freedom—your freedom. It is
right. When I man, I travel much. Good for learn better things my people."

I didn't kiss him good-bye, although I wanted to; I just ruffled his
hair, waved, and listened to the sound of hooves as he and his followers
rode away out of my life.

Just before I fell asleep, Growch already snoring at my side, Ky-Lin
at my feet, I asked the latter a question that had been bothering me.

"Ky-Lin . . . if plan alpha had failed, what was plan beta?"

"Plan what?"

"Beta. You told me—"

"Oh that. I haven't the faintest idea, but we would have thought of
something. Alpha, beta, gamma, delta . . . Now that really would have
been a test. . . ."

15

As far as I knew, we were never followed. It would have been difficult for the townspeople to trace our route, even if they had bothered. Probably it was as Ky-Lin had surmised: they would think I had had magic to help me escape, and you can't chase magic.

I slept—we all slept—for the rest of the day and the ensuing night, waking cold, hungry, but thoroughly rested. Tug had left us provisions, so we broke our fast with gruel and honey, cheese, and dried fruit.

Bear was eager to be away, declaring in his slow way that we were on the right road for his homeland. He sniffed the air, sneezed, then shook himself like a dog just out of water, his pelt rippling like a loose furry robe.

"Not far," he said, and sneezed again. "Air smells good. Woods, rivers, mountains."

Fine. The sooner the better as far as I was concerned, then we could take the more northern route to where I hoped I would find the Blue Mountain. Right at this moment, though, I couldn't see how we were going to move an inch further. I had repacked our baggage and rescued our money—including the gold from the palace performance—from Bear and tucked it away. I thought I could just about manage my pack, though how far I could carry it in one day was doubtful, but there was another problem. Tug had left us provisions, obviously believing we would find villages few and far between the farther we travelled, but now I looked with dismay at the sack of rice, the smaller ones of beans and oats, the pack of dried fruit, another of dried meat, a half of cheese and the three jars of salt, oil and honey.

Now there was no Tug or Dickon to share the burdens. I thought of Bear: he was big enough and strong enough to carry the burdens, but he was too unpredictable in his mode of travel. Sometimes he was content to lope along by my side, but he would often go off on his own for long periods of time, searching for grubs, roots, and honey. During one of these foragings he would be quite capable of forgetting his burdens, or dropping them, or just leaving them behind.

I scratched my nose; perhaps I could fashion a litter, or a form of sleigh, but they would have to be pretty tough to withstand the terrain. Perhaps Ky-Lin could think of something constructive.

But once again, he had read my mind and was now shaking his head from side to side in self-reproach. "Aieee! What a fool I am! If only we could all exist on fresh air . . ." He pulled himself together. "But we don't and can't, so there is the little matter of carrying the provisions is there not?"

"Not exactly a 'little' matter," I said. "There's enough there for a small pony!"

"Of course! Exactly what I had calculated. And I must now work twice as hard for not having anticipated all this, otherwise my Lord will be displeased. . . . You will excuse me for ten minutes, please?" and he disappeared into the undergrowth. Perhaps he had gone to look for some wood to build a litter, I thought; in any case, he had no need to reproach himself for anything; he had organized our escape, designed our performances and been a cheerful companion in all our journeying. And even now, running off like that, he had moved from stone to rock, in order not to even bend a blade of grass. His Lord was surely a hard taskmaster. On the other hand, the idea of not harming anything living if one could help it appealed to my soft heart. I should—

" 'Elp! 'Elp! Go 'way! Geroff!" and Growch burst into the clearing, barking wildly, closely pursued by what looked like a running rainbow, about four times his size.

I leapt to my feet and snatched up the cooking pot, now fortunately attached to the other implements, but at least it made a satisfactory clanging noise. Both Growch and the apparition stopped dead. Pulling out my little knife and wondering where the hell Bear had disappeared to, I walked slowly nearer.

"Now then, what do you—my God! Ky-Lin!—but you've *grown* . . . ! Growch, it's all right: just turn around and look!"

Instead of the puppy-sized Ky-Lin, there stood a creature the size of a small pony, perhaps as high at the withers as my waist. He looked extremely diffident, in spite of his new size, for parts of him hadn't grown as quickly as the others. No longer neat and petite, he was now large and untidy. The only completely perfect part of him was his plumed tail, with a spread now like that of a peacock.

He looked down and around at himself.

"It's a long time since I did this," he said apologetically. "Unfortunately it would seem that not everything changes at the same rate. Perhaps a grain or two of rice, or a little dried fruit . . . Thank you."

Almost immediately the shortest leg at the back grew to the right size.

"A little more?" I asked.

Ten minutes later and he was more or less all of a piece, except for a smaller left ear, a bare patch on his chest and extremely small antennae.

"A couple of days and everything will be as it should," he said. "I hope. . . ." He glanced at the packs of food. "And now, if you would load me up please? If you would put the spare blanket on first, I would find it more comfortable, and I could manage the cooking things as well."

I tried to balance the load as evenly as I could.

"Have you . . . ? Can you . . . ? Do you do this often?"

"Bigger and smaller? Let me think. . . ." I could almost hear the sound of the mental tally sticks flying. "This will be the seventy-ninth time bigger. Three times with you: figurine to mouse-size, then puppy-size and now what you want, pony-size. Smaller? Fifty-three times. I think that's right."

"Try notchin' yer 'ooves," said Growch. He was still behaving in a surly way, just because he'd allowed himself to be panicked, and had let me see it.

"I couldn't do that," said Ky-Lin seriously. "They are living tissue and I mustn't harm anything living, you know that."

"Funny way o' thinkin' . . ."

"Well then, what is your philosophy of life, dog?"

"Filly—what? Oh, you means what life is? Life is livin' the best way you can for the longest time you can manage. Grab what you can while you can, is me motto. An' that includes nosh. Catch me eatin' rice an' leaves when there's rats and rabbits! Anyways, it don' make no difference when you're gone."

What a contrast! One striving for (to me) an impossible state of perfection, the other living only for the day. And I suppose I was somewhere in between. But even I was having rebellious thoughts about what I had been taught. After all I had experienced I couldn't imagine a happy Heaven without my animal friends somewhere around. And think how sterile it would be without trees and flowers, streams and lakes, sun and rain. Hold it, I told myself, crossing myself guiltily. God knows what He's doing. Would the Jesus who considered the beauty of the lilies, who knew where to cast a fisherman's net and admired the whiteness of a dog's teeth expect us to live without natural beauty in our final reward?

Bear made no comment when he saw Ky-Lin's change of size. As I said, he was a very phlegmatic bear.

We set off west by north, using the Waystone and a fixed point every morning. We used mostly trails, but also the occasional road, though these were few and far between, only existing between villages, which also became scarcer. Money meant little out here in the wilds, so if we came to a village Bear danced for our supper, Ky-Lin keeping well out of sight to save scaring the children.

It was Bear also who was adept at finding shelter for our nights in the open: a cave, an overhang of rock, a deserted hut—we usually stayed warm and dry. Without realizing it, the turning of the year passed us by, and it grew imperceptibly lighter each day.

Careful as I was with our food, our stores diminished rapidly, for the villagers had little to spare and had no use for our money, relying on the barter system. Hens don't lay in winter, and their stores of grain, beans, cheeses, and fruit were all calculated to a nicety for their own needs. Now of course, Ky-Lin was eating as befitted his size and work load, so I sent Bear foraging. He seemed to find a sufficiency for himself, so I hoped for something to supplement our diet. Nine times out of ten I was disappointed because he either hadn't found anything extra, or had eaten it or just plain forgotten, but occasionally he returned with a slice of old honeycomb, a pawful of withered berries or some succulent roots which I baked or boiled.

There was one thing he was excellent at, however, and which helped our diet considerably, but we only found that out by accident.

One morning we came to a small river swollen by melted snows. It wasn't deep, perhaps three or four feet at most, but it was wide, probably a hundred feet across, rushing busily over stones around rocks, forming swirling pools and mini-rapids. I turned downstream to find an easier place to cross; no point in getting the baggage wet.

" 'Ey-oop! Just look at that!" Growch's voice was full of genuine wonder. I turned, just in time to see Bear flipping a fat fish from the shallows and swallowing it whole. "That's the second one. . . ." He was salivating.

I ran back along the bank, just in time to see Bear miss number three. He growled with disappointment and turned away.

"Can you do that again?"

He stared at me, his little eyes bright as sloe berries. "If I want fish."

"Well, want!" I said. "Did it never occur to you that we should like some, too?"

He stared at me. "You not like grubs and beetles I bring. Should ask."

"You eat our gruel and rice: we like fish. I ask now, to try."

He caught two more and I cleaned and grilled them over a small fire for our midday meal. They were delicious. After that, whenever we came across a stretch of water we encouraged him to go fishing. All he caught didn't look edible to me, but he wasn't fussy and ate the rejections as well. A couple of times we even had enough to barter for salted meat or beans, and we ate tolerably well.

The mountains came nearer to the north and west of us, the terrain was rougher and the air colder. Growch and I tired more easily, though Ky-Lin seemed unaffected, and Bear was positively rejuvenated. He bounced ahead of us most days, sniffing, grubbing, rolling in the undergrowth, snatching at leaves like an errant cub, splashing noisily through any water we came across, eating like a pig and snoring like one at night, too.

I reckoned we must have covered near three hundred miles since we left the Golden City when we stood on a wide ridge and looked down on a limitless land of forests, rivers, lakes and crags. Not a village or hamlet to be seen, no sign of human habitation for miles.

Bear sniffed deep, then reared up on his hind legs, to tower over all of us.

"My land," he said. "Start here, go on forever."

I smiled at his enthusiastic certainty. "Then we can leave you here?"

He sank down on his haunches. "Be with me until I find cave to sleep for rest of the cold, and I find you food to take with you. My country; I find fish and honey."

Near though the woodland had seemed, it took us two days to reach the forest proper, and as we came to the more thickly carpeted ground it was a difficult time for poor Ky-Lin, sworn as he was not to tread on anything living. Once under the trees it was easier for him; they were mostly pine and fir, and the dead needles made a nice carpet for his hooves.

Three days later Bear found his cave. Entered through a narrow cleft that widened out into a cozy chamber behind, it had not been occupied for years, judging by the thick drift of leaves that had piled up. The cave was situated at the foot of a bluff; in front the land stretched down to a thick stand of conifers and a stream trickled away to the right. An ideal hibernation place for a winter-weary bear.

He grunted with satisfaction. "Stay here till spring. You need fish. Go get, you light fire. Stay here tonight."

And off he trotted. True to his earlier word he had found us honeycombs and half a sack of nuts. He had obviously spied or smelled some water, so we could stock up with fish as well, God willing.

I dithered over lighting a fire inside the cave or out, but decided on the latter, reckoning that lingering smoke might disturb our night's sleep. There was plenty of wood and I filled the cooking pot from the stream and set it on to boil with salt, herbs, and some wild garlic I found growing nearby. It all depended on what Bear brought back, but if the worst came to the worst I could chuck in some rice and dried meat.

Just as I sat back on my heels, enjoying the warmth of the fire, and Growch had come to lean against me, there came a noise, and simultaneously my ring gave a sharp stab. Growch stiffened, Ky-Lin's antennae shot out in the direction of the forest and I sprang to my feet. It wasn't Bear, it was men's voices I had heard.

There it was again: voices, crackle of twigs, a laugh.

"Quick! Back in the cave, Ky-Lin. Growch, stay with me." There was no point in us all retreating to the cave; the fire was sending up a thin plume of smoke and whoever was out there would soon be coming to investigate. I didn't fancy being trapped in a confined space, but they might miss Ky-Lin if we hid him away. If we were lucky it might just be a couple of hunters, but my ring was still sending out warning signs and the hair had risen on Growch's back.

He growled. "There they are. . . ."

There was a shout, another, and three figures stood at the edge of the pine trees and gazed up the short slope towards us. I ignored them, putting more kindling on the fire and stirring the pot, although my hands were trembling.

"They look bad 'uns to me," muttered Growch. "Rough. Got weapons, too. Better run . . ."

Where to? The bluff was too steep to climb, the cave a trap.

"Just don't get into trouble," I urged. "Low profile . . ."

The strangers moved up the slope towards us, and now I could see them more closely my heart sank. They were ragged, dirty and unshaven with straggling moustaches and their hair tied up in bandannas. As Growch had said, they were armed; a rusty, curved sword, a couple of daggers, a club spiked with nails. They were used to this: as they moved up the slope they spread out, so they were approaching me from three sides, their dark eyes darting from side to side in case of ambush.

They came to a halt some ten yards away and I could smell the rank stench of sweat, excitement and fear. The one in the middle stepped forward. He spoke, but my heart was hammering so hard I couldn't hear him, even if I had been able to understand. Perhaps Ky-Lin was sending a translation from his hiding place in the cave, but I couldn't hear that, either. I could feel my knees knocking together.

"What—what do you want?" I asked in my own tongue, but my voice came out high and very unladlike. They glanced at each other, and the one in the middle muttered out of the corner of his mouth. He addressed me again. This time I heard Ky-Lin's translation.

"They are asking if you are alone."

I nodded my head foolishly, then could have kicked myself. Why, oh why couldn't I have indicated four, five others in the forest?

They grinned, shuffled closer, their hands resting on their weapons. The middle one squatted down in front of the fire, warmed his hands, pointed at the pot and asked a question.

"He asks if there is enough for all, and where is the meat," translated Ky-Lin.

I tried to smile, but my face seemed frozen. I shrugged my shoulders and waved at the pot, then at them. If you want meat, then go get it yourselves. . . . The leader leered at me, plucked a dagger from his belt and made slicing motions in the direction of Growch, who was growling valiantly. The man's meaning was plain: no ready meat, then the dog would do.

I backed away, pushing Growch behind me, still trying to smile as though it was all some huge joke—but I knew it wasn't. I thought even I might not be safe if they were especially hungry; I knew that in certain parts of the world human flesh was considered a delicacy.

"No," I said. "Please no! Let us alone. . . ." and I could hear myself whimpering like a child as I retreated with Growch until my shoulders were hard against the bluff behind me.

The bandits were laughing as they closed in for the kill, but suddenly there was a call from the forest behind, then another and another, as if the forest were suddenly full of strangers. My attackers drew back uncertainly, and at that moment Ky-Lin leapt from the cave, his tail seeming aflame with color. I snatched my knife from my belt and Growch attacked the legs of the man on the right. For a moment I hoped we could scare them away, but then I realized that Ky-Lin couldn't attack any of them: he could only frighten. Growch's teeth were sharp but not killers, and I had never used a knife on anyone in my life.

I say Ky-Lin dodge a sword thrust and then be clubbed over the head and crumple into a heap and lie still; Growch was still snarling and growling and snapping and had done some bloody damage to one of our attackers; then a boot caught him on the side of the jaw, he shrieked with pain and somersaulted through the air, to land with a sickening crack against one of the rocks. At the same time I was caught from behind, my arm was twisted behind my back and the knife clattered harmlessly from my grasp to the ground. I screamed, but the sound was choked off by the hand at my throat.

I could feel the blood thumping in my ears as the hand squeezed tighter. I couldn't draw breath, felt consciousness slipping away—

So this was what it was like to die, I thought: strange but it doesn't hurt that much, it's just uncomfortable. I was already rushing away down a dark tunnel, a long tube with a tiny light at the other end, when suddenly everything changed.

The pressure went from my throat, my breathing eased, but I could feel cold air on my body. As conscious thought returned I realized they must have been searching me for hidden moneys, but their rough handling had torn my clothes and revealed my true sex. Now their handling of me changed in character; they were eager for something other than my immediate death, they wanted to enjoy my body first.

I struggled now, really struggled, for the threat of rape seemed far more terrible than the certainty of death. I could feel the obscenity of their hands on my private parts, their hot breath on my face, something hard and thrusting against my thigh, and the more I fought them, the more they liked it. Despairingly I clenched my free hand, the right, and aimed for one of the faces above me. I missed, but felt another stab from my ring, my magic ring.

"Help me," I breathed, "please help me. . . ."

The hands still probed, my back was naked to the sharp stones on the ground, a mouth reached for mine, excited voices were laughing and urging each other on, then the whole world seemed to erupt in a world-shaking sound: an ear-splitting roar like a volcano.

Suddenly I was free. My attackers no longer threatened. The air was cold on my bruised flesh as I staggered to my feet, striving to cover my nakedness with the torn remnants of my clothes.

That dreadful roar came again, loud enough to make me cover my ears. I looked down towards the forest and there, coming up the slope towards us, was Bear!

But it was a Bear I had never seen before. . . .

16

Even I was frightened.

Bear stood on his hind legs, his great arms spread wide, the five oval pads set in a row on his front paws each sprouting a wickedly curved claw. The mane on his shoulders stood up like an extra fur cape, but the greatest change was in his head. Usually the fur framed his face rather like the feathers on an owl, his round ears pricked forward: now his ears were slicked back to his head, the ruff of fur was gone and instead there was a pointed snout with lips curled back in a snarl over a double row of pointed teeth. Saliva dripped down onto his chest and the little eyes were red with anger.

He roared again, and the sound seemed to reverberate from the rocks of the bluff behind me, then he dropped to all fours and bounded up the slope towards us.

Suddenly I was alone. The bandits were running helter-skelter towards the trees, their weapons scattered, the air full of their cries of terror. As one passed too close to the bear I saw a paw flash out and ribbons of cloth and skin flew from the gashed shoulder of one of my attackers. He shrieked and clasped his arm, blood dripping through his fingers, but he didn't stop running, though he stumbled now and again in his flight.

Bear reached me and reared up, his snakelike head twisting down till he nearly touched me. He sniffed, and almost too late I remembered how shortsighted he was.

"It's me, Bear. . . ."

He sniffed again. "So it is. Smell of them. Heard you call. All right? The others, then," and he whipped round and shambled off towards the forest, where the crashing sounds of the escaping bandits were growing fainter.

* * *

I pulled my clothes together as best I could, though needle and thread were urgently needed, found the pouch that had been ripped from my neck lying close by, then hurried over to where Growch lay, moaning a little. He wagged his tail however as I lifted his head to my lap.

"You all right?" As I spoke I was feeling him all over for breaks or wounds, but although he winced now and again there didn't seem to be anything broken, until—

"Ouch! Them's me ribs!"

"Do they hurt?"

"Reckon I cracked a couple." He struggled to his feet, shook himself, groaned, and spat out a couple of teeth, luckily not essential ones. "You all right? What about 'im?" He nodded towards the motionless figure of Ky-Lin.

He lay where he had fallen, utterly still. My heart kicked against my breastbone. No, not dear Ky-Lin! Not after all he had done for us. He had existed for so many hundreds of years, he couldn't suddenly end like this. I bent over him, the tears dripping off the end of my nose.

"You're wetting my fur," came a muffled voice.

"Ky-Lin! You're alive!

"Of course I'm alive!" Take more than a knock on the head to finish me off!" and a moment or two later he was up on his hooves again, shaking out his crumpled tail and straightening his twisted antennae.

"You all right? I heard your ring call the bear, and I presume he has chased them off. Oh dear . . ." and he sat down suddenly on his haunches, looking puzzled.

"What's the matter?" I asked anxiously, for his colors had also faded.

"Long years; lots of changes; body material not what it was . . . Would you be kind enough to examine the dent in my head? It feels quite deep."

It was, a cleft running from where his left eyebrow would have been to the opening of his right ear. The skin, or hide, didn't appear to be broken, but I wasn't happy about the bone beneath. Recalling the healing properties of the ring I drew it slowly and gently along the indentation.

"That's better; a Unicorn has great healing powers. Dog would benefit too, I believe."

And so he did. I found some Self-Heal growing nearby, mashed it into a paste, bound up Growch's ribs and Ky-Lin's head, and they both declared themselves much recovered, though Growch said the healing process would be accelerated by a spot of something to eat. . . .

I remade the fire, got the pot boiling again, and threw in rice and some rather desiccated vegetables in deference to Ky-Lin's tastes, Growch getting a strip of dried meat to chew.

Where was Bear? There was neither sight nor sound of him, and the sky was darkening into twilight.

"He'll be all right," said Ky-Lin. "Why not get out your needle and thread while you wait? Your clothes are falling to pieces!"

By the flicker of the flames I was able to cobble together my jerkin, rebind my breasts and renew the laces in my trews; my shirt was in ribbons, and I used it for binding up the animals, but I had one more in my pack. First, however, I scrubbed myself with cold water, determined to rid myself of any lingering taint from my attackers.

It was now full dark, and the dancing flames threw our shadows on the rocks behind, making them prance like demons. A larger shadow overtopped us all: Bear was back.

I hadn't heard him approach, but suddenly there he was, fur smooth once more, his face round and innocent, in his jaws a couple of trout.

He dropped them at my feet. "Took long time to catch."

I looked at him. He seemed as unconcerned as if he had been out for a stroll. Skewering the trout I laid them across the fire to broil.

"Have you eaten?"

"Trout. Roots. Full."

I turned the trout. "What happened?" I was dying to know how far he had chased them, but knew I would have to be patient.

"Long walk to lake. Take time to catch."

"No, not that! The men—the bad ones. Did they all go away?"

He looked puzzled, licked his paw.

"I called you: you chased them. . . ."

"Oh, them. Yes."

"They won't come back?"

"Not ever. Gone."

I breathed more easily. He seemed very sure.

"All dead. Lives for life. You help me, I help you. Will have some honey. . . ."

I carved him off a chunk, although I thought he had said he was full.

"But how . . . ?" I didn't know how to put it, was afraid of the answer.

"Men?" He thought for a moment. "In ravine. Long way down to rocks. All still." He turned to the pot. "Smells good. Small portion . . ."

And that was all I, or anyone else for that matter, ever got out of him, for the following morning he was so deep in his hibernating sleep that we couldn't rouse him even to say good-bye.

His deep, rumbling snores kept me awake that night—that and the various aches and bruises I nursed. I kept thinking about the complexity of the creature, if one could call one so simple complicated. The problem lay in me, I finally decided; I just couldn't comprehend a mind that thought in such straight lines. All that concerned him was food, sleep, and play. Like all simple souls he could only hold one thought at a time: once fixed, though, the idea was carried out ruthlessly, whether it was to catch a fish, scoop out grubs from a dead log, sniff out a honeycomb, chase a butterfly—or kill a man. And someone as simple as that would have no conscience, wouldn't know what one meant.

When we stepped out of the cave the following morning, we realized that Bear had the best of it, snoring away the winter in his drift of leaves, because the weather had changed for the worse. A nasty, nippy wind churned the ashes of last night's fire, whipping the tall grass into a frenzy and driving the tops of the distant pines into uneasy circles. The sky was gray, flat and oppressive, and looked as though it might hold snow.

We packed up quickly, then had to decide in which direction to go. I pulled out Suleiman's map and unscrolled it on a rock. Ky-Lin bent over it, doing his disconcerting bit of shaking his head from side to side with his eyes crossed.

"We are too far west," he said finally. "If we could all fly over the mountains for a thousand miles, it would be easy. But not even a dragon would go that way in this weather." His sensitive antennae traced a line to the northeast. "We need to turn east and find the Silk River, then follow it north to the headwaters. Then when the weather is better we find the Desert of Death, cross that, and we are within a few miles say, a hundred— of our destination."

"Yes," I said. It sounded simple, and also rather daunting. I didn't like the sound of that desert, and a thousand miles in a straight line meant many more afoot.

Ky-Lin glanced at me. "Don't be disheartened; think how far we've come already! The next few days, till we reach the river, will be tough; but once we get there, there will be plenty of villages."

He was right: it was tough. It took over a week of hard slog to reach any sort of civilization, and by that time we had run out of provisions and were footsore and cold and weary to the bone. The snow held off, but the winds were fierce and biting, shelter hard to find and our faces burned from several sharp showers of sleet. It might be February, but

the winter's hold was tightening rather than otherwise. Once we came
to the river it was easier.

Apparently it connected farther south with another, larger, which in
its turn coincided with the caravan routes, so the boatmen were used
enough to taking paying passengers up to the headwaters, especially
with the rivers being so low at this time of year.

The town at the head of the river was one that concerned itself with
the weaving of plain silks, ready for transport in great flat barges to the
caravan routes. During the winter months the river was too low for large-
scale transport, so the townspeople used this time to spin the silks, dye
some of the hanks and bale everything up for the first barges to come
through once the melting snows made the river navigable. We made our
way to this town by leisurely stages from village to village, with a lift
here, a boat trip there. Everywhere there were mulberry trees, the harsh
winter making the icicles that hung from their branches tinkle like wind
chimes.

The headwaters of the river were a disappointment. No waters gush-
ing from a spring, rather a seeping from a huge bog that stretched for
miles to the north. This was a smelly place, and I was not surprised to
learn that it had been the custom, years back, to execute their criminals
by tying them up with a hood over their faces and chucking them into
the marsh. But the bog got its own back. Eventually the bodies were
spewed forth again in the spring rains, to float away down the river,
providing their own curiosity, for their long immersion in the bog had
preserved their bodies like tanned leather. I saw one once; the clothes
were stiff and shrunken, but the whole effect was rather that of an ama-
teur wood carving. This practice of execution had been discontinued
some fifty years back, but the odd corpse resurfaced now and again.

The town itself was a prosperous one with everyone, from children
to grandparents, all engaged in work connected with the silk trade. At
one end were the weaving sheds, at another the huge barns where the
silkworms were reared, in artificial heat if necessary. In between were
the huge vats for the dyes, the boiling rooms, and the sheds of drying
racks. Nearer the docks were the baling sheds.

We rented one of the ubiquitous summer workers' houses; it was
like a thatched clay beehive, one large room with shelves built into the
walls for food and utensils, a sleeping platform, a central brazier and
smoke hole, and niches in the walls for lamps. The floor was covered
with rush matting and there were a couple of functional stools and a
low table. Clothes were hung from a pole above the sleeping platform.

No windows, and the door was like a heavy sheep hurdle, to be placed as one desired.

Once we reached civilization again Ky-Lin had decided to revert to a smaller size to avoid embarrassing questions, and now he travelled once more on my shoulder, ready to interpret if necessary. Coin was acceptable once more so there was no problem with food, nor with the warmer padded clothing I bought, the kind the locals wore. My hair had grown quite long, too, as it hadn't been trimmed since we were in the Golden City, and I adopted the local custom, used by men and women alike, of plaiting it into a pigtail.

For six weeks the weather pressed in on us; rain, sleet, snow, gales, frost and ice. The little house however was warm and dry, raised as they all were from the streets to prevent flooding, and there was plenty to keep me busy. Mending and repairing, bringing my journal up to date, going to the market, cooking and cleaning, buying off-cuts of silk for underwear—luxury!—and yet I yearned for action. To be so near and yet still so far from my objective kept me in a permanent fret for the better weather.

Growch, however, was in his element.

Fortunately for him, unfortunately for me, he had at last found his "fluffy bums." The town was full of them. It seemed that every family had one as a pet, and at the rate Growch was carrying on, there would soon be the same amount of half-breeds.

After the first complaint from an irate owner Ky-Lin and I put our heads together and decided Growch was one of the rarest dogs in the world: "He-whose-stomach-is-of-two-dogs-and-whose-legs-are-the-shortest-in-the-world." With a title like that, who could resist seeing what the puppies would be like? The bitches were soon literally queuing up and Growch was totally exhausted.

He came in one day, even filthier than usual, his fur matted and muddy, his stomach dragging on the ground, his tail and ears at half-mast, his eyes—what you could see of them—half-closed and his tongue hanging out like a forgotten piece of washing.

"Serves you right," I said unsympathetically. "It's what you wanted, isn't it? The reason you came all this way with me?" I jabbed my needle into the sandal I was finishing off, trying hard not to laugh. "Unlimited sex, that's what you wanted, isn't it? Well now you've got it, so don't complain!"

" 'Oose complainin'? I ain't. It's just—just I think I've gorra cold or somefin'. . . ."

"Dogs don't catch colds."

"Well, a chill, then. Think I'll stay in fer a coupla days. Have a rest."

"All right," I said placatingly. "I'll give you a dose of herbs, and if you have a fever we'll have to cut down on meat. Slops and gruel for you, my boy," and I bent over my sewing again and coughed to hide my giggles.

The transition from winter to spring, when it finally came, seemed to take place over a couple of days only. One moment a grim wind blew from the north and the ground was hard with frost, the next the sun shone, the ice melted and caged canaries were singing outside every door. It seemed thousands of little streams from the bog emptied into the river, which awoke from its sluggish sleep and ran merrily between its banks once more. Bales of silk were loaded onto flat-bottomed boats and set off southward, but the first trading boats didn't come upriver until the end of April, struggling against the swollen waters.

The whole town turned out to welcome the first string of barges, bearing long-needed supplies and the first of the seasonal workers, many of whom had relatives in the town. Ky-Lin and I had decided to start our journey north again within the week, so it was with holiday mood on me that I joined the rest of the town to watch the boats come in. I noted with satisfaction that the cargoes included dried fruits, grain, strips of meat and fish and cheeses, all goods that had been in short supply for the last month and that we would need for our journey.

Goods hauled ashore, passengers politely clapped and welcomed, bales of silk waiting to be loaded, we turned for our lodgings, content that the world had started awake again. In a few days we should be on our way.

"Got you!"

A hooded stranger, one of the passengers, had stepped from behind one of the warehouses and grabbed me by the wrist, so tightly I fancied I could hear the crunch of bone.

"Let me go! You're hurting me!" With my free hand I attempted to strike out at him, but he dodged the blow, holding me even tighter.

Growch growled warningly, and the stranger kicked out at him.

"You want to keep that cur of yours under control, Summer," came the voice again, but this time I recognized it, and my heart sank.

Dickon had found us again.

17

His explanation of what had happened to him since he ran away when I was arrested was very plausible; I think that after all the rehearsal it must have gone through he even believed it himself.

After I had fed him—and I admit he needed food; he looked half-starved—and had gone out for a jar of heady rice wine to loosen his tongue, he settled down on a stool by the brazier, a second mug of wine in his hand.

"I just didn't know what way to turn," he confessed. "I went chasing the bear, but he escaped me—where did he go, by the way? Never saw him again. Good riddance, I say. If it hadn't been for him murdering his master you would never have been arrested in the first place."

As I remember it, he had been running in a different direction from the animal; as for the reason for my arrest, how could I blame Bear? I had never had my feet scorched to make me dance. I didn't think it necessary to explain we had returned him to his own land.

"I couldn't find your dog, either, but I see you got him back. I saw that heathen boy and his friends carrying off your baggage, but there were too many for me to tackle. Once a thief always a thief, I say; I never trusted him."

He took another swig of the wine.

"After that I went back to the palace and demanded an interview, late though it was." Unlikely even a minor palace official would have bothered to get out of bed; besides, they were looking for him, too. "I begged, I pleaded to be allowed to see you; I even offered a bribe"—as far as I knew he had no money at all—"but they said I would have to wait until morning.

"I walked the streets all night, my mind in turmoil, turning over in my mind the options open to us. I had little money, no influence, and my command of the language was not as good as it should be. I thought of you, all alone and helpless in some underground dungeon—" he leant forward and patted my knee "—and I wept to think of your suffering."

I'll bet: he probably spent the night in a brothel. But now he was getting into his stride, aided by the wine.

"I went back to the palace at crack of dawn, to find everything in complete turmoil! I found that you had disappeared into thin air— 'flown up into the clouds' was the way they put it—but of course I knew that was rubbish, even with your magic bits and pieces and talking animals, so I reckoned that you'd had some kind of help. I thought, too, that they might recognize me as having been with you, so I decided to lie low for a while till things settled down; found a nice young lady who let me stay rent free for a while. . . ." His face grew dreamy, and he finished the mug of wine. "That's why I didn't immediately come looking for you. How did you escape, by the way? Bribe the guards? Pick the lock?"

"As a matter of fact," I said stiffly, "that 'little thief' as you called him, and his friends, pulled the bars from my cell and saw me safe on the road, together with my baggage, money, and extra provisions. He called it an exchange for the slavery I rescued him from."

"Oh . . . well, you never can tell, I suppose. Any more of that wine?"

"It's quite strong," I said, refilling his mug for the third time.

"I've got a strong enough head to take piss water like this. . . . Now, where was I?"

"Hiding," I said.

"Not for long, my dear, not for long! I found it very difficult to pick up your trail, though; no one had seen you go, though I realized you must have used one of the gates. After having questioned everyone I knew, and some I didn't, I remembered those maps of yours. You know the ones: 'Here be Dragons'?" I wondered whether he realized he had given himself away by confirming he had seen them. "I recalled the direction was north, but where? Here I was lucky." He tapped his nose. "I came across a mapmaker and—for a consideration—was allowed to take a peek and managed to copy a couple. Here!" He reached into his tattered clothes and brought out a couple of pieces of rice paper, the folds marked with the sweat from his body.

Gingerly I unfolded the scraps, still warm from his body. The first one was very like the ones I had copied at Matthew's house although with more detail: a couple more rivers and towns, more routes. The other was far more precise and Ky-Lin, viewing them from his hiding place on my shoulder, gave a little hiss when he saw it. I looked more closely. The Silk River was marked quite clearly, although in the unintelligible (to me) picture scribble they used. Here was our town, mountains to the north and west, and what looked like a plateau to the northwest.

Dickon was now nodding, his eyes closed, his body swaying on the stool.

"Keep that one," whispered Ky-Lin. "That is one we could use. If he won't part with it, we'll copy it while he sleeps."

But even as I prepared to tuck it away in my jerkin the mug fell from his lax fingers, his eyes snapped open and he reached and took the map from my hand.

"Oh, no you don't! I'm not having you running off on your own again. I have the maps, and we go for the treasure together!"

"There isn't any treasure! There never was!"

"Rubbish! What kept you going all this long time? We've been all through this before, and I know you're lying."

There was no point in arguing.

"If you really believe that, then go and look for it on your own. As for me, I am on a private pilgrimage to find a friend and there is no, repeat no, money at the end of it." I rose to my feet. "There is a spare blanket over there but you'll have to sleep on the floor. If you wish to relieve yourself there is a communal latrine at the end of the street."

Later I peered down from the sleeping platform; he was muffled up in the blanket on one of the grass mats, snoring gently. Slipping to the floor I made up the brazier and brewed myself a mug of camomile tea, an excuse in case he woke, though I usually had one before I went to bed anyway.

"What's so special about the map?" I whispered to Ky-Lin.

He sipped at the tea. "Nice . . . The map shows that we are on the right track. It also indicates the way we must take once we cross the Desert of Death."

I shivered. "We must go that way?"

He nodded. "If you can study that map you will see it is the most direct route. The only other way lies through the mountains, which are notorious bandit country."

I had had enough of bandits.

"Then we had better pinch the map and copy it. Is he fast enough asleep, do you think?"

"I shall make sure. . . ." He trotted across the floor. I saw him touch

Dickon's face with one of his hooves, there was a tiny puff of what looked like pinkish smoke, and he trotted back, nodding his head. "You can take it now; I gave him a little Sleepy Dust."

Together we studied the map. He pointed to where the town was marked: "We are here." With his delicate antennae he traced a way around the bog, shook his head and marked a path across the middle. "Quicker; as I remember there are markers."

I didn't ask how long it was since he had been this way. "What if they are no longer there?"

"We'll check first. After the bog the trail winds along that valley bottom to the desert. The Desert of Death," he repeated.

"Is it—is it that bad?"

He hesitated. "I have only been there once, and I was with my master and the others of my kind. Then it was not too bad, but you must realize that my brethren can manage on little water and food if necessary, and my Lord had reached such an exalted plane of consciousness that he could, I believe, have existed on air alone." He was perfectly serious. "Besides which, there was a town and temple halfway across."

"Isn't it very hot?"

"Yes, during the day. At night it can be equally cold. The terrain is difficult too. It is a bare, arid place, littered with small stones and rocks. It is necessary to carry all one's food and water; it is not called the Desert of Death for nothing. However if we take care and prepare ourselves properly it shouldn't be too difficult. I am sure I can find the temple again, and there we can stay for a while and stock up with fresh provisions; it is on the only oasis we shall come across."

He paused and his antennae flicked across the map.

"Once across the mountains we are in the foothills of the final range of mountains. Over them, just there, marked by a circle, is a Buddhist monastery. It looks over a deep valley, and in the center of that valley there is a conical hill—they say it could be the core of a long-extinct volcano—and because of the way the light falls and its distance, they call it the Blue Mountain. In the margin of the map is written: 'This is believed to be the home of Dragons.' This, by the way, and whatever your friend says, is an original map, not a copy."

"Then he must have stolen it. . . ." But I was not really concerned with that; all I could do was concentrate on that little hill on the map. It looked so near, but also, if the truth were told, so insignificant a thing to hold all my dreams.

"I saw it once in the distance," said Ky-Lin, "and it did look blue, but I did not know then that it was rumored a dragon lair. Come, you should make a copy before he wakes."

My hands were shaking so much both with anticipation and the discovery that my mountain did exist, that it took me longer than I had anticipated to complete the copy, but we managed to get the original back in Dickon's clothing without him waking.

"Ky-Lin," I whispered. "How soon can we go?"

He considered. "The weather is set fair, new provisions have come into the town, we have the confirmation of the map . . . two days, perhaps."

"Why not tomorrow?" I couldn't wait to leave.

"Provisions to buy and pack for a start; you need to make a proper list. Then we shall need a half-dozen water skins, more blankets, a length of rope and you could do with a new pair of strong boots. In order to carry all the baggage, I shall have to grow again, and you will have to alert your friend to my existence."

I glanced over at Dickon. "But he's not coming!"

"You don't want him to accompany us?"

"Certainly not! We've managed fine without him so far."

"He could be useful carrying the baggage. . . ."

"I—I just don't want him along, that's all." I couldn't explain it. It wasn't the sort of thing you could put into words. I could quote his cowardice, his obsession with the thought of treasure, his searching of my belongings, the way he literally seemed to haunt my every move, but it wasn't just that; it was something deeper and more frightening. Inside of me there was an unspoken dread of him: not what he was but what he might become. He posed a threat to my future happiness, of that I was sure, but how or why I had no idea. It was like waking to a day of brilliant sunshine and being convinced that it would rain before nightfall, but far more sinister than that. All I was sure of was that I couldn't explain it.

"Very well; if you can manage the purchasing tomorrow, and the packing, then we'll make it the day after. I'll tell you again what we need in the morning."

"Can you give him some more Sleepy Dust?"

Ky-Lin hesitated. "It is not good for humans to give them too much. Ideally there should be a twelve-month between each dose. But he did not take much tonight; perhaps a small dose will do no harm."

From the moment he awoke in the morning Dickon did his unintentional best to hamper all my attempts to organize our departure; he was a positive pain, following me round the town as I made my purchases.

"Why are you buying that? We've got a couple already. What do we need those for? When are we setting out? Where are you supposed to be going on your pilgrimage? How are we getting there? I hope you don't think I'm going to carry that. Are we going to hire some sort of transport? How much money have you left? Are we going to do another performance?" Etc., etc., etc., till I could have screamed.

But I knew I had to behave in a calm and rational manner, as if the last thought on my mind was to escape from him that very night, so I made up answers to those questions I couldn't answer truthfully, telling a heap of lies with a smile on my face and my fingers mentally crossed. Fifteen Hail Marys later . . .

By late afternoon I think I had persuaded him we would not be leaving for a few days' time, and I tried to make my frantic packing that evening look like routine tidying up. He eyed the sacks, packs and panniers with distrust.

"We'll never carry all that!"

"It's not more than we can manage; you carry your share, I'll carry mine."

"I shall just look like a donkey. . . ."

"No more than usual," I said briskly. "Now, what would you like for supper?"

We dined well, as Growch and I would be snacking until we had crossed the bog, and we didn't know how long that would take, so it was chicken soup with chopped hard-boiled eggs, fried pastry rolls filled with bean shoots and herbs, and chopped chicken livers in a bean and lentil pudding. I had camomile tea, Dickon had rice wine. I thought to allay further suspicion by begging for a further look at his maps, knowing what his response would be.

"Oh, no you don't! I'm not having you learn them by heart and then steal a march on me! Once we're on the road together you can take another look."

I yawned. "Have it your own way. There's no hurry. I'm for bed. The clearing-up can wait till the morning. Blow out the lamp before you go to bed, please. . . ."

I watched Ky-Lin scuttle out of the door to effect his "change," and lay down, convinced that I wouldn't sleep a wink, but my eyes kept closing in spite of it: must have been that heavy meal. Still, Ky-Lin would wake me as soon as he returned. . . .

I woke to broad daylight, Growch still snoring at my side and Dickon returning with a pitcher of water for washing.

"Wake up, sleepyheads!" he called out cheerily.

What in the world . . . Where was Ky-Lin?

The answer came from beneath my blanket. "I spend all evening changing to a suitable size, then find when I return that your ridiculous friend has so jammed the door tight shut that I can't gain entrance! So, I have to spend more time changing to be small enough to get back in again!" He wasn't at all happy.

"Sorry," I whispered. "We'll manage it better tonight, I promise."

But the matter was taken out of my hands by Dickon himself. That evening I left a stew of vegetables simmering on the brazier, and suggested we take a walk. I was hoping this would give Ky-Lin the chance for his change, since we had discovered that the house next door was empty, and he would hide in there while I ate less and didn't fall asleep before Dickon, so I could ensure the door was left open.

Dickon, however, had other ideas. We were wandering through the bazaar examining the goods without any intention of buying, when I straightened up in front of a stall selling slippers and found he had disappeared.

Not into thin air and not forever. On the other side of the road was a lighted doorway, screened by a beaded curtain still gently swaying as though someone had just entered. I crossed over and peeped inside. A waft of perfume, smoke from incense sticks, rustle of silks, a mutter of feminine voices. It was obvious what sort of place it was. I knew Dickon had no money, so wandered slowly off towards our lodgings, fairly sure he would seek me out. I was right; I had only gone a hundred yards when he caught me up.

"I say, Summer: got a bit of change on you?"

"No. It's suppertime. Come on, before it spoils."

"It's just that—that I saw there was to be an entertainment tonight and I thought I might take a look. . . . There's an entrance fee, of course, and I'd need a few coins for drinks. Come on, Summer! Life's short enough without missing out on all the fun! You're a real sobersides, you know: getting just like an old maid!"

Old maid, indeed! I should like to see anyone of that ilk who had travelled as far as I had, faced as many dangers, had two proposals of marriage and a dragon-lover! But I mustn't lose my temper.

I thought quickly. If he went to a brothel—place of entertainment as he preferred me to think of it—then he would roll home hungry at midnight and keep us all awake. On the other hand, if I could drag out supper till around nine, then give him extra moneys, he might well stay out all night, which would be perfect for our plans.

"Supper first," I said. "Then I'll see if I have a few coins to spare. Er . . . do you think it's the sort of entertainment I should enjoy?"

"Certainly not!" he said, and added hurriedly: "You might attract unwelcome attentions. It would be a shame if I had to escort you back just when it started to get interesting. . . ."

I made sure he had extra helpings of the meal, much to Growch's disgust, watched him finish off the rice wine and gave him more than enough coin to buy his choice for the night.

"Don't wake us when you return. . . ."

I waited until he had turned the corner, then went to the empty house next door to see how Ky-Lin was managing. Very well, he informed me, but was there a bowl of rice to spare? It helped the changeover.

I was too nervous to go to bed; I reckoned if Dickon was going to roll home before dawn it would be around two o'clock. At three he still hadn't arrived, so I went for Ky-Lin.

"Any reason why we can't leave right now?"

"We should wait for a little more light, but I expect we can manage. Light a lantern, and load me up."

Less than ten minutes later we were creeping through the deserted streets and, following Ky-Lin's lead, found ourselves in the poorer section of town. I kept the lantern as well shaded as I could, but in this part of town the streets were ill-kept, and we stumbled over rubbish and filth, so we needed the lantern on full beam. Ky-Lin was uneasy that someone would see us, but to me the streets were as quiet as the grave.

The ground beneath our feet became soft and spongy as we left the last straggle behind, and I was glad that my new boots had been thoroughly oiled.

"How much further?" We were splashing through pools of water now, and in the east the first graying of the sky announced the false dawn.

"Nearly at the causeway," said Ky-Lin, a large shadow ahead of me. "From there, about a mile to the first of the markers."

"Can't come too soon for me," grumbled Growch. "Me stummick is wet as a duck's arse and me paws full of gunge. When do we eat?"

Some time later we stood on a relatively dry pebbled causeway. Ahead of us lay a flat, steamy expanse of what looked like a vast, waterlogged plain, tinged pink by the just-rising sun. Tufts of grasses, the odd bush, a stunted tree or two, a couple of hummocks were all that interrupted the horizon, fringed in the distance by the ever-present and distant mountains.

Ky-Lin was concentrating: eyes crossed, head weaving from side to side.

"Well, this is it. I can see the first marker. Shall we go?"

18

I was soaked to the skin. No, I hadn't fallen in the water, nor had it been raining; it was just the all-pervading miasma of damp that rose from the bog that drenched us all as thoroughly as if we had jumped in. Ky-Lin's coat shone with droplets of moisture, like a spider's web heavy with dew, and poor Growch's hair was plastered down to his body as if it had been soaked in oil. I was not only wet, I was cold. Although there was a sun of sorts, it had to fight its way through the steamy mists it sucked up from the stagnant pools all around us.

The ground beneath our feet was solid enough, thanks to Ky-Lin's instinct; how he did it I couldn't even guess, for I had seen nothing to guide us. Around us the bog bubbled, seethed, slurped, belched and burped, an ever-present reminder of the dangers we faced if we stepped off the invisible path we followed.

No animals, no birds. Plenty of insects, though; whining mosquitoes, huge flies, buzzing gnats, all of whom welcomed the chance to land on my face and hands, and Growch's nose, eyes and bum. Ky-Lin they left alone, as if he were composed of other than flesh and blood.

We seemed to have been walking all day but the sun was at less than its zenith when Ky-Lin called a halt. There was a small, knee-high cairn to our left, and we shed our loads, sat down and I unpacked some cheese and dried fruit. Growch had a knuckle of ham which he chewed on disconsolately, deliberately dropping it into the muck every now and again to emphasize how hardly used he was.

Ky-Lin insisted we continue our journey as soon as we had eaten.

"To the next marker, and then perhaps another rest," he explained.

I sighed as I packed up again. "I haven't *seen* a marker yet! How do you know where they are?"

"You're sitting on one," he said. "Or were. The last one we passed was that pile of peeled sticks, and the first was that moss-covered rock."

"And the next?"

"The skeleton of a bird with one wing missing."

"But how can you see from all that way off?"

"Because my antennae give me enhanced sensibilities—like extra eyes, noses and ears; two are arranged so they see further ahead; two tell me what goes on at the side; two what happens behind."

I was busy counting. "You've got four pairs. . . ."

"The last ones are for seeing beneath the ground for a few inches, so I don't damage anything growing out of sight; a germinating seed, a worm, an incubating chrysalis: my master thought of everything."

"Then you could see where a squirrel hoarded its nuts?"

"Or a dog a bone," said Growch, interested in spite of himself in what he had considered up to now to be a very boring conversation. "Or a burrow of nice, fat little rabbits?"

"If I could, I shouldn't tell you," said Ky-Lin. "The eating of flesh—"

"All right, you two," I said soothingly. There could never be true accord between one who believed all killing was wrong, and another whose greatest pleasure was eating red meat.

We had walked perhaps a half hour more when we came to a division of the ways. To our left the track had obviously been repaired, and was neatly outlined with stones; the track we had been following continued ahead, but was now rutted and pocked, with pools of standing water as far as one could see. Ky-Lin was plodding along the old path, head down, so I stepped onto the new one and called him back.

"Hey! You're going the wrong way!"

He turned his head. "No. I'm not. That way may look to be the right road but it is a deception. Especially constructed to trap the unwary. Go down that road and you step straight into a quagmire which will suck you down into an underground river that would carry you to a subterranean tomb."

But I was tired of him always being right, tired of the seemingly endless bog, tired of playing follow-my-leader! "I don't believe you! The road you are taking is the one that looks like it ends in disaster; why, even now you are nearly hock-deep in water!"

He splashed back to my side. "Very well, have it your own way. We will take this road. But I warn you, you are wasting our time."

I felt exuberant, glad that I had shown an obviously tiring creature the correct route, and for a while, as the ground beneath us remained firm and dry, my spirits rose still further, especially as it seemed a more direct route to the mountains ahead, and although my ring had started to itch intolerably, I ignored it, telling myself it was just another mosquito bite.

I turned to Ky-Lin who was some ten yards behind. "I told you this was the right— Ow!" Walking backwards, my feet suddenly found the path had disappeared and, scrabbling at the air for balance, I toppled back into the slimy, sucking mess, dragged down still further by the weight of my pack.

A moment later I felt Ky-Lin's teeth in my jerkin and I was dragged back onto the path, a sticky mess smelling like a midden.

I looked back: the open maw I had so nearly been sucked down into was closing up again, and in less than a minute the path gave the illusion of being as it was before.

"Better get cleaned up," said Ky-Lin. "There's a small spring a little way back. . . . You're not crying, are you? Anyone can make a mistake."

"But you *knew* I was wrong: why didn't you shout at me?"

"Ky-Lins don't shout."

"Well they should!" I sniffed and wiped my eyes with my filthy hand. "We're friends aren't we? Well then: don't be sweet and gentle and kind and forgiving all the time. Next time I do or say or suggest something stupid or silly, say so! Loudly . . ."

"You shouts at me—" grumbled Growch.

"If I shout at you, then you deserve it!"

"Not always! I remember—"

"All right, you two," said Ky-Lin, in such a perfect mimicry of my earlier attempts to soothe him and Growch, that I couldn't help laughing.

"Sorry, Ky-Lin! And thanks for pulling me out. From now on you lead the way." And next time I would heed the ring, I promised myself.

After that interruption it was a real slog to reach the spot Ky-Lin had decided would be our night stop. Several times, when we reached a comparatively dry spot, I begged him to stop, but he was adamant.

"There we will be safe. The ground is dry, but more important is our safety."

"But there's nothing to threaten us—except mosquitoes," I added, slapping at my face and neck. "You're not going to tell me there are monsters down there!"

"I do not know precisely what is down there. But I do know that the place I seek will keep us safe from whatever could threaten."

So we trudged on. The sun sank below the horizon, the mist thickened and it grew more chill. All at once the air above us was darkened by clouds of great bats, obviously seeking the insects who had so plagued us during the day. They weaved and ducked and swerved only inches above my head, and I found myself wrapping my hands about my head, uneasy at their proximity.

"They will neither touch you nor bite you," said Ky-Lin peaceably. "Those are not the bloodsuckers."

Then as quickly as they had come, they were gone.

Everything was quiet; now the whine of insects was gone there was nothing to break the silence except the sound of our steps and an occasional suck or blow from the bog itself. It was eerie.

"You'd better light the lantern," said Ky-Lin, his voice loud in the gloom. "It's getting dark, and we still have a couple of miles to go."

Easier said than done. The air was damp, so was I, and when I opened my tinderbox I couldn't raise a spark. More and more frantic, my fingers now bruised, my breath dampening the dried moss, I was ready to cry with frustration.

"Here," said Ky-Lin. "Let me try." He breathed over the box, and miraculously everything was suddenly dry, and my lantern lighted us over the last stretch.

When we reached the marker it was not in the least what I had expected, although it was a place that was recognizable. There was the skeleton of a bird, hanging upside down on a roughly fashioned wooden cross, and the whole area, a paved rough circle some eight feet across, was surrounded by a raised rim of stones a couple of inches high. Within the circle were a couple of stunted shrubs, one with sharp, prickly leaves like holly, the other bearing hairy leaves with a sharp, bitter smell. In the middle was a symbol picked out in white stones, but I couldn't make out exactly what it was meant to represent.

"Right," said Ky-Lin. "We can have a fire now, dry ourselves out. The dry kindling and charcoal are in the left-hand pannier."

In a few minutes the fire shut out the dark, creating a cozy circle like a room. I reheated some rice left over from the day before, adding herbs, and also ate some cheese and a couple of sweet cakes. The food, though dull, put new heart into me. I was warm for the first time that day, and we were drying out nicely. Even Growch had stopped grumbling.

"How much further?" I asked Ky-Lin.

"If we make good progress tomorrow, then we should be across by nightfall."

"Can't be soon enough," said Growch. "Never bin so cold or wet in my life, I ain't. 'Cept for now," he added, stretching his speckled stomach to the glow of the fire.

"Throw on the last of the charcoal," said Ky-Lin. "And sleep. If you wake, or think you do, pay no attention to what you see, or think you see."

"Why?" How could you see something that wasn't there?

"This is a Place of Power," he said. "And as such attracts both good and evil. But we are safe as long as we stay within the circle." Searching the ground he found a couple of discarded leaves from the bushes and threw them on the fire, where they blazed brightly for a moment then smoldered, giving off an unpleasant smell. "Lie down, close your eyes. . . ."

I scarcely had time to wrap myself in my blanket before I was asleep and slipping from one fragment of dream to another. I played in the dirt in front of my mother's house, drawing pictures on the ground with a stick; I struggled through a storm to reach shelter; once, for a startling moment I was the father who was dead before I was born: I knew the tall smiling stranger was my father because I could see him from where I lay in my mother's womb. He had stretched out his hand to rest it on her belly and through his fingers I heard the resonance of the name he then gave me, that my mother later denied me: Talitha, the graceful one. My dragon had known that name. . . .

Another dream—no, this time a nightmare. I was shut in, enclosed, chained up in the dark, and something was there beside me, something with scrabbly sounding claws like a crab, something with fetid breath, something that was crawling nearer and nearer, something that had grabbed at my arm and was drawing me into its mouth— I screamed.

And woke.

And it was real, not a nightmare. Something had grabbed my arm, something I couldn't see, and it was dragging me over the edge of the rim of stones, down into the stinking depths of the bog. I screamed again, Growch barked wildly and suddenly there was light, a flashing light, my jerkin was gripped in strong teeth and I was dragged back to safety beside a fire blazing up a shower of colored sparks, nursing a bruised arm.

"What—what happened?"

"You tossed about in your sleep and your arm went over the edge," said Ky-Lin. "Whatever you dreamt about awakened one of the creatures in the bog."

"But—what was it?"

"Look." And there, in the extended light thrown by the still-spark-ing fire, I saw the waters of the mere surrounding us stir and shift as strange creatures broke the surface. Just a claw, a spiny back, an evil eye, the glimpse of a whiplike tail, then they disappeared again in bubbles of foul-smelling gas.

"Some of these creatures are blind, some deaf, but all are hungry. They are not necessarily evil—evil needs an active determination—and that is a concept alien to them. They will eat you or their fellow creatures, even each other, but they lack discrimination. You should be afraid of them, but also feel pity. Human beings have choice, most animals too. They have none."

I shivered. They were foul, distorted creatures and they made me feel sick. If I had been dragged a little further I should now be beneath that slime with mud in my lungs, being chewed into fragments. How could I possibly show pity for such? I wasn't a saint like Ky-Lin, full of his Master's all-forgiveness, I was just a frightened human being.

The rest of the night Growch and I huddled together, both for warmth and for company. I slept but little, for the creature who had grabbed me seemed to have woken all the rest, and the waters around us seethed and gurgled, every now and again throwing up a great gout of water. I heard the wicked snapping of teeth, splash of tails, queer gruntings and groans. Even worse were the lights. Livid yellow, sickly green, lurid purple, they shone both above and below the surface. I couldn't tell whether they were animal or plant or some other manifestation, all I knew was some of them hovered, some zipped through the air, others hopped in and out of water like frogs, with a strange whistling sound.

I must have dozed off eventually, because when Ky-Lin woke me it was light again and, apart from the mist, insects and unhealthy-looking surroundings, all was as it had been the day before.

"Let's get going," I said. I couldn't stand the thought of another moment in that place. We ate breakfast as we walked, stale pancakes and dried fruit, and made good progress, although the path, if you could call it that, was almost covered with water most of the way. At noon we halted briefly at the last of the markers, so Ky-Lin told us, though to me it looked just like a bundle of dried rushes. There was little left that didn't need cooking, but even Growch didn't grumble at the rice cakes and cheese.

But Ky-Lin ate very sparingly, and kept glancing back the way he had come.

"What is it?"

"Not sure. We were followed earlier—men and horses, but they have gone back. But there is still someone back there, I am sure."

"Can't you see anything?"

"No. The land where we rested last night is on a sort of hummock, and that is between me and our pursuer, if there is one. No one from the village comes further than the circle, where they used to hold sacrifices and ritual executions—"

"You never told me that!"

"Would you have felt any easier?"

"Worse!"

"So all I can think is—"

He was interrupted by a scream, a howl of pure terror. In that misty desolation it was difficult to tell what direction it came from, but as it was repeated Ky-Lin's antennae got busy, swivelling this way and that and finally pointing firmly back the way he had come.

There was a further shriek: "Help me! Oh God, help me. . . ."

"It's Dickon!"

I felt a sudden violent jolt of revolt. If he were in trouble, then let him get out of it himself. I didn't want him with us, he had no right to follow, and more and more I felt he was a threat to us all. I wanted to run away, put my hands over my ears and escape as fast as I could, leave him to die, but even as I wished it my reluctant feet were carrying me back along the path we had come.

He was sinking fast. He had obviously stepped off the path, tried to cut a corner where the trail twisted back on itself after a half mile and had been caught in a morass. Already the green slime was bubbling up around his hips, and the more he struggled, the faster he sank.

He was crying, tears of pure terror, choking on my name.

I pulled the rope from Ky-Lin's pack, put one end between his teeth and threw the other towards Dickon; it fell short, I drew it back, already slick with green slime. He started to flail his arms, and sank down further still.

"Stay still, you fool!"

This time he caught the end of the rope and Ky-Lin and I started to drag him out, but it was hard work, as at least half his body was now out of sight. We at last were making headway when the rope suddenly refused to move; we tugged again with all our strength and found we were not hauling one body, but two: tangled up with Dickon was a corpse, one of the criminals executed ages ago. The face had been eaten away, and as Dickon caught sight of the grinning skeleton skull he gave another scream and let go the rope.

I threw it again and this time we managed to pull him free, the corpse releasing its hold and sinking back beneath the slime, throwing up its arms as it disappeared in an obscene gesture of farewell.

Dickon at last lay on the path, gasping and groaning, covered in stinking mud and slime. He staggered to his feet, attempted to thank me, but I had had enough.

I walked away from him and didn't look back.

19

And what is more I didn't even speak to him until we had finally crossed the bog by last light and reached firm ground. I let Ky-Lin lead the way and followed close behind with Growch, paying no attention to the plodding footsteps behind, the whimpers and groans.

The bog finally petered out into a series of dank pools, bulrushes, bog grass and squelchy mud. The land then rose sharply into a stand of conifers and we moved thankfully into the shelter of the trees and were immediately enclosed in an entirely different atmosphere. The needles underfoot cushioned our tread, and the air was soft and full of the clean smell of resin, and the evening breeze soughed gently in the branches above.

I could hear a stream off to our right, so, after unloading Ky-Lin, I brushed aside the needles till I found some stones, then built a fire from pine cones and dead wood, before unpacking the cooking pot and going in search of the water.

The stream dropped into a series of little pools and, after filling the pot, I stripped off and stepped into the largest one, enjoying the shock of cold water, and scrubbed myself as best I could with my shirt and drawers, which I washed as well. Ky-Lin had followed me and drank deep, then stepped into the water and managed to surround himself with a fine cloud of spray, coming out as clean and fresh as ever.

I was about to don my clothes again, wet as they were, when he remarked: "The egg is ready to find another resting place: put it in your pouch for safety. Wrap it in a little moss."

I glanced down: it had certainly grown, and looked ready to pop out of my belly button any minute. I picked it up between finger and thumb expecting it to still give a little, but no. It was set hard and came away easily. I wrapped it in some dry moss, promising myself to make a proper purse for it as soon as I could. The pearly sheen had gone, and it now held a sort of stony sparkle, like granite in the sunshine.

A nose nudged my knee. "Where's the dinner then? Fire's goin' a treat, and all it wants is—"

"Clean diners," I said, picking him up and dropping him into the pool, leaving him scrabbling to get out and cursing me fluently.

Back at the fire, which I noticed had been replenished by a cowed Dickon, I put the pot on to boil, added dried vegetables, salt, herbs, dried fish and rice, and mixed some rice flour to make pancakes on a heated stone. A livid Growch came back in the midst of all this preparation and shook himself all over everything and everyone, so that the fire spat and sizzled and God knows what ended up in the cooking pot.

Dickon still cowered on the other side of the fire, a truly sorry sight, his clothes tattered and torn and covered with drying mud and slime, his face greenish under all the muck. I enjoyed my first words to him.

"You'd better go over to the stream and wash yourself. You stink! Wash your clothes out as well: you're not sitting down to eat like that. They'll soon dry out by the fire." Then, as he hesitated, glancing nervously at Ky-Lin, who was resting a little way away: "Go on; he won't bite you!"

"What . . . what is it?" he whispered.

" 'It' is a mythical creature called Ky-Lin. He and his brethren were guardians of the Lord Buddha. He is my friend."

His lip curled in a familiar sneer, obvious even through the layer of dirt on his face. "Oh, another of your only-talks-to-me creatures is he? Like the cur, the mad bear and the flying pig you once had—"

"Not at all!" I said sharply. "He understands you perfectly and talks as well as anyone. He's worth his weight in gold, and has been a perfect guide. If it hadn't been for him I could never have pulled you out of that morass, so mind your manners. Now, go wash!"

He told me later that the reason he had been able to find us was that someone from the seedy edge of town had seen us go, and he had persuaded a couple of horsemen to follow us as far as the Place of Power. But no further.

"I should have thought that by now you would have got the message," I said. "We don't need you; we can manage without your ceaseless suspicions and innuendos. The only reason you followed this time is because of your obsession with treasure, a treasure I have told you again and again doesn't exist. I am on a private pilgrimage to find a friend of mine and Growch has come along to keep me company."

"And—him?" He jerked his head in Ky-Lin's direction.

"I've told you that too. He is my guide and my friend, and I am his mission, if you like."

"Mission, suspicion . . . All a load of shit if you ask me. Anyway, who's this 'friend' you're looking for?"

"None of your business. And there is no place for you where I must go. I have a little money saved: I shan't need it where I am going, and I'm willing that you should have it if you will go back." I realized as soon as I opened my mouth that it was the wrong thing to say. By implying that I was unlikely to need money, it would only make him more convinced than ever that I was in expectation of finding more. I think my next remark made it worse, if possible. "I can give you ten gold pieces."

I still had the money Suleiman gave me, together with the coins my father had left me—but he wasn't having those.

I saw his eyebrows raise, but he was still staring into the fire, avoiding my eyes. The other two were already asleep, but I had stayed awake in order to have it out with him.

"If it is as you say," he said slowly, "then it matters little to either of us whether I go now or stay and see you safe. If I do the latter, then at least I can bear a message back to Matthew Spicer that I have left you safe and well. I can still be useful in fetching and carrying and I wouldn't feel I was doing my duty after all we've been through together if I didn't offer you my protection while I could."

Oh, very clever! I thought. Showing merely friendship and concern for my safety, but ensuring he kept his eye on me—and my money—right to the end. If I hadn't still had this indefinable feeling that only harm could come from his accompanying us, then I probably wouldn't have hesitated—but if I didn't know exactly what I was afraid of, how could I insist on leaving him behind?

"Very well," I said. "But I expect you to share all the chores and portage. And don't," I added, "grumble. Wherever you find yourself, or however tough it gets. I still think you're wasting your time."

"We'll see," he said, and by the next morning he was almost his usual cocky, arrogant self, just as if he had donned a new suit of clothes.

In fact more clothes were the first things we bought when we came across a decent-sized village. Our winter things had suffered badly in the bog, and besides the warmer weather was here and we needed thinner coverings. I bought us both loose cotton jackets and short breeches, reaching to the knees, and on Ky-Lin's recommendation, straw hats against the sun. I was going to buy sandals as well, but he advised me to keep my boots until we had crossed the desert.

As the villages we passed through were scattered, it didn't seem worthwhile Ky-Lin changing his shape or trying to hide, so we met a great deal of superstitious terror, but were better able to bargain: in many cases I believe they were only too glad to get rid of us!

As we worked our way through the foothills of the mountains towards our next objective, the Desert of Death, my spirits rose with each day that dawned, each mile we walked, each hour that passed. This was the last barrier to surmount, the last real test of our endurance. And with Ky-Lin to lead the way, what could possibly go wrong?

Suddenly, one day, there it was, stretching to the horizon as far as the eye could see. Even the mountains to the north seemed farther away than ever, misty blue in the haze that hung over the sand. There was no gradual approach; it seemed that one stepped off civilization into the wilderness like crossing a threshold. One pace and there you were.

We spent the night at the last village marked on the map, a tiny place squashed between two rearing crags, like a piece of stringy meat caught between two teeth. We were curiosities; very few travellers came their way, but even their awe at seeing Ky-Lin could not overcome their horror at the realization that we were intending to cross the desert.

At first Ky-Lin was reluctant to translate what they said, seated with us in the headman's hut that night, privileged guests, but I insisted, and he was honest enough to interpret literally.

Did we understand that it was called the Desert of Death?

Yes, we did.

Did we understand why it was called thus?

We thought so.

Did we know that no one returned from such a journey?

There was no call to, if they were travelling further on.

Then it was our turn to ask some questions.

Did the villagers ever venture out there?

Sometimes.

Why did they go?

To hunt desert foxes and hares.

Then there must be food for them, and water?

A shrug was the only answer.

How far did the hunters go into the desert?

Well provisioned they could last for a week, over a twenty-five-mile radius. After that there are no more animals to hunt.

What about other settlements?

Another shrug, then someone ventured that there were legends of a fabulous city, a great temple, but . . .

But what?

More shrugs. A long time ago, many lifetimes. No one came back to tell. Maybe it got lost under the Sand Mountains.

What are those?

Great hills of sand that march across the desert, eating everything they come across.

"Are you sure we're going in the right direction?" muttered Dickon.

"You can always turn around and go back," I whispered in return.

All the village turned out the next morning to see us off, and it didn't help one bit that they were burning incense, chanting prayers, and already looked at us as if we were ghosts.

"Don't worry too much," said Ky-Lin. "I assure you that out there, there is a huge temple and a thriving town: I've been there. It's situated on an underground river, but there is plenty of water. It was a while ago since I was there, but bricks and mortar and bronze and gold don't just disappear."

Comforted by his assurance we made our way to a line of scrub that, the villagers had informed us, marked the course of a now dried-up riverbed. Ky-Lin frowned a little as he gazed down at the river pebbles that lined the bottom.

"I remember a river running here. . . . Perhaps I was mistaken. Still it goes the way we want to, so let's follow it."

As the sun got higher in the sky the sweat started to trickle down my face, back and from under my arms. Five minutes later I saw Dickon drop behind and take a surreptitious swig from one of the water bottles he was carrying. He and I both carried four, and Ky-Lin another two, and these were meant to last us until we reached the temple: Ky-Lin's were for cooking and washing, ours for drinking. I was sorely tempted to copy him but decided to wait until Ky-Lin called a halt.

By my reckoning this must have been near noon, and we were now in a shimmering landscape, strewn with rocks under a baking sun. I blinked gritty eyes, but the shimmering persisted, like some curtain of gauze billowing out over a scene at best only guessed at.

"Right," said Ky-Lin. "Unload me, please, and then start digging."

I had wondered why we bought two mattocks some days past: now it seemed I was to find out.

"Digging?" Dickon and I queried in unison.

"Digging," said Ky-Lin firmly. "Every midmorning and every night you will dig a hole, or a trench, or whatever you prefer, to hide us from the worst heat of the day, and the extremes of cold at night. During the journey we will travel till noon, then rest until sunset. Then we shall march again till it gets too cold, and rest till dawn. That way we shall escape the worst extremes of temperature. First, a drink for everyone—only a mugful—and after the hole is dug we can eat."

Growch was so exhausted he just lay on his side, panting, his tongue flapping in and out like a snake tasting the air, so I served him first, letting him lap the lukewarm water from the cooking pot. He was so grateful that he showed us the best place to dig, and even helped for a while, the sand flying out between his hind legs far faster than we could dig. Once we had dug a reasonable trench we settled down in it and shared out the rice cakes, dried fruit, and cheese that was to be our midday meal from now on. At night we should have something cooked, and I would make enough rice cakes to eat cold at the next meal.

Propping a blanket across the trench, supported on the upended mattocks, I settled back to sleep for a while in sticky shade, but saw Dickon once again helping himself from one of his water skins, and was alarmed to see that he had almost finished one. Well, he'd get none of mine: I had to share with Growch.

I noticed that Ky-Lin had eaten but little and drank less; when the same thing happened that evening, I questioned him.

"I can manage for a few days; then I shall need rice, water, and salt in quantity."

"Salt? In this heat? It will only make you thirstier!"

"Not at all. Everyone needs salt, and you humans sweat it away in the hot sun. Without it you will become weak and dizzy, and your arms and legs will ache. That is why I insisted you bring salted meat with you: at least you will receive some that way."

We moved on again as the sun sank, a red ball, into the western sky, and kept the same routine day by night by day. It was very hard to reconcile the great extremes of temperature; at midday I would have given anything to be naked and blanketless, at night I could have welcomed two layers of everything. Once the shimmer of heat left the land at night, the stars were incredible; they seemed to be so much nearer, as if one could reach up and snatch them from the sky. It seemed some little compensation for the sting of sweat in one's eyes at midday, and the chattering of one's teeth twelve hours later.

Have you ever heard a dog's teeth chatter?

By the third day the mountains we had left had disappeared into haze, those we were moving towards seemed no nearer, those to the west invisible. The desert makes you feel very small: there is too much sky.

There is nothing to mark your progress, no trees or bushes or other landmarks, so you might just as well be standing still, or be an ant endlessly circling a huge bowl.

When I woke on the fourth morning and reached for the last of my water flasks, I found it was missing. I had been careful to follow Ky-Lin's instructions; it would be on the fifth day that we would reach the temple, and the water must last that long. There was a full day to go, and there wasn't a drop left! Frantically I shook the other skins: all empty. I couldn't have dropped the full one, surely! No, I remembered clearly the night before shaking it to make sure none had evaporated.

Springing to my feet I was just in time to see Dickon emptying the last of the water down his throat and sprinkling a few drops over his head and face. He started guiltily as he saw me.

"Sorry! I was just so thirsty. . . . Anyway, it's not far now. We can manage for a day. . . ."

I struck him hard across the mouth. "You selfish bastard! You had four skins all to yourself, and Growch and I had to share! I wish you had never come, I wish you were dead!"

"Hush, child!" said Ky-Lin. "Bring Dog over to me and close your eyes. I will give you some of myself. . . ." and he breathed gently down his nostrils onto our faces. "There! You will not feel thirsty for a while."

And it was true. Both Growch and I managed that day without needing water; somehow Ky-Lin had transferred liquid, precious water from his body to ours: I only hoped that it would not hurt him. Magic only goes so far.

That day we travelled faster and further than any day before, and the following morning Ky-Lin woke us early.

"By midday we should be there," said Ky-Lin encouragingly. "Just over that little ridge ahead and you will see the temple. And then water, food, rest, shelter . . ."

The struggle up that ridge was a nightmare. The sweat near blinded me, I ached, my limbs wouldn't obey me, my throat hurt, I was too dry to swallow. At last we topped the incline and, full of anticipation, gazed down on Ky-Lin's fabled city.

Only it wasn't there.

Nothing, except a heap of tumbled stones.

20

I gazed around wildly, thinking for one stupid moment that we were in the wrong place, but one look at Ky-Lin's stricken face told me the truth.

It was Dickon who voiced all our thoughts.

"Well, where is it then? Where's your town, temple, water, food, shelter, and rest?"

I had never seen Ky-Lin look so dejected. For an eye-deceiving moment he lost all color and almost appeared transparent, his beautiful plumed tail dragging in the dust. But even as I blinked he regained his color, and his tail its optimism. The only sign of disquiet was a furrowing of his silky brow.

"Well?" Dickon was panicking, his voice hysterical. "What do we do now?"

"What happened, Ky-Lin? There was something here once. . . ."

He turned to me. "I don't know. I wish I did. I told you it was a long time since I was here. Let's go down and see. There must be something we can salvage from all this."

At my feet Growch was whimpering. "Sod me if I can go no further. Me bleedin' paws hurt, me legs is sawn off, me stummick tells me me throat's cut and I could murder a straight bowl of water. . . ."

I picked him up, though my body told me I ached as much and was twice as thirsty, and we all stumbled like drunkards down the slope to the first of the tumbled wrecks of stones. When we reached them we found they were not stones but mud bricks, and as I looked around I could see this was the remains of what had once been a street of shops or small dwelling places, and as they fell they had crumbled and broken.

Ky-Lin prowled down the street, looking here, there, everywhere.

"No sign of war or pestilence. This place has been empty for many, many years, but it looks as if they went peaceably. Everything has been cleared away, no artifacts left about, no evidence of fire. . . . Let's take a look at the temple, or what's left of it."

Not much. We threaded our way through other deserted, tumble-down streets until we reached what must have been a courtyard. It surrounded a partly stone-walled temple, with now-roofless cells behind, which would have housed the monks. Sand had drifted deep on the temple floor, the roof had fallen in and the stone altar was empty. No idols, no incense, no prayer wheels, no bells. Only the wind, shush-shushing the sand back and forth across the stone floor in little patterns. On either side of the altar were a couple of stone lumps, now so eroded by sand, sun and wind that they were unrecognizable.

Unrecognizable to all but Ky-Lin, that was.

"Here, girl: come see what is left of my brothers. . . ."

Nearer I could see what must have once been their heads, their tails.

"Were they Ky-Lins too?"

He nuzzled the stones lovingly. "Once. But these two attained Paradise a long time ago, and the monks carved them to remind them of my Master's visit." He sighed. "At least it shows one thing, all this: the soul outlasts the strongest stone."

"How about getting your priorities right?" came Dickon's voice over my shoulder. "Souls belong to the dead: we're living. But we won't be much longer unless you find us something to eat and drink."

Without cooking I had a couple of rice cakes, some dried fruit, a little cheese.

"If you will unload me please," said Ky-Lin, "you will find one small water skin under the blankets. One mug of water each, no more; the rice cakes and cheese will be enough for now."

Strange: I had never noticed that particular water skin before, but then he was Magic. . . .

I shared my cheese and water with Growch, and although his share of the liquid was gone in half a dozen quick laps, I sipped mine as slowly as I could, running it over my parched tongue before swallowing, to get the maximum benefit; behind me I heard Dickon's water gone in a couple of quick gulps. I went over to Ky-Lin with some dried raisins and apricots.

"Come, you must eat something too; we depend on you to keep us going."

His forked tongue, ever so soft, lapped the fruit from my palm.

"Now get some rest. Go into the shade of that wall. I am going to reconnoiter. I shall return as soon as I can."

I settled back with my back against the stone. Just five minutes' nap, and then . . .

And then it was dawn. Someone had tucked a blanket round Growch and me, and further away Dickon was snoring softly. I was neither hot nor cold, hungry nor thirsty, and I felt rested and refreshed. Beside me was a heap of wood, smooth, bleached wood that had obviously been around for a while. Beyond, Ky-Lin was curled around, fast asleep, only the rise and fall of his chest showing that he was still alive.

A surprisingly wet and cold nose was shoved in my face. "What's for breakfast, then?"

I used half the water that was left to boil up rice, beans, dried vegetables and herbs, on Ky-Lin's advice adding the rest of the salted meat, and some rather desiccated roots he had found. They smelt oniony, and looked like water lily suckers. The wood burned brightly and too fast, with a sort of bluish flame, and I kept it down as much as I could, for now the sun was high and extra heat was unwelcome. Just before it was cooked I took the pot off the fire and clamped on the lid tight, then buried it in the sand so it would retain heat and absorb the last of the liquid, as I had seen it done in this country to ensure both tenderness and conservation of fuel.

"And now," said Ky-Lin, "we must find somewhere to shelter. I can smell wind, and that here will mean a sandstorm." He led us through the remains of a small archway to the left of the altar. Behind was part of a wall and domed roof, and a set of steps leading down into the darkness. There was remarkably little of the ubiquitous drifted sand.

"The way the wind blows here," explained Ky-Lin, "the sand merely piles up on the other side of the wall. Now, we shall go down the steps to better shelter. Once at the bottom, if we spread out the blankets, we shall be snug enough."

Something scuttled past my feet and I gave a stifled scream.

"Scorpion," said Dickon. "I'm not going down there, and that's flat!"

He kicked out at the creature, who raised its stinging tail threateningly and disappeared through a crack in the wall.

"The ultimate survivors," said Ky-Lin. "When everything else has disappeared from the earth, the ants, the scorpions, and the cockroaches will have it all to themselves. Don't worry," he added. "There are no more down there. Follow me," and he disappeared down the flight of stone steps.

"You're on your own," said Dickon, as I prepared to follow. "I'm not going down."

I fumbled my way down steps worn smooth by generations of monks. Once at the bottom the air was pleasantly cool, with only a fine layer of sand underfoot. The light from above was enough for me to see that this was a little cul-de-sac, but large enough to hold us all comfortably.

"Come on down!"

"Not on your life," came Dickon's voice, oddly distorted by the turn in the stairs, although Growch had already joined me quite happily.

"In that case," I yelled back, "you can go out and fetch in all the baggage. And the cooking pot," I added.

I knew he wouldn't, and it took the three of us to transfer everything to safety, Dickon grumbling all the while. By the time all was stowed away safely the wind had risen enough for us to hear even at the bottom of the stairs, and when I went out to retrieve the cooking pot it was really nasty up top. The wind was whining like a caged dog, gusting every now and again into a shriek, and with it the sand was spiralling as tall as a man, blasting into any unprotected skin like the rasp of a file. The very heaps of sand in the courtyard had changed position so much that it took me several minutes to locate where I had buried the cooking pot; it was still hot, and I had to take off my shirt and wrap it in that to carry it safely, the driving sand stinging my bare skin unmercifully.

I served out half the contents of the pot; a bowl each, my meat ration for Growch, and half a mug of water, and as I scoured out the bowls with the ubiquitous sand I wondered which of us was still the hungriest and thirstiest. Settling down on my blanket, I asked the questions that would probably mean the difference between life and death to us. Somebody had to ask; I didn't want to, but it was obvious Dickon wanted to hear the answers even less than I did.

"What did you find out, Ky-Lin?"

"I searched the whole of the ruins while you were asleep. I gave you all a little Sleepy Dust to ensure you slept for a day and a half—" He raised his left front hoof as we protested. "Yes, yes, I know; but you needed the rest, and I wanted time without your worries burdening me. I needed to let my senses roam free.

"This place was abandoned some eighty years ago. What drove them out was probably the threat of famine. From what I could determine, the wells on which the town depended for its water started to dry up, due to the river deep beneath the desert floor changing course. There may still have been enough for drinking, but certainly not enough for irrigating their crops.

"Added to this, there was the unprecedented advance of the Sand Mountains, a phenomenon peculiar to this desert. The villagers mentioned them, remember? They are formed by a combination of wind and sand, and move to any place they are driven. They may not be seen for a hundred years, but given special conditions they can build up within days, and overwhelm anything in their path. Such a disaster overtook this town. They had enough notice to move out in an orderly fashion, so everything portable was taken with them. The monks were the last to leave."

"And where are the Sand Mountains now?"

He shrugged. "Who knows? They were not here long, but time enough to destroy the fabric of the buildings, as you saw."

"Where did the people go?"

He shrugged again. "Probably west and north. The way we go. . . ."

Here it was, the question I had so been dreading. "Any—any sign of water?"

He looked at me with compassion, then shook his head. "No, I found no trace of water. Not yet, anyway. That doesn't mean there isn't any."

Dickon leapt to his feet. "No water, no food—what the hell do we do now?"

"We would do well to pray. Now, together. Each to our own God or gods." He bowed his head. "In any case it will concentrate our minds if we are quiet for a few minutes. Prayer always helps. Focus on our predicament and ask for guidance. . . ."

I wanted to pray as my mother had taught me: speak to God direct, she had always said. But she had sent me to the priest to learn my letters and the Catechism, and it was these familiar formulas, as comforting as a child's rhymes, that I now found filled my mind; the priest had taught me that God could only be approached through His intermediaries, those like Himself. My mother, on the other hand, had never been afraid to speak her mind, and she told me God was there to be talked to, just like anyone else, person to person.

I don't know whether she believed in Him; I think she only believed in herself. I recited three rapid Ave's under my breath, not thinking of anything really, except the comfort of the formula. I glanced at the others; Ky-Lin was obviously in communication with his Lord, but Dickon's hands were twisting as if he was wringing out a cloth, his eyelids flickering. No point in looking at Growch; his god, Pan, was a heathen.

But it was Growch who saved us.

I was in the middle of my third Paternoster when a sacrilegious interruption destroyed all thought of prayer.

"Bloody 'ell! Effin' little bastards!"

"Growch!"

"Sor*ree*! But what d'you say if'n you'd just been bit on yer privates by a bunch o' ravenin' ants?"

"Ants? But—"

Ky-Lin and I had the same thought at the same time. Ants in a town deserted for many years and surrounded by an arid desert could mean only one thing: ants, to exist, need both food and water, however minimal. So, somewhere there was water!

"Move, dog!" said Ky-Lin. "Slowly and carefully. The lantern, girl!"

At first the flames flickered wildly all over the stone floor because my hand was shaking so much, but as it steadied we all saw what had so rudely interrupted whatever Growch had been thinking about. A double line of ants, both coming and going, the ones advancing towards us laden with what looked like grains, the others empty-legged. I swung the lantern to the left; the laden ants were disappearing into a large crack in the masonry, obviously behind which they had their nest. The outgoing ones, where did they go?

I swung the light the other way, but obviously too far: no ants.

"Gently goes it," breathed Ky-Lin. "Back a little . . ."

And there it was. There was a long, straight crack in the floor, and down this the ants were appearing and disappearing without hindrance. I brushed away some of the sand, and there was another crack in the stone, this one at right angles to the first. Ky-Lin used his tail on the sand as well, and between us we uncovered a full square, some two and a half feet along each side. It was obviously an entrance of some sort to an underground storage area, but how did it work? I scraped away at the center: nothing! I blew at the sand, I scrabbled with my fingers, still nothing.

Ky-Lin's delicate antennae were probing the surface. "Try here," he said, indicating the corner farthest away. I brushed away the sand and there, recessed into the stone, was a rusty iron ring.

"That's it! That's it!" I was now in a fever of excitement. "There must be something down there, there must!" and bending down I tugged at the ring, but all I got was red, flaky dust on my fingers; the square had not budged.

Dickon had finally worked out what all the fuss was about, and exercised all his strength, again to no purpose except for rusty fingers.

"Let's try this scientifically," said Ky-Lin. "Neither of you is powerful enough to shift the trapdoor on your own and I cannot get a grip. Think my children; how can we raise it?"

I knew he had something in mind, but Dickon and I could only gaze at each other in perplexity. It was Growch, puffed up with his success in finding the stone trapdoor, who provided us with the simple answer.

"Well, you are a coupla dummies! Rope, that's what you want: rope."

Of course! And while the increasing wind raged outside and the sand trickled its way in little drifts down the steps, we found the rope in the baggage, looped it through the ring in the floor and, one end tied round Ky-Lin's neck, the other held by Dickon and myself, we tried once more to heave the square of stone from its bed.

"One, two, three, heave! One, two, three, heave!" We heaved, we pulled, we jerked, we struggled, but the damned thing wouldn't shift. We tried again and again, and finally there was a faint grating noise and it seemed the trapdoor shifted just a fraction.

"We've got it!" yelled Dickon. "Just one more heave. All together now—heave!"

Another minuscule shift in the stone, then it settled back into its square with a little puff of dust. The ants had disappeared, not surprisingly.

"Once more," exhorted Dickon. "Pull up and back this time. Now!"

We heaved as hard as we could, there was a sudden snap and we all three landed in a tangled bruised heap in the corner, the rope coiling itself round our legs. I pulled the length through my fingers, conscious of a bruised shoulder. "But it hasn't broken. . . ."

"No," said Ky-Lin. "It was the ring that snapped; it had rusted right through."

I burst into tears: I couldn't help it. "It's not fair! I'm so thirsty. . . ."

Ky-Lin nuzzled my neck comfortingly. "Courage. We haven't lost yet." He inspected the broken ring. "It was weak at this one point. Perhaps it could be repaired. Remember the bars in your prison, girl? Well this time we shall have to try the process in reverse. Give me some space; I shall have to think about this."

Obediently we moved back, and one look at Dickon's stricken face told me what I must be looking like too. True, we didn't know what we would find down there, but hope had been rekindled, only to be dashed again by a few flakes of rust. I had never felt so thirsty in all my life,

not even as a child in a high fever when I had cried and begged my
mother for the cool spring water she had trickled down my throat from
a wet cloth.

"Shut your eyes, children, you too, dog!"

Suddenly I felt the hair curl on my head, and even behind closed
eyelids I was near blinded by a brilliant light. There was a smell of
ozone, of snow, of wet iron. I opened my eyes to see Ky-Lin momentarily
surrounded by a haze of colorless flame. I shut my eyes again, and when
I opened them the ring was whole again, though considerably smaller.

I stretched forward to touch it, but Ky-Lin stopped me. "Not yet;
it is not yet cool enough. . . ." He looked tired, diminished.

I put my arms about his neck. "Rest awhile; we can wait."

But it seemed an age before the ring cooled enough to try; up above
it was full dark, and the wind still howled.

At last Ky-Lin nodded his head. "This time just keep pulling: no
sudden jerks."

Once more I looped the rope around his neck, once more Dickon
and I took up the slack at the other end. This was it.

"Now," said Ky-Lin softly. "Pull as hard as you can—and pray. . . ."

21

This time I didn't pray; I swore.

It made me feel better as I once more took the strain of the rope, endured the aches in my shoulders and arms, the rasp in my throat, the grit between my teeth—oh yes, I really enjoyed that swear, and I used all the bad words I had ever heard, whether I knew their meaning or not, and included the sort of things one sees written on walls. In fact I was concentrating so hard on remembering all the words, with my eyes shut, that I didn't see the stone begin to shift.

The first I knew was Dickon's mutter: "It's coming, it's coming. . . ."

There was a sudden slither, a grinding of stone against sand, and the rope burnt through my fingers. I collided once again with the other two, but this time it didn't hurt, and I found I was staring down at a black hole in the floor, revealing a triangular gap and the glimpse of more stone steps leading downward.

With the opening came a sudden breath of stale air, thick with the stink of rancid oil, dust, decaying meal—

"I can smell water," said Growch. "There's some down there somewheres. Faint, but it's there. Shall we go?"

A gap that would admit a dog wasn't large enough for two adults and a pony-sized mythical creature, so we had to push the stone trapdoor right away to one side before we could descend, Ky-Lin in the lead and Dickon and I with the two lanterns. Growch in his eagerness near tripped me up. I sat down hurriedly on one of the steps, noticing that even here the sand had penetrated, the only clear spaces being the lines where the ants had trailed up and back over the years. I had a sudden idea, which got shoved to the back of my mind immediately I reached the chamber.

It was a huge cellar in which we found ourselves, the stone roof supported by a row of pillars marching away into dark corners our lanterns didn't reach. The floor was flagged, and on either side stone shelves lined the walls. Empty shelves, no sign of containers to hold the water Growch still insisted he could smell. Slowly we walked the full length of the cellar, the lantern light sending our shadows into black giants that climbed startled pillars, crept along stone walls, trailed our footsteps like devoted pets.

To the left and right of us there were only empty shelves, dust and ancient cobwebs like dirty, disintegrating lace. The atmosphere was dry and choking and I sneezed involuntarily, expecting the noise to echo and reverberate, but the cellar had a peculiar deadening effect and the sneeze seemed to die at my feet. It was like being stuck behind the heavy curtains of a four-poster.

We reached the far end and there, ranged against the walls, were several tall clay pots, seemingly sealed with wax stoppers. My heart gave a bound of anticipation and I rushed forward, lantern bobbing wildly, my knife cutting hastily through the seals. I stepped backward, covering my nostrils as a dreadful stench seeped out.

"It's fermenting grain," said Ky-Lin. "Not fit to touch. Except for the ants," he added. "This is what has kept them going over the years. With luck it will last for many years more. They are sensible creatures and will not overbreed, so perhaps—"

"But where is the water?" shouted Dickon, coughing and choking, all control gone. "Don't you realize, you stupid creature, that we will die without it? Who cares about bloody ants? Fuck the ants!"

"I care about them," said Ky-Lin severely. "And so should you. I care for all living creatures, and if you would just realize that those little creatures can point the way to your salvation—"

"Fuck salvation!" yelled Dickon. "And fuck you too!" and flung his lantern full into Ky-Lin's face.

There was a burst of colored light—red, green, purple, orange, blue, yellow—then nothing.

Darkness. Even my lantern had gone out.

A brief moment of panic, angry sobs from Dickon, then a comforting nudge at my ankle.

"You stay 'ere, nice an' quiet, an' I'll nip up top an' get your lightin' things. Don' move now," and Growch's claws click-clacked away over the stone floor. A faint light came from the opening above, and I saw him disappear over the last step. A moment or two later he was back, and thrust the box into my free hand with his muzzle.

"Nice bit o' light, an' things'll look different . . ."

My hands were shaking so much it took two or three goes before I could light my lantern. I swung it over my head and saw Dickon, his face all blubbery with angry tears, the other lantern shattered at his feet.

"I didn't mean to hurt him," he whined. "It wasn't my fault! He shouldn't have riled me! Where's he gone, anyway?"

Where indeed? I rushed from one end of the cellar to the other, my lantern swinging wildly, but there was no sign of Ky-Lin. Perhaps he had gone up the steps?

Growch shook his head. " 'E's not up there. 'E ain't nowhere as I can see. Can't smell 'im neither."

I stumbled and fell to my knees, the lantern nearly slipping from my fingers. I had fallen over something, a stone, a pebble—

No, not a stone, not a pebble. A tiny little image, looking as old as the stone from which it had been fashioned. Tears stung my eyes as I recognized the pudgy little features, the plumed tail.

"He's here," I said. "What's left of him."

The stone was cold in my hand. There was no life here, no flicker of movement. Just the small shell of what had been a vibrant, loving, colorful creature. Even my ring was cold and dead, like Ky-Lin.

I felt anger rising in me inescapably, like the sudden jet of blue flame from a burning, sappy log. I thrust the stone figure under Dickon's nose.

"You killed him! You destroyed him with your evil temper! I hate you! I hate you! I *hate* you!" I sobbed, and swung my lantern at his head as he ducked.

"Steady on there," said Growch mildly. " 'E wouldn't 'ave wanted no 'istrionics. What's done is done. Nuffin's ever truly lost. 'E may be just a bit of stone in yer 'and right now, but what 'e was is still 'ere. What 'e taught you. Well then, try and think like 'e would 'ave wanted you to. Pretend 'e's still 'ere. If you concentrate 'ard enough it'll be like 'e's still speakin' to us."

I could feel my ring warming up again; looking down it had a pearly glow. Growch was right, wherever his doggy wisdom had suddenly come from. My anger evaporated. I kissed the little stone figure and tucked it in my pouch, promising it a better resting place when I found one.

What would he have done now? I shut my eyes and concentrated. Looked for water, of course. Just before we came down here, when I was sitting on the step, I had had an idea, a good one, I was sure. But what was it? Something to do with . . . Stone? Tracks? Ants? Yes, that was it. But how could it help? Think, girl, think! Ants, sand-covered stone, tracks, Ky-Lin saying they had to have water—that was it!

Rushing back to the steps I held the lantern high, searching for ant trails, but our comings and goings had made a complete mess of anything I was looking for, and the ants themselves were milling around in aimless circles. Half-shuttering the lantern, I settled down to wait.

"What the hell are you doing?" asked Dickon irritably. "We're wasting time. We should be searching for water."

"I am."

"What? Sitting on your arse?"

"Just shut up, keep still, and be patient."

"I know, I know, I know!" said Growch triumphantly. "Clever lady."

Which left Dickon in the dark, especially as he couldn't understand Growch, but seeing us both concentrating he lapsed into silence. The ants settled down and began their marching from the nest above. Down the steps in a double line, then—yes, my theory was correct. The line split into two, one set of ants going off to the darkness at the rear end for food, the other half turning left, and—

"Under the steps!" I called out. "We never looked there!"

Behind the steps was a man-sized space and three shallow steps leading down to a small cistern and—a thousand candles to Saint Whoever when I could afford them!—it was still a third full.

The water was clear, but littered with unwary ant bodies and with a layer of silt beneath, but nothing had ever tasted so good. We scooped it with our mugs into the cooking pot, then all of us drank till we were full and I for one felt slightly sick.

Growch rolled over with a grunt and a distended belly. "Near as good as a beef bone . . ."

A drink seemed to bring Dickon back to sense once more and cooled his temper for days to come. "We mustn't stir up the water too much," he said. "We need to fill the water skins with clean."

Looking at the cistern more carefully, wondering how the water hadn't dried up long since, I noticed a darker patch at the back which felt damp to the touch, so there was obviously seepage from some long-forgotten spring or rivulet behind. Not enough to keep the temple in water, just enough for the ants—and us. Praise be!

By now it was full dark above and the wind still whined and shrieked unabated, so we moved everything down into the cellar and I used what fuel we had left to cook up enough rice to keep us going that night and the following morning.

We fell asleep over the meal, but I had had sense enough to remove everything eatable from the ants though, remembering Ky-Lin, I sprinkled a few grains on the floor near their trail. Ky-Lin would have done the same if he had been with us, of that I was sure, making some gentle remark about it being a "change of diet" for the insects. Anyway, they deserved it: they had shown the way to the water.

The following morning the wind was gone as though it had never been and the sun shone brilliantly from a clear sky. We all wanted to get going as soon as possible, but now there was no Ky-Lin to help with advice and porterage, we were faced with real problems. The mythical creature had told us that the temple was "halfway," which meant there were at least five more days of travel to endure. He had consulted the maps and shown me the route we should follow, and with my Waystone I thought I could manage that. Burdened as we were, though, we should probably have to expect at least one more day's travel, bringing it to six, which would be over the limit for even the stretching of what food we had.

Well, we could go hungry, but not thirsty. I spread out everything from our baggage, hoping we could leave at least half behind to lighten our load, while Dickon carefully filled the ten water skins. I knew how heavy these were from bitter experience, but they were essential. But what to leave behind? The remaining food, blankets against the cold, and mattocks, these must come as well. Money in a belt around my waist, personal possessions (and the egg) in a pouch at my neck. Cooking pot, spoons and mugs (I had dismissed the idea of boiling everything up before we went: in the desert heat it would be uneatable in twenty-four hours); honey and salt were heavy to carry, but both were necessary. Likewise my few packs of herbs, the maps, sewing kit and oil: all had their uses.

In the end all we could reasonably do without was everything we were not actually wearing, the broken lantern, one blanket out of three, my writing things and my journal. This last went with me, I was determined on that; at worst if our skeletons were found in the desert, it would explain everything. I hefted the bundle we could leave: I could lift it on one finger. Well, two. So that wasn't going to make much difference.

"Dickon," I called out. "We'll never carry all this!"

He emerged with the last two water skins. "I've been thinking about that. The water is covered with a small grid the monks must have stood on to bucket up the water, and if you recall, there was a metal cover lying to one side. We could use both as sledges; why carry if you can pull? Both are metal, so they shouldn't wear away. The grid is no problem, and the metal cover has holes where it fitted over the cistern, so if we cut the rope in half you can pull the grid as it's smaller, and I'll take the cover. Right?"

So it was decided. We then ate, packed up and waited for the worst of the day's heat to dissipate, deciding to keep to Ky-Lin's order of march: early evening and dawn. While we were waiting I soaked some beans and dried vegetables for the following day, ready to cook. Fuel was going to be a problem, but I persuaded Growch to pick up everything we could burn during the march. Before we left we drank as much as we could take from the cistern, and I even took the luxury of a quick wash, soaking my clothes as well for a cool start to the trek. The water was all cloudy by the time I had finished, but it would soon settle back for the ants and I left them a few more grains and a dollop of honey as compensation.

We left the trapdoor open, in case other travellers came that way, and I took a soft stone and drew the universally recognized symbol of an arrow on the cellar floor to indicate the position of the cistern.

And so we left the temple to the ants and set off across the desert towards the dying sun.

At first our progress was slow but steady. The management of the improvised sledges was difficult to master. The metal cover travelled easier, but was more unstable. As we travelled the sledges became lighter each day, and now we took turns with each. The weather stayed clear, my directions appeared to be correct, for each day we persuaded ourselves the mountains we were headed for came fractionally nearer.

Then on the fourth day we ran into trouble.

The night had been overcast, for once, and we had overslept after a hard day's trek the previous day. When we awoke the eastern sky was bright and we cast long shadows ahead of us. We ate a hurried breakfast—not as much as any of us wanted, but rations were short by now—and set off at a good pace for a steep rise just ahead. We hauled the sledges up the rise, looking forward to the incline beyond and—

"What the hell . . . !" If he hadn't said it, I would. Ahead of us, about a mile distant, reared a sudden and unexpected range of mountains.

Sand Mountains.

These were the ones Ky-Lin and the villagers had warned us about, the giants who could stay in one place for years and then, given the right conditions, move across the desert floor at a terrifying speed, destroying everything in their path. And here they were, straight across our path, barring our way to the mountains. At the moment they were quiet, a range of sandhills some fifty to a hundred feet high at their lowest. And they stretched for miles. As we moved close an errant wind agitated sand on the tops into whirls and curls like smoke, and every now and again miniavalanches of sand fell down the steeper slopes.

For the rest of the morning we tried to climb those restless, shifting mountains, but for every stride up, we tumbled back two. The sledges became bogged down in the sand and we sank to our knees in it, like falling into quicksand, and twice we nearly lost Growch. Eventually we tried to find a way between, but the sand blew in our faces and filled our footsteps within seconds.

There was only one thing for it: we should have to take the long trek round them; the worst of that was we had no idea whether the way east or west was shorter, as they stretched as far as the eye could see in both directions.

Three days later we struggled round the western end and tried to pick up our bearings. We had wasted three days to find ourselves in virtually the same spot we had started out from and the real mountains seemed as far away as ever. On we tramped, our travelling time curtailed by our increasing weariness from lack of proper nourishment. Two days later the last of our food and water was gone and we piled all our goods onto the smoother sledge, pulling it in tandem to conserve our strength.

I began to see things that weren't there—houses, lakes, trees, camels, people—shimmering in the distance some feet above the desert floor, and beside me Dickon was hallucinating too. On the tenth day we put Growch on the sledge because he could move no further and lay there with his tongue hanging out like one dead.

Dickon and I now fell every dozen yards or so and our throats were so parched we couldn't even curse each other. At last we both tripped and fell together and I just wanted to lie there forever and forget everything. I was conscious it was high noon already and I knew if we didn't get up and seek shelter we should surely be dead before nightfall.

I rose to my knees and peered ahead, but all I could see was one of those fevered images again: a train of camels seeming to stride six feet above the sand and some half mile away. I collapsed, without even the energy to rouse Dickon, to offer a last prayer, and drifted off into unconsciousness.

But somewhere, somehow, I could swear I heard a dog barking. . . .

22

. . . a dog barking. Cautiously I opened my eyes. Normally in the desert Dickon and I slept within feet of each other, but now all my hands encountered was a blanket. There was a dim light over to my right, it must be the moon. No stars. And where was Growch? I was sure I had heard him a moment ago. I struggled to sit up, and there was a cold, wet nose against my cheek.

" 'Ad a nice kip, then? Thought we'd lost you at one stage. Feel a bit better?"

"I don't understand. . . . What's happened? I—" And then, suddenly, it all came back to me. The desert, the vast, terrible, unforgiving desert. Sun, heat, thirst, hunger, hallucinations, death already rattling in my throat, the last thing a dog barking . . .

I sat up slowly, stretched, wiggled my fingers and toes. I seemed to be all in one piece, but I was dreadfully stiff, my throat was sore and my head ached.

"Wanna drink? On yer right. On the table. That's it. Careful now, don' spill it."

Blessed, beautiful, clear cold water. The most wonderful liquid in the world. I drank it all, then burped luxuriously. I looked around me. I was obviously inside a house or hut, and the light I had thought the moon was a saucer oil lamp. I was on a pallet of sorts and it must be sometime at night. So, we had been rescued, but how and when? Where were we? And where was Dickon?

More than one question at a time flummoxed Growch. "I'll tell yer, I'll tell yer, but one at a time! Dickon? 'Is lordship is around and about in the town somewheres, and—"

"Which town? What's it called? Where is it?"

" 'Ow the 'ell does I know? A town's a town, ain't it? Same as all towns. 'Ouses, streets, people, dogs, food . . . We're still in the desert, but they got plenty o' water. Goats, chickens, camels. It was their camels as brought us in. I barked till I was 'oarse, managed to get over to the caravan, and they came back and picked you up."

"Oh, Growch! You saved our lives!" and I hugged him till he swore he couldn't breathe and why did I have to be so soppy? All the while his tail was wagging like mad, so I knew he was secretly as pleased as could be.

"An' afore you ask, all yer belongings is snug as well."

I felt for my money belt and neck pouch: all safe.

"Short and long of it is, they brought us in—gave you camel's milk out there, they did, an' you sicked it all up—" I was not surprised: the very thought of camel's milk made me ill again. "—then they gave you water an' things an' brought us 'ere. Got two rooms, an' I kep' 'is lordship away from all what is ours."

I stretched again, felt my headache lessening. "What time is it?"

"Middle evenin'. Sun down, moon not yet up."

"I must have been asleep for—nine or ten hours, then?"

"An' the rest! Four days ago it was when they brought us in. There's a woman been feedin' you slops an' things with a spoon."

"Four days!" I swung my legs over the edge of the bed, tried to stand up and fell back again. "By our Lady! I feel so weak!"

"Not surprised. Slops never did no one no good. Yer wants some good red meat inside of yer, like what I have." He smacked his chops. "Nuffin' like it. Treated me real well they 'as. Called me a 'ero . . ."

"And so you are," I said, giving him another hug. "Be a dear and go and find Dickon for me?"

Two days later I was up and about again, with an urge to get going as soon as we could. It was now well past Middle Year, we had been travelling for over fifteen months, and now I had recovered from my ordeal I felt a renewal of hope and energy. But it seemed we should have to wait a little longer. The nearest town, at the foothills of the mountains we were seeking, was a good four-day journey away by camel train—the same one that had rescued us—and they were not due to leave for another two and a half weeks, and strongly advised us not to try it on our own.

They were a hospitable people, and their town was clean and prosperous. Everywhere we went we were greeted with bows and smiles and clapping of hands, and though we couldn't speak a word of their language, we managed very well with sign language and the occasional drawing. As they existed solely on the barter system, our money meant nothing to them, and they insisted on treating us as honored guests. Which was lucky, seeing we had nothing to barter with.

Under the town was a river system that kept their cisterns full, with enough also for their crops of fruit and vegetables and the watering of their stock: goats, chickens, ducks, camels. They even kept ponds stocked with fish that looked rather like carp. The only goods they needed from outside were rice, clay for pots, and cotton cloth, and these they traded for with their own produce, which included pickled eggs, a special spiced pancake and other delicacies, desert fox furs, and exquisite carvings fashioned from the soft stone they found roundabouts. Once a month they journeyed to do their bargaining, and we agreed to await the next caravan.

There was plenty for us to do, however—for me at least, that is. Our clothes, what was left of them, were a disgrace, and I had spent four or five days doing the best I could with my sewing kit, when we had an unexpected bonus. Growch, investigating a tempting little bitch—what else?—had chased her into a store where cotton cloth awaited making up into the loose clothes the inhabitants preferred, and had been diverted by finding a huge nest of rats. He had set about them in true Growch fashion, and the grateful owner of the store had come to me, counting out at least twenty on his fingers, bearing also a roll of cloth sufficient to clothe both Dickon and myself.

Only when all my tasks were done, which included tedious things like washing blankets and mending panniers, did I keep a promise I had made to myself some weeks past. We had found out that the monks who had fled the destruction of the temple in the desert had found this town in time for survival, and had built a small temple to give thanks for their deliverance. This temple was now in the custody of one of the original monks, then a boy, now a blind old man of near a hundred. One of the village boys was his apprentice, and led him about the village with their begging bowls—always full—and assisted in leading the prayers.

One evening, when I knew the old monk and his acolyte would be dining, the sun tipping over the rim of the world had led to the lighting of the dried camel-dung fires for cooking and the last of the workers and herd's boys came tramping home, I made my way down the deserted streets towards the temple, the sad stone remnant of what had been Ky-Lin clutched in my hands.

It was only a small edifice, this temple, built from desert stone and mud bricks, but inside the floor was flagged, the air smelt of incense and oil saucers burned in front of the stone altar. Someone had left a garland of wildflowers by the crossed knees of the little smiling Buddha.

I had thought I would feel like an interloper, not knowing the language either, but it felt entirely natural to stand in front of the idol and speak in my own tongue.

I looked up at the statue, who stared above my head the while with empty, slanted eyes and an eternal smile, then I knelt down, as I would in one of my own churches, shut my eyes, and folded my hands around the remains of Ky-Lin.

"Please forgive me for not knowing your customs and language, Sir, but I have a special request. In my hands are the remains of a true friend, counsellor and guide, whom You lent to us to help us on our journey. He no longer has life, as You can see, but his death was a tragic accident, and he would have been the first to forgive.

"He was one of Yours, a Ky-Lin, who was left on earth to work off some trifling sins he had committed. Well *I* thought they were trifling. . . . Whatever they were, I assure You they must have been more than cancelled out by his care of us. So, will You please take him back? He spoke of a place where all was perfect and at peace: we would call it Heaven. Please allow him in Yours. Amen. Oh, and thanks for lending him to us. Amen again."

The Buddha had one gilded hand on his knee; the other was cupped on his chest. Reaching up as far as I could, I kissed the tiny stone that had been Ky-Lin and placed him gently in the cupped hand.

There: it was done. Ky-Lin could rest in peace.

I rose to my feet, bowed to the Buddha and backed out of the little temple. The idol seemed to be smiling more broadly than ever.

I had never ridden a camel before. It was extremely difficult to adjust to the rocking, swaying movement so far above the ground, and there was more than one moment when I definitely felt camel-sick. However, even the lap-held Growch agreed that it was better than walking, and in four days we were in a village in the foothills of the mountains where we said good-bye to our kind hosts, replenished our stores and set off in a direction of north by west.

At first we had an easy time of it; the tracks we followed led to other villages and small towns, where our money was accepted. We travelled easily into autumn, through reddening leaves, ripening fruit and the migration of small animals and birds: pint-size deer, foxes, squirrels; duck, swallows, swifts; the large butterflies flirting their just-before-hibernating wings on clumps of pink and purple fleshy-leaved plants. Peasants brought in the last of their harvest, stored their fruits, pickled and salted their meats, and the bats were coming out earlier and earlier to catch the last of the midges that stung us so heartily during the day. So, were the bats eating us, I wondered?

As we climbed higher the air became more exhilarating, and the streams were ice cold from the snowy heights above. All this, and the plain but adequate fare we ate satisfied me well enough, but Dickon was always grumbling, comparing our food with the comparative luxury he had enjoyed on the caravan routes.

"Nobody asked you to come," I said crossly one day, when he had been whining all day about not being allowed extra money to buy some more rice wine. "You're here because you wanted to be, remember?"

"And you're not being reasonable," he said, dodging the issue. "A man needs a bit of relaxation now and again, a sip or two of wine."

"You've already had a sip or four," I said. "And you said not yesterday that it was piss water, rotgut."

"Depends on the vintage . . ."

"This stuff doesn't have any vintage. They make it all the year round."

"I only want a nip. Set me up for the evening."

I flung him a coin. "Buy yourself a measure then. But only a small one, otherwise you won't be fit to go on."

I was right. That afternoon's trek was a complete waste of time. He swayed from side to side of the road, fell over twice, and when I went to help him up he made a grab at me.

"C'mon Summer: gi'e us a kiss!"

I kicked him where it hurt, and when he doubled up pushed him into a ditch and marched on for a half mile without him. By then, as I could see he wasn't following, I retrieved my steps, my temper near at boiling point, especially when I found him still in the ditch, snoring his head off. I was strongly tempted to leave him where he was and travel on alone, but common sense told me I couldn't manage the baggage on my own.

We climbed higher and higher, but the mountains we were aiming for, our last barrier, called on the maps Ky-Lin had explained to me the "Sleeping Giants," still seemed many miles away. Travelling during the day was still pleasant, but the nights were increasingly chill and we needed extra clothes plus the blankets to keep warm, especially if we spent nights in the open. A couple of times we slept under both blankets together, Dickon and I, but his behavior on these occasions worried and annoyed me. On both these times after I had dozed off, I awoke to find his hands where they shouldn't be.

At first I thought he was searching my person for money, but the intimate movement of his hands on my breasts and thighs persuaded me otherwise. I could not believe it was a personal thing, rather that he had been robbed of his usual visits to houses of pleasure, but in any case I found it highly embarrassing.

After all we had travelled together in enforced intimacy for many months, and in all that time, especially with all our differences, there had never been any hint of sexual familiarity. As it was, on both occasions I had turned away as if in my sleep, wrapping myself up tight so there was no way he could attempt anything further.

I tried to enlist Growch's help, but his views on sex being what they were—the more the merrier, whoever or whatever it was—I received little encouragement, until I slanted my argument towards the money I was carrying.

"I don't like him searching me like that when I'm asleep. Just think what would happen if he ran off with all our money!"

Growch knew what money meant: it meant food.

"Right, then. I'll see 'e don' touch you nowheres from now on. Sleep between you both, I will."

Which worked much better, especially as my dog by now smelt so high that Dickon and I slept back-to-back by choice. It was either that or holding our noses all night.

We came to the last village before the snow line of the mountains we planned to cross to our goal. I consulted the best of the maps. It showed a route that wandered away in the lee of the mountains to the east for what looked like a week's journey, before finding a gap into the valley beyond. There was another trail, however. This led almost due north from where we were now and, looking up, I could see, or believed I could see, past a thick stand of coniferous forest, the gap I was seeking, the first in the three-peaked range. This reminded me of the illusion/dream the old man in the market had engendered in me, when I had imagined I was a dragon flying through that very gap.

But when the villagers realized our intent there was an indrawing of breath, a lowering of lids, a shaking of heads.

"What's the matter with them? There's a trail that starts off that way. I can see it leading up to the forest."

Dickon shook his head. "They seem to be afraid of something up there."

"What?"

"How the hell do I know? Look at that old fool in the corner: he's been jabbering away for five minutes now, but I can't understand a word he's saying. Can you?"

"N . . . no. Not exactly. But he's making signs as well." I felt uneasy, not least because the ring on my finger felt uncomfortable, as if it was too tight. I went over to the villager and squatted in front of him watching his dirt-ingrained hands expressing alarm and dismay. Making signs that I didn't understand—oh, what I wouldn't have done for Ky-Lin's comforting presence!—I motioned him to slow down, hoping this would make him more intelligible. It didn't, but one of the brighter of his friends understood what I wanted and came to join us.

It went something like this—all in sign language, whether with hands, eyes, expression, body language, or sheer acting and mime.

Why can't we go that way?

Huge men up there. Giants.

No giants now.

Yes. They also eat people.

Cannibals?

They eat anything. Prefer meat.

Have you seen them?

Heard them howling.

Wolves?

No. Human voice.

How do you know they are human?

When they howl we leave them food at the edge of the forest.

How do you know they aren't animals?

Footprints.

What sort of print?

In snow.

Show me.

And that was the most puzzling of all. They drew in the dirt the outline of a foot, but it was no ordinary one. In general it followed the shape of a human foot, but it was two or three times as large. I drew one smaller, but they rubbed that out and drew an even larger one. What was worse, this foot had eight toes, with sharp long nails, if their drawings were to be believed.

I looked at Dickon. "Superstition?"

"Could be. They've never seen one of these creatures."

"Exactly. And if they've seen some prints in the snow—well, when snow melts so do the prints. Outwards. So a small print would look bigger after an hour or so. Right?"

"Could well be wolves, as you suggested."

"Wrong time of the year for them to be hungry. Shall we chance it? It'd save three or four days' travel. . . ."

"Why not? I'm game if you are."

"Of course!" At least I would have if my ring hadn't kept on insisting that somewhere ahead lay the possibility of danger. But this way would save so many days, and if we were careful . . .

In order to try and reach the gap before nightfall, we set off before dawn. None of the villagers came to see us off. At first it was easy, a clear track leading up towards the forest, which we hoped to skirt to the east. On the fringes we could see where the villagers below had started to clear the wood for fuel, for we came across chippings, a discarded and broken axe, a couple of sleds they used for transporting the wood.

Dickon pointed to one of these. "Why shouldn't we borrow one? It would make carrying all this stuff much easier. Quicker, too. The runners on the underside are obviously meant for snow."

Growch cocked his leg, then thought better of it. "Good for a lift, too, for those poor critturs as 'as short legs . . ."

"We can't just steal it. . . ."

"I said 'borrow,' " said Dickon quickly. "Once we get to the top we can send it back down. The slope'll carry it back."

"All right, we'll haul it unladen till we get to the snow line, to preserve the runners, then we'll load it up."

When we stopped to eat the sun was already high in the sky, and I reckoned we were nearly halfway to the summit. For some reason, although nothing stirred except a couple of eagles taking advantage of the thermals high above, we all felt irritable and uneasy. Dickon kept glancing over his shoulder in the direction of the forest we were skirting, my ring was getting more uncomfortable by the minute, although I reckoned any threat would come from the trees and we were giving them a wide berth. Growch said his mind felt "itchy." I knew exactly what he meant.

We carried on climbing. The forest thinned out to the left of us, and we came across the first patches of snow as the air grew colder. To our left the sun began its western descent and I realized it would be a race for the gap between us and the dark. We stopped briefly for food again, and this time we loaded the sled with everything portable, including Growch.

I looked up. Another couple of hours should do it, and there would be the valley I had dreamed of for so long, the valley that cushioned the fabled Blue Mountain. "Here be Dragons. . . ."

"Let's go," I said. "Let's go!"

Now we were crunching our way through real snow, unmelted all the way through summer, not the slush we had encountered on the lower slopes. The sled slid easily in our wake; we had attached the rope so that we could both pull it. The slope however grew steeper, and now we were bending forward, me at least wishing I had stouter boots: the cold was already striking through the soles and I had hardly any grip, but at least we were nearly there. The thinning forest was behind us and the gap was only some half mile away. The last bit looked the worst; the incline became so steep that it looked as though we should have to crawl on hands and knees.

We took a final breather; less than a half hour should do it. The breath plumed from our nostrils like smoke. Growch's eyebrows, such as they were, were rimed with frost. The sun was near gone, a red ball waiting to slide down the western mountains.

"Right," I said. "One more push should do it. . . . What's the matter?" Dickon was staring at something in the snow just ahead of us. With a sudden look of horror he backed away, his hands held out in front as though he was pushing the sight away from him.

"Look, Summer," he said. "Look there! It was true what they said!"

And there, clear as crystal in hitherto untrodden snow, was the print of an enormous eight-toed foot.

23

I clapped my hands to my mouth and stepped back in unconscious repudiation, but there was no denying what I had seen. It was as clear as the ice that lined it, reflecting the last of the red sun so it looked as though the giant that made the print had bled into the snow. Dickon pointed out another print, another and another. They came from just above us and then went away down towards the forest.

I swallowed, hard. Those footprints were just as large and terrifying as the villagers had indicated, and I couldn't begin to imagine the height and breadth of a creature who boasted feet that big. And eight toes . . .

Suddenly the sun was gone, like blowing out half the candles in a room at once, and a cold chill of terror gripped us all. Without realizing it Dickon and I were holding hands and a trembling Growch was actually sitting on my feet, his hackles raised, moaning softly.

"We—we'd better get going." I found I was whispering, although there seemed to be nothing moving in the snow. "It's clear straight up to the gap, and if we . . ."

My voice died away as a hideous ululating howl split the quiet around us, followed by another and another. With one accord we ran, sled forgotten, scrambling on all fours to find a grip. I could feel the hairs rising at the back of my neck and my heart was bounding like a March hare.

The howl came again, and this time it was answered by another— from ahead of us.

We came to a sudden, skidding halt.

"What the devil—!"

And Dickon's prophetic exclamation was answered by a horrific apparition that rose from behind a huge rock to our right. Nearly twice the size of a man, it was covered in fur—brown, black, gray—and its face was a twisted mask of hate, with huge fangs sprouting from its jaw. Slowly, lumberingly, it left the shelter of the rock and, with arms raised, came down the slope towards us, uttering that hideous howl we had heard before.

As one we fled down the slope toward the shelter of the forest, slipping, stumbling, falling, rolling, all thought gone save the urgency of escape, although something deep inside seemed to tell me to stop, not to run, but it was such a tiny voice that my fear drowned it.

Not looking where I was going I crashed into the trunk of a tree, knocking all the breath from my body, and I whooped and coughed with the effort to draw air into my lungs. I was aware of Growch gasping and panting beside me, and the inert form of Dickon a few yards away.

I struggled to my feet to see what had happened to him.

"Come on, Growch, we must get—"

"Too late!" he whimpered. "Look behind you!"

I turned, and found we were surrounded. Not by giants, but by strange, hairy humans holding stone axes and primitive spears. They were no taller than I, slightly hunched, and the hair on their bodies, thick on back and arms, was a reddish-black. Prominent brows and jaws, small eyes and noses, wide mouths with yellow teeth and long, tangled hair were common to all and they were mostly naked, though some of the women had bound their babies to their backs with strips of fur.

These creatures looked at us and chattered to themselves in a series of grunts, sibilants and clicks, and a moment later a couple of them dragged the half-conscious body of Dickon forward and dumped him without ceremony at my feet. He had a bruise the size of an egg on his temple. As I looked down he stirred, put his hand to his head and sat up, opening his eyes.

"Holy Mary, Mother of God!"

But he wasn't looking at the strange creatures who now crowded closer till I could smell the rank odor of their bodies; he was staring back up the hill the way we had come. I followed his pointing finger and gasped. Down the hill came striding the giant we had fled from, swaying from side to side, arms spread—Arms? What beast had four arms? I sank to my knees despairingly, clutching Growch for comfort, for surely the hairy people would have no defense against this hideous apparition.

From the giant came that dreadful wolflike howl again, and to my amazement it was answered with like from the hairy people around us, waving their weapons in the air in greeting with what could only be described as grins on their faces.

I scrambled to my feet, pulled Dickon to his. What the hell was happening? Surely the giant and the hairy people weren't in league with one another? Why didn't they—

Dickon and I gasped together. The giant careening down the hill towards us had been gathering speed in a more and more wild manner and now, suddenly, it broke in two! No, no, all in bits. Two pieces came rolling towards us, another sheared off to the left, one slithered to a stop against a tree—

And the hairy people were laughing, dancing, waving their spears!

"Laugh too," came a tiny voice from somewhere. "It's all a big joke to them. You've been had."

And I only realized just how much when two of the "pieces" came to a stop, unrolled, and became two more of the hairy people, one of them still wearing the misshapen boots that had made such a convincing giant's footstep. The other man went back and retrieved the mask that had so horrified us, plus the long cloak that had so convincingly covered one man riding on another's shoulders.

My heart sank even further as our captors, as they must be thought of now, closed in, pointing at the boots, the mask, the cloak, laughing and jeering and miming our terror, confusion and fear when faced with the "giant."

"Laugh with them," came that tiny voice again. "It's your only chance to get away. . . ."

But I couldn't. I tried; I forced the muscles of my face into what I knew was a hideous rictus, but I knew it only looked threatening, like that of a chattering monkey. I nudged Dickon, tried to make him smile, laugh, speak, do anything, but it was hopeless: he was almost rigid with fear.

One by one our captors fell silent, glanced at each other, at us, scowled: we weren't enjoying their joke. They muttered again, then gestured that we should follow them into the forest. Dickon fell to his knees again. Growch whimpered in my arms, and my ring felt as cold as ice.

"Do as they want," said the little voice in my head. "Don't despair!"

So on top of everything else, I was hearing voices. It must be all my terrified imagination, but the voice sounded so much like my dead-and-gone Ky-Lin that I could have cried. Perhaps it *was* his voice, perhaps his ghost had come back to comfort me. I could feel the tears, warm on my frozen cheeks.

"Help us," I whispered. "Wherever you are . . ."

Our captors hauled Dickon roughly to his feet and jostled us both along a narrow track through the trees. Too soon the last of the light was gone, forest gloom descended, and I had to hold one hand in front of my face to push aside the whippy branches I could hardly see. It was less cold under the trees, and the only sounds were the shush-shush of pine needles under our feet and an occasional grunt or snort from our captors, just like a sounder of swine.

After what seemed like hours, but can only have been minutes, we stumbled into a clearing. Other hairy people came out from the trees: the old ones and young children. About fifty or sixty surrounded us now, pointing, grimacing and, what was much worse, touching us; pulling at our clothes and hair, pinching our cheeks and arms, treating us as though we were strange animals instead of human beings.

I wanted so much to hear that ghosty voice of Ky-Lin's again, but, try as I could, the noise around us drowned all else. The sound of wood being dragged to the glowing pit in the center of the clearing, the hissing of the logs, the snorting grunts of those around us—I should have liked to cover my ears, but daren't put Growch down.

The women arranged a framework of sticks across the fire, and on these were spitted several small animals: squirrels, what looked like rats, a small snake. In baskets at the side were pine nuts, roots, wild herbs and a fungus of some sort. The smell of the cooking meat was hardly appetizing, nor was the sight of the filthy fingers that turned the sticks, poking the flesh now and again to see if it was cooked through.

Hands on our shoulders forced us down to sit a little away from the fire while the men went into a huddle, glancing over at us every now and again and then having some sort of discussion.

I poked Dickon, a rigid figure of fear. "It doesn't look too good, does it? Got any ideas?"

He shook his head, probably not trusting himself to speak, and I remembered what the villagers had intimated: these people were cannibals. I shivered, in spite of the heat from the fire, but the ring on my finger, though cold, didn't convey any threat of imminent danger; for the moment we were safe.

By my side lay one of the "giant's" boots; shifting Growch a little, I picked it up to have a closer look. It really was rather ingenious. The sole was made of two bear pads, sewn together, just four claws on each, making eight in all; the top was ordinary leather, the whole sewn over a wickerwork frame and padded, so there was just enough room for a human foot; it must have taken some practice to walk properly, especially with someone else perched on one's back.

One of the hairy ones saw me examining the boot, scowled for a moment, then nudged his fellows and brought over the other with a grin, miming their walk. He also brought over the mask for me to examine as well.

Near to it was quite crudely carved, I guessed from the hollowed stump of a tree, so that it fitted loosely over the head. The nose was a natural hooked beak of wood, stained red by some sort of dye, the eyes had been burnt out and were outlined in yellow. The top of the mask was covered with hair, real hair, and with a shock I realized it was human. Of course it could have been cut from someone's hair within the tribe but I had the terrible feeling that it came from some more reluctant source. They showed me the robe as well, and my suspicions were proved right: these were human scalps sewn together.

I pushed everything away with a sudden surge of revulsion, and they laughed as if it were the best joke in the world. Seeing them then one would have thought them a happy and harmless people, until one realized that their secrets would not have been shared if they had any intention of letting us go.

There was a diversion: apparently the meal was ready. Flat pieces of bark and large leaves were produced and filled with nuts, roots and fungi. Sticks were snatched from the fire and fought over, the meat on them charred on one side, raw on the other.

No one offered us anything.

They ate noisily, licking their fingers before wiping them on their stomachs, hair, each other, and the women spat out half-chewed bits to feed to the smallest of their scrawny brats. Too soon for us the meal was ended; they finished with the last of the unwashed pine nuts, crammed into their mouths so that the black, powdery stain covered their faces and hair, the grease on their skins spreading it still further

Now they were looking for entertainment—or was it more food? Several of the women were rubbing their stomachs, looking at the men, looking at us. My ring was throbbing again, so cold it felt as though it would burn straight through my finger. I looked around desperately, but we were ringed in on all sides. Suddenly two of the men separated from the rest and came towards us; Dickon and I scrambled to our feet and backed away, a trembling Growch hugged close to my chest.

Dickon was pushed unceremoniously aside and they approached me, great grins on their faces; in the sudden clarity that terror can bring, I noticed how stained their teeth were: fangs for tearing at the front, grinding molars at the back—

One of the men leaned forward, jabbering excitedly—and tried to pluck the terrified Growch from my arms. I had thought they came for me, and was quite prepared to take out my knife and hurt them as much as I could before I was overpowered. But Growch? No, never! Not my little dog spitted over a fire till his hair singed and the blood and fat ran spattering into the fire! I had rather slit his throat myself to spare him the pain and betrayal.

"Get away! Get your filthy hands off!" I was shouting hysterically. "Dickon, for God's sake *do* something! Help me. . . ." Now my knife was in my right hand. Growch still held with my left, and as one man advanced still further I connected with a lucky slash across his arm and he retreated with a grunt, sucking at the blood.

Dickon's voice came to me. "Give them the wretched animal, for Christ's sake! It's him they want. Give us time to escape. . . ."

I couldn't believe my ears! Give up Growch! In sudden anger I turned on Dickon and slashed out at him also, and saw the bright beads of blood spring from a cut across his cheek. Turning, I hit out again at my two attackers, and had the satisfaction of seeing them spring back from the arc of my knife. But now the others behind were closing in and I couldn't deal with them all—

"Help me! Help me!" I didn't realize I was screaming, or to whom, but all of a sudden everything changed.

"Leave this to me!" boomed a voice, and with a burst of firecrackers that would have done justice to a town celebration, into the clearing came bounding a huge creature, an apparition surrounded with light and noise and color and fire.

The hairy tribe scattered in all directions, sparks from the unguarded fire catching at their hair and stinging their bodies. For a moment I thought we had exchanged one horror for another, then I suddenly recognized the creature for who he was, larger now than I had ever seen him—

"Ky-Lin! But how . . . What did—"

"Follow me! No questions, just hurry!"

I can't remember much of that frantic dash through the trees, out into the snow and up towards the gap. I do remember finding the sled, Ky-Lin taking the rope between his teeth and dragging us all as hard as he could towards safety. I remember, too, the chill of terror when we heard the howls of pursuit behind us, as the tribe realized Ky-Lin provided no threat and they were losing a source of easy food. Their noise came nearer and nearer, a couple of ill-thrown spears skimmed past our heads, and we were there!

A gap as wide as a door, no more, a glimpse of a valley, more hills and we were through. Ky-Lin loosed the rope and the sled careened faster and faster down a slope of snow towards the valley below.

Now the moon was up, and through the tears of cold in my eyes and the wind whipping my cheeks a scene of beauty spread itself beneath, and there in the midst of it all was a coldly blue shape on the horizon.

"Look, look!" I cried out to Ky-Lin who had been left behind. "It's there, we've found the Blue Mountain—"

The sled veered, skidded, struck something hard and I was lifted into the air. Suddenly everything was upside down, and then my head hit something, lights buzzed through my brain, and everything went black.

Part III

24

The first thing I was conscious of was a pleasant smell: sandalwood, beeswax, pine, cedarwood. It reminded me of Ky-Lin. Then, what must have woken me, a dissonance, not unpleasant, of tinkling bells, and a faraway chanting, a deep resonance of a gong. For a moment longer I savored the light warmth of blankets tucked under my chin, then I became aware of a dull throbbing in my head and an unpleasant taste in my mouth.

I opened my eyes and sat up, immediately wishing I hadn't done either.

I closed my eyes and lay down again, but must have groaned, because at once there was a rustle of clothing and a woman was chattering away quietly by my side. Her hands were cool on my forehead; my head was raised and a feeding cup pressed to my lips. The drink was warm and fragrant, tasted of mint and honey and camomile and took away the nasty taste in my mouth. I wasn't about to open my eyes or sit up again, but there was a sort of puzzle that wouldn't go away: where was I, and indeed *who* was I? I couldn't remember a thing, so decided to think about it later. . . .

When I opened my eyes again the room was full of soft lamplight and shadows and I remembered who and what I was, what had happened before, but I had no idea where I lay. My head still hurt, but the pain was lessening. Putting up a languid hand I found a cloth wound tight about my forehead, the rag cool and damp to my touch. The last thing I recalled was riding at a giddy speed on the sled down the mountain, of hitting some obstruction and flying through the air to hit my head on something—it must have been quite a bump for me to feel like this.

Something moved up from the foot of the bed, and a sloppy tongue and hacky breath announced the arrival of my dog.

"Feelin' better? Thought we'd lost you again we did; glad we didn'. Gawd, what a place this is! All corridors, steps, passages . . . 'Nuff to turn a dog dizzy! Don't think much of the nosh, neither. All pap, no gristle, nuffin' to get yer teeth into. Still most 'portant thing is you're back with us. I said to meself yesterday, I said, if'n she don' wake up soon, I'm—"

"Growch!"

"Yes?"

"Can I speak? Can I ask you a couple of questions?"

" 'Course. Ain't stoppin' you am I? Now then, what d'you wanna know? Don' tell me, let me guess. . . . Where is we? Well, I ain't ezackly sure. It's a sort o' temple, high up in the mountains. Took us near a week to get 'ere, what with you bein' unconscious an' all, but that big beast, 'e pulled the sled wiv you on it all the way. 'Is lordship fancy pants weren't much use, 'e was all for stayin' in the first village we come to but Ky-Lin 'e said no, you needed special treatment and the best nursin'. Must say, though—"

"Growch?"

"Yes?"

"Where are Ky-Lin and Dickon?"

"Well, 'is lordship's next door, snorin' 'is 'ead orf, an' the lady what was tendin' you 'as gone fer a nap. Ain't seen much o' Ky-Lin, seein' 'e's special 'ere. 'E comes an' checks on you, then back 'e goes to them monks. They seem to think a lot o' 'im. 'E's the only one allowed inside their temple." He settled down on the pillow next to me, had a good scratch, licked my ear and continued.

"This place, bein' arfway up a 'ill, is sorta built in layers. The temple and the monks' part, they's at the top. This bit, the guests', is next down, then at the bottom is a 'uge courtyard, with goats 'n chickens 'n bees 'n things. All around is workshops—they weave these blankets down there; must say they're the softest I ever come acrost. Come from a goat wiv long hair what they combs. Cooking is done down there, too, an' the washin'. . . . Well, then: look 'oose 'ere!" and he jumped off the bed to greet Ky-Lin.

He seemed to have grown larger and more splendid than ever. His hide and hooves shone with health, his eyes were bright, his colors clear and vibrant. His plumed tail was truly magnificent and his antennae curled and waved like weeds in a stream. Bending over the bed he touched these latter to my head and immediately the dull ache lessened. I flung my arms about his neck in greeting.

"I thought it was you out there in the forest speaking to me—but then I believed I must have been hearing things! How did you come back to us? When I left you on that altar I was convinced you were—you were dead. Are you sure you are real?"

"Of course I'm real, silly one! I never really went away. I was hurt, yes, but we soon heal. A little rest, a word or two from my Master, and I was well enough to follow you. I was sitting in the lining of your jacket most of the time, staying quiet until you needed me."

I hugged him again. "Thank you a million, million times! Thank you for saving us, for bringing me here, for everything. Without you . . ." Words failed me. "But there is just one thing I don't understand."

"And that is?"

"When—when I thought you were dead . . ." I hesitated.

"Yes?" he prompted.

"I said a prayer for you. I said to the Buddha that I thought you had already done enough to go to your Heaven. Why didn't he listen?"

For the first time he looked embarrassed. He looked away, he looked back, his eyes crossed, he shook his head from side to side. Finally he mumbled something I couldn't catch.

"What did you say?"

"I said . . . said I was given a choice. My Lord was willing for me to go to rest with Him, or—go back and see it through. I'm afraid that for me there was little choice."

"How wonderful of you to choose the hard way!"

He raised a hoof, looked even more abashed. "No, no, no praise! It was partly selfish. I told you once before that I didn't think I would enjoy eternal peace and rest. Besides, I have grown used to this whole big, imperfect world. I actually enjoy being in it. I shouldn't, you know; it should be renounced, like anything imperfect." His head bobbed again. "My Lord said I was a child still, putting off the moment to go to bed."

The awkward silence was luckily broken by the entrance of Dickon, rubbing sleep from his eyes.

"What's all the noise about? Oh, you're awake at last, Summer. Feeling better? What's the matter? Why are you laughing?"

"What in the world are you wearing?"

"A nightshirt. What's so funny? You're wearing one too. . . ."

I had never seen him look so ridiculous. The high-necked gray garment had short sleeves and was slit down the sides, to end just below his knees, so that his thin, hairy shanks poked out below it, and if he moved incautiously, one caught a glimpse of dimpled backside.

Before I disgraced myself by laughing too much and gave myself a second headache the nursing woman bustled in, dismissing everyone except Growch—who retreated growling under the bed—gave me a bitter draught, blew out all the lamps bar one, tucked me up tight, and I had no alternative but to sink back again into a drugged sleep.

Three days later I was well on the road to recovery. My headache was gone, the cloth on my head had been removed, no more bitter draughts, and I was allowed out of bed to sit by the fire. There was a washroom down the corridor and at last I could have a tub of hot water to bathe in, although I had been sponged down while I was in bed.

Without asking, both Dickon and I had been provided with new clothes, the sort the peasants wore: padded jackets and trousers, with cotton drawers and undershirt and felt slippers.

The first thing I did, after a really good wash, was to check that all my belongings were safe, although Growch assured me that he had "guarded 'em with me life!" All was as he said, though I was surprised to see how much the egg had grown. One evening when Ky-Lin paid a visit, I asked about this.

"All the eggs I have ever seen stay their laying size: it's the chick inside that grows, not the shell. Why is this different?"

"The simple answer is that I don't know, but then I've never had to deal with a dragon's egg before. Obviously they don't behave like other eggs, but I can assure you that there are live cells in there and I can hear them growing."

It was exciting, awesome, and although I knew I should never see what was inside, I desperately wanted to. "Can your antennae see inside?"

"If they could—and I'm not going to try it—I wouldn't tell you. Some things are best left alone." And with that answer I had to be content.

However he did reveal something to me I hadn't suspected, perhaps to take my mind off the question of the egg.

"Have you looked at that piece of crystal lately?"

"The one the captain's wife gave me? No, not recently?"

"Then perhaps you should take another look."

"Now?"

"Why not?"

I unwrapped it carefully and laid it on the bed. "There's nothing

special about it—oh!" Ky-Lin had rolled it to the end where it caught
the light, and now it was as though a rainbow had entered the room.
The lamps caught the glass in a hundred, a thousand bands, strips and
rays; red, crimson, scarlet, orange, yellow, green, viridian, pine, cobalt,
ultramarine, mauve, purple, violet—and colors in between one could
only guess at.

"Hold it up," said Ky-Lin. "Let it find the light it has been denied
so long. . . ."

I was blinded by color; it was the most wonderful jewel I had ever
seen in my life. As I swung it between my fingers the light flashed
around the room ever faster, creating a gem within a gem, and we were
all patterned with color like strange animals—even Ky-Lin's tail was
dimmed.

"What *is* it?"

"Whatever it is, turn it orf!" said Growch. "You talk about *your*
'ead achin'. . . ."

"It is only a crystal," said Ky-Lin. "But beautifully cut. I've never
seen a better. Anyone would be delighted to own that."

I was reluctant to put it away, like a child with a toy. I must try it
again tomorrow. . . . Tomorrow? Why was I wasting time like this?

"Ky-Lin . . . are we in the right place? Is the Blue Mountain near?
Is that really the place of dragons?"

"Legend has it that this is one of the few places on earth where
dragons can still be found. The Blue Mountain is a half-day's journey
away."

"Then I must go there. Now. Tomorrow." But if this was the place
where my dragon-man had headed for, why was it I had no sense of
him being near? Surely my love was strong enough to sense his presence,
even over a half-day's journey. I couldn't come this far, to find I was
wasting my time! "Tomorrow," I repeated firmly.

"You may go," said Ky-Lin, "when you are completely recovered.
Not before. A week or so."

"But—but I want to go now!"

"At the moment you couldn't walk up a flight of steps, let alone
climb a mountain. Come now, be sensible! It has taken months to get
so far: surely a few days more won't change the world!"

"I shall be perfectly recovered in far less time than that," I said
firmly, although I was fighting a rearguard action, and knew it.

"We shall see," was all he said, but three days later he came for
me. Not to climb any mountains, but to speak to one of the monks, the
Chief Historian and Keeper of the Scrolls.

I followed him down a narrow, twisting corridor, following the curve of the hill on which the monastery was situated, narrow slit windows giving hair-raising glimpses of the sheer drop below. Once I thought I caught sight of the Blue Mountain itself, but couldn't be sure. Down some steps, up a lot more and then we found ourselves in a small chamber, scarce six feet by six.

Facing us was an intricately carved grille, decorated with red enamel and gold paint. Beside the grille was a small brass gong and a shallow wooden bowl with a red leather handle. The silence lay as thick as last year's dust.

"Strike the gong once," whispered Ky-Lin. (It was a room for whispering). "Wait a count of five and strike it twice, then once again."

"What is this—some sort of secret society?"

"Each monk has his own call; if you do it any differently you may get the Chief Architect, the Cloth Master, the Master of Intercession or even the Reader of the Weather. Every monk is trained to be an expert in one thing or another."

I wondered if there was a Master of Sewers and Latrines. . . ."

"Go on!"

I tiptoed to the gong—there was no need; the stone muffled even our whispers—struck it once, then stepped back hastily; it was far louder than I had expected.

"It won't bite," said Ky-Lin.

I struck the gong twice more, for a moment waited and struck it once again. As the last echoes died away, the silence seemed thicker than ever. Then came a faint creak, the distant sound of chanting, another creak, and the chant dying away. Another, more comforting sound; the flap, flap of sandals, a wheezy breath, a cough. Almost immediately a shadow formed behind the grille, a mere shift of light and shadow, and a thin high voice asked a question.

Ky-Lin answered, then turned to me. "If anyone knows of the dragons, he will. He has consented to speak to you through me. He is not allowed to speak to a woman directly. I will translate for you both. What is it you wish me to ask him?"

"Ask him how recently there were dragons here?"

Apparently the answer took some time, but eventually Ky-Lin translated. "He says it is unclear. There has been certain activity reported around the Blue Mountain during the last fifteen months, but these reports have not yet been substantiated."

"What sort of activity?"

"Strange lights, odd noises, a smell of cinders, an unexplained grass fire," he translated.

"And has it always been a tradition that dragons lived there?"

Apparently the records of the monastery only went back the three hundred years since its inception. At that time there was no direct mention of dragons, only a passing reference to the fact that the locals believed the Blue Mountain was "haunted." One hundred years later, when the monks had consolidated and had time on their hands, there were several references to a "Blue Monster," which had been reported many years back ravaging the crops in a particularly bad year for harvest. This particular monster apparently flew in the sky and breathed flame and smoke. There were no other sightings until another year of drought, when the creature was apparently spotted "drinking a river dry." Another time it was seen at night circling the valley, beating wings that "caused a great draught to blow the roofs off several houses, and the populace to take their children and hide them." Further sightings were reported over the years, but nothing recent.

"Is there nothing about dragons over the past two years?"

"He says not."

"Nothing at all out of the ordinary? However unlikely it might seem?"

"The Master has much patience, girl, but even I can see it is wearing a little thin. . . . However, I am sure he will give us a recital of every unusual or unexplained event that has come to his attention over the last couple of years, if I ask him."

Triplets, all of whom survived; a two-headed calf that didn't; a fish caught in the river with another fish in its belly; a plague of red ants; an albino child; another born with a full set of teeth; a rogue tiger carrying off villagers in the foothills to the north, rumors of a great battle to the east; the sudden appearance and disappearance of a stranger borne on a great wind; death of the oldest monk at the age of one hundred and twenty—

"Wait!" I said. "The stranger: does he know any more?"

Ky-Lin made his query, received his answer.

"Well?" I asked, for a tiny hope had started to flutter in my breast and Ky-Lin was looking puzzled.

"It seems . . ." He hesitated. "It seems all this happened in a village to the north of here, many miles away, and a report was brought in by visiting monks. There is doubt as to its authenticity as the only witnesses were children, yet there is no doubt that some unnatural phenomenon took place, for damage was done to buildings and many heard a strange noise. The children, a six-year-old boy and his three-year-old sister, went out early one morning to relieve themselves and suddenly there was a great wind and a man in a black cloak was standing by them. The children said he looked angry with himself, but then he laughed and spoke to them, but they don't remember what he said. They saw him run off down the street, then came the fierce wind again and they thought they saw a great bird in the sky."

I remembered a dark man in a black cloak, a man with a hawk nose, piercing yellow eyes and a mouth that could be either cruel or tender—

"That must have been Jasper!" I said excitedly. "He had to spend part of his life in human guise because I kissed him! Ask him—"

"Whoever—or whatever—it was, it won't be there now," said Ky-Lin firmly. "And you may have one more question and that's it. You are here on sufferance, remember? Now, what do you want to ask?"

I thought for a moment. "Ask him how long ago this took place."

"Do you have the coins I asked you to bring?" I nodded. "Then when we receive our answer, bow once, place the coins in that bowl and push it under the grille. Then step back and bow again. The monks need the money, you needed the information, and the bows are common courtesy here."

"What did he say" I pestered Ky-Lin as we walked back down the winding passage.

"He said that all this took place sometime during the winter before last, but the exact month is not known."

"But that means it could have been my dragon-man! He left me at the Place of Stones at the beginning of November and 'during the winter' could be anytime in the next four months!"

"Patience! There is absolutely nothing to indicate that he is here."

"But I've got to find out! And if you won't take me to the Blue Mountain, I'll go alone!"

25

"T he one thing Ky-Lins can't do," said Ky-Lin firmly, "is fly. Ky-Lins can change their size, their substance, their colors. They can run like the wind, go without food and drink, speak any language. They can produce Sleepy Dust, firecrackers and colored smoke. They also possess certain healing properties, but fly they don't!"

We were standing at the foot of the so-called Blue Mountain. So-called because close to it didn't look blue at all. It was a sort of blackish cindery gray, rising steeply from the valley floor. Conical in shape, it was almost entirely bare of vegetation, and I was quite ready to believe it was the core of an extinct volcano. It smelled rather like the puff of air you sometimes get from a long-dead fireplace.

Ky-Lin had explained not once but twice why it looked blue at a distance, but I had become more than a little confused with the principles of distance, air, refraction (whatever that was), and vapor.

"Well," said Growch. "It's as plain as me nuts as we can't climb that. We ain't ruddy spiders."

Now Growch wasn't supposed to be here at all. Three days after Ky-Lin had questioned the monk, he had come to me suggesting we visit the Blue Mountain the very next day. "I can carry you," he had said, "but even with what speed I can make it will take several hours. I suggest, therefore, that we set off before light, in order to be back before nightfall. I shall wake you when I am ready, and shall ask one of the cooks to make you up a parcel of rice cakes and honey, and a skin of water."

"Don' eat 'unny," said Growch. "You knows I don'. Bit o' cheese'll do. An' a bone."

"You're not coming," I said firmly. "This is my journey. After all,"

I added placatingly, as his shaggy brows drew down in a dreadful frown, "this is only a reconnaissance. I just want to know what's there."

"Never!" he said. "Not never no-how. You ain't goin' nowhere without you take me. You'd never 'ave got this far without me, and you knows it. Why d'you think I left the comfort o' that merchant's 'ouse to go with you? Not to be left behin', and that's flat! I bin with you since the day after yer Ma died an' you left 'ome, ain't I? An' if'n you even tries to go without me I'll bark the place down, that I will!"

Blackmail, that was what it had come down to, so he had come too, and to my secret satisfaction had hated every moment of Ky-Lin's erratic bounding from stone to rock to pebble, as he had borne us on his back across the valley.

So had I, if it came to that, but there's nothing like sharing one's woes, is there?

We had left well before dawn, Dickon unaware and asleep, and were let out through the gates of the courtyard by a half-awake porter. We had followed the twisting track down to the village below, and once on level ground I had climbed on Ky-Lin's back, taken Growch up in front of me and started the long journey across the valley floor.

At first, along the level bare tracks, it was easy, Ky-Lin skimming smooth and steady with scarce a jolt to disturb us, but when the trail petered out we had a much more adventurous journey. At first I couldn't understand why Ky-Lin was bounding about like an overgrown and demented grasshopper, but then I remembered his devotion to not even spoiling a blade of grass or errant ant. Obviously there must have been many such in our path, for we jigged and jagged our way across the plain till the breath was near knocked out of me.

"Sorry," said Ky-Lin at one point. "It's not all (bounce) that easy (leap) by the last light (swerve) of the (crunch) moon, but once the sun comes up (hop) it should be better." Bump.

I sure hoped so.

It was a relief to us all when we finally arrived at the foot of the mountain. Sliding off Ky-Lin's back I collapsed on the ground, dropping Growch as I did so, and we spent the next couple of minutes shaking ourselves together. We looked up at the mountain; smooth rock all the way to the top, no bushes, shrubs, trees, grass or foot- or hand-holds that I could see. Far, far above us was what could be a ledge of some sort and a hole in the rock, but it was too high up to see clearly.

"Now what?"

"Breakfast," said Ky-Lin, "and then I will scout around the base of the mountain."

He was gone about an hour, and appeared from the opposite direction.

"What did you find?"

"Better news, I think. Around the other side, to the south where the sun shines strong, there has been a certain amount of erosion over the years. The rocks are porous, and I think there is a way up, a narrow way that follows a crack in the rock. Up you get, and we'll take a look."

Perhaps because he had been this way before, our ride this time was easier, and the other side of the mountain provided a surprise. As Ky-Lin had said this side faced due south, and perhaps because of this the lower slopes were covered with vegetation—young pines and firs at the foot, and bushes, grass and scrub to about a third of the way up before it reverted back to bare rock. There were also numerous cracks, fissures and gullies worn away by rain, wind and sun.

I saw what I thought were several promising paths, but Ky-Lin ignored all these and led us about halfway round the southern side before stopping.

"Here we are: take a look."

I couldn't see anything, but Growch's eyes were sharper than mine.

"I sees it. Bit of a scramble, then there's a crack as goes roun' like a pig's tail an' outa sight roun' the other side."

"Does it go all the way to that ledge we saw?"

"Seems to," said Ky-Lin. "We'll have to try it. It's the only way I can see to get us there."

After the first "scramble" as Growch had put it, which was a hands and knees job, the first part of the narrow path seemed easy enough. We were gradually working our way round to the westward, and when I looked down the first time the plain still looked only a jump away, but by the time we were facing northwest it looked a giddy mile away, although we could only have been a thousand feet up. Now the path became more difficult. It narrowed, and some of the footholds were crumbling away; at one point, when I paused for a moment's rest and gazed down again, I felt so dizzy I had to shut my eyes and cling to the rock, too paralyzed to move another step.

"C'mon, 'fraidy cat!" It was Growch's ultimate insult. "If'n I can do it, so can you!"

I chanced one open eye, and there he was, perched on a rock some three feet above me. As I watched he leapt down beside me and then up again.

"Up you comes!"

Then Ky-Lin was beside me. "I told you not to look down. Come on, I'll give you a lift up to the next bit. Don't let us down now, girl: there's only a short way to go."

And, incredibly, he was right. With a leap of anticipation I saw the ledge we were heading for not a hundred yards away, and five minutes later we were there.

It was obvious that the ledge was part natural, part engineered. The natural rock jutted out like a platform, perhaps six feet, but its inner side had been painstakingly excavated to a depth of about ten feet further and smoothed down, making a natural stage some fifteen feet deep and the same wide. Stage? What about a landing strip for a dragon? Especially as, at the back, leading into the heart of the mountain was a dark, yawning passage.

Suddenly the strange, cindery smell was much stronger and I wanted to gag, so much so that I turned away and looked across the plain to where the faraway mountains raised their snowcapped heads. And with the sight came a scent from the distance, a hint of snow, thyme, ice, pine, a perfume to dispel the one that had so disturbed me.

Ky-Lin lay down with a sigh, hooves tucked under. "Well, we're here. Are you going in?"

I stared at him. "Aren't you coming?"

He shook his head. "Dragons are not—not within my commitments. It's like . . ." He struggled for an explanation. "It's like two different elements. The difference between a fish and a bird. Our boundaries just don't cross. I have my magic, they have theirs."

I thought of flying fish, of sea-diving eagles; for a moment at least they tried different elements. But Ky-Lin was adamant.

"This is your adventure, girl. I brought you here, I can take you back, but in there I cannot help you."

For a moment I hesitated. The passage looked dark and forbidding. I wished I had had the forethought to bring some form of illumination. I looked at Growch.

"You coming?"

His ears were down, his tail between his legs. " 'Course . . ." Not very convincing.

"Come on then: this is what I came for."

"What *you* came for! Orl right. Lead on. . . ."

But I didn't want to either. I closed my eyes, just to remind myself why I was here. The maps had shown a Blue Mountain, and I had no other lead to where my dragon-man had gone; he was the reason I had travelled so many miles, to try and find the one who had so roused my body and my heart to the realization that no one else but he would do. A dragon-kiss, that was why I was here.

I tried to recall the magic of that moment; the fear, the joy, the exhilaration of that moment nearly two years ago, when I had tasted what love really meant—but like all memories and the best dreams the edges were blunted by time, the sharpness rubbed off by recollection. However, this was why I was here, so how could I fail at the last moment, just because I was scared of a dark passage?

"You'll wait, Ky-Lin?"

"Of course. Just take it slow and easy. I don't believe there will be anything to fear except yourselves."

I peered down the tunnel. "It's very dark. . . ."

"You want a light? You should have reminded me humans cannot see in the dark like us. Here, pluck some hairs from the tip of my tail. Go on, it won't hurt you."

It might hurt him, though. I chose a small handful and gave a gentle tug; it stayed where it was.

"It won't hurt me either," said Ky-Lin. "As I say, I'm not a human."

I tugged harder and *pop!*—out they came, immediately fusing together into a minitorch that burned with a brilliant white light. I nearly dropped it.

"That won't hurt you either," said Ky-Lin. "You can even put your finger in the flame. It's really an illusion, like my firecrackers."

"How long will it last?"

"As long as you need it. Now, off you go: you're wasting time again."

Holding the torch high I stepped into the tunnel, Growch's wet nose nudging my ankles. Now that we had a light he didn't seem so reluctant. Step by step, my free hand against the tunnel wall to keep me steady, I stumbled along—stumbled because the way was littered with small stones, and even as we walked other stones and pebbles detached themselves from the roof and walls to complicate our passage.

At first the tunnel—some six feet wide—went straight, and if I glanced behind I could see the comforting daylight behind me. Then it kinked sharply to the left, to the right and to the left again, till the only light we had I held in my hand, except for a faint illumination I could not trace to its source. It was very still; the air smelled of rotten eggs and cinders, and it was strangely warm.

We seemed to have been travelling into the heart of the mountain for what seemed ages but could only have been a cautious five minutes, when suddenly the tunnel widened into a huge cavern. It was so wide and high that, even with the brilliance of Ky-Lin's torch, we couldn't see the roof or the far walls.

Two things I noticed at once: both the smell and the heat were suddenly increased, and as far as the latter was concerned it was like walking from winter into spring. The heat seemed to be coming from somewhere beneath our feet, as a hearthstone will keep the warmth long after the fire itself is out. It increased as we advanced further into the cavern, until we were halted by a great fissure that stretched from one side to the other, effectively blocking our way to the other side. It was from this great crack that the heat and the smell came.

Cautiously I peered over the edge, down into darkness so deep it was almost a color on its own. Up came a waft of hot air; Ky-Lin had said this was the cone of an extinct volcano, but there was certainly something down there still. No noise, however; no grumbling and bubbling, so perhaps I was mistaken.

I stepped back and held the torch as high as I could once more. It was like being in a huge cathedral, ribs and buttresses of rock rearing up into shadow. On the other side of the fissure, to add to the illusion, huge humps of stone could well be mistaken for effigies of long-dead knights. But giant knights these, in fact the shadows thrown by the torch gave these effigies of stone less than human characteristics: heads and claws and scaly backs.

"There's a sorta bridge here," Growch grumbled. It wasn't the sort of place to be too audible.

A thin arch of stone spanned the chasm; perhaps a couple of feet wide, it looked both daunting and insubstantial, and the thought of what might lie below was more than enough to make me decide not to chance it. Besides, I persuaded myself, there was nothing over there to look at, only misshapen lumps of rock and, now I noticed for the first time, some irregularly spaced heaps of pebbles, the sort of heaps a child might make while playing.

I felt terribly let down. All that travelling, the building up of anticipation, the hard times, the dangerous ones: was it all to lead to an empty, hot cavern scattered with stones and smelling of cinders? And where, oh where was Jasper? Where was my wonderful man-dragon? How could the maps, the legends, my own intuition, all be so wrong?

In sudden frustration and anguish I called out his name. "Jasper! Jasper! Where are you?" but the echoes engendered by my voice magnified his name into a frightening "Boom! boom! boom!" that bounced off the rocks, hissing on the sibilant, popping on the plosive, till I felt as if I had been hurled headlong into a thunderstorm.

Terrified, I clapped my hands to my ears, dropping the torch, but to add to the din Growch started yelping in fear and the noise was so dreadful it almost seemed as if the stones themselves were adding to the clamor. To add to the confusion the fallen torch was now pointing directly across at the misshapen rocks and I definitely saw one move—

That did it. I snatched up the torch, and with one accord Growch and I headed for the tunnel and fled as if the Devil himself were after us, never mind stones and stumbles, emerging out onto the ledge again with a speed that nearly had us over the edge.

"Well," asked Ky-Lin, comfortingly matter-of-fact. "Was it worth the climb?"

Out it all came, my disappointment, the way we had almost scared ourselves to death, the sheer empty futility of it all.

"I had thought it would be so different," I finished miserably. "Just great big rocks and heaps of pebbles."

"What did you expect?" he asked mildly. "A welcoming committee? Besides, rocks are rocks are rocks, you know. . . ."

I could have done without his homespun philosophy right then, especially as I didn't understand what he was getting at, and nearly told him so. Instead we wended our way down the mountain again and endured another bumpy ride, and it was well past dark when we arrived back at the monastery.

And the last person in the world I wanted to face was Dickon, but there he was, near hysterical.

"Where the hell do you think you've been? You've been missing all day! What on earth time is this to return?"

"Oh shut up, Dickon," I said wearily. I was exhausted, bumped, bruised, fed up and near to tears. "I'm tired. I want a bath and I want to go to bed. I'll tell you all about it in the morning."

"I know what it is: you went off on your own to find the treasure!"

"How many times do I have to tell you?" I yelled back. *"There is no bloody treasure!* There never was!"

"Oh, yes?" he sneered. "That's what you keep on saying, isn't it? Well, let me tell you this; nothing you say will ever convince me that you dragged us all this way for nothing—"

"Us? You mean *you!* Who dragged *you? You* insisted on coming. Each time we tried to go on alone, *you* insisted on following. *You* left the caravan to follow us, *you* travelled up the Silk River to find us, *you* tracked us across the bog—"

He evaded that. "But where did you go today, then?"

"Look," I said. "If you will leave me in peace right now, I have already told you I'll explain it all in the morning."

"Promise?"

"I said so."

"I can trust you?"

"It's your only choice." I shrugged. "If you believe I am going to lie, I can do it as well now as tomorrow. Think about it. Goodnight."

But even after a welcome soak and a bowl of chicken and egg soup, and a bed that welcomed like coming home, I could not sleep. I nodded off for an hour or so, then woke to toss and turn. I was too hot, too cold, itchy, uncomfortable. The longer I tried to sleep, the worse it became. I dozed again, with dream-starts that melted one into another. One moment the once-fat Summer fled an imagined horror, the next a huge moon was shining too bright on my face; now great bats chased across the sky, their wings obscuring the same moon. I woke fretful and pushed a too-heavy Growch away. I rolled down a steep mountain to escape the pursuing flames, a sudden wind rattled the shutters and I opened my eyes to see the oil lamp guttering. It must have been about three in the morning.

Growch stretched and yawned. "You goin' to tell 'im where we went?"

"What choice have I? And what does it matter anyway?"

And I burst into useless tears.

26

About two hours later I had had enough. Although it was still full dark I disturbed Growch again as I flung aside the blankets, donned my father's cloak and stepped outside onto the narrow balcony that served both my room and Dickon's.

Although it was October, the night was still comparatively warm and the stone of the balustrade under my fingers was no colder than the air. Below was a set of steps leading down to a small, ornamental garden, no bigger than ten feet by ten, facing south. I had sat there during the day a couple of times, on one of the two stone benches, amid pots of exotic plants, ivies, and those tiny stunted trees so beloved by the people of this land. Pines, firs, even cherry trees were bound and twisted into grotesque shapes no higher than my hand, yet it is said that they were as much as one hundred years old!

I wondered vaguely if it hurt them to be twisted so unnaturally, and whether it would be a kindness to dig them all up secretly and replant them in the freedom of unrestricted soil many miles away. Or were they so used to their pot-bound existence that they would perish without special nurturing?

The stars had nearly all gone to bed, those left pale with tiredness, but the waxing moon still held a sullen glow as it balanced on the tips of the faraway mountains. It was the color of watered blood, the warts and scars of its face showing up like plague spots. A faint breeze touched my cheek; false dawn would come with the going down of the moon. As I watched I could almost imagine it starting to slide down out of sight. My breathing slowed: I was in tune with the speed of the heavens.

Then, just as the jaws of the mountains gaped to swallow the moon, there came a lightening of the sky in the east. False dawn had turned everything dark gray, and somewhere a sleepy bird woke for an instant, tried a trill and fell silent once more.

And suddenly, like a stifling blanket being pulled off my head, came a lifting of both mind and spirit. I felt so different I could have cried out with the relief. But what had brought all this about? I gazed around at the fading stars, the sinking moon, a lightening in the sky to the east—no, it was none of these.

Then I looked back at the nearly gone moon and realized there was something different about the marks on its face. It was there, then it disappeared. I rubbed my eyes, but when I looked again the moon had slid away and so had the strange mark I thought—I imagined?—I had seen.

I wouldn't, couldn't allow hope to rise once more, only to be dashed. And yet . . .

I went back to bed and slept until midday.

And so, in the afternoon when Dickon again tried to question me about yesterday's activities I told him what we had done almost indifferently, as though it didn't really matter anymore. And at that moment it didn't.

"So you see we just went to look at the place the legends say the dragons live in, but after all that there was nothing there; nothing except an extinct volcano and heaps of rocks and stones, that is."

"Why didn't you let me come?"

"Ky-Lin carried us: he couldn't have managed you as well."

"I should like to have seen it. There might have been something you missed."

"Go see for yourself, then," I said recklessly, and described how he could climb up to the cavern. "But I tell you, it's a waste of time!"

"Then if there was nothing, and you didn't find this friend you told me about, why don't you just pack up now and go back to your tame merchant boyfriend?"

"Here's as good a place as any to overwinter."

"What about money?"

I shrugged. "I offered you some once. I still have it. I might even do a little trading myself. And you: what are you going to do with yourself now your journey is over?"

He looked aghast. "But—I understood we were together in this! I haven't come all this way just to be cast aside like an odd glove. I've got no capital! If you decide to trade, we trade together. What do you really know about buying and selling? Why, you can't even communicate with these people without that colored freak at your heels. . . ." He had always been jealous of Ky-Lin. "At least I have been learning the language in my spare time. You wouldn't last five minutes without me and you know it!"

"Well I shall have to try, shan't I? Don't worry, I shall manage. I shall stay around here for a while, and I shall stay alone. Apart from Growch, of course."

I felt mean, but somehow knew I had to shed him. I knew I had to be on my own, that whatever pass I had come to in my life, whatever awaited me, I had to meet it alone, free of the threat that someone like Dickon posed. No, not "someone like": it was the person himself I had to be free of. He had always made me feel uneasy, that was why I had tried so hard so many times to go ahead without him. And had failed. He was not evil, most people would just see him as a nuisance, and wonder why I had tried so hard to be rid of him. I couldn't explain it, even now: it was just something that was part of him that one day would do me great hurt, of that I was sure. It was nothing of which he was aware either, just as a straight man will not glance back to see he has a crooked shadow. . . .

I made one last try.

"My offer of the money still stands." I'd manage somehow.

"You can keep your ten pieces of gold—or were they thirty pieces of silver?" And he slammed out; as a parting shot it wasn't bad at all.

For the next hour I made a full inventory of my possessions. It was time I moved from the monastery, now I was fully recovered. I would try to rent a couple of rooms in the village below, rather than presume too much on the hospitality of the monks.

There wasn't much to take with me. A few well-worn clothes, sewing kit, leather for patching, monthly cloths, comb; my journal, writing materials and maps; a cooking pot, spoons, mug, and sharp knife; a bag or two of herbs. With a blanket to wrap it all in and my father's cloak, that was about it. Except, of course, for my money belt, in which I still had a little coinage from our performing days, Suleiman's gold, and the assorted coins from my father's dowry to me.

Lastly there were my special treasures: the Waystone, the beautiful crystal gem and, last but first as well, the dragon's egg. I took it out now and looked at it: even since the last time I had done this it seemed to have grown. I cradled it in my hands, marvelling at its perfect symmetry and the way the light caught the speckles that glinted like granite on its surface. I remembered what both my long-ago Wimperling and

Ky-Lin had said about the hundred years or so of incubation it needed before hatching, and was sad I should never see what it contained; I should have to find a suitable place to leave it soon, for it needed quiet and rest, to develop as it should.

There were three or four hours to go until dark, so Growch and I hitched a ride taking woollen cloth from the monastery down to the village, but we hadn't gone far down the narrow, twisty track when Growch announced that we were being followed.

"Who is it?" I asked, peering back up the track. I could see nothing.

" 'Is lordship. 'Oo else?"

"Hell and damnation! Why can't he leave us alone?"

"Wanna lose 'im?"

"Of course."

"Then when we gets to the first 'ouses, jump off quick an' follow me, sharpish."

Once on foot, I realized just how well Growch had used his time when he was off "exploring," as he put it. No doubt he had been in search of his "fluffy bums," but he had learnt the village like a cartographer.

He led me a swift left turn down a side alley, turned right into a courtyard and straight out again through someone's (luckily unoccupied) kitchen, across another street, into a laundry and out again, ducking under wet clothes; two sharp lefts, three rights and then helter-skelter up some steps, down others and into a stuffy little room, greasy with the smell of frying pork and chicken.

Growch trotted up to the cook, who had obviously met him before, because he aimed a halfhearted blow with his skillet, then fished out a pig's foot.

"C'mon," said Growch through the gristle. "Out the back."

This led out onto a street where the unoccupied ladies of the town held their nightly "entertainments." Everything was now closed, shuttered and barred, and backed out onto some unattractive garbage heaps, but I could hear awakening chatter behind the closed doors. Growch went over to inspect the rubbish, but I called him sharply back.

"That's enough! You'll be sick. . . ."

" 'Ow often you seen me sick?" It was a rhetorical question, and he knew it.

"Where now?" I asked, changing the subject.

" 'E's a'ead o' us now. Let's see what 'es up to. I'll scout, you follow close."

So we crept along the irregular streets, stepping in and out of afternoon-going-on-evening shadows, passing the elderly taking patches of sun, children playing primitive games with colored squares of baked clay, or chasing each other in the eternal game of tag. I ducked under lines of washing, stepped around rubbish, avoided the throwing out of slops. There seemed no system or plan to the village; it had just grown. Every now and then we passed through little squares, apparently there just because the houses had been built facing one another. Several lanes led nowhere.

Suddenly I heard Dickon's voice. He seemed to be involved in some sort of altercation and, rounding a corner, there he was, arguing with a couple of villagers over a tatty-looking horse. From the look of it he wanted to "borrow" the horse against future payment, but they were having none of it.

I ducked back into the shadows, but he had seen me. All that rushing around with Growch for nothing, but perhaps after all it had only been an excuse on the dog's part to pick up a snack or two. He wouldn't admit it if it was.

"Hey, Summer! Come here a minute. . . ." Dickon led me aside. "Look here. I've been thinking about what you said earlier: the parting of the ways and all that stuff. Well, I've decided to do something about it." He stood back and folded his arms. "I think it would be best if I took off for a few days, before the winter sets in. I could travel between the villages, see what opportunities there are for trade, check on what goods they are short of, that sort of thing. What do they import now? Rice, salt, oil, metals; those are taken care of, but there must be other commodities they could do with. Why, if I sat down and worked it all out I bet I could do substantial undercutting of the other traders."

"Very commendable," I said. Why was it I didn't believe him?

"Well, what do you say? I was just bargaining with these fellows for the loan of their horse for a few days, but they obviously want cash down. Now, if you want me to make a life of my own—if you still insist you don't want to come in with me, which is the most sensible thing to do, let's face it—then you can't deny me this chance. I just need a few coins to hire the horse and kit myself out—"

"How much?" At least it meant he would be out from under my feet for a few days.

He named a sum, but I shook my head. "Too much. I'll talk to them, or try to. . . ."

"No, no, no. No need. I'll do my own bargaining. Probably bring them down by half . . ."

Which meant he had been trying to con me out of some extra for himself. Apparently the men were satisfied with his revised offer, and I paid out a few coins from my money belt after they had shown us where the horse was stabled and included the hire of saddle and bridle.

We started back up the steep track to the monastery together, hoping for a lift on the way, but quite prepared to walk, though Growch would grumble long before the top.

"I suppose you were in the village looking for lodgings," said Dickon carelessly, when we had walked for about five minutes. "Any luck?"

"Not yet," I answered, equally carelessly. "Plenty of time."

"Oh. Yes, of course. Well you might as well wait now until I get back and I can give you a hand shifting your gear."

"There's not much to carry. Anyway, Ky-Lin can help me."

"How?"

"He can do the bargaining. Don't worry, just take your time. I'll be fine."

He hesitated. "In that case—I'll need a bit more money. For provisions."

I gave him a couple of coins. "That should be enough for some cooked rice and dried fruit."

He inspected the coins. "Not very generous, are you?"

"We've managed on less."

Just then we heard the rattle of the little wagon that carried goat milk down from the monastery twice a day coming up behind us, so we rode the rest of the way.

That he was determined on going somewhere there was no doubt; that night he was packed up well before bedtime, and had already arranged a lift down to the village before cockcrow.

Once again I couldn't sleep. Once again I went out onto the balcony, once again gazed out at the waxing moon. Had it been just my imagination that had showed me a fleeting shadow across that glowing surface? Was my sudden change of spirits due to no more than an illusion? And then, just as the moon touched the tip of the mountains I saw it again! No bigger than a distant leaf in autumn, it drifted across the face of the moon. I was almost certain now. Almost . . .

My heart thudding, not even bothering to throw a cloak over the nightshirt I wore, I ran down to the little garden below, my hands grasping the balustrade so hard they hurt. But there was nothing there, nothing.

Nothing other than the whisper of air across my cheek as though great wings were beating far above.

I waited and waited, but it seemed that was that. Despondently I trailed back to bed, and was just dozing off when there came a sudden rattling crash. It seemed to come from the direction of Dickon's room. He wasn't sleepwalking, was he? Or perhaps he had decided to get up extra early so as not to miss his lift to the village. Once again I hurried out onto the balcony; now the noise appeared to be coming from the little garden. The stupid boy hadn't fallen down the steps, had he?

"What the devil do you think you are doing, Dickon? Some of us are trying to sleep. . . ."

"Some of us can't sleep," came a voice from below. "And who the hell is Dickon? Not that stupid boy who stole your money all that long time ago, surely?"

27

Wimperling!" I called out joyously.

But no, it wasn't my little winged pig, the one who had flown me to safety all that long time ago, because he wasn't a pig at all, was he? He had almost broken my heart when he had burst to smithereens at my third kiss and left only a tiny piece of shrivelled hide that even now I wore in the pouch around my neck.

"Summer? Somerdai . . . my Talitha. Come here, my dear. Let me see you!"

A man, a tall man dressed in the colors of the night, was leaning on the balustrade in the little garden. I knew who it was although I couldn't see his face, of course I did, but was I still asleep and dreaming?

"Come on down! It's been a long time. . . ."

And many, many wearisome miles. Heat, cold, exhaustion, near starvation, danger; and my imaginings of it had not been at all like this, a hidden-faced stranger who lolled against a balustrade and called my name as though we had only parted yesterday. The memory that had sustained me had been of a snatched embrace, a burning kiss, a wrenching away. Quick, violent, fraught with emotion for both of us.

"Do I have to come up there and fetch you?" It wasn't a soft, warm voice like my blind knight had used in his seducing mood, nor the comfortable town-burr of the merchant, Matthew Spicer; it had a harsh, nasal quality, a sort of scraping reluctance for the words to form. A disturbing voice, a compelling one, but not necessarily a very nice one.

"No," I said. "I'm coming down."

And slowly, almost reluctantly, I moved down the steps till I stood on the bottom one, clutching the neck of my nightshirt as if it could be the one gesture that kept me from being stripped naked.

"You're thinner," said the voice. "And your hair is shorter. But your eyes are just the same; great big wondering eyes, mirrors of your soul. Why don't you come nearer? Are you afraid?"

"I—I don't know. I don't remember . . . I didn't think—"

"If you don't know, remember, think—then why are you here?" The voice was gentler now, as if it was getting more used to human speech, and there was even a hint of amused tenderness. "And why don't you use my human name?"

Jasper. Master of Many Treasures. The dragon-man, man-dragon I had travelled half the known world to find. And yet I couldn't even use his name. Why? I was frightened, shy, now uncertain of those feelings I had been so certain of before. Or thought I had. Even while I cursed myself for my stupidity I could feel the tears welling up in my eyes, spilling down my cheeks, blurring my vision, till the figure before me wavered and dissolved.

Something touched my face, and the corner of a cloak caught the tears as they fell, absorbed them as they coursed down my cheeks, wiped my nose.

"Blow . . . That's better! Am I so terrifying? Why you're trembling. . . . Here, wrap my cloak around you. There, isn't that better?"

As he was still wearing the cloak himself—yes, it was. Suddenly, very much better. But he didn't press it; he had one arm round my shoulders now and with the other hand he lifted my chin, but we were still inches away from a proper embrace. Physically, that is; emotionally, as far as he was concerned, I could see it was miles.

"Open your eyes: look at me! I don't bite."

"Dragons do," I said, still feebly resisting the temptations of his sudden nearness.

"I'm not a dragon all the time. I've learnt a lot in the time we've been apart, including how to keep my two selves separate—usually. I make mistakes, of course—and I still find it difficult to land on narrow balconies at night, as no doubt you heard. . . ."

"Have you been a dragon all the time till now?"

"Mostly, but not all. So now I am owed a little man-time."

"Three months in every year," I said, remembering.

"And all because you kissed a rather ugly little pig three times—"

"You weren't ugly! I mean the Wimperling wasn't! You—he— wasn't exactly beautiful, I suppose, but very endearing."

"More than me, I suppose! Perhaps I'd better reverse the process."

"You can't, can you?" Forgetting to be shy I opened my eyes properly and looked up at him.

It wasn't fair: I had forgotten just how handsome he was. The dim light threw half his face into darkness, but the dark, frowning brows, yellow eyes set slightly aslant, strong, hooked nose and the wide mouth that could express both harshness or humor, strength or tenderness, they were quite clear. Tentatively I raised my fingers to the hand that cradled my chin; two years ago it had been cold, with the traces of scales still evident, but now it was warm and smooth.

"Remember me?" He was teasing.

"Of course I do, but—" I lifted a finger to trace the thin line of moustache, the short hairs along his jawline. "You're not quite the same."

"Neither are you, my dear. You're grown up." He tipped my chin higher. "There are great shadows under your eyes, your mouth is firmer, you are much slimmer. . . . Was it bad, your journey? No, don't tell me now," and his mouth brushed mine so gently it was come and gone like the touch of a moth's wing. "We have plenty of time to talk." His lips met mine again, lingering there longer, exerted a stronger pressure. "I can't tell you how nice it is to see you again. And what a surprise!" The next kiss still teased, though it was more like a proper one. "You know something, my little Talitha? You are practically irresistible! Tell me something; how did you manage to end up here, of all places in the world to choose from?"

For a moment the meaning of what he had said didn't sink in, but when it did I pushed away from him and stood there, bewildered. His question meant that he didn't realize that I had come all this way just to seek him out; he didn't know how much I loved him. How could I now betray my foolish hopes, my enduring love, to someone who obviously thought of me just as a temporary plaything?

The hot blood rushed to my cheeks and I was about to cover my shame and confusion by muttering something utterly inane like "looking for treasure," when I was saved from making a fool of myself by glimpsing a sudden flash of white on the balcony above.

I tugged at Jasper's sleeve. "Quick, you must go! Dickon—yes, the same one—is up there on the balcony, and he mustn't see you!"

"Then I shall come again tomorrow night. Earlier."

"He's away this morning for a few days—"

"Good." He leapt up on the balustrade. "Tomorrow. Midnight . . ." He paused for a moment, then plunged over the edge.

My genuine cry of fright was echoed by a yell from Dickon above. I rushed over to the void, terror-stricken, my heart in my mouth, then I heard the *crack*! of opening wings and saw my man-dragon soar away into the darkness.

Dickon, who had seen nothing of this, joined me at the balustrade. "Who was it? What happened? Where did he go?"

I was still trembling, though he didn't notice this, and I tried to keep the shakes from my voice as I answered.

"I've no idea. A thief, a voyeur? I heard a voice, got up and came down here. I tried to talk to him, find out what he was doing—" how long had he been listening? "—but when he saw you he jumped down to the rocks below." I leant over the edge. "There's no sign of him now."

"You must be more careful! Are you sure that money of yours is safe? Bar your door and your windows. Get that lazy dog of yours to stand guard out here at night." He seemed genuinely worried, though whether it was me or my money he was more bothered about it was difficult to say. "Promise me you won't do anything—foolish—while I am away?"

No, I wouldn't do anything foolish. I had done enough of that already, including coming here in the first place, following an impossible dream.

"I promise," I said. "I shall be here when you return, safe and sound. And—" the thought coming to me unbidden and forcing itself into speech "—and I may change my mind about staying here after all."

"You mean . . . go back to the merchant?" He sounded incredulous. Then, suddenly, suspicious. "You have found what you seek, then?" I could almost see the picture of a heap of treasure in his mind, followed by the thought: where has she hidden it?

"Why not? There I was safe and secure. A good marriage . . ." I shrugged. "Or I could still go into trade somewhere else. It's not entirely a man's world, you know; there are women physicians, builders, painters, herbalists, farmers, metal workers, writers. . . . And now I'm going back to bed. Have a good journey."

It was a relief to be rid of him, but unfortunately this also gave me too much time to think. Over and over again I reviewed in my mind Jasper's visit, what he had looked like, what he said, and, more important, what he didn't. I had been stupid, shy, tearful, but he had been—different. I suppose it was ridiculous of me to suppose we could pick up just where we had left off over two years ago, for that had been a moment of such high intensity it could not be repeated, but I had expected him to understand why I had travelled all this way to see him again.

Instead he was treating me with an amused tenderness, just as you would a particular pet, indulging my tears and stupid behavior. But hadn't he said I was now grown-up, too? And did he truly not know why I was here? Long, long ago he had warned me against loving him: was this because he knew he was incapable of such emotion? Or was it that he no longer found me attractive?

Had my journey been in vain, then?

I'd be damned if it had! My pride wouldn't let me just creep away without a fight. I hadn't come all this way to be brushed aside. As for being attractive—well, just let him wait and see!

Off I went down to the village and when I returned spent the rest of the day with scissors, needle and thread, warm water, the opening of this jar, that bottle.

Ky-Lin visited me at around six. I hadn't seen him for days, but it seemed he knew, somehow, of Jasper's visit.

"Was it how you imagined it, girl? Was it worth all the journeying?" He looked around at my preparations. "You know, I remember something my Master used to say to his disciples: 'Be careful on what you set your heart, for it may just be you achieve your desire.' "

I didn't understand; surely to get what you wanted was the ultimate goal.

He looked at me steadily, his plumed tail swishing gently from side to side. "You will understand someday, I think." I had never seen him look so sad. "Do not forget I am still here to help you, if you need me."

At last I heard the monks chanting their evening prayers, the dissonance of their softly struck bells. Soon it would be midnight. I slipped the green silk gown I had made that afternoon over my head. There was no mirror of course, but it felt good, the dress swirling round me in soft, loose folds, as it did so catching the perfume of sandalwood oil I had used in my bathing water. On my feet were a pair of green felt slippers I had hastily cobbled once the dress was finished, and I had a green ribbon in my hair.

I had told Growch whom I was expecting and asked him to please not interrupt our meeting.

"Din' last night, did I? You goin' to do naughties tonight, like the first time you met?"

Ridiculously I felt myself blushing: fancy being embarrassed by a dog! "None of your business what I'm going to do!"

"You looks nice," he said unexpectedly. "Quite the lady . . ."

Probably I was now wearing the most beautiful dress I had ever possessed, and after what Growch had said, I wished, I wished I had a mirror. It would be nice to see a beautiful Summer, just for once, especially as I had spent so much of my life as a plain, fat girl nobody looked at twice.

I left a lamp burning in my room, took the lantern from Dickon's room and set it on the balcony. Tonight was overcast, the moon hidden behind a scud of cloud. There was a sudden sound behind me: only a moth, banging helplessly against the oiled paper of the lantern. I brushed it aside, although the flame was well shielded.

Suddenly it was cold; a chill wind came rushing from the snow-capped mountains to the north and whirled around me: my skin shivered into goosebumps and the breeze lifted the hair on my head into tangles. Winter was giving its warning—or was it something else that made me think of a dying end?

The wind ceased as suddenly as it had risen, the clouds parted and the moon shone clear and bright. I twisted the ring on my finger—strange, it seemed much looser; perhaps I was losing too much weight—but it was warm and comforting, and I pushed any dark thoughts from my mind as a shadow flicked across the edge of my sight and swooped away beneath.

I ran down the steps to the little garden and there, just climbing over the edge, was my man-dragon, his cloak flapping behind him like wings. He stopped when he saw me, one foot still on the balustrade.

"My, what have we here, then? A strange fair lady!"

"What—what do you mean?"

"To what do I owe this honor, beauteous maid?" Stepping down, he gave me a bow, his hand on his heart. "I swear you are the very vision of loveliness . . ."

For a moment I truly believed he didn't recognize me, then he laughed, came forward, and took my hands

"You look absolutely wonderful, Talitha! I wouldn't have believed it possible!" Did it depend so much on the clothes I wore, I wondered? "Of course you are beautiful anyway, always were, but that dress frames your loveliness perfectly! Did you make it especially for me?"

"Of course not!" I lied too quickly. (Never let a man think you've tarted yourself up just for him, Mama used to say. They are big-headed enough as it is. A little disarray is perfectly acceptable.) "It's just something I had put by."

He turned over my right hand, brushing his thumb across my index finger. "With fresh needle marks? You're not a good liar, my dear—no, don't be angry. I am deeply honored, believe me," and he sang a little song I used to be familiar with in my own country.

"Silver ribbons in your hair, lady;
"Golden shoon upon your feet.
"Crimson silk to clothe you, lady:
"And a kiss your knight to greet!"

Only he changed all the colors to "green," and I got a kiss at the end of it, a proper one this time.

In an instant my arms went around his neck and my body curved into his, so you couldn't have passed a silken thread between us. I felt as though I was melting, fusing with him until we were metal of the same mold. I couldn't breathe or think, all I could do was feel.

Then at once everything changed. Suddenly I was standing alone, scarcely able to keep my feet for the trembling in my limbs, shaking with a frustration I had no words for, an ache that came from the deepest parts of my body.

All I could say was: "Why?" and I didn't even realize I had spoken out loud.

"No," he said. "No, my very dear one, no."

I didn't understand. "What's wrong? What have I done?"

"Done? Nothing, nothing at all. But we can't let this happen again. It was bad enough last time, against all the laws of nature, and I was the one who let it happen. No, now don't cry. . . ." He came forward and held my hands again. "Remember this: we are different, you and I. You are human, through and through, and nothing but. I am three-quarters, nay more, of a completely different creature. Normally I have a different form, different morals, different view of life, different future. There is no way, absolutely none, in which we could ever have a future together, even for a few days, and anything less wouldn't be fair to you. Don't you understand?"

"What about the quarter that isn't dragon? What about the times when you are 'He who Scrapes the Clouds' or whatever is your dragon name? What about the man who stands before me now? What happens to Jasper?"

"Jasper," he said, "may be the Master of Many Treasures, but not of his own soul—if he has one, that is. He is ruled by his larger part and that is dragon; he is subject to dragon rule and dragon law. He may make no important decisions contrary to those that are already laid down, unless it is first referred to the Council for consideration. And unless this Jasper is a Master Dragon, which he is not, then there is no hope of changing the laws or of making any appeal against them. . . ." He was speaking in a dull, monotonous way, like a priest bored with the service.

I tried to humor him. "What is the difference between an ordinary dragon and a master?"

"Treasure. The gathering of enough to satisfy the Council. The last master brought five great jewels, still much admired. An emerald from a rainforest on the other side of the world, a sapphire from an island in the warm seas, a diamond from the mines of the southern desert, a ruby from a temple of the infidel, and a priceless freshwater pearl from the Islands of Mist."

"How long ago was that?"

"Some five hundred years."

I gasped. So long ago! "Then how long can a dragon live? And what is the Council?"

"A fit dragon can live for a thousand years, perhaps more. Once there were hundreds, all over the world, together with other similar creatures of all sorts, shapes and sizes. Now their bones lie scattered, for our legends say that a disaster came from the sky, a great ball of fire that brought with it a breath of death that destroyed millions of creatures, the dragons among them. Some survived, but very few, and those only in the high mountains, where the contamination couldn't reach them. Other pockets of safety conserved other creatures, mainly small ones: lizards, tortoises, lemurs. Then the world gradually changed, mammals growing strong at the expense of the dragon." He glanced at my indignant face. "That is what our legends say; yours are probably rather different."

"God created the world," I said stiffly. "And Adam and Eve came before dragons. I think. If He ever created them; some say they come from the Devil."

"Who's he?"

He didn't know? "And in any case I don't think Noah would have been able to cope with a pair of dragons in his Ark. It must have been difficult enough putting lions and sheep with rats and camels. . . ."

He was laughing now. "Oh Summer-Talitha, you take things so seriously, so literally!"

I was so happy to see him back to normal, as it were, that I couldn't take offense. I knew what was right, so what the dragons believed in didn't matter. "And the Council?" I prompted.

"All the Master Dragons who survive, eleven in all."

"And where is the Council?"

"You've seen them."

"I have?"

"Of course!" He smiled again. "Let us say they saw you, and the dog. They told me so."

"The Blue Mountain?"

"Yes."

"But there was nothing there—except rocks and stones and pebbles and dust and a nasty smell."

"Rocks and pebbles? Are you sure?"

I remembered something Ky-Lin had said: "Rocks are rocks are rocks, you know. . . ."

"You mean—the cavern was full of dragons? The rocks . . ."

"Yes."

"And the pebbles?"

"Treasure. Heaps of it."

So Dickon had been right after all! There *had* been a fabulous treasure waiting at the end of our journey. . . .

I was silent for a moment. "How do they hide—look like rocks?"

"A mist of illusion. Easy stuff."

"But don't you think it's an awful waste having all that treasure just sitting there doing nothing?"

"It's very pretty. A delight to run between one's claws, to taste with one's tongue. Did you know all jewels taste different? Like bonbons do to humans . . . Myself, I prefer the tang of a fire opal."

I thought he might be joking, but a glance told me he wasn't.

"I still think it's a waste."

"Why? What about all those kings and princes, merchants and misers who do precisely the same thing? They have rooms full of treasure that never see the light of day. What about those who bury treasure so it is lost forever? What about those vandals that actually destroy what you would call treasure, just for the joy of it? Why should a few ageing dragons be denied their simple pleasures? Which is worse: to steal a jewel every now and again, or to take lives in the name of religion, or whatever?"

"But dragons eat people, too!" I remembered the tales of my childhood; beautiful damsels chained to rocks, children offered up, young men stripped naked to fight with a wooden sword a battle they could not hope to win.

"Perhaps some did, once. There were many more of us then. Now we eat seldom, and then only to fuel our fires, speed our wings. And there are not many of us left who undertake journeys of any distance."

"Why?"

"Most of them are too old, some well over the thousand-year norm.

All they want is a little heat, a little sleep, and their memories. They are great tale-tellers. To them the puny adventures and battles and wars of humankind are like a breath, soon expended."

I wondered. Sometimes he spoke of "us," sometimes of "them." Was this because of the life he was forced to lead? A quarter man, three-quarters dragon? I must try and keep him thinking of dragons as "them," and concentrate on making him feel like a man.

"Well, waste or no, I didn't come all this way for treasure," I said, choosing my words carefully.

"Why, then?" He released my hands and slipped an arm about my waist. "Adventure? Curiosity?"

No, Love, you great idiot! I thought, but of course didn't say it. "A little of both, I suppose," I said. "All that travelling we did, while you were still the Wimperling, gave me a taste for it. Besides which, I have had a chance of earning my own living. Real money . . ."

"And where did you pick up that little thief, Dickon, again?"

I explained. "I kept trying to leave him behind, but he persisted in believing that I was after treasure, dragon treasure. Thank God he has given up that idea and gone off for a couple of days looking for trading opportunities."

"Oh, I don't think he has given up. Did you tell him about your visit to Blue Mountain?"

"Yes, but—"

"I flew over his encampment earlier, frightened his horse off into the bush. Take him the best part of a day to catch up with it again."

"You don't mean . . ."

"I do mean. He's camped at the foot of the Blue Mountain, and tomorrow, if I'm not much mistaken, he'll be climbing the path you took, looking for the treasure!"

28

The crafty devil! Telling me he was looking for new opportunities, and making me pay for yet another treasure hunt! I should never have told him about the Blue Mountain; it was obvious he hadn't believed me.

"He won't find anything; will he?"

"No more than you did."

"Well, I hope he falls off the path!" I said crossly. "He's been nothing but trouble ever since we met up again."

"Tell me . . ." and he spread out his cloak on the stone flags of the little garden, sat cross-legged and pulled me down beside him. "I want to hear everything that's happened to you since the Place of Stones."

I glossed over that dreadful journey back to Matthew's, for after all it wasn't his fault I had near starved to death; I told him of my decision to turn down Matthew's offer (but not the real reason), made him smile over my forgeries of the merchant's signature and running off dressed as a boy to seek my fortune. I made my adventures as amusing as I could: storm at sea, ambush, imprisonment, the bog, bandits, the Desert of Death and the hairy people.

When I had finished he ruffled my hair, leant forward and kissed my cheek.

"I reckon it was a good job you had your friend Ky-Lin with you. I have heard of them, but never seen one. You could have easily died a dozen times without him. . . ." He frowned. "But all this doesn't explain why you left the caravan trails and came this way."

Ah, Jasper, my love, this was the difficult part. . . .

"I wanted to see you again," I said lightly. "Man-dragons are a little out of my experience, you see. Added to that, the coins my father left me led me all the way across every country to this one. And on Matthew's maps this part was marked: 'Here be Dragons.' Simple as that."

"Was it? Was it really?" He slipped his arm about my waist again. "You know something? I went back to look for you after I made my initial journey here. I worried that you would find it difficult to find your merchant's house again. But you had vanished from the face of the earth! Nice to know you were all right." He cuddled me closer. "Well, now that you've found your man-dragon again, what do you want of him?"

"A couple of kisses," I said promptly. "Proper ones. Not no-commitment-it's-dangerous-you-mustn't-get-entangled-with-a-dragon-man. Neither should it be let's-have-a-laugh-and-a-kiss-and-say-good-bye! I want you to pretend," I snuggled up closer, "just for a moment, that I am the most desirable woman in the world. . . ." My hand stroked his cheek. "I am a princess under a spell, and only you can break the ice about her heart." Had I gone too far? "It's not a lot to ask, it can't threaten your life! You're not going to change back into a pig, or anything like that—"

"I should hope not!"

He was chuckling; that was encouraging. At least there was no outright rejection.

"Well, then?" Now for it; my heart was beating uncomfortably fast and loud. "Or can't you pretend?"

"I don't need to pretend," he said, and gathered me into his arms.

At first he just held me close, his hands stroking my hair, my cheeks, my hands. Every time he touched me my inside tangled itself up into knots and I feared he would hear my heart, but he hummed a gentle little droning song, as soothing as the sound of a hive or the turning of a spinning wheel. Gradually the tune and his gentle touch calmed my mind, but not my body.

I was aware of my skin, my blood, my bones. I could see his shadowy face bent over mine; I could hear his soft voice, with the slight grating tone in the lower notes; in the air was the pungency of the rough-headed autumn plants in pots in the garden, the night-wind smell of Jasper's clothes, and a certain slightly musky scent that seemed to come from his skin. My whole body was stimulated to a point I had not thought possible, and now came the taste of his lips.

I thought of the tang of burnt sugar, the bitter black heart of an opium poppy, the smoke from autumn bonfires, the cold, iron smell of ice and snow, newly washed linen sun-dried, the sharp bite of a juicy apple, a snuffed candle—then I didn't think at all.

At first he was experimenting with my lips and tongue, but gradually as he pulled me closer I knew that at last it was me, me, me! that he wanted. I didn't care if it was lust without love, desire without commitment, I just kissed him back with all my heart. His hands found my breasts, his body was full of a hard urgency that found a response in my yielding form.

"Summer Talitha," he murmured. "My little love . . ."

For answer I pulled him down so we rested together on his cloak, our bodies inhibited only by the clothes we wore. For a brief instant it seemed he might think better of it, but then I took over the caressing, my fingers moving on his chest and stomach, untying the laces of his trews, my mouth thrust up hungrily to his. . . .

And then it was too late for either of us.

I remember the rip of silk as my dress parted company with its stitches; I remember the feel of his crisp, dark hair under my fingers, the rasp of his beard against my cheek; I remember stifling my cries in the soft skin where his neck met his shoulder; I remember, oh I remember the hard thrusts I welcomed with fierce ripostes of my own; I remember—but there are no words to describe the cascades of delight that followed, never will be. No words, no music, no painting: nothing can adequately portray raw emotion like that. Until you have felt it you will never know, and if you have you will realize it is beyond description.

Afterwards we lay in each other's arms. Only now did my cheeks sting where his heard had rubbed them; only now was I conscious of the uncomfortable rucks of the cloak beneath us; only now did my insides ache with an inward tension as though they pulled against a cat's cradle of tiny inside stitches. I was sticky and sweaty, but so was he, and it didn't matter.

He stirred, sighed, stroked my hair. "You are a witch, girl: you know that?" He leant up on one elbow and gazed down at me. "You realize I had no intention of that happening?"

"I know." I put up a finger and traced the line of his nose. "But I did." I sat up. "And you wanted it too."

"Maybe. But it was wrong, wrong! We shouldn't have done it."

"Why not? Who are we hurting?"

"Ourselves." His voice was bitter. "In time I could have forgotten you and, whatever you think now, you would have forgotten me too. But now I shall always want you. You will always want me. If we looked for love elsewhere, or tried to do without, we should both think only of each other. We have forged a link that can never be broken."

"But that was the way I wanted it—"

"You didn't understand what you were getting yourself into. We can

never be together, don't you understand? And you will suffer more than
I. In my dragon form I can forget you for three-quarters of the year, but
you—you will never forget!"

"Then I shall wait for the quarter-year you are a man," I said ob-
stinately. "Wherever it is. That will be enough for me. Three months
with you is better than none at all."

He rose to his feet in one swift movement and crossed to the balustrade. His whole posture was stiff, his hands clenched on the stone,
his shoulders raised, his head bent.

"It's impossible."

I went to stand at his side, clutching at my torn gown, aware all at
once of a chill wind that blew from the north, making the stars shiver
in sympathy. The moon was down, but a pale light had followed her
descent, a trace of silver on the permanent snows.

"Why is it impossible? Don't you want to see me again?"

He glanced at me, but I couldn't see his expression. "Of course I
want to be with you, as often as I can—but that is just the point. It's
not possible!"

"But *why,* if you want to? What's to stop you?"

He turned, gripped my shoulders. "It's not as simple as you seem to
think! If I could know for sure, say to you: all right, my dear, my love, I
am yours from November until January. Find us a house where we can
be one for those three months of the year. . . . Or if I could say: I can be
with you in March, May and September, find me that house etc."

He released me, leant over the balustrade again. "But it doesn't work
that way: I wish it did. I just don't have those certainties. These—" he
gestured at himself "—these remissions, if you can call them that, give
me very little warning. At first, they gave me none at all and it was
dangerous. Then I had no idea how long they would last either: five minutes, five hours, five days. . . ."

He traced the line of my jaw with his finger. "That was one of the
reasons I gave up looking for you; it was too unpredictable, the time I
could spend asking questions, and twice I nearly got killed." He sighed.
"It has become easier, like changing to come and see you. I can control
it for a couple of hours or so, and if it is going to be longer, a week or
so, I get a warning beforehand, a sort of painless headache. But I still
don't know how long it will last."

I was devastated. "But—"

"No," he said firmly. "I couldn't live with you all the time. My
dragon side is too unpredictable. Nor could you keep me in a shed at
the bottom of the garden betweenwhiles, just waiting for my nicer side

to come out. I think the neighbors might object," he added, with a smile.
"Oh, come on darling: we'll think of something!"

"But what?" I was close to tears.

He shrugged. "Right now I have no idea. I shall consult the Council,
though I warn you they are finding it difficult to accept that I am not
completely dragon. No precedent, you see. Plenty of legends, but no
firm records. At the moment I am something of a celebrity, but there
are those who wish to cast me out." He shook his head. "I should have
a better case to argue if I could bring them the jewels they so desire—my
permit to become a Master Dragon. But that, of course, will take time."

"So it is just some jewels they need?"

"To become a Master Dragon and not a mere Apprentice—as I am
now—I have to be able to perform the usual flying tricks: spirals, hovering, steep dives, flying backwards, backspins, and I also have to contribute something of value to the Hoard. It can be of gold or silver, but
they prefer the easier-to-handle glitter of jewels, cut or uncut."

"Do there have to be a certain number of these?"

He shook his head. "Recently—within the last thousand years or
so that is—it has become traditional to bring in a selection, but the
foremost criterion is that of color. Sometimes one stone is enough; we
possess, I believe, the largest uncut emerald the world has yet seen. As
big as your fist, Talitha, but too fragile to cut."

An idea was forming in my mind. "Do they have light in that cave
of theirs?"

"Of course. There are a number of small openings that let in both
sun- and moonlight, and with a blast or two of fire they can light
semipermanent torches. Why?"

"Just wait a moment. . . ." Running up the steps I found what I
wanted in my room, disturbing a sleepy Growch, then went back out
again, picking up the lantern as I rejoined Jasper in the garden. Setting
the light on one of the benches I opened my fist and slowly twisted the
crystal the captain's wife had given me in front of the flame. Even with
that relatively dim illumination the crystal threw a thousand rainbow
lights across the garden, the balcony, our faces and clothes, the wall
above, the rocks beneath, and we were almost blinded by reds and
greens, yellows and purples, blues and oranges.

Jasper took it from my fingers. "By the stars! This is the most
beautiful . . . Where did you get it?"

I explained.

"Do you know what it is?" He sounded excited.

"A crystal. Nicely cut, but—"

"But nothing! This has been cut by a master! In fact—" He looked at it more closely. "In fact I believe this may be one of the thirteen lost many hundreds of years ago when pagan hordes overran the city of the Hundred Towers. . . . So far six have been traced of the thirteen that were made by the Master of Cut Glass—one for each lunar month, you see—and this might well be the seventh." He was handling it as reverently as I would a splinter of the True Cross. "We—the Council that is—already possess one of these, but to have a pair . . . Do you realize what this means? If you let me take it to them, that will mean automatic Dragon Mastership!" He wrapped his arms about me. "And that would mean I could be equal to any, and they would be bound to consider any request I made!"

"They could agree to—regularize your changes?"

"Yes! I can also ask to spend my man-time with you."

He was fairly dancing around the small space of the garden, holding me up high against his chest. "We can find somewhere. . . . Why, I've just remembered the very place! There is an island set in the bluest of seas, miles away from the trade routes, where the sun shines warm year round and the land is peopled by the gentlest of natives, who would welcome us both. Everything you planted would grow, and there are fish in the sea—"

"It sounds like Paradise," I said wistfully. I could see it now. Yellow sands running up to the greenery of a forest, cool streams running between moss-covered stones, hills blue in the distance, huge butterflies feeding from the trumpets of exotic lilies, trees alive with the chatter of multicolored birds. A little hut set in a clearing, not too far from the sea, lines set out for fish, a net for the collection of shellfish, a patch of ground for the vegetables, another for a few chickens and a goat; a hammock slung between the trees, and Growch for company when Jasper had to be away . . .

His kiss prevented any further daydreaming.

"And now I must go, and quickly; I can feel a change coming over me already. Forgive me, my dear: I shall hope to see you tomorrow." He kissed me again. "And I shall keep an eye on your Dickon. . . ."

"Not *my* Dickon!" I protested, but Jasper had disappeared. Instead a black dragon hung on to the balustrade: scaly body, gaping jaws, huge leathery wings outspread, yellow eyes burning in a bony skull. I was afraid, but not so frightened as I would have been two hours or so earlier if Jasper had suddenly appeared in his dragon shape without warning.

The intelligence in those yellow eyes was benign, I was sure of that, so I had no hesitation in picking up the crystal and placing it in one outstretched claw.

"Godspeed, my love," I said, then stepped back hurriedly as the wind of his wings blew hair, dress, leaves, petals around me like a whirlwind.

All that long day I was in a fever of impatience. I mended my green silk dress, sorted out my belongings for the umpteenth time, brought my journal up to date, couldn't eat; snapped at Growch, then hugged him; washed my hair and set it; didn't like the result and washed it again to hang loose, and sun-dried it.

Ky-Lin paid a visit around midmorning, looked at all my preparations, fluffed the tip of his tail up like a peacock and retired, remarking: "I hope you know what you are doing. . . ."

Of course I did! I was getting ready for my love, shedding what I did not need, preparing for the time when we would both be together forever, even if only for part of each year. Nothing was more important than this, yet the day seemed to crawl by, the sun standing still in the sky on purpose, the hours marked only by gongs, dissonant bells, and the soft, monotonous chant of the monks.

Several times I went out onto the balcony and looked in the direction of the Blue Mountain, wondering how Jasper was presenting his case to the Council; I wondered, too, if Dickon, that handsome treacherous boy, had reached the cave, only to be as disappointed as I had been.

At last the sun really did start to slide down the sky to the west. I supped some broth and bread, tasting nothing in my impatience, took a warm bath, slid into my mended dress, combed my hair until it sparked out from my head like a halo, then sat down by the door to the balcony to wait.

And wait.

The moon came up, near full now, and flooded the countryside with light, the stars pricked through their cover; at midnight a small wind blew up; at one it died down again, and I was yawning; by two I was half-asleep and must have drifted into a dream, because I thought I was talking to my old friends Basher, Traveler, Mistral, and the Wimperling, when suddenly the latter took wing, swung around in the sky and came back to land at my side, only this time he was a man.

"Jasper!" I started up, suddenly wide awake once more. "What did they say?"

"I am now a Master Dragon, thanks to your gift!" Glints like rain-drops or tiny diamonds seemed to surround him. "But . . ."

"But what? Will they let you go?" I ran into his arms.

He kissed me, but there was a constraint in his manner. "They are considering it, yes. But they want to see you: face-to-face."

29

I drew back, shocked and horrified. "B—but I can't! They might eat me!"

He drew me close again. "Nonsense! They are so pleased with the Dragon Stone that a whole village full of desirable maidens could parade in front of them and they would never notice! They were so euphoric they gave me the accolade of Master Dragon at once, without asking to assess my flying skills. Just as well: I think I would have failed on the backspins. . . ." He kissed my brow. "Then I asked for leave of absence from my dragon form for a fixed term each year. They wanted to know why, of course." He frowned. "It was very difficult for them to understand. To them, fair maidens were for dining on, not living with—in the legends, of course," he amended hastily.

"There must be lady dragons," I said. "Couldn't you have explained it that way?"

"There are no 'lady dragons' as you call them. There may have been once, I suppose, but now many of those left are bisexual. There are others, like myself, who are totally male, who can fertilize the bisexuals, though most of them manage on their own. It's a bit difficult to explain, because it just—just happens. You don't think about it."

He was right: I didn't understand at all. Except the bit about him being totally male. I wouldn't like to think I had been making love with a bisexual. Then I suddenly remembered something so important I couldn't get the words out straight.

"Supposing . . . if it's as you say . . . the dragon's eggs . . . your being a male . . . it isn't possible, is it? I mean you and me . . . Ky-Lin was so sure!"

"What in the world are you talking about?"

But I had second thoughts; my ring had given a warning tingle. Don't tell him yet: wait and see.

"Nothing. When were you thinking of taking me to see them?"

"When? Right now."

"Now? But I'm not ready. I've nothing suitable to wear, how do we get there, I don't want to—"

"Now!" he said firmly. "The sooner the better. Trust me—you do trust me, don't you? You would have trusted the Wimperling, as you called him, with your life, wouldn't you? Good. Go get your cloak and wrap yourself up tight: you're going to be dragon-borne tonight!"

And it all happened so quickly I had no chance to argue. One moment I was standing there in my silken dress, terrified at the whole idea, the next I was back on the same spot, swathed and hooded in my father's cloak.

Jasper held me close.

"You are not used to riding on the back of a dragon, and now is not the time to teach you properly." I could feel him laughing a little. "So we'll do it the easy way. I shall carry you—no, don't panic! You won't know much about it. Close your eyes and relax. I am going to make you go to sleep for a little while, long enough to get you safe to the mountain. I don't want you struggling at the wrong moment."

His lips came down on mine and I surrendered to his embrace as his fingers came up to my neck. A little pressure—in my mind or my body I wasn't sure—and I slipped into a sort of waking unconsciousness. I didn't dream, or anything like that, but the sensation of flying was curiously dimmed, though I could sense wind, the clapping of wings, a cindery smell. . . .

My stomach gave a sudden jolt, like the leap of a stranded fish.

"Sorry about that: I came down a bit sharply and changed early. You can open your eyes now, my love."

It was lucky his arm was around my waist, otherwise I might have tumbled to the ground. I was shaking and cold and my hair, in spite of the hood of my cloak, felt as though it had been attacked by a flying thornbush. I thought my eyes were open, but everything seemed as black as pitch. I blinked rapidly a couple of times and tried again. Looking up now I could see the stars and the moon illuminating the ledge on which we stood, but I had been staring straight at the entrance to the passageway that led to the cavern, and this still remained ominously dark. How could we possibly negotiate that without a light?

"Come," said Jasper. "Take my hand."

I pulled back. "It's so dark. . . ."

"I know the way, just as easily as you would in the dark of your own home without a candle. Besides, there is some light. Wait and see."

I allowed him to draw me into the passage, but closed my eyes like a child, only to be told to open them once we had passed the first turning.

"If you don't I shall let go your hand!"

Promptly they were open, to be faced with a faint silver glow from the rocks around us, like a seam of precious metal running through the stones. It was not so much a light as an emanation, and only extended a few feet in front and, glancing back, the same behind. As we paced it kept step with us.

"What is it? Dragon-magic?" I whispered.

He pressed my fingers. "No, it's a natural phenomenon; a kind of phosphorescence that is activated by the heat of our bodies as we pass."

The ring on my finger was tingling gently; no immediate harm, but a warning to go carefully; I wondered for the second or third time why it seemed to be getting so much looser.

The last time I had been in this passage I had cursed at the twists and turns, eager to reach the end; now I wished it would go on forever.

It didn't, of course. In less time than it takes to tell we had rounded the last corner and there was the cavern, lighted now by a broad spear of moonlight that shafted down from an opening in the roof of the cave and lit a pile of rocks—or were they? I gripped Jasper's hand more tightly.

Gently he loosed himself and stepped forward. "You are speaking with animals, so your ring will translate," he said to me. "Pay careful attention to what is said, and remember your manners. These are creatures as old and venerable as any in the land."

Then he spoke again, but this time it was in a series of creaks, groans, hisses, sighs, and rumbles.

"I have brought her. . . ."

I could understand what he said, the ring translating in my mind as he spoke. I had been staring straight ahead at the rocks, expecting some movement, but as he spoke I glanced to my side, and was horrified to see it was no man who stood at my side but a full-grown dragon! My heart gave a great jerk, then steadied. Didn't I say I would trust him? In spite of this I had backed away a little, but my ring, though still throbbing, had not increased its warnings.

The dragon at my side—black, with tiny pinpoints of light illuminating his wing tips—turned his bony face towards me, the yellow eyes still surprisingly kind. The rumble of dragon talk started again, but thanks to my ring, Jasper's own voice came through, warm and comforting.

"Don't be afraid: it's better that I appear to them this way. Come, stand by my side. And toss aside that cloak. I want them to see you as you really are."

I was quite glad to throw the cloak aside. It was very warm in the cavern. The fissure that divided us from the other side was throwing out a summer's night heat, and I found I was perspiring. I stepped to Jasper-dragon's side, aware once again of the cindery smell and the roughness of the stones beneath my feet. And now came a sound, a sort of stirring, slithery scrape—

"What is it?"

"Watch . . ."

Across the chasm something stirred, a general sort of shifting; rocks altered their shape—round, square, oblong, irregular, jagged—and also changed their position relative to each other. A few pebbles rattled against each other. I could feel the hair rising at the back of my neck, although Jasper-dragon stood calm and quiet beside me. My ring gave a warning twinge, but no more.

I thought I saw a claw, a bony head, a wing, decided I must be mistaken, then all at once everything seemed to shimmer, like the sun on a long road on a hot day. No, not quite like that; perhaps more like glancing down into a swift-flowing stream, trying to make out what lay on the bottom through the uncontrollable shift of the water.

"Here be Dragons," I thought stupidly, and suddenly they were there.

Still half-veiled, distorted, shimmery, around a dozen of the huge creatures bestirred themselves, yawning, stretching, unwinding long sinewy tails, opening dark eyes, extending claws and wings. With them came color and light; it seemed they emanated their own illumination, for now I saw gleams and sparkles at their feet. The piles of pebbles, so dull and uninteresting before, now started to glow and sparkle with an unquiet riot of colors as the dragons stirred them with their claws. Ruby, beryl, garnet, fire opal, coral, rose quartz, topaz, peridot, emerald, sapphire, amethyst, aquamarine, agate, jet, bloodstone, jasper, opal, pearl, diamond—they were all there, plus gold and silver. Then I saw that the light that shone over all did not come from the heaps of gems, nor from the dragons, but rather from the shaft of moonlight catching the facets of a jewel that hung in the air above all: the crystal I had given Jasper.

He stepped forward and then came that confusing rumble of speech again that my ring sorted out for me.

"I have brought the girl, the giver of this gift that now shines above us all." A soft hiss from across the chasm.

"Bring her forward."

I was nudged forward by one of his wings. "Don't be afraid. . . ."

I went forward hesitatingly till I stood at the lip of the chasm and felt as well as saw the flickers of light that flashed across from the moonlit crystal; now everything I looked at had a strange unreality.

"I'm here," I said unsteadily. "What do you want of me?"

For a moment there was silence and I thought perhaps they had not understood my human speech, although the ring should be translating to them as well, but then came a low, grumbling growl, like Growch magnified ten times. I thought about turning and running, right away back and out to safety, but in spite of an involuntary step backwards, I otherwise stood firm.

The ring on my finger was still throbbing, but it was an encouraging feeling rather than a warning. I repeated my question.

"What do you want of me?"

When the answer came, it was not what I had expected. "You gave this Dragon Stone as a gift to our colleague. He-whose-wings-scrape-the-clouds?"

They must mean Jasper. "I did."

"And what do you hope for in exchange, daughter of man?"

I squared my shoulders; all or nothing. "When your new Master Dragon was in his first incarnation, I saved his life; I ask you now for the price of that life. Let him spend his man-life time with me, a quarter of each year that we may have together."

Another growling roar, louder this time. "You are impertinent!"

"I do not mean to be. If I had not been in that place, at that time, assuredly the growing creature that was to become your splendid He-whose-wings-scrape-the-clouds would never be standing here in front of you, an addition to your—your . . ." (what on earth was a collection of dragons? A flock? A gathering? The ring gave me the answer) ". . . your doom of dragons. I admit that I kissed the creature he was then three times, causing this—this, to you, malfunction in his makeup, but that was a human manifestation of what you would recognize as kinship. . . ." Where were the words coming from? This wasn't me talking! Thank you, ring! "As it is, if you agree to my proposal, for nine months of the year you will have his company and his services, those of a Master Dragon. Can you afford to lose these? If you refuse our request—and it is his as well as mine—he will merely be sulky and uncooperative and absent himself from your meetings.

"There are few enough of you left: your distinguished race has been declining noticeably during the last thousand years. Do you want this to go on happening? I rescued one for you: surely you can grant me a quarter of his time?"

There was silence. And silence. The air in front of me shimmered and the lights went out, one by one, as the moon passed beyond the opening high in the cavern. The dragons disappeared and so did their jewels till only the rocks and pebbles remained.

I blinked back the tears. "Why didn't they listen to me?"

"But they did." He looked across the chasm. "They just haven't made up their minds, that's all. You were magnificent, by the way. . . ." If he had been in his human form, I'm sure he would have been smiling. "What's a day or two to a dragon, who measures your years as ten to his one? Give them time, my love, give them time. . . . And now I must take you back. Put on your cloak and wrap it tight. Close your eyes. . . ."

Once again I felt the pressure on my neck, his breath on my face and then I was asleep with the wind on my face, the flap of wings in my ears, the smell of cinders in my nostrils, the dizzy descent—

I was lying in my own bed and a voice whispered in my ear: "See you tomorrow."

"You gonna sleep the 'ole day away?" said Growch peevishly. "S'long after my breakfast . . ."

I sat up, blinking, to find the sun fingering its way through the shutters and the sound of chanting.

"What time is it?"

"Dunno. Near enough noon, I reckons."

I looked down. I was still wearing my green silk dress, my father's cloak. I remembered what had happened during the night, and I sighed. There must be something I could do to persuade them. . . .

"Enjoy yer trip?"

So he had been watching. "What? Oh, yes. I suppose so . . . Sorry, Growch, I've been neglecting you, but I've got a lot on my mind."

"That wouldn' include food, would it?"

I sighed again, but I loved him, grotty foulmouth that he was, and his devotion deserved some reward.

"I think that would do us both good. Let's go down to the market in the village and see what they've got."

And over honeyed and spiced roast ribs, egg noodles and sweet-berry tart I made final plans for the strategy I had been planning for the last couple of days. As far as I could see there was only one sure way of granting that which I wished for both Jasper and myself.

Tonight I would tell him my plan.

First, though, there was plenty to do. Practical things like hanging my dress free of wrinkles, taking my sheets down to the laundry woman in the courtyard, washing my hair free of wind tangles, warm water for a bath, bringing my journal up to date with last night's happenings. Certain things to be specially packaged, two letters to write. The first, to Matthew Spicer, was finished quickly. The other, to his agent in Venice, Signor Falcone, took longer. And I must have a talk with Ky-Lin.

And what if it all went wrong? The letters were easily torn up, but the rest? I wouldn't think about that.

Something else had been niggling me for days: I had been neglecting my prayers. Of course there was no Christian church within a thousand miles but God was God, wherever worshipped, so at the next call to prayer in the monastery I knelt and closed my eyes, offering up my heartfelt thanks for all that had gone before, and my various deliverances from evil. I prayed for those dead, my mother and my father, and for those I hoped still lived: the no-longer blind knight, Matthew and Suleiman, Signor Falcone, the sea captain and his big wife, little prince Tug, even Dickon. Then there were the animals. Jesus had been a shepherd to his people, so surely He would understand the prayers to those creatures I had loved and lost to their new lives: Mistral, Traveler, Basher, Ky-Lin, of course, even Bear, and my darling Growch. Last of all there was Jasper, my one and only love, Master of Many Treasures. Easy enough to pour out my prayers for the man, but how did one pray for a dragon? I suppose if one owned a lizard that grew out of all proportion, turned nasty, started to fly around all over the place and charred all it ate, then one could pray for a dragon.

I tried my best, but even the patience of God must have been tried by my ramblings.

I took out the egg. It had grown even larger. I placed it on the clothes chest against the wall and covered it with my shift. I looked around the room: all seemed ready. Bed freshly made with clean sheets, my dress free of creases, a skin of honeyed rice and two mugs on the side table—

" 'Spectin' 'im in 'ere, then? Where does you want me to go?"

Oh, poor Growch! But I had thought about him earlier. A large bone awaited him in Dickon's empty room next door.

"You goin' to do naughties again?"

I nearly cancelled the bone.

30

The rest of the day dragged by on leaden feet, and two or three times I found myself pacing restlessly around and around my room like a caged animal, chewing my nails, until Growch planted his tail under my foot and I had to spend a quarter-hour apologizing.

The sun went down and I tried to stay relaxed, knowing that Jasper would not come till moonrise, for dragons don't like flying in full dark, and the few stars were still lie-abeds, reluctant to leave their day's sleep.

The night was chill: no wind, no clouds. I took to twisting my ring about my finger; it was definitely looser today, and with a pang I thought I knew the reason why. This was one of my few possessions I had not taken into account on settling my affairs. I must see Ky-Lin. There was also an addition I must make to Signor Falcone's letter.

I could leave it until tomorrow—no, I would do it right now. So it was with pen in hand, paper in front of me, legs curled up beneath, and my tongue between my teeth (normal position when I was writing) that Jasper found me. I had my back to the balcony door, which was open, in order to sit as near as I could to the candles, and the first I knew was when he dropped a light kiss on the nape of my neck.

I jumped up, scattering paper, pen and ink; there was a huge blot on the paper which no amount of sand would soak up.

"Jasper! How did you manage to be so quiet?"

"You were busy!" He kissed me again, this time properly. "Catching up on your correspondence?" He was only joking, but it was too near the mark for me. I gathered up the papers, turned them facedown.

"Something like that . . . oh, I am glad to see you! I thought the moon would never rise."

He drew me out onto the balcony. "Well there she is, near full.

Whatever they call the days and months here, do you realize that to-
morrow night it will be two years since we returned to the place where
I was hatched at that farm by the Place of Stones? All Hallows' Eve . . .
Remember?"

As if I could ever forget. That was the night when my beloved Wimperling had turned into an even more beloved man-dragon. Fiercer, more
unpredictable, someone to fear as well as love, an unknown quantity in
many ways, he had still captured both my imagination and my heart. I
had watched him fly away that night knowing he had taken part of me
with him.

And that feeling of loss had never grown less. This was why I had
travelled so far to find him, knowing that no other man would do for
me. My thoughts scurried back to another All Hallows' Eve: the night
I had found my mother dead and had left my home forever to seek my
fortune. That had been three years ago, but it seemed more like ten. So
much had happened to that naïve, ingenuous, then-plump girl who had
believed that all she had to do was travel to the nearest town to find a
husband! So proud I was then, I remembered, of my book learning and
housekeeping skills. The ability to read, write and figure had been useful,
especially when travelling as Matthew's apprentice, but as for my skills
in cheese making, embroidery, rose-hip syrup, possets, headache pills,
smocking, elderflower wine, besom making, green poultices, patchwork,
face packs, spinning and weaving—none of these had ever been exercised.

The fine sewing had descended to plain sewing and mending, the
cookery to tossing whatever there was into the pot on an outside fire,
and the fat girl had slimmed down dramatically and was lithe as a boy.

So here came another All Hallows. I felt a tiny prick of forebod-
ing—whether it came from the ring or not I wasn't sure—but after all,
the saints had seen me through so far, and there was no need for the
superstitions of a hag-ridden night to disturb me now.

"Yes, I remember," I said, in answer to his question. "I reckon they
are lucky for me, those dates."

"Me too!" He hugged me tight. "Don't you want to know what the
Council said?"

No, I had been too frightened to ask. "Yes, of course I do! Tell
me?"

"Well, it's not bad, and it's not good. They are still deliberating, but
although it seems they will probably agree to my spending my man-time
with you, they are still divided on whether I can have three months at
a time. Most of them would prefer one, I think."

I pretended to consider, all the while knowing that I had something priceless with which to negotiate. "Yes, I suppose that would be better than nothing. April, August, December? Then I would have you for late spring, full summer and the snows of winter."

"Good." He was kissing my throat and shoulders now, and it was difficult to concentrate. "They want to see you again, tomorrow night, to hear their decision. That's good, because I don't think they would waste their time seeing you once more if they intended to refuse."

"Perhaps they mean to serve me up for supper," I said lightly.

My dress fell to my ankles; those shoulder ribbons were too easy.

"I told you, sweetheart, they don't eat damsels anymore—if they ever did."

"I believe you," I said obediently. My hands went to his head, feeling with pleasure the strong bones under my fingers as he bent to my breasts, the exquisite reactions this engendered almost unbearable. The rest of my body was shivering with anticipation—that or the night wind, I had no idea, nor did I care, for a moment later he had swept me up in his arms and carried me to the bed. As I felt his weight press down on me, his mouth on mine, his hands busy elsewhere, the rapture I felt surpassed anything I had ever known. But even as I lost myself in his embrace I thought I felt a faint tingle in my ring, and somewhere a dog barking—

But a moment later all was forgotten with his body in me, with me, by me, part of me. . . .

Later, much later, we lay in each other's arms, at peace. It must have been near dawn, for the last, low bars of moonlight lay aslant the floor and the candles were burning low. I snuggled closer, feeling his body stir in sympathy.

"Jasper?"

"Mmmmm?"

"Do you—do you . . ." But no, I couldn't ask him. Women always wanted the answer to "that" question, if it hadn't been volunteered before; men always tried to avoid committing themselves. That much my mother had taught me.

"Do I—do I . . ." he mimicked gently. "Of course I do! Why do you think I am here? But you want to hear me say it, don't you my love?"

"It doesn't matter, truly it doesn't—" Liar!

"It matters to both of us," he said gently. "You see when I saw you again and realized just how far you had travelled to see me—I know you pretended otherwise but it didn't work—I felt guilty. Then my conscience took over; my man-conscience, because dragons don't have one you would recognize. That conscience told me you would be far better off without me, so I tried to play it casual. I wanted you to think I no longer cared for you, because I knew I could never give you the sort of life you deserve—"

᾿ "But you have! I—"

"Hush! Let my finish. This sort of life we hope to wrest from the Council isn't anywhere near perfect. You could do much better: go back to your merchant. At least there you will be safe, secure and loved for twelve months of the year."

"I don't love him, I never did!"

"I know, I know! As the Wimperling I knew; as myself I know. But my conscience—that damnable thing that a certain young woman encouraged in a pig once upon a time—won't let me capture and keep you without a struggle. Dragons are totally selfish: sometimes men are not. I love you so much I want what is best for you."

There. He had said it. "And I love you, as you know. All I want is to be with you, even if it's only for a day a year, so don't let's have any more trouble from your conscience. Go ahead: be selfish!"

He smiled wryly. "I knew it wouldn't work. . . ."

"But I have something that might. . . ." I slipped from his side and, naked, crossed to the clothes chest, peeled back my shift from the egg, picked it up as if it were the finest porcelain and carried it back to the bed. "There! What do you think of that?"

He sat up, slowly at first, then suddenly, as though he had sat on a pin.

"What's this?" He answered his own question. "It's a dragon's egg, or I'm—I'm a pig again! Where did you find it? How long have you had it?"

"I've had it for about a year. But it was hidden for a year before that, and it has grown a good deal since it first saw the light. When I first saw it, it was about the size and color of a freshwater pearl, but it was quite soft to the touch. So I kept it safe and warm until it hardened. Since then, until now, I have kept it in a pouch round my neck. Pretty, isn't it? Somehow I never thought a dragon's egg would look like this. . . ."

"Where did it come from?"

"Guess!"

He scowled. "I don't want to guess. I want to *know*! This is important, don't you realize that?"

"Of course I do! It is our bargaining power: it's the most valuable thing we have!"

He leant forward, took it in his hands. "This is incredible! The Council can surely refuse us nothing now. But I must know where you found it."

"Oh, it has an impeccable pedigree." I was enjoying this. "Like a mug of rice wine?" He shook his head impatiently. "It is a Master Dragon's egg, no less."

"How do you know that? How could you know . . ."

"Because it's yours, that's why!"

"Mine!" I watched the various expressions chase their way across his face: amazement, disbelief, doubt, hope, puzzlement, and, finally, a sort of bewildered joy. "But—how do you know? How can it be?"

"That time at the Place of Stones. Remember? You held me in your arms, you kissed me, you changed back and forth from dragon to man, man to dragon, and all the while you were—you were . . . You made love to me."

"But—it couldn't happen that way! It's impossible!"

"You told me dragons could self-procreate and that's difficult for me to believe. If that can happen why couldn't you have produced a life of your own for me to hold?" I leant forward and kissed him. "All I am sure about is that it is yours, and that I held it within me for a year. I had no usual monthly flow during that time, and it was Ky-Lin, the creature I told you about, who helped me with the pain of producing it. Since then I have been normal. So, I truly believe we share it."

"Mine—and yours," he said wonderingly. "They say there is nothing new under the skies. . . . What do we do with it?"

"It belongs to those who are left: the Council, to guard and nurture until it is time for the hatching. Many years too late for me, my love . . . But surely, with a gift such as this, you can persuade them to give me your lifetime as a man to spend with me? Not a week, a year, our time as man and woman together. When I am—gone—then you can be theirs again. In return for the egg, another dragon for them."

He rose from the bed and took me in his arms.

"My dearest dear, my little love, there is nothing would please me more! I'm sure they will agree—and that island I promised you still waits for us!"

He drew me tight and showed me just exactly what I had to look forward to.

It was nearly dawn, the first flush of light was graying the outlines of the shutters as I opened my sleepy eyes. Jasper had left me as the last rays of the moon slanted across the valley, promising to put our request to the Council. He had left the egg with me.

"Tomorrow night we shall go together with the egg, and exchange it for our freedoms—don't worry: they will want our egg more than any jewel in the world: it is their promise of continued life. After tomorrow night, the world is ours! We can be an ordinary couple—-even go to one of your churches and become man and wife. Would you like that?"

So, there were—how many hours? Perhaps sixteen. And everything to do. And nothing. I stretched luxuriously and turned over on my back. I would have just five minutes more, then get up and go down to the market and buy something special for Growch, to make up for sequestering him in Dickon's room all night.

It can only have been a couple of minutes' doze when I heard the door to the balcony creak open and soft footfalls on the matting. A moment later a hand stroked my shoulder. Jasper must have come back. I turned over to face him, my eyes still closed, my arms outstretched in welcome, disregarding the sudden prickle of my ring.

"Forgotten something, my love?"

A breath on my cheek, a fumbling hand and then a weight, an alien weight on top of me, a strange mouth grinding down on mine and an insistent knee pushing my thighs apart. I struggled violently, but an arm was across my throat, a hand pinioning my hands above my head. His sweat was rank in my nostrils, his knee grinding my thighs, his mouth and tongue a-slobber all over my face. I jerked my head aside, took a gulp of air and yelled as loud as I could.

Instantly the arm across my throat pressed down harder and now I was choking. My ears were full of a roaring sound, my eyes felt as though they were popping out, I couldn't breathe, but I knew I couldn't resist much longer

There was a yell of surprise, a frantic growling and all at once I was free, gasping for welcome breath, and my assailant was rolling in agony on the floor, flailing and kicking ineffectually at a small dog, whose sharp teeth were fastened firmly on his left buttock.

I couldn't believe my eyes. "Dickon!" I croaked. "How could you! What in the world were you thinking about?"

"Get the bugger off me, damn you, get him off!"

I took my time, pulling down my green dress, wiping my face with the hem, spitting his taste from my mouth. "All right, Growch, let him go. He doesn't deserve it, but thanks anyway. Where were you?"

"Shut me in 'is room. Came out through the winder. E's bin askin' for that 'e 'as! Pretty boy won' be able to sit down for a day or two. Let 'im try showin' that to the ladies! Now if'n I'd got 'im at the front—"

"That's enough, Growch," I said hastily. Standing up, hands on hips,

I glared down at Dickon, who was trying to examine his bites, a near-impossible task without a mirror. I was glad to note that all other pretensions had withered into insignificance.

"Now then," I said. "Why? What have I ever said or done to make you think you would be welcome in my bed?"

Dickon rose to his feet, rather unsteadily, but his chin was jutting out dangerously. "It's rather what you haven't done! All the time we've been together you've been playing the little virgin, Mistress-Hard-to-Get, and at the same time you've been giving me those come-hither looks, little enticements, half-promises—"

I was astounded. After doing my utmost to discourage anything like that! "You must be mad," I said finally. "Utterly mad."

"Don't kid me! I've seen you—it's been all I could do to keep my hands off you! Touching me, making suggestive remarks, all but stripping off and asking for it . . ." He ranted on, while I tried desperately to remember if I had ever given him the slightest encouragement, knowing all the while I had not. But the more I heard him, the more I realized that he truly believed what he was saying. In some part of his twisted mind his sexual psyche had convinced him that he was irresistible, so if I didn't fling myself at him it was my fault, all my refusals merely stimulating his desire still further.

"Why do you think I kept on going to those brothels? Because if I hadn't I wouldn't have been able to keep my hands off you!" His voice was rising, he was on the verge of hysteria.

"Dickon, I never meant you to believe—"

But he was past listening to anything except his own twisted logic.

"I worshipped you! I believed that one day, if I waited long enough, you would come to me, say you loved me, ask me to be with you while we worked together. That's why I followed you! Not for any treasure that doesn't exist: *You* were my treasure, my unspoilt, virgin bride!" He was so far out of control by now that his hands were tearing at the loose robe he wore.

"And then I come back unexpectedly and what do I find? You in the arms of a stranger as soon as my back is turned, all decency and decorum forgot! What do you think I felt, seeing your abandoned behavior? You, whom I thought above reproach behaving like a strumpet! Why, you're nothing but a whore, a bloody whore!" Saliva was trickling from the right corner of his mouth, and his eyes were glazed.

It took only a couple of steps and I had slapped him hard on both cheeks.

"Don't you *dare* speak to me like that! You don't deserve an expla-

nation, but I think you'd better know that the man you saw is my betrothed. He is the one I have been seeking all this long time, the 'friend'
I told you I sought. My journeyings have all been towards this end and
have never, ever, had anything to do with treasure! And now we have
found each other again, we are going to spend the rest of our lives
together." I paused. He had reeled back when I struck him, and now he
was regarding me with a bemused expression on his face. But at least
now he looked sane. "Now, isn't it time you apologized?"

"I—I—I . . ."

"I—I—I!" I mocked. "And you are supposed to have the gift of
tongues! You'll have to do better than that."

He tried to pull himself together; it was a visible effort. "Of course,
I didn't realize . . . but now you've explained . . ." He seemed to draw
into himself; his eyes hooded any expression, his lips drew back into a
thin line. "I am sorry," he said formally. "I was obviously mistaken.
What are your plans now?"

I was surprised by how quickly he was back to normal. "I was going
to see you later today if you were back," I said. "Or leave a message
with Ky-Lin. But if you like we can talk now."

"Let's get on with it. Tell me." He sat down on the stool, drawing
his confidence around him again, like his tattered clothes.

So I told him I was leaving that night with Jasper for another life
in another place, where no one could follow us. I explained that I had
not forgotten him. He was to have all the moneys I had left (excluding
my father's coins, which were to go to the monks) on condition he took
a package of letters and my journal and delivered them to Signor Falcone
in Venice. This gentleman, I explained, would reward him handsomely
for his efforts, but only if the packet was delivered intact.

"You will do as I ask?"

He stood up. "I have no alternative."

"Then I will leave it on my bed, together with my blanket, the cooking things and anything else I don't need. Do with them what you will."
I held out my hand. "Thanks for your help. No bad feelings?"

Ignoring my hand he suddenly embraced and kissed me, then as
quickly stepped back, so abruptly I nearly fell.

"No bad feelings," he said. "But you can't blame me for trying."

And that was the last I saw of him.

Ky-Lin visited me at midday. He knew without the telling what I
was planning to do. He looked at me gravely, asked me once more if I
truly knew what I was doing. Of course I reassured him, told him of

my happiness, our hopes for the future. He looked so down, not like his
usual ebullient self, that I feared he might be ill.

"Ky-Lins are never ill."

"Then what is it, my dear? You don't look at all happy."

"I cannot answer that. Ky-Lins are always supposed to be happy."

"I know—it's because your task is finished, isn't it? You've seen
me through, done all you had to do—"

"No. I have not. But I am not allowed to interfere."

"I don't understand. . . ."

He must have seen my distress for he came forward and laid his
head against me. I bent and kissed him, stroked his sleek hide.

"I wish you could come with us."

He drew back. "I told you: we do not deal with dragons. There is
a rule. It is like your Waystone; there are laws that repel, others that
attract."

Although I didn't understand what he was saying, that reminded me
to tell him what I had done with Dickon, and how I had enclosed the
Waystone in my package to Signor Falcone, asking him to deliver it to
the captain's wife, telling her that the crystal she had given me had been
a gift to my betrothed's kin. "Rather neat that, don't you think? After
all, it has gone to Jasper's dragon relatives!"

But he didn't smile.

Later he took the pouch into which I had placed my father's coins,
promising to deliver the money to the monks. I asked him if he would
give Growch a tiny pinch of Sleepy Dust later, to make his flight to the
Blue Mountain easier, and this he promised to do around suppertime.

The cloak I shall leave behind. Its color, weave and texture are the
same as the cloth of the monks' robes, and now I am sure that the father
I never knew once lived here. He probably committed some sin and had
to leave; this would explain why the Unicorn's ring would no longer fit
him and also why the coins of my "dowry" led me across the world to
this place. So it is fitting that it remain here with the coins.

This is the last I shall write. Half an hour ago Ky-Lin left me, having
given Growch his "dose." My dear dog is fast asleep on the bed now,
snoring gently. I have told him nothing except that we are going on a
trip, but have fed him all the things he likes best, in case it is a long
journey.

Myself, I cannot eat. Surprisingly, I feel depressed. Perhaps it is
something to do with my ring. It had been a part of me for so long that

I felt a real sense of loss when it just slipped from my finger when Ky-Lin was here.

At first I couldn't believe it. I just stared at it, then picked it up between finger and thumb. It was so light, so thin, just a sliver of horn so delicate I could crush it between my fingers. . . . I tried to put it on again, but somehow it had curled around itself so that now it was too small.

"You have no need of it anymore," said Ky-Lin gently. "It cannot go where you go. Let me take care of it. I shall keep it safe until there is another who needs it."

"But aren't you due to go to your heaven?"

"My task is not finished. You have your future, but others . . . There is another who will need me for a while. And afterwards?" He shrugged. "Time is a relative thing."

"Don't talk in riddles! So, where will you keep my—the ring?"

He bent his head. "It will have a home on the horn of my forehead. Like to like."

Again he was being abstruse, but I placed the ring as he had said, and it fitted at once as if it were a part of him.

"And now, good-bye. It has been an interesting time. I shall miss you, girl, but I shall pray for you. Now if you cry like that, you will get my hide all wet, and Ky-Lins don't like the damp. . . ."

It is All Hallows' Eve, not far from midnight, and the moon, a blood-red full moon, has just risen. The piece of paper on which I am writing this I will tuck away into the package at the last moment.

It is strange, writing like this in the present; I have been used for so long to write in the past, catching up on my journal, which I hope will explain to Signor Falcone—and Matthew if he passes it on—exactly what has happened to me. I hope they will understand how all my life for the past two years has led to this moment, how this is the culmination of my dreams.

How do I feel? Frightened a little, yes, but once Jasper is here all fear will go. The egg is by my side; I have sewn it into the scrap of skin that was once the Wimperling, the outer self of Jasper. Two years ago, to the day, we created this egg; a year earlier I started on this travelling, and now that I was about to lose it I had a sudden flood of maternal feeling for the egg and had to tell myself it was only a stone, even though within it lay hidden a tiny creature that was certainly a part of Jasper and perhaps of me too. But even if I kept it I would never see it hatch . . .

It has been a long, long journey. God keep all those I have loved.

Moonlight floods the room: out with the candle. The light that is the love of Jasper and myself will illuminate the rest of my life.

A last prayer . . .

Away with this. He is here!

Epilogue

To the illustrious Signor Falcone: greetings. This by the hand of Brother Boniface of the Abbey of the same name in Normandy.

Sir, I introduce myself as the Infirmar of the Abbey. Recently I took under my care a traveller by the name of Ricardus. When he was admitted to the Infirmary it was obvious he suffered from a low fever, with much coughing and spitting of blood. We kept him close, administered plasters to his chest, doses for the ill humors and bled him, but a practiced eye could see that the Good Lord was the only one who could intervene in a terminal illness.

Alas, this was not to be, our prayers being unavailing, and the Lord moving in mysterious ways.

Two days before the patient died, fortified by the rites of Holy Church, confessed and given the Last Rites, he asked to make a deposition that was to be forwarded to yourself. He had given us the last of his silver for Holy Church and was currently in a State of Grace, so I placed a young novice who writes in the shortened form by his bedside. He took down the words of Ricardus, later transcribing them into proper form, the result of which is here to your hand.

A great deal of what the patient said was not understood, and towards the end he rambled a great deal, but the words are his and will doubtless mean more to yourself, illustrious Signor.

I am dying: they told me so. They don't mince words, these monks. All that chanting; reminds me of a monastery where—

To be fair, I asked them, but then I think I knew, anyway.

I am accursed. . . .

At first, after I delivered Summer's package to you, and went on with the letter to Master Spicer, everything was fine. With the moneys you both gave me I set up in business for myself. For the first ten years

I travelled the Western World and had ample compensation for my outlay. And yet . . .

Some years ago I caught a disease in a brothel in Genoa—God curse it!—which no medicines, poultices or prayers could assuage. Another infection caused my hair to fall out and great boils appeared on my body. Then, to add to all this, I contracted the Great Itch on my arms and legs and great sores in my groin that caused me much discomfort. Because of these afflictions I remain covered at all times, and have had to confine my business to the colder northern clime where such garb is accepted all year round.

Yet still did I prosper, enough to buy me those pleasures not readily available to those in my unfortunate condition, but during the last couple of years, due to unwise investment in cargoes that foundered, all my fortune has dwindled away, and now I only possess the silver in my pocket and a certain object which I shall ask to be forwarded to you. Of that, more later.

I lied to you, you know. When I brought Summer's journal, fifteen years ago, I made it sound so romantic, didn't I? And you have probably believed all these years that she flew off into the sunset with her man-dragon and lived happily ever after.

But it wasn't like that. That night didn't go as any of us expected, least of all her. Why didn't I tell you the truth? Because I thought you and Master Spicer would pay more for good news than for bad, that's why.

I fancied her myself, did you know that? When she turned up in that boy's gear, with those long legs and all . . . Respected her, too. All that reading and writing, the way she trained those animals of hers, the ladylike way she spoke. She never paid any attention to the men, either; always kept herself to herself, never flirted. She behaved like a virgin and I treated her like one. I mean, I never really tried it on. Not really. Not until the end, that is, when I saw her with that fellow of hers—

No more now, I'm tired. Leave me a candle. It'll be full dark ere long.

The patient worsened overnight, with much coughing up of blood and loss of breath, and was not well enough to dictate in the forenoon. In the afternoon we were afflicted with sudden gales, which stripped the last of the fruits in the orchard and loosened the roof on the guest house. These strong winds seemed to stimulate the patient, who indicated he wished to continue his deposition, albeit in a more disjointed and rambling way. . . .

* * *

Where was I? Oh, yes.

I fancied her, yes, but I doubt I would have left the caravans to follow her unless I was sure she was after treasure. There were the maps, you see—and who was right in the end?

She told me there was nothing, and I know now she believed that, but I thought she was trying to con me, wanted it all for herself. The thought of treasure can do strange things to your mind. . . . *Radix malorum est cupiditas* . . .

She talked your monk tongue, learnt it from an old priest. . . . But you met her, you know what she was like. No, not you, him . . .

God, I'm thirsty, give me wine! Gnat's piss . . .

Of course I didn't know about him then, her pig-man-dragon, did I? How could she prefer a man like that? All dark, with yellow eyes like a wolf! The girls have always said I was handsome, well endowed—still am, and know how to use it too—

Heard them that night, saw them as well. Disgusting, from one I had thought so pure! Tried it on after he'd gone, but she wasn't having any; set the dog on me, she did. Hated that dog!

But I knew what I knew then, didn't I? Knew that what I'd seen wasn't what it seemed. Heard enough to know where to go that night—

Moon was red as blood, bats flying like witches. Alone . . .

For Christ's sake, can't you stop that wind? I'm fucking dying, and I want some peace! Ahhh . . .

The patient being in obvious distress he was dosed heavily with poppy juice till he quieted and enjoyed an uneasy sleep. He continued late that night, when he awoke, although his testimony became increasingly disjointed.

I was there before them, knew where to hide, they didn't see my horse. They came down on the ledge and she had that blasted dog in her arms. One moment he was a dragon—near shit myself—then just the fellow she slept with. Followed 'em down the passage, not too close . . .

Got to the cavern. Hid in the entrance. They walked to the chasm, he said something and the whole place lighted up. Talk about fucking rainbows! There was this light. . . .

Thirsty: any more of that wine? God, how you drink it, I don't know! Now if you were me, travelled all over the world, tasted the wines of— What was that? Bells, bells, bells! Same in that monastery. Bloody monks . . .

The jewels! Never seen anything like those jewels! Piled up like mountains they were. Forgot to be afraid of the dragons. Gold, too. Enough to buy you and your trading empire out a thousand times. Dazzled . . .

There was a lot of growling and hissing and roaring and from what I had heard last night they were going to try and exchange that obscene thing she called a dragon's egg for him, her fellow, to stay human. Well, she brought it out from behind her back, held it up for them to see, then laid it on the ground together with her sleeping dog. It all went quiet, I tell you!

Then Summer and her boyfriend walked over a kind of bridge and there was a sort of ceremony, lots of spitting and hissing and roaring, and then they started to walk back, with smiles on their faces like they got what they wanted. It was their own fault, I tell you! They stopped in the middle of the bridge and started kissing and cuddling and I couldn't stand it no more!

Couldn't get near the jewels, but if that egg thing was that important, why shouldn't I have a piece of the action? Never meant no real harm, just a bit of a threat; hold it over the chasm, they'd give me enough of the loot to keep me going.

Crept forward, had my hands on the thing, when that bloody dog woke up and started barking—

How was I to know they thought it was a plot? How was I to know they thought she and him was in it too? I didn't mean no harm, honest! No one can say I haven't suffered for it neither. He was trying to shout something and she was clinging to him like ivy when it happened—

Oh, God, Jesu, I can see it, hear it, smell it, now!

I swear I didn't mean to. . . . The fires of Hell, I can feel them now! I'm burning, burning! Christ Jesus, I never meant to hurt her! I loved her, God curse it, I loved her. All right, so I was jealous; that too. But you don't hurt those you love, do you?

What time is it? Time for me to go. Creep into a dark corner, like an animal. Like the bloody dog . . . The rainbow creature came for him afterwards, all bloody and singed as he was, took him away and healed him. But you can't heal a mind, can you? She loved them both, more than she ever cared for me. . . . Hated them!

The fires, the fires! Have you ever smelled singeing flesh? She screamed, so loud it burst something in my heart. Couldn't feel anything for anyone after that.

It seemed the top of the world blew off. They were in the middle of the bridge when it collapsed, he had her in his arms and the flames came up and caught their hair. I saw him change man-dragon, dragon-man, so quick you couldn't blink and he wrapped his wings about her and then they were gone as though they'd never been!

That scream . . . she knew it was me. She looked at me. Just once. Oh, Summer, it wasn't my fault, it wasn't, I swear it!

Dark, it's dark; why don't you light the candles?

The patient became delirious, then relapsed into a coma; he awoke for the last time just before midnight. He was given wine, but was unable to drink it. He asked the time, day and date.

All Hallows' Eve? I might have known it. She had her revenge after all. Fifteen years . . . Oh, Lord: was it worth it all?

Ricardus lapsed again into a coma, the storm returned to harass us, and then, just before midnight, he woke once more, sat bolt upright in bed and uttered his last words.

But I did get something out of it! And now those dragons can search till Doomsday, God curse them and curse you all! Do with it what you will—

This is the testimony the man Ricardus asked us to forward to you. If you feel so disposed, our messenger will willingly bring moneys back to us for Masses to be said for the deceased's soul, for I fear he did not die in a State of Grace.

In fact any donation towards the upkeep of the Abbey would be most welcome. . . .

I also send with Brother Benedict whatever poor possessions Ricardus carried with him: his few clothes were distributed to the poor, as was his staff and mug and plate. There was, however, a certain object he referred to in his disposition and kept in a pouch around his neck; a round pebble wrapped in hide, and a scrap of paper. Although the object appears to be worthless, no doubt it will prove of sentimental interest to yourself. As you can see, the piece of paper bears the misspelt legend: "This be Dragonnes Eg."

Postscript

In the Indian Ocean there is a small island, situated well off the trade routes. It was charted in the eighteen thirties by the Portuguese, who mapped it as Discovery Isle. Many years later the missionaries arrived and once they understood the native language, found that the inhabitants had always called it "Dragon Isle." When questioned, the islanders related the legend that accompanied the name.

There were two points of consistency, otherwise the tale had obviously changed with the years and recollection. The points of agreement were that one day in the distant past a great black dragon, sore wounded, had arrived in the skies from the northeast bearing a burden. It had circled the island three times before alighting somewhere in the hills to the north. The other point of agreement was that the creature eventually left in the same direction, after circling the island in the same fashion.

Between these two "facts," there were two different versions of events. The first had it that the dragon laid waste to the forests of the island till the air was black with the fires, then he buried whatever he carried in a cave high in the mountains before flying away again.

The other version had the dragon again alighting in the hills with his burden and three days later a man and a woman, both badly injured, coming down to dwell among the islanders. This story would have it that the pair recovered and lived for many years at peace, the woman communing with the beasts of the field, the man a master of weather. In the fullness of time the woman died, and the man bore her body up into the hills and buried it, then the great dragon appeared again and flew away, sorrowing. . . .

Dragonne's
Eg

This is for you,
Sam,
with my special love!

Acknowledgments

My thanks as usual to my husband Peter, whose patience appears to increase as mine decreases!

Thanks also for the support of the "Baen Family" always there if needed.

Last, but not least, as a reward for his persistent interest, I shall dedicate this book to Sam, my own "Beau Thai". . . .

Book One

"Where there's a Will there's a Way"
—William Hazlitt

1

Birthday Girl

Please, Miss! Ern's 'avin' a fit again . . ."

Birthdays shouldn't be like this, I thought savagely as I squeezed along the narrow row between the desks to where Ernest was jerking uncontrollably. I held him tight for a moment, glad to see that he hadn't bitten his tongue; as his spasms lessened and he started to snore I scooped him up in my arms and carried him out of the class, down the corridor and into the kitchen, where there was a pallet in a corner for emergencies. I stripped off his soiled pants, chucked them into a bucket and rinsed them out, my nose wrinkling as I draped them over a fireguard to dry.

Ellen turned from the stove, where she was stirring the soup.

" 'Im again? Just cover 'im up, I'll keep an eye on 'im." The smell of the soup made my mouth water. On the table the bread was already sliced. Ellen saw my face.

"All counted out, miss—but come 'ere . . ." She took a knob of crust from the side and dipped it into the soup. "Careful, it's 'ot!"

And absolutely delicious. I crammed it into my mouth all at once, in danger of choking.

"Thanks, Ellen. Only an hour to go . . ."

"Thank God it's Sat'day!"

"Amen to that!"

As I made my way back to the classroom, making sure no crumbs would betray my scrounging and wiping my mouth on one of my second-best handkerchiefs, one used to mop up childish tears, snot or blood from cuts and grazes, I reflected that I should have a full two hours extra this afternoon to celebrate my twenty-first birthday.

School was from eight in the morning till six at night, Mondays to Friday, but on Saturday we broke two hours earlier. Fine in summer, but in winter it made little difference, the nights closing in early. Just two hours longer shut away in my room, a smoky little fire in the grate; just two more hours mending or trimming or studying. Once a week I would call at the local lending library, but I read so fast and so voraciously that I had to ration my pleasure to an hour a day. One penny a week was all I could afford, this being the going rate for borrowing.

I preferred to save a penny or two here and there and browse through one of the second-hand bookshops. This way I had built up my own little library: by now I had some of the novels of Mr. Dickens, Miss Austen, the Misses Brontë, Mrs. Gaskell and Mr. Thackeray, a Treasury of Poetry, the collected Histories of Mr. Shakespeare and *The Commonplace Cook*. This latter I could not really put to the test, as the fire in my room would only hold one pan at best and cooking in one's room was discouraged, but if some day I had a home of my own I should, theoretically, have knowledge enough to produce good, nourishing meals.

In the meantime I, like pupils and teachers alike at the Reverend Ezekiel Moffat's Charity School, lived on just that: the posthumous generosity of our founder. Founded sixty years ago in the early 1820s, the worthy minister had envisaged saving the souls of London's poorest children with his four "R's": Religion, Reading, 'Riting and 'Rithmetic. His daughter, who now ran the school, had added another "R": Refreshments.

For many of these children of the streets the food they received at school was their only sustenance. On arrival each child was given a slice of bread and dripping and a drink of milk and water. At lunchtime there was a bowl of Ellen's soup and another slice of bread and at hometime a slice of bread and scrape and another drink of milk and water. We teachers shared the same diet, which made the twenty-six pounds a year we received go a little further. It meant I only had to buy supper during the week, and could spoil myself on Saturday nights and Sundays.

Still, ten shillings a week didn't go far. Four shillings a week for rent, plus a penny for hot water. One penny a day for the emptying of my slop bucket. This last was definitely worth it, not having to tramp down two flights of stairs to use the revolting, fly-infested privy in the backyard. That made five shillings and four-pence. Three-pence for laundry, a penny for the library, which left four shillings and four-pence for everything else, which included clothes, coals, sewing materials and ribbons, soap and, of course, food.

At present I was managing to save one shilling a week towards the cost of material for a winter dress and new boots, and another shilling went into the Co-operative Bank. Then there was the collection at church on Sundays and a penny for the Missionary Fund, which left me two-pence a night for a meat pie or a couple of sausages. This week I had bought wool to knit mittens and a muffler for the winter, but I had the princely sum of nine-pence left with which to indulge myself tomorrow.

In the fine weather I would make a packed lunch and take it out into one of the parks, but when it was wet or cold on Saturday nights I would visit the butcher for a couple of chops, then the greengrocer for potatoes and some apples or an orange, plus a loaf from the baker and perhaps a chunk of cheese from the grocer. Saturday night was cheapest too, as all was closed for the Sabbath, and the later you went, the better the bargain.

Back in the classroom my pupils were in disarray. Obviously those who could had scratched their versions of "Cat, Rat, Mat, Hat, Sat" onto their slates, and were now teasing one another, throwing things or fast asleep. I hurried over, apologising to Miss Hardacre and Miss Hepzibah Moffat for the possible disruption of their Middle and Senior classes, clapped my hands for order, tapped a few heads with my ruler and hurriedly wiped the blackboard with a damp cloth and substituted "Dog, Log, Hog, Bog, Fog" for the earlier words. I then moved down the aisle, praising where I could, as blame was no use with these deprived children.

Some of them were patently ineducable, others would never get further than adding the simplest of numbers and writing their own names, but there were exceptions, like Jude and June, half-caste brother and sister who held the glimmerings of something better. These two now presented me with "The Cat sat on the Mat" and "The Cat in the Hat" respectively. Next term I would recommend them to Miss Hardcastle's Middle Class, who were now monotonously reciting their seven times table.

Having all three classes in the same room was difficult at the best of times, but usually two were either writing or listening so we teachers didn't have the added strain of shouting above each other.

Of course there were always more girls than boys. As soon as they were old enough the latter were out on the streets for their parents, thieving, running errands or, if they were lucky, 'prenticed out to coal merchants, chimney sweeps, dockers, lightermen or costers. The girls, if they were presentable, usually ended up on the streets at puberty or helping out in laundries or cookshops. We did have some successes: some of the children had been properly placed, boys to printing presses and the retail trade, even one to the Christian Church; the girls out as milliners, seamstresses, nursery governesses or placed in respectable households. But these alas, were few and far between.

I had been here in London for three years now. My parents had died within a week of each other of a low fever while I was still at boarding school. We had never been well-off—it was said my mother had married beneath her to a humble watch-maker and repairer—but they hadn't stinted on my education, more than they could have afforded; but once all debts had been paid and most of the furniture sold from our rented cottage, I found all I had was enough to keep myself for six months, a few sticks of furniture and fond memories of a pretty, merry mother who was a hopeless housewife, and a gentle, retiring father who waited for work rather than seeking it out.

So, Miss Sophronisbe Lee would have to find a situation, fast, but for an unattached girl of nineteen with no special skills and only the recommendation of her headmistress to back her applications it wasn't easy. At first I was picky, answering only those advertisements that appealed to me, but as time passed I grew more desperate as most of my applications were either unanswered or were curt rejections, the general consensus being that I was both too young and too inexperienced.

So I no longer applied to those advertisements for a "genteel children's governess," or "Lady F. requires experienced ladies-maid," rather was I driven to replying to seekers of companions for the elderly, or housekeeper in a "large and boisterous household." These came to nothing as well, if you discount an interview I actually undertook with hope concerning a "disabled gentleman" requiring a young lady for reading aloud, writing letters and other "light duties." Unfortunately he was not too disabled to chase me all over his study and he made it very clear what the "light duties" would entail. . . .

This went on for nearly three months until I had almost decided to apply for a straightforward domestic post, when I had an unexpected bonus. One of our neighbours had paid a visit to an aunt in London, and brought back a morning paper which contained ten suitable posts. Although the paper was a few days old I answered all the advertisements eagerly, then sat back and waited. And waited.

Of the ten, four never answered, and I had five replies turning me down, but the last letter was different. This was from the headmistress of a Charity School offering a teaching post. "Young person, male or female, to teach class of five- to eight-year-olds in poor district. Wages: twenty-six pounds per year. Some food supplied. Only serious and dedicated applicants need apply." Her advertisement had been last on my list because of the low wage, but somehow the tone of the letter I received fired me with an uncharacteristic enthusiasm.

"I note that your qualifications are more than adequate for our Junior Class, but you must realise that the possession of knowledge is not, in itself, the only requirement in a good teacher. It also involves patience, a liking for your pupils and, above all, the art of communication.

"You are young, but that cannot be held against you: you will not have had time to form bad habits or hard opinions. I note from your headmistress's recommendation that you have a mind of your own and are not afraid to express your views: I prefer this attitude to that of a milksop-miss.

"If you decide to take the post you must be prepared to live in an insalubrious district and deal with children who are poor, ill-clad, unwashed and often apathetic. The position is not an easy one, but it might well prove rewarding if you manage to improve the lot of only one of these deprived children."

So, my youth and inexperience didn't matter! Even my assertiveness was accepted as a sort of virtue. Was I patient? I thought so. Could I like the unlikeable? Probably—after all, children were children the world over. Could I communicate? Definitely!

And so, a fortnight later, the remaining sticks of furniture sold, apart from my father's comfortable wing-chair, my mother's writing desk and embroidered footstool and a mantel clock that I had had in my bedroom since I was a child, I took the stage to London and a new life.

And here I still was, nearly three years later.

Perhaps if I had had the faintest idea of just how tough those years were to be I would not have come, but, perversely, I was glad I had. Financially I was badly off; I lived in squalid conditions and probably didn't eat enough healthy food, and the teaching was mind-blowingly monotonous and unrewarding. It seemed my nostrils were always full of the smell of unwashed bodies, urine, chalk, smoke and fog.

Against all those was the plus of living in London itself. It was a wondrous, vibrant city, full of museums, galleries, ancient monuments, theatres, parks and beautiful churches, all of which fed the hunger for beauty and learning which I hadn't realised had lain dormant in me for so long. The fantastic wonders of the Crystal Palace, the military bands, the Palace with its changing of the guard, the gaily dressed people, the shops crammed with goodies—

Of course there was the other side as well. London was like a beautifully dressed woman with dirty underwear. Horrendous slums, depraved and deprived lower-classes, running sewers, a pall of choking smoke most of the year; the blind, the crippled, the lame begging on every street corner and the prisons full of debtors, thieves and worse.

But these three years had toughened me. I was now far more self-reliant, realising just how sheltered, pampered and protected I had been as a child. Now I believed I knew far better how to extract the best from the simplest of pleasures. I also realised how our little school shone out like a bunch of bright weeds against the dull poverty around us.

Only one in ten of our little charges really benefited from the education we offered, but at least they were off the streets, were fed, warm and, if necessary, clothed. Miss Moffat and her sister were adept at visiting some of the better neighbourhoods, especially if a child in the household had died, and begging for charitable cast-offs. Most of the bereaved were only too glad to be rid of unpleasant reminders. Otherwise we took advantage of any scraps of cloth we managed to gather and cobbled together what we could. Every Christmas and Easter each child was presented with a bright new penny, (birthdays being out because few of the children knew their birthdate), and at the New Year there was a bag of sweet biscuits.

The headmistress and her sister were as unalike in appearance as could be. Miss Moffat was tall, slim and severe-looking; Miss Hepzibah was small, round, wore wire-rimmed glasses, and sighed a great deal: Ellen told me she had been disappointed in love. There was one other member of their household: Madeleine, a remarkably quiet and composed young lady of about nineteen who filled in as a teacher when necessary, and was apparently adopted by the Misses Moffat as a baby. When I expressed to Ellen my admiration for their generosity, she shrugged her shoulders.

"There's some as would say they didn't have much choice," she said, and left me to work it out for myself. I guessed Madeleine must be at least a distant relation, for she bore a remarkable resemblance to a younger Miss Hepzibah. . . .

There was a bustle at the back of the classroom and every childish head turned to where Ellen was carrying in the cauldron of lunchtime soup. She was followed by Madeleine with a tray of bread and a bundle of spoons. Next came the enamel bowls and a bucket of soapy water and a rag, for every child had its face and hands washed before eating. I slipped out to the kitchen to check on little epileptic Ernest, and found him already seated at the kitchen table with soup and bread. On the way back I passed Miss Moffat, who gave me a nod before striking the brass gong outside the classroom to signal luncheon, a sound quickly drowned by the scrapes of chairs and stools, excited squeals and the rush of feet as the children formed into class lines. As usual there was much pushing and shoving, seeming that every second without food was life-threatening, but the routine was well established, and as soon as Miss Moffat entered the room and called for order she gained it within a half-minute.

Madeleine wiped hands and faces, I handed out bowl and spoon, Ellen ladled out into the former and Miss Hepzibah and Miss Hardcastle doled out the bread. The children went back to their desks to eat, before returning their bowls, having their hands and faces wiped clean again and escaping to the yard at the back for a half hour, to play tag, leapfrog, Fairy Footsteps or Hopscotch and visit the privy.

Then, and only then did we teachers repair to the kitchen to eat our luncheon and toast our toes, with the added bonus of a cup of hot, strong tea to follow. This was also the time when we discussed any especial problems with the children; those who needed extra clothes, who appeared to be sickening for something or who showed signs of maltreatment or abuse.

This half-hour always whizzed by, and today the children were even more difficult to control, but this was usual on a Saturday. My class were supposed to be doing the simplest of simple arithmetic, but even the effort of adding one and one together seemed beyond them, let alone two and two. At least three of them were fast asleep, heads on desks, and the rest of them were either yawning or wanting to pick a fight.

The classroom seemed to be getting darker and darker, although it was only the first of October. Glancing up at the long windows, so high up they had to be opened (rarely) and shut by a hooked pole, my heart sank. So far autumn had been bright and fairly sunny, but now the first yellow wraiths of fog were rubbing against the grubby panes. It seemed I shouldn't be spending my afternoon tomorrow after church strolling in the park. At least I had a good book to read: I had re-borrowed Miss Anne Brontë's *Agnes Grey* from the library. A failed governess maybe, but in the end she had gained her man.

Of course I had to enjoy her final success vicariously, for I had never had even the sniff of a proper suitor. One couldn't count the boisterous schoolboy who had tried to steal a kiss on my fourteenth birthday,

nor yet the young curate with the sticky-out ears who was always begging me to come and see his pressed-flower collection. In London the
pattern had been the same. I discouraged the approach of strangers, and
the only man of my acquaintance had been the student on the floor
above at my lodgings. According to my landlady he originated from
Dublin, in Ireland, and he certainly had the gift of the charm and volubility of his race, and he insisted on writing me reams of doggerel which
he shoved under my door nearly every day. I ignored his knockings—no
visitors after six o'clock, no gentlemen in ladies' rooms and vice versa—
and either returned the "poems" the same way they had come or, if I
was feeling particularly vicious, they were useful for laying the fire.

But this was not the limit of his attentions. Although he never did
nor said anything improper, and hardly spoke at all except for the conventional greeting now and again, he seemed to shadow me everywhere.
He peered over my shoulder at the baker's, the grocer's shop and the
butcher's; he was in the seat behind me at church; he checked on my
choice in the library; he was behind me in the park, at museums and
galleries, and he even peered through the railings when I was ushering
the children in and out.

Then, after some three months he disappeared, owing my landlady
for the last two . . .

I jerked awake. Goodness, I was succumbing like my pupils to a
Saturday afternoon lethargy! I looked around to see what had disturbed
me and saw that the door to Miss Moffat's private apartment was open,
and Miss Moffat was beckoning Toby (one of our successes: it was he,
the youngest member of our laundress's family, who usually escorted
me home) from his place in the top class. Of course everyone stopped
whatever they were doing to listen to the exchange, although the actual
words were inaudible.

I tapped my ruler on the desk. "Come, children: anyone who has
finished please bring your slate to me . . ."

I looked up. Twelve- or thirteen-year-old Toby was threading his
way through the desks, heading straight for me! What could he possibly
want? What dread rule had I broken that the headmistress needed to see
me urgently at three o'clock on a foggy Saturday afternoon?

"Miss Sophy?"

My throat was suddenly dry and I swallowed convulsively. "Yes,
Toby?"

"Miss Moffat asks that you 'tend her in her office, most partickler.
Seems there's a gennulman to see you . . ."

2

The Bequest

How often do the most innocent among us imagine themselves guilty! During that long walk from my desk, through the crowded classroom and down the corridor to Miss Moffat's study-cum-sitting-room I felt I was experiencing all the terrors of Mr. Sidney Carton on his way to the guillotine, the voices of the children, the chant of the mob—

Yet what could I have done? My thoughts rushed around like a rat in a maze, seeking some explanation and finding none. And who was the gentleman who wanted to see me? Was he from the police? Had someone I knew done something dreadful? Could it be a forgotten creditor of Papa's?

I could feel my heart beginning to race, my whole body to tremble, and it was only when I raised my hand to knock on Miss Moffat's door that I remembered to discard the half-sleeves I wore to protect me from chalk-dust and pat my hair into some sort of order, though as I had inherited Mama's unruly curls it was merely a case of tucking them hastily into my snood.

I could no longer put it off; whatever lay on the other side of that door I would face with my head held high—so high, in fact, that when I knocked briskly and walked in, not waiting for an answer, I remembered too late the tatty rug that lay just inside the door, a trip-trap for the unwary.

Miss Moffat rose from behind her desk. "Watch where you put your feet, child! And please straighten your collar."

I rose from my knees, smoothing down my skirt, cursing under my breath at my clumsiness.

"Sit here, beside me."

It wasn't only the chill in the room that had me clasping my hands tightly in my lap—there was a perfectly adequate fireplace, but to Miss Moffat winter only began with the first snows—no, it wasn't the cold, it was the figure lurking in the shadows whose face I couldn't see that had me trembling.

Miss Moffat addressed the shadow. "Please be seated, Mr. Swallow," indicating the Windsor chair across from her. She turned to me. "This gentleman is from the firm of Goldstone, Crutch and Swallow of Lincoln's Inn. He has a legal matter to discuss with you." She half-rose from her chair. "If you wish I shall leave you to—"

"Oh, no, please!" I clutched unthinkingly at her sleeve. "I should much prefer you to stay." This although the ogre of the shadow proved to be only a slight, middle-aged man with a bald head and half-glasses. He sat down, laid a bundle of papers on the desk and cleared his throat.

"This is she?"

Miss Moffat leaned back in her chair, patting my arm reassuringly. "Yes."

He coughed, rearranged his papers. "Well, Miss Laye—"

"Lee," I corrected automatically.

"Of course, of course . . . Miss Lee. I am here to reveal some of the terms of our client's Last Will and Testament. I say 'some,' because a part is left for you to discover." He shuffled the papers again. "I must say it has taken some time for us to discover your whereabouts, as the private detective who was hired to trace you is—was—behind bars. A matter of a small debt which we were obliged to disburse, as the gentleman was a trifle obdurate in the matter of your address until we had—ah!—freed him."

Client? Will? Private detective? Prison? It sounded as though I was caught up in some travesty of a novel, a combination of Mr. Dickens and Mr. Conan Doyle. Miss Moffat saw my bewilderment and patted my arm.

"Mr. Swallow," she said. "You have me a trifle confused and, I believe, Miss Lee even more. Do we have a name for this client of yours whose Will you are executing?"

The solicitor looked faintly astonished. "Of course. I assumed—that is I believed—that Miss Lee would know of whom I spoke."

"No," I said. "I'm sorry, but I haven't the faintest idea.

He smiled, but it was a thin smile. "Perhaps I had better begin again. . . . He extracted a document from the heap in front of him. "I have here the Death Certificate of one Algernon Charteris Lyle, the eminent archaeologist, who died some six weeks ago and is buried in the local village church . . ." He looked at me expectantly.

I shook my head. "I know no-one of that name."

His eyebrows shot up. "Mr. Lyle of Hightop Hall in Dorset? I speak of your uncle, Miss Lee!"

My uncle? But I hadn't got an uncle. I said so. "I'm sure my father . . ." I faltered. Wasn't Lyle my mother's maiden name? I was sure now that I had seen it on my parents' wedding certificate, which I kept with other important papers. But my mother had never mentioned that she had a brother, never talked about her family at all. I searched my memory; hadn't she once handed Papa the newspaper, remarking: "Read that article, my dear: it seems our Algy is making quite a name for himself . . ." Papa had said: "Not enough to seek out his relations," and Mama had said quietly: "You know how they felt about us—" but Papa had interrupted: "Not in front of the child, dearest . . ." and that had been that.

"Was he my mother's brother?" I ventured.

"Exactly!" He rubbed his hands together, as if I had got ten out of ten in some obscure test. "I gather your mother's family were not without some standing in the county of Dorset, but when their only daughter ran off to marry a humble clock-repairer—" he contrived to make it sound a profession slightly lower than that of refuse-collector "—they cut her off without a penny and broke off all further communication."

"I'm sure she didn't mind!" I said hotly. "My parents were devoted to one other! We didn't have much money but we were a very happy family. And Papa wasn't just a clock-repairer: he was a qualified watchmaker, with letters after his name!"

"He was also, I believe," said Mr. Swallow, "of Eastern origin?"

I was silent. I saw Miss Moffat glance sharply at me and then look away.

"My father's true name was Henry Li," I said at last, spelling it out. "His mother was French, his father Eurasian. His parents settled in Switzerland after they married, and that is where my father learned his skills. When his parents died he decided to try his luck in England, where he changed his name to Lee by deed-poll." I turned to Miss Moffat. "I'm sorry, ma'am. Perhaps I should have told you. It wasn't a deliberate omission, I've grown up with the knowledge all my life."

"It would have made no difference," she said firmly. "It must be interesting to consist of so many cultures. For myself, I have always had an interest in the East . . ." She recalled herself, to glare at Mr. Swallow. "But I do not see what this line of questioning has to do with the matter in hand."

"I apologise for any embarrassment," he said. "But I believe it to have relevance. During their lifetimes, Mr. Lyle's parents forbade him to communicate with his sister, for this very reason. It seems they were somewhat . . ." He hesitated.

"Prejudiced," supplied Miss Moffat.

"Precisely. While they were alive our client respected their wishes, but with their deaths he made enquiries and was satisfied that your parents were reasonably well off and happy with the birth of a daughter. He purchased Hightop Hall the better to house the many artifacts he brought back from his travels and these were added to over the next few years as his activities were extended." He coughed, and shuffled the papers again before continuing.

"Unfortunately he contracted malarial fever at one stage, and once at home recuperating suffered a mild heart attack, which gave him cause to reassess his future. He decided to leave your mother a small legacy, but when he tried to contact her he found both your parents were dead, Miss Lee, and that you had moved to London, address unknown. He commissioned us to search for you, but we had no success." He sniffed and glanced around the rather shabby little room. "Obviously we were looking in the wrong places.

"As his health worsened he decided to take matters into his own hands and advertised for a private detective, payment on results. In this he had greater success, as the young man was quite enterprising. He has a very—persuasive—way with him, and once he had ascertained from one of your former neighbours that you had applied for various posts from a particular newspaper, and the approximate date thereof, it did not take him long to narrow down the search. To cut a long story short, he not only found you, but furnished your uncle with such precise details of your looks, character, likes, dislikes and situation, that he immediately added a codicil to his Will." He extracted a paper from the heap. "I must say we found it a trifle unusual . . ."

Unusual? The whole matter was unbelievable from my point of view. During the last half-hour not only had I found—and lost—a forgotten relative, it appeared I had also been left a legacy! I could not mourn a man I had never known, but I could be grateful that he had tried, at the last, to make up for the prejudices of his parents. Mama would have been comforted to know that her "Algy" had thought about her at the end, and that he had also considered his niece. I wanted to know what my uncle had looked like, his manner, but now was not the time for questions: Mr. Swallow was still talking.

". . . insofar as it is incomplete. I am not in possession of the full facts, as I believe your uncle has left you a choice. There is a letter awaiting your perusal at Hightop Hall, and I have moneys here for you to travel there and read the same. So far, his instructions to us are clear. So is the fact that he has left you the contents of a small, locked cabinet in what was his study. I have the key here." He handed it to me. "All the rest of his artifacts have been left to various museums, his books, writings and manuscripts to his Cambridge college." He paused and cleared his throat again. "Although his housekeeper and her husband have been left a small legacy, I cannot promise you that you will have much money as your lot. During his last years he lived on his capital and the house and grounds grew more and more neglected, although the Hall itself has not suffered any structural decay.

"So, do not expect to live in luxury. I suggest you keep your present post for the time being, travel to Dorset to see what is in your uncle's letter, then decide what to do next. You will give her permission to take the trip, Miss Moffat?"

"Gladly. The child has taken no holidays since she has been with us, except for the usual weeks at Christmas and Easter, and of course her post will remain open." She said all this, but she knew the real reason I had taken no leave was because (a) I needed the food and (b) I had nowhere to go. She turned to me. "Take all the time you need. Your wages will still be paid, and Madeleine will cover for you."

"Then when will you be ready to travel, Miss Lee?"

I thought rapidly—everything was happening so quickly. Still, the sooner the better. I glanced at Miss Moffat. "Monday?"

She nodded.

Mr. Swallow shuffled his papers together for the last time. "In that case I will have one of our staff down there to meet you and help out if necessary. We shall reserve a seat on the train and arrange for a carriage for the last part of your journey. Our representative will reside at the local inn and you may do the same, or stay at the Hall if you prefer. I will telegraph the housekeeper to expect you. All costs will be borne by your uncle's estate.

"If you would call at our offices in Lincoln's Inn at nine-thirty on Monday morning—number 22A—we shall have all ready for you."

We shook hands—his were clammy and cold—and Miss Moffat escorted him out. Through the open door I could hear the clatter of nailed boots as the last of the children made their way home, and the noises from the kitchen as Ellen cleared all away for the weekend. Through the net curtains behind the desk I could see the fog thickening.

I glanced at my fob-watch: five minutes past four. An hour and five minutes and my life could have changed completely.

I leant back in my chair. It had all happened too quickly for me to grasp the implications. Sure, I knew what I had to do next, how and when, but it just didn't add up to anything concrete. My mind and body were still attuned to a Saturday at the school; time now I went home, did some shopping on the way, picked up my laundry, lighted my fire, collected my hot water and had a wash, ate my supper, did some mending and then relaxed with my library book before undressing and going to bed. Tomorrow, Sunday, my best dress and church. Perhaps a walk in the afternoon, a visit to one of the parks, a halfpenny ride on one of the open-top horse-drawn trams . . .

I realised I was trying to push my new knowledge away, instead of both accepting it and trying to make sense of it. The fact was, I was afraid. So far there had been so few changes in my life—going away to school, the death of my parents, finding this post in London—that I was ill-equipped to deal with sudden advances or retractions. It was only now that I was beginning to realise what a rut I had got myself into in the last three years; well, here was a situation I had been forced into and I felt the first stirrings of anticipation. Perhaps this was the beginning of something new and exciting—

There was a knock on the door and Ellen brought in a tray of tea.

"Miss Moffat said as 'ow you'd missed your bread and jam you might like to join 'er in a cuppa. She'll be back in a minute, just locking up." She hesitated in the doorway. "She said as 'ow you're off on Monday to look at your uncle's place and might not be back. Just like to say as 'ow we'd miss you. And if you ever need a cook, I'll be there like a shot." She slipped out the door, then poked her head round it again. "Young Ern 'as gone off with 'is sister, but master Toby says as 'e'll wait in the kitchen to see you 'ome . . ."

Dear Toby! Like the rest of my laundress's children, he was not certain which of his various "uncles" was his father, but he was no worse for that, being one of our most promising pupils, determined to better himself. Realising that my lodgings were within a stone's-throw of the laundry, he had offered to show me a quicker way home.

This had opened my eyes to the darker side of the city. Narrow alleys with houses leaning crazily in all directions, gutters running with ordure, shouts, screams and rantings from behind open doors with no hinges; windows nailed up with sacking; beggars with no hands, no legs, no eyes. Rats as big as cats scuttling in and out of the heaps of refuse, some of which latter came alive as we passed, gnawed fingers grabbing for my skirts, Toby's ankles. We crept through the filth of courtyards where dogs prowled and snarled and fought and copulated and half-naked children played listlessly with rags and pieces of string. We passed low taverns, stinking of sour beer and wine and the sweet decay of vomited gin, men and women staggering out, their faces bloated and blotched, swaying and falling into the gutters. We went by the painted women, some not even yet women, but boys and girls no older than Toby himself. Lines of people waited for the pawnbroker to open for the evening so they could "pop" their few possessions from one week to the other. Flies fastened on our hands and faces, greedily seeking salt; we stepped aside for the rag-and-bone man with his cart: rags for paper, bones for glue, bottles for reuse. The night-soil people never came here and slops thrown from the windows stained the house-fronts and caked the cobbles.

The sights, the sounds, the smells, all combined with the thick, murky air, revolted me: it was like a walk through Hell. But Toby walked through it all with the assurance born of familiarity. With him I was safe. He knew the streets and many of the people, warning off the urchins who would have crept up behind me to snatch at my reticule, bonnet or even cloak. I saw that he carried a small sharp knife, besides the short, weighted stick stuck in his belt. After that first time I never wanted to tread that way once more, but he persuaded me every now and again. I never came to any harm, and gradually he introduced me to his especial friends: the old-clothes dealer, Simeon, whose face reminded me of the illustrations of Fagin in "Oliver Twist"; Pegleg Pete, a crippled ex-sailor, who hawked matches; Old Nell, who had a houseful of felines, spending whatever she earned with the cat's-meat man; Sal, a prostitute whose moneys kept not only herself but her three young siblings and an invalid mother and my favourite, little Em, a crippled child with the sweetest singing voice I had ever heard.

This night, with the fog closing in, we would go by the longer route. I decided that supper would be a celebration, not only for my birthday but also for my uncle's legacy, whatever that might be, and that I would invite Toby to share it with me.

Miss Moffat came back and shut the jingling bunch of keys away in her desk.

"Well, that's that for a couple of days," she said briskly. "Pour the tea, child, while I wind the clock. It only needs attention once a week, and Saturday is as good a day as any other . . ."

I poured out the way Mama had taught me: milk first, the first cup for the guest, second for the host, in case the tea grew too strong. This was never a problem with Miss Moffat's tea; Ellen brewed it as she liked it, pale and straw-coloured. I picked up the tongs and added the rare pleasure of two lumps of sugar to mine. The headmistress drew the drugget curtains, turned up the lamp, accepted her cup and saucer and took a couple of sips before seating herself in the chair next to mine.

"Well, this afternoon was a surprise, wasn't it?"

"Yes, ma'am. I'm afraid it hasn't quite sunk in yet."

"No more it will child, until you find yourself on that train on Monday morning."

"I've never travelled on a train . . ."

"Then you have both a treat and an experience in store! I well remember the first time I travelled so . . . The speed! Why, we must have reached at least thirty miles per hour! The worst things were the smoke and smuts and the hardness of the seats . . . Make sure you visit the Ladies Room at the station before you board the train: there is nothing worse than travelling in discomfort. Try and find yourself a 'Ladies Only' carriage: you will be safe from tobacco smoke and any unwelcome attentions."

"But surely, ma'am, no gentleman would venture to light a pipe or cigar in front of a lady without first requesting permission?"

She sniffed. "Once upon a time, yes, but times are changing, and not for the better." She leant over and squeezed my knee. "Besides, if you are in a 'Ladies Only' you will feel less inhibited when you unwrap your sandwiches or pie."

I was becoming more and more bewildered. "I shall need to take food with me?"

She nodded. "It would be wise. You will probably have just a crust for your breakfast, then you will have to walk to Lincoln's Inn. From there I presume they will provide transport to the station, but you will have to wait for the train. It is possible, I believe, to obtain a cup of tea there, but you will still have a long journey ahead. I cannot see you arriving at your final destination much before the middle of the afternoon, and who knows then what comforts, or lack of them, will await you? You would not wish to arrive in a distressed or fainting condition, would you?"

"N—no," I said. "Thank you for your advice, ma'am. I shall certainly take some refreshments with me. May I pour you some more tea?"

"Thank you. And please help yourself. I think we should try Ellen's seed-cake as well . . ."

Another cup of tea and two slices of cake later I felt far more relaxed. As I put down my empty cup and saucer she leant forward once more and squeezed my knee again, quite hard this time. "Have you given thought to what you will do in the future?"

"I suppose—I suppose it all depends on what is in my uncle's letter." I faltered, feeling uncomfortable all of a sudden.

She released her hold. "Of course. But if you find only a small amount is involved—will you consider returning here?"

"Of course," I reassured her. "In spite of everything, I have still enjoyed my time here. And I should miss the children sorely—"

"And us?"

I puzzled. "I don't know Miss Hardacre very well, but Ellen is a dear! Miss Hepzibah and Miss Madeleine are always very pleasant and you have shown me every consideration—"

Suddenly she stood up and loomed over me, her shadow huge on the wall, then she bent forward and cupped my face in her hands. "I should have realised where you got those eyes from," I thought she said, but couldn't be sure, because the blood was beating so strongly in my ears. She bent closer: she smelt of stale powder. Without any warning she kissed me full on the lips, as my mother might have done, but this wasn't a motherly kiss.

I pulled my head away and stumbled to my feet, knocking over my chair. When I had righted it and turned back, hoping my cheeks were not as flushed as they felt, Miss Moffat had her back to me, fiddling with something on the mantelpiece. Her back was very straight, but I noticed that the hand I could see was trembling. Her voice, however, was as firm as ever.

"Ask Ellen to collect the tea-tray, will you?"

3

Journeying

I was so busy puzzling over Miss Moffat's uncharacteristic behaviour on the way back to my lodgings, that it wasn't until we were nearly there that I realised that Toby had hardly uttered a word. Normally he was that delightful mixture of child and young adult which comes at the onset of puberty; one moment he would be darting ahead, leaping up to pull a leaf from a tree or somersault over some railings, the next he would engage me in serious conversation, asking impossible questions like "What does the Prime Minister *really* do?" or "Does the Queen wear a different pair of shoes every day?" or even "How far is it to the Moon?"

Very often I was stumped for a sensible answer. He was a naturally inquisitive child with an affectionate nature, though I sometimes wondered whether this had anything to do with the fact that he always managed to coax a sausage or pie from me on Saturdays . . . Not ever by direct asking, but the wistful face and appreciative thanks always touched my heart.

Being the youngest in the family at home he ran errands and delivered the laundry. His two eldest sisters were married and the younger two worked with their mother, although one was crippled. Of his brothers, one had run off to sea and the other was serving three years for assault. The "Missus" of his mother's title was purely a courtesy one. She had a fancy for soldiers and sailors: easy come, easy go. This I had learned from Ellen, who was expert at putting two and two together.

All the children had been to the Charity School at one time or another, but Toby was the only one to have shown any aptitude. He could read and write, although the latter was largely phonetic. He wrote as he spoke with all dropped or substituted aitches: "Hay" was " 'ay"; "afterwards" was "halfterwoods." His arithmetic was exceptionally good, in fact he was way ahead of his teachers, and used the abacus with bewildering speed.

But this afternoon there were no questions, no skipping ahead, no jumping the piles of leaves that swirled with every passerby. The fog didn't seem to be getting any thicker, but the gas-lamps had a smoky nimbus and people loomed up in shadowy insubstantiality to disappear again almost immediately, and the cries of the street vendors and the rattle of wheels had a muffled quality.

I tried to make conversation, but there was either no response, or he replied in monosyllables. As we reached the turn to my lodgings I fumbled in my purse and extracted a three-penny bit.

"Here, Toby, this is for my laundry. Don't bother to bring it back for a couple of hours, but when you do please tell your mother I would like your company for a while as escort. Clean face and hands, please!" I patted him on the head. "And please try to look a little less miserable! It's my birthday today . . ."

He looked up at me, his expression unreadable. "Happy birthday, Miss."

The clock of St. Michael and All Angels church nearby struck five. "Well then . . . See you about seven. Do you want to borrow my lantern?"

He shook his head and darted away. I made my way up the steps to my lodgings, still wondering what had upset him. Once in my room though, I was too busy to dwell on a mystery which was probably just a storm in a teacup anyway.

Putting on my apron I lighted the candles, laid the fire, collected yesterday's ashes in the coal-scuttle, put two weeks' rent in my pocket and went downstairs to find my landlady.

Explaining that I would be away for a few days due to the death of a relative, I also added that if I decided to stay longer I would send for the rest of my belongings, and arrange for their transportation. To this end I would give her two weeks' rent, the second in lieu of notice if I did not return. She was full of questions of course, but I pleaded distraction and escaped upstairs with my ration of coals and the promise of hot water within the hour.

Once swept, dusted and polished I looked around my little room with an affection of sorts I had not known I possessed. After all, it was the only place I could call home, and the unknown was always daunting. For three years, not altogether easy ones, this place had been my refuge. Over there was the bed with the patchwork quilt I slept under; there was the rickety table where I ate my meals; there was my mother's desk where I wrote up my diary, there was the window-sill where crumbs were placed for the hungry London sparrows and over there was the little shelf where my books were placed, next to the hooks for my clothes.

Books! What in the world would I have done without the escape they offered? My imagination had soared away from the confines of four walls—into the marshes with Hereward, fleeing the destruction at Pompeii, crusading with Ivanhoe, tasting the quieter gossip at Cranford, or enjoying the ecclesiastical in-fighting at Barchester . . . How often had I wished I had been a part, a real part, of the stories I read!

I gave myself a mental shake. After all the adventures I had yearned for, what was I doing clinging to a dingy little room, when on Monday my whole life might change!

Come on, young woman, I told myself. Today is your birthday, your coming-of-age. Tonight you will take Toby out for supper, a treat for you both. In the meantime go out and buy something you want—not something you need—find an extravagance.

Three-quarters of an hour later I returned with bread, bacon, pies and two oranges for Sunday, and my birthday presents to myself: a bottle of shampoo scented with orange-flowers and a bar of soap to match, rare luxuries, and two second-hand books: "Our Mutual Friend," by Mr. Dickens, and "Westward Ho!" by Mr. Kingsley. I should take them both with me on Monday. I had also bought some sprigs of rosemary and lavender to pack amongst my clothes, and had withdrawn all my savings. Not that I had any intention of spending them, but they might be useful in an emergency. I could always put them back afterwards—after *what* I wasn't quite sure.

My hot water arrived, I had a thorough wash, put on a clean white blouse and sponged my dark-blue skirt and cloak and polished my boots. Then I pinned two rosettes of white ribbon to my bonnet. Mama had taught me the importance of matching the colours of my dress discreetly, without drawing undue attention to it. "A lady is not known by her dress but by her manners," was one of her favourite sayings.

I peered at myself in the scrap of cracked and blotchy mirror above the mantelshelf, holding my candle close, but my face looked mysterious, far away. Without conscious thought I tried to focus my eyes, which had apparently inspired Miss Moffat to such uncharacteristic behaviour, but they looked exactly as they always had to me. Greeny-hazel, with thick black lashes—perhaps it was a slight tilt upwards at the outer corners that had intrigued her? Papa's eyes had had the same tilt but his eyes had been dark brown.

I shivered of a sudden and slammed the candle down, wax dripping into the hearth. Rubbing my mouth I tried to wipe away the memory of that kiss, unasked and resented. Would it happen again if I returned to the school? I hoped not: there had been something unsettling, wrong about it.

Footsteps on the stairs, stumbling a little in the dark, and a knock on the door. I opened it and there was Toby, my escort for the night.

Only he didn't look as if he was going anywhere. Thrusting the bundle of laundry into my arms he turned to go, face dirty, hair uncombed.

"Toby! What's the matter?"

"I'm not coming!" Tossing the laundry onto the bed, I seized his arm and drew him into the room.

"What do you mean, you're not coming? Won't your mother let you?" I laughed. This was incredible! He must know I intended to feed him and he was always hungry.

"Just why don't you want to come? Are you ill? I thought we could find somewhere pleasant to eat and—"

"And *I* thought you were my friend!"

"Of course you are my friend. Why should you think otherwise?"

"Because you're goin' away, that's why! And you're not comin' back neither, only you won't admit it. You're not just cel'bratin' your birthday, if that's what it is, you're cel'bratin' goin' away! And you didn't even tell me!" He looked as if he was about to stamp, throw something or burst into tears, and I didn't want him doing any of these.

"Toby! I'm surprised at you. That's one of the reasons we are going out tonight, so I can explain, just to you. Instead of waiting to hear what I have to say, you've obviously listened to some half-heard story from Ellen, who—"

"I listened! I listened at the door when you were with that lawyer fellow—"

"You shouldn't eavesdrop! It's wicked, and—"

"But that way at least I knows what's goin' on! Didn' hear it from anyone else. Straight from the 'orse's mouf."

I thought for a moment. "And did you hear my conversation with Miss Moffat later?"

He shook his head. "Saw me in the corridor, she did, an' sent me back to class."

"Then you didn't hear her ask me what I had decided to do in the future, and whether I had thought of returning?"

He shook his head again.

"Mr. Swallow said my uncle left very little money, did he not? Well, when Miss Moffat asked whether I had thought of returning, I told her it all depended on what I found when I went down there, and what was in my uncle's letter. So, what's the problem? Come on now, pull yourself together. I shall probably be back within the week."

"If'n you say it like that . . . Cross your heart and hope to die?"

I obliged. "Now then, what about that chop-house round the corner?"

"Nah . . ." He shook his head dismissively. "Ma does their linen, and I gets to see the food. Cat's meat. Flies all over." He brightened. "Tell you what: I know of a place 'bout quarter-mile away. Nothing posh, but the grub's good an' you gets value for money. Maggie May's. You game?"

"Maggie's" proved to be an Irish quarter-mile distant: more like a half. The fog was thickening, but Toby had the lantern and guided me safely enough, though I near jumped out of my skin when a bell clanged at my elbow, but it was only the muffin-man, wooden tray on his head, ready to cry out his wares. There were few people about, and we passed the chop-house I had suggested with only a small sigh of regret from me, for Maggie's sounded much more fun. It was.

We descended steep steps to a basement lit by oil lamps, with a large open hearth at the far end. It was warm, smoky, but cosy. Being early to dine, not long after seven, there were few tables occupied, these by quiet, respectable-looking people. Looking more closely at my surroundings I saw the floor was of worn, well-scrubbed red tiles, the walls were distempered white, and it would seem that none of the tables or chairs shared a common origin, although the former were spread with clean and cheerful red gingham cloths and starched napkins.

A small, round woman wearing a large white apron came bustling out from the back.

"Why, Master Toby! How nice to see you . . . And you have brought a lady-friend with you!" Her black eyes, darting from one to the other, had probably summed us up correctly even before Toby introduced me as his teacher, whom he had brought here for her birthday treat.

" 'Cos you makes the best 'n' freshest food in Lunnon," he added.

She wiped her hands on her apron. "Well, that's very kind of you,

Master Toby. We shall have to make sure we live up to your recommendation, shan't we?" She led us over to a table in an alcove near the fire,
where it was warm enough for me to discard bonnet, cloak and gloves.
"Now, what can I get for you? My standards are up on that blackboard
over there: tripe and onions, steak and kidney pudding, mutton with
caper sauce, rabbit pie, liver and onion sauce, stewed eels, and a treat
from India, vegetable curry. What do you say?"

"Rabbit pie for me," said Toby, "Though the tripe and onions sounds
great . . ."

"Leave it to me," she said and turned to me. "And how about you,
miss?" She looked at me speculatively. "I can tell you aren't a tripe and
onions lady, nor yet one for eels . . ." The very thought of either put me
right off. "If you don't mind waiting a little while, I'm sure I can come
up with something to suit," and off she whisked back to the kitchen,
her large apron spreading like the sail of a ship.

Five minutes later a serving-maid brought a bowl of tripe for Toby
and some toast and paté for me, accompanied by a large jug of lemon-
barley water.

"Starters," she announced.

The paté was delicious, with a hint of brandy behind the chicken
liver base. My first hunger sated, I glanced around the restaurant once
more. It was filling up nicely; some single gentlemen, married couples,
a pair of lovers and at least two families. Nobody seemed to mind the
mismatched furniture nor the odd pairings of cutlery.

Toby followed my gaze, scooping up the last of his sticky, glutinous
tripe with a slice of bread. "Mostly clerks as come here," he said. "They
finishes late, and it's a good place to bring the fambly. Mrs. May does
the cookin' and her daughters wait on. Mr. May works at the docks;
good man, but a bit dumb. She's the one as keeps them all goin'. Used
to work as cook to a titled gent till 'e went bankrupt."

But bankrupt her dishes certainly were not. Toby's rabbit stew came
with carrots and turnips and I was served with a mouth-watering plate
of Beef Wellington, the pastry light and flaky, the meat pink and tasty,
the mushrooms complemented by the tender French beans served as my
vegetable. We both finished with apple pie flavoured with cloves and
cinnamon and dressed with a rich custard. It was probably the most
delicious meal I had had in years, and much cheaper than I had expected.

A satisfactory end to a very odd day.

4

The Journey

After church the following day I started my packing. There was probably no need to parcel everything up, but even if I were to be away only a couple of days, my belongings would be safer packed away. So, into my father's old cabin trunk went my clothes (what there were of them), the patchwork quilt, spare bonnet, best boots and linen. In the tray at the top went writing materials, sewing things, books and the gold-rimmed, rose-patterned cup and saucer that had been my mother's favourite. I strapped up the trunk and labelled it, then also labelled the writing-desk, chair and footstool.

My dirty linen would go to Toby's mother on Monday, for return on Wednesday, and I prepared a label for that as well. I would travel in my working clothes, but in my travelling valise went clean underwear, nightdress, dressing-gown, slippers, washing things, an apron and my best blouse, skirt and jacket, plus the two books I had not yet read. It was so heavy by the time I had finished, I was glad I would be met at the other end.

I broke off to eat bacon sandwiches for lunch, and later warmed a pie for my supper, with an orange with each meal, but the time went so swiftly that it was after seven before I asked for hot water, one lot for washing my hair with my new shampoo, the other for an all-over wash. It seemed years since I had seen a proper bath-tub.

I asked the landlady to call me at six, plenty of time to clear out the grate, bundle up the washing, take it to Toby's mother, Mrs. Jugg, buy fresh bread and ham for sandwiches, plus a couple of bottles of ginger beer.

I had thought I would spend a sleepless night, worrying about the morrow, the future in general, but surprisingly I slept like a top, was ready in plenty of time and was five minutes early at the offices of Messrs. Goldstone, Crutch and Swallow of 22A, Lincoln's Inn.

Mr. Swallow was waiting for me.

"Ah, Miss—er—Lee. All arrangements have been made. You will catch the ten-thirty train from Waterloo, which will arrive at three at Deepling Crossing. There, our representative, Mr. Cumberbatch, will have arranged transport to Hightop Hall. The caretaker and his wife have been advised of your travel plans, and you will stay at the Hall until these matters have been—ah—sorted out satisfactorily. Mr. Cumberbatch will stay at a nearby hostelry, to be contacted when you are ready for your next move."

He handed me an envelope. "In here you will find your ticket and some travel expenses." He shook my hand. "I wish you luck, Miss—er—Lee."

Outside the office, treading through the fallen mulberry leaves, I opened the envelope. Inside was a first-class ticket for a "Ladies Only" compartment and twenty bright shillings. A fortune! There were no cabs in Chancery Lane, so I crossed to Kingsway with better luck.

At the station there was over an hour to wait, so I bought a buttered scone and a cup of coffee, all the while marvelling at the great glass and stone edifice, echoing with the huff and puff of the engines, the shriek of whistles, the clatter of the hurrying passengers, the call of the newsboys and the announcements, through a megaphone, of arrivals and departures.

The air was thick with that rotten-egg smell that seemed characteristic of steam engines, and the ground strewn with debris, amongst which pigeons and sparrows rooted for crumbs. I hesitated over buying a newspaper, but decided I had been prodigal enough. Besides, I had my books in my valise to read. After checking the platform from which my train left, and confirming the time, I retired to the Ladies Room, remembering Miss Moffat's advice and visiting the washroom.

In spite of all this time seemed to be crawling, not helped by the fact that I was checking my fob-watch every three minutes, or so it seemed. The waiting-room was nearly full; a woman with two grown daughters, a market-lady with two baskets of eggs, a severely dressed, thin woman with a satchel full of leaflets and another reading from her

Bible. Small children ran around, whining at the delay, eager to escape
and look at the engines.

Eventually, with still twenty minutes to go, I decided to see if my
train was at the platform. It was, and a helpful guard showed me the
way to my compartment and indicated my reserved seat, a corner one
facing the engine. No-one had briefed me as to tipping, but he seemed
grateful enough for the penny I offered.

It was all more comfortable and clean than I had expected from
Miss Moffat's reminiscences, but perhaps she had not travelled first
class. My seat was well sprung, there was a sunblind at the window and
a small upper window that could be slid open. I put my valise on the
netted shelf above my seat, took off and folded my cloak and adjusted
my bonnet in the mirror opposite. Then I sat back and watched the
passengers hurry past my window; all shapes and sizes, men, women
and children, laden and unladen, purposeful or hesitant, smart or shabby.
Seeing the numbers, I was glad I had the luxury of a reserved seat.

In the event I was joined only by two nuns and a languid lady with
a lorgnette, who shut her eyes and apparently dozed off as soon as the
train started. The sisters meanwhile occupied themselves with their ro-
saries and reading their psalters, so I was not obliged to even open my
mouth during the whole journey.

I had thought I would treat myself to a chapter of Mr. Dickens and
one of my sandwiches, but I was too engrossed in the journey. The
speed, the smooth motion, except when we passed over points, the ever-
opening vistas of town and country that flashed past the windows entranced me, punctuated as they were by the chuff-chuff of the powerful
engine and the diddly-dee, diddly-dee of the wheels on the tracks.

Once we had crossed the slow-moving Thames and cleared the
smoke-grimed tenements of south London we emerged into a world I
had almost forgotten: the green and pleasant land of rural England. I
had not realised how much I had missed the fields, trees, streams and
cattle that were so much a part of my childhood. I found my hands were
so much a part of my childhood. I found my hands were clenched in
my lap and I was filled with nostalgia as at one moment we plunged
into a cutting with bosky woods stretching up on both sides, their leaves
turning red, yellow and brown and fluttering down in the wake of our
passage. Then we would have a straight run through fields bisected by
neat hedges in which brown and white Herefords grazed or ponies galloped away, pretending panic at our passage, their tails held high.

There were long, low farmhouses, sheep dotting their fields; over
there they were burning the stubble, smoke mushrooming up and drifting

away north with the breeze; here they were already ploughing, the patient Shires straining against their collars as the straight furrows grew behind them.

Sometimes we rode high on an embankment, the sun throwing our shadow like a toy train onto the fields on our right. Now and again I would catch a glimpse of a stately home, in white or yellow stone, usually set on a knoll and backed by carefully cultivated woods. These set me to wondering what my uncle's house was like. With a name like Hightop Hall it ought to be grand enough, and at least I would be spending a couple of days there in greater luxury, I hoped, than my London lodgings.

This was a stopping train, as opposed to an express, and we halted at every station, from those that serviced small towns to those that were only to offload milk-churns for a farm across the fields. I kept careful count of the number of stops, as Mr. Swallow had written in pencil on my ticket that mine was number sixteen.

Deepling Crossing, when it came, was just another halt, and I was the only one alighting or getting on, and I felt rather lost as I watched the train puff its way round the curve and disappear.

I looked about me. The downside platform on which I stood had no exit and was backed by fields. Across on the upside however there was what looked like a ticket booth, a gate and a lane leading away into the distance—but no sign of any transport. I glanced at my watch: the train had been on time, but perhaps punctuality in this part of the countryside was more lax. After all, even in these advanced times, many people didn't own a timepiece of any kind, in or out of the home. Farmworkers relied on light and dark in the passing of the seasons, those in towns or villages on the striking of the church clock.

No point in just standing around. I walked to the end of the platform where it sloped down, crossing the line carefully in case another locomotive appeared suddenly, and walked up to the ticket booth, checking on the way that "Deepling Crossing" was clearly painted on the signs on both platforms: right place, right time.

I tapped on the closed shutters of the ticket booth, but there was no answer. I tapped again, a little louder this time—still no reply. I walked around to the back—but there was none! It was just a three-sided shelter, containing a stool, a broken clay pipe and two or three ancient ticket stubs: obviously the ticket-collector didn't have much call for his services.

I walked over to the wicket gate and peered down the lane: still no sign of transport. Well, I could wait a little longer, but after a half-hour pacing the platform, I began to feel worried. I decided the best thing to

do was have something to eat, because I was feeling distinctly hungry.
I took the stool out of the booth, found a patch of sunshine and sat down
to enjoy half my ham and chutney sandwiches, washed down by one of
my bottles of ginger beer. I could have eaten the rest, but thought it
wise to keep them for emergencies—like the non-appearance of any
form of welcoming party.

By the time an hour had passed since the arrival of the train—during
which time two expresses had roared through the station, one up, one
down, causing me to shrink back as I was buffeted by their passage, I
had decided that enough was enough. There was only one way out of
the station so I would walk in that direction, to meet whoever had been
sent out to fetch me.

I returned the stool to the booth, picked up my valise, opened the
gate and walked out into the lane. I then decided it would be wisest to
relieve myself before anyone turned up, found a gap in the hedge and
a nettle-free patch, a lesson I had learned early as a child when running
around the fields and lanes, too far away from home to seek our bathroom.

Thanking the good Lord that I was wearing my stout boots, kilting
up my skirt against the dust in the lane and picking up my valise I started
off again.

The lane wound and turned on itself, obviously following some
long-forgotten sheeptrack, and as I walked, changing my increasingly
heavy valise from hand to hand, the land rose and fell on either side. I
passed the entrance to two farms, but the houses were so far down the
access roads that I didn't dare risk asking for directions or aid, in case
I missed my intended transport. I passed a couple of cottages too, but
one was derelict, and the other housed a zany old man who apparently
had never heard of Hightop Hall.

At last I came to a cross-roads. There was a sign: to the left DOR-
CHESTER THIRTY-SIX MILES. To the right just the one word: LONDON. Putting
down my valise, I stood irresolute. Left, right, straight ahead? I looked
at my watch: four o'clock, two hours since I had alighted from the train.
Spreading my cloak out on a grassy bank, I sat down to review the
situation. Here I was, apparently miles from anywhere, it was October,
night would be descending soon, and—

Cartwheels? I stood up and peered across the road to the lane's
continuation and slowly a cart came into view, the driver and horse
looking half-asleep, their heads nodding in unison.

Springing to my feet I ran across the road and waved my arms
frantically to halt the cart. The driver hauled on the reins and the cart

came to a stop: "JOS. CARTER. CARRIER" I read on the side. Breathlessly I asked if he knew the way to Hightop Hall.

He looked at me suspiciously, then nodded. "Yerss."

"Is it that way?" Pointing back the way he had come.

"Yerss."

"How far?"

"Depends . . ."

"On what?"

"Whether you takes the high road or the low road."

"Which is the quickest?"

"High."

"How far that way?"

"Ten mile, give or take."

"Do you know where I could get a lift?"

For the first time he seemed to look at me properly. "You wanting to go there?"

I could have screamed. "Yes, I do. Urgently. It was my uncle's house."

His face brightened. "You be Miss Lee?"

"Yes!"

He scratched his head. "Be you sure? You supposed to be at the station—sent to meet you, I was." He scratched his nose this time. "Why bain't you at the station?"

I explained, as patiently as I could. "I thought I would be met by a young gentleman from London—did he send you instead?"

He nodded.

"Didn't he tell you the time of my train?"

"May have done. But I be a carrier. Old Nan, she wanted that chair delivering from her daughter's. Jones wanted them stores early. Got to keep in with the regulars . . ." He pursed his lips. "You coming then?"

The cart turned as slowly as his conversation had been, and as cautiously. There seemed to be no attempt to help me up, so I hoisted my valise aboard and climbed into the back via a wheel and a flurry of petticoat. Not that the driver took the slightest notice. I settled myself on a pile of dusty sacks and off we went. After a few miles we turned off the lane into another, even narrower.

I tapped him on the shoulder. "Is this the high road?"

He shook his head. "The low."

"But I thought you said the other way was shorter!"

"And so 'tis. Horse prefers this way . . ."

After that I gave up, ate the rest of my sandwiches and drank the

other bottle of ginger beer and even dozed a little as the miles slipped
away with the creak of wheels and the clop of hooves. Two hours later
I woke with a jerk as the cart pulled up.

"Are we here?"

"Yerss."

I lowered myself and the valise to the ground. The sky was already
glooming over and the wind had turned chill.

"That'll be five shillings, miss."

"I beg your pardon?"

"Five shillings to the station and back."

"But you didn't—" I caught myself in time. "Didn't the young
gentleman from London pay you?"

He shook his head. "Said it was up to you. Said you'd have money."

I had been caught napping, literally. A good job Mr. Swallow had
been generous with my travelling money. I paid the carrier and he trun-
dled off down the lane.

I turned to survey my temporary lodgings. Open double gates, a
small lodge, and a weed-infested driveway that led through tumbledown
parkland uphill towards—

The most hideous mansion I had ever seen.

5

Hightop Hall

It looked as though three different houses had been welded into one.

In the centre was what must have been a perfectly pleasant Queen Anne three-storey home. Red brick, with a grey slate roof, it was approached by a shallow set of steps leading to double doors. Two large windows on either side of the door indicated perhaps a withdrawing room and dining room, and behind these would be morning room, study, music room and, attached at the back, the kitchens and dairies. Above, on the first floor, were slightly smaller windows, bedrooms, I guessed, and dressing rooms. Above these were eight dormer windows, like surprised eyebrows, which would be for the servants. So far, so good.

But look to the right and the whole aspect changed. Sir Walter Scott would probably have approved of the grey stone castle, complete with towers, turrets and battlements, that was attached to the main building. Not on the grand scale maybe, but nonetheless this modern copy was utterly incongruous among its older settings. There was even a round tower. . . .

If that was not bad enough, then glance to the left. On the other side of the main building was what looked like a white stone Regency town-house, whose front door was approached by a pillared portico like a temple. Again, on its own it would not have been out of place, but the two-storey building, pleasant enough of itself, only served to accentuate the horrendous amalgam of the whole.

I stopped first at the lodge, of course, but the shutters were down and there was no answer.

My heart sank, nevertheless I trudged up the long drive, hoping against hope that it would be better inside. But the windows gazed back at me blankly, and on either side what must have once been attractive parkland was full of tall grass, rank weeds and neglected trees. The only sign of life anywhere was a thin plume of smoke rising from one of the chimneys on what I had already mentally christened "The Temple."

At last, cold, out of breath, I stood in front of the doors of the main house. There were doorknockers of greeny-tinged brass lion's heads, and a bell-pull to the right. I hesitated, then knocked first. No answer. I knocked again and used the bell-pull for good measure. Still no reply. Then I noticed, stuffed into the left-hand lion's mouth, a scrap of paper. Pulling it free, I studied it by the failing light.

"Miss Lee," it read. "Please go to the other door on the left." That must be the front door to the Temple. Well, at least someone was expecting me!

Picking up my valise I scurried across the front of the main house, my bonnet flapping in a sudden quixotic wind. It felt like rain, too.

Arriving at the other door I was grateful of the shelter of the portico as I searched for a knocker, but there was none, so I thumped on the door with my gloved hand. I waited a moment and thumped again, and less than a minute later I heard bolts being withdrawn and the door swung open to reveal a middle-aged couple carrying candles.

"Miss Lee? Come in, come in, you must be perished!" The woman drew me in, relieved me of my valise, which she handed to her husband, then preceded me down an unlit corridor towards an open door at the end. "You are late: we were expecting you much earlier."

I explained as best I could, and the woman tut-tutted. "You were picked up by that lazy, good-for-nothing Josiah? I'm surprised the lad from London chose him . . . But of course he has been finding the cider at the inn a trifle heady, so I hear. Sooner he gets back to where he came from the better!

"Now, miss, if you don't mind the kitchen I can have you warm and fed in a trice. If you wish to wash up, here's a candle, and it's the second door on the left out the back."

I recognised the euphemism, and was glad to relieve myself and wash the grime from hands and face. Returning to a roaring fire, I found my bonnet, cloak and gloves put away neatly.

"Thank you, Mrs. . . . . Er?"

"Early. They calls us Early and Late, Bill and me, 'cos I was Lattey before we was wed." She obviously expected me to laugh, so I did. "Now, miss, here's a mug of mulled ale. Do set yourself down by the fire and I'll have something for you to eat in a minute."

Mrs. Early bustled about, laying a place at the scrubbed pine table, lighting a couple of oil lamps and stirring the contents of various pots and pans, while her husband brought in more wood to replenish the fire, till I had to draw back my chair to avoid getting scorched. He filled a copper with water—which I guessed would be for washing—smiling and nodding all the while, but speaking only in monosyllables.

As people they were physically alike; medium height, round and rosy-cheeked with smooth dark hair. Their only real difference, apart from being opposite sexes of course, was the volubility of the one and the taciturnity of the other.

I liked them both immediately, and never had cause to change my mind.

I sat down to a simple but tasty repast: julienne soup, cottage pie and peas and blackberry tart and cream. As I ate the housekeeper bombarded me with questions about London: was it as big as they said, the largest city in the world? How many people lived there? Was the weather any different? (She had heard about the fogs.) Did lots of titled people live there? Did they eat different food? What did the river Thames look like?

I answered as best I could, but once I had finished my meal I was caught out by a half-stifled yawn. She noticed at once.

"Well now, my poor dear, here's me rattling on and you must be fair wore out! I thought as how you might like a warm bath before you goes to bed, so Mr. Early will carry up some hot water while I shows you where everything is." She lit two candles and handed me one. "There's more in the bedroom and a fire lit, too. Now, if you'll just follow me?"

Leading me up a flight of stairs that curved onto a landing above, she opened the second door on the left. "This whole part of the Hall was once the nursery wing, but when your uncle bought the place he decided to use it as the guest wing, being small and easy kept up and warm." She moved into the room and lit candles on the mantelshelf, above a cheerful little fire, and on the bedside table. "Had some peculiar ideas your uncle did; liked nothing better than to sleep in a blanket outside on the hill: said it reminded him of abroad. No wonder he was always getting the shivers!"

I wanted to ask her more about him, but she was still rattling on.

"Your bed has been warmed, but I'll put in another stone. I'll draw

the curtains—there'll be rain before morning, Mr. Early says." She suited
the actions to the words, then opened a commodious wardrobe. "This
is for your clothes. Hangers on one side, shelves on the other." As if by
magic her husband arrived with my valise, although I thought my poor
possessions would be lost in that piece of furniture. "There's your dressing table. Bath, commode, wash-bowl and hot-water jug are next door,
first on the left." She bustled about, turning down the bed, putting more
wood on the fire. "Will a call at eight in the morning suit? I'll see there's
hot water for you next door.

"Now, don't you worry about a thing. Sounds as though Mr. Early
has filled up the bath. If you want us, we're downstairs, left off the
kitchen. Tomorrow I'll show you the rest of the premises."

"My uncle left a letter—".

"Everything's in the study across the landing, which used to be the
day-nursery. Best leave it till morning when you're refreshed. I'll show
you then. Now, anything else you need?"

After they had gone I unpacked my valise, put away my belongings
and ventured into the bathroom next door, where I found a large, enam-
elled bath half-full of hot water, plus two jugs of cold, towels and soap.

Shedding my clothes I climbed in gratefully to soap and soak, until
I felt my eyes closing.

Back in the bedroom I set my mantel-clock above the fireplace
where I could see it; this was one of the things I couldn't have left
behind, even for a couple of days. It had been a gift from Papa for my
fifth birthday and was set with miniatures of my parents in the stand.

I drew back the curtains and pulled up the sash window; outside it
was raining softly and the air was full of the sweet smell of wet earth
and decaying leaves. The fire had sunk to a red glow. I blew out the
candles and groped my way back to the high double bed and climbed
into the starched linen sheets smelling of lavender. My toes found the
renewed and wrapped stone hot-water bottle; I remembered, just in time,
to say my prayers, and fell asleep before I could form another
thought. . . .

I was awoken by the curtains being drawn back on a sunny morning.

"I left you for an extra half-hour as you were sleeping so sweetly,"
said Mrs. Early. "I see you're like your uncle in preferring an open
window. . . . Hot water's ready next door. I took the liberty of laying up
in the kitchen as it's warmer, but if you prefer to eat alone I can bring
you something to the study next door?"

I assured her that the kitchen was fine. Had I really slept for twelve hours? It must have been the first time in memory.

"Afterwards I thought you might like to take a walk around the grounds with Mr. Early, and I could take you round the rest of the Hall before lunch, then you could have the afternoon to yourself, to see what your uncle left you . . ."

It all sounded fine to me, and as any dissent would probably have prompted Mrs. Early to further vociferous efforts, I agreed readily enough.

Breakfast was oatmeal with cream and sugar—how long it was since I had had porridge!—bacon and mushrooms, toast and marmalade and a pot of strong tea.

Afterwards I donned boots, cloak, bonnet and gloves and prepared to follow Mr. Early around my uncle's demesne. He started at the back door to the Temple, which led out to a cobbled yard. To the left were greenhouses and a well-cultivated kitchen-garden, and beyond that a stand of firs and pines, sloping down towards the road, to what must be the western end of the property. Good for both firewood and carpentry.

Turning towards the back of the main part of the house, I noted that there were still onions, broccoli, cabbages, sprouts—these waiting for the first frosts—carrots, turnips and swedes ready to be harvested in the kitchen garden. Beyond was an orchard, blessed with apple, plum and cherry trees.

At the back of the main house were the stables, empty except for a pony for the all-purpose trap, but a score of chickens pecked among the cobbles, and a half-dozen ducks doused their beaks in the pond at the rear. Farther on was a herb-garden, still cultivated, and the remains of what had been an ornamental garden surrounded by a neglected box-hedge, where tangles of late-blooming roses rioted amongst dead-headed phlox, delphiniums, oriental poppies and michaelmas daisies.

Behind the Castle part of the property was what once had been a shrubbery, and sprawling bushes of rosemary, sage and lavender. It should have been sad amongst all that neglect, but it wasn't. Nothing was actually dying away, all was still living and lusty. The soil was obviously fertile, and I longed to be amongst the most neglected: pull up the weeds, prune the roses, trim the shrubs. . . .

With goats and sheep to crop the grass, which would mean milk and cheese, this place could be almost self-supporting. A couple of bee-hives, perhaps, some pigsties and a stretch of potatoes—

Mrs. Early came out to call us into luncheon, mutton and caper sauce, with a milk pudding to follow. It had taken longer than I had expected, that exploration of the grounds, and I hadn't yet seen the interior of the rest of the house. Time seemed to whiz by, far faster than it had in the metropolis.

After luncheon Mrs. Early suggested that she show me over the rest of the Hall while it was still light enough to dispense with candles. The full tour took two hours.

We started in the Temple: across from my bedroom was the study, and farther down the corridor two more guest rooms. Downstairs, apart from the kitchen and Mr. and Mrs. Early's rooms, there was a sitting-room, dining-room and morning-room. A nice, comfortable home for a couple with two children . . .

The rest was very different.

The main house was very much as I had imagined: withdrawing-room, dining-room, morning-room, library, music-room and a small ball-room on the ground floor, plus the outhouse kitchen and dairies. There was also a cellar with empty wine-racks. On the first floor six bedrooms, two dressing-rooms, two bathrooms, and in the attics accommodation for a staff of at least twelve. A large house for a large family fond of entertaining.

As for the "Castle"—small, odd-shaped rooms, unexpected steps and stairs, low ceilings, slit windows, a superb view from the battlements and a baronial hall that could have seated a hundred, complete with a minstrel's gallery! Children would love it; their imaginations would run riot, and scrambling up and down inconvenient turret stairs would be an added bonus. A perfect place for a school, I thought. Or an orphanage . . .

The houses, apart from the Temple, were sparsely furnished. A few tables and chairs, including a vast table in the "baronial hall" to seat at least sixty, and a couple of dozen decrepit beds, wardrobes and dressers.

"Nothing left of any value," said Mrs. Early. "All the good linen, pots and pans, carpets and rugs, china and cutlery went to where you is staying now. The curtains in the rest of the place fell to shreds, and he sold the silver and gilt. Said he didn't need it no more."

I think the most incongruous items in the whole of the main house and the Castle were the artifacts, labelled and wrapped, that were still waiting to be collected. In the hall of the main house were row upon row of Greek statues, Roman mosaics, Egyptian mummies, Sumerian stone friezes, European arms and armour, Mayan idols, French tapestries, German carvings, Italian glass, Celtic crosses, Russian icons, coins from around the world, and the housekeeper assured me that this was only the remnants of my uncle's collection, still waiting to be collected.

In the bookless (sad!) library were scrolls, manuscripts and stacks of papers. Everything was neatly labelled.

"He wanted everything to be catalogued," said the housekeeper. "Right down to the smallest item. Although he collected all his life, and took great pleasure in his collections, spending hours just looking at a statue or a piece of writing, after he became ill for the first time he had a change of heart. He said things like what he had collected weren't just for one man, they should be shared by everyone. That's why he sent a lot of the stuff back to where it came from, if they had museums and things to put them in. Rest goes to museums and libraries here. This lot is the last waiting to be collected.

"You seen enough, miss?"

I had, indeed! My feet ached, my head buzzed and I felt as though I had spent three days in one of the London museums without a way out. How could anyone have spent most of his life collecting avenues of stones, miles of statuary, piles of papers and heaps of coins? I would be glad when they were all gone and the house was empty again. At least my uncle had had the sense to realise that history belonged to everyone—but then I realised that thinking like this I was treating the place as my own, not as something that would probably be sold under my nose.

Back again at the Temple, Mrs. Early ushered me upstairs to the room my uncle had used as his study in his last few years. A large, square room facing southwest, with blue Chinese-patterned wallpaper and a Chinese carpet to match. To the right a bright fire burned in the grate and opposite the door a long, now-darkening window looked out on pastureland and the pine wood. Immediately to the left was a long, low map-chest; on the left wall was a curio cabinet, the one I presumed my uncle had left me. The centre of the room was filled with a pine table about six feet square with two chairs, and over by the fireplace was what looked like a comfortable Windsor rocker, with cushions whose colour matched the curtains, a burgundy that contrasted pleasantly with the blue and white of the wallpaper and carpet. An empty bookshelf occupied the left-hand side of the fireplace.

On the mantelpiece was a large manila envelope . . .

"Why don't you slip out of that skirt and blouse and put on your dressing-gown?" suggested the housekeeper. "I'll wash the blouse and iron it in the morning, and sponge the skirt at the same time. It's heavy with the dirt from outside and the dust in, I can see that. I'll bring you a tray of tea, and you can have your supper up here later. That way you can have the evening in peace to read your uncle's letter."

A half-hour later, two cups of tea, muffins, egg-and-cress sand-wiches and fruitcake eaten and drunk, I took down the envelope from the mantelpiece, snuggled up in the rocker, opened the seal and started to read my uncle's letter.

6

My Uncle's Letter

At first it was difficult to follow the crabbed, small hand that helter-skeltered across the pages, but I took it slowly and methodically, realising that my uncle had probably written it during his last illness.

"My dear Niece," he had written. "It is one of my regrets that we shall never meet, although I have the advantage of knowing a little of what you look like, and also have an idea of your disposition."

Out from the letter fell a small pencil sketch. No way was it me—I thought I recognised a copy of a soap advertisement that graced the hoardings in London, but the girl had my curly hair, large eyes (even to the tilt) and wide mouth.

"As far as I can see, you have inherited your mother's hair, short nose and mouth; the rest must come from your father. I have had nothing but good reports of you. My solicitors wasted six months trying to discover your whereabouts and I had almost given up hope, when I saw an advertisement by a fellow calling himself the head of a Lost-and-Found Bureau. I had him visit me here and was both surprised at his youth and charmed by his manner, which was obviously his intention.

"However I decided to give him a try, though payment was to be by results only—I have often found this is efficacious, especially when hiring porters, guides etc. abroad. To cut a long story short, the young man found you through a combination of common sense and good luck far sooner than I had hoped. During this time I suffered another heart attack and realising that the next would be the last, I paid him for finding

you and suggested another payment for sending me a detailed report as
to your character, disposition and interests.

"You must forgive this second-hand snooping, but I felt there was
such a short time left to decide exactly how to dispose of what little
there is left. I learnt of your poorly paid post, your earnest endeavours
with the children and your especial care of a young boy called Toby
Jugg—why do parents not think harder before they burden their children
with names that will invite derision? I say nothing of the name you were
burdened with, you notice! I was told of your scrimping and saving,
your regular attendance at church; I was also given a list of your reading
matter, and the museums, concerts and galleries you attended. All of
these I thoroughly approved of—even down to your regular feeding of
the sparrows on your window-sill!"

I put down the letter in bewilderment. How on earth could this
person he hired have found out all this—even down to the sparrows? I
got up to stretch my legs and to both pull the curtains and light the oil
lamp on the table; candles, unless right at one's elbow, are not ideal for
reading. It must have been difficult for Miss Austen and the Misses
Brontë, I reflected. I put a couple more logs on the fire, and the pine
spat and crackled cheerily.

I moved over to the table to continue reading.

"I am of the opinion that you have inherited the courage and love
of life that characterised my dear sister and also the patience and attention to detail that must have contributed to your father's success as a
watch-maker, and probably both a compassion and love of learning that
has nothing to do with either.

"But I digress. This letter was meant to explain why I have been
so dilatory in contacting my only surviving relative. Let it be said here
and now that I was weak not to stand up to my parents, and initially it
was pure escapism that made me choose a life abroad, but gradually I
became absorbed in exploration, and discovered a real affinity for the
objects I excavated, so much so, in fact, that collecting rapidly became
an obsession that took over my life, even after the hold my parents had
over me was loosed by their death. *Mea culpa!*

"It was only after my bout of malaria, which recurs even now, and
the first heart attack and consequent enforced convalescence, that I began to see how selfish my life has become. Of course some of my work
has been worthwhile, especially the research, but a great deal has been
downright stealing, the theft of historical objects that rightfully belong
in their countries of origin. So I determined to return the majority of
the artifacts from whence they came, but where this was either unwise

or impracticable, I would leave them to museums here, so that they might be enjoyed by all. Research material and papers go to my old college, in the hope that they may inspire future students to follow my profession, albeit with a greater sense of responsibility.

"Part of my regret, as far as you are concerned, is that all that travel and acquiring of artifacts have left me with very little money, and during these last few years I have been living on my capital. My solicitors inform me that once the last artifacts have been shipped, funeral expenses paid, an annuity (which they richly deserve) left to Mr. and Mrs. Early and their own charges disbursed—avoid solicitors like the plague, Niece, if you can: they will bleed you dry!—there would be only the Hall and less than five hundred pounds left. And if they say 'less,' then that is exactly what they mean.

"And now I come to the nub of the matter. There remains in my estate four or five hundred pounds and the Hall. I offer you a choice. You may either take the money and walk away to, I hope, a better life, in which case the solicitors have instructions to sell the Hall to endow an archaeology scholarship at Cambridge, or you may inherit the Hall and do with it what you please. In this case the moneys awaiting will be used for you to undertake an expedition very dear to my heart, which I am now too old and ill to contemplate. This latter choice will not be easy, but I am convinced that if any woman can do it, you can. If you decide to take the money I shall not blame you, but give it to you with my blessing. If that is your decision, inform the solicitors and it is yours at once. However if the other alternative has any appeal please read—carefully—the rest of this letter . . ."

I sat back in my chair. Four or five hundred pounds was a fortune! I could give up work, rent a small cottage and even afford a cleaner. . . . Or, if I went back to work, I could buy some decent clothes and find a better position. Whichever way, the money would last for a long, long time—at least ten years. I found I was smiling with relief and pleasure; how very kind of my uncle!

But he had mentioned an alternative: something about an expedition? Although I was sure I had made up my mind, I owed it to him to at least read on.

"Ah, I see you are either not satisfied with a little security, or else are filled with a natural curiosity in that you continue with this letter. Good. I should tell you that I hate to leave any matter unfinished, and there is one problem I have been unable to solve during my lifetime. If I may beg your indulgence to explain further?

"I visited many out-of-the-way places in my journeys, but it was on a routine stopover in Venice that my curiosity led me to visit a local auction, the contents of a crumbling palazzo that was being pulled down to make way for a more modern building. There was little to attract my attention, except for a box of miscellaneous items, amongst which was a rather fine blue glass vase. I already possessed one, so bid for the box, paying less than a tenth than I thought it worth.

"I caught the transport I was awaiting, leaving the unopened box in store, and almost forgot to retrieve it when I returned some three months later, and did not fully examine it until some year later, when I finally returned here. The blue Etruscan vase joined its sister—they are some of the few items I kept: you will find them in the morning-room downstairs. Most of the rest of the items I threw out as chipped, broken or worthlessly modern, but right at the bottom I found a package wrapped in an old cloak. It contained a round object like a small cannon-ball, a crumbling bundle of manuscript, an ivory figurine of some age and a twisted piece of horn.

"At first I could see no connection between the disparate objects, but a closer scrutiny revealed that around the round object was wrapped a piece of material which read: 'This be Dragonnes Eg.' Of course I treated this statement with the scholarly contempt it deserved, but by now I was intrigued enough to examine the manuscript more closely. I found it was written in a kind of mediaeval shorthand, but once I had cracked the code I found it contained the remnants of an interesting tale. Remnants only, alas, because many of the pages were worm-eaten or had fallen into dust, or the poor ink used had faded beyond deciphering.

"That part I could translate contained the story of a brave young woman who undertook some sort of pilgrimage, firstly to find a husband, and then trace her lover, who, according to the story, was a dragon-man. According to the narrative she covered many hundreds of miles in her searching and the story is unfinished. I dismissed it as pure fiction at first, but when I had finished the translation, with its sorceries and magics, talking animals, shape-changing and flying pigs, I found many of the details as to places—a desert I recognise, towns that still exist miles from anywhere, rivers and mountains that are readily identifiable—so convincing that the writer must at least have visited these places.

"A couple of scraps of map accompanied the manuscript, and these I have redrawn. My translation together with these and what remains of the original are locked away in the cabinet to which you have the key."

I glanced across at the cabinet; the key was in my reticule and I was dying to open it and take a look, but I would see what else my uncle had to say first.

"I could not immediately see any connection between the four objects in the bundle, but then I recalled mention of an 'Eg'—the product of a liaison between the heroine and her dragon-lover—being stolen. There was also mention of a 'Unicorn's ring' and a shape-changing creature called 'Ky-Lin,' a mythical creature from the Buddhist religion.

"Once I realised, however, that whoever had collected these articles believed in their being kept together because of their relevance, I examined them more closely. I weighed and measured the so-called 'Eg'— typical mediaeval phonetic spelling—then attempted to break it open or crack it, but it resisted all my efforts. One thing I did notice was that it was not as cold as stone. It seemed to hold the same warmth as of that fossilised resin, amber. The little ivory figure is exquisitely carved, obviously Chinese, but shows no sign of the 'life' attributed to it in the manuscript. As for the twist of horn, presumably meant to represent the so-called 'Unicorn's Ring,' it would fit none of my fingers nor those of Mr. and Mrs. Early.

"So I put this puzzle to one side for two or three years, occupied as I was with other matters. When I returned to it, of a mind to retain the manuscript and the figurine and dispense with the stone and the twist of horn, I made a startling discovery. On picking up the stone it felt heavier and larger than previously. Unwilling to trust my senses, I checked both weight and size against my earlier notes, and indeed, if I had calculated correctly initially, the stone was not only four ounces heavier, it was also two inches larger!

"Now I am not a superstitious man, any more than other scientists, but here was something strange. I was due to travel to the Valley of the Kings, a journey I could not delay, but as soon as I returned I again weighed and measured the stone, to find it had gained another couple of ounces and another inch in diameter. This time there was no mistake, no miscalculation, which I had rather hoped for as a rational explanation. And it was still relatively *warm*. . . .

"I wonder if you can have any idea of the turmoil this discovery threw me into! Here was I, a dry-as-dust scientist without an ounce of imagination, forced to re-evaluate all my previous theories as to the state of the universe! At first I clung desperately to the theory that what I held was merely some large reptile egg, of a species as yet unknown, but yet was not a dragon a reptile? Was there some truth in the manuscript? Were the times so different then that what we now dismiss as sorcery and magic did exist? I am no longer sure of just how true scientific facts are: all I am sure of is that something mighty strange is going on. I have left a list of measurements of the egg—or stone, who knows?—in the cabinet, together with the measuring instruments, and I'm willing to wager you will find an increase.

"Explain it I cannot, except that I do now believe that the object will not get any rest or fulfilment until it is returned to the place from whence it was stolen. Perhaps it will hatch out into something so incredible that our modern, nineteenth-century minds cannot encompass it.

"If I were still alive and well I would make this my last expedition, but, as you will realise as you read this, I am not. I would ask that you, my niece, might undertake this task. An arduous and tall order, I agree, but as I said before, I cannot bear unfinished business. If you do decide in favour of this suggestion, then the moneys you may receive as a lump sum will have to be used for travelling expenses, especially as someone from the solicitors' office would have to accompany you, and I would wish the young 'detective' who found you to travel with you as well, as extra protection.

"I have another, more quixotic, condition: that this expedition must be completed within a calendar year. So, my dear niece, you have a choice: either accept what little moneys I have left, or embark on an adventure you may never forget. It is up to you, but before you decide I would ask that you read my transcripts, look at the maps and examine the contents of the cabinet. Also remember that if you do succeed you will receive Hightop Hall, to do with as you will. Hideous, I agree, but it would make a good school or orphanage . . ."

Strange . . . exactly what I had thought.

"When you have read the transcript, then read the last pages of this letter—"

There was a tap on the door.

"Suppertime, Miss Lee," said Mrs. Early. "Hope I'm not intruding—goodness me, you've near let out the fire!" Rapidly she laid the table from a tray she had brought with her, then poked and coaxed and replenished the fire till it was once more a cheerful blaze. "I'll be up with the soup in a moment—"

"Don't go, Mrs. Early." I hesitated. "Tell me—you knew my uncle for—how long?"

"Thirty-five year," she answered promptly. "Not to know him as we did when he moved here, but I went as under-housemaid to his parents when I was thirteen, and have been with the family, as it were, ever since. Mr. Early was gardener's boy when I first met him, and—"

I tried to stem the flood. "What I really wanted to know was what he was like as a person—"

"Just you wait one moment . . ." She clattered away down the stairs to reappear with a magazine, which she opened at a well-thumbed page.

"See this? It were a sketch some artist did for a posh magazine, and it's him to a T!"

I must confess I had expected a tall, burly man, with probably a full beard, but the reality was quite different. He had been clean-shaven and balding. In the drawing he looked nervous and had his hands clasped behind his back. The man I was looking at was unused to the niceties of social life and preferred objects to people. No, not preferred: felt more comfortable with. A lonely man . . .

"Would you say my uncle was an imaginative man?" I asked, handing back the magazine. She looked puzzled. "I mean, was he easily persuaded into believing superstitious tales, for instance?"

She shook her head vigorously. "Quite the opposite, miss! Very sceptical, he was. Never took nothing for granted. Always weighing and measuring and labelling things. Liked everything just so, he did." She paused. "Only time I ever saw him upset was over something in that cabinet; something about measurements that weren't as they should be. Even had us trying to put some old bit of horn on our fingers to prove something or other, but it didn't work." She paused again. "Come to think of it, it was that time he asked us if we believed in magic. Strange, coming from him . . ."

"And what did you say?"

"Said of course we didn't; after all, that's what he wanted us to say. Not true, of course; anyone who lives on or near the land knows all about witches and such, though he never noticed the hag-stones as are hung near the back doors, nor that the nearest trees are rowans . . . Still, him being so generous and all, couldn't destroy his beliefs. Why, if I was to tell you that Mr. Early and I were courting for twenty years before he asked us here, and that he not only attended the wedding but gave us the gift of a full twenty pounds to set ourselves up with, well then you'll know that—"

There was another knock on the door and Mr. Early came in with some more wood. He nodded to me and spoke briefly to his wife. "Tatties is done," he said.

This signalled the end of Mrs. Early's reminiscences, and the appearance of supper: tomato soup, cutlets, roast parsnips and potatoes and a helping of local cheese and biscuits to follow. When she came up to clear away the dishes she brought me a hot toddy, and asked if her husband should bring up my bathing water in a couple of hours. I looked at my watch: eight-thirty.

"That'd be fine, thank you." A couple of hours should be long enough to read my uncle's transcript, but I must admit it was with a rapidly beating heart that I fetched the key to the cabinet from my reticule and fitted it in the lock.

It turned easily and the door swung open. There were two blue-velvet lined shelves. Picking up the lamp from the table, I peered inside. On the top shelf was a bundle of papers in a leather folder, a small curiously carved creature and a twist of horn. The lower shelf held a box of hard, dry vellum, some measuring instruments and a large, round object that glinted in the lamplight.

This must be the fabled "Dragonnes Eg" that had so perplexed my uncle. I touched it gently—as he had said, it wasn't cold like stone. I wanted to pick it up, test its weight, but decided that first I would read the transcript, so I took the folder back to the table, turned up the lamp, put another log on the fire and settled down to read.

As my uncle had said, it was an intriguing story. As I sipped my toddy, redolent with cloves and cinnamon, I followed the adventures of a girl called Summer who left home when she was orphaned to find a husband, but it seemed she found everything but; it pictured her with a magic ring, which enabled her to understand the speech of animals, but it didn't stop her from ambush, ghosts, starvation and a flying pig. Much of the story was missing apparently, but my uncle had tried to make her journey clear through mediaeval France, then a series of petty kingdoms. The first part ended with reference to a "dragon lover."

There was more in the second part of the narrative. Apparently the girl decided to pursue her missing dragon lover, accompanied by her dog, also mentioned in the earlier narrative. She travelled many miles towards a fabled Blue Mountain, where she hoped to find her lover. On the way (this bit wasn't quite clear) she produced a small dragon's egg. She found her lover, but the egg was stolen at the last moment by Ricardus, one of her companions, only to be returned on his death to a merchant in Venice who had inherited Summer's memoirs. What happened to her afterwards wasn't clear either.

I sat back in my chair.

Of course the whole thing was ridiculous! Dragon lovers, flying pigs, talking dogs . . . And yet while I was reading it I had almost been persuaded that it was true. I shivered, and noticed the fire was nearly out. I could hear Mr. Early clumping upstairs with the first of my hot water. Hastily I returned the transcript to the cabinet and locked it. Time enough to examine the other objects tomorrow, when daylight would show everything in its true light, I hoped. In the meantime I looked forward to a good night's sleep . . .

Which I didn't get.

All night long I tossed and turned, dreaming of dragons: tiny ones scurrying about the carpet, medium ones stalking the corridors of the Hall and large ones landing on the roof—

And all of them crying with one voice: "Bring us back our egg!"

7

More Revelations and
a Visitor

I had asked Mrs. Early to call me at eight-thirty, and at a quarter to nine I was seated in the kitchen, gritty-eyed and pale of face, tackling kippers and toast. It was a big pot of Assam tea which finally pulled me round, that and a brisk walk as far as the orchard, where I finished off with a Cox's Orange Pippin.

Back to the study, where a fire was already blazing. Once again I opened the cabinet; first I looked in the box where what remained of the original manuscripts were housed, taking care not to handle the pages too harshly—even as I looked they seemed that they were crumbling away before my eyes. It was a miracle they had lasted this long, anyway. If my uncle were right, some six or seven hundred years!

I put my uncle's letter and his transcript on the table and looked at them again, paying attention now to his footnotes, where he had identified various towns and places, and glancing at the maps he had drawn to interpret, as far as he could, the route the girl Summer had taken.

It looked an awful muddle, with a lot of guesswork thrown in. . . .

Now for the egg—or whatever it was. I had forgotten to pack my shawl, but I went and fetched my cloak, so it wouldn't roll around the table. I made it a kind of nest, then went to take it out of the cabinet. It was far heavier than I had imagined. I had never seen a round egg before, though I understood the ostrich and most reptiles preferred this shape, but as far as I knew those were all white in colour, whereas this one was definitely a greyish colour with a metallic sheen and little sparkly bits that caught the light.

Back to the cabinet to get the measuring calipers and the scales, with the measurements my uncle had already made, some dozen in all. Luckily the basin for the scales was round, so the egg wouldn't tip. I looked at the last figures my uncle had quoted for weight and width and decided to work from those. Not that I expected any increase in either, but at least it would set my mind at rest. Dragon's egg, indeed! First the weighing . . .

Some ten minutes later I sat back in my chair, my hands trembling. Somehow, in the six months since my uncle had last recorded his findings the what-ever-it-was had gained a full seven ounces in weight and an inch in width!

What was this—this *thing* that sat on the table in front of me? I found I was pacing around the room, my arms wrapped tightly around my chest. How could something like that grow larger by the month? Nay, the day, the hour, the minute? My heart was pounding, my mind racing. Perhaps the scales and the calipers were wrongly set, perhaps my uncle's figures were fictional, perhaps I was hallucinating, perhaps . . .

But I ran out of perhapses, which were getting more ridiculous by the moment, and calmed down a little, just enough to decide to examine the other objects in the cabinet. Forget about the Thing for a while.

First I lifted out the yellowing ivory figurine and examined it closely. It was obviously meant to represent some sort of mythical being, for it contained elements of more than one creature. A horse or deer, buffalo, fish? For sure it had never walked the earth in that guise! But then, hundreds of years ago, who could have imagined an elephant, giraffe or kangaroo? But no, this was definitely from the imagination.

Next I went back to the cabinet for the scrap of material that was supposed to be from the horn of a unicorn, another mythical beast. An insignificant scrap it was too, almost transparent in its triple curl. I put it down next to the Thing and the little figure. Now I had all the pieces of my uncle's puzzle together with the story they were supposed to come from, but what to make of it all?

I touched the "Eg" again and noted its warmth, I turned the figure this way and that; I picked up the ring once more—

There was a sudden knock on the door, I started, and the ring I was holding in my left hand slipped out of my fingers and dropped over the middle finger of my right. Mrs. Early came in, looking flustered and wiping floury hands on her apron.

"You've a visitor, miss! It's that young gentleman"—she said the word as if it were a bad taste in her mouth—"from London as is staying at the Lamb and Flag in the village. The one from your uncle's solicitors . . . D'you mind if I bring him up? There's no fire lighted downstairs, 'cept in the kitchen."

I was about to say that would be fine, when said young gentleman appeared in the doorway behind her, followed by an angry-looking Mr. Early.

"Wouldn't wait," he said tersely.

"It's all right, Mr. Early," I said. "Come in, Mr. . . . ?"

"Cumberbatch, Claude Cumberbatch. Junior clerk in the offices of Goldstone, Crutch and Swallow of Lincoln's Inn." He presented me with a card. "And you must be Miss Sophronisbe Lee." Without a by-your-leave he dropped into the chair opposite mine and gazed around the room. "Servant's quarters?"

"Not exactly, Mr. Cumberbatch." I tried to control my temper: he was probably younger than I was. "I find it most congenial . . ." His expression indicated that it wasn't the sort of place he expected to be received in. "And now that you have finally found me . . ." I paused to let that sink in; after all I had arrived two days ago and had not had so much as a message. ". . . may I offer you some refreshment? A cup of tea, perhaps?"

"Oh, I think something more lively than that, miss! Tea is for old biddies. Let's see, does this establishment boast a bottle or two of sweet sherry?"

I shook my head, just in time to see Mrs. Early nodding hers. I glanced at my watch. "I feel that eleven in the morning is a trifle early for spirituous liquors—"

"Oh, maybe for school-mistresses, but for us men of the world . . ."

I glanced at Mrs. Early: perhaps she had something in mind. From her smug expression I realised she had.

"Perhaps the young gentleman would like to give me his opinion on some rather strong turnip and ginger wine we have been saving for special guests? With some salted biscuits, of course . . ." It must be poisonous! "And you Miss Lee? China, or Russian with lemon?"

"China if you don't mind. And a couple of your sweet cakes, please."

While she was gone Mr. Cumberbatch—what a mouthful, I thought—got up and wandered round the room, peering through the window, poking the fire, gazing into the cabinet, setting the rocking chair tipping back and forth, fingering the velvet of the curtains. He then sat down again and poked the Eg with his finger, setting it into a dangerous wobble.

"Be careful!" I said sharply. "I don't want it to roll off!"

"No problem, miss!" He reached out his hand for the ivory figurine, but I was there before him. Somehow I didn't wish him to touch it; I was glad I had the twist of horn on my finger temporarily—he would probably have snapped it in half.

I studied him as he sat in his chair, cracking his bony knuckles. He was probably in his late teens or early twenties, thin almost to the point of emaciation, with a pasty complexion and straight fair hair, rather greasy, worn long down to his collar. He had pale blue eyes, a large Roman nose, a lot of teeth and a rather weak chin. In fact his facial structure was that of someone you might see in one of the *Punch* cartoons as representing the last scion of a degenerate aristocracy. His voice would have betrayed him, however: it held decided echoes of the East End of London.

He was dressed in the latest fashion of high collar, tight jacket with checked waistcoat, baggy trousers and pointed shoes and even wore a pair of the hideous yellow gloves that were all the rage, but his linen wasn't the freshest and from where I sat I could smell the scent of the tavern: greasy food, stale ale, whisky and tobacco. Indeed right at that moment he extracted a leather pouch from his pocket, pulled out a cheroot and lit it with a vesta, which he threw at, and missed, the fireplace. I rose immediately and opened the window then crossed to his side, took the cheroot from his fingers, and tossed it on the fire.

"You didn't say you didn't want me to smoke! Cost me four pence—"

"And you didn't ask!"

Luckily for us both Mrs. Early knocked with a tray of tea and little sponge cakes for me, and a jug and large wineglass plus a plate of salted biscuits for our guest. "Let me know if you want anything else, miss . . ."

What she really meant was that it was unorthodox for me to receive a gentleman in my rooms, but that she would be handy (probably just outside the door), ready to rush in and defend my honour . . . I hadn't the slightest doubt that that would be unnecessary.

Claude Cumberbatch filled his glass to the brim and took a long draught. There was a peculiar expression on his face when he put the glass down, and he took a hasty mouthful of biscuits.

I was letting my tea brew. "To your liking, Mr. Cumberbatch?"

"Er . . . Very unusual. I've never tasted anything quite like it . . . Home-made, I venture to guess?"

"Certainly. Not for the faint-hearted, I agree, but excellent for warding off the chills of inclement weather. It is, of course, a man's drink. Another glass? Do help yourself." I poured out a cup of tea and sipped it.

"Was there some especial reason you wished to see me, or is this just a social call?"

"Huh? Oh, yes." He fumbled in his pocket. "Got—got a 'munication from the firm s'morning." He was already slurring his words, to my delight. That wine must be strong! He slurped another draught. "Want to know when—when you're ready to go back—back to Lunnon . . ."

"Who said I wished to return to London?"

"Well, you must: no—no-one in their ses-, sesnes, would want to live in the w-wilds . . ."

"I do have a choice, Mr. Cumberbatch."

He finally produced the letter, all crumpled, and waved it at me with a shaking hand. "It says—Mr. Swallow says—as the most 'venient train would be twelve-fifteen on Friday, or ten-thirty Sat'day. Take a trap from the inn . . ."

"Sure you wouldn't prefer the carrier?" I couldn't keep the sarcasm from my voice, but he didn't notice.

"Oh, no, far too s-slow. Never get there . . ."

"Does Mr. Swallow say anything else?" From where I sat the letter looked at least two pages long.

"No, no, no . . . Just some 'structions for me. Private . . ."

He filled his glass from the jug, draining it down to the last drop. "Goo' stuff this . . ."

"I'm sure it is," I agreed, "Now, as to the letter of Mr. Swallow's—"

But he wasn't listening; in fact he wasn't hearing anything at all. His head was down on the table, his hands hanging loose to the floor and he was snoring heartily. I rose to fetch Mr. Early to dispose of him, but decided that Mr. Swallow's letter came first. As I scanned the first few lines it occurred to me with a certain surprise that even a few days ago I wouldn't have dreamed of reading someone else's correspondence. But things had changed dramatically, and this concerned me and my future life, so blow the conventions!

The letter read as follows: *Mr. Cumberbatch, as our representative I ask that you visit Miss Lee, enquire as to her health and well-being, and assure her that if there is anything we can do to facilitate her en-*

quiries, to let us know. I do not expect her to be precipitate in her decision, as I judge her to be careful in her considerations. Please inform her that her employer, Miss Moffat, is happy for her to take as much leave as she wishes. If for any reason, she wishes to visit London before she has made up her mind, please inform her of the times of the trains, buy her a ticket, and escort her to the station. Please assure her of our best attention at all times." It was signed in an indecipherable squiggle.

So much for being expected to accept my uncle's offer of cash and return to London the day after tomorrow! Just because Claude Cumberbatch couldn't stand the countryside, I was supposed to fall in with his plans and return him to London!

I stuffed the letter back in his pocket and went downstairs to find Mr. and Mrs. Early, suggesting they dump him just outside the gates to the Hall, but Mr. Early harnessed the pony to the trap, saying he would deposit him with the landlord of the Lamb and Flag.

"Punishment enough with the head he'll have on him," he said, in a rare burst of confidence and volubility. "Yon's strong stuff."

Mrs. Early arranged that, not to waste the journey, he could bring back various items she was short of: sugar, flour and oil. "And you'll be needing a new yard-broom and a bag of nails," she reminded him.

When they had gone she suggested that I take a closer look at the rooms in our part of the house. "There's some nice bits and pieces, and they'll all be yours if you decide to take on your uncle's dare."

"Dare?"

"Well, it's like that, isn't it? He did talk to me a bit, you know. About that Egg-thing. Wanted it to go back to where he thought it belonged. I expect it worried him because it didn't fit in with all his theories; men like him always like things neat and tidy." She paused. "You don't have to say, miss, but I reckon as how he's given you a choice: take what money's left and the Hall's sold, or try and take the thing back to Chiney, or wherever, and get the Hall when you gets back."

I didn't deny it. "Put like that it isn't much of a choice, is it?" I said with a smile.

"I agree, but not the way you think. I reckon it depends on the person. Were I your age now, knowing what I know, I wouldn't hesitate. But thirty years ago I would have chosen different. Then I was just an under-housemaid, glad for a roof over my head, reasonable food, a small wage and a day off a month. If then someone had suggested I give it all up and travel abroad—me, who hadn't been farther than twenty miles from here in my life—and get my own cottage if and when I returned, I'd have turned it down flat. I'd have taken the money."

She looked at me shrewdly. "Circumstances is different, but the situations much the same, I'd say. As I said, depends on the person concerned . . . Now, shall we take a look at the rest of this place properly?"

The remainder of the floor I was on consisted of bedrooms, adequately if sparsely furnished with beds, wardrobes, chests of drawers and dressing tables, with bright rugs on the polished floors; a large window at the end of the corridor gave a good light.

Downstairs it was different. The fanlight above the front door threw bars of sunshine across the black-and-white tiled floor and a couple of small sidetables were bright with vases of autumn leaves. The first door on the left revealed a pleasant dining-room, mainly in blue, down to the seascape over the sideboard and the Passion-Flower patterned crockery and china candlesticks. "Your uncle said all the furniture in here were by a man called Chippendale," ventured Mrs. Early. "He preferred it to the modern stuff." So did I.

The next room on the left was the morning-room. Here the emphasis was on the colour green with a couple of touches of dark blue—I noted the Etruscan vases on the mantel. The room was still full of the morning sunshine, with its two tall windows facing southeast; two small sofas, half-a-dozen chairs, a gaming-table, two pretty landscapes and plenty of room for a writing-desk like my mother's.

Across the corridor was the withdrawing-room, this in rose and green. Longer than the other two rooms, it had a fireplace at either end. One half was obviously meant for cosy relaxation by the fire, with sofas and occasional tables, and the other for perhaps cards or even dancing, for there was a piano and two card tables with chairs. On the walls were a dozen gold-framed prints of those deliciously scented French roses, and over both the fireplaces, in rose-veined marble, were large, ornamental Italian gilt-framed mirrors, which made the room seem even larger than it was.

The last room was smaller than the others, but was fully shelved, except that on one wall hung a huge oilcloth map of the world, pierced by a multitude of coloured mapping pins.

"This is where your uncle kept his books and manuscripts," said Mrs. Early. "That map on the wall showed all the places he'd been. In his last illness he had a pallet bed brought in here, because he found the stairs difficult. Liked to lie and look at the map, he did." And the map should be kept right there, I thought, a fitting memorial. But it would be nice to fill the bookshelves once again, and my father's wing-chair would do well beside the fire . . .

There was no carpeting in here, apart from a Persian rug by the fireplace, and the polished wood flooring was echoed in colour by the table, leatherseated chairs, curtains and copper candlesticks.

"Did he die in here?" I asked, noting that the pallet had been removed.

"Oh, no. He died outside, up on Bracken Hill. He would have wanted it that way. Mr. Early found him up there, one day when he missed luncheon. All peaceful he looked, like he'd fallen asleep on a pleasant dream," and her eyes filled with tears, which she mopped with her apron.

I was most impressed with the arrangements at the Temple: as I had thought before, it would be ideal for a small family—but I must stop mentally furnishing it with my own bits and pieces, I told myself, because I most certainly would not be staying!

As soon as Mr. Early returned we had luncheon—toad-in-the-hole, minted peas and gravy, with apple crumble and custard to follow—and as it was a sunny afternoon I took another walk around the grounds, kicking up the piles of leaves like a child in a park, the scent of a bonfire Mr. Early was tending tickling my nostrils with its evocative scent.

After tea I did some necessary darning, only noticing as I finished that I was still wearing the ring. I tried to pull it off, but it wouldn't budge. I even used soap, but it stayed just where it was, on the middle finger of my right hand. Actually I didn't mind it being there at all; it felt warm and comfortable. It would have been nice if it had been gold, or contained a precious stone, but I had never had a ring before and was pleased to see that if I looked closely there were little sparkles of colour in it, rather like an opal.

I had supper with Mr. and Mrs. Early in the kitchen, and went upstairs again determined to make a "Pros" and "Cons" list so that I would be absolutely certain I had made the right decision to take the money my uncle had offered, rather than attempting that ridiculous expedition, but I got no further than the headings on a sheet of paper before I found myself yawning prodigiously.

Country air was very enervating, I decided, as I put the Eg, figurine and transcript in the cabinet, locked it but left the key there. I asked for hot water and a half-hour later was tucked up in bed with one of Mrs. Early's hot toddys. I read the first chapter of *Westward Ho!* but couldn't keep my eyes open any longer. Blowing out the candles I laid my head on the pillow and slept dreamlessly.

Called at eight-thirty, refreshed and hungry, I ate my breakfast hurriedly then went upstairs, determined to concentrate on my listings. I got out the Eg and placed it on the cloak once more, then reached inside the cabinet for the ivory figurine—

It wasn't there!

8

Pros and Cons

I couldn't believe it! It couldn't just disappear like that! Frantically I searched the cabinet again: the manuscript in its box, the transcript, the egg—they were all there, and the ring was on my finger. Could I have left it on the mantelpiece, the shelves, the table or one of the chairs? I knew I hadn't, yet I searched the whole room methodically and even went into my bedroom in case I had left it in there.

Mrs. Early had lived up to her name and the study had been swept and dusted, yesterday's ashes removed, a bright fire was burning and the wood-basket had been replenished. The cabinet had been locked, but I had left the key there. Was it possible the housekeeper had removed the figurine for cleaning? It seemed extremely unlikely, but I must ask—

Could there have been a stranger in the house? I remembered young Cumberbatch's visit: could he have . . . ? But no, I distinctly remembered refusing to let him touch it. And I was still convinced that I had put it away last night, safe and sound.

I crossed to the door, but as I opened it I heard a faint rustling noise behind me. I stopped, listened. There it came again. I looked back across the room—no, it must have been the fire crackling, a log falling . . . I heard it again, and for one wild moment thought I saw a corner of the curtains twitch, as though a mouse had run behind it. Or a rat . . . It twitched again—that did it! I didn't mind mice, but rats (and cockroaches) were right off my list of tolerances.

I raced downstairs and flung open the kitchen door.

"Mrs. Early! Mrs. Early . . ." She was kneading dough on the marble slab. "Do we have rats in the house? And have you seen that little ivory figurine? It's gone missing. I just thought . . . you might . . ." I sat down heavily at the kitchen table, my heart pounding. "And have there been any strangers in the house? I mean, in this part of the Hall? Or could they have got in from another part?" I was trembling.

She smacked her hands together to rid them of the flour, rinsed them in a bowl of water on the side, then wiped them on a cloth. "Now, Miss Lee dear, just start again, tell me what's the matter . . ."

So I tried to be coherent and rational. I explained how I had found the figurine was missing, and as I had left the key in the lock overnight, wondered if she or her husband had removed it for cleaning? She shook her head. I asked, had anyone else been in this part of the house? Again she shook her head. I explained that I thought I had seen the curtains move, but everything I said made the whole thing sound sillier and sillier. I sounded like a hysterical female of the worst kind.

But she didn't laugh at me. Instead she opened a cupboard and put a glass of sweet sherry in my hand.

"Now, sip this down, Miss Lee, and calm yourself. . . . We neither of us ever touched nothing of your uncle's, unless he asked us particular. That answers your first question. As to others in the Hall, the only strangers, apart from that lawyer fellow yesterday, have been those packing up and removing the artifacts, and then we always keep the door from the Hall through to here locked, as it is today, as is the front door. Back doors bolted at night, otherwise there's always one of us in the kitchen. That's number two. As for rats or mice or anything else like that, I pride myself there's nothing in this part of the house like that."

I sipped the sherry, already feeling better. "Sorry, Mrs. Early, but it was a bit of a shock to find it missing."

"Not to worry. Howsomever, we'll take a besom up there and if there's anything or anyone as shouldn't be, they'll get short shrift. As for the ivory, it's probably fallen down behind something . . ."

Once upstairs she attacked the curtains, but there was nothing there. She turned to the cabinet. "Now show me exactly where you put it."

I pointed to the top shelf, but I saw it even before she did. Not on the top shelf but the bottom, next to the manuscript. And I knew, I *knew* I had searched that shelf!

"Why, there it is!" She picked it up and handed it to me. Even as I took it in my hand I knew it had changed. It was surely nearly twice as large as before. "You must have misplaced it." She smiled at me.

"Well, all's well that ends well, that's what I say! Luncheon at the usual time?"

I sat at the table in the study. On the table was the Eg, the ring was on my finger, the ivory in my hands, and I was looking at each in turn.

Here was a mediaeval round-shaped object, warm to the touch, that kept on growing; a ring that wouldn't come off, reputedly part of a mythical Unicorn's headgear, and an ivory figurine that disappeared and then reappeared, larger than before. And all this was somehow tied in with my uncle's wish that I return this egg to wherever it was supposed to belong. Against all this was the attractive alternative of taking whatever money was left and abandoning all these strange objects to their fate.

All except the ring: it still wouldn't budge. . . . And yet I liked the feeling if it on my finger. I would have preferred to find out what the egg contained, although I didn't want a baby dragon deposited in my lap, and the ivory looked friendly. . . .

I had never been abroad and there would probably never be another chance, unless I settled down and took a post as a governess who took children to a place like Brittany for the summer, or perhaps worked for a family who wanted a chaperone for their daughter at a German spa.

Stop daydreaming, I told myself severely: you're not likely to do better than the Charity School, although with the extra money you could live far more comfortably.

Right. Pros and Cons. I drew out a sheet of paper, took ink and a pen. I made two headings: Plan A, take the money; Plan B, take the Eg back. Then I subdivided each into two sections, for and against.

I started with Plan A. Immediate money, which would either keep me a lady of leisure for a few years, or supplement any income I received for longer. Either way, freedom from penury for a while. So much for the pros. I turned to the second column and tried to be fair. How long would the money last? Would it be so little, after all, that I would have to go on working, whether I wished to or no? What if I became ill or crippled? Then came a line which seemed to write itself: Did I really want the rest of my life to be so dull, predictable, plain *boring?* I looked down at what I had written: was my life dull and boring? It certainly wasn't now.

I thought back on my life at the Charity School. Life had been ruled by the seasons, although the same lessons came round time and time again. Only the children had been different, but not much. Different faces, different names, but the same poverty, apathy and hunger, the latter not for knowledge, only Ellen's soup.

I did love London, however. Apart from the museums, galleries, parks, libraries, concerts, churches and buildings, there was the teeming life and the magical way everything changed with the seasons. Spring, with its hope; crocuses springing through the grass in the parks, the glorious scent of violets and narcissi in the baskets of the flower-sellers, the first house-martins swooping over the rooftops and the urgent chirp of nesting sparrows—in such a season it was torture to be shut up in school all day. Then came summer with roses falling over the railings of the houses and the welcome warmth; but summer could also be over-hot, dusty and sticky, with the smell of sewage and rotting food perco-lating even to the schoolroom—in such a season it was torture to be shut up with the smells all day. Autumn was crisp and colourful with falling leaves, the scent of bonfires and blowy skies. On those days I longed to escape the confines of the school: torture to be shut in all day. Winter could be cold, foggy, with frost and snow, but still there was the comfort of a warm fire, the taste of roast chestnuts from the corner vendor and the lights and celebrations of Christmas. In such a season it was torture to be shut in all day. . . .

I couldn't remember thinking like this before. I don't believe I had ever analysed my feelings in this fashion—perhaps deliberately. Maybe I had been afraid of admitting to myself what I really felt like, because I couldn't change my situation, so would have to accept it without whin-ing to myself that I wanted something different. Of course my work was worthwhile, and I knew I did it to the best of my ability, but I now knew it wasn't the only thing in the world.

Had I always been so fond of my freedom? I had loathed the re-strictions of my boarding-school, though I had submitted in order to please my parents. At home I had been happy enough, although I was always escaping to the woods and fields, or into other worlds with my books. Our village, Ditchling in Sussex, was pretty and friendly enough, but sometimes I had stood at the crossroads and watched the Brighton express coach go thundering past, or its counterpart stop at the inn to let its caped and crinolined passengers alight for refreshments before the continuation of their journey to London, I had often wished I could just jump aboard and leave everything behind, to glimpse what lay over the hill. . . .

All this had nothing whatsoever to do with the lists I was trying to draw up, I told myself. A little boredom and frustration are common in every life. Security, and perhaps to be needed, that was what mattered. I looked at my watch: time for luncheon.

Afterwards I decided to walk off a little of the pork, stuffing and applesauce by strolling the couple of miles or so to the village. The first building I came across was the Church of the Good Shepherd, where I ventured in to pray for guidance and leave an offering in the box near the door. The church was obviously old, and owed much to the trade in wool, judging from the carvings in wood and stone. There were some pretty stained-glass windows, all reflecting Christ's life as the Good Shepherd.

The village itself held little to speak of: the Lamb and Flag, a butcher's, chemist, grocer, and green grocer, ironmonger's, general store and forge. I bought some black darning wool for my stockings at the store, but was careful to scurry past the inn with my bonnet pulled forward, as I had no wish to encounter Mr. Cumberbatch.

I dawdled on my way back to the Hall, collecting brightly coloured sprays of berries to put in the study, so the sky was already darkening as I reached the driveway, but I noticed that Mr. or Mrs. Early had hung a lantern by the front door of the Temple to light my way: it was almost like coming home.

I drank a late cup of tea in the kitchen, put my berries in a glass vase, went upstairs and placed them on the mantel, then settled down with my list of pros and cons. I had put a sheet of paper with Plan A on it aside as completed, but as I glanced at it I noted that I must have added something I didn't remember to the "cons" side. "How can I find true fulfillment if I stay at home?" I must have written it, because it was in my handwriting—but it wasn't my style.

I decided not to worry any further about it, but to concentrate on the pros and cons of Plan B, the expedition and the chance of inheriting Hightop Hall. I picked up my pen, wiped it with the pen-wiper, dipped it in the ink-pot and hesitated, then under "pros" I wrote: "Foreign Travel." After another two minutes: "I like the place." Another minute: "It was what my uncle really wanted," and lastly: "It would make a pleasant school or orphanage."

Unfortunately the "cons" column was far easier to complete. Never been abroad before, didn't know where to start or whether the money would last out, women just didn't go on expeditions, I would have to suffer the proximity of two people I didn't know, I only had a year in which to do it . . . Besides which there weren't any such things as dragons or unicorns, so what was the point? I finished with what I should probably have started with: even if I succeeded, I wouldn't have enough money to keep up the Hall. It would have to be sold; a pity, but there it was.

I sighed and laid down my pen. There, it was easy enough to make a decision if one was logical and systematic about it. Better safe than sorry.

It was now Thursday evening—I had been here three full days!—and I decided I would write a letter to the solicitors later tonight and get Mr. Early to deliver it to Mr. Cumberbatch tomorrow. If a reply was received in time, I could travel back to London on Saturday, otherwise it would have to wait until Monday. I hoped so: I rather fancied a few more days being cosseted in what was, to me, the lap of luxury.

I wondered what would happen to the Eg? I had already decided to take the ivory with me—it would look nice on my mother's writing-desk, and the ring seemed to be a fixture. I would throw away the original manuscript, but keep the transcript and read it again one day, for fun. The Eg? Perhaps I could take it down to the beach at Brighton, where my parents had taken me as a child, and roll it down the pebbles into the sea. Or I supposed I could give it away—but who would want something that looked like a cannon-ball, was warm to the touch, and kept on growing?

I decided I would have supper in the kitchen with the Earlys, so I could quiz them about their memories of my mother, but I wouldn't tell them of my decision to take the money until tomorrow or the next day.

They both remembered my mother as a harum-scarum, pretty girl with a mind of her own, easily bored and with no mind to her lessons. Apparently my maternal grandfather was much like my uncle, a recluse, and it was my maternal grandmother who ruled the roost. She was fond of entertaining, was highhanded with the servants, a stickler for routine and a strict disciplinarian with her children, which didn't suit my mother.

"First chance she got, she was off," said Mrs. Early.

"You mean—when she met my father?"

Mrs. Early nodded. "He came to the house two, three times to do a routine check on the clocks. There must have been—oh, twenty or more in those days. The usual clock-minder fell ill, and your father happened by chance in town at just the right time. Nice young man. Only saw him twice, quiet and respectful. But your mother fell for him head over heels, she did. He stopped at an inn nearby, and turns out later she let herself out of the house several times and met Mr. Lee outside.

"Your grandmother was fit to turn purple when she found out and shut your mum up in her bedroom, and kept the key under her pillow. This went on for three weeks, and all the staff were real sorry for the poor lass. Your father was dismissed on the spot and she tried to persuade your grandad to put a whip across his shoulders. Luckily for your father your grandad believed it was six of one and a half-dozen of the other. Perhaps he knew his daughter better than most gave him credit for . . .

"And then one day your mother disappeared."

"Disappeared?" This was all news to me. My parents had never discussed their earlier life in front of me. They were absorbed in each other, so in love, even after all those years, that even I felt sometimes excluded.

"Yes, disappeared as though she had never been! Your gran paid her a visit before breakfast, to give her her usual lecture, unlocked with the only key, and found her daughter gone! You can imagine the state she was in! Everyone was questioned, but had she not had the only key I think she would have dismissed us all. Then she got a note from your mother, signed in her married name of Lee. Not that we would have known about it but that she screwed up the letter and threw it away, and one of us, er—found it."

"What did she say? How did she escape?" I was on the edge of my seat.

"Seems the two young lovers were more resourceful than we thought. Your mother knew that your gran would blame everyone but herself, so she explained how it was done. She had torn a petticoat into strips and attached it to some ribbons, so she could lower it out of her window at night and exchange letters with her lover, your father. He told her what to do: save some candlewax and keep it soft, and when your gran came in to lecture, take a quick impression of the key, which she always left on a side table. She lowered the wax out of the window, your father had a key made and hey presto! They were away!"

I leant back in my chair. My parents had been so inventive, so daring. But it was difficult to think of them as a pair of star-crossed lovers.

Was I lacking in their initiative, I wondered as I went upstairs again? Surely not, I thought as I replenished the fire, just because I had chosen security over speculation. I must write to Mr. Swallow at once before I was tempted to change my mind.

I took a fresh sheet of paper and dated it. "For the attention of Mr. Swallow," I wrote. "Dear Sir," but then I noticed something out of the corner of my eye. The ivory figurine had gone missing again!

I looked under the table, back in the cabinet, on the shelves, behind the curtains but it wasn't there. I sat down again at the table. What in the world was happening? I glanced at the papers on which I had written my pros and cons and suddenly was on my feet, my hand to my mouth.

On the sheet of Plan B where there had been a long list of cons, there was now a mess of spilled ink. On the left, against the few pros, had been added a couple of lines in flowing capitals: "YOU WILL HAVE HELP, YOU KNOW."

9

Ky-Lin

I didn't scream. I didn't faint. I didn't panic.

I could have done all three quite easily; why didn't I? Perhaps because I was too frozen with shock, perhaps because a curious calm seemed to be descending around me, which appeared to emanate from the ring on my finger. I looked at it. It was more sparkly than ever and seemed to be throbbing a little, in time with my heartbeat. Then I looked again at the mess of spilled ink and those alien words in an alien hand and I suppose at that stage I wasn't really surprised to see that they were fading even as I watched, and now were gone.

Even three days ago I would have been utterly fazed by all this, but I felt my whole life was changing by the minute and that shortly I shouldn't be surprised if someone told me that the earth was flat and the moon was made of green cheese. Perhaps that is why I found myself talking to something that couldn't possibly be there.

"All right," I said. "Fun's over. Come out, come out, wherever you are . . ." It was like being back at the Charity School again, looking for some child who had hidden rather than return home.

There was a pause, a log settled on the fire; I went and put on another, and returned to the table.

"I'm going to close my eyes," I said, "And count to ten, slowly. When I open them again I expect everything to be back to normal. If so, I won't take any more action. But if it isn't, and there's a coach or train tomorrow, then you won't see me for dust."

"That would be a great pity," said a tiny but perfectly clear voice, (in my head, of course), "after all the trouble we took in getting you here in the first place."

I closed my eyes, and kept them firmly shut. Of course! I told myself, there's a perfectly simple explanation to all this. You had a good supper of chicken and stuffing, stayed on to hear Mrs. Early's reminiscences of your parents and fell asleep as soon as you started your letter to the solicitors. You are dreaming now, but in about half an hour Mr. Early will be bringing up your hot water and Mrs. Early your toddy. You can go on dreaming until then, so why not enjoy it? See what happens. Play along. People this room with elves and fairies. Let yourself go. Pretend this is a palace and you the princess. Fly out of the window—no, *not* a good idea, what if you were sleep-walking?

"I'm going to start counting now," I said. "One, two—"

"Buckle your shoe . . ."

My eyes snapped open, then I closed them as quickly. If it came to playing games, then I could play with the best.

"Three—"

"What will you see?"

"Four—"

"Knock on the door."

"Five, six—"

Silence. Then: "Do you really want things as they were?"

"Of course! Have you any better suggestion?"

"Yes," came the tiny voice. "Open your eyes and see things as they could be."

I considered, my eyes still shut. "No. Four, five—"

"Look alive! You've already said that . . . Just try. It can't hurt. Stop counting and open your eyes."

"I'll open my eyes when I've finished counting, and not before."

"And you want your dull, lonely, cramped, circumspect life to continue as it was?"

My eyes flew open. "It wasn't—isn't—dull and circumspect! Who are you to judge, anyway?" I shut my eyes again. "Five—"

"You've said that."

"Right!" I was getting distinctly annoyed. "Six, seven, eight—"

"It could be too late . . ."

"Rubbish! Nine—"

"Rise and shine!"

"Ten!" I opened my eyes, expecting to see everything as it had been before I started dreaming. Some dreams you can control, make them turn out the way you wish, and at first sight this looked like one of those, but, unfortunately, it held one or two surprises. The ring pulsed on my finger, the Eg glowed in the lamplight, and the pros and cons lists were as they had been originally. And there, in the middle of the table was the missing ivory figure—

Only it wasn't. It was neither ivory nor a carving. It was alive! There might have been a superficial resemblance to the original figurine but it *was* only superficial.

About the size of a clenched fist—my fists were clenched right at this moment—it had the body and hide of a deer, the hooves of a horse, antennae flicking back and forth on either side of its mouth, a mini-horn in the centre of its forehead and a long and sumptuous buffalo's tail, with a large plume at the tip, almost as big as itself. This was now waving back and forth like the tail of an annoyed cat.

But it was the colour that was the most arresting.

Legs and tail were dark grey, it had a bright yellow belly, the antennae were pink and the hide on its back bore various shades of blue, purple, brown and rose. The plume of its tail was the brightest of all: crimson, green and gold.

"Who on earth are you?"

The creature regarded me with bright, brown eyes. "I am a Ky-Lin."

The name sounded familiar, though for a moment I couldn't place it. "What's a Kiling?"

"Lin. Ky-Lin." He nodded. "I am in the transcript your uncle made. I am a mythical creature, if you prefer it that way. My Master is the Prince Siddhartha, whom men call Buddha, and I come from China. When my Master graced the earth with his presence he had a group of my brethren as his companions, his disciples, his bodyguard. We were trained by him to respect life in any form, right down to the ant in the grass, the grass itself. We were taught never to injure or kill anything living, however insignificant it might seem to be . . ." He broke off and coughed delicately. "Might I trouble you for a bite to eat? My throat is rather dry after all these years . . ."

What did you give a creature like this in your dreams? I glanced around wildly. "I'm afraid I only have—er, ink or water in that vase. Or a bit of—candle?"

The creature shook its head. "Not really sustaining . . . Now if you would lift me up onto the mantel—no, better still, if you would bring the vase down onto the table, then I can break my fast."

I went over to the mantel and fetched the vase containing the sprays of berries and watched, fascinated, as the creature chewed the pulp from the hips, haws and blackberries as if they were manna from heaven, though I noticed he spat out the seeds tidily onto the piece of paper I had intended writing to the solicitors on.

He saw my look. "I am leaving the seeds so that you may sow them in the garden tomorrow, to make other plants."

If he imagined I was going to—but he obviously did. Better humour him. "But of course. Would you kindly tell me what you are doing here, after all these years?" Thousands, if he really had anything to do with the Buddha.

The creature hesitated for a second. "There is always one bad apple in the barrel. My companions attained Nirvana, but I wasn't good enough. I was careless and broke some of the rules: truth was, I liked the world and wanted to stay in it. My Master gave me a chance to expiate my sins by helping a young girl called Summer to attain her Quest. After that I thought to have rest, but received a message that my task wasn't done. You could call it a piece of unfinished business, I suppose: Summer's egg must be returned to the dragons." He put his head on one side. "And you are the person to do it."

"Rubbish! I'm not the only person in the world! What you need is an experienced traveller, someone like my uncle was—"

"What we need is you!"

"Why *me*? And who's 'we'?"

" 'We' is me, the Egg and the Ring." He pushed the rejected seeds into a neat pile, fluffed out the plume on his tail and sat down on his haunches. "If you have a little patience, I'll tell you how we all fit in. Firstly, I accompanied young Summer to the place this is destined to go, so I know the way—"

"But that was *hundreds* of years ago!" I was glad to note that, although this was all a dream, I was answering logically.

"Years, your years, mean nothing to such as we. We are all some centuries old."

"But why does the Eg have to go back right now, after all this time?"

"Because, after lying dormant for many, many years, it has started to grow, and this means it will soon be ready to hatch. If you have read your uncle's transcript you will know that this egg is the product of a liaison between Summer and her dragon-lover, and that she and Jasper, for that was his name, took the egg to the Blue Mountain, where the remnants of the dragons live, to trade it for a promise that Jasper might retain his human shape during Summer's lifetime. As you also know, it all went disastrously wrong when the egg was stolen at the crucial moment. Summer lost her life, together with that of her lover, or so I believe, and the dragons lost their egg. If they know where it is, and that it is about to hatch, then they will come to find it, and that cannot be allowed to happen . . .

"Er . . . Could you possibly tip the vase a little? I find that talking after all this time is thirsty business . . . Thank you."

"You say you know the way, but there are maps . . ."

"I can grow larger, large enough to carry burdens on my back. I speak all the tongues known to man, and eat and drink very little. I also know the places to avoid, the dangers one might come across."

"In that case," I said frivolously, "you and I and the Eg could set off tomorrow, and you could carry us there and bring me back in a week or so!"

He shook his head. "It would take far longer than that . . ." Didn't he have a sense of humour? "Besides, you forget we have to take someone from the solicitor's to ensure fair play, and that young detective as well."

"And if they took one look at you," I said, "either large or small, they would swear off spirituous liquors forever and refuse to go anyway!"

"Not necessarily. I can change in a few seconds—or at least I will be able to after a little more practice; more than a few years in any one shape and one grows somewhat stiff."

"Have some more berries," I suggested.

"Not at the moment, thank you. I have had an elegant sufficiency."

"This size-changing—is that how you disappeared yesterday?"

"Of course. When I opened the cabinet—metal-bending is one of the things one learns early on—I found difficulty in the latter stages of the change. That is when I had to whisk behind the curtain and you found me resembling a rat. So, regress again and back to the cabinet."

"But I looked all over for you!"

"Down and around, yes, but not up. I was on the ceiling."

"Oh." There was no answer to that. I went back to the beginning again. "But why especially me? I know my uncle had this bee in his bonnet, but—"

"Because you are the Chosen One: the Ring-Bearer." He sounded as though that explained everything.

"This? This tatty bit of horn?" I held up my finger.

He looked scandalised. "That's not just a 'tatty bit of horn,' as you call it! That is a precious sliver from the horn of a fabulous Unicorn, who lived over a thousand years ago, and sacrificed his immortality for a love you couldn't hope to comprehend! He left behind the Ring to future generations to use for the good of the world. It has been passed down from generation to generation. Summer used it on her travels, and when she had no further use for it she left it in my safe-keeping. And the next wearer is you."

"But anyone could wear it—"

"Your uncle couldn't, neither could the housekeeper or her husband. The Ring chooses its own wearer. If you don't believe me, try and take it off."

"I can't. It seems stuck."

"Exactly!"

"What do you mean?"

The Ky-Lin sighed. "As I intimated, the Ring only fits those it has chosen. You could offer it to anyone in the world, of any race, colour or creed, large or small, male or female, fat or thin, young or old, and the Ring would still discriminate. I have no idea why it chooses whom it does, but it selects that person who is most fitted for the task to be undertaken. And it has special properties, you know."

"Such as?"

"It can warn you of danger. It can calm you down, make you think logically. It conserves your energy, keeps you young. Most and best of all, it allows you to communicate with the animal world. And if you weren't wearing it now, you wouldn't understand me."

I looked at it with more respect. I believed what he said—one did in dreams. Magic ring . . . "Does it do anything else? Can I have three wishes, for instance?"

He looked disgusted. "You're not being serious!"

"Oh, I am! This is the best dream I've had in *ages!*"

He bounced over the table towards me. "You're *not* dreaming! Listen to me. Everything points to you being the one to return the Eg. Your uncle bought us all at auction, in a lot I had taken care to be included in. Although he wasn't the one we looked for, he translated the manuscript and realised we should all be kept together. *He* couldn't solve the problem, but something told him you could."

"But he didn't even know me! How could he expect me to do what he could not?"

"I don't know. Perhaps because he knew and admired your mother's—his sister's—spirit of adventure. Perhaps because he knew your father must have had special qualities to keep her happy all those years. Perhaps because he liked what he heard when he had you investigated." He hesitated. "Perhaps just because you were family . . ."

Footsteps on the stairs, the clank of a bucket. Mr. Early bringing up my hot water. I gathered the papers on the table together, the sheet with the seeds on top, turned up the lamp, put away the pen and ink. In came Mrs. Early with my hot drink. She glanced at the table.

"Been busy, miss?"

I was awake again, and yawning. "I think I dropped off for a while," I said. I picked up the Eg and the ivory and put them back in the cabinet, locking them in and putting the key in my pocket.

The following morning I checked the study before I went down to breakfast. Mrs. Early had cleaned, dusted and laid the fire, but everything else was as I had left it. Even as I checked, I had allowed myself to acknowledge that I had almost been persuaded by that dream last evening to believe I had held a conversation with a small creature with a colourful tail called a Ky-Lin, and that I wore a magic ring that allowed me to talk to animals . . . How ridiculous! I looked for the seeds, but they had gone, of course.

I decided to try out the ring on the kitchen cat, a fat, lazy creature who spent most of its time by the fire. "Good morning, cat! How are you this morning? Caught any mice lately?"

The cat stared hard at me, as well it might, then stomped off, its tail twitching irritably. So much for magic rings, I thought triumphantly. So much for dreams . . .

"Anything special to do today, miss?"

I shook my head. "Nothing planned, Mrs. Early." I peered out of the window. "Looks like a nice day; I might go for a walk, to clear my mind."

"Good idea, miss. Nothing like fresh air, your uncle used to say. They are coming for the rest of the statues and papers today, so I've got two girls from the village to give everything a good scrub now the place will be empty. Would you mind cold cuts for luncheon?"

"That'd be fine . . . Tell you what: I could take out a picnic, like I used to do in London. Some sandwiches and lemonade, perhaps."

"No sooner said than done, miss! I'll have a basket ready for you."

I went upstairs to change into my serviceable boots, to hitch up my skirts some two inches higher and collect my cloak. No need for bonnet or gloves, as the sun was shining and there was little wind. I decided I would explore the pine wood and search for mushrooms in the pasture behind the Hall. I would take *Westward Ho!* with me and read of the further adventures of Amyas Merion. I would have a day in which I worried about nothing, put letters and decisions to one side. I would just be holidaying . . .

Picking up my book and giving it a hug in anticipation of the plea-sure it would bring, I crossed over to the study, just to make sure ev-erything was as it should be before I left for the day. Downstairs I could hear Mrs. Early giving instructions to the village girls, with much clank-ing of buckets; Mr. Early had gone out to the orchard earlier to prune the cherry trees, and no-one, apart from Mrs. Early's cleaning, had been upstairs, not even the cat, which made it all the more frustrating to find that someone—or some*thing*—had ripped all my papers to pieces; pros and cons, the start of the letter to the solicitors. Torn them all into bite-sized pieces and scattered them on the neatly laid fire, and that since breakfast!

Running back into my bedroom and snatching the key from my reticule, I went back into the study and opened the cabinet. Inside all was as it should be, but I was so angry that I picked out both the Eg and the ivory and dumped them on the table, shouting: "I've had enough of all this! You're mine to dispose of as I will, and that is exactly what I am going to do!"

And with that I picked them both up again and, wrapping them in my cloak, stormed down to the empty kitchen, snatched up the picnic basket and set off past the kitchen-garden and orchard, feet stamping so hard on the path that I saw Mr. Early suspend action with the pruning-shears and scratch his head in puzzlement.

I set off to climb towards the back of the wood, but before long I was hot and sticky, so I transferred the ivory and the Eg, which seemed to weigh a ton, into the corner of the picnic basket, taking care not to squash the sandwiches.

The wood was stifling. Inches of dead pine-needles hindered my feet, red squirrels dashed the branches overhead, chattering angrily at my intrusion, and the trees only offered intermittent shade from the bars of suddenly hot sunshine that struck down on my bare head, so that I felt sick with heat.

At last I broke through into the open, and I saw ahead of me to the right a bracken and gorse-covered hillock. It could have been part of the grounds of the Hall or not, but at that stage I didn't care. I climbed a stile, ripping my skirt as I did so, struggled a few yards up the hill and then sat down, exhausted. The head-high bracken, with its fusty-dusty smell and autumn russet dress almost met over my head and golden gorse was still a-buzz with bees . . .

I lay back and closed my eyes. "Kissing's out of fashion, when the gorse is out of bloom," I recited sleepily, relaxing at last, with only the hum of insects and the plaintive cry of a curlew to disturb my rest.

I don't know how long I slept, but when I looked at my watch it was a quarter to midday, and for a moment I felt disoriented. Then I remembered where I was and what I had to do. Struggling to my feet I hitched up my skirts into my belt, picked up the basket and started to climb the hill again, hampered by the strands of bracken. At last I reached an out-crop of rock near the top, which I thought would serve my purpose.

I undid the straps to the picnic basket and there was the Eg, glinting in the sunshine. I hesitated for only a moment, then picked it up, still marvelling at its weight and warmth, and then deliberately let it tumble from my hands down the hill, where it cut a momentary swathe through the bracken before the reddish stems closed behind its path. Something stabbed at my right hand, but I ignored the sting—a mosquito, perhaps, or more likely a midge, this high up.

"Goodbye and good riddance!" I called out after the vanished Eg. "Hatch your dragon out here if you feel like it! I'm not travelling half round the world just for you . . ." A flock of pigeons flew overhead, probably from some stubbled field, the clap-clap of their wings disturbing the air with a momentary chill.

I paused for a moment, then picked the ivory figurine from the basket. "And as for you . . . !" But words failed me. "Just disappear from my life, that's all!" and with all my strength I hurled it away, till it disappeared into the heart of a distant gorse-bush. There was another stab on my right hand. If I climbed right to the top of the hill the insects probably wouldn't bother me so much.

Once there I found I was looking down on the back of Hightop Hall. The stick-like figure in the kitchen-garden must be Mr. Early, and way down the drive I could see two horsedrawn pantechnichons apparently carrying away the last of my uncle's artifacts. A plume of smoke rose from the kitchen chimney, but that was the only other sign of life. I opened my book, but the sun hurt my eyes, and my stomach felt empty, although it was only twelve-fifteen.

I felt better for doing as I had, of course I did, so why did I feel so—so empty?

Of course it couldn't be guilt, could it? I had done nothing to feel guilty about, had I? Absentmindedly I opened and ate my sandwiches: home-boiled ham with mustard, egg and pot-grown cress, late, sweet tomatoes, an apple and a slice of plum cake. I finished with a drink of lemonade, but after it all I still felt empty, and everything seemed to have tasted the same. I must have been sickening for something.

I looked for mushrooms, but only in a desultory fashion, and found none. Afterwards I left the basket and my book at the top end of the orchard and walked down the drive, turned left and walked until nearly sundown. Once back I retrieved the basket and went towards the kitchen door. Two pigeons were cooing to one another on a corner of one of the outhouse roofs; they glanced at me as I passed.

"C-r-oo-l," said one.

"Th-r-oo them away," said the other. "S-a-a-a-w her . . ."

I dropped the basket onto the cobbles.

10

"Repent Ye . . ."

I heard the tinkle of broken glass as the basket hit the ground, but it scarcely registered. I stared up at the pigeons—ordinary grey ones with the sheen of green on their necks, dark bands across their wings—as they strutted above my head. They nodded to one another, fluffed up their feathers, nothing more.

I stooped to pick up the basket, then it came again.

"Croo-oo-ool," came the soft voice. "Too-oo-oo coo-oo-l for the Eg."

I was trembling violently. Now I was hearing voices! As if in answer the ring on my finger started to throb. I looked down at the ring, up at the pigeons, remembered a flight of them passing over when I threw away the Eg into the bracken. Could it . . . ? No, it couldn't. But the Ky-Lin had said . . .

There was no-one about, no humans anyway. "Right," I said out loud to the birds. "If you're so clever, just tell me exactly what I'm supposed to have done?"

"Yooo-oo-oo know," crooned the pigeons. "Yooo-oo-oo knoo-oo-w!"

It was true! Either that or I was mad or dreaming. I pinched myself: no dream. And I didn't think I was mad. Then all that fantasy the other night must have been true. That little creature that called itself a Ky-Lin must have been speaking the truth.

To say that I was devastated was an understatement. I was terrified, exhilarated, awed and humbled at one and the same time. Being a logical girl, or so I believed, I had accepted fairy tales as just that: pretty fiction. To suddenly find that there was another dimension demanded a tremendous leap of faith, a conversion into the suspension of disbelief.

I needed to give myself time to think; routine things first. I picked up the basket and took it into the kitchen, emptying it carefully on the table. The glass tumbler was broken, as was the plate. I wrapped these carefully in the sandwich paper and put them on the draining board. Luckily the stone lemonade bottle was intact. That, together with the knife used for paring my apple, I placed in the sink, and the apple peel on the fire, remembering too late that Mr. Early might have used it on his compost-heap.

So far, so good. I was calmer now. Perhaps I should put the kettle on the stove and make myself a cup of tea. Mrs. Early should be back soon, and—

The kitchen cat walked past, her tail in the air. "Murderesssss!" she hissed.

I sat down at the kitchen table and burst into tears.

After a lonely evening, trying to read and failing, and a restless and disturbed night, I awoke the following morning with stomach pains. Of course I knew what it was, the curse of all women, but this time the gripes were worse than usual, so much so that I declined breakfast, but once Mrs. Early had found out what was the matter she insisted I spend the rest of the day in bed, with hot stone bottles, a drop or two of laudanum and a light diet.

"Used to suffer the same way myself, miss, and in those days there was no excuse for not carrying on with your jobs. Swore that if I ever met someone the same, I'd treat them different."

No point in telling her that this didn't happen every time, that I believed in my heart that it was some kind of retribution for my doings of the day before. But of course she didn't know the Eg and Ky-Lin were somewhere out on the hillside, open to all the vagaries of the weather. Now I really knew what it felt like to feel guilty!

And it didn't help that the sermon the following morning appeared to point directly at me: "Repent ye, for the Kingdom of Heaven is at hand . . ."

We went to church in the trap, tying the pony to the rail outside. The church, probably Norman in origin, was comfortably full, but to my surprise the churchwarden led us to a private pew near the front, which had belonged to my uncle. I saw many of the congregation turn to each other and murmur as we took our places. I was wearing my best skirt and jacket in navy blue, and had trimmed my bonnet with black rosettes and ribbons in deference to the mourning for my uncle. Once the service started I was soothed by the familiarity of the words, and comforted by the sunlight striking through the stained-glass windows and casting patterns of soft reds, greens and blues on the aisles. These did much to soften the harshness of the half-hour sermon, which seemed to strike at the root of my guilt, and I found myself wriggling uneasily.

Once the service was over, as was the custom, those in the closed pews at the front left the church first. Most of the congregation was soberly and sensibly dressed, with the odd coloured ribbons or checked jacket, but the party I now saw for the first time might have been dressed for a garden party or a wedding. As they passed our pew there was no disguising their curiosity. They stared quite openly. A middle-aged couple, two somewhat older, two young men, three young ladies, followed by probably a ladies' maid and a governess, all looked at me as if I were an exhibit in a sideshow.

Only a week ago I would have blushed and lowered my gaze; today as my uncle's representative I returned their gaze steadily enough, inclining my head infinitesimally in acknowledgment of their interest. Mr. and Mrs. Early and I were a few paces behind their party as we moved towards the church porch, so I was in a perfect position to hear the following exchanges; there was no attempt to lower their voices.

Taller of two young men: "Quite a nice looking gel, wouldn't you say, Mater?"

Mother: "Passable, I suppose, if you like that somewhat sallow complexion. But remember, she hasn't two farthings to rub together. From what I heard, her uncle left her penniless."

Smaller young man: "Have to sell up, I suppose. There's a nice piece of rough shooting at the back."

Older man: "Reasonable stand of timber, too . . ."

Father: "We'll see, we'll see. Shouldn't think she'll quibble over a price."

One of the girls to the others: "My dears, did you see that *awful* bonnet? And she was wearing *boots* . . ."

By now I was crimson with both embarrassment and anger, conscious that everyone within earshot must have heard. How dared they!

But Mrs. Early was whispering in my ear. "Take no notice, miss. Both families made their money in trade, and can't keep staff above a week or so."

But unfortunately that was not the point. They had the money, so believed they could behave as they wished. One thing was for certain: if ever I was in a position to have any say in the disposal of Hightop Hall, then the very last people to be allowed to bid for it would be the people who had behaved so condescendingly.

I needed a diversion. "Will you show me where my uncle is buried?"

Mrs. Early led me down a side-path in the churchyard to a secluded spot shaded by an ancient yew tree. Here were no urns, vaults, stone angels, crosses with wreaths or elaborate railings; just a green mound, the turves beginning to knit together, and at their head a curiously shaped slab of stone, rather like a broken tooth. It was streaked and striated with green, and could have been malachite. On its surface were some deep indentations, which if looked at from a certain angle could have formed a cross. Inset in the stone was a small bronze plaque bearing my uncle's name and dates of birth and death, nothing more.

Mrs. Early considered it, her head on one side. "I'm getting quite used to it, but it looks—looks . . ."

"A bit pagan," I supplied with a wry smile.

"I'm sure that was the word I was looking for," she agreed. "Brought that stone back from his travels, he did, many years ago. Set it up against his bedroom wall and said: 'That's my headstone, Mrs. Early. I expect the vicar will object, but that's what I want. You can see it bears the symbol of the cross.' Morbid I thought it was, having it there, and I couldn't dust it without a shiver. Looks better in the open."

As it was still fine I elected to walk the couple of miles home— strange, "home" was now its name in my mind—and I picked sprays of hips and haws and a twist of Old Man's Beard to replace those depleted by Ky-Lin two nights ago, and put them in a silver-rimmed glass in the centre of the study table, before changing into my working-clothes for Sunday lunch.

"Rain later," said Mr. Early, coming in to wash his hands. "Wind's getting up. Cold snap coming—more berries'n usual."

I hoped the rain would hold off until I had done what I had to do.

I found I had a good appetite from my walk back, and tucked into a typical Sunday luncheon: Brown Windsor Soup, roast beef and horse-radish sauce, Yorkshire pudding, roast potatoes, gravy, boiled cabbage and carrots, with apple tart to follow.

As I climbed upstairs I could hear the wind getting up: I must hurry. Putting on my cloak and boots, I decided against a bonnet, "awful" or not—it would probably blow away in the wind. I should be gone at least a half-hour, so decided to check that the fire in the study was made up before I left.

But this was not the first thing I noticed. To my utter astonishment there, on the table, finishing his second rose-hip and fishing out the seeds and laying them out in a neat row with his delicate antennae, was Ky-Lin!

"Absolutely delicious!" he said enthusiastically. "How nice of you to think of me. Someone threw out the last lot of seeds, but we will save these to plant when we go out—"

I rushed forward and picked him up, hugging him fervently. "You came back!"

"Of course. I—"

"You knew I would come and look for you, didn't you?"

"I knew you were very upset—"

"I was all mixed up! I didn't realise that what you had said was the truth—about the ring and the Eg. But then I heard . . . How did you get back, anyway?"

"Pigeon Post. This morning . . . Er, do you think I might get down? I'm afraid I'm not used to being hugged."

I apologised and set him back on the table. "But how did you get up here?"

"The pigeons dropped me off—literally—in the stable-yard and the cat gave me a lift upstairs, carrying me as she would one of her kittens. A little hazardous . . ." A tiny forked tongue came out and flicked fastidiously over his hide.

"I was coming to find you before it started raining," I said. "You and the Eg." I explained how I had become convinced he had been telling me the truth about the ring. "I felt—sort of guilty. I shouldn't have lost my temper. So you needn't worry, I'll make sure you and the Eg find a safe haven, wherever and whenever."

He looked inordinately pleased. "I was sure you would decide correctly," he said. "I must thank you in advance."

I waved away his thanks. "Please don't do that: it may take some time to get you both settled."

He nodded. "Then shall we go and pick up the Eg before the weather worsens? I know exactly where it is—I watched over it in my larger guise last night."

I tucked him in my cloak till we were away from the hall, then he sat on my shoulder as I climbed the hill.

"Exactly how big can you grow?"

He considered. "About pony-size, maximum. Normally I travel round as small as I can, and in the most convenient material: ivory, stone, wood, amethyst—I have been all those."

I couldn't think of anything to say. If he were to be believed—but why not? Everything he had said so far was apparently true.

"Here we are," said Ky-Lin.

I lowered him to the ground and he darted off through the bracken. As I followed I noticed he avoided actually touching living growth, just jumping from pebble to bare earth to stone. I stooped down and picked up the round Eg and examined it as best I could.

"It hasn't come to any harm, has it?" I asked anxiously.

Ky-Lin waved his tail dismissively. "Take more than a roll down a hill and a night in the open to harm that. Whatever is in there is well insulated. Your uncle tried to break it and crack it with a hammer, but it wasn't hurt."

By the time we reached the orchard the rain had started to fall, and Mr. Early was so busy fetching in the last of the wood and Mrs. Early the washing, that neither of them noticed that I was carrying something in my cloak, so I had time to arrange everything nicely on the table in the study, including paper, pen and ink, before Mrs. Early came in with my tray of tea. Even Ky-Lin had reverted to his ivory shape, but as soon as she had gone I was witness to a remarkable transformation.

First his outline seemed to blur and soften, then expand. For a moment it trembled on the brink then suddenly his head, then his body, emerged from its covering like a chicken from its egg. Last of all were legs and tail; he was having trouble with his right fore-leg however, which initially seemed reluctant to grow as long as the others but finally, after an all-over shake, all the pieces came together.

"Getting better," he said. "Only twenty-five seconds."

"Would you like a sip of tea, after all that exertion?"

"China?"

"Lapsang Souchong."

"A sip would be nice."

I let it cool in the teaspoon before I offered it to him, then watched as the forked tongue, each side working independently, emptied the teaspoon without spilling a drop.

"What do you eat and drink at home?" I asked.

"A little rice every now and again, cheese, nuts, windfalls—that sort of thing. We Ky-Lins are not allowed to eat flesh or pluck anything that is actually growing."

"And can you fly?"

He shook his head. "We leave that to creatures like the dragons, among us so-called mythical creatures. They fly, we don't; they eat meat, we don't; they collect treasure on earth, we don't; they are aggressive and unforgiving, we are not. Different outlook. Different life-style."

He hesitated, then continued. "But I'm afraid I can't tell you much more about them than that. I have seen them flying in the distance, usually at night, although they normally keep away from human habitation. I think that nowadays they are afraid that with all the modern ways you humans have developed for killing, they may one day become targets themselves. While once they were fearsome enough to terrify whole towns and villages, their shape and brain-size hasn't developed from what you would call their 'prehistoric' days, whereas you humans have changed with the times." He added, "I've never seen one close to, nor do I wish to, and I believe their language is incomprehensible."

"Then why . . . ?" I hesitated.

"Did I become involved with the Eg? I thought I had explained. First, it is Summer's egg: unfinished business. Secondly, I volunteered. Unofficially, of course. Besides, it's an egg, not a dragon—yet." He sat down on his haunches. "And now that the explanations are done, hadn't we better get to work? You'll need paper, pen and ink."

"What for?"

"To plan our strategy, of course. Better to have it all written down. And then there's the letter to your solicitor—"

A step outside, a tap at the door, and Mrs. Early entered, carrying a small packet wrapped in oilskin.

"I'm sure I don't know what that young gentleman is about, sending young Jem from the inn out in this weather! Like a drowned rat he is, and told he's to wait for an answer!"

"What is it?"

"A letter from that Mr. Hamperhutch, the one from the solicitors!"

I opened the letter. *"Miss Leigh,"* it read. *"Today is Sunday, and tomorrow will begin the second week you have sojourned at Hightop Hall. May I remind you that your stay was only intended for you to confirm the acceptance of the moneys left by your uncle. My employers await your decision with some impatience, in order that they may arrange your return to London. If you will do me the honour of inscribing a few lines to the effect of your intent, I shall ensure that the letter leaves on the stage in the morning. Your humble servant, Claude Cumberbatch."* Hmm, a bit more polite than the last. But there was a postscript. *"PS: If you would be kind enough to give the boy, the bearer of this, a couple of pence, I should be obliged."*

"The cheek of the man!" I crumpled the note in my hand angrily, then thought for a moment. "Mrs. Early, the boy—would you see he dries out by the fire, please? And perhaps a glass of your raspberry cordial and a slice of cake . . . Any chance of the rain slackening off?"

"Mr. Early says perhaps a half-hour or so, though it'll be back before morning."

"Then I shall write an answer to this immediately!"

As soon as the door closed behind her I drew a sheet of paper towards me, grabbed a pen and opened the inkwell, to see out of the corner of my eye what had been an ivory figure a few minutes ago, turn once more into a living creature.

"Right, Ky-Lin! Just for that young man's impudence I shall stay until Saturday at least!"

He looked flabbergasted. "But we can't possibly be ready by then! It'll take at least a fortnight longer!"

I turned to him, puzzled. "To do what?"

"To get ready to take the Eg back to China, of course . . ."

11

Surprise! Surprise!

I paused, pen in hand, not quite sure I had heard correctly. A large blob of ink spoiled the first page.

"*What* did you say?"

"I said we would need more than a week to prepare for the journey."

"Which journey?" But even as I asked, I think I knew the answer. Another, smaller drop of ink fell on the paper. The earth and the moon . . .

"The one we were talking about earlier," Ky-Lin explained patiently. "You said you were prepared to do your utmost to get the Eg and I back where we belonged. Remember?"

I recalled saying something to that effect, but he had interpreted it quite differently from my meaning: I had meant him to understand that I would find somewhere nice for them to settle down in, *not* take them all the way back to China!

"But I didn't mean—"

"No, of course you didn't realise how much there was to be done. You will have to resign your post at the school—that letter can be written tonight, together with the one to the solicitors. They will have to arrange for your bits and pieces to come down here, and of course find a member of their staff to accompany us, to make sure we actually carry out our quest."

"But you don't understand—"

"Of course I do! Anyone in your position would be a little apprehensive about the journey. But we'll have a good look at the maps, and don't forget I speak most of the languages and can guide you over the last part easily."

"But I haven't said—"

"That you'll need new clothes? That's another thing we must arrange. At this time of the year, for the first part of the journey at least, you will need much warmer wear. And of course we don't know how soon that mysterious young detective your uncle used to find you will take to reach us."

"But—"

"No, of course I will travel incognito, at least until and unless the others will accept me. I can travel quite comfortably in one of your pockets. A nice, new travelling jacket should have plenty of those for a compass, chocolate and Ky-Lins!" And he wagged his tail at his own bit of alliterative nonsense. "Oh, and you must get a passport."

I laid down my pen very carefully and sat back in my chair. I had run out of buts or, more correctly, knew whatever I said, Ky-Lin would chirp in with some enthusiastic idea for the promulgation of the journey. *His* journey. Not mine.

I knew very well I was being manipulated; I also knew that I had very little chance, apart from fleeing into the night and seeking Mr. Cumberbatch's unwilling protection, of getting out of this. And even then the mythical creature would probably reassemble itself into a pony and come galloping after me, or grab the attention of a passing owl and get there before I did.

At the beginning of the afternoon I had been fully determined to go back to London, resume my post at the school until I could find something better, invest my uncle's money and live a more comfortable life. But there had been my sense of guilt, exacerbated by that uncompromising sermon; I had been really happy to see Ky-Lin again, to the extent of an uncharacteristic hug; I had been upset by the odious conversation I had overheard at church about the proposed disposal of the Hall, which I now realised I was very fond of, and the final straw had been Claude Cumberbatch's letter.

Crumpling up the spoiled sheet of paper I got up and tossed it onto the fire, then crossed to the window, pulled up the sash and leaned out to smell the resin from the rain-soaked pines. Crossing back to the table I pulled out a fresh sheet of paper, wiped the nib with the pen-wiper and dipped it into the ink.

"Right, Ky-Lin, you win!" I said. "First the letter of resignation. Want to dictate?"

An hour later, with both letters written, I realised that this was what I had wanted all along: a clean break, a new life, the spice of adventure.

I felt myself grow stronger and more positive with every line I wrote, as if a weight had suddenly lifted from my shoulders. I remembered a game we had played at boarding-school: you put your arm straight down against your side, then leant against a wall, pressing the arm as hard as you could for three or four minutes, then stepping away. Your arm rose into the air of its own volition, like magic.

My spirits were rising, just like that arm, so when Mrs. Early arrived to inform me that the rain had stopped and to collect the tea-tray, I was able to greet her with the sort of smile I hadn't felt like giving since I arrived.

"I have two letters here, Mrs. Early. Please give the boy this six-pence for his trouble." I knew that she would puzzle over the addresses before she handed the letters over, so I thought I would anticipate any confusion. "This one is to my previous employer, announcing my resignation, and the other is to my solicitors, asking them to forward my luggage from my former lodgings and advise me as to what arrangements need to be made before we set off."

Her face lighted up, then she frowned. "You're not stopping then, miss?"

"For a while—until we are organised. By the way, sometime in the next week or so there will be two gentlemen staying here, the ones who are to accompany us—cr, mc."

"You're going to take that stone ball all the way back to Chiney? Well, I never . . . Not that I thought you wouldn't, mind. And then you'll come back here and make this place something to be proud of. Hcavcn be praised!" And she meant it.

"What do we do now?" I asked Ky-Lin, once she had gone.

"We wait," he said, "We wait . . ."

In the meantime there was plenty to do. I sent off for catalogues of men's and women's travel-wear, and with Ky-Lin's help picked out stout, high-laced boots, thick gloves, leggings(!), a leather cap with ear-flaps, warmer underwear, a money-belt, a man's tweed jacket (small size) and a wicked-looking "hunting-knife." I didn't dare ask what that was for. From another catalogue we picked out a warm blanket, which I sewed up to form a sort of sleeping bag—we were going to sleep in the open? And a lightweight haversack.

All these items were, of course, cash on delivery, but I was relieved when Mr. Swallow paid us a visit in person on Thursday. I wouldn't have wanted to pay for all those items out of my own money.

I was pleased to be able to receive him in the morning-room, with a bright fire blazing and a vase of autumn leaves on the games-table. He raised his eyebrows at his surroundings, obviously impressed. Mrs. Early brought in sherry and sweet biscuits, and as he sipped and nibbled, and confirmed that he didn't need accommodation as he had booked into the inn for the night, I could see that he was revising his opinion of me.

He produced a folder full of documents, brushing the crumbs from his waistcoat as he did so. "I have here your uncle's instructions if you were to choose his alternative plan—which action on your part Miss, er, Lee, I must admit, rather surprises me—and he confirms that he wishes the expedition outward to be completed within one year. The time of your return is immaterial." He managed to make the latter sound unlikely.

"On the outward journey I should budget for one pound per day. There are moneys for outfitting included. Any moneys not used can be utilised for your—er, return." He consulted his papers. I have contacted a certain—er—Mr. Danny Duveen, whom it was your uncle's wish should accompany you. I gather you will be able to accommodate him? I believe he is out of funds again."

I nodded. "We have room enough. What about your own representative?"

He seemed faintly embarrassed. "We are having, ah, a little difficulty in choosing the right candidate, I am afraid. But I expect to confirm the position as soon as possible." He shuffled his papers together. "When he—this person—arrives, he will bring the moneys with him, together with a receipt, of course, and his luggage. I can also confirm that your own personal belongings will be dispatched by train tomorrow and I have arranged for them to be picked up at the station and transported here—"

"Not by the village carrier, I hope!"

He raised his eyebrows. "Why, yes. Our Mr. Cumberbatch assures us he is an excellent man."

"Excellent, nothing! He is lazy, idle and forgetful! Can't you find somebody else? Or at least hold back my possessions until we find alternative transport?"

He shook his head. "Firm arrangements have already been made. The luggage will have left your lodgings long before I can contact anyone to stop it. Can you not find someone to accompany him and make sure he is on time?"

"What about Mr. Cumberbatch?"

He looked embarrassed again. "He has already returned to London, I'm afraid, as his presence here was no longer required."

I thought for a moment. "What time does the train arrive? Is it the same one I travelled on?" He nodded. "Wait a moment, please . . ." I went and had a quick word with Mr. Early, who seemed glad enough to oblige, then returned to Mr. Swallow. "Please ensure that the carrier is here at ten-thirty in the morning. Mr. Early, the housekeeper's husband, will accompany him to the station, making sure he is on time for the train and that the luggage is properly taken care of. Do I have to pay him again?"

"But I understand that Mr. Cumberbatch . . ."

"Then you understood wrong." I rose to my feet. "And now, if there is nothing else? Mr. Early will drive you back to the village."

"It has been a pleasure to do business with you, Miss—er—Lee." He stood up to shake hands. "I must also say that I would not have believed at our initial interview that you would have the determination and will to undertake this task, although I know your uncle had great confidence in you."

I was flattered. I had always thought of myself as something of a mouse. True, I had tackled the hard work and poverty in London pretty well, but what choice had there been? Come to that, what choice had I had here? I thought there had been, but what chance did I have against a magic ring, a close-to-hatching dragon's egg, and a fast-talking, persuasive, wily little Oriental creature of myth?

"Thank you, Mr. Swallow. I am grateful for your help. If—if our expedition proves a success, I presume you will have the papers ready to sign over Hightop Hall to me?" Nothing like sounding confident.

"Of course." He bowed. "I look forward to your return, Miss—er—Lee."

That evening Ky-Lin and I pored over the maps I had taken from my uncle's map-chest: Europe, Russia, Northern China.

"Is this the way you went with Summer?"

He shook his head. "Our way went further south. She travelled from Venice, through Turkey and Arabia into Persia, which is where I picked her up. We then used a caravan route through Northern India and Southern China, across the Gobi desert, then up the Altai Mountains to there—" He touched the map with his hoof. "All modern names, of course. Then, many of them were different, together with the boundaries. Of course, then time didn't matter: now it is of the essence. I suggest the northern route will be quicker."

"But—at this time of year—won't it be colder?"

"Probably; that's why I suggested the warmer clothes. But if we initially use the rivers—Rhine and Danube and across the Black Sea to Georgia and the Caspian, then we can cross the Khirgiz Steppes and bypass the Gobi: the Desert of Death they called it in those days—it will be cheaper. We can use commercial barges up the rivers. The only alternative . . ." He hesitated.

"Yes?"

"The way your uncle would have taken. Straight by ship to India, then north by camel-train. It would be quicker and infinitely more comfortable but we couldn't afford it."

Then that's out, I thought disconsolately. I looked at the mileage graphs at the bottom of each map, measuring them off a thousand miles at a time against my thumb joint, and—

"It must be five or six thousand miles!" I gasped.

"Double that," said Ky-Lin. "We're not flying, you know."

Double? That would make it twelve thousand miles! It wasn't possible! I couldn't do it! Nobody could . . . The dismay must have shown on my face, for Ky-Lin plumed his tail reassuringly.

"We *can* do it. Just about . . . Don't worry, girl. But from now on, until we leave, I want you to practice walking in your new boots, with a rucksack weighted with stones on your back. If you do that, it will be easier when the time comes."

"*Walking!* I thought you said we were travelling by river!"

"Have you ever found a river that you only had to step across to find another? There will be travel between all the waterways and beyond. If we can't find wheeled or animal transport, then we walk, and we carry our food and belongings with us."

"It's all right for you!" I burst out. "You're going to end up being carried in someone's pocket!"

He waved his tail. "When the time comes I shall do my part, I promise you."

"All right! I understand you will translate, guide and advise us, but what about the hard slog we shall have?"

He was silent for a moment, then: "Please put me down on the floor near the window and stand back . . ."

I did as he asked. For a moment or two nothing happened, then I saw something I would not have believed had I not seen it. Turning from mouse-size to rat-size was one thing, but what Ky-Lin managed was incredible. His outline became cloudy and there was a sort of creaking noise, followed by some popping ones and he grew up in size, first one leg and then the other; a thickening of the body, enlarging of the head, and finally his tail shot up into the air, the plume larger than ever, and his outline became clear and distinct.

I stepped back, suddenly scared. He was now as pony-sized as he had once boasted.

"Hey, there, don't be frightened!" His voice was the same, although it had deepened in tone. He stepped towards me, and his hooves clicked on the wooden floor, the plume of his tall swishing back and forth, creating a current of air that brushed me like a caress. "You see? If necessary I can carry burdens as great as any human. As I said, if we have to walk then I will do my share."

I opened my mouth to say something, to apologise, when we both heard footsteps in the corridor outside: Mrs. Early with my hot toddy!

"Open the window!"

I rushed to do his bidding, there was a hiss like air escaping from a balloon and a flurry of curtain and Ky-Lin had disappeared.

Mrs. Early bustled in, setting my hot toddy on the table by the maps. "Been plotting your journey, have you? Many's the time I'd see your uncle with not only the table but the floor covered with— Why! You've got the window wide open! It's raining again and you'll catch your death in that draught! I know your uncle was one for fresh air, but enough is enough . . ."

She began to cross towards the flapping curtains, but I stopped her.

"It's all right, Mrs. Early. I opened the window because some smoke blew back into the room. I'll close it in a minute."

"As you wish. Mr. Early will be up in a few minutes with your hot water . . ."

As soon as she had shut the door behind her I rushed over to the window to find a diminished-to-his-normal-size Ky-Lin shivering on the window-sill. Lifting him inside I pulled down the sash and put him down on the rug by the fire to dry out. I was trying hard not to laugh, he looked so bedraggled.

"Here, have a sip of my hot toddy . . ."

He did, then pulled himself together in a small, dignified way. "I bet you would fare no better if you'd been out there in the rain, and had to change back so quickly . . . Yes, thank you, another sip or two would be most welcome!" A long drink. "Er, this *is* alcohol-free, I suppose?"

My luggage arrived the next day, mid-afternoon. Jos. Carter, Carrier, came trundling down the drive with Mr. Early next to him in the front seat. The men carried my mother's writing desk into the morning-room, where it was unwrapped and polished by Mrs. Early. My grandfather's wing-chair went into what I had christened the library, where it received the same treatment from the housekeeper. The books went into the study, and my trunk into the bedroom, where I unpacked what little I had and put it away into the wardrobe and chest of drawers. The patchwork quilt I spread over my bed, bringing a bright patch of colour to the room.

Mrs. Early commented on what I had brought. "Two nice pieces of furniture, miss, and the chair matches the curtains perfectly. Is the quilt your own work?"

I explained it was my mother's handiwork, and she was full of praise. "By the way, miss, I've taken the liberty of putting the laundry basket in the kitchen. It was that heavy, Mr. Early said, that I thought you might have something special in it."

Laundry basket? My meagre laundry usually came in a brown paper parcel. Surely Mrs. Jugg hadn't wasted one of her hampers, which usually went to those with a far bigger laundry than mine? And heavy? I would go down and take a look.

But first I tried out my father's chair in the "library," letting its soft curves and soft cushions wrap me into remembered ease, but suddenly there was a loud scream from the direction of the kitchen.

Rushing down the corridor I opened the kitchen door and found Mr. and Mrs. Early looking at a medium-sized laundry hamper in the middle of the floor.

Mrs. Early was armed with a poker. "It moved," she cried. "I'll swear it did!"

"Saw it too," said Mr. Early, armed with a cudgel.

I gazed in alarm at the hamper, which bore a label addressed to "Miss S. Lee, Hightop Hall, Dorset. By Rail."

Suddenly the whole basket jerked and creaked and we all jumped back. One of the leather straps snapped, and there was a faint groaning noise.

"There's something inside," I said. "Perhaps it's a dog . . ." I was scared stiff, but reckoned we couldn't leave whatever it was trapped in there for ever. Making a quick decision I moved forward and fumbled the other strap free, then moved back quickly.

Mr. and Mrs. Early clutched their weapons more tightly.

"Come out!" I said loudly. "At *once*!"

The lid lifted, fell back, and out of a tangle of laundry stepped—

"Toby!" I cried.

12

Toby

Toby!" I repeated. "What in the *world* are you doing in there?"

He looked a real scarecrow: tangled hair, tousled clothes, a smeary face, filthy hands—and most of this had come off on my laundry, in which he had been wrapped.

Mrs. Early lowered her poker. "You *know* him, miss?" She made it sound like a crime.

I started to explain, but he turned a pitiful face in my direction and clutched the front of his trousers.

"Wanna piss, miss!"

I snatched at his sleeve, rushed him out into the yard and pointed him in the direction of the outside privy. When he reappeared, looking much better, I hauled him back into the kitchen.

"Would you be kind enough to give him a mug of milk, Mrs. Early?" He downed it in one gulp, sighed, and put the empty mug on the table. "There's more where that came from," I said, "when you have explained yourself!"

"Where'd you want me to start?"

"At the beginning. Just a moment though . . ." I turned to Mr. and Mrs. Early and finished explaining who and what he was. "Not my idea," I said.

"And just look at what he's done to your laundry!" Mrs. Early snatched out the sheets, pillowcases and towels. "Need more than one boil!"

"Right, Toby!"

"Er . . . I ain't et nuffin since—"

"How many times do I have to tell you? 'I haven't eaten anything since . . .' Repeat it after me—and leave out that whine . . . Good. Carry on. You can eat after you have told me why and how you are here. The truth, mind."

I was fiercer with him than usual, largely because his appearance had been such a shock, bringing back the environment I had come from with painful clarity, now when I had decided to give it all up.

He hesitated. "I hid in there because I wanted to be with you. When—when I heard as you weren't coming back—"

"*That* you weren't—"

"That you weren't coming back, I grew desperate. Me Mam's latest—"

"*My—*"

"My Mam's latest hates me, he does. Doesn't want me in the house no more—"

I sighed. "*Any* more. Come on, Toby, you can talk better than that!"

"He told me as—that—I reminded him of a frog. Me—my Mam—was always saying as—that my dad was the best lover she ever had."

I looked at his filthy face. Large, long-lashed eyes, straight nose, determined chin—"You don't look a bit like a frog—or a toad, come to that."

"Not a *frog* frog, a Frenchie Frog. Me—my Mam—let slip he came from a town called Paree."

All Mrs. Jugg's children had different fathers, I knew that. Beside me Mrs. Early's eyes were like saucers.

"But how did you get in there? And when?"

"Miss Madeleine. From the school, remember? I went and told her everything, how I wanted to be with you, an' all. She went and saw my Mum. My Mum's got the hots for this new fellow—"

There was a gasp from Mrs. Early: such things just weren't mentioned.

"—and she said as it—that it was probably for the best if'n I joined you. For the time being, at any rate."

"But why the laundry basket?"

"Miss Madeleine ain't—hasn't got no—any—money, seeing as—that she's only Miss Hepzibah's by-blow—" Another gasp from Mrs. Early. "—so it was my Mum's idea, to save the fare. Miss Madeleine got permission to check that your things were all packed proper—properly—and she shut me in and labelled me this morning before they came to take everything to the station."

I wanted to laugh, but kept my voice severe. "And how do I know all this is the truth?"

He fished about in his pockets. "Got a letter from Miss Madeleine."

Taking the crumpled envelope I opened it and rapidly scanned the contents. It seemed that Madeleine Moffat had hidden depths. Not only did her letter confirm all that Toby had said, but she added a few details about Toby's new "uncle" that Toby would never have told me, which also made me glad that he was away from home. She hoped I could find him a good position, suggesting that he deserved it and would benefit from further education. She closed by regretting she had not had the chance to bid me farewell, and wishing me well in my new life. In a hastily written postscript she added that she had taken over my position at the school, "Although I shall not, of course, be receiving any wages!"

So here I was, a sort of surrogate aunt, charged with finding Toby a secure position and a temporary home, on top of everything else I had to think about! I looked at the filthy, forlorn-looking boy and felt a rush of sympathy. It must have been quite an experience, being humped and bumped around on carts and trains, upside down or right way up, without food or water and never even sure if he were going to arrive safely.

"Does he stay, miss?"

"For the time being, Mrs. Early, until we can find him a suitable position. I realise this will mean extra work for you—"

She shook her head. "Think nothing of it. Just a bit more food on the stove, for I'll bet he has an appetite . . . An I might suggest it, he could do with a bath!"

He certainly could. It was warm in the kitchen, and even where I stood I could smell the unwashed children stink of the school . . .

But Toby had turned to me in something like terror. "A barf? I ain't 'ad a barf since Gawd knows when!" Obviously the very thought had washed away any attempt at correct speech.

"Now listen to me; you came here uninvited and I could send you straight back to London, if necessary in custody. Don't think I'm not pleased to see you, but if I let you remain, then you must do exactly what I say, is that understood?" He nodded. "Now, Mrs. Early will give you something to eat—" Indeed, she was already ladling soup into a large bowl. "—And then you will have a bath, as she suggested. I myself bathe every day, and I shall expect you to do the same. Understood again?" He nodded once more, as if he couldn't trust himself to speak. I realised he must be feeling that perhaps he had made a mistake in leaving home, so I softened my tone and added: "And as soon as Mr. and Mrs. Early have dealt with you, you can come upstairs and we'll have a talk by the fire and tea and cake."

The housekeeper cut a large hunk of bread and set that and the soup on the table, pulled up a stool and motioned Toby to eat. He needed no further invitation. He fell on the food like a starved dog, and ate as untidily, stuffing the bread into his mouth until his cheeks bulged, and slurping the soup noisily. I opened my mouth to remonstrate, but behind his back Mrs. Early shook her head, conveying without words that she understood his hunger. He was obviously in good hands.

"I'll send him up when he's ready, miss. Don't worry, he'll be all right. And if you hear a noise or two, just ignore it. I doubt he's seen soap and water in a good while . . ."

So I ignored the yells and screams I heard some time later, as I brought Ky-Lin up to date with what had happened.

"I shall be curious to see your little friend . . ."

But I don't think either of us was prepared for what came up shortly after Mrs. Early's tea-tray, now with a bigger tea-pot and two large slabs of cake.

"Mr. Early will be up with him in a minute, Miss," she said without preamble. "We had to burn his clothes, they were that flea-ridden. Once the eggs get into the seams, there's nothing else to do." She looked uncharacteristically hot and bothered, with wisps of hair escaping from under her cap. "So, begging your pardon, we've put him in one of your uncle's old nightshirts, not having anything else to hand. Your uncle wasn't that tall, but the garment reaches his ankles, and we had to stuff the slippers with paper. He wouldn't wear the combies . . ." She turned to go, then came back and lowered her voice. "Thought you might like to know: poor lad was covered in bruises and two burns. Not where they would show, mind. Reckon it's a good thing he's away from all that."

Poor Toby! But I had expected as much from Madeleine's letter.

She turned to go again, but hadn't quite finished. "By the by, the nightcap was your uncle's too, but we thought it best to cover his head against the cold. It was the lice as well, you see . . ."

I didn't immediately, and it was only when Mr. Early ushered the boy in a couple of minutes later that I realised the extent to which he had been "done over," as he would have put it.

I had always seen him as a healthily tanned, curly-haired boy with a ready grin, but what I saw now was someone I hardly recognised.

A thin pale-faced lad with freckles on his nose, wearing an absurd nightshirt and a nightcap with a bobble on the end, shuffling across the floor in over-large slippers. His eyes were big, dark-rimmed and frightened.

"Toby? Come and sit down and let me pour you some tea." He smelt of good, strong carbolic soap, and even his bitten nails had been scrubbed clean. "My word! I hardly recognised you. It's nice to see you so—so clean and tidy! Aren't you glad to get rid of all that London dirt and grime?"

He looked at me resentfully, his lower lip trembling, then suddenly snatched off the nightcap, to reveal that they had shaved him completely bald. "Just look what they done to me hair! Bald as a coot, I am!"

"It'll soon grow back," I soothed, even as I tried to hide my dismay at the loss of his normally luxuriant mop. He saw my expression and flushed angrily.

"See? You don't like it neither! Looks like a freak I does, a bloody freak!"

"Toby! Don't swear—"

" 'Nough to make a saint swear!" I heard a tiny snigger from the hidden Ky-Lin. "You ain't never 'ad your 'ead shaved, 'ave you? Bloody cold it is too: you'll 'ave me catch me death!"

"Oh, come on," I said placatingly. "I think it makes you look sort of—sort of *distinguished*. Like one of those marble busts we saw in that museum once, remember?" For sometimes I used to take him with me on my expeditions in London.

"They was wearing stone wigs," he said disgustedly. "And I ain't wearing no wigs, stone or otherwise. Right fright I'd look!"

I forebore to say that he looked a "right fright" at this moment. Leaning forward I touched his skull; it was strange to study the true shape of the head, so often hidden by hair, with its unaccustomed slopes, furrows and hollows. I examined my own head later, discovering for the first time my own bumps and lumps. Phrenology was an emerging science, I learned.

"Listen, Toby! Once your hair grows back—and it will, and quickly too—there'll be no more lice, no more nits, no more scratching. Doesn't that make any difference?"

"Not when you're as bald as an egg! Not when folks are goin' to look at you as if you came from a freak show! Not when the wind is whistling past your ears fit to freeze off your balls!"

"Toby!" I expostulated, though I was grinning inside, and there was another snigger from the hidden Ky-Lin. "That's enough of that! Tomorrow I will have you kitted out properly in the village, including a nice cap to hide your baldness. Now, drink your tea and eat your cake and I'll show you where you will sleep."

He ate his slice, and mine, and drank three cups of tea, with six lumps of sugar in each. Afterwards he looked much better, with a flush in his cheeks and a sparkle in his eyes.

I leant back in my chair, waiting till he had finished, initially loath to spoil his mood, but it had to be done.

"Look here, Toby, at the risk of repeating myself, I didn't invite you here, and I'm afraid you have come at rather a busy time as I shall be going away on a long journey very soon. Before I go, however, I shall find you somewhere to live and, hopefully, some job or other to keep you busy. However, if I agree to take on the responsibility of doing this, you must promise to behave yourself, and keep your bad language to yourself. Understood?"

He nodded, and I relaxed. Not for long.

"Reckon I'll go with you, miss."

"Oh, no you don't!" I said. "This is nothing to do with you. I'm not taking you on an expedition to China!"

"Chiny? Must be a third of the way across the world!" His eyes were now dangerously bright. " 'Member that map we had in the classroom?"

Indeed I did. Probably about six feet by four, a Mercator projection, it was primarily meant to glorify the British Empire, with all the red bits showing that we seemed to have conquered half the world. Actually its most useful function was to hide the badly stained plaster of the wall, for as a map it was pretty useless. The greasy brown oilcloth had dimmed so that the red was pale pink, the blues and greens and yellows all dulled to a sort of dun colour, smearing the world into an ancient hoarding, rather than the bright tapestry it should have been.

"Used to look at that map all the time, miss, 'specially when the lessons were boring. I was nearest, see. Got to understand what the different shapes were: ours looking like a little old lady in a bonnet riding a pig to market; Italy like a posh boot, kicking little Sicily, France and Germany big squares—and Chiny and Roosia so big they could swallow up 'most everybody else, 'cept the triangle of India. And the rivers, miss! Like wriggly worms, they was—sorry, were—so it must take a long time to travel along them, though it looks shorter in a straight line . . ." He ran (temporarily) out of breath. I was fascinated; I had never heard him so animated, and had no idea he was so keen on geography—unless of course he was making the whole thing up in order to impress me and book his place on our expedition. If so, it was a very adroit performance, especially as it seemed to be spontaneous.

"I never knew you were so keen on maps and things," I said carefully.

"Oh, yes! I used to look at Miss Madeleine's sometimes when she took over if Miss Hardacre were—was—off. She's like you, buys books second-hand, but they got maps mostly, and plants and animals. Helped me make up my mind what I'm goin' to be: a 'Splorer."

"An explorer?" Small chance, Toby, I thought. You need to have a private income for that sort of thing.

"Yes, however long it takes. Reckon I could get a job, save a bit, then volunteer to join an expedition. Cook, carrier, collector—whatever, till I gets—get enough to strike out on me—my—own."

In spite of my misgivings, I was impressed. If his actions matched his determination, then he would succeed.

"China is out of the question, I'm afraid, but tomorrow or the day after I'll tell you where I'm going and why. It's quite a story . . ." I doubted he would believe it though. "Ah, here's Mrs. Early to tell us supper is ready . . ."

After seconds of mince and dumplings and treacle tart, I gave him a candle and showed him to his bedroom, explaining that I was just across the corridor, and introduced him to the commode in the bathroom.

"No guzunder?"

"No . . . ? Oh, I see. No chamber-pot! Relieve yourself now, and I'll see you into bed."

I could see he was overawed by his bedroom, with its spruce single bed and the fire that had been lighted to air the room. He allowed me to tuck him up, but when I turned back to say good night I saw he was out of bed and standing on the rug.

"What's the matter?"

"It's so *clean,* miss! And—and too *quiet!*"

"Rubbish! You'll soon get used to it. If you are going to be an explorer you have to get used to anything, and this will then seem like luxury. Blow out the candle and go to sleep . . ." A little harsh, perhaps, but it wouldn't do to accept everything he said at face value.

When I got back to the study Ky-Lin was nibbling at a couple of hazelnuts which I had collected for him earlier.

"Well, what do you think?"

"Not bad at all. A *little* more time in the sun, perhaps, but nice and sweet just the same . . ."

"No, not those. Toby!"

"We can take him with us," said Ky-Lin. "He's a likely lad."

"We can do no such thing! He's only a child."

"He's a bright thirteen- or fourteen-year-old, and a trip like ours can only be good for him. Who else at his age and background gets a chance to travel like that? Where else would he hear different languages and have the chance to observe other life-styles? How do you know that the expedition wouldn't be an inspiration for him to follow his dream of being an explorer? Would you deny him all that?"

Put like that I was behaving like the classic wicked stepmother, denying a deserving child the chance of a lifetime because I was too protective, couldn't be bothered, didn't want the responsibility, saw too many drawbacks.

"He's not very strong. I said weakly. "It's a long way . . ."

"He's tougher than you think. You are a model for the sort of woman he has never known before. I think it would do him more harm if you leave him behind. Don't forget you are the only secure point he has in his life at the moment. One day he may go back to his own family, but from what the housekeeper said he's better off here for the time being. The boy needs affection, praise, most of all to feel he's needed. Here's your chance to make something of him; a year or so travelling could make all the difference. He's at a difficult time of life physically, too, just growing up. The discipline of a long trek will add muscles and inches, just wait and see." He paused. "I don't say there won't be moments when we shall want to throw him over the moon, but I still think it's worth it. Besides," he added slyly, "how do you know you will get on with your other travelling companions? At least you know Toby will be on your side . . ."

I had lost, and I knew it. "What about telling him everything—including you?"

"The sooner the better," he said briskly. "Save me all this chopping and changing. Er . . . could you possibly find some more of these splendid nuts tomorrow?"

I bathed, then sat up and read for a while before seeking my bed. I decided to check on Toby before I turned in, but was horrified to find his bed was empty. Rushing down the stairs to find Mrs. Early, I collided with her at the bottom. She had her finger to her lips.

"Hush, Miss . . . Just take a peep at this." She opened the kitchen door quietly and I peered in. At first I could see nothing untoward and then I glanced at the fire: there, wrapped in one of the blankets from his bed, the cat cuddled to his chest, was Toby, fast asleep on the rug.

Mrs. Early had a smile on her face. "Reckon a soft bed and being on his own is something he'll take a time to get used to. Don't worry, I reckon he'll do just fine!"

13

Educating Toby

In the morning I had to deal with an increasingly impatient Toby, forced by his lack of clothing to stay indoors, but Mrs. Early had given me an idea. I asked her to look out all the clothing my uncle had left, and she produced woolen shirts and sweaters, tweed jackets, caps and leggings, mufflers, gloves, shoes, a double set of underwear still in its tissue paper, handkerchiefs (ditto), and a lined cloak.

"I gave all the well-used materials worn next to the body—socks and underwear and such—to the Church for the poor, after I'd washed them," said Mrs. Early.

"You did right," I told her. "And you may do the same with those shoes and gloves, but I think we can make something of the rest for the lad." And after a tape-measure and a list for Mr. Early, he set off for the village and returned before luncheon with boots and felt slippers, socks and mittens for Toby, plus the village seamstress. She spent the afternoon, with Mrs. Early's help, cutting and snipping and sewing and altering. Although Toby was two or three inches shorter than my uncle, width-wise they were about the same, so it was only a case, for the most part, of shortening sleeves and hems and lifting waistlines. They also made a good job of altering the caps to fit, so that by dark Toby had a full set of clothes. The seamstress took the rest back with her to alter at home, promising to return them by Monday.

Toby was as pleased as Mr. Punch, and strutted around in his finery, trying to catch glimpses of himself in any mirror he could find, but insisted on wearing his caps back-to-front, with the brims at the nape of his neck.

"All the fashion in Lunnon," he said. "Wish me mates could see me now!" He wanted to rush out straightaway and parade himself but luckily it started to rain.

He ate like a horse at all meals, but was reluctant when reminded about his daily bath.

"I had the scrub to end all scrubs yesterday! Why, I'll bet I lost most of my skin as well, see, I'm a diff'rent colour! Me—my Ma didn't believe in baths. Laundering, yes; bathing, no. Why, I might even shrink! Clothes do, sometimes . . ."

I had to smile. "Toby, people don't shrink from bathing! Don't you see, if you hadn't had a good scrub you would have dirtied the sheets on your bed and the nice clothes you're wearing? Just like you ruined the laundry in the hamper . . . I can't tell you how happy I am to at last have the stink of London out of my nostrils, and don't have to look for fleas or lice anymore. And you look and smell so much nicer now!"

He looked at me, then grinned, a smile that was both cheeky and endearing at the same time.

"Just testing . . ." He thought for a moment, then added: "Thanks for the clothes, and for letting me stay," and gave me a quick, embarrassed hug. Which was enough to forgive him everything—for the time being.

The following day being Sunday I was in two minds about taking Toby to church with us, guessing that the only previous religious teaching he had received were the prayers and Bible readings we had had at the school, but he seemed to think it was natural to accompany us. I told him he must sit quiet, listen to the sermon and behave reverently through the prayers and lessons.

"Din' I sit quiet for five years in that school? Din' I listen to every— well, nearly every—word that was said? Did I ever not behave myself?"

He was right. Many of the children that had a spark of life left in them, apart from eating enough to keep them alive and wearing enough to keep them warm, became bored and restless. Toby had been less trouble than most, because we had all given him books to look at and extra work to do; the others wanted to be entertained, rather than providing their own amusement.

In any event he behaved himself perfectly in church, absorbing the ritual bowings and scrapings only a half-second behind, following the prayers and lessons in the prayer-book I lent him, and singing the one hymn he knew lustily. This week the snobbish families weren't present—

perhaps they had satisfied their curiosity the previous Sunday—so we were greeted with friendliness untainted with condescension.

Toby and I decided to walk back to the Hall and, freed from the restrictions of the service, he reverted to pure boy. He kicked at the heaps of leaves, whistle-copied the song of a robin, hunted the hedgerows for old nests, while I picked some more bright foliage and lingered here and there to find some more hazelnuts for Ky-Lin. I hoped it would be sooner rather than later that he revealed himself to the boy, because it was becoming increasingly difficult for us to find time on our own to plan our journey.

After luncheon it started to rain again, so I took Toby on a tour of the rest of the Hall to keep him occupied. Now all the rest of my uncle's artifacts had been removed it was possible to appreciate just how much space there was. Our feet echoed on the bare wooden floors, on marble tiles, clattered up and down endless stairways. We went, on Toby's insistence, from cellar to attic and back again. Not that the place was entirely empty; ordinary, plain tables and chairs, a few bedsteads, cupboards, wardrobes and chests had been left behind, as were some threadbare rugs and runners and a pile of mothballed blankets.

He was enchanted with everything. Watching him dash about I realised what little space he had had in London, just tramping the same streets day after day. To be sure there were parks and grassy spaces in town, but he had never been encouraged to use them, except when he rarely accompanied me on a picnic, and in the large buildings like museums he had to behave sedately. Here he romped on the way back from church and was now behaving as if he were attending a party. Although the place was as clean as Mrs. Early and her girls had been able to get it, he still managed to end up happily grubby.

As we went back to the door leading into the Temple and tea, he slipped his hand into mine.

"You know what, miss? I reckon as this place would make a wonderful holiday home for poor children—or even an orphanage . . ."

After tea I pretended my eyes were tired, and had him practise his reading by telling me a couple of stories from my *Fairy-Tales by the Brothers Grimm*. He seemed to enjoy "Rumpelstiltskin" best. After supper we had a hand or two of cards and I sent him to bed at half-past nine, with a length of string, to practise some cat's cradles I had shown him.

I settled down with Ky-Lin, tracing-paper and one of the more detailed maps to plot the first part of our journey. We decided to take the railway to the coast, first ascertaining where we would get a ferry across to Holland, travelling on deck as it was cheaper, and then to the mouth of the Rhine where it debouched into the sea and on by barge or boat to southern Bavaria and then cross overland to the Danube in order to continue our journey eastward.

I had the tracing-paper in place, cut into strips like the old-fashioned ones, where you only concentrated on the bit you wanted to travel, with Ky-Lin holding down the farthest end with his hooves, when there was a light tap at the door and Toby entered.

"Couldn't get to sleep, miss: reckon it was those apple dumplings we had for supper. Can I come in for a bit?"

I glanced at Ky-Lin, expecting him to have changed into a figurine; instead he was just the same, except that he was perfectly still. He winked at me.

"You can come in for a few minutes," I said. "Kindly shut the door."

He sat down opposite me, and I could see he was about to ask about the maps, but then he caught sight of Ky-Lin.

"Gosh, miss, you've got a cuddly toy! Where'd you get him from? Never seen one like that before . . ."

"And you aren't likely to. This—this is a representation of a creature who comes from China. In the mythical past he and his brethren were guards and guides for a holy person called the Buddha. Part of his teaching was that you could be reborn again, depending on the way you lived this life, and that every living thing was trying to do the same. In other words even the smallest living thing is trying to better itself, and you must never destroy anything alive, plant or animal. A fly can be reborn as a bird, from there to a rabbit, and thence to a man . . . But if you are bad, then you regress."

"So you don't stamp on an ant in case it's on its way up . . . I see." He leant forward. "Can I touch it?"

I glanced at Ky-Lin: another wink.

"Yes, but gently. He's fragile."

Toby reached out his right index finger and stroked it down Ky-Lin's spine. He drew it back, a look of surprise on his face. "Why, he's quite warm!"

"Yes."

"But toys aren't warm . . ."

"Well, he's not exactly a toy—"

As if in answer Ky-Lin winked at me again, then proceeded to act exactly like a mechanical toy. He made a whirring noise, then rose on his haunches to all four hooves, swinging his head from side to side, then stepped slowly and jerkily round to face Toby, this time nodding his head, then sat down on his haunches again.

Toby's eyes were as round as the saucer-eyes of the first dog who guarded the treasure in the fairy tale, and he must have been holding his breath, for he let it out in a great sigh and a low whistle.

"Woweee! He's like those mechanical toys we saw in that museum once . . . Must be worth a bundle!"

"Irreplaceable," I agreed, trying not to giggle. "As far as I know, he's the only one left in the world."

"Did your uncle bring him back from his travels?"

"Yes, together with a couple of other things that I have inherited. Tell you about those in a minute."

He nodded towards Ky-Lin. "Does he do other things too?"

"Loads!" I was enjoying this and, from the look of it, so was Ky-Lin. "What would you like him to do?"

"Er—turn a somersault?" He put out his hand. "Hadn't you better wind him up again?"

"No. He goes for quite a long time without—without any external influences, don't you, Ky-Lin?"

The little creature nodded, obliged by starting his whirring noise again, and turned a grave and well-controlled somersault. Then he executed a pirouette and fluffed out his tail to its fullest glory.

Toby clapped his hands, then frowned. "But how do you tell him to do these things? How did he know to do a somersault next?"

"Ah, that's part of his magic!" Ky-Lin sank back on his haunches, making a noise like a coiled spring running down.

Toby said: "You were going to tell me about the other things your uncle left? Are they toys as well?"

"No, definitely not." I looked across at Ky-Lin who gave me an almost imperceptible nod. "Listen, and I'll tell you a story." I fetched the manuscript out of the cabinet, where I had kept everything since Toby arrived, and gave him a potted version of Summer's story, explained about my uncle's will and told him of the choice I had made. He didn't seem at all surprised.

"Just what I would have decided, miss. Where's the egg then that we're taking back to Chiney—er, China?"

"The Eg *I* am taking back to China . . ." I brought it out of the cabinet and laid it on my shawl on the table.

"Does that do tricks as well?"

"Not as such, but it is growing larger every day, it's warm, and my uncle believed it holds something living. He also couldn't smash or crack it, so it is somewhat unusual. Pick it up . . ."

He did, although it was heavy, and examined it carefully, rolling it around in his hands.

"It *is* warm . . . So that's what a dragon's egg looks like." He turned a puzzled face towards me. "But there aren't any dragons, are there, miss, so how can that be a dragon's egg?"

"Most people would say there wasn't such a thing as a Ky-Lin, but there he is on the table." I took pity on him. "No, I didn't believe in dragons or Ky-Lins or magic either when I first came here, but I have a more open mind now. Circumstances have forced me to reconsider, put it that way. My uncle didn't believe either, but he changed his mind."

Toby continued to examine the Eg, shaking it, scratching it with a bitten nail, even touching it with his tongue. He held it to his ear, and suddenly his face lit up.

"You're right! It *is* alive!"

"What do you mean—alive?"

"I can hear something inside. A soft, kind of fluttery sound. Listen!" He handed it to me, but I could hear nothing. "Can't you hear it?" I shook my head. "Well, I can! It may not be a baby dragon, but there's something in there, sure as—sure as eggs is eggs!" And he laughed at his own joke.

"That settles it," said Ky-Lin unexpectedly. "He comes with us."

Toby stopped laughing and looked at me. "What did you say?"

I shook my head. "Nothing. Not a word."

"Somebody said something . . ." He picked up the Eg, listened. "Not this." He looked at Ky-Lin. "Does he talk as well?"

"Sometimes . . ."

"Can you make him speak?"

"He speaks when he wants to—but only to me."

"Why?"

"Because I have a magic translator."

He was silent for a moment. "Where's the key?"

"What key?"

"The one to wind him up."

"There isn't one."

He frowned. "Then how do you make him work?"

"*I* don't. *He* does . . . Watch . . . Now you see him—" I covered Ky-Lin with my hands and willed him to change back to his ivory shape, which he did in about ten seconds: "—and now you don't." I parted my hands and there was the figurine.

Toby picked it up, looked at my hands, under the table and examined my sleeves.

"All right: where's he gone?"

"He's there." I pointed to the ivory.

"You're joshing me! It looks a bit like him, but it ain't him. That's not alive like he was. That can't move."

I sat back. "Don't be too sure! All right, Ky-Lin, show him!"

And in front of Toby's astonished gaze the ivory turned back to the "live" Ky-Lin, slowly and carefully, like a conjurer explaining a trick.

For a moment or two Toby was dumb, then: "If'n I hadn't seen it with my own eyes . . . Guess I'll believe anyfink now." He rose to his feet and bowed reverently as if he were in church.

"Tell him not to be an idiot," said Ky-Lin. "Tell him also that we are taking him with us."

I translated, and Toby's face lit up like an instant lamp. "I'm going with you? Gee-golly-gosh-an'-green Gorgonzola!" He jumped to his feet and did a little jig round the room. "Thank you, thank you, thank you!"

"Tell him the terms and conditions," said Ky-Lin, and I translated as he told me.

"Ky-Lin says I have to tell you that we have a long and difficult journey ahead of us. There will be two other companions with us, as yet unknown, and you will have to fit in with them. It will be well over a year before we return, if we're lucky. There will be dangers to face and it is not a task to be undertaken lightly. If you wish to change your mind about coming, no-one will blame you . . ."

"No way! I'm coming! I'll do anything, just anything! I'll carry the egg all the way to Chiney—China! I'll . . . I'll . . ."

"All right, that'll do! Come here and sit down." This was me talking. "Now, you said you would do exactly as you were told?"

"Yes, miss! Whatever you say . . ."

"And I say bed. Now. Immediately!"

"A little help," said Ky-Lin, and he bent forward and blew gently into the boy's face. "A little Sleepy-Dust . . ."

Within seconds Toby's eyes were drooping, and three minutes later he was in bed and sleeping soundly.

"Another of your tricks," I remarked to Ky-Lin as I fished a handful of hazelnuts out of my pocket.

"Thank you. Nothing special," he remarked modestly. "The Sleepy-Dust I mean, not these excellent nuts . . . I didn't want the lad to get over-excited."

"I hope you know what you are doing, taking him with us."

"So do I," he said. "So do I . . ."

The following morning Toby, clean, fed and shining, came and asked me if he could take Ky-Lin for a walk.

"Oh, I don't think that's a very good idea . . ."

His face crumpled. "But he *asked* me!"

"He did?"

I fetched the figurine out of the cabinet.

"But he hasn't been out of here today. How could he?"

"He asked me—sort of in my mind. Out loud in my mind. Honest!"

"He's right," said Ky-Lin, coming to life again. "I didn't know, however, whether he had understood."

"But what do you want to do?" I asked, the tiniest stab of jealousy prickling. After all, he had never asked me to take him out.

Toby answered for him. "He wants to practise," he said, frowning to himself. "He wants—he wants . . ." and he held his hands out in front of him like a fisherman demonstrating his catch. "He wants to practise growing big."

Ky-Lin nodded at me. "The boy's a natural. If we go up Bracken Hill, then perhaps I can get rid of this stiffness. I'm afraid I'm a little rusty, as you would put it. And if you would ask the boy to look out for a few nuts or berries?"

"Right, Toby." I described where he was to go, and the search for food for Ky-Lin. "Blackberries—you know what they look like—and haws and hips. Dark red smaller ones, and large orangey ones." I had a good idea. "As it's a fine day, how about me asking Mrs. Early to make up a picnic basket, and I'll join you at lunch-time?"

So, later in the day, after a morning mending, sewing and making lists, I walked up through the bracken with a basket filled with cold egg and ham pie, Russian salad, cheese and onion pasties and Conference pears, with a flagon of ginger beer.

When I reached the top of the hill however, there was no-one to be seen. I was sure, however, that I had heard a giggle from Toby as I climbed up, so I sat down and let the breeze cool my cheeks and ruffle my uncovered hair, content to await whatever surprise was in store. I didn't have to wait long. There was a sudden war-whoop and onto the rocks over my head sailed a pony-sized Ky-Lin with Toby on his back.

They teetered for a moment on the summit, then Ky-Lin gained his balance.

"Great, ain't it?" said Toby, slipping off Ky-Lin's back. "What's in the basket, then?"

Ky-Lin folded himself down to a reasonable size, and we all tucked in, Toby and I with the hamper, Ky-Lin with an assortment of nuts, fruit and berries Toby had provided. I was just packing the hamper with the empties when Toby said: "I wonder who came in the carrier's cart . . ."

"When?"

"When you was climbing the hill. Came down the drive with a couple of people in it, and now there's smoke coming out of another chimney. Look down: you can see it from here . . ."

"Could be our fellow-travellers," said Ky-Lin to me.

"I'd better go see," I said. "Toby, bring back the picnic basket," and gathering up my skirts, I ran back down the hill, to find a flustered Mrs. Early in the kitchen, her mouth drawn down, brewing a large pot of tea.

She didn't wait for my questions.

"Two of them. Says they're the ones what's going with you. Their luggage is in the hall. Shall I make up the other two bedrooms?"

"I'd better have a word with them first . . ."

"Doubt whether you'll be best pleased," she said, looking more disapproving than ever. "Not what I'd have chose myself . . . I lit a fire in the morning-room. You want me to bring the tea in there?"

"Yes, please . . ." I couldn't understand her ill-humour, until I tidied my hair, changed into slippers and walked down to the morning-room and opened the door.

Then I understood part of her temper immediately.

14

Unwelcome Guests

Mr. Cumberbatch!" I was aware I was repeating myself, but I couldn't help myself. And after I had thought to get rid of him forever, here he was turning up again like the proverbial bad penny!

"Your servant, Miss Lee." He rose from the fireplace, where he had been warming his hands. "I have here a package of money and a letter from Mr. Swallow." He handed them over. Taking a paper-knife from the writing-desk I slit the letter open.

It read, after the usual salutations: *"I am sending you Mr. Cumberbatch to accompany you on your journeys, on behalf of our firm, under your uncle's instructions. I have decided to send him as the other members of our firm are more advanced in years, and he is both young and fit, I might add, however, that he is unwilling to undertake this task, but I hope he will become reconciled as time goes on. We have equipped him as well as we could for his travels. He carries with him the moneys for your journey, which I must ask you to receipt as provided.*

"He will be accompanied by the private investigator your uncle also insisted upon, a Mr. Danny Duveen. He has been provided with moneys for his travelling outfit." He ended up wishing us well.

I put the letter and the packet of money down carefully on the writing-desk, realising that I was prolonging the moment when I would have to turn around and face my unwelcome fellow-traveller. He didn't want to go, and I didn't want him either! What a pickle . . . I couldn't imagine a more dreary companion: dreary and useless.

Mrs. Early provided the diversion I needed by bringing in a tray of tea, so I was able to greet him pleasantly enough, offer him a cup of tea and assure him his room would be ready as soon as possible. All this while I had half an eye on the other occupant of the room, seeming intent on examining one of the prints on the wall. He was wearing a heavy caped coat reaching almost to his ankles, as if he wasn't very tall. I wasn't sure whether his turned back was indicative of boorishness, politeness as I spoke with Mr. Cumberbatch, or shyness.

"Did you both have a pleasant journey?" I asked, preparing to pour the tea.

"Not particularly. Dem' smoky carriage and the dem' carrier was late—"

"Mr. Cumberbatch: we do not use language like that in this house, nor will I tolerate it on the journey. You are not in the office now."

My other guest clapped his hands as he turned round. "Well said, Miss Lee, well said! I always say you have to watch your mouth in front of the ladies, so I do!"

I nearly dropped the milk jug.

"You! What on earth are you doing here?" The man who now faced me was even more familiar than Mr. Cumberbatch: it was the importunate young "poet" who had lived for a while at my lodgings, and who had both pestered me with his poems and followed me round wherever I went. What was his name? Random, that was it: Richard Random.

He came forward, flung his coat off over a chair and extended his hand.

"Hello again, Miss Lee! Danny Duveen at your service . . . Mine's two sugars and only a splash of milk."

"But—but you're Richard Random!"

"Was, Miss Lee, was! That was only an alias, if you know what I mean. In my line of work it is essential that you move along and leave no clues behind you. So, the name changes with the job, and so do the disguises. If you had any idea how hard it was to write that dreadful doggerel! I did say two sugars, did I not?"

So this was the man on whom my uncle had depended for his report on me! And I had always thought it was my hidden attractions . . . I had to admit he had been both clever and persistent. As for "disguise," he looked little different: unshaven, untidy, unruly black hair falling over his forehead, very blue eyes. His clothes, too, had seen better days. They were decidedly grubby, ill-fitting, a little out of date, with a compensating touch of the exotic: a multicoloured scarf, a sporty yellow waistcoat, a green handkerchief hanging out of one pocket, a flashy red-stoned ring. He looked as if he had rummaged very quickly through Old Sol's second-hand clothes shop, or was about to take his turn at a provincial music-hall, singing Irish ballads.

Still, it had been my uncle's wish that he accompany me, and at least he had more spirit than the lack-lustre Claude. Meanwhile the tea was not getting any warmer, so I lifted off the cosy and poured to suit them both; it didn't surprise me one bit to find that Claude preferred his very weak with no sugar.

Mrs. Early tapped at the door to inform me that fires had been lit in the bedrooms, and was the luggage to be taken up?

"Please. Have you seen Master Toby?"

"He's in the kitchen with us, miss."

"Would you have him join me in here? And we will have supper in the dining-room at seven, if that is not too inconvenient?"

"No trouble at all, miss. I'll have hot water sent up to the gentlemen's rooms a half-hour before."

In came Toby a couple of minutes later, obviously having been taken in hand by Mrs. Early, for his hands and face were clean and his hair combed.

"Gentlemen, I would like you to meet Toby, my ward. He will be accompanying us on our travels. Toby, the gentleman on my right is Mr. Cumberbatch from the solicitor's office, the other—"

"But I know's him!" cried Toby, pointing at Danny Duveen. "He came round my ma's a couple of times, asking all sorts of questions 'bout you! He's just a snooper, miss!"

"And your ma sent me away with a flea in my ear, didn't she Toby me boy? Or rather a soapy fist round my head . . ."

"Only after you kicked over a bucket of lye!"

" 'Twas an accident, me boy, a pure accident! Tripped up over the damn' thing, didn't I? Could hardly see a hand in front of my face, down in that steam-filled basement you call a laundry—"

"Mr. Duveen! Toby! That'll do . . . And my remarks about swearing to Mr. Cumberbatch apply equally to you, Sir! Is that understood?"

"Slip of the tongue, Miss Lee, slip of the tongue . . . Won't happen again, I assure you!"

Now why was I so certain that it would?

Supper was an uncomfortable affair. In spite of the fire the room was chilly through lack of use, and although I was used to correct table manners, it was obvious my two guests were not, and their sloppiness affected Toby. Not only was he overawed with the formality of the room, the best china and cutlery, the attempts at polite conversation, he was also thrown by the fact that both men picked up their chicken bones and chewed them, quite contrary to the instructions I had given him only a day or two since, that one only picks up the bones of game-birds.

As a consequence of all this he managed to slurp his soup in one of the many silences, spilled his gravy on the cloth as he was pouring it, one of his roast potatoes shot across the table and onto the floor and he ate it instead of leaving it, he forgot and tried to eat his peas off his knife, so that by the time we came to the tapioca pudding he was too disheartened to choose five of the stewed plums to go with it, to make sure he was the "Rich Man," living in a mansion this year and clad in silks although that game he had always enjoyed working out.

Not that the conduct of the other two was any better. Claude's manners showed some promise, although using his cheese knife to pare his nails was an excruciating sight and he drank his wine in great gulps as though it were water or ale. Danny insisted on second helpings, and left half of them; he kept his elbows on the table and his cutlery at either side of the plate and talked with his mouth full. They both belched.

At the end of the meal I rose to my feet and surveyed the debris.

"Right, gentlemen! Pigs usually eat from troughs, but I will be lenient and elevate you to the kitchen from now on! I cannot have you setting my ward a bad example. I will ask Mrs. Early now to serve you tea or coffee in the morning-room, and will expect you for breakfast—in the kitchen—between eight-thirty and nine. Good night. Come, Toby!"

And I swept out leaving them looking as though lightning had struck.

The following morning Toby and I enjoyed our breakfast of porridge, bacon and eggs, toast and marmalade in peace and warmth. Afterwards we went up to the study and I taught him a little more about the maps we would use, and he helped me with the tracing. I had asked Mrs. Early to light a fire in the morning-room and left a message for Claude and Danny that I would meet them there at eleven for coffee. I learned later that Claude turned up for cold porridge at nine-forty-five, and Danny didn't appear at all.

At eleven-fifteen I was still waiting for them to appear, seething inside, but when they eventually arrived I saw at once what had held them up. They were unshaven, apologetic and obviously under the influence. Either one or both had bottles in their rooms.

I took the cold coffee back to the kitchen, ordered some more, extra strong, and left Mrs. Early with a special directive. The coffee sobered them up a little, but as I tried to explain our expedition, even showing them some maps, I might as well have been talking to my five-year-olds at the School. At last I gave up, instructing them both to take a walk to the village and back to "freshen up" (though I didn't mention the fact that I knew they had hangovers) and instructed them to return in time for luncheon.

This was a big mistake.

Neither of them turned up for the meal, and it was growing dark by the time they staggered up the drive, full of song and strong ale. It was no use reprimanding them, they were past it, so I asked Mr. Early to "escort" them up to their rooms, supperless, making sure there were chamberpots under their beds. He was to call them at seven-thirty in the morning, informing them that there was plenty of hot water for bathing and shaving in the bathroom, and that they were expected to be down for breakfast at eight-thirty prompt.

That morning we all breakfasted together. A couple of pale, shaky, but clean-shaven young men spooned down their porridge with little enthusiasm but the kedgeree went down better and by the time they reached the toast and the second pot of tea was on the table, they were at least communicating, even if it was only "pass the butter/any more toast/where's the sugar/another cup of tea" type of speech.

After that it was a lot easier as they apparently had very little spare cash left, and the stores of liquor they had brought with them rapidly diminished. The instruction I had given Mrs. Early on that first morning was to examine their luggage—snooping perhaps, but I was a young woman on my own, charged with leading an expedition with two unknown men as my escorts, and no chaperone. So it was up to me to find out as much as I could about my erstwhile companions before we started.

It appeared that Claude's luggage, apart from a couple of bottles of sweet sherry, was of the conventional sort—well-worn but clean and mended underwear and a couple of rather threadbare suits. He obviously was a mother's boy, because his pocket-handkerchiefs were embroidered in blue with his initials, a jar of menthol and eucalyptus cream and another of corn-cure were wrapped in tissue, there were lavender sachets and a silver-framed photograph of a beaky-nosed matron, the spit of her son. The travelling clothes the solicitors had provided were adequate, though when I checked them later with him, it was obvious he needed stronger boots and a travelling cape.

Danny Duveen's luggage, such as it was, was a different matter altogether. While Claude's clothes and effects were in a battered but well-polished suitcase, Danny only possessed a crumpled cardboard case which, according to Mrs. Early, contained the sum total of six whisky bottles, three empty, three full, two dirty shirts and some unmentionables, also filthy, two electro-plated hip-flasks (empty), a packet of what appeared to be recommendations for jobs, all in the same hand, two marked decks of cards and another envelope of what Mrs. Early described as Dirty Photographs in capital letters and a reddened face. (For the record I examined these later and can only report that I had a good laugh.)

What Mrs. Early appeared to be most shocked about in Danny's luggage was not the dirt or the photographs, but the lack of nightshirts: apparently it was a crime above all others not to go to bed decently clad. I forebore to tell her that I had done just the same in those stuffy August nights in London when the only relief was to cast everything off and open the window to one's nakedness.

So. Claude was more or less provided for, apart from stronger boots and a cloak, but Danny had nothing, as far as I could see, and was probably a con-man, a gambler, fond of the bottle, had little use for hygiene, and was not above indulging his lower tastes with a little wishful thinking.

I discussed all this with Ky-Lin, who had met both Claude and Danny, via Toby's pocket, a couple of times. He was the one who advised me to treat them as a couple of recalcitrant schoolboys who wouldn't learn their tables, and now advised me to go through what remained of my uncle's clothes for Danny, remarking that he was afraid I would still have to use some of my own money to kit them out.

"Of course," he added helpfully, "if that Irish fellow decides he doesn't want to go, then we can discount him, quite legally, I believe."

No chance.

I had agreed with Claude to furnish him with stouter boots and a cloak and, I must say, he was properly grateful, but when it came to Danny . . .

First of all I asked why he had not come properly equipped and got the sort of answer I expected: no list and no money. "Then what happened to the moneys supplied to you by the solicitors?"

"Oh, that . . . Well now to tell you the truth I thought those were to sort of set me on me way. Pay off the odd debt or two, you know . . ."

"Instead of which you got drunk as a skunk and gambled the rest away," I said equably.

"How did you—? Oh, come on now, Miss Lee. Darlin' girl, a lad has got to have his bit of fun before going on a life or death expedition, now doesn't he?"

"Not with somebody else's money," I said firmly. "And I am not your 'darling girl': please remember that. And may I ask where your ordinary clothes are? Shirts, suits, shoes?"

He spread his arms wide, with what he hoped was a disarming grin. "In rags or in hock, truth to tell!"

"That's better. I prefer the truth. Now, if my uncle hadn't considered you capable of undertaking this journey . . . You can, of course, back out if you wish to, and no hard feelings?"

He looked horrified. "Oh, no, I'm going with you! Otherwise I don't get—"

"You don't get what, exactly?"

"The fifty quid the solicitors said your uncle promised."

So that was it. Right, Mr. Duveen would get just as much as he deserved and no more. I went through my uncle's belongings once again and found that he and Danny were of a size—had that been an added attraction I wondered—and that I could provide Danny with nightshirts, combinations, shirts, jackets, socks, caps, gloves and even shoes which needed no further alteration and which, luckily, Mrs. Early had not yet passed on. There was even a little-used pair of walking boots. So, in the end, all he would need was a travelling-cloak and, like Claude, a haversack and blanket. I heaved a sigh of relief.

Having sent off for the last of our requirements, I settled back for a few days, with Ky-Lin's help, trying to make our guests better prepared for the journey. By now they were what I would call "house-trained"—in other words they were bathed, shaven, appeared on time for meals, were polite and (more or less) tidy. That they were bored was quite obvious. Neither of them were readers or walkers or naturalists and the idea of helping Mr. Early in the garden was anathema to their town souls. There was no doubt they missed the metropolis. Most of the time they spent playing cards, probably with Danny's marked decks, so Ky-Lin and I decided a little further education was necessary.

One morning after breakfast I brought them up to the study, for a lesson in map-reading.

Their reaction was unexpected.

"What do we need to look at maps for?" said Claude, covering his mouth at the last minute over a tremendous yawn.

"So as you can find your way should we get lost on the way," said Toby, unfortunately catching the yawn and repeating it.

"Why then should we get lost?" asked Danny. "Sure the way is plain enough, is it not?"

I had a feeling of misgiving.

"Tell me," I said. "What have you two been told about the journey?"

Claude was the first to answer. "Mr. Swallow told me that you were taking one of your uncle's artifacts back to where it came from, that you were given a year to do it in, and that I was to accompany you to make sure the conditions were fulfilled."

"Did he tell you where we were going?"

He shook his head. My heart sank.

"And you?" I asked, turning to Danny.

"The solicitors said that I would get fifty pounds for acting as an escort while you went on a journey for your dead uncle."

"Do *you* know where we are going?"

"No, but at least it'll be better than here . . ."

I threw up my hands in despair and even Toby looked disbelieving.

"Mean to say as you two gents don't know we're walking to Chiney and back with a dragon's egg and a—" He clapped his hand over his mouth just in time; I had warned him not to mention Ky-Lin.

"Chiney?"

"I believe the boy means China, Claude me lad," said Danny. "Full of little yellow men."

"But isn't that a long way away?"

"Nearer than the other side of the moon," said Danny. "And they've probably got a decent rail service most of the way."

"I hope it's not too hot," said Claude. "I always get hay-fever in the summer."

"It's the thought of the rice that's putting me off right now. I never fancied rice pudding, even with a dollop of me mam's gooseberry jam . . ."

"Can't you send it by post?"

I decided it was time to intervene, but before I could open my mouth Toby took over.

"Let me, miss. Reckon I could put it straight and quicker." And he did. He explained as you would to under-fives about my uncle's will, got the original manuscript from the cabinet and briefed them on Summer's journey and ended by saying that my uncle believed the Eg, which he also produced, belonged to the dragons. He ended by dashing Danny's hopes of a rail service and Claude's of using the post, explaining to the latter that a dragon's egg was far too precious to entrust to a postman, and anyway they probably didn't have them in China.

I couldn't have put it better myself.

They both looked rather white when Toby had finished, though Claude tried a last-ditch stand.

"But there aren't any such things as dragons," he said. "We all know that!"

"This is what we have all been taught," I said. "Dragons don't exist and never did. Like fairies, elves, gnomes, brownies, goblins, trolls, ogres, giants, witches and wizards. If so, why are there so many legends, myths, folk-tales? I admit that I now have an open mind, and an open mind, gentlemen, is what you will need if you are to journey with us!"

"We've come all this way to—to take a lump of stone to China? Was your uncle out of his senses?"

"I don't believe so, Mr. Duveen. As I said, I have an open mind, but certain happenings, which I am not at liberty to discuss, have convinced me that there is more to this 'lump of stone' than we imagine. Besides I am bound to this journey now, else I renounce all hope of inheriting Hightop Hall. So you see, I have a vested interest." Perhaps that would appeal to his mercenary instincts.

It did. "Would there be any treasure at the end of all this? If you're talking about legends, then they all had it that dragons were hoarders of fabulous jewels . . ."

"I doubt it," I said. "I think our rewards will be less substantial. If we succeed, I shall inherit this place; Toby will have had the adventure he's always wanted; for you, Mr. Cumberbatch, this is just part of your job, but it should prove more interesting than sitting behind a desk all day; Mr. Duveen, it means you will be free of debt for the time it takes to get there and back. That should be some incentive." I looked round at them all. "Now, shall we have a look at the maps?"

The next two weeks were pretty hectic. Eventually everything I had ordered came through, including two lengths of lightweight rope, a compass—"In case I'm not at hand all the time," said Ky-Lin—containers for salt, tea, sugar and water and tin plates, mugs and cutlery. It all sounded dreadfully Spartan and rather intimidating.

"Are you sure we hadn't better take a frying-pan and a stew-pot?" I said to Ky-Lin, intending frivolity, but he answered me seriously enough.

"I don't believe we shall need those, initially at least. And in order not to weigh us down too much, I suggest we buy them on the way."

Instead of heavy leather suitcases I had ordered two wicker ones, lined with oiled silk against the rain. They were much lighter, and it was agreed that Claude and Danny would share one, Toby and I the other, keeping items to a minimum, which meant underwear and spare shirts and sweaters, and any personal items we couldn't do without. Toby and I were easy, but the other two quarrelled until the day we left over what they considered essential.

As for the haversacks, it was agreed that Toby would carry the Eg, wrapped as usual in my shawl, and extra towels and toiletries; the men would take the ropes, plus the crockery and cutlery, and I would carry the maps, papers, sewing things and a small pair of binoculars. We also carried a blanket each. I was encumbered with a moneybelt, which I had no intention of handing over to either of the two men, although it was heavy, once I had changed the money into smaller coin.

Strangely enough getting all the paperwork through had been the most difficult. To get passports and all the requisite permissions from the embassies in London had proved frustrating. France, Germany and Bavaria were easy enough, and Russia came through at the last moment, but from China we heard nothing.

The date was agreed, we booked ahead on the overnight ferry to Holland and, through the same firm, a trip by ferry on the first stage of our journey up the Rhine. Mrs. Early packed whatever she could that would last us through at least part of our journey: salt, tea, sugar, dried fruits, shelled nuts, apples, long-lasting fruitcake and parkin, pickled eggs, a tin of cocoa, Liebig's extract of meat, packets of pepper, a jar of ready-mixed mustard, home-made chutney and pickles and a well-smoked ham. By the time these had been distributed between our haversacks, we were all visibly sagging.

That was not all—for the first two days of the journey the housekeeper had made sandwiches, pies, tarts, cakes, buns and biscuits, and included two large flagons of lemonade and barley water, which meant we had to burden ourselves with a huge hamper as well, but at least it would save money.

Hiring a small carriage from the village we made good time to catch the four-fifteen slow train to the coast, boarded the ferry and settled down on deck later in the evening. Leaning on the rail, I looked back at the lights of the coast and the still-shining blur that I took to be the white cliffs of Dover, a popular landmark.

It wasn't a cold night, nor was there much sea running, yet I had been shivering. I found it difficult to believe that we were really on our way and that here I was taking a trip by sea for the first time.

Toby joined me, and Ky-Lin leapt from one of his pockets to stand on the rail between us.

"Not superstitious are you, miss?"

"Don't think so . . . Why?"

" 'Cos tonight's All Hallows' Eve—Samain, they used to call it."

"A good omen," interrupted Ky-Lin. "That was the night Summer set off on her travels, so she told me . . ."

But in spite of his optimism, I found myself shivering again.

Book II

"Over the hills and far away."
—John Gay

15

Slow, Slow, Quick-quick Slow

I threw my corsets into the upper reaches of the Rhine, and watched them bob up and down in our wake, their strings trailing behind like the tentacles of an octopus.

It was strange to feel a cotton shift next to my skin instead of thinly covered whalebone, even stranger to know I could wriggle about without restriction. I had worn stays or corsets ever since I could remember— probably five or six years old—and the only relief had been at night when I could curl up in my nightdress and rub away the marks left on my skin. But over the years I had grown so used to lacing myself up each morning that it had become as automatic as brushing one's hair or teeth.

I shivered a little—not from cold, for I had plenty of layers of wool on underneath—but from my daring. No lady went around without her corsets. I wondered if that had led to the term a "loose woman."

Toby joined me at the rail, handing me a cup of coffee and a hunk of garlic sausage on rye bread. The corsets were still in sight.

"Cor! Me mam wears them!"

"Those. . . ."

"Those, then. Bet they was—"

"Were."

"Were uncomfortable. Pinchy. Me mam was always getting bits of her stummick stuck in the laces . . ."

"Yes, well . . ." I shivered again.

"You chilly, miss? Can't've been that warm . . ."

"No, they weren't. Just feels strange without them."

"Better, I hopes, seein' as they's gone forever. Less you wants to swim for 'em that is."

I gave up trying to correct him. Usually he was very good, but if something unusual happened he tended to slip back into Cockney.

"No, no swimming . . ." I wouldn't have lasted two minutes in that water anyway. Thin sheets of ice broke off against the sides of the string of slow-moving barges as we chugged up the narrowing river, soon to reach the limit of navigable waterway.

It was now mid-December, and we had had a mixed journey. We had slipped easily through Holland, watching the windmills with their slow-moving sails, imagining the flat fields blossoming with tulips in the spring and admiring the ingenious Dutch in their efforts to keep the ever encroaching North Sea at bay. Our transport had been comfortable, with good food and clean linen, but unfortunately that part ended at Koblenz. Apparently the ferry ran no farther at this time of year, a fact that the firm that booked us had omitted to mention.

We complained and protested (through Ky-Lin) that we had paid to be carried farther, but the captain just shrugged his shoulders and referred us to our tickets which only specified transport up the river, "according to the usual rules and regulations." So we would have to find something a lot cheaper, to make up for the money we had lost. Thus the barge we were on now.

We had switched from one mode of travel to another, as and when we could find it, but mostly by river transport, although a couple of times we went along the bank by wagon, cart or stage, rather than waste time waiting for a barge or ferry. The trouble was, it was all too slow for our purpose. True, there was time to admire the wonderful scenery and marvel at the fairy-tale castle perched impossibly high on the cliffs above the river, but I was conscious all the time of how swiftly time was passing.

"We take to the road tomorrow," said Ky-Lin, appearing from my pocket. "Then we should travel faster. Don't give up yet!"

He seemed to be able to read my thoughts, was always encouraging and had been invaluable in translating our wants; he would perch on my shoulder, hidden by scarf, and make my requests in my own voice whispering the reply so only I could hear it! All I had to do was pretend I was talking and try to synchronise my actions. Magic as good as I had ever seen.

Both Claude and Danny, knowing nothing of Ky-Lin, were amazed at my linguistic prowess. Although I was still "Miss," we were now on Christian-name terms. This had come about after we had crossed the English Channel for they had both been as sick as dogs in spite of the calm sea, and all pretence of male superiority went overboard together with their suppers, and "Miss Lee" had disappeared in "Please help me, Miss Sophy!" and "Mr. Cumberbath" in "Shut up, Claude, it's not as bad as that!" and "Mr. Duveen" became "Serves you right for making such a pig of yourself, Danny!"

"How will we travel?" I asked Ky-Lin.

"Well, there will be some public transport—coaches and the odd railway—but I think it might be better to hire a coach partways."

"But surely that will cost the earth!"

"Not necessarily. Much more convenient and we can travel by a more direct route; there are plenty of posting-houses between here and the Danube, and that is our next target."

It started to snow, great blobs whirling out of the grey sky, and we slipped and skidded on the icy deck as we made our way to our cabins. Claude and Danny were in the saloon, a polite term for the place where we ate as well. They were playing cards, Danny wrapped up to the eye-balls in coat, cloak, scarves and mufflers, while Claude, who seemed to have developed a permanent sniff and a drip on the end of his nose, was complaining bitterly about Danny's winning streak. I suspected that the latter cheated, but there was no way of finding out.

We retired to my cabin, where I continued as best I could with Toby's education, with Ky-Lin's help. He knew more about everything than I did, anyway.

The following day we disembarked at a small town called Schwarz-berg, which Ky-Lin said meant Blackhill, after the mountain behind; al-though it belied its name, being now covered with last night's snow. We visited all the livery stables, but found there was no private transport to be hired, so we repaired to an inn by the quay for luncheon, and to discuss our next move.

Toby was gazing out the window at the barge unloading when he suddenly made a rather crude exclamation, which I didn't bother to try and understand, but obviously he had been struck with some idea.

"Look out there, folks: what do you see?"

"Barges unloading," said Claude, wiping his nose for the umpteenth time. "Why?"

"Yes, but what's waiting to be loaded up?"

Danny craned his neck. "Looks like logs of wood to me . . ."

"Exactly!" Toby was obviously bursting to impart his theory. "And what did we bring on the way up?"

"Sugar, dried fruit, flour, toys, barrels of wine, hunting rifles and ammunition, thick eiderdowns . . ." I was beginning to see which way his mind was working.

"Exactly," he said again. "Don't you see? They brings up what they needs up here, stuff they can't make themselves, and vikky-verky—sends back their wood in exchange."

"So?"

Toby was still patient. "So, Master Claude, just where does all that stuff from the barge go to?"

"Sure it goes into the shops here, I suppose." said Danny.

"Place ain't big enough. And what about all those parcels and packages they was carrying?" I let him tell it his own way, though by now I was smiling.

"There must be lots an' lots of small towns and villages round here what wants the goods, and someone got to take them there, and that is why we couldn't hire no transport!" He was flushed and bright-eyed. "So all we've got to do is find a carrier who's going our way and beg a lift!"

After that it was easy. Ky-Lin and I found a man who was taking a covered wagon to the next village on our way, staying overnight with his brother, then travelling on to the next town, and was glad of our company, promising to find us overnight accommodation. When we attempted to pay him for his troubles later, he refused, adding: "The more the people, the fewer the wolves," which Ky-Lin and I didn't bother telling the others, not sure whether the wolves he referred to were human or lupine. I did notice, however, that he carried a loaded rifle by the driver's seat. What he did accept, however was the offer of Mrs. Early's empty food hamper, which we still carried with us, explaining that it would be useful for carrying his racing pigeons.

And so it went on. We accepted lifts when we could, used public transport when there was any, hired the occasional chaise and were sometimes holed up for days by bad weather, spending Christmas in a cheery little inn in a forest and stuffing ourselves silly with roast goose, sausages, pork and masses of potatoes: roast, boiled, baked, grated and fried, or mashed. We also ate vast quantities of cabbage, fermented with white wine, which they called "Sauerkraut," and of course there were trays of gooey cakes, sweet biscuits and candies. There was also a tree, decorated with pretty bows, a custom the Hanoverian-born Prince Albert, the late husband of our dear Queen, had apparently introduced to England.

By the middle of February we were well on our way, the snows had begun to melt, the going was much easier and traffic on the roads more frequent. I was still worried about the money situation, but our spending had slowed down somewhat. We were all in good health—thank God!—although Claude still nursed his perpetual sniffle. Danny still sneaked off for the occasional drink—I had to give them a little pocket-money for their regular needs, but while Toby saved his and Claude spent his on luridly coloured picture-postcards to send home to his mother or on throat-lozenges, Danny spent his on strong beer or spirits.

Nevertheless, both men were improving: Claude was becoming less stuffy and staid, and Danny could be the life and soul of the party, if he chose. Toby was growing and filling out by the day, making a real bonny lad, and every day to him was a new discovery.

In February we reached Bavaria and the upper reaches of the Danube, and with the better weather we made good progress from Neuburg to Ingolstadt, Ingolstadt to Regensburg, then Straubing, Deggendorf and Passau. In March we crossed the border into Austria and really felt spring had arrived. If Bavaria had been charming, Austria was even better. The people were warm and welcoming, indulging in music at the least excuse; pipes, flutes, fiddles, trumpets and drums all sounded from one house to another, and even the school-children carried their recorders to school.

We spent three days in Linz, due to the unwelcome return of late snows, but we took the opportunity to repair our wardrobes: stockings and summer underwear for me, thinner shirts and socks for the men and Toby. As the touring season had now begun, we decided to take one of the tourist boats as far as Vienna, which we had heard was the most beautiful city in Europe.

A tour of the city was included in our tickets, although it passed so swiftly it seemed we were whirled past the fine buildings and statues without a chance to get more than a glimpse, but we did also get tickets to a concert in the evening, dominated by the divine waltzes of the brothers Strauss. Although the favourite was apparently the "Blue Danube"—a misnomer if ever I heard one: it was a sort of brownish-grey—my favourite was the "Emperor" with its full, sweeping tones and at times I could almost imagine being clad in silks and being borne around a vast ballroom in the arms of one of the handsome, uniformed officers who seemed to twirl their moustachios on every street-corner . . .

Their uniforms were so figure-hugging, the girls at boarding-school would have gone into swoons over them—

For almost the first time in my life I felt longings of a strange kind, a sort of yearning to be held tight in masculine arms; I wondered if it had anything to do with throwing away my corsets. Did I miss their tight restrictions, or was it more the general looseness of body bringing on a looseness of the emotions?

I subdued these feelings fiercely.

We left Vienna at the beginning of April, and had now been travelling for over five months. I asked Ky-Lin how much farther we had to go. "Are we halfway yet?"

"Well . . . Not exactly."

"But we've been travelling for ages! If we are to get there in time—"

"We will, we will. Up until now we have been travelling relatively slowly because of the terrain. Once we get to the steppes—"

"The what? The stairs?"

"Steppes. With two P's and an extra E. Now we have to get to the mouth of the Danube—perhaps another couple of weeks—then across the Black and Aral Seas—"

"You never told me all that!"

"You saw the maps."

"But—but—"

"You did."

I was silent for a moment. "It—it all looked—sort of smaller . . ."

"Maps usually do."

"But you're sure we're on course?"

"Sure. Sure as I can be . . ."

And with that I had to be satisfied.

Soon after we left Vienna we took to the roads again, traffic being faster and cheaper. We even took advantage of the infrequent railways, although the farther east we travelled, the more primitive they became, with frequent stops and delays, and with the warmer weather they could be stiflingly hot, and the wooden bench seats were exceedingly uncomfortable. If one tried to open the windows to get some air, they either wouldn't open or one got covered in smuts, most of the engines being wood- instead of coal-fired.

We passed through parts of Hungary, Slovakia, Croatia, Romania and Bulgaria with little time to absorb or enjoy the differences in each. The plains of Hungary and Croatia, mountains and forests of Slovakia,

Transylvania and Walachia blurred into one another, the only distinctions being the differences of language which I was not clever enough to distinguish between, though Toby apparently could, according to Ky-Lin.

"The boy has a musical ear, and pace intonation and the particular lilt of language means much to those so gifted."

"What language did Summer speak?" I asked on impulse.

He considered for a moment. "Mostly Norman-French, and some Market-Latin, which was of course widely accepted in the west. I helped her with the Oriental languages of course, and she talked to the animals through the Ring which you now wear."

Now that he had answered one question about a person he normally seemed reluctant to discuss, perhaps he would satisfy another. "What was she like?"

"She was a very brave, considerate young woman. Over-impulsive, perhaps, but she was full of ideas, loyal and caring."

I had really wanted to know what she looked like: all females are curious about their predecessors or rivals. "Was she beautiful?"

He wrinkled up his nose, curled and uncurled his antennae. "Beautiful? My Master taught us that all Life was beautiful, from the leaf on the tree to the tooth of a shark. But if you ask me about the length of a nose, the shape of a mouth, the formation of one figure as set against another member of the human race, then I cannot tell you. Could you tell me that one ant is more 'beautiful' than another? No. Another ant is the only one who would know. I am a Ky-Lin, and things like this do not concern us."

He must have seen the disappointment on my face, because he added: "She was about three inches shorter than you"—I was five feet six inches—"but then people were shorter in those days. Her hair was much lighter, and her eyes much bluer and a different shape, too. The formation of your bodies was similar." He thought for a moment. "And she smiled more often than you do."

Was I really that morose? Still, what did I have to smile about . . . Just to please Ky-Lin I essayed a grin, more a stretching of the mouth over the teeth. "That better?"

He shook his head sadly.

16

The Suitor

If the so-called Blue Danube was brown, then the Black Sea was definitely blue; dark, deep blue—my paint-box would have called it Prussian. As we stood on the dockside waiting for the ferry to start loading, it was sparkling like a jewel. The sky was clear, except for some small, fluffy clouds, the May sun was warm, and we were all in good spirits. Once we had crossed this sea we should embark into the real unknown. The rest of the journey, apart from a short journey up the Don, would be overland.

The gangplank was lowered and we climbed aboard with the other passengers. Some of them had brought their own food and would sleep on deck, as we had done when we crossed the English Channel, but the cost of a cabin was outweighed by the extra comfort. Or so we thought . . .

We had booked two doubles, Toby and I to share one, the men the other, but when we located them they were far from ideal. They held two, short, tiered bunks, both tiny and hard, with one thin blanket; there was also a hook for hanging clothes, a hanging lantern and a deeply recessed wash-basin and jug, which looked faintly ominous. A small porthole gave a restricted view, and Toby and I found it difficult to squeeze past each other in the confined space. In the end the one who wasn't washing, changing or looking out of the porthole had to tuck their feet up on one of the bunks.

It was complicated by the fact that there was no room for our haversacks or suitcases, which had to be stored in the hold, so everything we would need for the two days of sailing had to be extracted and stowed away somewhere. The Eg we kept with us, plus night wear, washing-things and our cloaks, but when we went to check on Danny and Claude we found the latter complaining that there was no room for his legs and Danny swearing at his clothes hook, which had just fallen off the wall. On every available space on the ferry were printed, on yellowed, faded paper, in English, French, German and Russian the Rules and Regulations. Breakfast, luncheon and supper would be served in the dining-saloon at—and there was then a list of "bells," which repeated ringing was apparently the way sailors measured their time. Each meal was the equivalent of two shillings per head. No-one was allowed in the engine-room or on the bridge, otherwise passengers were allowed the run of the ship. Canvas chairs were available for those who wished to sit out on deck. In inclement weather all would be expected to remain below, deck-passengers in the saloon. In the case of several blasts from the ship's sirens, we were all to assemble on deck, prepared to board one of the two lifeboats.

From the elevation of the deck we looked out at the calm blue sea, the mountains in the distance, and wondered what all the fuss was about. The weather seemed set fair, the air was balmy, our fellow-passengers seemed cheerful enough and the sailors unconcerned. Rough weather, alarm signals and life-boats could safely be ignored, I reckoned.

"I do hope it won't be choppy," said Claude apprehensively.

"Of course it won't! The sea's like a mill-pond."

"All right for you, Sophy. You didn't get sick last time." The "Miss" had finally disappeared. I didn't mind.

"And you won't this time," I comforted him. "It's all in the mind, you know: *think* sick and you'll *be* sick."

"Up and down, up and down, up and down," intoned Danny mischievously, suiting actions to the words. "Up and down, and—"

"Shut *up!*" said Claude, clutching his stomach.

"Give over, Danny!" I said. "Or you'll catch yourself with your own shenanigans."

"Just listen to the girl! And isn't she catching on to the Irish just like crabs to a piece of bacon rind!" The very mention of food made Claude look anxious again, as Danny knew it would. "Now I remember when I was a wee one, and I had a stomach upset, Mam used to make me sick by tying a piece of bacon rind to a length of string and—"

"Come on Claude," I said firmly. "You can walk me round the deck." I glanced back to where Danny was standing with a huge grin on his face. "Don't forget you will be sharing a very small cabin, and the only toilet is way down the corridor, in case Claude feels . . . un-well."

The smile was wiped off his face as if it had been sponged.

The meals were adequate, if uninteresting, consisting mainly of cold cuts, pickles, hard-boiled eggs, black bread and preserves, with weak coffee. On that first day the steamer chugged across a smooth sea, and gradually the coastline receded behind us. Up on deck the engines didn't sound too bad, mainly a sort of throbbing beneath one's feet, but both in the dining-saloon and more markedly in the cabins the constant clatter and thrust of the machines could give the more sensitive a racking head-ache. Of course we all knew it was only for two nights, but what with the noise and heat below decks and the inconvenience of the tiny cabins by the following morning we were all short-tempered, and the thought of another night in the same conditions was daunting.

At least no-one had been sick . . .

We spent most of the day on deck, enjoying the warmth and sea-breezes. Now at the mid-point of our voyage, there was no sight of land, except for the occasional smudge of smoke, one of which heralded the crossing of the ferry's sister-ship to port of us. There were a couple of small fishing boats in the distance, but the real excitement of the day was provided by the passengers crowding to the rail to watch some great fishes diving and surfacing again alongside, like giant needles tacking the hems of the water. There were eight or nine of them, it was difficult to count, as their black backs gleamed for only a moment before they plunged back down again.

"What are they?" asked Toby excitedly, leaning over the rail so far I felt constrained to grab his belt.

One of the passengers, a well-dressed man with a fair moustache, answered his question, in rather drawly English.

"Why, they are dolphins, my boy, and they are mammals, not fish. They are sociable creatures, and often follow ships in and out of harbour, no-one is quite sure why."

"I wouldn't have expected them here," I said without thinking, re-alising too late that the gentleman might think me too forward for joining in the conversation without an introduction. "I thought they lived in warmer seas. It must be very cold here in winter."

"Oh, in winter they go back to the Mediterranean," said the gen-tleman, raising his hat politely. "The Black Sea isn't landlocked, unlike the Caspian. To the south it flows out near Constantinople." He bowed.

"May I introduce myself? Archie McCall at your service, on leave from my regiment." He didn't say which one. "Just an idle tourist, I'm afraid."

He looked at me interrogatively and although I had no wish to involve us with a stranger, it would have been bad manners not to reciprocate.

"Miss Lee, and my—my brother, Tobias."

He smiled, smoothing his moustache. "On holiday, like myself?"

I opened my mouth to agree, but Toby forestalled me.

"Oh, no," he said seriously. He was still watching the dolphins, but I could see the mischievous look on his face. "We're on a sort of pilgrimage."

"Pilgrimage?"

"Yes. We're going to China with a Buddhist to look for dragons!" And with that he turned and grabbed my hand. "C'mon sister dear, let's see if there are any dolphins on the starboard side!" But once out of earshot of the bemused Mr. McCall, he turned on me. "What are you always telling me? Don't never—"

"Ever . . ."

"Don't ever talk to strangers! That's what you've always said, and what are you doin'? Chattin' up the first likely gent who eyes you up!"

"I wasn't 'chatting up' anyone!" I was amazed at his vehemence. "It was you he was talking to, about the dolphins."

"Just an excuse, *sister* dear! He's been following you around looking for a chance ever since we came on board. Last night at supper he was swooning over every mouthful you took."

I was surprised. "I never noticed . . ."

"You was too busy gobbling that cabbage-stuff."

"Toby! I don't gobble!"

"Well, perhaps not. But you know what I mean."

"No, I do *not!* I do not invite attentions from anyone, male or female, and I never have . . ."

And this was entirely true. Not that there had been any males at boarding-school, and when I had come to London to teach I was just another shabby little school-marm who spent nine hours a day in the class-room and the rest either in her lodgings or else in decorous visits to an art gallery, concert or museum, and who would look twice at such? As far as being out alone in the metropolis, I never left the school in the dark without Toby's escort, to discourage unwelcome attentions. In the summer I kept to the more populous ways and scurried along with my head down, finding it easy to blend in with my surroundings like the blandest of wallpaper. That was why Miss Moffat's strange behaviour had so upset me.

"Well, this gent's been following us round all day. And he's got his eye on you."

"You're wrong, Toby—"

"No, I ain't! He's comin' over here now . . . You just leave him alone. He's bad news. Don't encourage him. Don't even pass the time of day . . ."

But I had had enough. I wasn't going to let a child—and that was all Toby was, after all—dictate to me whom I should or shouldn't talk to. I was a responsible adult and could trust my own judgment to choose my own acquaintances. Besides, after the exclusive company of Claude, Danny and Toby, it would be nice to hold a conversation with somebody different. And if he proved to be a bore, then we were reaching our destination tomorrow, and that would be the last I should see of him.

After all, I was free to do with my life as I wished, once this expedition was over. I could marry a tramp, live in sin with an artist in a Parisian attic, join a harem, live as a gipsy, settle down to a respectable spinsterhood. Freedom of choice was an intoxicating thought, so when Mr. McCall approached me again I accepted the offer of his arm for a turn about the deck, ignoring Toby's furious scowls.

He was an agreeable companion, telling me of his recent trip to Australia, where he had studied closely the strange marsupials—kangaroo, koala, and wallaby that I had seen pictures of, but never come across even in a zoo. He also spoke of the Aborigines, the primitive natives of that continent, but I was rather taken aback by his attitude towards them, dismissing them as feckless, dirty and backward, fit only to be driven away into the bush.

"But surely those people, who were there before the settlers arrived, should be given the consideration they deserve?" I asked rather more warmly than I should. "I myself contribute regularly to the Mission Society, and our members believe most strongly that these children of God—and this includes the native Indians of North America and the Negroes of Africa—should be treated like any other member of the human race. After all, it is only ignorance that restricts them from becoming useful members of society, and ignorance can be cured by education."

"Your sentiments do you credit, Miss Lee!" he declared. "I am amazed that such a pretty and demure young lady should be so emancipated! You are to be congratulated on your humane outlook."

I blushed with pleasure. It was comforting that such a widely travelled gentleman should be willing to listen to my views. I felt quite exhilarated, and glanced up at him with gratitude, being reminded, unfortunately, of Red Riding Hood, for his teeth, when he smiled, were rather large . . . But he *had* called me pretty.

"I am so glad to have made your acquaintance, Miss Lee. It is rare to meet someone who is both charming and erudite."

If possible, my blushes grew even deeper, but I averted my gaze, and hoped my bonnet hid the most tell-tale of them.

"You are too kind, sir. Any erudition I have acquired is entirely due to my profession as a schoolteacher, I am sure."

"A school-marm? I might have guessed." I glanced up at his face, fearing disappointment or ridicule, but it was perfectly bland. "But I cannot guess what such a talented young lady is doing so far from home and during term-time too . . . ?"

It was a clear invitation to declare my true mission, but I side-stepped his enquiry with a noncommittal answer.

"Like yourself, Mr. McCall, I am taking some leave."

"With your brother? I believe you have two other companions as well?"

"Mr. Cumberbatch and Mr. Duveen are escorting us, yes."

I was becoming a little annoyed by his questions, but as if sensing this he turned the conversation to other matters. At luncheon I found the attentive Mr. McCall on one side and a scowling and uncooperative Toby on the other, who constantly tried to monopolise the conversation, and when that didn't succeed, exhibited dreadful table manners, for which I had to reprimand him, thus gaining his objective of my attention.

Afterwards Mr. McCall commented on our relationship. "Your brother . . . He doesn't seem—quite in tune with you?"

How to answer this time? "He's . . . he's not exactly my brother. He's my ward, although we enjoy a brother/sister relationship."

"Ah," he nodded. "That explains a great deal. A different upbringing obviously. A special pupil, no doubt?"

I nodded too, and changed the subject. Time for a question on my part. "How long do you expect to be away from your regiment, sir? I do not think you mentioned the name?"

He looked at me and mentioned a town: Aldershot, which he could see meant nothing to me, and then a regiment, which meant even less. Shortly afterwards I excused myself to take a siesta, pleading a poor nights rest, and down below I found a furious Toby drumming his heels on the top bunk.

"I tol' you not to get too friendly with that—that—"

"That'll do! I don't want any of your back-street obscenities, nor do I want any criticism of my behaviour! I do what I please with my life, and I might remind you that you are only here on sufferance anyway!"

To my dismay the child that was still in Toby burst into tears and I moved at once to comfort and hug him, chastising myself for being so harsh and unfeeling. A quarter-hour later we were friends again, but he was still adamant in his dislike for Mr. McCall. We agreed to differ, especially as I reminded him that we docked tomorrow and would probably never see the man again.

"And now you must promise not to spoil the rest of the day with scowls and anti-social behaviour. Understood?"

He nodded, but I wasn't convinced. However he seemed to be as good as his word, going out of his way to be pleasant at supper-time and not making the usual objections when I sent him to have a good wash and bed at ten. As I left Mr. McCall put a hand on my arm.

"A little stroll around the deck later on? We can round off a pleasant acqaintanceship by watching the moon rise . . ."

I demurred. "Such behaviour is not possible on our short acquaintance, Mr. McCall—"

"Miss Lee, we are just ships that pass in the night . . ." Now where had I heard that before? "Why lose the chance to exchange a few pleasantries, an episode to press like a flower in the Book of Life?" He was certainly mixing his metaphors!

I'm afraid he took my quickly suppressed smile as encouragement.

"Come, Miss Lee—Sophy—have pity on a lonely bachelor who desires no more than a pleasant memory to carry back to his exclusively masculine and lonely life in barracks . . ."

At that moment, poised between yea and nay, I was rescued by Danny, who reminded me I had promised a hand of cards, so I had no chance to give Mr. McCall a definite answer. However, several hands into the game, I was surprised to learn that both Claude and Danny had noticed his attentions.

"Shouldn't pay too much attention to that chap," drawled the former, apropos of nothing in particular. "Not the right sort at all. . . . My trick, I believe?"

"Sure and begorra and you're right!" added Danny, studying his cards with a frown. "Wouldn't trust the beggar as far as I could throw him." He had been drinking again, and in consequence was losing. "He's a smooth-talking rogue, so he is!"

"It takes one to know one," I snapped. "My gamc!" and I threw down the three remaining trumps. "And now I am going to my cabin to read. Good night, *gentle*men!" and off I flounced indignantly. First Toby and then them! What right had they . . . If I had stopped to consider I might have realised that they were trying to shield me from any trouble, but I was beyond reasoning. The disadvantage to me lay in the fact that I had had to grow up too quickly, make decisions before I had the experience to judge their effect beforehand, and had mislaid something that was essential to a young woman in my position: feminine caution.

In the cabin Toby was apparently asleep on the top bunk, so I took off my bonnet, shawl and moneybelt, loosened my hair and lay down on the bunk, prepared to read another chapter of *Westward Ho!* but after awhile the lantern started swaying to and fro erratically and getting up to peer out of the open porthole, the glitter of waves from the navigation lights seemed to be rising and falling more energetically than earlier. Perhaps we were in for a storm.

I could have gone down the corridor to the bathroom and had a good wash, then tucked myself up, but I didn't feel sleepy. In fact I felt more wide awake than I had all day. I shouldn't have had that siesta earlier. Perhaps a turn on deck would settle me down; it would be nice to get a breath of fresh air.

Without trying to analyse my decision or make excuses I picked up my shawl, turned down the lamp and made for the door—

"Where are you going?"

"I thought you were asleep!" I said, nearly jumping out of my skin. "Just for a short stroll on deck, that's all."

"You're going to meet that man!"

"Of course I'm not! I have no arrangement to meet Mr. McCall. You should know me better than that."

I turned to the door again, but there was another voice.

"Be careful out there; the wind is rising and the deck could be slippery with spray."

"I'll be careful," I said. "Thank you, Ky-Lin."

I closed the door, but his voice came muffled through the panelling. "Remember the ring; remember what it tells you . . ."

Why the ring, I wondered, as I walked down the corridor and climbed the companionway to the deck, having to clutch at the rail as I did so. I peered in at the lounge: all was quiet, a late foursome of cards and an old man dozing in a corner the only occupants. No sign of Mr. McCall—not that I was looking for him, of course.

The card-players finished their game, the steward came round with offers of coffee and brandy, but I declined. A gust of wind rattled the doors of the lounge: if I was to take a turn around the deck, I had better hurry. As I rose I felt a twinge in my finger, and looked down at the ring, so much a part of me now that I scarcely ever noticed it was there. Did that signal mean that I shouldn't go out on deck, or perhaps that I should be extra careful?

No further warnings, so I mentally shrugged my shoulders; just a quick foray. But outside the wind caught my shawl, almost tearing it from my shoulders, and loosened my hair still further so it lost its last pin and streamed back from my face. I made my way to the rail with a shiver, for the air was suddenly colder. Below me white caps were crowning the waves, and the bluff bows of the ferry were throwing up spray as they dipped and rose on the swell. I pulled my shawl tighter and knotted it behind: I had had enough. Sleepy or no, I would be better off in the cabin, but I had to cross a third of the deck to reach the way down and didn't want my hands encumbered.

As I inched my way along the rail towards safety, I found the ring was itching and throbbing on my finger; I paused for a moment to rub my hand against my skirt, and suddenly a pair of arms slid around me from behind, fingers slipped familiarly up towards my breasts and I caught the scent of bayrum hair oil, brandy and cigars.

"Well met, my little school-marm," said a voice in my ear.

"Mr. McCall! Let me go this instant, sir! What on earth do you mean by this—this extraordinary behaviour?"

Twisting away from his grasp, I tried to reach the doors of the lounge, the nearest refuge, but he caught my arm and dragged me back towards the rail, pressing his body against mine in a most suggestive manner.

"Oh, come on, Sophy! Don't pretend that you don't want this! You've been giving me the nod all day—"

I freed one arm and aimed a slap at his face, which he easily evaded. "Mr. McCall! I demand that you—"

"Call me Archie, m'dear . . ." and he bent his head and attempted to kiss me, but I wrenched my head aside, at the same time trying to push him away, but I had underestimated the strength of a man all fired up as he was. My struggles only seemed to bring us closer together, and I realised that this was exciting him still further.

I opened my mouth to scream, but realised I would have no chance of being heard. By now the cumbersome ferry was rearing and plunging in the increasing storm, the wind was whistling through the wire struts of the rigging, and smoke from the two stacks was being whipped away to starboard. There was a light up on the bridge, but the windows on this side were shuttered and my struggles would not be seen.

How I wished I had never come out here! How I wished I had listened to Toby, Claude and Danny! I knew, however, that this was mostly my fault; I had, however innocently, encouraged this monster to believe I had an interest in him. I had to admit I had enjoyed his earlier attentions, being both flattered and intrigued, stupid, naive young woman that I was! Now all I wanted was to gain the safety of my cabin without harm.

"Leave me *alone!*"

"Oh no, my little temptress! Not now I've got you where I want you . . . You're going to deliver the goods, I promise you! If we go down to one of the lifeboats we'll be nice and snug inside . . . That's right! Give us a bit of a struggle: I like a girl with spirit . . ." As he spoke he was dragging me down towards the stern of the ship, his hands gripping me fiercely.

The ring on my finger was throbbing really hard now, and I remembered Ky-Lin's words: could it help me now, when I hadn't heeded its earlier warnings?

The ship gave a sudden lurch, as if the captain had decided to change direction to ride out the storm, and my attacker and I were both thrown over onto the deck, now slippery with spray. I tried to roll away, but in a moment he had followed and thrown his weight on top of me. One arm was across my throat, near choking me, while his other arm slipped down to my rucked-up skirt and his hand groped upwards. Instinctively I brought a knee sharply into his groin and he rolled off me with a groan and a couple of obscenities.

I tried to get to my feet, but the now-slanting deck prevented this, so I started to crawl towards the rail. To my horror I saw Archie McCall scrambling after me, his face twisted with fury. I grabbed the rail with one hand, but a moment later a fist smashed into my face and I lost my hold. The ship gave another lurch and I found I was sliding under the rail. With scrabbling fingers I tried, terrified, to cling to whatever I could: at one stage I had hold of Mr. McCall's sleeve, but I couldn't hold on. To his credit, once he realised I was in real danger, he stretched out a hand to me, but it was too late.

The last thing I saw before I fell over the side was a night-shirted figure skidding across the deck towards us, and a small object seeming to fly through the air. There was a moment when, my mouth open in a silent scream, I seemed to be suspended in midair, then I hit the water with a thump that knocked the breath from my lungs, and I went down, down, down . . .

17

Treasure Island

Down, down, down . . .

Down into the freezing, dark water, choking and gasping, mouth and nose and ears full of water, lungs screaming for air, arms and legs flailing, pressure of water and weight of clothes pulling one down still further, the accelerated thump of one's heart-beat—

God! Dear God! I didn't want to die! I went on struggling, not even sure which way was up and which down. Suddenly my head broke through to the surface and I took a great gasp of air, a draught sweeter than any I had ever tasted. Then once more I was beneath the waves, struggling to reach the surface again: another gasp of air and then back, drowning a little more each time, my clothes growing heavier and heavier as I tried vainly to tear them off. I started to pray, hopelessly, then I heard God answer me, a tiny voice in my ear, a voice that transcended even the bubble and pop of water that clouded my hearing.

"Stretch out your hand," said the voice. "And hang on tight!"

The power of prayer! Like a trusting child I did as I was told and found I was grasping a chair-leg. A chair? Out here? I was dead, or dying, or at best hallucinating. I stretched out my other hand and found another leg. A chair, or perhaps a table. Well whatever it was, it was keeping my head above water and I was no longer gasping for breath. Moving forward I got my elbow over the seat of the chair, or the top of the table, whichever it was, only to find that it immediately overturned, and I had to start all over again, having luckily kept a hand on one of the legs—

"Steady on, Miss Sophy!" said Ky-Lin. "I haven't quite got the hang of this yet!"

"Ky-Lin!" I gasped, on a gulp of water. "How on earth did you get here? I thought you were . . ."

"Something else?"

"I thought—I thought you were a chair, or a table." I couldn't tell him about God. "Is it really you? You're all stiff and—and wooden."

"How else could I support you in the water? I'm the wrong shape for a lifebelt . . . Sorry I was so long in changing, but I haven't tried this before. I knew I could change into different materials, I knew I could grow larger or smaller, but I didn't know whether I could combine the two at once. Apparently I can. One lives and learns . . . Which reminds me, if you want to live, because we are getting nowhere right now and you are getting colder and colder, I think we need some outside help. Besides which I think I am getting water-logged. Wrong wood, obviously. Please twist the Ring on your finger and ask for help.

"How? What help?"

"Just do it. We need swimmers, because Ky-Lins don't swim. Come on, before you freeze to death and I forget how to turn back again . . ."

So I moved my hands together on one of Ky-Lin's wooden legs and turned the Ring, with some difficulty because my hands were freezing and swollen. "Help us," I murmured. "We can't swim. Please help us . . ."

At the same time I heard Ky-Lin give half-a-dozen shrill, burbling whistles. I waited for a moment. "What's supposed to happen?"

"Just wait . . ."

It could have been five minutes, it could have been longer and my legs had gone numb and it had started to rain, when the choppy waves around us grew even more disturbed and suddenly we were surrounded by surging bodies and a high-pitched whistling such as Ky-Lin had produced.

"Good," said Ky-Lin. "They heard us . . ."

It was the dolphins, and within seconds I was borne up on one of the backs and surrounded by the others, the air thick with talk I could understand through the Ring.

"Bear her up, brother, she can't swim . . . poor girl, we must help . . . we heard the Ring . . . cannot stand the cold . . . mustn't sink . . . can't catch the ship . . . nearest land . . . the sacred one is with her, keep them together . . ."

I was clinging, spreadeagled, across a hard, thick-skinned back, and rolling up and down on the surface—not always, for sometimes my water steed darted a few feet below the surface, to rise again a few seconds later—but at last feeling safe. It seemed easier, too, to try and ride the back of the dolphin as I would a horse; at least that way I kept my mouth above water most of the time. My ride wasn't helped by the fact that the other dolphins kept close order, sometimes jostling each other in an affectionate, boisterous way.

But where was Ky-Lin? For a moment I panicked, then there was a small voice in my ear.

. "Safe and sound. Don't worry: we are being taken to the nearest land where we will wait for rescue. Toby will have alerted the captain to you going overboard, but in this storm he would be powerless to turn the ship to search for you. But the lad knows I am with you, so he won't be unduly worried."

Perhaps a half-hour later the dolphins' ceaseless chatter, and the rhythm of the waves, both changed. The sea became choppier and shallower and by the occasional light of a moon that appeared to be racing the clouds I could see a darker blur to my left. The dolphins stepped up their commentary among themselves.

"Coming in to land . . . a little to the left . . . watch the rocks . . . run them up onto the sand . . . gently does it . . . she'll feel heavier as we lose way . . . touch down!"

My watersteed grounded gently on a stretch of sand and then wriggled up higher so that I could step off dry-footed—my slippers had long gone—and I turned to face my rescuers, now sliding back into the sea. I knew that if I could understand them through my life-giving, life-saving Ring, then they would understand me as well.

"My friends," I said, standing as tall as I could in spite of the shivers and shakes of cold and exhaustion, "I and my friend Ky-Lin thank you for coming to our rescue. We shall be forever grateful!"

"Grateful . . . grateful . . ." I heard. "The human is grateful . . . we are grateful too . . . do not often have the chance . . . most do not understand . . . one day we will speak together without the use of Rings . . . we will teach humans how to communicate . . . we will have the art of healing . . . give us the human children . . . they will understand . . ."

"I hope that will be soon," I said sincerely. Walking forward into the surf I laid my cheek in turn against the forehead of each dolphin. "Bless you, my friends . . ."

One by one they slipped back into the sea, their bottle-shaped snouts bobbing up and down in a kind of farewell. When they had gone I stumbled back onto the sand and sat down suddenly, thoroughly exhausted, feeling as though I couldn't walk another step.

Ky-Lin came up behind me and nuzzled my shoulder. He was now back to his "living" self, but pony-sized still. "Come on, let's get you off to sleep. We can't do any more till morning."

I allowed him to lead me back amongst some trees, away from the rain, and tuck me up in the shelter of an overhanging rock, after insisting that I discard all my clothes apart from my shift and hang them on an overhanging branch. I was now even colder than ever, my teeth were chattering and I was shivering, but Ky-Lin lay down beside me, and with my back against his stomach, I began to respond to the warmth of his body.

He shifted a little. "Turn your face towards me for a moment . . ."

"Why?"

"Sleepy-Dust."

I turned my head obediently and he breathed into my face and nostrils a scent like that of sandalwood boxes in the sunshine . . .

When I awoke, after a night and half a day of dreamless sleep, I found myself lying on the beach, both warm and dry. The sun was high in the sky, interrupted by a few fluffy clouds, and the breeze came warm from the south. One could not have believed the storm of the night before, except for the debris I now saw cast up on the shoreline. And amongst all this debris was an industrious Ky-Lin, sorting out pieces of jetsam.

He looked up. "Feeling better? I thought you would be better in the sunshine so I rolled you down here. Come and give us a hand: we need some dry wood for a fire."

Between us we built a small cone-shaped heap of kindling, at the base dried moss and strips of birch-bark. I sat back on my heels.

"How do we light it? I haven't any vestas."

"The way your ancestors did, of course." He gave me two differently shaped stones. "Strike these together till you get a spark, and hold it near the moss. When it catches, blow it into a flame."

But I was hopeless; if I got a flame, it wouldn't catch. In the end Ky-Lin sat on his haunches beside me, forbade me to blow, and got the fire going almost on his own. Anyway, it was soon blazing away merrily upon which we had to gather damp seaweed so that it would give off smoke as a signal.

"What if nobody sees it? What if nobody comes? What if they think I am dead?"

"Oh, they'll come," he said confidently. "This may be a deserted islet with no water, but there is far more traffic across than there used to be all those years ago when the pirates fought here and people called it the Accursed Isle.

"Accursed? Then no-one will come, and if they do they won't pick me up!"

"Course they will! You've only got to run down to the beach in your shift waving your petticoat and they'll be queueing up to take us off!"

"How do you know about the pirates?"

"I'll show you." He led me across the islet to a small cave, and there were the skeletons of two men, two swords and a dagger.

"Obviously they fought, over what I do not know, and both died." said Ky-Lin. "But this place is so seldom visited that no-one bothered to bury them."

"Then let's do it now," I said, and I found a thick fallen branch to loosen the earth while Ky-Lin's hooves moved so fast I could hardly see them as he shovelled out a shallow grave. I had thought I would not wish to touch the bones, but when it came to it, it was no different than shifting a bundle of sticks: blessedly, something inside of me had rendered me numb to the revulsion I had thought to feel.

Once the earth covered them I stuck the swords and dagger in the earth beside. "Shouldn't we say a prayer?"

Ky-Lin nodded. "I shall pray that they may find a better way next time, and you that their sins be forgiven and that they gain eternal rest. Strange, we both wish them well, but in different ways."

We stood silent for a moment, then I asked Ky-Lin how he knew the island was called "accursed."

"Places tell you things," he said. "Stones, rocks, caves, houses can retain an image, a feel, of any unusual action. Some of you humans seem to have a stronger feeling for this: they can sense at once when they enter a house whether it has had a sad or happy past." I nodded: I knew what he meant; my mother used to call it "atmosphere," and I knew now that Hightop Hall had a good one, whatever its past.

As turned to go back I stubbed my toe. "Damn! Er . . . Sorry, Ky-Lin. An echo of Toby, I guess."

He nodded. "Do not forget the boy knew nothing better before. You do. But that must have hurt. Let me see? Ah, a little touch with my horn—so—and it is better." Poking about with a hoof, he unearthed a pouch of shrivelled and desiccated leather. "Open it up, Miss Sophy."

I wrenched apart the stiff ties and tipped the contents out onto the ground. "Pearls? But what strange colours . . ."

Ky-Lin examined them, his forked tongue flickering rapidly over each one. "Fifty. All genuine. All beautiful." He examined the pouch. "And they have not been here that long: perhaps twenty years. So this is not what those two were fighting over. Probably someone hid them where he thought no-one would search."

"How do you know—the number of years? And why are they such funny colours? Look: black, pink, yellow, a sort of green . . ."

"I know the years through the decay of the leather they are in, and also because the colours have not faded: they tend to fade with exposure and age. The colours? These are very rare, precisely because of that very thing. They will fetch good prices. Put them back into the pouch until we can find something safer to carry them in."

"We're—we're not going to keep them?" I said, scandalised.

"Why not?"

"Because . . . because they don't belong to us. The person who put them there will come back for them one day."

"Unlikely after all this time. Besides, I have felt them, and there is no sense of ownership. They are like goods laid out on a stall, waiting to be bought. You are very lucky."

I didn't understand how he knew all this, but then there were a lot of things about Ky-Lin I didn't understand . . .

We trudged back towards the beach, and by now I was feeling distinctly hungry and thirsty, but Ky-Lin pointed out a scoop of rock that held a cupful of rain water, so at least I slaked my thirst. My clothes were damp-dry, so I dressed as well as I could in the crumpled, salt-stained garments. I was just fastening the buttons on my blouse when there came a shout from the direction of the beach. I snatched up my shawl and prepared to run, but there was a hiss from Ky-Lin.

"Wait for me! And do up those buttons . . ."

He was rapidly shrinking before my gaze, and a few seconds later was back to his figurine self, which I picked up and put in my pocket.

"Sorry . . ." I prepared to run again.

"You've forgotten the pearls . . . And when you get to the beach, stagger about as if you are on your last legs. I'll do the interpreting: just keep your face turned away."

I did as I was told, trod falteringly towards the fire, which was still belching smoke, and sank to my knees, shading my eyes and staring out to sea in the best "Robinson Crusoe" tradition.

"Don't over-do it," muttered Ky-Lin. "On the other hand they are only simple fishermen, so your histrionics are probably appreciated . . ."

There was much excited jabbering from the boat, about two hundred yards from the shore. I stood up and waved: they waved back. No-one made a move to come nearer and I realised, without Ky-Lin's prompting, that they were superstitious about landing on the islet and also, thanks to the dolphins, I remembered there were rocks close inshore. So I kicked sand over the fire to put it out, and then waded into the sea.

Immediately two men jumped into the shallows and waded to meet me, and in a minute or two I was hauled aboard, showing a deal more leg than I would have wished, to lie on the bottom boards of a boat that stank of fish. Not that I cared: at least I was safe, and by the time Ky-Lin had spoken through me, explaining my dramatic escape from drowning and the dolphins help in guiding me to dry land, everyone's mouths were open in admiration.

I was given bread and cheese, which I wolfed down, and chicory coffee which they brewed on a small brazier on deck. I thought-asked Ky-Lin whether they would take us to harbour and he said they would for a large bribe, which was the way they did things here, and that they had had a poor catch because of last night's storm.

"Promise them what they want, I just want to get to dry land and see the others again . . ."

Dusk was falling as we approached the harbour where I should have docked early this morning, and as we chugged towards land I could see the quayside was lined with people. We were followed by the scream of the gulls chasing our boat, as they did with all fishing boats, and in their exuberance my fisherfolk flung their meagre catch overboard to feathered appreciation.

Once we docked and I was helped up the steps to the quayside, I was met by Toby, Claude and Danny, who hugged and kissed me in a very satisfactory manner. It appeared they had at last persuaded the captain of the ferry to turn back to look for me, but of course he had been unsuccessful. It also meant that they had only docked some two hours earlier, and since then they had tried to persuade a flotilla of boats to go out looking for me.

"Only we didn't have the lingo," explained Toby. "Reminds me: you got you-know-who?"

"In my pocket," I said. "Hush . . ."

Toby had rescued my money-belt from the cabin, so it was easy to pay the fishermen well, and we left them recounting my rescue to the rest of the townsfolk, doubtless to the accompaniment of free hospitality for many days to come. We found a comfortable hotel where I luxuriated in masses of hot water to wash the salt from my hair and skin, sending my clothes out for laundering.

We took a table downstairs for supper, away from other diners, where we enjoyed kebabs with a fruity red wine, followed by sticky pastries and coffee. I felt we needed a celebration, especially since I now held the secret of the pearls.

I suddenly remembered something important.

"What happened to Mr. McCall?"

The others glanced at one another. "He skipped ship as soon as we docked," said Danny. "Last seen heading for the back streets, sans luggage."

"We tried to hang on to him," said Claude. "But no-one would listen."

Toby thumped his fist on the table. "I knew he was no good from the beginning!"

"All right!" I interrupted. "I should have listened to you all."

"Don't blame yourself, Sophy," said Claude, going pink. "You couldn't have known." He patted my hand.

"We understand," nodded Danny. "Sure we do. Slimy feller like that . . . Takes experience to recognize that sort."

I hid a smile.

I had told the others that the dolphins had guided me to safety, and I hoped the townsfolk would now be more tolerant towards them, but I brought Toby more fully up to date later.

"And Toby," I finished, "just stop me from doing anything foolish like that again!"

Two days later, fully recovered and freshly kitted out, we joined a caravan of travellers moving east. I knew we were starting the second, more wild stage of our journey by Ky-Lin's reminder the day before.

"Time to buy that cooking-pot, I think . . ."

18

A Very Unusual Cat

There were no border guards, no flags, no lines drawn in the sand, no indications whatsoever, but I knew immediately when we left Europe and crossed into Asia. It wasn't that the terrain had changed: for days now we had been travelling through undulating countryside, past pretty little villages, snow-capped mountains in the distance, the forests on either side full with June leaf. Then one morning when the ground grew steeper and the ground stonier and I caught the scent of pines on the warm air I knew we were at last in Asia. To be sure I asked Ky-Lin. "To humans the extent of countries and continents are lines drawn on a map," he said, "and as such have little importance. But yes, if you were now standing on a map, you would be in that part which has 'Asia' written on it."

I felt as excited as if I were a real explorer. Not in the sense of being the first in unknown territory, but in the knowledge that everything from now on would be different, my senses bombarded with new impressions: touches, tastes, smells, sights and sounds. So much to absorb, so little time to do it. I didn't keep a journal as such, but I had a small sketchbook in which I did some quick drawings and jotted down anything I wanted to remember: "flocks of small brown birds" I had written at one point; "grasshoppers," "lop-eared sheep" and "woman in red scarf" at others. I just hoped it would all mean something when I looked at it in the future.

I left it to Claude to record our progress, which he did faithfully, every day putting first the date and day of the week, then where we were (if we knew), how far we travelled that day, any unusual incidents, approximately how much we spent, and the state of the weather. He had twelve black notebooks, one for every month we spent away, and this was for the benefit of the firm, to prove we had been there and back. I would have found it all very boring.

We had hired a wagon, a driver and two spare riding horses before we joined a caravan, as I had got very good prices for three of the smaller yellow pearls, and I thought we deserved a little luxury. Ky-Lin advised us to carry our own food, so I had to do a quick mental re-cap of the cookery book I had left behind: not that that prepared me much for the cooking of rice, couscous, dried salted meat and fish, dried fruit and vegetables, nor for the making of unleavened bread. Surprisingly, my best help was Claude, who confessed to a liking for cookery, saying that after his father died and they had been "temporarily embarrassed," he had helped his mother with the cooking.

To my mind this more than made up for his dire performance on horseback. I had ridden as a child, and the small, stubby, hairy horses we had now were not much different from my ponies. Danny, being Irish, had an inborn gift for riding almost anything, and he showed un-characteristic patience in teaching Toby, who was an apt pupil. So three out of the four of us could ride, which would be necessary on the next stage of our journey, and I realised we would have to persist with Claude, who still rode (or fell off) like the proverbial sack of potatoes—or, con-sidering his build, more like a dislocated skeleton, in spite of the fact that his feet almost touched the ground.

We kitted ourselves out for the warmer weather with leggings, loose cotton shirts and, in my case, a divided skirt for easier riding. The men had haircuts—yes, even Toby, whose locks were now almost as long as they had been before—and I decided on drastic action for myself. But when I arrived back from the hairdresser, I was greeted with silence.

"Well?"

Luckily the silence had been of approbation, rather than otherwise, for they came crowding forward and touched or ruffled my unfashion-ably cropped head, springing already into soft curls. Claude decided it was sensible, Danny that it didn't spoil my beauty, and Toby said it suited me much better than those "dull plaits and buns and things."

It certainly felt much lighter and cooler, and was far easier to wash and keep clean.

In the sunshine we all wore woven straw hats against the sun and we only rode early in the morning or towards dusk. At night our wagon-driver curled up outside, near to his tethered ponies, and Toby did the same. Danny and I did sometimes, Claude never. I always seemed to find the ants. Normally we flung back the front and back openings to the wagon, making sure it had the benefit of the prevailing easterlies. Even so, it was rapidly approaching the hottest part of the year, and we all welcomed the occasional stream, river or lake in which to cool off, even fully clothed.

The caravan plodded on, ever upwards, our pace that of the slowest, those who brought their herds of sheep or goats for sale further on. If we had forgotten anything it would have been provided for, for there were the usual entrepreneurs who took their places in the caravan. One family brought a dry-goods wagon, laden with pots, pans, firewood, rope, boots, blankets, harness, nails, hammers, spare wheels and axles for the wagons and whatever else one needed in that line. Another brought food, including crates of chickens, and a third provided ready-cooked food. And all charged exorbitant prices.

What they carried back in return was anyone's guess, but Ky-Lin remarked that there was a profitable trade in opium and also in the handwoven rugs and blankets the tribespeople made.

The countryside through which we passed was completely different from the mostly cosy European villages, hills, woods and forests. Here were vast stretches of open grassland, rippling in the breeze, with mountains dim in the distance. The air was thinner, sharper, more difficult to breathe, and we needed time to become acclimatised. One good thing was that Claude's "hay-fever," or whatever it was, seemed to have dried up.

Sometimes we saw no-one else for days, heard nothing different from the dump of hooves, the clink of harness, the cries of the drivers and herders, the bleatings of sheep and goats, the shush-shush of the wind through the grasses, the twitter of flocks of finches as they harvested seeds and the occasional lonely cry of a solitary raptor, circling overhead. Other days we would pass another caravan on the return journey, or see a group of herdsmen with horses or sheep, or a family trudging in single file, laden with packages and parcels, the men in embroidered felt caps, the women in headshawls or scarves.

We didn't always pass through grassland; sometimes we descended into mini-deserts of rocks and stones, and once or twice into the pleasure of a fertile valley with fresh fruit, grain and meat and the sheer bliss of mountain-cold water. To me the tracks we followed were barely discernible in the now-July grass, but Ky-Lin told me that this was part of the old Silk Road, which every traveller knew well enough from centuries ago.

Sometimes our fellow-travellers took out long, unwieldy-looking guns or even sling-shots to try and vary their diet, but although they sometimes came back with a few small birds, the shy Saiga antelope evaded them, standing on the skyline just out of range.

The weather was warm, sixty-five to seventy degrees during the day, and the nights pleasant, and in spite of my clothing, I was becoming as brown as a gipsy. Once we reached our first sizable town I was determined to dispose of my skirt, much as I had chucked away my corsets, and ride breeched like Toby and the men. No-one would care.

Ky-Lin kept me entertained with reminiscences of his travels with Summer and was the ideal travelling companion: compact, easy to feed and full of stories.

And the Eg continued to grow. . . .

At the end of July we reached our first objective, the town of Azumak, which straddled the most important trade routes for hundreds of miles. There was the way we had come and its continuation east; another road swung north towards the Russias, yet another southwest towards Persia, while the one we wanted went southeast towards the mountains of northern China.

To call Azumak a town was flattering it. True, there was a large market-place surrounded by ware-houses, eating-houses, lodging-houses and stables; farther out was a small mosque, ditto a Buddhist temple; there was a tiny Greek Orthodox church and an even tinier Christian shrine, whose wooden effigy was so worn it was impossible to tell whether it was male or female, but the streets of the rest of the town were a hugger-mugger straggle of mud huts, tents, stalls, goat-pens, chicken-houses, sheds, yards and night-soil pits.

We found lodgings in one of the inns facing the square, and it was quite the noisiest location I had ever tried to sleep in. Morning, noon and night there were shouts, screams, yells, the rumble of wagons, the squeak of axles, quarrels, arguments, sellers extolling their wares, drums and pipes—and all this without the bleats, grunts, groans and squeals of the animals. Plus the all-day all-night barking of the dogs . . .

We had no intention of staying in this maelstrom of noise, dirt and dealing, but there seemed to be no choice. I had thought one night, perhaps two, before we found a caravan going our way, but it appeared no-one wished to travel that particular road. The rewards of such travel— opium, silk, jade, mohair, certain herbs and spice—were easily available on the longer but safer and more populous Silk Road, for which caravans were made up every two or three days. Travellers for Persia left approximately every two weeks, for Russia there were few takers except in the fur-trading season.

We—Ky-Lin and I—enquired everywhere, but no-one offered. It seemed so frustrating to have come so far, just to kick our heels. We tried to change our lodgings, but there was nothing better available, although we did manage to change our rooms for those at the back—at a higher price, of course. We had to eat out and this wasn't cheap either, and each day we were spending well over our budget. After three days of this I was beginning to despair, in spite of Ky-Lin counseling patience. He also advised me to use some of the waiting time finding us warmer clothes. This seemed ridiculous with the August heat pressing down on us, but he assured me that now was the cheapest time to buy.

Fur jackets, padded trousers (me as well), fur caps with ear-flaps, fur mitts and stronger boots, this set us up, together with the what was left of the winter clothes we had worn last winter through Europe. For all of this, and for the price of the journey ahead, it was necessary to sell more pearls, which Ky-Lin counseled me to bargain for through a back-street trader, rather than travellers from a caravan. I wasn't convinced, but after he had taken me through both options, I had to admit he was right.

On the fourth morning I was thoroughly restless and decided to take a walk round the market on our doorstep. I left Claude and Danny over one of their endless games of cards (on the second night I had made the mistake of giving Danny and Claude money to buy their own meal, and they had come home reeling and reeking of some rot-gut called arrack, or something like that, were thoroughly sick, which served them right, and stank of anise for twenty-four hours afterwards, so now we all went out together, or not at all). Toby had set off with Ky-Lin in his pocket, having perfected the art of Ky-Lin speaking through his mouth, Ky-Lin doing the prompting by fine nudges in his pocket. So, although Toby couldn't understand anything, Ky-Lin could report back to me. I rather suspected Toby's first call would be at the camel-lines outside the town. We had both seen a sad-looking specimen in a zoo in London, and a string of them on the skyline while we were in the caravan, but he was always fascinated by the varying animals and birds we came across.

The market was its usual crowded, smelly, noisy self. Jingling the few loose coins in my pocket, for I had no intention of buying anything, I wound my way past the fresh food stalls—meat, vegetables, fruit—to the dry goods—fish, rice, beans, sultanas and raisins—then to the salt and spices. Next came the sweet things: sugar, honey, cakes. On to the cloth: silk and ready-made clothes, thread, needles, scissors, tape and ribbons. Then there were pots and pans and crockery, the latter ranging from the cheapest to the finest Chinese porcelain. One section was devoted to furniture, mostly bamboo and Chinese, and Persian rugs and carpets. Of course there were stalls for the sale of arms: swords, spears, rifles and percussion revolvers. Jewellery, from the exotic and expensive to the cheap and tawdry—I didn't see any pearls as good as mine. Toys for children, wooden mechanical monkeys, dolls with porcelain faces; one stall devoted entirely to soapstone and jade, the latter from spinach through rose to the pale "mutton-fat." I passed quickly through the stalls selling dull things like hides, saddles, boots, baskets, rope and tents, likewise past those selling tobacco, snuff and hashish, and finding a patch of shade, bought a refreshing cup of sher-bert, deciding that enough was enough and that the rest of the stalls could hold no further surprises.

I emptied my tin cup and hung it on my belt, to be rinsed when I returned to the inn. We all had one: it was common sense not to share in the cups and ladles supplied by the drinks vendors, especially when one saw the diseases and sore mouths among the population.

Rather than try and battle through the middle of the market, I headed for the side, knowing that two corners would see me back at the inn. Now I was passing those stalls that faced the buildings surrounding the square. These were mostly small, some of them selling second-hand goods. This was the part where one found the bargains, if anywhere, but although I looked at a couple of embroidered purses I had no Ky-Lin to bargain for me.

Now I was at the last corner before the inn and I hastened my step, but suddenly an almighty great racket broke out just ahead to my right. Squealing, screeching, barking, howls of pain and the crash and splinter of wood. Hurrying forward I came across one of those sorry little stalls that sold "pets": mainly exotic birds, but also reptiles and the occasional dog or cat, although these latter were such prolific breeders that the streets were full of mongrels and feral cats already that no-one wanted anyway.

It seemed that this stall was one of the typical, cheaper ones: cages of pink-dyed canaries and colourful finches, a few somnolent tortoises, a couple of half-grown Saluki crosses and—a cat? At least that's what it sounded like. Half the cages were on the ground, the birds fluttering up and down, a tortoise lay on its back, claws waving helplessly, and the dogs were barking furiously and straining at their leashes, their fury directed at a creature crouching right at the back of the stall beside a cage whose door had literally been torn off. The animal was spitting, snarling and growling, while the stall-holder was stabbing furiously in its direction with what looked like a small, two-pronged pitchfork, cursing and yelling and out of control.

I became aware that the Ring on my finger was throbbing madly, so much so that it was actually hurting. I was supposed to do something or avoid something, but what? I stepped forward and turned over the tortoise which crawled away to safety, righted the bird-cages, avoided the snarling dogs, but still the Ring hurt. There was a sudden scream of pain from the corner of the stall and the stall-holder had the cat, or whatever-it-was, pinned down beneath the pitchfork, was picking up an iron bar and obviously moving in for the kill.

Without further thought I moved forward and snatched the pitchfork from the stall-holder's hand, and a moment later wrenched the bar from his suddenly slackened other hand, throwing both to the ground. He raised his fist at me and I stepped back as he picked up the pitchfork again, prepared to have another go at the animal.

I was in an awkward position. I couldn't understand him, nor he me, but I knew without doubt that I was meant to rescue the animal, now growling quietly in a corner and licking at an injured side. It now looked more like a cat to me, although I had had little to do with them, except as rodent-catchers in barns and stables. I wasn't even sure I liked them very much, although I had never really been able to find out. My parents had never considered pets to be essential to a household. I rode a perfectly pleasant pony, the doctor had a snappy little terrier, there was an aloof striped cat next door and my headmistress had a pair of blue lovebirds, but that was it. I had never stroked or cuddled any animal, and when I saw how obsessed their owners became with them, I decided I wouldn't bother to have one. But I wouldn't see one needlessly hurt.

The trouble was, I had only a few coins in my pocket, and nothing else to bargain with . . .

Still, it was worth a try. I tried the universal gesture for money, rubbing my right thumb and first two fingers together and raising my eyebrows interrogatively.

At once his attitude changed. He fawned and chirruped like his birds and burst into a flood of Arabic, putting down the pitchfork and obviously extolling the virtues of his beautiful cat. When he saw I didn't understand he threw in a few phrases of guttural French for good measure. Through this I gathered that the cat was unique and came originally from Siam.

"Look at his princely form, his unusual colour, his thick soft fur, his extraordinary eyes . . ." Words to that effect, but as I could see nothing but a dim form, a snarling row of teeth and a red-eyed glare I took his rhodomontade with the large pinch of salt it deserved. After five minutes or so, a sum of money was mentioned, which was far beyond my reach.

I shook my head and mentioned a sum commensurate with the few coins I had in my pocket—coinages were some of the terms one learned in all languages, and quickly—but he spat in disgust and waved me away. I knew some of the moves and pretended to walk away, waving my hand as though I had no further interest. The stall-holder caught at my sleeve and now his price had halved, though it was still more than I had.

I mentioned the same sum, he held his nose as though I was a bad smell, I pointed to the still snarling cat and the broken cage, as if it was he who had the worst of the bargain; I even poured my few coins into his palm, but I could see it was no use. I knew also that even if I managed to convey that I would bring back more money, he would have lost patience before I returned, preferring to get a good price for an animal for the pot; many people ate dog, cat or even rat, considering them a delicacy.

But there was nothing else I had to offer; I turned out my pockets and came up with a lump of fluff and a length of string. As a last resort I tried the secret pocket I had made in my new leggings and found the smallest pearl I had brought to change yesterday but kept as we had got enough with the other six—Eureka!

With the air of a conjuror I handed it over to the stall-holder who took it as though it would bite, demonstrated its smallness, tasted it with his tongue to see if it was genuine and again shook his head, though I noticed the coins had disappeared and he kept the pearl between his fingers.

At that moment the cat took matters into its own paws.

There was a sudden blur of movement, it sailed past my left ear and a moment later I yelped with pain as a heavy weight settled on my shoulder and several sharp bits dug into my skin as the creature regained its balance and turned around, so that out of the corner of my eye I could see an ear, an eye, a furry muzzle.

The stall-holder moved forward as if to interfere, but the cat spat and growled so savagely that he retreated, waving his arms and cursing, no doubt glad to be rid of the pair of us at a profit, for that pearl was worth twenty cats and more.

In the meantime I was frozen on the spot. Having only seen the formidable animal growling, spitting and snarling and feeling the weight and the claws—admittedly now sheathed—I was scared stiff the cat would turn on me if I so much as shifted an inch. I had such a picture in my mind of its savage aspect and menacing growls, so that when it started to purr against my ear I at first thought it was the prelude to imminent attack.

However, just in time I realised the Ring was no longer throbbing, rather was it exuding a kind of soothing warmth. So when the creature rested its head against my cheek and a cold nose tentatively touched mine, I felt I had fulfilled the Ring's intention in freeing the creature. I moved slowly and gingerly away from the animal stall and made my way down the alley towards the inn, a little bowed under the weight. Coming to a wall a little higher than I, I patted the top invitingly.

"Here you are, pussy-cat. Now you are free to go." I was glad there was no-one to hear. "I expect you can catch plenty of mice and—and things. Off you go now, and keep away from cages . . ."

I had thought it would understand, at least in part, through the Ring, but it was obviously deaf or something; it just settled down closer on my shoulder, purring more loudly, its tail tapping gently on the back of my shoulder, as if to say: "Keep on going . . ."

Of course! It was probably hungry. Well, I could probably get something for it at the inn. Reaching the courtyard I stepped over to the outside stairs which led to our rooms, ignoring the curious glances of those who always haunted the place, squatting around a small fire or leaning against a wall in the shade. I walked up the stairs very carefully, so as not to jolt the cat from my shoulders, or have his claws digging in once more.

Reaching my room I first opened the shutters then moved over to my pallet, sitting down gingerly. At last the cat cooperated, leaping down onto the blanket and licking a paw.

"I'll go and get you something to eat," I said, feeling foolish. "A little fish and a drink of milk, perhaps . . ."

I had my hand on the latch when I heard a quiet voice behind me.

"Not raw, if you don't mind. Lightly poached with a sprig of tarragon, and water, not milk . . ."

19

An Addition and
a Subtraction

I whirled round, convinced someone was playing tricks: Toby, perhaps, hiding under the bed or perched on the roof outside, but the cat and I were alone, and the former had its attention firmly fixed on the other paw. I shook my head to rid it of the cobwebs. All this had been too much; it was just an accumulation of stress, that was all. I was thinking for myself, not the cat. I wouldn't eat raw fish, so obviously I had arranged a recipe in my mind and spoken it out aloud. But the voice hadn't sounded like mine. . . .

I went down to the kitchen with a few coins in my hand and arranged for the fish and tarragon. I drew a fish in the dust on the floor, mimed the filleting and picked a few leaves of dried tarragon from the selection hanging from the rafters. I then pointed to the pan and water, and supervised the poaching, indicating when I considered it done. By then I was so hungry myself that I bought a leg of chicken and ate it on the spot.

Opening the bedroom door the cat leapt off the bed and advanced to meet me, tail held high and gently waving. I set down the dish on the floor and removed the cover, the enticing smell making my mouth water.

"It's hot," I said unnecessarily, for the poor thing was obviously deaf, like all blue-eyed cats, but it had the sense to sit back and wait for the steam to disperse. Risking scalded fingers I knelt down and examined the fillets, pulling out a couple of bones that had been missed and discarding the tarragon. "There, nothing left to choke on. I'll put some water in the cover . . ." Stop talking to yourself, Sophy!

After a couple of minutes it started to eat, delicately: a gourmet rather than a gourmand, obviously. As it ate I had leisure to study it more closely. It was completely unlike the chunky tabbies, gingers, blacks, black-and-whites and tortoiseshells I had seen in England, nor had it the snub-nosed appeal of the Persian. Neither did it resemble the shabby alley-cats we had come across abroad. For a start he was much bigger and undeniably elegant, slim and streamlined, with a pointed muzzle and long ditto tail, this last with a tiny kink at the end. His colour was the most striking, of course, dark chocolate at the extremities and a cream body. Without touching him I could see that the fur was dense and soft. His claws looked shorter and blunter than most cats, but it was those beautiful blue eyes that I found the most appealing; not a dark blue, rather that translucent pale blue of the tiny flowers we used to call "babies' breath" when we were children—pity about the deafness. Then I noticed that his ears flicked back and forth from every noise outside, and I wondered . . . perhaps he spoke some strange tongue that was not transmitted through the Ring.

Finished, he drank deeply, gave me a glance as if to say "thank you" and leapt back onto the bed to give himself a thorough wash from head to toe, wincing a little as he licked his side, where I could see the skin had been broken, probably by that wretched pitchfork. I put the dish, cover and bowl on the rickety table under the window. I was deathly tired after my expedition, but the bed was occupied, and I didn't want to risk those claws, remembering what I had seen earlier.

"Er . . . Could you move up a bit? I'd like to have a rest." But how could I expect it to understand?

"Sure," said the cat in my sleepy head, moving to the foot of the bed, and without thinking any farther I lay down and immediately fell asleep.

"What on earth is *that?*" asked Toby, bursting into my room, but as the answer was perfectly obvious he didn't wait for one but instead launched into an enthusiastic account of how he and Ky-Lin had found a man willing to guide us to his brother's village, some one hundred and fifty miles on towards our destination, and that his brother would be sure to take us the rest of the way.

"Apparently the guide has goods to deliver to his brother, knows where he can hire half-a-dozen ponies, and Ky-Lin says—at least I *think* he says—he nodded anyway and only did a bit of the bargaining—that the price was reasonable. What do you say to that?"

"I say you've done a wonderful job," I laughed giving him a hug. "Both of you!" For of course it had been Ky-Lin who had found the man and done the bargaining through Toby's mouth. "When do we start?"

"Tomorrow at dawn," said Ky-Lin, jumping from Toby's shoulder to mine. "We meet him outside town at the beginning of the track south-east. Each of us will have a pony, and there will be two for transporting our food and blankets and clothes, etc."

"Well, we'd better get going, then! We have to get packed, buy some food and—"

"And I'm *starving!*" interrupted Toby. "Haven't had anything since breakfast . . ."

I discovered I was starving too, and went down the corridor to rout out Claude and Danny. We partook of a hasty meal of fried fish, meat and rice, then set out to do the serious shopping: firewood, rice, salt, oil, dried meat, fish, vegetables and fruit, and extra water-bottles. What with packing and organizing, I completely forgot about the cat, though when I at last returned to my room at about nine that night I felt an uncomfortable pang to find that he had gone through the still unshuttered window. He had chosen his freedom. I just hoped he would be all right.

Ky-Lin had already hidden under my pillow, so I took down the dirty dishes to the kitchen and had a quick wash under the pump in the yard and then sought my bed, where I had no trouble falling asleep.

To be awoken by a thump in the middle of my stomach.

"Ouch! What the hell . . ." Sophy! Language . . .

"Sorry! Missed my footing . . ."

Voices in my head again. I turned over and looked at my fob-watch by the moonlight coming in through the open window. Three A.M. At my feet the cat had curled himself up.

"Thought you had gone . . ."

"Just exploring . . . And using the usual toilet facilities. May I ask you a favour? I am afraid that my side is quite painful. I would not wish it to become infected."

I stumbled out of bed and lit the lamp, still convinced I was dreaming, but then one did strange things in dreams. Like talking to injured cats. I dampened one of my diminishing store of clean handkerchiefs and bathed the contusions on the cat's ribs. The skin was broken, weals breaking out on the surface where the fur had been torn away.

"There . . . That better?"

"Let me," said a voice from my pillow. Ky-Lin spoke to the cat. "If you will allow me?"

In my increasingly confused dream the cat nodded, and Ky-Lin moved down the bed and touched his little pink horn to the cat's side. Immediately the skin seemed to heal, the swelling going down.

"Thank you, Sacred One . . ."

"No problem," said Ky-Lin. "And now let's get some sleep. We have a long day ahead of us tomorrow." He blew out the lamp and lay by my pillow, while the cat curled up at my feet again. I slept without further dreams until Ky-Lin nudged me awake just before dawn. We had paid our dues the night before so started to carry our luggage down the stairs and into the street, where it piled up formidably. Toby and the others were to carry it down to our rendezvous, but it took three journeys, and a sleepy sun was reddening the grey dawn as we finished loading our ponies, Mustaq, our guide, muttering at our tardiness.

Even though it was so early, people were already stirring, and I paused to pick up some savoury pancakes from a yawning stall-holder. On either side of these alleys bedding was already being hung out to air on the balconies, cooking fires being lit, sleepy children carrying buckets to the nearest well, bundles of rags coming to life again as vagrants and beggars.

Juggling the hot pancakes in my hands, I saw that the cat was following me. It wasn't coming with us, that was for sure, but it was probably hungry. Carefully I dissected the coolest of the pancakes and laid it on the ground.

"There you are, pussy-cat; goodbye and good luck!" and off he trotted to join the others and hand out the pancakes. The guide provided us with some revolting coffee, which wiped any lingering sleep from anyone's eyes. I was just shortening my stirrups ready to mount, Danny having already lengthened Claude's, who was looking extremely uncomfortable and quite precarious, when I felt a nudge on my right leg. Oh, *no!* Not the cat again!

"Shoo!" I said. "Go away! Look I gave you something to eat, your hurts are better and cats fend for themselves."

"Just a moment," said Ky-Lin from my pocket, which he had swapped from Toby's a few minutes past. "How many are we, counting the Eg?"

Peculiar question, given the circumstances. "Er . . ." I counted on my fingers. Me, Toby, Ky-Lin, the Eg, Danny and Claude. "Six. Why?"

"Summer had seven with her on both her first and second journeys, at least for part of the time. So did the One before her, but that was a long while ago. But the Ring remembers."

And as if to echo his words, the Ring gave a tiny, painless throb.

"You mean that seven is a lucky number?"

"It is considered to be so by some."

It was now obvious which way the conversation was leading. "You want us to take the cat?"

"My wishes have nothing to do with it. I was just trying to remind you of your options. I neither want you to ignore the obvious, nor to make a decision you might later regret. I also believe you should not pass up on any luck that comes your way."

I thought about it. It had been the Ring that had urged me to rescue the cat, and I had to admit it had been no trouble. But it couldn't run behind a horse —

"It can perch quite comfortably on the pony carrying the luggage," said Ky-Lin, reading my thoughts for the umpteenth time of our acquaintance. I looked down at the subject of our conversation, and a pair of beautiful blue eyes gazed back at me.

"I won't be any bother," it said, quite clearly.

"I thought you couldn't—didn't—"

"He was shy," said Ky-Lin.

When we rejoined the others the cat leapt gracefully onto the back of the luggage-carrying pony and settled down, wedged comfortably between the haversacks.

"Is he coming with us?" asked Toby.

"I suppose so."

"What's he called?"

"Cat," said Danny.

"Tom," said Claude, accurately.

"No," said Toby. "He deserves better than that. He's very beautiful—no, I suppose you would call it handsome for a boy."

"Beau," I said. The cat raised its head and looked at me.

"Near enough," it said, and settled down again. So Beau-cat he became, fulfilled his promise of being no trouble, and was seldom far from my side when we were on the ground.

So off we went into the unknown, through the undulating steppes, always tending higher and higher. Sometimes we rode through grass as high as the horses' withers, and other times over stony ground, and I would have been lost in five minutes, but Ky-Lin assured me we were headed in the right direction.

We progressed more or less uneventfully. I cooked for us every night, leaving enough cold for breaking our fast and a lunch-time snack with, as I said before, the competent help of Claude; he seemed to be a loaves-and-fishes man—able to make a little go a long way. Having watched the sort of herbs our earlier fellow-travellers had gathered, I was able to vary the taste of the ubiquitous rice and couscous a little. This was nothing to the spicy smells that our earlier guide, Mustaq, conjured up, although when I begged a pinch of his mixture, it nearly burnt the roofs off our mouths.

At night he erected a kind of tarpaulin for us, and we slept on the ground, wrapped in our blankets and with our cloaks for pillows. It was the first time I had slept on bare ground and I'll swear that every pebble and stone in Turkestan, or wherever we were, was digging into my hips, spine and shoulders, but after the first couple of nights I became used to it, having the sense to clear the space and scrape out a small depression before I lay down.

I must admit that I was intrigued by the sight of the night-shirted men, for they bore no resemblance to the statues and paintings of gods and athletes I had seen in various art galleries and museums in London. When we had travelled earlier in the wagon, there had been a blanket slung between them and me, but now it was amusing to see the strategems they underwent when they were changing: hiding behind the pony-lines, running off a couple of hundred yards and crouching down or doing as we used to do at school—undressing under our nightgowns. They were not as adept at this as I was . . .

Of course many of the workers we had passed in the fields, and some of the herdsmen also, wore the minimum of clothing, merely a brief loincloth, but this seemed normal and natural in the native population—but Claude and Danny had such skinny shanks! And without regular exposure to the sun, these limbs looked like white pipe-cleaners, especially Claude's!

The village we were headed for was some hundred and fifty miles distant and we reached it in just over a week. All the while we were gradually climbing, so gradually that sometimes it wasn't until we stopped for a meal or overnight camp and looked back the way we had come that we saw how far we had climbed. Now we could see the mountains we were aiming for; just a bluish suggestion on the horizon, but day by day gaining shape. Ky-Lin reckoned we had about another five hundred miles to go before we found a suitable pass though the mountains, which sounded pretty daunting, especially as we were well into September. Now that we were that much higher, the grass was not as tall, which made the going easier for the ponies, and we were instead passing through mini-meadows of blue, yellow and white flowers, dancing in the perpetual easterlies.

We spent two days in Mustaq's brother's village because, like many other horse-owners, their ponies grazed well away from the village and had to be rounded up. In the meantime we were lodged at one end of a smelly stable, divided from the sheep and goats by only a wooden paling. We ate well, though: pancakes, unleavened bread, cheese, lamb kebabs and spicy fried vegetables.

Mustaq's brother, Makub, was as like his brother as could be: small, dour and uncommunicative, with the same droopy moustaches. With the help of Ky-Lin we agreed a price, half down, the other half when we reached the mountains.

I bought provisions, though of course the price was much higher so far from a town: more rice, oil, dried meats and vegetables and fruit, firewood, plus some hard and rather smelly cheese. The poor pony carrying the food looked swaybacked by the time we had finished, but we knew these foods would have to last us three weeks at least, till we got through the mountains, as there were no more settlements on the way.

We made good progress during the next few days and Ky-Lin whispered that we had covered at least a third of our journey to the mountains.

The ground was becoming more broken up, and several times we crossed small gullies and streams, and even came across the odd tree. On the evening of the fourteenth day since we had left the village, our guide, Makub, suddenly became more convivial, and suggested he join us for supper, bringing a couple of spicy dishes to serve with our rice.

I didn't entirely trust this sudden change of heart, and something—perhaps it was the Ring—warned me against his food, and more particularly against the flask he offered round afterwards. I couldn't consult with Ky-Lin, as he had crept off some time before to forage for some fallen seeds he had seen earlier, but it was with a sinking heart that I saw even Toby take a draught from the flask, although he made a face and refused more. When it came to my turn I merely raised the flask to my lips and pretended to swallow, out of courtesy, but to my dismay Claude and Danny set to with a will until the flask was empty. They then broke into raucous song, music-hall ballads with dubious lyrics, some decidedly risqué, and I regret to say even Toby joined in.

It was very late when I managed to get them to bed and by then was exhausted myself and could only give the returned Ky-Lin an abbreviated version of what had happened. I fell asleep to the sound of loud snoring which drowned out the more pleasant sounds of the night.

It was still dark, though dawn wasn't far away, when I was awoken by a panicking Toby.

"Sophy, Sophy, wake up!"

I rolled over. "Whassa matter?"

" 'E's gorn!" It must be bad: he was back to Cockney again.

"Who's gone?"

" 'E 'as. The guide! I went out there to be sick, cos me stummick's fair terrible, and there's nothin' an' nobody there. There's nothin' but us! The dirty git's run orf with everythin'! Ponies, gear, the lot!"

20

On Our Own

I tried to spring to my feet but fell to my knees, tangled in my blanket. Furiously I scrabbled free and went out into the pre-dawn, the skies already paling and the stars fading one by one. Toby was still retching, but Ky-Lin and Beau-cat were anxiously awaiting me. I gazed around: nothing. Toby was right. Makub had left us and taken everything with him. Even the Eg . . . A thief in the night.

What on earth were we going to do? Without food, water or transport we would surely perish, and even if Ky-Lin could guide us back to the village it was doubtful if we could make it. Besides which, the object of all this journeying had gone: without the Eg, what was the point of going on? I sank to my knees in despair, but there was a nudge from Ky-Lin.

"Get dressed," he hissed. "Quick as you can. Wake the others if you can, but I doubt it."

The first quickly done, the second impossible. They lay there and snored and snored and snored, and no amount of shouting, shaking or even kicking made the slightest bit of difference. I ran out of the shelter again to find Ky-Lin rapidly changing into his pony-size mode, as always in fits and starts, ending with the last shortened foot and a crumpled ear. Beau-cat was watching impassively, but Toby was still retching. Ky-Lin finished "changing" and briefly touched Toby's stomach with his horn.

"That should make it better . . . Tell him, girl, to stay here and get the others on their feet—if necessary drag them over to the stream and dunk them in it."

"What's the matter with them?"

"A powerful drug in that flask he gave them. The food was probably contaminated as well. You and Beau here had neither, which is why you are well enough." He paused. "Well, come on then . . ."

"Come on where? What are we going to do?"

"Go after him, of course! Climb on to my back and hang on tight."

"But we'll never catch him! He's been gone five or six hours. He must be at least twenty miles away!"

"With eight ponies? Probably only five or six. Come on, we're wasting precious time."

In fact it was a good ten.

Toby had had the dubious pleasure of riding Ky-Lin before and enjoyed it—I say dubious, because he wouldn't touch a living organism, so the progress was a hair-raising behind-bumping teeth-jarring nightmare—but to me it was an experience I preferred to forget, especially as Beau-cat had decided to accompany us, and was clinging on for dear life to the back of my (luckily) thick jacket. True, when we came to suitable stony ground Ky-Lin trotted instead of bounding, but when he finally drew to a halt I slid off his back, groaning and aching in every joint.

"Hush!" said Ky-Lin. "He's not far away . . . Where does it hurt?"

"Everywhere," I groaned, but quietly. Even the cessation of movement was a treat.

"Sorry," he said. "But if we had left it any longer or been any slower he would have gone too far, and we must retrieve the Eg, or else I will entirely forfeit my time in Nirvana. Lie still." And quickly and expertly he dabbed me with his little pink horn, and immediately I felt better. Beau-cat seemed all right, although he was carefully straightening his claws to their correct alignment.

"Thanks . . ." I stretched and wriggled about a bit and discovered I was still in one piece. I started to get up but Ky-Lin stopped me.

"Stay down. I told you he isn't far. Move forward to that large rock over there and take a quick peep."

By the time I reached the rock I had already seen the plume of smoke over to our right and when I cautiously raised my head I could see that Makub had built a small fire in a little dell, having tethered all but his own pony to a lone tree nearby.

"He reckons he's safe," breathed Ky-Lin in my ear. "What with the drug and the distance."

"What are we going to do? He's got a gun."

"Come back a bit and I'll tell you." Obediently Beau-cat and I followed him until we were out of earshot of the guide. "Now listen you two—"

I pointed at Beau-cat. "Will he understand?"

"We are both animals—" He stopped. "On second thoughts, put your Ring-finger on his collar—"

"He hasn't got one. A collar, I mean."

"Just because you haven't seen it, doesn't mean he hasn't got one."

I pushed my fingers into the soft fur around Beau-cat's neck and, sure enough, I could see a tatty brass-coloured chain, studded with green glass stones. I thought it might be too tight, but my finger fitted quite easily underneath.

"Now listen, and listen carefully, because we haven't time to go over it more than once. He will soon have finished his coffee . . ."

And he told us what we had to do.

We didn't get back to the others until the sun was on its way down. What with rounding up the ponies, who had panicked, broken their halters and were anything up to a mile distant, and indulging ourselves in a scrappy meal, plus walking the beasts back, I wasn't surprised to see Toby had come a couple of miles down the track to look for us.

He was overjoyed to see us again, mounted one of the ponies and listened intently as I told him of our successful foray. He declared it was better than a play, but added: "Won't you have to tell the others about Ky-Lin now?"

I looked across at Ky-Lin, who was trotting, pony-size, among the other steeds.

"Well?"

"Probably as good a time as any. It would have to happen sooner or later, anyway. I'll stay behind while you explain, otherwise they'll probably die of fright. Break it to them gently; at least now there are no other humans around."

Claude and Danny were in a sorry state. They were still stumbling around half-dazed, alternately clutching at their heads and their stomachs. While Toby hobbled the ponies, ensured the Eg was safe, and looked out some rations, I built a small fire and heated up couscous and vegetables, telling the two disgraces to go down to the stream and not to return until they were sober, clean and presentable. This took some time, but eventually they returned as the moon rose and accepted a small bowl of food and drank water.

"Perhaps that will teach you to be a little more abstemious," I said severely. "You could have died, you know."

"I shall never, ever again touch strong liquors," said Claude. "Not ever." And as far as I know, he never has.

"What was it?" asked Danny. "Food poisoning?"

"Man poisoning. Makub was going to abandon us, steal our ponies and make his way to the village, where he probably had an arrangement with his brother to take our belongings back to town and sell them. He's probably done it before, on the less-frequented routes."

"You mean—he meant us to die?" asked Claude.

"Well, with no food and no transport, what else?"

Toby looked at me and I nodded. "Tell us then, dear Sophy, how you managed to get the horses back . . ." This we had rehearsed.

"Well," I started, "I couldn't have done it without the help of my friend Ky-Lin . . ." I turned my head and called out into the darkness. "Are you there?"

And out trotted Ky-Lin into the firelight.

A quarter-hour later, when Toby had found Claude cowering a couple of hundred yards away and I had caught up with Danny, and persuaded the pair of them that there was nothing to fear, I introduced them to the mythical creature, explaining that Toby had known about him from the beginning.

"And there were none of your stupid hysterics from him," I added. "Toby took him for what I said he was: someone sent to help us. And before you ask, my uncle bought him many years ago. If you remember I told you part of Summer's story, and he, Ky-Lin, accompanied her on part of her journey and was there at the inception of the Eg we are here to return."

I wasn't sure whether they were listening to me properly, and I must admit that a Ky-Lin by the fire in all his shimmering glory was a sight to behold.

"I might add," I said, "that he can also change his size. That is why you have not seen him before. He has usually been either in my or Toby's pocket. Show them, Ky-Lin."

Obediently, slowly, carefully he shrank back to dog, cat, rat, mouse size and scuttled across to my side.

"See?"

Claude and Danny scrambled back to their places by the fire.

"But how do you'se two understand each other?" asked Danny, a question I had been dreading.

"We have a necessary bond," I said carefully. "A sort of built-in interpreter." I was unwilling to explain the Ring fully, even to Toby. "Now would you like to hear how we beat Makub at his own game?"

"Er . . . You don't have one of your headache powders left, do you?" asked Claude.

As it happened I did, and dosed them both, before settling down to tell them of our Marvellous Adventure.

I explained Ky-Lin's plan to make the thief believe he was surrounded, which meant that we three had to move to different points, and then one by one make as much noise as possible. Beau-cat screamed as only a full-blooded Siamese cat can (which I admit made me jump out of my skin), I was to yell the Arabic for thief, something like "Harami!" then move a hundred yards to my left and groan loudly like a ghost. Then I was to return to my original position and yell "Thief!" again. And so we alternated, Ky-Lin making a sort of screeching noise like a giant eagle owl. By the time we had done this a half-dozen times Makub had had enough. After the first couple of shouts and yells he had fired his long Afghan rifle, then struggled to tip in more powder and shot, but as it was a muzzle-loader he only got off one more wayward shot before Ky-Lin burst on the scene in all his glory, and Makub took one terrified look before leaping onto his horse and heading north at a gallop.

"Will he get back?" asked Danny.

"Very probably. There is plenty of water, and his horse has grass. Ky-Lin says he will be very hungry . . . Perhaps it will teach him a lesson. Of course he will have a good story ready, telling them how we were ambushed by bandits, and he only just escaped with his life."

"Serve him right," said Claude. "Haven't we got an extra horse?"

"His baggage pony. A bit of food and some items we might use for bargaining, if necessary." I didn't tell them this latter consisted of tobacco, hashish, alcohol, opium and, of course, the rifle and ammunition.

"So, what do we do now?" asked Claude nervously.

"We go on, of course. We have food, transport and Ky-Lin will be our guide. He knows the way."

"Are you sure?" asked Danny.

"Of course," I said. But I wasn't. It wasn't that I had no faith in Ky-Lin's guidance, rather I had my reservations about our endurance. We still had a long way to go.

Ky-Lin guided us a little more east of the southeast we had been travelling so far. Now we were higher than we had ever been, the air was thinner and the dawn and dusk closer together as the year waned. Gradually we were assuming our winter clothes: no more night-shifts, rather sleeping in our underwear. The sun was still fierce at midday but the stars burnt cold at night. Consequently we started off each morning shortly after dawn, rested at midday for an hour, then pressed on till well after sundown.

Ahead of us the mountains reared like fearsome, jagged teeth, their tops snow-covered already, wreaths of powdered snow blown westward from their tips like ladies' shawls in a wind. Already we were near enough to see that the lower slopes were covered with thick pine forests, and could glimpse the glitter of the many small streams that cascaded down through ravines and gullies.

I had to admit we were making good progress, but for the past few days I had the feeling that we were being watched or followed. We had glimpsed a couple of herds of shaggy horses, and once I was sure I had caught sight of a mounted horseman. Both times the Ring had given a tiny jolt but nothing to suggest that danger was imminent. Beau-cat was also uneasy, his tail twitching irritably every now and again, but Ky-Lin kept his own counsel.

One night before we unfolded the tarpaulin and made a pocket of it on the ground, for greater warmth and protection, I asked Claude, busy making notes in one of his little black notebooks, what date it was?

"October fifth. Twenty-six days to go." I wished he hadn't sounded so cheerful.

Perhaps it was the thought that we only had three weeks and five days to go, perhaps it was because I had indulged myself with some cheese, but that night I found it difficult to sleep. My dreams were snatches of rubbish, and I couldn't get comfortable.

So, shortly before dawn I gave up all pretence at sleep and went and relieved myself, accompanied by an equally restless Beau-cat. We teamed up again on the way back to camp, but suddenly everything changed. The Ring gave an enormous stab, and Beau-cat lifted his head and hissed. "Quick! Run! Strangers are coming . . ." and he bounded away in the direction of the camp to alert the others. But before I had gone a dozen yards or so I was knocked to the ground from behind, my head wrapped in a thick covering and my hands fastened; I was then lifted from the ground and carried away.

21

The Shaman

It was hot and stuffy in the felt tent, or yurt, and the smoke took its time leaving the animal-dung-burning brazier and finding its way out through the small hole in the roof.

My hands had been untied and I sat with Toby on one side, the men on the other and Ky-Lin tucked away in my collar, unseen. There was no sign of Beau-cat, but I comforted myself that of all the seven of us, he was best equipped to look after himself.

We had been given a space, rather like prisoners in a dock, but the rest of the yurt was crowded. Both men and women were dressed alike, in trews, short skirts, thick jackets and caps, the latter rising conically to a point, with embroidered ear-flaps. They were all swarthy, with plaited black hair and slanting eyes, the men with wispy beards and moustaches.

They didn't seem particularly menacing, although all the men wore knives in their belts or stuck in the tops of their high boots. The tent was about fifteen feet wide, roughly circular, and supported on thin wooden poles, and there were already some twenty-five people squatting on either side of us. Directly opposite us was a high stool, painted in bright colours and boasting an embroidered cushion, and the people kept glancing at the open tent-flap then the stool, as though expecting an honoured guest.

All at once there was a loud rattling noise and a thin, ululating cry, midway between that of a strangling dog at the end of its chain and an owl with a cough, and through the tent-flap came one of the tallest men

I had ever seen, thin to the point of emaciation. He had to bend his bald head to enter, leaving the beams of sunshine outside to dance with motes of dust and pollen.

Everyone straightened up as he entered, and all talk ceased abruptly. He was dressed in skins and a loin-cloth; around his neck was a rattle of bones, from his pendulous ears dangled the same, and in his right hand he held a staff with a triple row of feathers. His face was decorated with a smudge of blue on both cheeks, a yellow line down his nose and a red chin.

He stood for a moment in the centre of the yurt, then raised his arm and rattled his staff deafeningly. All his people bowed their heads as if in worship, and he took his place on the stool like a king ascending his throne. Unfortunately he smelt like a midden.

"Local witch-doctor or shaman," murmured Ky-Lin in my ear. "Very important. We can ignore all the others. He is the one who will decide what happens to us."

"Is he very powerful—as a shaman?"

"Not particularly. Probably got the job because of his genetic defects—all that height and hairlessness. But don't underestimate his power over his people."

"Then what do we do?"

"First of all we listen. If I am not mistaken he is about to give us all a speech: I only hope his is a dialect I understand . . ."

Right on cue the shaman rose to his feet, pointed a finger at us (all his nails looked as if they had never been trimmed, yellow bits of corrugated horn that spiraled away from his finger-ends like corkscrews) and started off in an accusatory tone.

"Good," muttered Ky-Lin. "The dialect is based on Kurdish, and one I can now understand, although I didn't when I travelled with Summer, to my shame, but I have made myself fully conversant since then . . . He is asking who we are, where we came from, where we are bound, why we are in his tribe's grazing grounds. All this wrapped up in flowery persiflage to impress the rest of them. When he's finished he will invite us to reply, which I will do through you. Keep your head down, then he won't notice we don't synchronise. Tell the others to sit still and not interrupt or look bored."

I watched the shaman working himself up into his final frenzy, bones clanking, eyes rolled up into his head, spittle flying from his mouth. His audience was obviously impressed as he finally sat down, there was a hiss of approval. But he hadn't finished. After a moment to seize his breath, he stood up again, reached into a leather pouch at his waist and threw something into the glowing embers of the brazier. There was a flash and a bang, and a cloud of coloured stars filled the space in the roof of the yurt, to fall back and singe the carpets on which we sat.

We all jumped, except for Ky-Lin.

"Third rate," he observed. "All right for children. Poor quality gunpowder, mixed with sand and grit, and little plugs of barium nitrate. We can do better than that . . . Now it's our turn. Stand up, bow to the shaman, keep your head down, and do a regal wave now and again if I give you a nudge. Just to emphasize a point . . ."

Now Queen Victoria I was not, although I had seen her once driving in a London park with two of her daughters, and her "regal wave" had consisted of a languid black-gloved hand being raised an inch or two and doing a quarter-turn in the air.

"Right," I said. I turned to the others and repeated Ky-Lin's instructions, then rose to my feet. It didn't help that one of them had gone to sleep, but to disguise this I did a little shuffle-like dance turning in a circle before facing my audience. My heart was beating like a captured bird, but after ten minutes and Ky-Lin was still droning away in my voice, I relaxed a little. I mouthed, I nodded, I shook my head, I waved my hands every now and again on cue. As I gained confidence I overdid it.

"Steady on," murmured Ky-Lin. "You'll never make Covent Garden at this rate . . ."

In between "our" speech, he told me what he was saying. We were on a special mission, but had left our trail on purpose to meet the great and fabled horsemen of the Plains, who were in a position to help us, if they so wished.

Of course the fame of the shaman had also preceded him, and we had brought a couple of gifts as appreciation for receiving us so cordially.

"Tell Toby to go to Makub's horse and unearth a packet of hashish—just one, mind—and ditto of tobacco."

After a moment or two of indecision he was allowed to go, escorted of course, and when he returned he reported that our gear had not been touched, but that the ponies had been hobbled and were grazing.

"Good," muttered Ky-Lin. "That means they are still undecided how to deal with us."

To say the shaman was pleased with his gift would have been an understatement. His eyes gleamed, his tall bean-pole body gave a little shimmy, but of course his words were less effusive. He thanked us as if we had merely gifted him a half-dozen eggs, but his fingers were trembling as he pulled out a kind of pipe from his tatty clothing and proceeded to pack it with a lot of hashish and a little tobacco, lit it and puffed contentedly, until the sweetish smell of the drug over-rode all other odours.

I could see the other members of the tribe sniffing appreciatively. Was it possible, I wondered to myself, to become affected by the smoke?

"Very unlikely," murmured Ky-Lin, reading my thoughts again. "But any noxious fumes from that sort of thing can harm others . . . Now I am going to demand breakfast!"

It worked. Ten minutes later we were presented with bowls of a milky porridge, followed by a sort of blood-sausage wrapped in rice-flour pancakes, and bowls of pale tea. Everyone was eating with us, and I noticed their appreciation was expressed by loud belchings.

"Tell the others to copy," said Ky-Lin. "Bad manners not to."

Toby managed well enough, so did Danny, but Claude and I, try as we would, couldn't even manage the tiniest burp. Having been brought up to repress any such manifestation of bodily functions, I found I was now surprisingly embarrassed at *not* being able to!

"Wait for it," murmured Ky-Lin. "First Master Claude . . ." A moment later Claude apparently obliged, looking as startled as if he had sat on a thistle, wondering where the sound had come from. "Yes," said Ky-Lin. "I can throw my voice. Useful sometimes. Your turn . . ."

My expressions of appreciation were more genteel, but still I blushed.

"Now down to business," said Ky-Lin when the debris had been cleared away. "First we'll soften them up with a story . . . Ready?"

He proceeded to tell them the story of the little slave-boy Summer had called "Tug," because she couldn't pronounce his name, whom she had rescued and taken with her on her journeying, until he had been fortuitously re-united with his tribe.

Ky-Lin's account however, differed a little from the fragment I remembered from my uncle's summary. "Once upon a time, many, many moons ago, before your father's father's father's time, a prince was born to your people. At that time your herds stretched from dawn to sunset across the plains and your people were as numerous as the stars in the sky . . ."

The shaman was half-asleep, but everyone else shuffled forward on their heels, and the light from the tent-flap was dimmed as those outside leant in to listen too. It seemed that like children all over the world, there was nothing these people loved better than a story.

"This prince, Xytilchihijyckntug—" There was a great gasp from the audience and several of them nudged each other, so perhaps Ky-Lin had got it right. Even the shaman now had one eye open. "This prince could outrun the wind, outride the greatest horseman in the world, throw a spear farther than the eye could see and charm both men and women with his wit and wisdom. He visited other peoples to bring back to his own people the best of other cultures. He lived to a great age, outliving his three wives and was survived by fourteen sons and seven daughters. When he died it seemed the whole world mourned his passing, for the sun withheld his face for seven days, the moon was veiled, the winds were hushed and the clouds wept for sorrow . . ."

In other words, it rained for a week.

"But the story I have to tell," continued Ky-Lin (and me), "concerns a time when the prince was only a young boy, some ten or eleven years old . . ." And he went on to tell the story more or less as I knew it. How the boy was captured, sold and re-sold until Summer bought him at auction, being the nice girl she was, and how they travelled together until they came across some of his tribespeople performing at a fair, when he went back with them. Not as briefly as that, of course, but with much verbiage and colourful episodes which served to show the young prince's promise, even at that age.

Our audience were quiet as mice, except for now and again a little "hoo!" or "ha!" of appreciation.

There was no mention of the Ring, nor how Tug had repaid his debt by rescuing Summer from jail, instead I heard to my astonishment that *he* had taught *her* his language, instead of the other way round, which is why I could speak it now. Apparently too, Summer had put off her own journeyings in order to return him to his people without delay.

I began to see where all this was leading: the idea of a long-ago debt that now needed repaying—but Ky-Lin was winding up his peroration.

"They finally parted with tears of regret, the prince swearing a solemn oath on the bones of his forefathers that if ever Summer, her heirs or friends needed help from him or his tribe, in the however distant future, that help would be forthcoming. And now," said Ky-Lin simply, "we are here to collect the debt."

But how, I wondered, were we going to persuade these people that we were Summer's heirs and assigns after all this time?

Our audience glanced at one another, not sure whether they had heard aright and the shaman suddenly snapped upright on his stool and glared at us suspiciously.

"Before you presume to collect this so-called debt—" (Ky-Lin translating) "—I should first want proof that you are what you say you are . . ."

"Of course!" Ky-Lin and I interrupted. "You could not believe we would offend your hospitality by impersonation? If you will be patient for a moment or two longer we will present our credentials. I must tell you a little more about the girl, Summer, who rescued your prince from a life of slavery and degradation . . ."

Skipping over the awkward bits, Ky-Lin and I told of how Summer, while with the prince, had been entrusted with a fabulous dragon's egg— gasp from the audience—which, after she had seen the prince safely back with his people, she had carried to the dragon's lair in a certain Blue Mountain.

As she attempted to return the egg, it had been stolen by a traitorous companion, and she had lost her life in consequence. (Sympathetic groans from the audience.) For many moons the egg had been lost, but it had now been found, and the dragons wanted it back. They had given my brother and me and our two servants until the next full moon to return the egg, otherwise they would issue forth from the Blue Mountain and lay ravage to all the lands within their reach, carry off the young women and children, kill the men and the horses.

We had been abandoned by our guide, who had run off with food and transport, so we needed their aid to reach our objective in time, before the dragons revolted. . . .

How were Ky-Lins allowed to tell such awful whoppers, I wondered? Perhaps they crossed their hooves, like we crossed our fingers behind our backs.

Our audience were impressed, no doubt about that, but the shaman hadn't finished with us.

"And where is this fabulous egg?" he demanded, rattling all his bone decorations. "And how is it that you came into its possession?"

Ky-Lin had obviously thought about this one, because the answer came pat enough. "Because I inherited from Summer the ability to recognize it for what it is, and also because I can converse with animals, as she could, and as your prince will have told you."

The shaman could obviously neither confirm nor deny this last, but demanded to see the egg, so off Toby went once more and fetched it back wrapped as usual in my shawl. As he unwrapped it I could see just how much it had grown since the last time I saw it. It must now weigh at least twelve pounds, and seemed to be glowing slightly. There was a definite warmth there too.

I invited the shaman to come forward and inspect it. He walked around it, leant over and peered at it closely then finally, very gingerly, poked out a bony finger and touched it, then snatched it away again, obviously surprised by its warmth.

I/we invited him to listen to it, see if he could hear anything. He knelt down with a rattle of bones and applied his left ear to the Eg. At first he shook his head, then suddenly stiffened, touched a finger to his own heart and then leant forward again, only to shoot back in a surprisingly agile somersault, his mouth an O of amazement and awe.

"I added a hiss or two," murmured Ky-Lin. "And a very little roar . . . Don't worry: he was the only one who heard it."

I turned my chuckle into a cough. Surely now we had convinced everyone! The shaman, however, wanted one last try.

"You said that this—Summer?—could converse with animals? And that you have inherited that gift?"

I nodded, panicking. How to prove it?

"Beau . . ." murmured Ky-Lin.

"But he's—"

"Here," said Beau-cat, nudging the back of my knee. "Been hiding."

I knelt down and whispered. "That silly old wizard over there wants proof that we can communicate. It's very important. Could you forget your dignity for a moment and, say, walk in a circle, sit up and beg, and lie down and roll from side to side?"

He looked at me with those beautiful blue eyes. "What's it worth?"

I blinked. It was unlike him to ask for favours. "What do you suggest?"

The answer, when it came, was so unexpected that I almost forgot where we were.

"How about a kiss?"

I was scandalised. "One doesn't kiss cats."

"Oh, well: worth a try . . . Now, what was it you wanted me to do again?"

Strolling into the middle, he gazed around the audience with that haughty air that some cats seem to be able to summon at will. The people shuffled back, obviously not used to such a large animal—he certainly had grown since I had rescued him: almost twice as big, I reckoned.

He looked back at me. "Now?"

"Please . . ."

He went through the routine with an air of the utmost boredom, as if humouring a group of children, and when he had finished he sat down and washed his face, to some applause.

The shaman hung on, however. "How do I know this is not a well-established routine?" He rattled his bones menacingly.

"Then you choose something you want him to do, and I will instruct him . . ."

"Tell him, then, to jump over the brazier. And back again."

This would not be easy. The brazier, on its tripod, stood perhaps four feet from the ground, and it was glowing with heat.

I explained to Beau. "Can you do it?" I asked anxiously. "I don't want you to hurt yourself."

For answer he stood up, backed away a little, eyed his target and then leapt, not once but four times: twice there, twice back. The audience burst into spontaneous applause and Beau-cat retreated to my side.

"Satisfied?"

"Not bad—for a cat," said Ky-Lin. "Now, Miss Sophy, let's finish this with some fireworks of our own. Raise your arms above your head, bring them down slowly, then point your index fingers at the fire."

The resultant display of coloured balls, stars, ribbons of smoke and tongues of fire almost emptied the yurt, but to their credit Toby, Danny and Claude stayed where they were, with the cat.

I looked around for the scorch-marks on the rugs that lined the tent but there weren't any.

"Pure illusion," said Ky-Lin. "They saw what they wanted to see. And now," he added briskly, "I think some luncheon is in order!"

Pancakes, cheese and milky tea later and we were ready to go. We had fresh, tough-looking little ponies, extra food, fuel and blankets, and two guides, only too anxious to get going.

Ky-Lin reminded me that we shouldn't need any of Makub's hashish or opium anymore, so we left the majority for the shaman, keeping some back for our guides.

We didn't see the shaman again; I think he had retired to bed with a headache. Of one thing I was sure: he was glad to see the back of us.

Later that night after we had made camp and had eaten some more of the delicious blood-sausage I had warmed up, I congratulated Ky-Lin on his strategy, and Beau-cat on his bravery.

"I knew we were all right if we survived the initial attack," said Ky-Lin. "All children love a story, love to be frightened by tales of dragons and such-like, and adore fireworks. And that's all they were: gullible children."

"Well I, for one," said Claude, "will miss their delicious food. The milky tea was most refreshing."

"I prefer less milk in mine," said Danny. "But these sausages are the best I've tasted in an age."

"Good," said Ky-Lin. "You'll probably get offered some more before this trip is over. The pack-ponies are mares, and the other ponies have already been cupped more than once."

Toby and I understood at once, I think, but the other two had to have it explained to them.

"How else would they get fresh milk and blood, except from their horses?" said Toby, though he was looking a bit green. "It obviously doesn't harm the horses, otherwise they wouldn't do it."

I remembered something I had read once. "I believe they prefer their milk fermented: they say it's a nice refreshing drink . . ."

Without a word the other two got up and disappeared in different directions, not coming back for sometime . . .

Our guides didn't believe in wasting time. They hurried and harried us from dawn till dusk, determined to be rid of us as soon as possible.

They were probably scared that the Eg would hatch out while we were travelling, and woke us up before dawn, curtailed our lunch-break and had us on the move until long after the sun had gone down.

The little ponies were more than equal to the task, and even Claude didn't fall off so often. Rapidly the mountains drew nearer, and fearsome they looked, with sharp inclines, jagged tops, steep cliffs and great icicles hanging hundreds of feet up.

It was much, much colder, and we were glad of the extra blankets at night. We were already wearing most of our winter gear, and Beaucat's fur was growing longer and thicker.

On the sixth day we left the plains for good and started to climb through increasingly dense forest of pine and fir, their thick, resinous smell with us all day. It was also getting difficult to breathe again with the increased altitude. Their was no definite path to follow but our guides were adept at finding the easiest way, sometimes having to hack a gap for us with their little axes.

We all felt a little odd: Claude had a couple of nosebleeds, Danny started talking to himself and I had a slight headache, but Ky-Lin told me that this was just a touch of mountain-sickness, which affected different people in different ways, and it would pass as we became more acclimatised.

We climbed for three more days, more slowly as the ascent grew steeper, and Ky-Lin worried as to how we would carry our food and gear once our guides had left with their horses. Toby suggested that we try to build a sledge, so for two nights we laboured, with the aid of the guides and their efficient axes, who chopped pine and spruce, until we had a reasonable enough sledge, capable of carrying at least our food, fuel and any extra gear. All the rest would have to be carried in our haversacks.

At last we reached the head of the pass and made camp in one of the most bleak and exposed places I had ever seen, open on all sides to the weather.

"They should call this Four-Winds Crossing," said Danny, shivering like the rest of us as we huddled round a sparse fire. What he said was true: wherever we sat or crouched, there was an icy wind at our back. I crossed over to the guides and handed them some hashish and a couple of pellets of opium for helping us. They accepted with grunts, but I could see all they were waiting for was their departure in the morning.

In the event they didn't wait for dawn, but were packed up and gone without a goodbye by the time we had struggled awake.

"Right," said Ky-Lin. "Now for it!" and he stretched and creaked and popped until he was once more pony-size, which still made Danny and Claude nervous. "Told you I would pull my weight. Load up the sledge then, and let's get going. It's all downhill from here . . ."

22

River of Ice

What Ky-Lin didn't say was that going down could be quite as painful as climbing, for you were using completely different muscles; also falling upwards wasn't as perilous as falling down a slope—in fact some of that first descent was so steep that we had to hold the sledge back rather than pull it behind us.

That initial way down wound irritatingly between interlocking spurs of the mountains, so although we moved as fast as we could, as far as losing height was concerned it was a slow business. We stopped for a quick mid-day snack, cheese and dried fruit, and then pressed on. Later a few flakes of snow drifted down, and the sky was a greyish yellow.

Ky-Lin looked anxious. "There's a lot more snow up there—we'll need shelter tonight. These hills are mainly limestone, so there should be caves farther down."

By sundown we had managed to find a small scoop in the hillside, surrounded by boulders, with an overhang of rock. I made a fire and boiled up enough rice and fish to last until the following night and, at Ky-Lin's suggestion, put the pan outside to catch any snow for filling our water-bottles.

It was a miserable night. Quite apart from the moaning wind that seemed determined to seek us out, both with noise and cold, and the rattle of stones intermittently falling from the rocks above, we all ached all over. Ky-Lin touched us all with his healing horn and that alleviated the pains a little, but did nothing for the cold; however I was comforted by the warmth of Beau-cat, who crept under my blankets and snuggled up against my back.

It had been snowing heavily overnight; as we progressed the sun melted most of it away, but the ground was slippery and several times I ended up on my behind. One consolation was that the spurs of the mountains were widening and our course downwards was faster and easier, although the going was very uneven: smooth rock, stony clefts, thin soil.

At last we rounded the last spur of the mountain and there before us, some five hundred feet below, was a wide valley, sloping gently towards the horizon, the midday sun glittering on what looked like a sliver of river, that grew larger as it progressed southward.

"Great! Now we can float the sledge down the water," said Danny, clapping his hands together; he was tired of dragging on the ropes.

"Not on there we can't." said Ky-Lin. "And tell him, tell them all, not to make any sudden loud noises." He glanced up at the mountains on either side. "There's enough snow up there to give us all a nasty shock."

"Why can't we float the sledge?"

"Because that isn't a river of water: it's a river of ice. A glacier."

A glacier! I had heard of them, read something about them many years ago. Rapidly I translated Ky-Lin's words to the others, who gazed down at it with a wonder equal to my own.

"Well, if it's a river of ice, why can't we slide the sledge along it?"

"Not on that surface," said Ky-Lin. "At least, not for more than a short distance. It is like a badly iced cake, and is rough with stones, rocks, whatever has got caught up with it over the years. Also, it moves, albeit slowly, more towards the middle and the edges tend to pile up with rubbish. You'll see when we get there."

I translated again, and then we began the steep descent, which was quite the most hazardous part of our journey so far; it was far steeper than we had had to cope with so far, and at one stage we were literally clinging to the rocks with the sledge dangling beneath us. All the while Ky-Lin was trying to educate me with talk of moraines, ablation, neves, sublimation, crystallisation, firn and crevasses, but I'm afraid I was too busy trying to get down in one piece to pay much attention. Afterwards I wished I had, but by then it was too late.

The glacier started like a thin tongue of ice, but gradually widened until it filled most of the valley. As Ky-Lin had predicted, it was very difficult to walk upon. Not only was it both skiddy and slidy, it was also gritty, fissured and uneven. The sledge was more difficult to manage than before, because we had to seek out the smoother bits all the time, or lift it bodily over ridges as high as my waist. Of all of us, the terrain was toughest on Beau-cat. Not because he wasn't far more agile than the rest of us, but because of the tenderness of his paws; he could manage stones and rocks, but the gritty surface of the glacier scratched and tore at his pads, so for the most part he rode on the sledge.

The one bonus we had was to realise how we were definitely moving downhill, cheered at our pause to eat at mid-day to see the highest mountains receding behind us.

"Another two or three days," said Ky-Lin.

We took turns with the sledge, generally an hour at a time, although Ky-Lin, pony-size, always did a double stint. After eating that day it was Toby's and my turn, it being easier with two at once, each with a length of rope. Suddenly Toby stopped on a smooth stretch, so abruptly that the sledge ran into the back of my legs.

"Ouch! What's the matter?"

"Quick, over here everyone!" he shouted. "Just look at this!"

"Hush!" said Ky-Lin, sharply. "We don't want to bring the snows down on us."

"What is it?" Claude, Danny and I were over by his side in a moment, for he was pointing downward through the ice.

"Look," he breathed. "Just look at that . . ."

Generally the ice was cloudy and we could not see more than an inch or so beneath the surface, but here we could see far farther by a freak of the glacier's movement. What we saw was like something out of a book of faery. There, trapped beneath the ice, were the antlered heads of two enormous stags, locked in a battle of death. Anywhere else their bones would have long ago vanished, but here they were forever immortalised. We could only clearly see their heads, part of their shoulders and one leg, but they were so large, even at this distance beneath the ice, that I found it hard to believe they had ever existed.

"Giant elk," said Ky-Lin. "Some call them Irish elk, because their remains have been found in the peat bogs of that island. Peat is a good preservative."

"Why the two of them together?" asked Toby. "Did they kill each other at the same time?"

I translated Ky-Lin's reply for him. No, one would die first, but because their antlers were locked solid, the other wouldn't be able to free itself, and would die later of wounds or starvation, as sometimes happens even now with the red deer of Europe.

I shivered, not only because it was cold, with the bitter north wind chasing us down the valley, but also because it was sad to think of death coming that way—the victor becoming the vanquished. Somehow for a brief moment a thousand years, two, three became now and they were here—

I shivered again.

"Come on," said Ky-Lin gently. "We've a way still to go before nightfall. *They* are history: *we* are now. Their reincarnations will have passed through many stages by now." I had forgotten he was a follower of the Buddha.

That night we found a better cave, which seemed warmer, but this, we discovered, was because of the snow which had again fallen overnight. The wind seemed to have increased and was pluming the snow on the tips of the mountains into puffs of what looked like mist, and drove icy particles skittering unpleasantly across the ice of the glacier.

All night long we had been aware of the creaks and groans of the glacier as it moved in the centre at an average of one foot per day. Fresh-fed by spring melts it would flow faster, also in the heat of summer, but now it was almost static. Despite this it still made the most weird noises as the ice rubbed against the banks, or thrust up a barrier in the centre.

What happened later was meant to be, perhaps not. All I know is it changed our journey irrevocably. It was a mistake, my mistake, and a costly one.

It was Toby's and my stint to pull the sledge, the last one before our midday halt. We had done a half-hour when Toby went off to relieve himself. The sledge was much lighter now, because of the food and fuel we had consumed and I didn't find it too burdensome, but the Afghan rifle kept getting in the way. Danny had insisted on bringing it with us, saying darkly that "it might come in useful," but so far it had just been a nuisance. For the dozenth time it hit me in the back of the legs and I lost patience. Tugging it free, I sent it skidding across the ice in Danny's direction.

"If you want this, then carry it yourself . . ."

"Now don't get in a paddy, darlin' girl . . ."

"For the last time, I'm not your darlin' girl!" and I pulled away as fast as I could. Not far to go now: another couple of days or so and our journey would be over. I fell into a reverie of just what I would do when I got back to Hightop Hall, and saw that I was falling behind with my daydreaming. Seeing a nice long, smooth, stretch of untrodden snow, sloping down for at least two hundred yards, I thought: perfect! Why pull when one could ride?

Gathering up the ropes I went to the back of the sledge and gave it a shove, then ran forward and jumped on as it gathered speed. My weight made it go even faster and I waved gaily to the others as I drew level. Toby waved back, but it was with both arms and urgently, while Ky-Lin started to bound across the ice towards me. I waved again, to assure them I was fine—

Then the world disappeared.

One moment I was accelerating along the fresh snow trying to keep the sledge in a straight line, as I had when a child, delighting in whizzing down the slopes near the village, to tumble off at the bottom and be scooped up in my father's arms, the next I was falling into oblivion, my mouth full of snow, blocking out my shout of panic. There was a bump that nearly knocked the breath from my lungs, a knock on my head and momentarily I lost consciousness.

I opened my eyes again to a blur of white, pain, a dragging sensation in my left wrist, piercing cold and complete disorientation. There was a creaking, crunching noise in my ears, the falling of stones . . .

"Stay still, stay perfectly still . . ." It was Ky-Lin's voice in my ears, thought rather than the spoken word. "Just don't move, however much it hurts. We're coming to get you. No, don't look up: just *wait*. Don't try to talk . . ."

I did as I was told, desperately fighting all my instincts to move, to yell out my terror, to wriggle free of whatever held me fast. I was shivering like the leaves on an aspen tree, my teeth chattering like the proverbial castanets. All I could see from my prone position was a wall of ice, layered like a giant sandwich: white, grey, stony, clear, cloudy, thick, thin. Even the strips were wavering before my eyes, for my shivering was growing uncontrollable.

All at once there was a creaking noise above me and instinctively I cowered, fearing a fall of rock, but a moment later I saw a pair of feet followed by the attached legs, and a moment later there came the reassuring voice of Toby.

"It's all right, Sophy: just lay still."

Idiotically I wanted to correct his English. "Lie . . ." I whispered, but I'm sure he didn't hear me.

"Keep still. I know you're cold and you hurt, but for the moment you are best just laying there while I set things up. You're on a ledge—that's why you mustn't move—and I'm going to land just beside you. The sledge-rope is still attached to your wrist, and I'm going to cut it loose so they can haul you up. Meanwhile I shall stay with you." He was speaking in a very low voice, as if he feared he would bring a further fall down on us.

It seemed to take an age. I could feel his feet nudging my body, hear the sawing of the rope, and then suddenly my wrist was free, the pain started to subside and a creaking, bumping noise told me the sledge was being retrieved. I was now so cold my teeth no longer chattered: they felt as though they were glued together, and I was sure that if I bit my tongue I wouldn't feel it.

There was another slithering noise and then Toby was fastening the rope around my waist. He thrust my hands around something, but I couldn't feel what it was.

"Now, hang on and don't struggle. You'll be perfectly safe. Don't look down . . ."

There was a sudden jerk, and I screamed as I found myself spinning and twisting in space. For a long moment I panicked, as the rope slipped from my waist to my chest, and I was afraid of the disgrace of soiling myself but luckily I had to concentrate on just breathing, for my weight was tightening the rope cruelly. At last I realised I was moving upwards and, risking a look, I saw a ring of faces above me, spinning slowly round.

It seemed like forever, but it could only have been a couple of minutes later that my front was being scraped painfully across the lip of the crevasse into which I had fallen, as I was finally hauled to safety. I was pulled away across the ice to safety, and a moment later Danny was rubbing my arms and legs, and as Toby was hauled to the surface by Claude and Ky-Lin, all joined in carrying me to the edge and wrapping me in blankets, while a warm, furry blanket wound itself round my neck and proceeded to lick at my ears and nose. I attempted feebly to push away Beau-cat's rasping tongue, but Ky-Lin stopped me.

"Let him. Best thing for you: we don't want frostbite."

Ky-Lin pronounced that there were no bones broken, just bumps and bruises and a slightly sprained wrist.

"No more travellng today. Stay where you are, and I'll scout around for a decent shelter." No words of blame for stupid behaviour: if I had been wider awake I would have realised there was some good reason why the rest of the party had been on a completely different course. I was lucky to be alive, I knew that now, and I tried, inadequately, to thank them all.

I felt even worse when I discovered that the sledge was a write-off and that we had lost a lot of the heavier provisions: rice, fuel, honey, the axe and larger cooking-pot. We still had one spare blanket, a small pan, some flour, dried meat and fruit, but it was a pitifully small heap. Thank goodness there were only a couple of days or so to go. . . .

Ky-Lin found us a roomier cave than usual, and once we had everything inside it started to snow again, so we probably wouldn't have got far even without my "accident." Claude and Danny were trying to wrest apart the shattered remains of the sledge, but they needed the missing axe.

"Pity!" said Danny. "It would have made a broth of a fire."

"The wood's damp anyway," said Claude. "No, it's hopeless."

I was still shivering, and there was a tightness in my chest. Ky-Lin glanced at me anxiously.

"Claude is wrong," he said. "Nothing is entirely hopeless . . . Tell them to stand back from the sledge."

Somewhere at the back of my mind I seemed to recall a fragment of Summer's journey: was it something to do with Ky-Lin splitting rocks, or metal, or something?

There was a sudden flash of light, a scrunching noise, chips of wood seemed to fly everywhere, then rearranged themselves into a neat heap of firewood in the corner of the cave.

"Wow!" said Danny and Claude in unison.

"How did he do *that?*" asked Toby.

"Tell him," said Ky-Lin, "that it is literally the triumph of mind over matter."

"Magic?"

Ky-Lin shook his head. "No magic. Just a simple matter of disassociating various elements into their separate constituents and reassembling them into a combination more acceptable to our present needs."

I tried to translate this but failed: I hadn't the slightest idea what he was talking about. I glanced at Ky-Lin and thought I detected the fragment of a smile—obviously he didn't want me to understand, or he was making the whole thing up and it *was* magic.

We lit a small but warming fire and Claude took over the cooking, producing pancakes with the last of the flour and pouring melted cheese over them. Everything else would have to be divided up between us and carried in the haversacks, but we decided to leave this until morning, especially as Ky-Lin had diminished in size, explaining to me that splitting the wood had weakened him somewhat. I made sure he ate part of a pancake and some dried fruit, then he curled up in a corner and slept till morning, when he seemed almost fully recovered.

That afternoon while Claude soaked some dried meat to add to a supper of rice, we played desultory word-games, several times looking

out to see whether it had stopped snowing, but it hadn't. The tightness
in my chest didn't seem to lessen, and that night I kept waking up with
a troublesome little cough.

In the morning everything was covered with a fresh fall of snow
that squeaked its protest underfoot and dogged our footsteps. We had
parcelled out what remained of our goods, Toby being in charge solely
of the Eg, which was by far the heaviest individual burden.

"Take care now," advised Ky-Lin, now nearly back to pony-size.
"If we keep to the edge of the glacier, the snow will have cushioned
the rough places."

We made reasonable progress, and before long I was perspiring. I
looked across at the others: they too were mopping their brows and
Danny, now using the long Afghan rifle as a walking stick, had undone
his jacket.

Ky-Lin lifted his nose and sniffed the wind, which had swung round
to the south. "There's a temporary thaw coming," he said. "We shall
have to take extra care. This will activate small streams and rivulets and
may well loosen the snow above us. We'd better move out into the centre
of the glacier, just in case."

We ate a frugal luncheon under an overhang so we didn't have to
sit on the snow, then moved out again. We had been plagued by thin
wisps of mist all morning as the sun sucked up moisture from the snow,
but suddenly these cleared temporarily and we all saw it at once. There,
admittedly at least a day's journey away, was a green valley.

We gazed at it disbelievingly for at least a minute before the mists
closed in again, then we all started talking at once.

"Are you sure that wasn't a mirage?"

"We should be there tomorrow!"

"What a relief to see a bit of green again!"

"At last some proper food . . ."

Then what should have been the impossible happened.

Danny, in his exuberance raised the Afghan rifle in the air and
mimed what we had seen the tribesmen do in reality: firing a round into
the air. He pulled the trigger twice, mouthing silent "Bang-bangs."

Then three things happened simultaneously. Ky-Lin whispered an
urgent "No!" The Ring gave a tremendous stab, and Danny pressed the
trigger for the third time. There was a terrific bang that ricocheted from
side to side of the ravine, then a horrible hush.

Danny threw the rifle away, whispering: "I didn't know it was
loaded!" and we all glanced at each other in terror. For a moment it
looked as though we might have got away with it, but the Ring was still

stabbing away furiously and Ky-Lin was herding us urgently towards the edge of the glacier.

"Find us a cave, a large one, Master Beau!"

Then it came.

At first it was a rumble so low that it was almost under the threshold of sound, but it grew in pitch and intensity until it drowned all other sound. We ran as fast as we could, but the clinging snow impeded our progress, and it was like trying to run in thick, dry sand. We were only halfway to the edge when Ky-Lin left my side and went back the way he had come, and to my horror I saw Toby had fallen. I ran a few more faltering steps and then glanced back. Toby was hobbling and Ky-Lin took him up on his back and started back towards us, but at that very moment a huge slab of ice came skating down the glacier towards them.

I stifled a scream, saw Ky-Lin leap aboard the ice, carrying Toby, and then the vanguard of the avalanche was upon us.

With a huge rumbling roar and an icy blast of air the snow bore down on us like huge waves on the sea-shore, turning over and over, curling and spuming, cresting impossibly high. I looked for Toby and Ky-Lin but couldn't see them, forgetting my own danger until hands grabbed me from either side and dragged me away.

I couldn't see for the tears in my eyes. Gone, probably for ever, were Toby, Ky-Lin and the Eg. Not that the last mattered against the lives of the other two: people I had loved, my especial friends. I would have given anything to have them back beside me.

A moment later I was pulled into a black hole, the rumbling and crashing behind me intensified, I was thrown to the ground and then utter darkness . . .

23

The Caves

The dark . . .

Darkness and pain and partial deafness, choking on dust, the rumble of stone, panic of emptiness—

"I'm here, I'm here!" A brush of fur against my hand. "Don't panic! Just get your breath back and sit up. We are in a large cave and are safe for the moment. Claude, Danny, you and I. And nobody's hurt; just a few bruises, that's all. I'm going to leave you for a moment to explore but I'll be back in a few minutes."

It was the longest speech he had made through the Ring: I realised that, even in my distressed state.

A wail came from somewhere to my right. "Jesus, Mary and Joseph! My *head!*"

"Your head! It was my head you hit with yours!"

"And whose fault was that, may I ask? Where are we, anyway? And where's Sophy?"

"I'm over here, to your left. Stop arguing and come and join me . . ."

Scrabbling, scraping sounds, suppressed swearing and we were all together. A quick hug all round, and then the questions. I wanted to know if they had seen any more of Toby and Ky-Lin than I had, the answer no, and they both wanted to know where we were.

"Sure, and they were together," said Danny. "And a canny old thing like Ky-Lin knows how to survive."

"He won't let Toby come to any harm," comforted Claude. "They are probably looking for us now. . . ."

I told them what Beau had told me, and a moment later he was back, rubbing against my knees.

"No way out the way we came in, I'm afraid. The fall brought down part of the entrance tunnel, and it must be blocked by at least twelve feet of debris."

I could hear the panic in my voice. "You mean—we're trapped? If there's no way out we'll die!" Without thinking I had spoken the words aloud, instead of by thought-process through the Ring, and immediately I could hear the others muttering hysterically.

"Now look what you've done," said Beau-cat. "I never said we were trapped."

"We're in a cave, aren't we, and you said the entrance was blocked— shut up you two—so we must be trapped . . . mustn't we?"

"I said we couldn't get out the way we came in, yes, but that doesn't mean there aren't other ways out. This is a large cave—just sing a couple of lines of your favourite hymn. Yes, go on!"

"All things bright and beautiful . . ." How inappropriate! Danny and Claude must have thought I had completely lost my mind, but as my voice strengthened I understood what the cat had meant. It was not like singing in an overstuffed sitting-room, far more like being in church. "You're right . . . But how do we know there are any passages leading out?"

"Trust me. Stand up and turn around slowly. See if you can feel any difference in the quality of the air. No, I'm not joking. . . ."

I did as he said, then repeated the manouevre. Sure enough I felt a slight difference in the movement of the air. I pointed to the two directions I thought it was coming from, forgetting of course that we were in darkness. But it seemed he could see me.

"Correct. Well done. As it happens I have already found our first passage and it leads in the right direction."

"How do you know?"

"Because we want downwards and as far as possible east of south. That way we have a good chance of finding the ultimate way out. And, yes, before you ask, I do know my south from my north!"

I was quite sure this new, masterful Beau-cat did. I told the others why I had been singing and the fact that Beau had found a passage for us to follow, at which they cheered up considerably.

"Now," said Beau, "retrieve your haversacks and let's see what we have. Yours is a little way to your left. I believe there are some candles in there."

He was quite right. There were a half-dozen ordinary ones and four

long-burners, plus vestas. I wasted a couple of the latter before I managed to get a candle going, then bent to light some more.

"Steady on," said Beau. "One at a time. We don't know how long
those will have to last."

So, by the light of one small candle we emptied our haversacks
and took stock of what we had. It was a pitifully small heap. We each
had a blanket, mug and water-bottle, the latter full. Then there were
two coils of rope, a quantity of firewood, the small cooking pot and
a ladle. As far as food was concerned, it was a small quantity of everything. A little rice and couscous, but not much; a pack of dates,
another of dried figs, a few dried vegetables, some nuts, cheese and a
handful of raisins. I would have said that would give us one meal, but
not much more.

"Now that we haven't got Ky-Lin with us, it is up to you to take
charge. Those two need leading, they can't do it on their own. So, I will
help you, and you must be positive and firm. Every day I will scout
ahead and find the best way forward—"

"Every *day?* I thought we'd be out of here by tonight!"

"Sorry, Sophy, but I think it will take longer than that. These hills
are honeycombed with caves, but they don't all lead the right way; some
are dead-ends and others may be too small to traverse. So, come on and
give your first orders. Pack up everything except the shorter rope, get
fastened together so we don't get parted. I'll lead the way, you follow
with a guarded candle. We'll keep going as long as we can on this first
stage."

He paused for a moment. "Tell me: how is the Ring?"

"The Ring?" I looked down at it. "It's fine. . . . Why?"

"Then that means we are doing the right thing. Let me know if it
starts playing up, won't you?"

I nodded. After that first stab when we tumbled into the cave it had
been quiet, so perhaps things weren't quite as bad as they seemed.

I decided to take Beau's advice and be positive, so I organised the
others as he had suggested. "What time is it, Claude?"

He looked at his watch, shook it, looked again.

"Just after two in the afternoon, Sophy. I would have thought it later
than that."

So would I: just over a half-hour since we had been entombed,
because I had checked my fob-watch minutes before the avalanche.
"Well, that's a bonus: means we can travel further . . . Right! Off we
go! At least it isn't cold . . ."

In fact, after the sub-zero temperatures we had had to endure, it was almost pleasantly warm; I presumed these caves retained more or less the same temperature, like cellars: cool in summer, warm in winter, although it didn't do anything for my cough.

We started out with high hopes, but after an hour or so of stumbling along a stony, unlit, uneven, twisting passage, anchored only by a rope that we had to adjust because somebody either trod on somebody's heels or was jerked forward painfully, we were all short-tempered and much less sanguine. The passage was also not uniformly wide, nor did it slope down evenly. Once there was a sudden drop of about three feet; once a rock-fall almost blocked our way completely: another time we had to lower our heads to avoid bumping our heads on the roof—especially Claude!

We conversed in whispers—why whispers? Because it is a known fact that one always whispers in churches, cathedrals, libraries, museums, catacombs—anywhere one feels awe, unease or fear. Anything was possible in these caves; I would not have been surprised if they brought forth all the things which used to give me nightmares as a child: bats, ogres, witches, trolls, statues-which-came-to-life and giant cockroaches.

"Rubbish!" said Beau's thought-voice. "Don't you think that I would sense those things? Stop worrying!" And he rubbed his face against my thigh. Goodness, he certainly was growing. . . .

"You almost sound as if you are enjoying all this!"

"Why not? Better than giving up and crying! Think of it as a game, a puzzle, a maze to solve. We'll get out, never fear, but it may take a day or two. At the moment we are travelling at a snail's pace, but when we get into some of the larger caves we should move faster. Don't forget you have to measure this stumbling around in semi-darkness with what we achieved in the open. Twenty miles outside, what with twists and turns as well, will take four times as long in here."

An hour and a half later we reached the end of the passage, which debouched into a small chamber, before splitting into two exits. While Beau searched ahead we took a well-earned rest, ate a couple of mouthfuls of nuts and dried fruit, then pressed on again. This time the going was easier, but there were several halts as we passed other passages which Beau had to scout. At one, tantalizingly, there came a breath of outside air, but the cat reported that it was only a narrow funnel that even he couldn't struggle through.

At last, after we had used three of the ordinary candles, we reached a larger cavern, and I decided that enough was enough and called a halt for the day.

"We're not going to spend the night in here?" asked Claude fearfully.

"You're not going to tell me that you really thought we would be tucked up safe in some cosy inn, are you?" said Danny. "Are you frightened of the dark, then?"

"Of course not," he answered hurriedly. "It's just that . . . that . . ."

"We're all in the same boat, and we're all together," I said. "So be a good lad and help me prepare something for supper."

We made a small but comfortable fire and boiled up the rest of the couscous with a scrap or two of the fish, and finished with some dates. Hardly satisfying, but better than nothing. We were all physically exhausted, but sleep didn't come easily: our bodies were tired, our minds wide awake. Not only was the ground uneven and stony, but everyone must have been worrying the same way I was: how long would we be in here? What would happen if the little food that was left ran out? Worse, how about using up all the candles? Would we wander endlessly until we lay down and died?

Danny sat up suddenly. "This is no use, you know. I'm not a bit sleepy. Why don't we have a sing-song or something?"

"Or a story," suggested Claude, who couldn't sing.

"A story it is then; who's to start?"

"You can, Danny," I said.

To his credit he told us an amusing folk-tale about how an enterprising Irish family finally outwitted a couple of ill-intentioned leprechauns.

Claude then told one of my favourites, "Stone Soup," how a cunning traveller and his dog conned a fat and lazy cook out of dinner and a gold coin. But of course this talk of food made us feel hungry again, so when it was my turn I steered away from all that and started to tell the tale of the "Princess and the Pea," but before I had finished I had the strong suspicion that I was talking to myself (and Beau).

"They're asleep," I said.

"Five minutes ago. An interesting tale. My governess never told me that one. But normal princesses aren't as tender-skinned as that."

"Cats don't have governesses, Beau. And how would you know how princesses feel?"

"Young princes have tutors or governesses, and they also have princesses as sisters."

"But you're not a prince—"

"Who says? Want to hear my story?"

I hesitated. The Ring was warm on my finger, the candle was out, what remained of the fire a couple of embers, but I was still not sleepy enough and my chest felt tight. What on earth would he invent to entertain? "All right, then . . ."

"Lie down, tuck yourself up, and I'll tell you just how a handsome prince was turned into a lowly cat . . ."

I see: it was one of those. A fairy-tale. At least "Stone Soup" could have had a basis in fact—just with a clever enough man and a stupid enough woman . . . But even thinking about that and my stomach started to protest, so I shut my eyes and concentrated on Beau's tale.

"Once upon a time," I murmured. "All the best fairy tales start that way. . . ."

"Once upon a time," he began obediently, "if that's what you want. But this is fact, not fiction."

"Anything you say . . ."

"This story begins in the country of Siam some few years ago," he began, and I snuggled down to listen through the Ring. "The current king had many wives and innumerable concubines, so there were plenty of royal princes and princesses—eleven of the former and twenty-three of the latter, if I remember correctly . . ."

I found myself drifting.

"The king decided he had to do something about it, as the palace was getting definitely overcrowded. All the royal children had had English governesses, and that is why I speak your language so well, but the king decided to give his sons the chance of further education, and arranged advantageous marriages for the girls. The princes were sent to foreign universities—"

"Oxford and Cambridge," I murmured sleepily. "Harvard and Yale . . ."

"And the Sorbonne, of course. That's where I went, and that is why I was pleased when you called me 'Beau,' the French for handsome."

"But you are a cat, not a prince!" I interrupted, waking up.

"Fiddlesticks, as you English say! You haven't heard the rest of the story . . ."

"Sorry, I won't interrupt again."

"Well, when I came back from the Sorbonne I found that my father had decided it was time that I got married. I was then twenty-four years old and in no mood to settle down. I asked him to send me abroad again for a while, to one of our embassies perhaps, but he was adamant. Until all of his sons had produced a son he would not be satisfied, for he had not yet decided whom to make his heir.

"That might have been acceptable to my other brothers, but not to me. I had always been a rebel, so I took off on my own with a purseful of money and some jewelry to enjoy the fleshpots of the world. My wild way of life led me into some very peculiar situations, but none so strange as an encounter I had in Spain. It was fiesta-time, and I had watched a very beautiful girl dancing all evening. It seemed she had noticed me, too, for when the dancing was over—and very late it was—she caught up with me as I was returning to my lodgings, and invited me to her place for a last drink. I was already stumbling-drunk, so it didn't seem at all unusual that a young woman like that was not chaperoned.

"As it was, I'm afraid I disappointed her, for immediately I entered her apartment I was sick, then fell asleep on the floor. Waking some time before dawn I found I was immensely thirsty, and wandered down a long corridor looking for the kitchen. On my way I became aware of some strange chanting coming from a room to my right, whose door was partially open. I peered in, intending to apologise to my pretty hostess and beg a glass of water, but what I saw drove all thoughts of thirst from my mind . . ."

He paused, and sighed. "We can finish the tale tomorrow. You must be very tired."

By now I was sitting bolt upright and the thought of sleep was far from my mind. "No, no, go on!"

"All right then . . . Where was I? Ah, yes. I peeped into the room, and I couldn't believe my eyes. An old crone, bent almost double with age, was hobbling round a bubbling cauldron on a brazier, muttering spells and charms! At first I thought it must be some ancient relative of the girl I had met earlier, then I noticed she was wearing the same dress, and in her ears were the same earrings! Even as I watched, I could see the spells begin to take effect; from looking about a hundred years old she was gradually straightening, and her hair was turning from white to its previous colour . . .

"I must have made some sound for suddenly she turned towards the door and saw me."

"Couldn't you just have run away?"

"I suppose I could—I certainly should have! But I suppose it was the residue of the drink talking, but whatever it was I stepped into the room and accused her of being a witch!"

"What did she do? What did she say?"

"At first she was surprised, then she was very angry that she had been found out, and told me to get out and never darken her doors again!"

"And did you?"

"No, I was an idiot. I did the very worst thing I could have done. She looked so stupid half-changed—"

"Half-changed?"

"The top half was nearly the pretty lady again, the bottom half was still the old crone. I couldn't help myself: I laughed at her."

There was silence.

"You don't believe me, do you?"

"I'm just suspending judgment, that's all," I said carefully. "Of course I don't believe in witches—"

"You should! It was she who made me what I am now. Apparently she knew perfectly well who I was all the time, and had some hare-brained scheme of seducing me into becoming her puppet and then persuading my father to make me his heir.

"I said something to the effect that she must be jesting if she thought I would ever agree to anything like that, saying that she was just a silly old woman and I wasn't the least afraid of her spells and curses. I'm afraid that did it."

This was better than the Arabian Nights! He had a terrific imagination. "Couldn't you still have run for it?"

"She had fixed me where I stood. I could move neither hand nor foot. Some kind of hypnosis, I suppose."

"Couldn't you have struck out at her? Shut your eyes and unhypnotised yourself? Yelled for help?" I was getting involved in his fairy-tale.

"One, she was out of reach and I couldn't move; two, I tried looking away, it didn't work; three, who would have heard me? Anyone else in that apartment would have been her creature anyway.

"Then she started to threaten me, everything that could hurt me most—blinding, laming, impotence—but I gathered from her mutterings that these spells lasted only for a specific time, and I reckoned I could put up with any form of disability for a short while. My spirits started to rise, and at last I found a tongue in my head, tried to defy her.

" 'I don't believe you have any powers at all!' I said. 'Why, if you could work any spells, you would have turned me into a dog or a toad or a crow long ago!' A foolish boast to make, for at once she started to circle me, muttering in a strange tongue, and a rhythm I realised was a primitive form of spell-casting.

"Suddenly I felt a horrid shrinking feeling, and realised the floor was coming up to meet me. I found I was on all fours, and that my feet were turning into clawed paws! The room was expanding, my mouth became full of pointed teeth, suddenly I had sprouted a tail, my body had become covered in fur, and there I was, crouched on the ground amidst my discarded clothing. The only thing from my other life that I still retained was the necklace I had been wearing—an insurance against the need for money—which I still wear."

"You mean the one you're wearing now? The tatty one of coloured glass and brass?" I snorted with derision. "I suppose you're going to tell me it is really gold and emeralds!"

"Of course—when she changed me she changed that as well, without realising it. She laughed at me, gave me a lusty kick, and opened the window. 'Out you go, tom-cat; roam the alleys until you die, or else find a virgin who will give you three human kisses of her own volition. And this you must do within the year, else you will turn to dust!'

"I leapt from the window and fled." He paused. "And that's it. That was four months ago; I won't bore you with my aimless wanderings, nor my capture by that stall-holder you rescued me from. You are the one I have been looking for, the one with the Ring, the only one I can explain this to." He paused again. "So how about it?"

"About what?"

"A kiss, freely given. The first . . . Or more, if you feel like it."

I drew away and tucked myself up again. A story was a story, but as to believing it—

"I don't kiss cats," I said. "Sorry. It was a good tale, though. 'Night . . ." And I turned over and went to sleep almost immediately.

24

The Last Barrier

I woke from a wonderful dream, instantly forgotten as I realised nothing had changed, that we were still imprisoned in this maze of caves. But the good feeling persisted, which was just as well, because the others, except Beau, were distinctly querulous and grumpy. It took me time to get them going, to make them believe that a breakfast of a handful of nuts and raisins and a drink of water from a brackish pool was sustaining.

However we made good progress that day, led by the indefatigable cat and heartened by the fact that the passages we followed all seemed to slope downwards and lead in the right direction. Then around five in the evening, we came across an unexpected hazard.

Beau came trotting back to announce that a few hundred yards farther on the passage dropped away some thirty feet after a recent subsidence, and it would be difficult to climb down.

"We mustn't get too near the edge: it's still crumbling away."

"No other way round? An alternative passage?"

"Sorry, no."

We proceeded cautiously, but there was no doubt when we came to the edge of the landslide, for there were still rattles of stone and pebble, and the ground felt crumbly beneath our feet.

"How do we get down?" said Danny.

"Not sure," I said. "Beau is going to take a look . . . Take care," I muttered to him. "We don't want to lose you . . ."

"Give us a kiss, then . . ."

"Shut up! Sorry . . ."

"Apology accepted. Don't worry: cats have nine lives, you know, even if they are princes in disguise . . ."

His fur slid under my hand and he disappeared. Claude, Danny and I huddled together, listening to the slithers still occurring.

"How long has he been?" I whispered to Claude.

"Nearly five minutes," he whispered back, and after that I must have asked him to consult his watch every thirty seconds, until he told me gruffly to stay still and wait. But the waiting seemed intolerable and it was with the greatest relief that I heard a scrabble of claws and a panting Beau arrived back.

I overwhelmed him with questions until he tapped his paw against my thigh. "Hush up! Let me get my breath back . . ." A couple of minutes later he told me what he had found. "Now you won't like it, but it isn't impossible. It's farther than I thought, some sixty feet or so, and it is more or less sheer all the way down. And before you ask, no, none of you could expect to climb down unassisted."

"Then how in the world did you manage it?"

"Have you ever watched a cat climb down from high up in a tree? No, I thought not. They spread out all their claws and come down backwards, paw over paw, back ones hanging on, front ones finding the best purchase, then, when they reckon they are near enough to the ground, they twist around, kick off with their back feet and land right way up."

I translated the essential bits to the others.

"All right for cats, but how do we manage?" said Danny.

"Find a witch, and we can all be cats." I said facetiously. Beau was the only one who knew what I was talking about, and he wasn't best pleased.

"Serve you right if I left you to work it out for yourselves!" he hissed. Of course he didn't mean it, and between us we planned a viable solution. We had a rope fifty feet long, which would have to be looped securely at the top; this would make it too short to reach the ground at the other end, but if we added a couple of blankets that should lengthen it enough. Unfortunately the nearest knob of rock to which we could attach the rope was some way back down the passage, so it meant tying our jackets together by the sleeves to get the extra length. At last Beau declared himself satisfied with our knots, and I only hoped the seams in our now rather tatty jackets wouldn't split.

"Well, who's first?" I asked. "Afraid I've never climbed down a rope before."

"Neither have I," said Claude.

"Sure and I have," said Danny. "Many's the time my pa and I went—"

He stopped suddenly as if afraid of saying too much. He shrugged. "I'll go first. Give us a candle and vestas, and it'll light the rest of you down." He spat on his hands and rolled the sleeves of his woollen shirt down over the palms. Grabbing the rope he swung himself over the edge accompanied by the rattle of stones and pebbles. He disappeared into the darkness, and there was only the creak of the rope and an occasional muffled exclamation to show us he was still there.

There was an agonising wait, then a *thump* and an "Ouch!"

"Are you all right?"

"Sure, fine and dandy!" His voice had an echo. "Apart from a broken leg and a lump on my head the size of a duck's egg . . . Only joking. The rope is still about three feet short: difficult to see where you're landing. Haul the rope back and send down the haversacks next, while I light this candle."

Looping the straps through Claude's scarf, which gave us the extra length we needed, this was accomplished successfully, then it was my turn.

My palms were sweating. "I'll never make it!"

"Of course you will," said Beau. "Make a proper loop from the scarf and Claude will lower you down. You're not heavy, and it isn't very far."

After all that it was easier than going to the dentist; there was a moment of utter panic when I was lowered over the edge, but luckily I kept my mouth shut. Claude lowered me jerkily, hand over hand, but as I had my eyes firmly closed it wasn't until I found Danny's hands around my waist that I realised that I was safe. He set me down gently as I disentangled myself from the scarf.

"All right, Sophy?"

I nodded, exhaling a breath I hadn't realised I was holding.

Now it was Claude's turn. The rope started swaying, Danny grabbed the end to hold it steady, and soon enough I saw the soles of Claude's boots by the light of the candle some ten or fifteen feet above me. Then everything went wrong. There was a snapping, tearing sound and he fell the last six feet, bringing the scarf and my jacket, minus the right sleeve, to land heavily with his left ankle twisted underneath him.

He let out a cry as he tried to stand and crumpled back down again. Even by the sparse light of the candle I could see that his face was white and twisted with pain.

"Think I've broken it—swelling up like mad!"

I unlaced his boot carefully, before the ankle swelled up too much to get it off; casting about for something to wrap it up I saw the very thing: his own scarf. Pouring water from my water-bottle I handled the ankle carefully: there had been plenty of sprains and breaks in the school at which I had taught, and I could see and feel that there was no break, but sometimes a sprain was more painful. I wrapped it up tightly until he looked like a man with a bad case of gout.

"Just take it easy. I'll give you a headache powder to ease the pain a bit."

"Always knew his brains were in his feet. . . ."

"Don't be cruel, Danny . . ." although I was smiling to myself. I telegraphed Beau to unhook the rope and send it down, moving us out of the way. It snaked into a neat coil at my feet, closely followed by the cat himself.

I insisted that we carry on, although Claude was in considerable pain. Perhaps I was being hard, but I knew just how little food there was left and God only knew how long it would take us to find a way out. We did stop early for supper and sleep, although both were in short supply.

I lay awake longer than the others, trying to control my troublesome cough.

Next day we moved as fast and as far as we could, although Claude found it difficult to keep up, even though the passage was now mostly wide enough for Danny to walk alongside and hook his shoulder under Claude's. I was really worried; we were down to a mere handful of food, although there were plenty of little streams and rivulets to slake our thirst. Most worrying of all was the situation as far as the candles were concerned. There were only two and a half left, and while we could manage without food for a while, we couldn't stumble about in the darkness.

I was just about to suggest settling down for the night, having turned to see the exhausted faces of Danny and Claude, when Beau came bounding up the passage.

"Another half-mile and there is a large cavern. No way out, but a glimpse of the world outside."

Intrigued, we followed him into a cave, the largest I had ever seen, stretching away into a darkness too great for our feeble candle. Not only did it stretch away on either side, it also soared up like the roof of a cathedral, and even our whispers were tossed back in mini-echoes. It was awesome and I felt a bit like tip-toeing. It was the sort of place one would expect to find stalactites and stalagmites marching away like the pillars in a church.

We walked along the left side until we found a relatively smooth patch to settle down on. I dished out most of what was left—only a handful of dried fruit for breakfast, and that was it—then renewed Claude's bandage. As soon as we were finished I blew out the remains of the candle, hoping it would last us for a while in the morning.

Then it happened.

There was a glow in the cavern, a soft light that came and went. We all looked up in the same direction at once and there was a collective gasp of recognition.

"The sky!"

"Moonlight."

"Clouds!"

"And the stars—how absolutely wonderful!"

Stumbling in the dark, but drawn irresistibly by the light, we walked into the centre of the cavern, and stood under the jagged hole that scarred the southern wall of the cave. No way could we climb up there: it must have been a hundred feet up, but from where we stood we could feel the occasional breath of fresh, colder air. Heavy clouds interrupted the westering moon, now near full, and I felt a sudden alarm when I realised the Eg had to be delivered on the night after the full—

"Reminds me of home," said Danny. "The roof's leaking. Anyone got a bucket?" and he pointed to the shaft of light, down which drifted a few desultory snowflakes.

We awoke to light, real light, day-light.

None of us had passed a particularly good night. There was the uneven dripping of water from somewhere nearby; it was colder than it had been and the blankets were not much help; worst of all there were certain cracking and rumbling noises, mostly far off, although the echoes in the cavern were distortive, and my chest felt tight and uncomfortable.

"Sounds as if the whole complex is falling to pieces," I muttered to Beau.

"Nothing of the sort! Every now and again, especially when the temperature changes, or when water has built up and seeks a way out, then you get a rockfall or two: that's what you can hear. Go back to sleep. . . ."

And now, like all mornings in the light, the night fears and dangers were chased away. The dawnlight coming down through Danny's "hole in the roof" was still grey, but quite strong enough for us to see to eat the handful of food left.

"That's it," I said unnecessarily.

Beau, who had eaten nothing for two days, now came and nudged my elbow. "Come and see something that might cheer you up."

He led me over to a spot almost directly opposite the soft light coming through the jagged hole. I peered at the wall: it looked as though there were faint scratches in the stone.

"What is it? Why is it important?"

"It's hope. Our first. Wait a minute until the light grows stronger, then look closer."

I did as he suggested, then I could make out what looked like pictures of animals, but the sort of animals I had never seen before. A long-tusked elephant with a thick coat of hair, a tiger with down-pointing canine teeth, horses with thick, stubby legs and manes, deer with enormous antlers, just like the ones we had seen in the ice . . . And among them all were sketches of fur-clad men with spears and clubs. Some of the animals were pictured lying on the ground, stuck with broken spears—

"What does it mean?"

"It means that once upon a time, perhaps thousands of years ago, men lit fires in here, cooked, ate, slept and raised their children—and they couldn't have done that unless there was a way in and a way out. Those pictures you see were their record of the animals they hunted and how."

"Then why did they leave?"

"Probably an Ice Age, like the one that created the glacier. They were meat-eaters, so would follow the migration of their food farther south. It could have been tribal warfare or disease, but there are no bones. I've looked."

"You said yourself that could have been thousands of years ago! The way could well have been blocked long since!"

"There are signs of more recent occupation, if you move a little farther along—there! Put out your hand: what do you feel?"

It sounded very silly when I said it. "Big toes?"

"Right. Step back some way and then look up."

I saw what looked like six statues, some twenty feet high, carved into the rock. The light from the roof was stronger now and a shaft of sun struck momentarily against one of the eroding faces: slanted eyes, a calm flat face, curved lips.

"The Six Immortals, I guess," said Beau. "This place must have been some sort of temple some three or four hundred years ago. If you look between each pair of feet you will find a niche or bowl for offerings. So the worshipers had a way in and a way out."

"Then why did they stop coming to worship?"

"That I don't know. What I do know is that we cannot be far from the way out now, and the quicker we get going, the quicker we get out."

I told the others what we had seen, we packed up and started off, but it took longer than we thought. Claude's ankle had stiffened up, and we had to adapt to his slower pace, so that it was well past mid-day when we had traversed the full length of the cavern, some two miles, and left what there was of the light behind, lighting our penultimate candle in the only passage Beau could find.

It seemed claustrophobic being in a passage again after the size of the cavern, but we stumbled on as best we could, and I reckoned we had made another mile when the passage turned a corner and widened abruptly. At the same time the sound of running water we had been hearing intermittently suddenly intensified until it almost drowned speech, and the candle-flame bent back on itself. The only encouragement was that there seemed to be a slight lessening of the darkness ahead.

Now the walls on either side of us were dripping with water, and as we rounded yet another turn we saw why: across our path raged a roaring torrent of water, effectively blocking our progress.

We had come to the end of the road.

25

Dangerous Crossing

I sat down hard and burst into tears. Anger, disappointment, frustration and fear: to have come so far and to be finally denied our freedom. A further cruelty were the chinks of light that came through a crack in the roof above, showing us just how impossible a crossing would be. At some time or another water had built up against a wall of the cave until the rock had given way and the water had roared through, digging itself a deep channel over the years, to disappear underground once more.

One by one we retreated to the first bend in the passage, where at least we could hear ourselves speak.

"I—I can't swim!" blubbered Claude, his tears, like mine, mixing with the fine spray that had drenched us. Indeed we were all shivering, and it was this, more than anything, that brought me back to my senses.

"Neither can I," I said. "But there must be some way across."

"Not through that water," said Danny, his usual optimism dampened. "You're not on your own, Claude, you great lob-lolly, so pull yourself together and get that brain of yours working. We'll think of something." But he didn't sound convinced.

I looked around. "Where's Beau?" I wiped my face, ashamed of my earlier outburst.

"Here," he said. "Just been reconnoitering." He was dripping; his fur clung to him in clumps, bare skin showing through the darkened pelt. "All may not be lost." He spoke to me through drying licks of his fur. "This must be the reason (lick) that the cavern was finally abandoned. (Lick) We can't get out at the far end (lick) where the water exits (lick) because there is a risk (lick) that we would be sucked down and lost."

"It's all impossible!" I burst out. "We can't wade or swim across: we'd be dashed to pieces on the rocks. There must be some other way out!"

"Probably, but it might take days to find it (lick) and even then it could leave us stranded (lick) high up on some mountain. (Lick) Besides we have no food and no candles. (Lick) And Master Claude's ankle is not getting any better. (Lick) No, this is the best we can do. Let me think . . ." He continued to tidy himself finishing with a comb to his whiskers. Right-handed, or pawed, I noted . . .

The tiny bit of candle in my hand gave a flare and collapsed back, a reminder of how little time we had left.

"Could we catch some fish?" We all gazed at Claude without speaking and he sighed. "Just a thought."

"Rod, line, hook, bait, net?" said Danny, his voice heavy with sarcasm. "Besides which there probably aren't any, and if there were they would be uneatable. What kind of fish live in a cave all their lives?"

Suddenly Beau started to pace back and forth, his tail twitching from side to side. We all watched him, not really in any kind of hope, but with a wish that he would suggest something, *anything.*

At last he stopped his pacing and looked at me. "We still have the rope?"

I nodded. "About forty feet long."

"Should be long enough. Tell them to tie a loop about a foot across at one end." I relayed his instructions, dying to know what he had in mind, but not wanting to be disappointed by some cat-brained scheme that couldn't possibly work. "Now," said Beau to me, after inspecting the knot, "make a bag out of the jackets, one strong enough to hold me, but leave the two ends free."

I was more mystified than ever, especially when he trod around the scoop of leather and declared himself satisfied. "It'll do."

"Do *what?*" I just had to ask. Beau looked up at me, his blue eyes gleaming in the last of the candlelight.

"The only thing we can do," he said. "You are going to catapult me across to the other side!"

It sounded like complete madness, stated like that, but once Beau had explained a bit more to me, I could see that there might, just might, be a glimmer of hope, although it was an awful risk for him. All his calculations had to be exactly right, and if he failed the consequences for all of us were too horrible to contemplate.

He sensed my reluctance. "What alternative is there? Come on, let's get it over with. The others understand what they have to do?" I nodded. "Your job is to hang on to the other end of the rope and pay it out: don't lose the end!"

"What happens if . . . ?"

I couldn't say it.

"Then you will have to pray—ask the Ring to help you, if I cannot."

That was a strange thing: the Ring wasn't jabbing a warning. It seemed as cool as ever. Perhaps it was because I wasn't yet in any real danger. I gave it a quick rub, praying it to help Beau.

He led us back to the roaring waters and in moments we were all soaked once more. The path alongside was neither even nor of uniform width and very slippery underfoot; at one moment we could walk two abreast, the next we were hugging the wall, terrified lest we slip, the weak illumination from above making it even more difficult as we slipped from light to shadow almost step for step.

At one point a large chunk of rock broke away behind us: glancing back I saw it had taken the path with it and shivered with fear: no way back!

Beau, who was leading the way, stopped and looked at me. This was the spot he had chosen. Although the torrent was not at its narrowest here, still some twenty feet across, at least the ledge on which we stood was wide enough to swing a cat—what an awful expression to think of, given the circumstances!—and on the other side was another, not as wide but at least clear of obstacles.

Beau indicated that Claude and Danny should spread out his "sling" on the ground; he climbed in and settled himself comfortably, shaking himself first like a dog to rid his fur of excess water. I knelt down by his side.

"Are you sure?"

His only answer was: "Going to wish me luck?"

"All the luck in the world!" and without thinking I leant forward and kissed his wet muzzle.

There was a sudden gleam of light, blue light, as though a spark had been lit behind those beautiful eyes.

"One down, two to go . . ." He nodded at Claude and Danny. "Tell them to start swinging; not too fast at first, but higher and stronger bit by bit, like a child on a swing."

My mind momentarily confused by having actually kissed an animal, a thing I thought I would never do, afeared by the dreadful position in which we found ourselves, numbed by the terrible cold, dazed by the roar of the torrent and nursing the thoughts of everything that could go wrong, I found it difficult to start everything off. I remembered at the last moment, thank God, to wrap the other end of the rope around my wrist, ready to pay out the rest. The loop I settled around Beau's neck and stepped back. All was now ready. I muttered a swift prayer for all of us, my heart beating like a hammer, and making my breathing more difficult than it had become over the past few days.

At last, still reluctant, I nodded at the other two.

Slowly at first they achieved some sort of rhythm. Beau was now about the size and weight of a large dog, and it took some time to get the swing effective, back and forth, higher and higher. I could see the cat was clinging with all his might to the cloth, to avoid being shaken off too early; he must be feeling pretty sick.

The sling went higher and higher, until eventually at its highest it reached the height of Claude's shoulder. Suddenly on the next outward swing there was a flash of fur and in a seemingly endless arc Beau sailed through the air, a blur of movement against the spray. I followed his progress with agonised attention: like all such moments, it seemed to be happening at half-speed. As I automatically paid out the rope all I could think was. "He isn't going to make it, he isn't going to make it—he couldn't!"

For an agonising moment he landed and then teetered unsteadily on the ledge on the far side, then he gained ground and with a surge of relief I saw him safe and upright on the ledge he had chosen. The boys let out a cheer, which I doubt he could have heard, but I was too busy with my tears of relief to join in. At least one of us was safe. . . .

"Congratulations, dear Beau!" I thought across to him.

"It was the kiss that did it!"

I was glad to see that he still had a sense of humour.

"Listen, Sophy: I think I can smell fresh air. I'm going to go to the end of the passage and find out. In the meantime put a loop on your end of the rope and move a bit farther down. I'll loop mine over here."

Beau stopped some fifty feet farther on, shucked off his loop and passed it over a pinnacle in one easy movement. He then looked through the spray at me.

"Find something similar over there, and get the rope as taut as you can. Back in a bit."

When he did come back, some ten minutes later, he was still soaked through, but he held his tail at a jaunty angle. "It's there," he called out to me. "The way out. About half a mile farther on. So let's get going. Send the first one over!"

We had discussed this before. Danny, being the most lithe and agile among us would be first, so he could help anyone in difficulties from the other side. We had the rope stretched as taut as we could, so it didn't dip into the water.

I relayed Beau's good news. "So, just a quick hand over hand," I said in a shout to make myself heard. "Ready, Danny?"

"Easy as fallln' off a log," he shouted back. "When it comes to your turn grasp the rope firmly, cross your ankles and hang upside down. One hand at a time and don't look down. Just concentrate on getting across as quick as you can."

"Wherever did you learn all that?"

He leaned close, his curls flattened against his head with the wet, and spoke in my ear. "From me da'. And wasn't he the best housebreaker in all Ireland?"

At least that's what I *thought* he said. But I might have been mistaken.

A moment later he was off, swinging across the gap like a monkey, although he was soaked through in a second, and I could see the spray was getting in his eyes. It took about two minutes to cross the twenty-foot wide chasm, but he stepped off the other side safe and sound. He checked the loop at their end, then gave us a cheery wave, meaning: "Next one!"

I had already decided this should be Claude, because I knew that if he was left until last, he would never have the courage to start out. It wasn't his fault: he was just like that. He would always need someone to pull him and someone to push.

Just before he set off Beau thought to me: "Now we've found the way out we won't need the haversacks, so leave them behind. Just get anything you want out first." I knew Danny would have nothing, but had a look just in case. A pack of cards, some of those silly photographs, a couple of dice: I tucked the first and last into an oilskin pack in which I kept my sewing things, fob-watch and Bible. At the last moment I tucked my monthly rags and clean handkerchiefs into my pockets: they would dry out. Claude retrieved his notebooks, also in oilskin, and tucked them into his jacket, together with his chronometer and photograph of his mother.

Then I took at least five minutes arranging him on the rope. His legs were so long that he didn't seem to have grasped the concept of hauling himself across with his ankles hooked over the rope. First one then the other fell off, and when I had got them properly aligned I found he was hugging the rope to his chest instead of hanging by his hands. In the end I got quite cross with him, and told him I would go myself and he would be left on his own if he didn't pull himself together.

At last he started off at a snail's pace, his eyes tight shut and a sort of moaning noise coming down his nostrils. As he got farther across the rope sloped downwards, aiding his progress; at last he seemed to be getting the hang of it. I checked the loop at our end: it seemed to be holding all right, although his slow, swaying progress was threatening to fray the edges a little.

If only he would just hurry up! He was now two-thirds of the way across, and I was just beginning to think I would have to steel myself to follow him very shortly, when it all happened.

His feet became unlocked and slipped down, until he was only hanging by his hands from the rope. He was making no attempt to right himself, and his mouth was open in a silent yell for help. I started forward, but Danny was quickest. In a moment he was back on the rope inching his way towards Claude. By now the whole thing was swaying wildly and I knelt down to hold it steady, hoping to God that it would hold, but it was swaying and jerking so much with both men on it that there was little I could do.

Eventually Danny reached the panicking Claude and leaned down to place his feet and ankles round the rope again and tried to tug him forward, but Claude wasn't having any. He doubled his arms around the rope and just hung on, making no effort to go either forward or back. I could see Danny was shouting at him, getting more and more exasperated, tugging at his collar and his belt. At last he jerked one of Claude's arms free and placed it forward on the rope, and pulled at him again. This time he moved, but only fractionally. Danny repeated the process again and again until he backed up on the ledge and inched Claude up as well.

Then he kicked him good and hard, on the behind—

In the meantime I could see Beau pacing anxiously back and forth. As soon as Claude was safe, he thought-yelled at me to hurry up. "And check the rope," he added.

I turned and saw to my horror that a couple of the strands had snapped, due probably to the extra weight of Claude and Danny together. But there looked to be plenty of thickness left, and I was now so cold that I couldn't have re-knotted the rope. I said a quick prayer, then lowered myself over the edge, pulled my sleeves over my hands, grasped the rope by guess rather than feel, because I was so numb, hooked my ankles over the rope as Danny had instructed and started to haul myself across.

He had made it look so easy, but I found it very hard. The weight of my body made it a real effort to pull with my arms, and my feet didn't help at all. All at once the Ring started to throb urgently, even though I had hardly any feeling in my hands. For a moment I gazed back, dreading that the loop was about to give way, and saw to my horror that the piece of rope to which Beau must have alluded was the one that hung over the river; it had sagged so much it was now badly frayed, and even as I looked a strand snapped and curled towards me.

For a moment I was frozen with fear, then the urgent pricking of the Ring got me going as fast as I could towards safety. Halfway there, at the lowest drop of the rope, almost touching the roaring waters beneath—

The rope broke.

Half a second later I found myself in the water.

This was not water as I had always known it, this was a battering ram, a great thumping that drove the breath from my body, bruised my arms, legs and ribs, banged my head with great cuffs, poured itself down my mouth as if it had forced my mouth open and then held it in a dentist's vise. My screams were literally washed away, and I was a piece of flotsam that wasn't sure which way was up and which was down.

Suddenly I was brought up by an agonising jerk round my waist, and for a second or two my head was above water. I took great gulps of air and promptly vomited before being sucked down again, frantically trying to rid myself of the constriction around my waist, only to find that it was the frayed end of the rope that had snapped and whipped around me.

I realised that this rope was possibly my only hope. It was firmly looped at Beau's end, so if I could hang on perhaps, just perhaps, I could pull myself towards the far side. I wrapped the loose end as tightly as I could around my arm. My mind was starting to blank out, and in another few minutes I should start to lose consciousness forever—

Another kind of painful jerk almost pulled my arm from its socket: had the rope snagged? Another jerk, I swallowed another mouthful of water, got a sudden gasp of air, choked, vomited again. Now I was dragging across rocks, my head took a painful blow, then at last my head was above water and the roaring pounding waters were receding. My shoulders were clear, my waist, my hips; my legs were being scraped against something and suddenly I was in a different dimension, flat on my stomach on the rocks on the far side where the boys had hauled me.

Anxious hands were patting and pummelling me and my ears ringing and bubbling with water and distorted voices.

I tried to sit up, but firm hands were pressing me down, pumping the rest of the water from my lungs. I dribbled for a bit and then tried again. "I'm—I'm fine," I managed at last. "But so cold . . ." Somebody's jacket was put round my shoulders and I was helped to my feet, shaking and trembling, Danny on one side and a limping Claude on the other, and led away from the roaring torrent.

There was a faint mew ahead. "Follow me," said Beau. "The light from behind will guide you to the turn in the passage, and then you will be able to see where we get out of here. Just take it easy: there's no real hurry right now."

I was crying however, and couldn't seem to stop, and the three of us stumbled along that ill-lit passage like a trio of drunks leaving an inn at closing-time. I was still shivering, my head ached, my chest hurt so much I wondered whether I had cracked any ribs, and I was still coughing up what I supposed was water.

It took us an hour, that last half-mile, but at last I could smell fresh air, sharp and cold, and see a patch of daylight ahead, growing bigger as we stumbled and swayed towards it.

A moment later and I blinked: something was obscuring the light, something that grew larger and larger until it filled my vision. A creature radiating warmth and comfort and reassurance—

"*Ky-Lin . . . !*"

Book Three

"Journeys end in lovers' meetings."
—Wm. Shakespeare

26

The Return
of the Eg

He seemed to fill the passageway, bringing with him a sort of aura
of light, I flung my arms around his neck and hugged him convulsively.

"Ky-Lin! You found us! Is Toby all right? Where's the Eg? Where
are we? Where's the Blue Mountain?" I was stopped by a convulsive fit
of coughing and a pain in my chest, the worst yet.

He leaned forward and touched me with his little horn, and instantly
the pain abated somewhat.

"Dear girl, you are soaking! Here, climb up on my back and I'll
carry you outside. Master Claude with an injured ankle?" He bent
forward and touched that, too. "Better? I cannot carry you both, but
make your way outside and I will arrange for transport. Come, Miss
Sophy . . ."

"But where is—"

"Just do as you are told. Answers as we go."

Off we trotted towards the widening oval of light, with it coming
the first intimation of ice, cold and snow, but Ky-Lin radiated heat and
I snuggled down against his warm hide as he bore me down the passage
and out into the open.

Once outside I opened my eyes to their widest and breathed in the
sharp air as deep as I could, although it hurt my chest to do so. We were
at the foot of the mountains among the broken rubble of the outermost

rim of the glacier, among what I believe Ky-Lin had referred to once as a "moraine."

And there, a basket at his feet, all bundled in scarves and a cloak, was Toby!

He helped me off Ky-Lin's back, exclaimed at my damp clothing and wrapped me in his cloak. I hugged him happily and started off with all my questions, which had so far remained unanswered.

"Let the lad tell his own story," said Ky-Lin as he turned back to help the others. "It'll be quicker!"

Ky-Lin was gone about ten minutes, but during that time it seemed that Toby never drew breath. Apparently the avalanche that had nearly cost us our lives was the most exciting thing that had ever had happened to him. "Awesome," he called it.

They had initially outraced the front of the avalanche on their slab of ice, but as it caught up with them Ky-Lin had taken Toby and the Eg on his back, managed to steer them closer to the side, then given an almighty leap that landed them safe on a ledge away from the rolling, boiling mass of snow. Once everything grew quiet again they had made their way down to the valley, and a small Chinese village some three miles from where we now sat. They had made this their headquarters, coming back every day to try to find us. They had even already explored the pass we had emerged from, but had decided that the torrent of water would have been too difficult for us to cross, after going back to the spot where we had disappeared and satisfying themselves that we couldn't escape that way either.

They had examined every exit they could find, mostly farther west, but Ky-Lin had insisted they came back to this one that morning. "I reckon he had this sort of sixth sense, being a sort of magical creature."

I guessed the Ring might have had something to do with it, but didn't say so.

I gazed around; the sun was already setting towards the west, and I couldn't help my shivers. Our goal, the Blue Mountain, couldn't be so far away. I switched my gaze to the south, and there it was! It should have been tinged by the setting sun, but it wasn't. It held a cold blue light of its own. I suppose it had once been conical, the cone of some extinct volcano, but the top had caved in years ago—wasn't there something about that in the long-ago journal of Summer?

I sprang to my feet, or tried to, yielding to a bout of coughing.

"That's it! Where is the Eg?"

"Here." He pointed to the bundle at his feet. "Heavier than ever."

"We must go there. Now!" I coughed again. "We must have wasted so much time wandering around those wretched caves. I must take it *now!* Help me to pick it up and carry it—"

He rose to his feet. "Be reasonable, Sophy! You're in no fit state to carry anything. You can't just run off like that, anyway. The mountain is miles away!"

"I must! Don't you understand? This is what we all came here for—"

"You're just not well enough! And it'll be dark soon. We'll never find our way for starters . . ."

"Well, Ky-Lin will just have to carry me, or something . . ." I sat down again and burst into tears. "How can we be so near and yet so far?"

"Now then, what's all this about?" Ky-Lin was back, with Beau. I explained as best I could, and to my surprise he fell in with the idea without any objections. "If you are set on it, I will help you all I can. I have left the others at the entrance to the cave, where they will be sheltered from the cold, and will send back litters for them both. We shall go down to the village, where you will get something to eat and a change of clothing. It will take a half-hour for me to get you to the village, and then you must rest. We'll set out for the mountain about three hours before midnight, then you will have fulfilled your quest. You're sure it must be tonight?"

I nodded. "I've got this sort of urgent feeling . . ."

He nodded. "Let's get going then." He looked at Toby and Beau. "Can you two make it? If you fall behind, Toby knows the way . . ." I translated quickly to Toby, and he nodded.

"We'll go at our own pace."

Then Ky-Lin and I were off. I was still shivering but, as he promised, within a half-hour I was snug in a village house, supping a bowl of chicken-noodle soup. Strangely enough, even after so many days practically starving, I didn't really feel hungry, but I drank three bowls of fragrantly scented pale tea, and felt much better.

The villager's wife gave me hot water to wash in all over, plus clean my hair, and then she took away my tatty, torn clothing and provided me with typical village wear of padded blue jacket, trousers of the same material, felt slippers and a cap with ear flaps. I should have felt warmer, but I still shivered, so she tut-tutted and led me to a small pallet. Making me lie down, she covered me with a coarse blanket, bringing the brazier which heated the house nearer. Putting her finger to her lips she mimed sleep and carried the lamp—a wick floating in a stone jar of oil—farther from my eyes.

I must have dozed off, because the next thing I knew was the arrival of the others, about an hour later. Toby and Beau must have been fed and rested at one of the other houses, because they turned up a few minutes later, yawning and stretching, but otherwise looking ready for anything. I wished I did.

Within minutes Danny and Claude were guzzling large bowls of chicken and rice, and slurping their tea, belching politely afterwards, which I suppose I should have done also.

Ky-Lin breezed in and asked if I was ready, asking me to tell Danny and Claude that washing water, dry clothes and beds would be ready for them shortly.

"Why, where are you going?" asked Danny.

"To return the Eg, before the time runs out. I have a sort of feeling it's got to be done tonight."

Claude frowned, and glanced at Danny. "But I thought you said—" to receive a sharp dig in the ribs.

"Never mind, never mind," said Danny hurriedly. "We'll talk about it later . . ."

Claude rose to his feet. "Are you sure you're all right? You look a bit pale to me."

"So would you if you had nearly drowned! Now, don't try to stop me, because I have to be there before midnight." But they still looked uncomfortable.

A couple of crude litters stood outside; basically they were just hammocks suspended from bamboo poles, with lanterns slung at either end. Toby looked dubious, ready to argue, but I told him, from Ky-Lin, that he had done enough running about already, the Eg needed safe transport, and anyway he would have to help me once we got to the mountain.

Beau joined me in my litter, but before long I think we both felt it would have been better to walk, apart from the fact that it was too far. The combination of both jogging unevenly at the same time as swaying from side to side made me feel slightly sick, together with the dancing of the lanterns. In spite of that I dozed off again, but Beau excused himself to run alongside for a while.

I seem to remember disembodied dreams with no sense to them: a huge clock ticking away the minutes at an astonishing rate; a calendar whose pages flipped back and forth at the bidding of a wind I couldn't feel; rocks falling all around me and bouncing at my feet soundlessly; a gargoyle spouting water detached itself from a wall and marched towards me, leering; trees burst into bloom in the snow and died in the sun.

"Hey there, wake up!" said Ky-Lin, touching my face with his antennae. "This is as far as they will go."

I climbed stiffly out of the litter, the nasty taste of the dreams still in my mouth, coughing a little with the effort. Bright moonlight, piercing cold, and in front of me a dark mass rising smoothly from the plain, crowned with a gap like a broken tooth.

The Blue Mountain.

"How do I get up there?" I was shivering again. It looked very forbidding, dark and threatening, and I couldn't see any way up. And I had to carry the Eg, and presumably the lantern as well. "And—and what do I do when I g-get there?"

"You just leave the dragons their egg," said Ky-Lin gently. "Summer told us there was a cavern up there, remember? Just get up there and come straight back." He nodded at Toby and Beau. "They'll go with you."

Obviously Toby had picked up the sense at least of what Ky-Lin had been saying, for he held up the sack in which he was carrying the Eg. "I have this safe, and we'll take a lantern and go slow. Any idea where we start off?"

"Around the other side," Ky-Lin explained to me. "I'll carry you as far as I can, but I'm not allowed to go any further; our people do not deal with dragons—it has always been so. Each of us pretends the other doesn't exist. It is easier that way."

Around the other side the moon illuminated a steep and rocky climb leading to a sort of path that snaked around the mountain. Ky-Lin carried me as far as the beginning of the path and promised he would wait as we set off, Beau in front in case of hidden obstacles, then Toby with the Eg and the lantern, and me bringing up the rear, stopping now and again to catch my breath.

I had thought that the climb would be difficult, but in fact it was surprisingly easy; the path was more or less smooth and the gradient not particularly steep. I suppose it took us about a half-hour to reach the end of the track and the mouth of a dark passage. I shivered again: surely I didn't have to go into the unknown darkness of a cave so soon after our escape!

Toby started forward but I grabbed his arm. "Do we have to go in there?"

He turned and gave me a grin. "Sure, it's the way in, isn't it? This was the way Summer went in, and I bet she was scared, too."

"But the whole place was supposed to have blown up: how do we know the passage isn't blocked?"

"Only by going in and finding out. And if it *is* blocked, then we give the dragons a shout and tell them where we've left the Eg."

I was sure he was joking. "What if there aren't any dragons left?"

"I don't believe it really matters if there are or not. All your uncle wanted you to do was bring the Eg back to the Blue Mountain wasn't it? Well, here you are, and you've carried out his wishes. If the passage is blocked and there are no dragons, we'll just tuck the Eg up snugly and it can hatch itself. Come on: five minutes and the job's done and we can all go home again!"

"I'll go first," said Beau to me. "I don't sense any danger. What does the Ring say?"

Just a steady throb: nothing life-threatening. A warning, but not a definite danger. "Right," I said. " 'Lead on, MacDuff!' "

After a few yards we turned a sharp corner and at once there was a different quality to the light. A sort of phosphorescence seemed to be seeping from the walls; it was like the luminosity you get from decaying plant life, but without the stench. But there was a smell ahead: a sort of cindery, sulphurous stink that made me pinch my nostrils. We turned a couple more corners and then stepped out into what resembled an arena.

It had once been a large cavern, but now the roof was gone, leaving the jagged edges looking like the overhanging eaves of a decayed mansion. The high moon showed that where we stood the ground was smooth, but on the other side of a central chasm was a jumble of rocks and stones, like a giant's playground.

But there was no sign of any dragons . . .

It was warm in there, but not a healthy heat; it was like the embers of a fire not quite out. We moved forward until we stood on the rim of the chasm, from where the heat was coming. Gazing carefully down, we could see, far, far below, what looked like the ruby heart of sullen coals, with a spark traveling now and again from end to end. Obviously if this had once been the heart of a volcano, then there was still life down there.

There was a sudden puff of heat-laden air from below, with the rotten-egg smell of steam-trains and we retreated rapidly, gasping and choking.

"Let's get out of here," said Toby in a low voice. "You're coughing badly."

"But—but where do we put the Eg?"

"Don't know. Perhaps we can find a place where it won't roll about."

"Why are you whispering?"

"I'm not . . . Dunno. Anyway, you are too."

I shrugged. "Let sleeping dragons lie is my motto."

"There's a sort of egg-shaped dip over here," called out Beau. "Look as though it would be a good fit, too.

On my instructions Toby carried the Eg over to where Beau was sitting, and sure enough there was a depression in the ground that looked as if it were made on purpose. Taking the Eg out of the sack, he made a kind of bed for it with the same and then laid it down like putting it in a nest.

I gazed down at it. It was even bigger than I remembered, and must weigh at least fifteen pounds. I wondered how much larger it would be before it hatched, and when that would be. . . . In the moonlight it still held its own sparkly radiance. I patted it gently.

"Good-bye Eg, and good luck. May your hatchling be something very special. . . ." It ought to be, I added to myself, after all these years! "I've carried out my part of the bargain: now it's up to you." I stepped back. "Right. Time to go."

Beau nudged my knee. "Hadn't you better say something polite to the dragons?"

"What dragons? There aren't any."

"Are you sure?"

"Of course!" I had forgotten about whispering and gestured all round the cavern. "Nothing but a jumble of old stones and a few embers. How can I talk to things that aren't there? I'd just feel silly."

"I still think you should try. Just tell them how you came to undertake this journey and that the Eg has now been restored to them."

Toby looked at me with surprise as I gazed out over the chasm to the jumble of rocks which was the only place where dragons could possibly hide, and gave a potted version of why we had come and what we had brought. I finished on a bout of coughing, but decided on one last attempt to find out whether I was talking to thin air or something solid.

I looked back at the stones. Was it my imagination, or had they rearranged themselves a little? I was suddenly afraid. "Listen here, dragons," I said. "Of course I don't necessarily believe there are any of you out there, but if there are, it would be polite to show yourselves and perhaps say thank-you. . . ."

Nothing.

I turned to go, but at that very moment there was a strange kind of hissing noise, like the noise a gas lamp makes when it is turned on too high, and a hot choking blast of air; not air from the chasm, this smelled quite different, more like an overdone roast. At the same time Toby's lantern dimmed right down, so we could hardly see a thing, only being able to distinguish the entrance to the passage with difficulty by its darker outline, as the moon was also temporarily hidden by cloud.

As we gained the beginning of the passage I glanced back one last time, to print the memory firmly on my mind. The moon was now westering and a beam touched the rocks and struck off one—no, two—points of red. And surely there were two more? But those were green—

Another blast of burnt-fat air nudged us down the passage and once again the lantern burned low. We reached the entrance to the path outside and I took deep breaths of the fresh air, or tried to, as my lungs felt stuffed up.

"Come on, Sophy, let's get you—" but Toby never finished his sentence because there was a sudden clap like thunder directly above us. I glanced up and was sure I saw the silhouette of a dragon above us. Not that I had ever seen one before, but it looked just like the ones in my children's books; huge sweeping wings, four taloned feet, a twisted tail and a coruscating flight. It could be nothing else.

"Look Toby, Beau: a dragon!"

"Where, where?" They gazed around, but it must have been in the wrong direction, because they shook their heads.

"Up there! Above us . . ." But even as I spoke the dark shape drifted away out of sight. "It *was* there," I insisted. "I *saw* it!"

"Yes, yes I'm sure it was," said Toby soothingly. "Come on, Sophy, you are not at all well. You look a bit feverish to me."

Indeed I now felt dreadful. I had been artificially buoyed up by the incentive of getting the Eg to its destination, and now we had succeeded and no further effort was needed all I wanted to do was lie down and sleep, for a week if necessary. My chest hurt, I had the shivers again but my head felt as if it was on fire. I followed them down the path, my hand on Toby's left shoulder, because my feet had suddenly developed a tendency to wander off in the wrong direction.

Finally I made it to where Ky-Lin was waiting; he took one look at me then touched me briefly with his horn, as usual alleviating the pains a little. I don't recall any of the journey back to the village in the litter, though when we dismounted I looked back at the Blue Mountain and quite clearly saw two shapes like outsize bats wheeling above the mountain.

"Look, Beau! Dragons . . ."

He gazed up into the sky. "Yes," he said. "Dragons . . . Come and lie down Sophy: you'll feel better in the morning."

I thought I was so tired I could have fallen asleep on one of Toby's mother's clotheslines, but it wasn't as easy as that. I was hot, I was cold, tossed and turned, couldn't get comfortable, and at one point got up to see if the dragons were still there.

Ky-Lin appeared at my elbow. "Back to bed Sophy, and I'll give you something to help you sleep . . ."

As I lay down again he breathed over me gently: a scent of spring, a breath of autumn, stimulating and soothing at the same time. I closed my eyes and slipped into dreamless sleep.

27

A Day Too Late?

I don't remember much about the next few days: ten, to be precise, as I was told afterwards. During that time I drifted in and out of consciousness, never quite sure what was reality and what was dream—or nightmare.

Once there seemed to be an interminable, jolting journey; I was either burning hot or freezing cold; there were bitter brews to drink. Sometimes there were voices whispering in my ear, words I could not understand; at other times it sounded as though a crowd was shouting somewhere in the distance, and always, always there was the struggle to breathe, as if I were running a perpetual race I couldn't win.

Whenever I opened my eyes there were shadows: the sun chased them across the white walls, the candlelight made them rear and sway like demented devil-dancers. Then there were the dreams. Once, when I was so cold I couldn't bear it, I went for a walk and found myself at the back door of the little cottage I used to share with my parents and they were there at a wicker table under the apple tree, just as I remembered them.

My mother looked up and smiled. "Come and join us," she called. "We've been waiting for you!" But then my father put his hand on her arm and shook his head. It was all in slow motion, as it sometimes is in dreams. His voice, when it came was oddly distorted. "It's not time yet," he said. "Go and check the clock." I started to move towards them, but he held up his hand, palm forward. "Go and check the clock!" I turned back into the cottage and there beside the door was a clock I didn't remember having seen before. I looked at the face, but instead of the usual hours and minutes and numbers of one to twelve there were figures of one to seventy-five and a single hand, which pointed to twenty-two, just my age.

Was this supposed to measure my life-span? I turned back to ask my parents, but they were gone, just a few petals falling from the apple tree, to remind me of what I had once known. . . .

That was the only dream I remembered clearly, but there were others, less pleasant.

Once I awoke, or thought I did, to hear Claude and Danny arguing outside. I didn't know what it was all about, but I thought I heard Danny say: "If you won't tell her, then I will! You can't go on letting her believe she's won!" To which the reply was: "You're not to tell her! If it's any-body's task, then it's mine!" and "But you know how much it means to her—"

I don't recall any more, but I do remember wondering who the "she" was they referred to.

I didn't "come to" apparently for a few more days, but one morning, after a particularly restless, sweat-soaked night, I awoke to diffused moonlight on whitewashed walls, a clear head and the ability to breathe without wheezing and choking. A woman was bending over me and I indicated that I was thirsty, and a couple of minutes later I was gulping the best drink in the world: a cupful of ice-cold, clear, pure, mountain water. Five minutes later I was chair-lifted by two of them to the bath-room, where I relieved myself, and was then given a warm bath and hair-wash and dressed in a clean shift. My bed had been changed and re-made as well, and the women fussed and twittered around me in their own language, until I pointed to my mouth and rubbed my tummy, in-dicating that I was hungry.

Five minutes later there arrived a bowl of warm gruel; it tasted of nuts and honey and I spooned it down eagerly, not realising just how hungry I had been. I tried to ask where the others were, but it wasn't until I repeated the name "Ky-Lin" a couple of times and they nodded, and one of them spread her fingers a couple of times to indicate twenty minutes, that I knew she had understood.

I fell asleep again while I was waiting, to wake to the dissonance of bells and the sound of distant chanting, to find Beau at my side, purring.

"You awake? Feel better?"

I yawned. "I think so—to both questions . . . Where am I? How long have I been ill?"

"We are being cared for in a Buddhist monastery some ten miles from the Blue Mountain. It is high up on a hill, and it is where Ky-Lin normally lives. And yes, you have been ill, very ill for quite a long time. They said it was pneumonia. At one stage we thought—even Ky-Lin thought—that you wouldn't make it."

I felt very uncomfortable. It doesn't help to be told that one had been near death. "I suppose it was getting wet in the caves?"

He nodded. "Apparently." He padded up the bed towards my pillow. "But now you're better!"

I hugged him. *"Much* better! Where are the others?"

"They'll be here in a minute." He pushed his wet nose against my cheek. "Give us a kiss . . ."

I pushed him away, laughing. "I told you, I don't kiss cats!" He was even bigger than I remembered.

"You have done already—"

But he was interrupted. The door was flung open and in came Claude and Danny, the latter clutching a bunch of wild chrysanthemums. I was embraced, congratulated on my recovery, told how much they had missed me, and then subjected to a detailed account of the monastery, where they had been, what they had done.

"For six days we weren't even allowed to tip-toe in to see you," said Danny, "and when we did you looked half-dead already! And now here you are, sitting up and taking notice, just as if nothing had happened at all, at all!" He had gone Irish. "Ten days it was since you went up the mountain and you were all but lost to us!"

Lying back in bed I tried to calculate. "Then it must be the eleventh of November . . . We missed Bonfire Night, boys!"

There was a sort of uneasy silence, and then Claude blurted out: "Actually, it's the twelfth."

I stared at him. It couldn't be. Even I could count. There was another even more uncomfortable sort of silence, broken eventually by a crimson-faced, embarrassed, uncomfortable Danny.

"What he's trying to tell you," he said heavily, "is that you were one day late depositing the Eg."

"And I'm telling you I'm willing to lie and change my notebooks," protested Claude. "You won't lose out, Sophy. I'll tell the solicitors—"

I burst into angry, frustrated, hopeless tears.

"Hey, what's all this?" Ky-Lin came bouncing into the room, his antennae as pink as raspberries. "Welcome back to us, Miss Sophy! But why the tears?"

There was a flurry of explanations.

"Well, well, well. Just sit back and think before you all jump to conclusions. Don't you have some sort of nursery rhyme about how many days there are in every month?"

In a sort of ragged chorus Danny, Claude and I recited the following:

"Thirty days hath September,
April, June and November.
All the rest have thirty-one,
Except for February alone,
Which hath but twenty-eight days clear,
And twenty-nine in each leap year."

"Excellent!" said Ky-Lin. "Now then, what year is it in your Western counting? Well, Master Claude?"

"Er . . . Eighteen-eighty-four." He ventured.

"And is that number divisible by four?"

He nodded.

"Then this year was a leap year, wasn't it? So, Miss Sophy was in time after all!"

"I was? I am? I did it after all?" In spite of my weakness I bounced up and down on the bed.

Claude went red, then white, then red again. "Apparently yes, Sophy. All my fault," and then he disappeared, presumably to alter all the dates in his little black books, from the twenty-ninth of February onwards . . .

Danny raised his clasped hands above his head. "Glory be!"

"Knew it would be all right!" purred Beau.

Completely forgetting my previous vows I leant forward and on impulse gave him an exuberant hug and kiss, to feel a strange constriction in my stomach, a sort of breathlessness that had nothing to do with my recent illness. His lovely blue eyes dilated, then he let out a sigh more human then feline.

"Two down," he said clearly. "One to go . . ."

After that it should have been easy, and home again before Easter, but Ky-Lin, the nurses who had been tending me and the monk who made up the noxious potions I had drunk, all insisted that I convalesce for a while longer, until all traces of congestion were gone. So I twiddled my thumbs through the rest of November and into December, when of course the snow and the icing up of the rivers made traveling impossible until the spring thaw.

During my extended stay at the monastery I spent a great deal of time on the balcony-garden outside my room. A set of steps led down to a tiny paved garden, full of button-chrysanthemums and bonsai plants, protected at night by straw matting. When the sun shone it was pleasantly warm out there during the day, but at night I was only too glad to snuggle down under my feather-filled coverlet.

On one such day I was sitting outside with Ky-Lin and Beau; Claude and Danny had walked down to the village that nestled at the foot of the steep hill on which the monastery stood, because it was market day.

I shaded my eyes against the strong sunlight. "Ky-Lin, what's that lump?"

"Lump? What lump?" He had shrunk a good deal because, as he explained, being larger was hard work; he now about the size of a small terrier. "I don't see any lump . . ."

I laughed. "Perhaps it isn't a lump then." I pointed. "Over there: that piece of stone on the rail of the balcony."

He leapt up to the two-foot rim and nosed what I had referred to. "You mean this?"

I nodded. "What is it?"

"This—this *lump* you referred to—this is a memorial to my friend, my dear friend Growch, Mistress Summer's traveling companion."

"I remember! In the translation my uncle made he was meant to stay behind when she went to the mountain. Did he disobey?"

"He did, and he got badly burnt when the mountain blew. I nursed him back to health, but the damage to his emotions I could not cure. He loved Mistress Summer and served her well, and could never forgive himself for not being there when she—disappeared."

"The account never mentioned what happened to her after-wards . . ." I hesitated. "Did she—did she die with her lover?"

"No-one knows. Some say they both escaped and flew away to a far-away island, but I must admit I did not sense her presence later. But then, of course, I was busy caring for the dog."

"You loved him?"

"Ky-Lins do not 'love,' as you understand it. We are capable of affection and respect, and for Growch I had a great deal of this. He was an amiable companion and we talked much of many things. When he passed away to another plane I was very sorry, but one of the monks, a devoted admirer of his, carved a stone statue of a dog asleep in the sun. This is what you see, but hundreds of years have softened the stone and rounded the statue."

I reached out and touched it, warm from the sun.

"I wish I had known him . . . And Summer."

Ky-Lin seemed to have recovered his composure. "I was glad to know them both. He was a real 'character' as I think you would put it. He taught me a great many words that I am sure my Master would not approve of, but with him they just seemed natural."

I moved forward to lean over the parapet: to my left was the Blue Mountain, ahead the valley stretched away towards the river we should take on the first part of our journey, and towering above us to the right were the mountains.

"What will you do when we are gone?"

"Wait here for my Master. He will decide whether I have expiated all my sins, or whether I have to stay here a little longer, to be of use to someone else."

I tried to question him about his "sins," but he shook his head, only murmuring something about "carelessness" and "pride." It seemed it was very difficult for a Ky-Lin to become, and stay, perfect. . . .

The proposals came a few days after that. I had noticed both Danny and Claude behaving oddly during the last few days—arguing in fierce whispers, going into corners with pieces of rice paper, brush and ink, nudging each other and looking at me and then away again. The first time this latter happened I thought I was blemished in some way because of my illness, but a mirror reassured me. Thinner-faced perhaps, but otherwise unchanged. So, when I came across them tossing best-of-three, then best-of-five, then best-of-seven, I decided to leave well alone. If they wished to behave like a pair of overgrown schoolboys, that was up to them.

So, one afternoon when Claude tapped on the door of my room and asked if he could have a word, I thought it was some kind of advice he needed about his acne, perhaps, or a request to mend his combinations, which he still insisted on wearing. Whatever it was, it was clear he was highly embarrassed, red as a turkey-cock's wattle and perspiring profusely. I offered him a cup of water and led him out onto the balcony, where there was a welcome breeze and we could stare out over the scenery instead of having to look at each other eye to eye.

"How can I help, Claude dear?"

At first he hemmed and hawed, then all at once the words came tumbling out like a string of broken beads, and as difficult to match together. Apparently I would never be fulfilled until I had known the joys of married life with all it entailed. I needed a husband to care for and protect me. Money was no object, because two could live as cheaply as one. He said, obliquely, how much he had always admired me etc. etc., that I was the only one, true, suitable mate to share his life with, so would I accept his hand in marriage? He was sure his mother would find me acceptable, he added, only I must never reveal I had ever worn, er, trousers. . . .

"No, I won't," I said firmly, "because the situation will not arise. I am both grateful and honoured by your proposal, but I have to tell you that marriage plays no part in my future plans, at least for the foreseeable future." I stifled my giggles with a fit of coughing. During his declaration I had veered between surprise, repulsion and amusement. The latter was winning, but I was glad to see he looked relieved, not tear-stricken.

"Well, if you're sure . . . ?"

"Absolutely." I felt an imp of mischief ready to jump out from the corner. "Did you toss for who should be first?"

He half-rose from his chair. "How did—how did you know?"

"It didn't take much! Don't tell him I know, just say you failed in your endeavour." I relented, rose and kissed him on both cheeks. "Claude, this doesn't mean I'm not immensely fond of you, and will never forget your company during our expedition. Go and find a girl more worthy of you—and your mother—and be happy!"

After that I didn't have to wait too long for Danny. Perhaps encouraged by Claude's failure, he appeared on the scene only a few minutes later.

This time it was quite different. He came armed with a bunch of flowers and a mouthful of Irish exaggerations, his tongue making the words flow like a lively stream over rolling pebbles (and as near unstoppable). Apparently I was the most beautiful, talented, desirable creature on earth, and the best prospect a man like him could hope to find. He even went down on his knees to propose, but this time the amusement couldn't be held back.

He sprang to his feet. "You're laughing at me!"

I shook my head, tried to stifle my giggles. "No, my dear, not at you, just the methods you use! I'm very flattered that you asked me, but I'll tell you what I told Claude: I've no plans to marry for quite a while."

At first he looked cross, then as relieved as Claude, then finally he laughed, too. "Worth a try, girl!"

After they had both gone I turned to Beau, a silent and hidden witness to both proposals.

"Did I deal with them properly?"

He yawned and straightened luxuriously. "Of course. Neither was right for you."

I laughed again. "And I suppose the prince-you-are is?"

"Of course. Wait and see."

When I had fully recovered we left the monastery, after a well-deserved donation of a couple of pink pearls, and rented a small house in the valley below until the spring. It was really one large room with niches for sleeping, a primitive stove and a large brazier. There was a well outside in a little square, a woman to do our washing, an annex that served as a bathroom, and a market twice a week, so we did pretty well, with frequent visits from Ky-Lin.

Of course we couldn't celebrate Christmas as we would have wished, but we did the best we could, with paper streamers, chicken stuffed with what we could get—rice, nuts and dried fruit—and we let off some firecrackers. Afterwards we decided to sing a couple of carols, so the boys stood outside and serenaded me through the open door. A heavenly choir it was not, although it awakened in me all sorts of nostalgia. Some of the villagers came out of their houses to listen, and the dogs *loved* it, joining in with enthusiasm. . . .

Once we heard that the ice was breaking up on the river, we knew it was time to go. Ky-Lin accompanied us. He was back to figurine size and I carried him either in my pocket or on my shoulder. We decided to walk rather than ride: walking was the way Summer had done it, though in the opposite direction. As we left I took a last look at the Blue Mountain; in the daylight it looked like a harmless, bluish lump rising from the plain, and I found it hard to remember that terrible trip to restore the Eg. I hoped it was all right.

On the way I looked in vain for the deadly swamp that had nearly ended Summer's expedition. We were walking along a paved causeway at the time, with neat fields of rice, vegetables and fruit on either side.

Ky-Lin anticipated my question.

"This is it," he told me. "A lot can happen in a few hundred years. Gradually it was drained, the land was fertile, the population grew, and now it is as you see it today. There are still some outlying patches that remain to be treated, but they will be done, in time."

Ky-Lin acted as translator when we arranged for our passage down-river, also when we sold off a few more pearls to see us on the first part of our long journey. I would have dearly loved him to come with us, but as he explained his part of the story was over and he had to return to the monastery to await his Master, the Buddha.

"How will you get back from here?"

"A pocket here, a pouch there. I shall wait till someone goes in the right direction."

He bumped his knobby forehead against mine, a sort of goodbye, I supposed. "Don't worry about me. Good luck attend you and your Prince of Purloiners." But before I could ask what on earth he was talking about, he was nodding at the middle finger of my right hand. "I don't believe you will be needing that any more."

I looked down at my finger where the little ring of horn, the Unicorn Ring, had been getting looser and looser over the past few days. In fact I now had to screw up my fist or trap it with my thumb to keep it from falling off.

"It *is* a bit loose . . ."

"Which means you no longer need it. When you relied on it to help you with this expedition you couldn't take it off. Now it is ready to await its next wearer, one who will need its magical powers to help them on another worthwhile adventure. The Ring chooses its own wearer, you know that. Why don't you take it off and put it round my neck? I have been involved with it before and we trust each other. What do you say?"

I hesitated; it had been so much a part of me for nearly eighteen months . . . But I knew I had no permanent right to it. "But—but how will I understand animals, how will I know when danger threatens?"

"Your own common sense and the new life you will lead makes both these needs superfluous."

"What about understanding Beau?"

"He will make his feelings known to you, with or without the Ring. You two have grown close enough not to need words. Trust me . . ."

Slowly, reluctantly, I drew the Ring from my finger. Once off, it seemed to have a life of its own, for in an instant there it was nestling round Ky-Lin's neck. All at once the world seemed a duller, greyer place, birdsong muted, the bales of silk waiting to be loaded a paler colour, the sun behind a cloud. Momentarily I closed my eyes on the disappointment, something brushed against my eyelids and when I opened them again everything was back to normal. Everything that is, but one. Ky-Lin had gone. . . .

28

"Prince of Purloiners"?

After that it was a leisurely voyage home, by sea when we could, by coach when we couldn't. We swapped a river-barge for a bouncy junk, a smoky coaster, a dhow (not much room in this), a river-boat, and finally the cross-channel ferry. During the long days and gradually warming nights I washed and mended all our clothes—what there was left of them—bought pen, paper and ink and wrote down an account of all our adventures so that perhaps one day my children might read it.

Once we were in "civilisation" again I had to go back to wearing a skirt, and I found I had enough to refit us all cheaply, and to give the boys a little pocket-money. Danny promptly bought packs of cards and small, smelly cigars, Claude some more handkerchiefs, although his permanent sniffles were now minimal. He had already, with the money he had managed from the little I had given them before, bought a length of purple silk for his mother. Toby saved his money right until the last, when he came across a very good second-hand compass in a shop, just before we joined the cross-channel ferry that would take us on our last lap.

My purchases were books, of course; second-hand copies of Mr. Browning's poems—and a real delight they were: it was almost as if he was talking to you, acting out the part of Fra Lippo Lippi, for instance—and a very tatty copy of Mr. Verne's *Around the World in Eighty Days*, another interesting tale.

During our voyage home, Danny and Claude had become close

friends, as though the trials we had been through had done much to smooth over their differences in lifestyles and outlook. Perhaps it was more accurate to say that that they accepted the differences, and tried to assess how they could work to their mutual advantages. So much so, that they ventured to me that they were thinking of combining their talents and opening a detective agency.

"If Danny does the detecting, then I'll do the books and the house-keeping," Claude told me. "He's got lots of good ideas. . . ."

I was sure he had. . . .

Having exchanged the few pearls I had left—apart from the half-dozen most beautiful: a huge pink one and five perfectly formed blacks, guessing that I would probably get a better price in London—we still had enough to telegraph Mrs. Early of our imminent return, the price of a hired coach and two cabins on the ferry. The boys shared one, Beau and I the other, although the captain had looked askance at Beau.

"No wild animals," he had said dismissively.

I could understand his hesitation. Already Beau was the size of a panther, and appeared to be expanding every day. I assured the captain that he was perfectly tame, and that I would pay for any damage he caused.

It was true what Ky-Lin had said: we got along fine without the Ring though of course we couldn't converse the way we used to. I talked to him, though, and he appeared to understand everything I said, so we were a comfortable couple; I was going to say there were no disagreements, but I had learnt enough about cat body-language to understand what a lashing tail meant!

We had dined well, the sea was smooth and it was a warm, early June night, with a thin silver moon curving up from the sea through our open porthole. Although I was excited at the thought of our long journey at last coming to an end and thought I wouldn't sleep, in fact I succumbed within minutes of lying down on my bunk, leaving Beau gazing out of the porthole. It seemed only minutes later that I woke—in fact the moon didn't seem to have moved at all—to find Beau padding back and forth across the cabin from my bunk to the porthole and back again, obviously with something on his mind.

"What's the matter, Beau? Can't you sleep? It won't be long now; when it gets light we should see the White Cliffs, and before you know it we'll be on our way home!"

"Your home . . ." I thought I heard him say.

"And yours to share."

"Not the same . . ."

I sat up. Yes, I was sure he had spoken. Right, so I was dreaming: no wonder I thought I had only been asleep for a few minutes. Well, dreams could be interesting, and it was nice to talk properly to Beau. His head was on my pillow, and the moonlight, thin though it was, showed me a beloved face whose every change of expression I had become used to; the angle of the ears, line of mouth, depth of cheeks, attitude of whiskers, arrangement of fur, the set of the eyes, the dilation of the pupils—the whole look now was one of misery, depression and resignation.

"Of course it won't be the same as your beautiful palace in Siam," I said, pretending to fall in with his absurd stories. "But I will try to make it as comfortable as I can for you—I promise you will eat well and have the run of some lovely countryside. Lots of rats and mice . . ."

"Princes don't eat mice," he said. "All I want is that kiss you promised me, before it is too late."

"I didn't promise you anything of the sort," I said. "I told you, one doesn't kiss cats. The fact that I forgot a couple of times has nothing to do with it!" But I was angry with myself, just for being angry. I paused. "What do you mean: 'before it is too late'?"

"Because my year is nearly up. If I cannot receive that kiss then I am condemned to spend the rest of my life as a cat. And that I could not bear, however kind you would be to me. I am a *man,* not an animal!"

Because I was still angry with myself I hit out at him.

"You know perfectly well I don't believe that rubbish you told me, don't you? Princes and palaces, witches and spells—a load of rubbish!" I had forgotten I was still dreaming. "And that story of that tatty collar of yours being made of precious stones . . . Pah!"

There was a little silence. "I thought it might come in useful with that orphanage you were planning," he said at last.

How did he know that? I had never discussed it with anyone, even Toby, although it had been much on my mind on the way home.

Somehow that touched me as nothing else had.

I was beginning to realise just how much I valued his comradeship, his company, his constancy. Would it hurt me so much to kiss him once more? Of course it wouldn't! But there was a reason for not doing so, I realised. What would happen if it didn't work? If he had been wrong all along? Supposing that third kiss left him as he was—a cat? What would he feel like? Wouldn't it be better that he blame me, rather than face the humiliation and distress of defeat?

If it meant I could guarantee that he would turn back into the prince he thought he had been, then I would kiss him all over, for as long as it took. . . . But I just couldn't risk it.

"Listen my dear, I just can't do it. I don't want to disappoint you." I patted the bunk. "Don't let's spoil our last night's travel. Come up and have a cuddle!"

Suddenly there was no room to spare; I was surrounded by cat: warm, furry, purring. This latter was a deep-throated rumble, in-out, in-out, on different notes, a semitone in between, and a trifle more *forte* on the breath out. It was soothing, soporific: I closed my eyes . . .

"Of course it may be that you are afraid of being confronted by a prince," said Beau, as if continuing a conversation we hadn't had, and effectually jerking me out of my dose. "What would you say if I told you I was not the scion of a noble house, but rather the bastard son of a waterfront woman, and a thief as well?"

I sat up. "What on earth are you talking about?"

"I am saying that perhaps I should have told you the truth right from the start, instead of trying to romance it up a bit, but I thought you might accept me more readily as a suitor if you thought—"

"A suitor? How on earth could you have thought—"

"That you would countenance a cat? But I keep telling you—"

"You keep telling me about a witch and a ridiculous spell—"

"But that was the only part that was true! The rest I made up, just to impress you!"

It took me a minute or two to digest all this, but once I realised I was still dreaming I decided it wouldn't interrupt the dream if I heard what he had to say.

"Perhaps you had better tell me the truth then," I said. "Not that I will necessarily believe you, of course. And not that it will make the slightest difference to my decision," I added.

He nodded. "Understood. But I will feel better to have told you. . . . The story begins before I was born. In the country of Siam there lived a rich widower, a merchant, with one child, a beautiful girl with hair the colour of the night, eyes the brown of autumn leaves and a skin like ivory—"

"How do you know she looked like that? You said this was before you were born!"

"Don't interrupt! All will become clear . . . Being a rich merchant and trader her father had several warehouses and a counting-house down by the waterfront, and his daughter, who was also gifted with figures, helped her father in the latter.

"One day her father was attending other business and his daughter had occasion to do business with an English ship which was carrying a cargo of tin. During her supervision of the unloading she noticed a young sailor, a handsome young man with fair hair, blue eyes and a smile to melt one's heart, so she told me later. Apparently over the next couple of days they fell deeply in love, and by the time the sailor had to rejoin his ship some couple of weeks later, she was already pregnant. By the time her condition became obvious, she swore to her father that the sailor had promised to come out on his next voyage to marry her, and that he had already sent a letter ahead to his parents telling them of his decision. But her father was so angry and humiliated that he threw her out of the house.

"She waited in vain for her lover to return, for his ship foundered on the voyage with all hands, but her son was born before the news reached her."

"How cruel! First being thrown out of the house and then losing her lover! How did she survive?"

"Although her father refused to see her again, he gave her a small annual income, enough to keep her and the boy from starvation. He also gave her a necklace that had belonged to her mother, a magnificent example in diamonds and emeralds . . ."

Where had I heard that before? "You were that boy?" In my dream . . .

"Yes, that is how I can remember how beautiful she was. She told me that if she had been on her own she would have cast herself into the sea to die as her lover had, but that I had given her something to live for. She taught me all she knew about book-keeping and mathematics, and managed to save enough to hire me an expatriate Englishman to teach me to speak, read and write in my father's language."

He paused. "And so it went on until I was about fourteen or fifteen years old. . . ."

"Go on . . ."

He sighed. "The next bit I always find difficult to even think about. My grandfather, the merchant, married again, a wicked woman who tried to persuade him to cut off my mother's allowance. When he refused he became ill, and was dead within a year of his marriage. Our allowance was stopped, my mother became ill and my wicked step-grandmother sent round the police for the necklace, saying my mother had stolen it. She had bribed them, of course."

He sighed again. "Those were the hard times. My mother needed medicines, and the care of a doctor. I applied for job after job, but always my applications were turned down—my step-grandmother again."

"So what did you do?"

"The only thing I could do: I turned to thievery." He saw my look of shock. "What else could I do? And I was good at it; it wasn't too difficult, with all the goods passing through the port. I was quick and agile, and I was never caught. I found a couple of fences willing to buy whatever I could not take home—jewellery or clothes—but food and delicacies I bought for my mother every day. I don't know whether she realised what I was doing, for I told her I had a good position, though she must have marveled at the strange hours I kept—but perhaps she just didn't want to know.

"She was only thirty-five when she died; I believe she was longing to be re-united with her English sailor, reckoning that I was now old enough to take care of myself: her death hit me hard. For a while I had no wish to live myself. I grew neglectful of my appearance, forgot to eat or wash. Eventually though I pulled myself together and, not wanting to continue a thief and waste my life, decided to follow my father's profession and went to sea. This was a big mistake: I'm afraid I hated every minute. Businessman, yes, given the chance: sailor, no.

"I reckoned my mother had left me two things she wished me to do. My father had told her of his parents address in England, and she asked me to visit them some day; the other was my determination to retrieve the necklace. To this end I took to spying on my step-grand-mother in her villa, and it wasn't long before I discovered that she was a witch; I watched her cast spells to entrap young men and make up the most subtle poisons and potions.

"I waited one night until I reckoned she was asleep, then used my thieving skills to enter the villa and steal back the necklace. Once found I put it on, and was just leaving the villa when my step-grandmother jumped out at me. Apparently her powers had told her I would come."

He stretched, quivered, and settled back. "The rest you know, more or less; there is no need to go over it again. She used her powers to bewitch me into what you see now, and laid the curse of the three kisses on me. Since then I have spent months of my life trying to escape cap-ture, starvation, degradation, and it was only when you rescued me from that murderous stall-holder that I began to hope once more.

"But now my time is running out. It took a great deal out of me learning to eat and hunt like a cat, and also to avoid capture. A couple of times it was only my tough claws that got me out of trouble. I was trapped a number of times by the enticement of food, but luckily my captors had to sleep and I remembered the ways to open doors and unlatch windows."

I knew I was dreaming, I must be, but why would someone like Beau alter his story, so that the desirable prince became an undesirable thief? Surely if anyone was going to be idiotic enough to believe his story they would rather look forward to a princely suitor than a commoner!

I had one more thing puzzling me. "You said you liked it when I called you Beau, but you never really explained why. Was it a pet-name?"

"Depends on how you spell and say it. My father's name was David Bowe and my mother named me after him—only she called me 'Davey.' "

"I *see!*" I thought for a moment. "Can I go on calling you 'Beau'?"

"Of course. Well?"

"Well what?"

"Does it make any difference to your decision? The truth, I mean."

"How can I be sure it is the truth?"

"You can't. Any more than you can tell whether a kiss will turn me back into the man I once was. You'll just have to trust me . . ."

I turned to him, hugged him, stroked him. "Look, I'm quite happy with you as a cat. Why do you want to tempt fate? I love you. . . ."

"I love you too, but I'd rather love you as a man. . . ."

I sat up abruptly. I had never thought that if he really was a man— But I was dreaming, and silly thoughts do come with dreams.

"You aren't, you know," said Beau. "You are as wide awake as I am. Look, if you are so convinced it won't work, I promise to absolve you from all blame if anything goes wrong—but it won't."

So, tired of arguing, and praying against all reason that he was right and I was wrong, and that I wasn't dreaming, I leant forward and kissed him full on his mouth.

29

The Wedding Gift

T old you so," murmured Beau, a.k.a. David Bowe. He took off the emerald and diamond necklace and clasped it round my neck. "There you are: my wedding present. We can use it to finance the orphanage, if that's what you want." He leant over and kissed me, a proper, human, deeply satisfying kiss. "And now, if you don't mind moving over a bit, my darling?"

30

A Year Later

My husband and I leaned on the gate that led to the playfield, the baby asleep in a basket at our feet. A year after our return another June breeze riffled the corn in the farmer's field next door and stirred the waist-high bracken on the hill, bringing with it the scent of summer flowers, honey, lime-blossom and the richness of warm pine trees. The children, eight girls and three boys so far, although Toby would be bringing us more the next day, were chasing a soft ball across the grass and, judging by the shrieks of laughter, thoroughly enjoying themselves.

Behind us in the old stable-yard, drying linen flapped and cracked in the wind, and through the kitchen window I could see Ellen and her widowed sister Jeannie were making the final preparations for luncheon: cold chicken and summer salad, with fresh, warm bread and milk pudding to follow. All the produce was from Hightop, apart from the flour and yeast, for we now had two dairy cows, were fattening a couple of pigs and had increased the numbers of ducks and chickens and extended the kitchen garden by half as much again, and Mr. Early was busy carpentering a see-saw and swings for the children.

The choice of children we had left to Toby—he knew better than any who needed help—but at first I had been full of worthy schemes for their education—globes and improving books in the room we had designated as the schoolroom. But it was Ellen—who had left the school and Miss Moffat after being accused by the headmistress of not being economical enough with the poor fare the children were offered, which was absolute nonsense, as well I knew—who had put me on the right path.

"Listen, miss—sorry, missus, but it's difficult to think of you as a married lady—you ain't teachin' in a school no more, you're goin' to run a Horphanage. What them children need is food, more food and lovin' care, not books, leastways not at first. Once you've got them clean and tidy and rid of the bedwetting and have taught 'em to use a knife and fork proper and say yes please and no thank you, the next stage is bedmakin', dustin' and polishin', layin' fires and blackleadin'. Then into the kitchens to prepare vegetables and learn to wash up. After that comes simple stitchery, which my sister can teach 'em, 'cos she earned what she could as a seamstress. Then you can teach 'em enough to follow a receipt, sign their names and add two and two so they aren't cheated when the tradespeople call."

She saw the dismayed look on my face, and I could see she was trying not to laugh.

"Oh Missus Sophy, don't look so worrit! They'll come to your learnin' soon enough, but first things first! Now, the first thing is what they's to wear. It's summer, so vests and cotton shirts and leggings for the boys, and vests, short dresses and pantaloons for the girls. Something cool, comfortable and easy to put on and take off. As this is a Horphanage, perhaps it would be better if they all wore the same colour: how about brown for the boys and blue for the girls? That way there won't be no nonsense about one wearing something better than someone else . . . And that's another thing: they'll have to learn washin' and ironin' as well. And I forgot the butter and cheese makin'.'"

"But Ellen, some of them will be only five or six years old!"

"Never too young to learn. Fact, the younger the better. Now, when we've got them to rights, the boys can help Mr. Early with the kitchen garden and the animals, and I'll have the girls in the kitchen. Tell you what, you have them in the mornings and we'll take them for the rest of the day. Don't forget, you're not teaching future Prime Ministers and lady librarians, you're trying to make the girls fit for service in good positions and the boys 'prenticed well. That's all. If on the way you find someone to take further, like Master Toby, well and good, but don't expect it!"

She was perfectly right, of course, but I found it difficult to absorb, no more so than on the day we welcomed our first arrivals and I watched horrified as the new arrivals were taken out into the yard, stripped bare, had their heads shaved, girls as well as boys, and were then dumped, one by one, into a large tub of warm water and scrubbed with carbolic soap until all the London grime had gone for good. Two of them were too cowed by their earlier life and the newness of their surroundings to do anything but submit, but the other three yelled and shrieked and fought all the way through and Mrs. Early, Ellen and her sister had their work cut out. Bathed and disinfected, they luckily fitted into the clothes Jeannie had already sewn. They were then fed—outside—just to see about their manners which were, mostly, nonexistent. So that was the first chore . . .

Play-time was before luncheon and before supper. In the winter months we had to spend a good of time indoors, and at those times we used the schoolroom, which I made as bright and welcoming as possible, to hear many stories and play games of blindman's buff, hunt the thimble or musical chairs from the old piano, together with the quieter dominoes, draughts and hands of cards. Two of the downstairs smaller rooms were turned into indoor privies and washrooms. We bought new beds, put up hooks for clothes, provided cutlery and crockery and hung curtains. After we had just about become used to our first arrivals, Toby brought six more, and we started all over again, luckily helped by the first lot, determined to show their superiority.

We had decided that about thirty children was about enough to cope with, replacing after that those who got good positions. We had sold the pearls in London for an excellent price, and the necklace had been bought at our inflated asking price by a certain "Royal Personage" for his mistress! That money was invested in railways, cotton and munitions, which Beau said people always need, and were paying good dividends.

He himself had found a position as consultant with a city Merchant Bank dealing with the Far East, and went up to town two or three times a week. We had given Claude and Danny a hundred pounds each to set them up, because they were still determined on the detective agency.

We had found Beau's grandfather and grandmother living quietly in Plymouth, and although wary at first they had soon accepted their grandson and his wife as welcome additions to the family, and were delighted to learn they were soon to be great-grandparents.

As for Toby, we had offered him a lump sum but he wouldn't take it, asking us instead to put a bit aside whenever we had any to spare and invest it, so he would have a bit put by when he kitted himself out for his first expedition. He was still determined to become an explorer, and to this end was studying every book he could find on the subject, besides searching out the most deserving cases for the orphanage. With the five he was bringing us tomorrow, it would bring the count up to eighteen, with Jeannie's two little girls. He explained that we would always have more girls than boys, because the latter were better able to look after themselves on the streets, and adapted readily to being part of a gang of young thieves.

Another piece of news was that Miss Madeleine from the Charity School was planning to join us next week. Apparently Miss Moffat had found a rather attractive young lady to fill my post, and Madeleine wrote that she was just twiddling her thumbs and would I take her at a low wage? Between the lines I could read that she was desperate also not to end up as an old maid, and immediately bethought myself of the young curate at the village church, who came faithfully every Sunday to lead us in prayers and tell the children Bible stories. Beau was happy for her to come, saying I would have more time with our daughter if I had someone else to do the teaching.

We three lived at the "Temple," as I still thought of it, looked after by Mr. and Mrs. Early. Our bedroom was the one I had first occupied, the baby's Night Nursery next to it, the Day Nursery the room in which I had prepared for our journey, which still left three bedrooms for guests. If Madeleine had one of these, Toby could have one and Claude and Danny double up, if they all arrived for a visit together.

Thinking of those two made me grin, and Beau turned to look at me.

"Share it?"

"Just thinking of that first success of 'Cumberbatch and Duveen.' "

"Typical Danny . . ."

Indeed it had been, but it had opened all sorts of doors for them, so now they had moved from their original lock-up to an office with a room behind for eating, cooking and sleeping and an outside privy, with two let floors above, from which they collected rent. Their first "scoop" had been, as Beau said, "typical Danny." As I saw it, it was ten out of ten for opportunism.

It appeared that he had witnessed an accident in which an expensive-looking carriage had overturned, discharging a small beribboned dog who yapped and dodged between the legs of the passersby. Danny seized his chance, grabbed the dog and bore it back to their lodgings. In spite of Claude's protests he fed it and cleared up its messes and bore its petulant barking, until he could study the papers the next day, and saw as he expected, a reward of ten pounds. He waited until the next day when the reward had risen to fifteen pounds, then had visited the bereaved dog-owner, a hysterical dowager, and offered his services to "find" the dog, hinting darkly at a dog-stealing gang, and the dangers of trying to penetrate their fastnesses, and had been offered the reward, plus five pounds per day if he could return the dog. Obviously he had been successful, but it had taken him five days. . . . Forty pounds to the good, plus the recommendation of a grateful dowager! Danny had a lucky touch, or a four-leaved clover.

Behind us the bell clanged outside the kitchen door and the children ceased their play and streamed for the gate, which Beau swung open. Ten minutes until luncheon, time for the children to wash their hands and tidy up. Beau closed the gate and dropped a kiss on the tip of my nose.

"Saturday afternoon, sweetheart . . ."

"So?"

"So the children are going on a nature ramble this afternoon with Mr. and Mrs. Early. Neither of us will be needed between, say, two and five. I suggest we—" and he bent and whispered in my ear.

I blushed. "In the open?"

"Why not? The sun is good for you, and I like to see my wife in daylight. You are beautiful in any light, my sweet, but the sun is something we can't often take advantage of . . ."

I adored him, of course. Strangely enough, his cat-colours had come through to his human body. His skin was the creamy-beige of his cat-coat, his hair the chocolate of his mask and paws, and his eyes the same startling blue; his body was as lithe and strong as his cat-body. And he loved me too . . .

I nodded down at the wicker-basket, where Serena had just opened her eyes and was stretching and yawning her toothless mouth. Her fist went to her mouth, obviously ready for *her* luncheon. "What about her?"

"Go and feed her, and then let Ellen have her for an hour or two. You know she dotes on her. . . ."

Serena opened her eyes, the same blue as her father's, and yawned again, and my heart turned over with love for them both, my husband and my daughter. Just now, life was good. Doubtless there would be hard times, bad times in the future, but our love would see us through, of that I was sure.

Beau put his arms about me. "Any regrets, my darling?"

"None at all." But then I remembered something that was still nagging at me. "Well, yes: I suppose there is something . . ."

"Tell me!" He kissed me again. "I'll cure it if I can."

"You can't, nobody can . . ."

"But what is it?"

"Well, it's just that . . . Sounds silly I know, such a small thing really . . ."

"What?"

"I just wish I knew what happened to the Eg . . ."

Epilogue

Ky-Lin could have told her . . .

As soon as the Travellers had left, the dragons flew, one by one, across the chasm to where the Eg, their Eg, their long-lost treasure, lay in the niche in the ground long reserved as the official Hatching-Ground. They flew in order of precedence; first the senior Master-Dragon, the Brown, followed by the Orange, the Green, the Grey, the Purple, the Yellow and finally the Blue, his mere twelve hundred years making him the most junior.

One by one they approached the Eg reverently, muttering a suitable welcome, until all seven were grouped round in a circle, admiring, longing to touch, to examine more closely, to guess the weight, estimate the date of hatching. It was for the senior dragon to make the first move, followed by the others in order of seniority. Although it was not encouraged, there were inevitable side-bets; these were safer than quarrels, and they only used trinkets as stakes: a silver platter or two, a small string of pearls, an amethyst brooch—the sort of wagers they laid in their endless games of chess, checkers, Mah-Jong etc.

The dragons' colours glowed with excitement. Although naturally of a neutral colour, the lozenges of scales on their chests reflected their "true" colours, which only dyed their skins when they were excited, as now, or were injured or ill, when the colours seeped into the neutral patches and dyed the whole dragon with a paler shade of the original. This had happened hundreds of years ago to the Blue, at a bad time when he had temporarily mislaid the jewels that would make him a Master-Dragon.

The dragons were more or less agreed. The hatching would take place around Middle-Year, and the weight was about fifteen pounds at present, of which three pounds were the shell. It would be a large baby dragon.

In the meantime there was plenty to do to prepare for the new arrival.

Firstly the Eg must be kept warm and comfortable and turned regularly. One after the other the dragons provided comforts. Yellow filched a padded quilt from the bush where it had been drying, though when he had tried to accelerate the drying process with a puff or two of dragon-fire it was not quite as it should have been, although the scorched bits didn't show once the quilt was folded. Blue concentrated on a layer of dried grasses for the floor of the Nursery, Green fashioned a beautiful teething-ring from bone and coral, Purple picked out the finest jewels for the baby's first toys and Orange wove a basket to hold them, while Grey fashioned wind-chimes from the smallest bones in their collection.

As senior dragon, Brown was in charge of the arrangements and supervised the rota for the weekly turning of the Eg and the continual Hatch-Sitting.

Winter passed, spring brought new life to the crops and countryside and the dragons did their annual Turd-Out, as they called it among themselves, although Brown frowned on this and preferred it to be referred to in his hearing as Spring-Clean. This year it was more important than ever that the whole cave was as pristine as possible, pending their New Arrival, so they all set to with a will, using their wings to sweep all the debris down into the accommodating chasm, so that detritus, dried faeces and general rubbish went up conveniently in a puff or two of greasy smoke and a couple of sparks. Their Hoard was sorted, examined, cleaned, stones polished and arranged to their best advantage; the silver and gold on stone shelves at the back, the jewels each in their own piles of colour: rubies, garnets, beryl, blood-stones, rose-quartz, carnelian and fire-opals; topazes, agate, amber and tiger's eye; emeralds, peridot and jade; sapphire, aquamarine and amethyst; diamond and crystal; pearl and moonstone and opals, and all set off nicely with bands of jet.

Now all was ready, and only three months to go . . .

Unseen and unregarded, the Travellers who had returned the Eg started their long journey home, and at the monastery Ky-Lin welcomed the spring sunshine and spent much of his time snoozing on the parapet of the balcony where stood the stone replica of his friend Growch. Some time soon his Master would arrive and take him to his rest, although He had so much to do it might be later rather than sooner. After all, he,

Ky-Lin, was one of his Master's most unimportant servants, and must wait his turn.

Truth to tell he had rather enjoyed his extended time on earth. Without becoming too puffed up with pride, he had at least helped both Summerdai and Sophronisbe to attain their goals. He, too, wondered what had become of the Eg. He couldn't miss the fact that there was more than usual activity among the dragons, some of them flying by day, which was most unusual.

He wondered, too, how far his friends had travelled homewards, and whether that rogue of a Beau-Cat had managed to persuade Sophy that he needed a final kiss to transform him, when he knew perfectly well that the spell only lasted a year anyway. . . .

It had been a long journey for all of them, as had the earlier one with Summer: he hoped this one would have a happier ending. He had thought the Eg would have hatched earlier than this; there was certainly life in there, even after all the vicissitudes it had been through; both he and the boy had heard the somewhat puzzling sounds from within. Still, he felt that everyone would be left in no doubt once it had hatched.

Not that he knew much about dragons. They were creatures of another, earlier time, some of the survivors of the Great Darkness he had been told about, when the Black Star fell on earth and shut out the sun for aeons. He and his brethren were of a later time, direct creations of their Master, devoted to the preservation of life in all its forms, unlike the careless, fire-setting, meat-eating dragons—although their reputation as man-eaters was erroneous. Perhaps this one would grow up differently, although if Growch had been there he would have said: "No chance, mate. Once a dragon, always a dragon . . ."

March had gone, April and May came and went, and now the days had lengthened until it was no sooner time to go to bed than time to get up again, or so it seemed to the peasants toiling on their land, although in the monastery the monks enjoyed the indulgence of the sun on their shaven skulls as they moved from one duty to another.

Up in the Blue Mountain the dragons jostled one another for the privilege of Eg-Sitting now the time was drawing near for the hatching, sometimes only giving their predecessor five minutes before shoving him aside and taking over. The Eg grew warmer and larger, and now it weighed over eighteen pounds. What a baby it would produce!

As Middle-Year appeared to accelerate towards them, all the dragons vied with one another to provide their baby with the very best. Orange scorched his tail down in the chasm while smoking the tenderest pieces

of meat for the baby dragon's first meals; Grey almost choked on the fluff
he collected from plants for bedding; Yellow was badly scratched searching for shards of glass to reflect the moonlight; Green was nearly exhausted when he arrived back from the south with a length of the finest
silk for covering while the baby's scales hardened; Purple blunted his
claws tearing out suitable white stones from the moraine to fence in the
Hatching-Ground and Blue took one of the silver spoons and filled several
golden bowls with the finest spring water for drinking and washing. Of
course dragons used to roll in dew or snow for their twice-yearly bath,
but the baby would be too young for a while even to be flown out for this.

Nobody cared for bumps and bruises. Their baby dragon hatching
safe and healthy was all that mattered. The years since the last hatching
were legion, and the surviving dragons were not growing any younger.
There must be other dragon eggs scattered throughout the world but these
were in forgotten places and might never have the right conditions to
hatch, but this one was here, it was real, it was live and it was about to
hatch.

The sun rose higher in the sky, the air grew warmer, and at last it
was the eve of Middle-Year-Day. There was an overnight full-moon
which bathed the Hatching-Ground and the waiting dragons in silver
light. It seemed that the moon was reluctant to miss the hatching, for it
was still a pale disc in the sky when the sun rose in the east, and now
all the dragons were gathered in a circle around the Eg, most of the
side-bets having been paid out already.

One hour before mid-day the tapping began.

At first it was so faint that the dragons had to hold their breath in
unison to hear it at all, but then the noise gradually grew in volume and
faster and faster, until it was perfectly audible. Tap, tap, tap; tap, tap, tap.

But the shell of the Eg resisted. The tapping grew more frantic,
punctuated by what sounded like tiny thumps, as if a small fist was
joining in with the disposable egg-beak attached to the jaw of the baby
dragon. The noise crescendoed, and then gradually died back as though
the creature within was exhausted, was losing both strength and heart.
The dragons glanced anxiously at each other, then turned to the Senior
Dragon, Brown.

He thought for a long moment; all sounds had ceased. Then he
nodded slowly. "Show claws . . ."

One by one the dragons raised first their left then their right front
claws, which were carefully examined by Brown. All the dragons were
supposed to keep their claws sharp on the specially imported granite
Sharpening Stone, but some of the older ones skipped the chore, so

consequently it was the youngest, Blue, who was chosen to help their baby out of his prison of shell.

Brown indicated where he wanted the cut made. "But not too deep; just hallway through. Be very, very careful . . ."

All held their breath as Blue extended the middle claw of his right front foot and held it poised over the Eg. They noticed he was trembling. He took a deep breath, then as delicately but decisively as a glass-cutter etching the thinnest balloon glass, he traced a fine line two-thirds around the breadth of the Eg.

For a moment there was no response, and then the tapping started again, louder this time, the accompanying thumping as well, and now through the crack in the shell a thin mewling sound. Like a miracle the crack widened fractionally until there was a minute glimpse of movement. By now all the dragons' heads were circled above the Eg, a living dome of bony heads and hissing breath.

Noon, and the sun at its zenith on this Middle-Year-Day. A shaft of light suddenly burned down on the dragons' skulls and they all drew back as if scorched. They believed that the sun's rays were harmful, would burn through their skulls and scramble their brains. Now the rays of the sun shone on the cracked Eg and the noise and activity within increased a hundred per cent. The membrane which divided the outer shell from its contents stretched and stretched, thinner and thinner as the crack in the Eg widened until suddenly with a ripping *pop!* it burst apart, the Eg-shell opened into two distinct halves like a two-petalled flower, and its contents were revealed . . .

Ky-Lin heard the roar from where he lay in the mid-morning shadows among the bonsai trees on his little balcony. He sprang upright, thinking for a moment that the fires in the Blue Mountain had erupted again, but recognized immediately that the noise came from the harsh, cacophonous voices of the dragons. Whatever it was, they were clearly upset.

Gradually the noise subsided, rising once more into a brief crescendo every quarter-hour or so, but this merely increased Ky-Lin's sense of unease. He could not imagine what could have occasioned such an uproar, audible so clearly across the miles that separated the monastery from the mountain. Had something happened to the Eg? If it had hatched normally he would have expected something other than this howl of both anger and bewilderment. Was there something wrong with the baby dragon? Could it be malformed? Sick? Dead? And if it were any of those things, wouldn't the dragons blame both him and the Travellers for not taking enough care with it? If so, what could they do? Would they take to the air and pursue Sophy and Company and wreak a terrible vengeance? Or would they seek him out and pulverize him, raze the monastery to the ground?

No, he couldn't let that happen. He must journey towards the mountain and meet them half-way, try to undo whatever damage had been done before it was too late. Accordingly he did a quick transformation into pony-size and made his way through the monastery, down the track to the village and turned north onto the plain. He trotted along in the afternoon heat, carefully avoiding damaging any living growth, his hooves throwing up little puffs of dust.

He made good progress, and as he neared the Blue Mountain the dragon voices grew louder and more discordant. He wished he could understand just what they were shouting about—

He skidded to a sudden halt, realising all at once what an utter idiot he was. Because of the unspoken ban against any congress between his people and them, they had always ignored that the other creatures existed, and of course there was no way he could communicate with them if they came face to face. They were such primitive creatures that thought transference was out, too.

He sank down on his haunches, in his misery shrinking down a size or two. He could not remember ever feeling so miserable, even when . . . But no point in remembering that. He and his brethren were not supposed to feel sadness—nor anger, hatred, love, pride or impatience. Perhaps he had been in the world too long, for he knew he had felt all these emotions at one time or another, most of them only momentarily. His downfall had originally been his pride, and luckily he didn't really know how to be impatient; but he had felt affection for Summer and Sophy, and for the boy Toby, but probably the greatest had been for Growch.

There was only one thing to do. He closed his eyes, bowed his head, gazed inwards and sent a prayer to his Master—not a request for direct aid, that would be wrong, rather a prayer for guidance on what to do next. One had to rely on oneself for action.

He was deep in meditation, sinking into that limbo where the body no longer mattered or responded to outside influences, when he was jerked back into the real world by a sudden clatter of leathery wings above. Claws seized his shoulders and he was borne upwards into the air with a whoosh! and a sinking lurch in his stomach. All his senses returned with a rush as he saw the plain beneath him disappear with alarming speed. Whatever in the world was happening?

He realised that he had been pounced on by one of the dragons and was being carried higher and higher towards the north-east, but to what purpose? Was he to be dropped from a great height, to be smashed to smithereens? Made into a snack for the dragons' dinner? But perhaps they had something less violent in mind: to show him something perhaps? To demonstrate why they were so angry?

Whatever the eventual outcome they had obviously seen him coming and decided to collect him, although it was unusual for them to fly in the heat of the sun, so it must be urgent. Lifting his head a little he saw they were approaching the Blue Mountain, swinging back behind it to the shady side, but when it seemed they must literally brush the rocks his carrier-dragon shot straight upwards, making Ky-Lin dizzily wish he had not indulged in those few extra grains of rice that morning. They must be all of three thousand feet high . . .

The next moment they started to drop like stones, plummeting down so fast that Ky-Lin was thrust back momentarily against the dragon's bony chest. Beneath them the black maw of the mountain rose up with frightening speed: a dark blot, an inky puddle, an ebony lake—the mouth of Hell itself!

The dragon braked sharply at the last moment, then did a neat landing in the middle of a circle of six scaly others, dropping Ky-Lin unceremoniously to the ground. All around was the stench of cinders, old bones, stale air, sulphur. Ky-Lin choked and gagged and his eyes started to run. Something shoved him in the back, propelling him forward; blinking he tried to clear his streaming eyes, conscious of the dragon-voices grumbling and growling all around him.

His eyes clearing, becoming used to the dragon-stench, he peered ahead of him. He was in a small enclosed space surrounded by a fence of stones and—yes—there was the Eg, or rather one of the neatly bisected halves. Moving nearer without hindrance, he peered down and there, cradled in the egg, its tiny claws clutching a strip of smoked meat which it was attempting to chew with its razor-sharp baby teeth and making contented little mewling sounds, was a baby dragon.

Its blue eyes gazed up at him curiously. Blue eyes? Did they change as the dragons grew, like puppies, kittens or human babies? He peered closer. It seemed healthy enough: four legs, claws present and correct, two vestigial wings, tail, nose, eyes and ears all looking in the right places. Just for a moment it bore a fleeting resemblance to a little piglet, especially as its tail was tightly curled.

And it was pink . . .

Presumably all dragons started that colour, together with the blue eyes, and they lost that ridiculous tuft of blond hair like chicken-fluff that grew on top of its head as they matured.

He was saved from further guesswork—if the baby dragon was healthy and happy then what was all the fuss about—by a violent nudge, one which knocked him sideways out of the ring of stones and onto a bare patch of ground, on which lay the other half of the Eg.

Now all the dragons were hissing, instead of the crooning-growl they had made over the baby dragon, but suddenly a thin, angry wail cut across all other sounds, pitched as it was at a higher frequency; rapidly it grew into a horrendous, ear-piercing screech, a sound compounded of anger and despair, grating on the ear like a giant chalk on a giant blackboard. Ky-Lin moved over to the other half-egg and gazed down. And there . . . ? There was a baby.

A *human* baby!

The little girl, tufts of black hair sticking up all over her scalp, eyes screwed up in temper, toothless mouth agape for another wail, arms and legs pumping, was quite obviously not a dragon, although she was behaving like one. So, the Eg had held its surprises after all—twins! one dragon-baby, one human one.

No wonder the dragons were so upset. At last Ky-Lin had an inkling of why he was here. He realised that the dragons thought he was partly to blame for this mess: after all hadn't he helped first Summer and later Sophy to deliver a flawed Eg? Sure, they had their baby dragon, but here was a lively, lusty reminder of their renegade dragon, Black Jasper, who had broken all the rules and fathered an Eg with his human love.

Now he was left in no doubt as to his role. He glanced over to where the baby dragon lay—no eye contact with his captors, kidnappers, hostage-takers, hijackers, whatever they were: this only incensed them, apparently—and he saw the baby dragon lifted tenderly from his half of the Eg and cradled in blunted claws, while a padded quilt was ripped in half by another, sharper claw. Half was tossed across to land at his feet, a scorched, charred half, while the other, unmarked half was the dragon-baby's new cradle.

Another dragon tossed the half-shell with the baby girl onto the damaged quilt then brought the corners together into a rough knot, and moved back. Another pushed him forward again till he was standing over the bundle. So, he was expected to carry it away. He opened his mouth, took the knot into his mouth and tugged, but the cloth slipped away. He tried again, but once again his ruminant's teeth could not get a grip, and he knew that even if he grew to pony-size he would never be able to carry the bundle away. He stepped back and shook his head, was nudged forward again, attempted it again, but only succeeded in trying so hard that he merely let go too quickly and landed with an undignified bump on his rump. And if dragons could be said to snigger, they were sniggering now.

The baby had been quiet for the last few minutes, but now she started up with another piercing wail, rising to an indignant shriek. The dragons shrank back, and he realised that the noise actually hurt their ears, accustomed as they were to their own much deeper voices. There was hissed conversation above his head, then suddenly he was grasped once more by strong claws and borne aloft; out of the corner of his eye he saw that a second dragon had grabbed the baby-bundle and was bearing it aloft also.

Once more the vertigo, the churning stomach, the rush of wind over his hide, but now he was surprised to see it was already dusk and that there was much cooler air in the upper reaches, although the further they descended heat from the baked earth beneath came puffing up like an open oven.

Ky-Lin looked down, expecting to find the plain rising up to meet them, but they appeared to be swinging further south-west. He saw the monastery looming up, and already he could see the twinkling lights of the cooking-fires and lanterns in the courtyard. What were the dragons doing? Almost immediately there was that sickening drop of hundreds of feet and then a lurch as his dragon pulled up just short of the balcony. So they knew just where they could usually find him . . .

A moment later he was dropped unceremoniously beside the bonsais, and the bundle followed, a little more gently, to lie in front of him. Above them the dragons hovered for a wing-beat or so, their downdraught flattening the hair on his plumed tail and smelling of cinders, then they were up and away, their raucous cries fading away as they swept back towards the Blue Mountain.

The bundle beside him stirred. Awkwardly Ky-Lin worried the knot loose until the baby girl lay revealed, wriggling uncomfortably, her mouth squaring itself for another gappy yell. Soon someone would come to investigate, on the excuse of bringing him his supper or lamp, but before then he would have to seek help, make a plan.

Despairingly he nosed the lump of stone that represented his old friend, Growch, and let his thoughts wash out over the stone. "What shall I do next? I've never had to deal with a baby before. . . ."

He didn't expect an answer, but at once, in his mind, he heard a voice: a hint, a murmur that sounded so like Growch that he shook his head in disbelief.

"Come on, mate? Think . . . Babies is no different from pups. At this age they needs milk, warmth and a lick or two to keep 'em clean. Once they starts to grow, then they needs training, care, an' lots of love. Start 'er off right: after that it's up to you . . ." The phantom voice faded, died away.

Of course! A wet-nurse from the village to care for the babe until she was weaned. That took care of the next few months. But then? The voice that had seemed to be Growch's had said "after that it's up to you . . ." but there was always a choice, wasn't there? And if his Master came for him soon . . . But if he didn't?

He glanced down at the baby girl again. She had decided to calm down, but she was still frowning, sucking at one of her fists; then she stretched out her other hand towards him and for a moment her face smoothed out and she was still and there was a sudden fleeting resemblance to . . .

He sighed. Yes, there was always a choice—but then he had just made his.

Hadn't he?